HOODED MAN

An Abaddon Books™ Publication
www.abaddonbooks.com
abaddon@rebellion.co.uk

This omnibus published in 2013 by Abaddon Books™,
Rebellion Intellectual Property Limited,
Riverside House, Osney Mead, Oxford, OX2 0ES, UK.

10 9 8 7 6 5 4 3 2 1

Editor-in Chief: Jonathan Oliver
Desk Editor: David Moore
Cover Art: Mark Harrison
Design: Simon Parr
Marketing and PR: Michael Molcher
Publishing Manager: Ben Smith
Creative Director and CEO: Jason Kingsley
Chief Technical Officer: Chris Kingsley
The Afterblight Chronicles™ created by Simon Spurrier & Andy Boot

ISBN: 978-1-78108-168-6

Printed in the US

AN OMNIBUS OF POST-APOCALYPTIC NOVELS

HOODED MAN

PAUL KANE

WWW.ABADDONBOOKS.COM

The Afterblight Chronicles

INTRODUCTION

As MUCH AS *The Afterblight Chronicles* are a series of action-packed novels set in the aftermath of the apocalypse, as much as they are about cultists with guns, heroes with attitude and epic journeys across the wastelands of a world gone to hell, they are also about legends.

For in the ashes of Earth, new legends will be born, as those who have survived seek to put back together the broken pieces.

But what we have here is not only a legend, he is a legend reborn.

I'm from Robin Hood country myself, having been born and raised in Nottingham, so I'm somewhat familiar with the stories of the Hooded Man and his coterie of rogues. So when Paul Kane, a writer whose work I was familiar with from horror fandom, came to me with the idea of a post-apocalyptic Robin Hood, it was too good an opportunity to pass up.

Paul has steeped himself in the myths and legends of Sherwood, but what he gives us here is a fresh take on a familiar figure. He reminds us why certain legends endure and his novels in the series speak about the need for heroes, and what heroes are, in a way that raises this trilogy above your run-of-the-mill action adventure.

That's not to say there isn't plenty of thrilling escapes, frantic gunplay and brilliantly-executed set pieces within these pages, there's lots and lots of that. But Robert is far more than a hero that tackles violence with violence – at the heart of his crusade is a desire for justice and fairness to return to a wrecked society.

So these then are the new legends of the Hooded Man, a hero for the end-times.

Jonathan Oliver
Oxford, March 2013

ARROWHEAD

Original cover art by Mark Harrison

For Mum and Dad who helped me find my path
through the forest, and for my darling Marie
who coaxed me out of it.

The spirit of Robin Hood
Lives forever in Sherwood Forest
And in the hearts of those who seek him...

CHAPTER ONE

THE ARROWHEAD EMBEDDED itself in the wall just millimetres from his left temple.

Thomas Hinckerman had screwed up his eyes as the crossbow was raised, flinching only slightly when he heard the impact; in one way relieved to still be alive, in another wishing this ordeal would be over soon, one way or the other. The apple on top of his head wobbled slightly. There was a wetness running down his face; he assumed it was sweat. But when he opened his eyes and looked down – carefully, so as not to dislodge the fruit he was balancing – he saw the spots of red on the floor. The bolt had nicked his skin...

And seconds later there was pain.

Not that he could feel it much – this latest wound paled into insignificance compared with his others: the bullet hole in his shoulder, for example, the fingernails dangling off, pulled with pliers, the missing teeth, or how about the cigar burns on his stomach? Still, he'd fared better than Gary and Dan. Their bodies were still cooling on the floor near the entrance to the station.

It had been his idea initially, taken from those stories of refugees trying to enter Britain simply by walking, long before the virus came and took its toll. Before the Cull. Back then, those people had wanted in, but now it seemed like a much better idea to get out of the country before things grew even worse.

Thomas suggested it to Gary, a former scrap metal dealer, and Dan, who used to be a butcher, who both felt the same. He'd met them at the local impromptu meetings early in the Cull, when everyone was still trying to figure out what could be done about their loved ones, their neighbours, those who were dying all around them. They weren't the kind of folk Thomas would have mixed with before all this, not the sort of men you'd see hanging out at the library where he had worked. But fate had thrown them together, and they'd stuck like glue: through all the madness that had followed.

Now they were dead. Just like he would be soon. Thomas was under no illusions about that, not after he'd seen them murdered in cold blood. His last memories of the men he'd trekked thirty-one miles with, sharing adversities he never would have thought possible, were Dan's brains exploding all over his own shirt, feet still twitching as he hit the ground, and Gary dancing like a puppet as he was riddled with bullets from a machine gun.

The three of them had emerged from the tunnel and into the station at Calais that morning, their torches almost out of batteries, supplies exhausted a day ago, glad to be free, glad to be back above ground. They'd passed dormant trains, their yellow noses rusting, glass at the front smashed. They'd seen no one, not until they reached the station. There Gary spotted a lone figure sitting on one of the benches inside the foyer.

They must have been watching from the start, though. As the trio walked over to make contact, Dan was already dropping, a bullet coming out of nowhere to blow half his head away. And then the other men emerged – a half dozen or more, heavily-armed; one with silver hair carrying what looked like a sniper's rifle. That's when they'd pulled Gary's strings...

They'd been waiting, too, he found out. Waiting for someone like him to come. Thomas had been left alive – just clipped with a bullet – to tell them what he knew.

He was dragged to his feet by two men, one with a paunch, the other smoking a cigar. Their leader wasn't a huge man, but carried himself well. He had the air of someone much larger. He was dressed in grey and black combats, and was wearing sunglasses. When he took them off and stared into Thomas's face, he saw that the man's eyes were just as black as his glasses. There were jewelled rings on most of his fingers. He spoke with a French accent, and his first question was: "Are you in pain, Englishman?" When Thomas nodded, the man smiled with teeth as yellow as the noses of those trains. Then he stuck two of his ringed fingers into the hole in Thomas's shoulder. His whole body jerked, but he was held tightly by the men on either side.

When Thomas had recovered enough to speak, he whispered: "What... what do you want from me?"

"Information," said the man.

"A-about what? I don't know anything."

He smiled again. "We will see."

Thomas was introduced to a broader man with olive skin and short, cropped hair. Thomas was told that his name was Tanek. "When Tanek was in the army," the man in combats told him, "his speciality was making people talk." The Frenchman nodded firmly, and that's when the pliers had come out. Tanek had gone to work on his fingernails first, grasping the little one on his right hand firmly and yanking it off, the nail splitting and cracking as it went.

Thomas let out the loudest scream of his life. Even getting shot hadn't hurt like that. Through the tears, he saw the outline of the Frenchman's face again. "I need to know about the place you've come from," he told Thomas.

"W-What...?" Another nail was pulled. "*Yaaaaaahhhh...*"

The Frenchman slapped his face. "What is the situation in England? Do you understand me?"

Thomas shook his head.

"How organised are the people over there? Are there communities? Are the defence forces still operational?"

Thomas laughed at that one, which earned him another lost nail. "Everything's gone to shit," he shouted back at the man. "It's chaos. Fucking chaos! Why do you think we came through the tunnel? It's like being back in the dark ages."

The Frenchman chuckled this time. "I see."

They continued to question him for at least a couple more hours, asking him everything he knew about Dover, where they'd entered, about the surrounding areas of Kent, what he'd heard about London and other regions of England – which was very little since the Cull. Thomas had no idea why they were putting the questions to him, but he answered as honestly as he could, especially when Tanek pulled out his molars, then snatched the cigar from one of the men holding him and used that too. He'd cooperated as well as he was able and his reward was to be handcuffed to a notice board, ruined fingers dangling limply, while some of the men took it in turns to play 'William Tell' with a crossbow Tanek handed around, and an apple – a fresh golden apple that would have made Thomas's mouth water had it not already been filled with blood. And had his mouth not been taped over because they were sick of hearing his cries.

As he opened his eyes now, he saw motorcycles being wheeled into the station, six or seven in total. He also heard one of the men call out their leader's name: De Falaise.

The man came to join Tanek, just as another bolt was clumsily fired from the crossbow. It wound up in Thomas's right thigh. His muffled grunt caused much amusement amongst the group.

De Falaise raised a hand to stop the game for a moment, walking towards Thomas. "I thank you for your help, it was fortuitous that our paths should cross," he said. "It would appear there is much in the way of opportunity for people like us in your land. Unlike the situation we leave behind... Your people are weak; we are not."

It then dawned on Thomas what he had in mind. De Falaise and his men were going to use the bikes to make the same trip he'd done, but in reverse, shooting up the tunnel and into England just like one of the bolts from Tanek's crossbow.

"In return, my gift to you, Englishman," said De Falaise. Thomas looked into those black eyes, and thought for just a moment the Frenchman might let him live, let him go. Then he saw that smile on De Falaise's face, and struggled against his bonds, the apple falling from his head. De Falaise stepped aside and there was Tanek, with his weapon now fully loaded – aimed at his head. Unlike the others, he would not miss.

Then it was over, and De Falaise was already giving the order to move out, to take the bikes down to the tunnel so they could be on their way. Tanek paused before leaving, to pick up the apple and take a bite.

"Come," said De Falaise, laughing again as he led the way. "There is much to do, much to see. And a country ripe for the taking."

CHAPTER TWO

THE HUNTER HAD been crouching in the undergrowth for almost two hours when the creature finally wandered into the clearing. His prize. He'd been tracking it for the best part of a day, and this was one of its favourite haunts. This would be the place where he'd look into its eyes, where he'd feel that familiar adrenalin rush from bagging such a fine catch.

So he'd settled himself down to wait.

He was a patient man. And, besides, it wasn't as if he had anything else to do, was it? No going down the pub for a pint and game of darts, no cosy nights in front of the TV. Those days were long gone now, a distant memory... most of the time. The problem with waiting was that the mind needed ways to amuse itself. Against his will, he found himself drifting back, remembering. Thinking about the man he used to be and the life he'd once led. It felt like a dream.

"Read to me some more, Dad... please..."

He tried to shake the memories from his head, in much the same way his old Golden Retriever used to shake himself dry. How little Stevie would laugh when Max did that – he could see the boy's face now on that holiday in Wales. They'd left the campsite and taken a walk down by a long river. Then they'd let the dog off the lead to run around and he'd immediately jumped in the water to chase a fish he'd seen. After swimming with his head held high, Max had finally realised there was no way on Earth he was going to catch the thing. He'd sprayed them all when they ran across to him. Stevie had laughed and laughed, as Joanne held up her hands to...

"Robert... Robert, come back to bed. It's Sunday morning."

They were random, these recollections. That one was from back when they'd first got married, back when they used to lose themselves in each other every weekend. Back before Stevie came along and would climb in with them on a Sunday morning, bringing the papers with him. His son would read the comics while Robert took the sports section and Joanne would comment on what was happening in the world; which usually involved some soap or pop star spending thousands on rehab when everyone knew they'd be back on booze and drugs within a month.

"Listen to this: the government are stating categorically that there's nothing to worry about, Rob... That the people infected are 'isolated incidents,' and there's only a slim chance of it becoming airborne."

He squeezed his eyes shut, but the images didn't disappear. Robert went way back now, to his graduation from training college. Remembering how proud his parents had been of him that day; at least he'd given them something before the crash two years later. And he had to admit to feeling a swell of pride himself as his name was called.

"Would you please step forward, Constable Robert Stokes." He could see the crowds of people, the flashes of cameras as they snapped pictures. The applause was deafening. He thought he could change the world back then, make a difference.

Fast forward to the riots when the system was breaking down. The stones and half bricks that were hurled, terrified people hitting them with lead piping, with sticks. So many faces, so much panic.

Robert and his family had moved out of the big city a long time ago, when Stevie was only four. Joanne had argued that she didn't want her husband on the streets facing gun crime and goodness knows what else. She didn't want Stevie growing up without a father (a sick joke, when he thought about it now).

"You ready?"

"Push the swing Dad, come on!"

"Okay, you asked for it."

"Higher, higher! Can we go on the roundabout next?"

"Sure thing."

"You're the best, Dad. The best."

Of course, he'd argued that there were pockets of violence everywhere, but he could see it from her point of view as well. In the end he'd listened and they'd upped sticks from the place where he was born and bred. But he hoped to return one day.

They hadn't really gone that far. Robert put in a transfer to a market town north of Nottingham called Mansfield, taking out a mortgage on a house between there and Ollerton. They'd been so happy there. He enjoyed community police work well enough and they lived in one of the most beautiful areas of England, only a short distance from rolling green fields, from woodland and forests – plenty of places to take Max out for walks. Yet close enough to 'civilisation' that Joanne could go shopping if she wanted, and pursue her ambitions to run her own accountancy business now that Stevie had gone to school. She always had been a whizz at maths, even when they were young...

"Hi, my name's Robert – I'm in the class above you."

"Joanne. You're friends with Tracey's brother, aren't you?"

"Yeah, that's right. A bunch of us are going out on Saturday, to the pictures. I was wondering...Well, do you want to come?"

The violence and the death found them all the same, all those years later. But it was the same countrywide in those dark days just before the Cull.

If the time before that had been a dream, then surely what came next was a nightmare; one from which he was constantly praying he'd wake. As friends on the force stopped turning up for work, as kids from Stevie's school were kept off sick, as more bullshit about the virus appeared in the papers and on the TV news... Nobody had taken it that seriously at first, not after all that business with SARS and Bird Flu. All that changed when they were smacked in the face with it.

Grimacing, Robert relived that night when Joanne had suddenly begun coughing in bed. Turning on the bedside lamp, he'd rolled over to find her holding a tissue up to her mouth. When she brought it away again, there was a bright patch of red there. And her eyes, *God in Heaven, her eyes...*

"You've got the most beautiful eyes, do you know that?"

"Charmer."

"It's true."

She was looking at him, petrified. They both knew what it meant – had seen enough about it to recognise the symptoms. Then they'd heard the coughing coming from Stevie's room as well.

The scene was playing out in his mind in slow motion: slamming open the door and snapping on the light; seeing crimson splattered all over the ten-year-old's duvet; Stevie crying because he didn't know what was happening to him; Max barking at the foot of his bed.

He'd bundled Joanne and Stevie into the car, knowing it was no use phoning for an ambulance. He and some of his colleagues had waited four or five hours for one to show up just a few days before. Tearing down the country roads, and thankful for all those lessons driving at speed when in pursuit, Robert was soon brought to a halt when he reached the nearest hospital.

The car park was overflowing. People had left their vehicles on grass verges, double and triple parked; wherever they could. He'd had to abandon his vehicle half a mile away from the building itself, then he'd carried Stevie on his shoulder, holding up Joanne with his other arm as they made their way to the Accident and Emergency department. The place was heaving, packed to the rafters with patients, some on trolleys, sitting or laying down – or both – and some making do with a couple of chairs for a bed, but most were strewn around the reception area and the corridors like beggars hoping for a handout. It was like something out of those history books from school, monochrome etchings showing people suffering from the Black Death. Doctors and nurses wearing scrubs and masks flitted about in front of him, until Robert grabbed the nearest one and demanded that the man examine his wife and child.

"Look around you, mate – all these people need attention, and they were all here before you."

"I'm a police officer. I –"

"You think that matters anymore?" shouted the man in scrubs. "You think it matters whether you're with the police, the emergency services or... or..." The man coughed. "People are dying... people..." He coughed again, except this time it was loud and wracking, chorusing with the others. The doctor pulled the mask away from his mouth, revealing the blood inside it. Then he looked up. "Oh, Jesus," was all he said.

It was at that moment the penny dropped. It really didn't matter anymore: nothing did. Because they were all fucked. The medicos didn't have a clue how to stop this; not even the government – of this country or any other – knew what to do.

Reluctantly, Robert returned home with Stevie and Joanne, made them as comfortable as he could, trying to force cough mixture and paracetamol down them as if they had a common cold or a dose of the flu. Robert waited it out with them, just like he was waiting here today. Knowing that any minute now, exposed as he'd been to the virus as well, he'd start coughing up blood. They'd all go together if they were going to go at all. He watched his wife and son pass their final few hours back in bed, in each other's arms, heaving up their liquefied lungs, fighting for breath. Max lay beside them on the mattress, whining as if he could sense what was about to happen. Robert had spent his whole life trying to protect people, and now he couldn't even protect his own family from the microscopic bastards ravaging their bodies. As they slipped away from him – Joanne first, taking a final, wheezing breath, followed by nothing; then Stevie, as he stroked the boy's blond hair, not knowing how to answer his questions about why he felt so ill or why Mum wasn't coughing anymore – Robert cried until he thought his tear ducts would burst.

"Help me, Dad... it hurts... make it stop!"

Max licked at Stevie's face, trying to bring him round. The boy didn't move.

Robert slumped over their still bodies, clutching their clothes, screaming at the universe, at God, at anything and everything, before finally exhaustion took him. Conversely now he didn't want to wake, to face what had just happened. But when he did at last, realising that this was all real, wrapping them in the blankets they'd died beneath, he held on to the one and only shred of hope left.

"Stop wriggling about, Stevie, you're taking all the covers. And let your Dad read his sports section."

"Kay."

Robert waited again, it must have been days... maybe even a couple of weeks, but he didn't feel the passage of the hours. This time it was his own death Robert anticipated. He willed the cough to come, the blood, for the virus to take him. He was ready for it. Oh, was he ready.

Robert existed on what was left in the house – tinned food, mainly, that Joanne had squirreled away; she was a terror for keeping the cupboards overstocked. Though he hardly felt like eating or drinking, his survival instinct was too strong to simply let himself starve to death. He fed Max, but left the door open so the animal could supplement his diet elsewhere if he chose. Or perhaps for another reason altogether.

"You're going to have to find a new owner soon, boy," he'd tell the old dog daily. "I'm not going to be here for much longer."

Then even that was snatched away from him by the men in gas masks, the hooded yellow-clad figures in their wagons, sent to scoop up the dead that littered the streets in a vain attempt to halt the spread of this infection. Even this far outside the towns and cities, the pavements were covered. The men broke down the doors of houses, checking inside, coming for the victims of the virus, spraying crosses on walls of buildings to be gutted with flamethrowers. Robert heard them approaching down the street, the megaphones blaring, but it hardly registered. Not until they were actually inside his house, waving their guns around, did he acknowledge their presence.

Max leapt at one of them, clawing at his plastic suit. The man struck the dog on the side of the head with the butt of his automatic rifle. Max fell to the floor with a whine and lay there twitching. Robert jumped out of his chair, but when a rifle was swung in his direction, he froze. He watched anxiously as a couple more men ascended the staircase. Was this what had become of the authorities in his absence, Robert wondered? Bully boys throwing their weight around?

"Two of 'em up here," came the muffled call from upstairs. "Been there a while as well, by the looks of things."

"Leave them where they are," Robert warned the man pointing the gun at him. "I'll be joining them soon enough."

The fellow gave a cold laugh. "You not seen the news lately, or what passes for it these days? If you haven't got it by now, chances are you never will. You must be O-Neg."

"O-Neg?" Robert gaped at him.

"Completely immune, you lucky bastard. Though it's a wonder you haven't caught somethin' else off them stiffs."

He couldn't take it in. He wasn't going to die after all – leastways, not from the virus. But Robert felt far from lucky: he'd lost everything he ever cared about and now he just wanted this all to end.

The men came back downstairs and told him he'd have to go with them. They were looking for people like Robert, apparently. Someone in 'power' thought they might actually be able to develop an antidote from them.

"And what... what's going to happen to Joanne and Stevie... My house?" Robert asked.

"Same as all the others with infected dead inside. *Poof*," said one of them, opening his fist like a flower in bloom. "The rest of us can't run the risk of catching it when we've gone to all this trouble."

Tears welled in Robert's eyes as a man to his left grabbed his arm, attempting to drag him outside. "I'm not going anywhere," he told them.

"Oh, yeah?" the first man brought up his rifle, aiming at Robert's head. He took a step towards the barrel, pressing the cold metal against his forehead.

"Do it, get it over with."

They all looked at each other. "He's too valuable," said the second man, shaking his head.

"Don't you understand? I don't want to live anymore!"

"Tough shit," said the third man, and they began to drag him out through the door. Robert elbowed one, lashed out at another, but all this earned him was a punch in the stomach.

Outside, two of them held Robert while the third sprayed a red 'X' on the front of his house and signalled to a truck behind. Robert looked on through the tears as more men climbed out with flamethrowers, tanks strapped to their backs. While he struggled, the 'firemen' disappeared inside, only to emerge moments later, leaving a trail of flames in their wake. And then, as if the rest of it hadn't been enough, something crawled from the spreading conflagration, looking for all the world like a demon emerging from Hell. Fur alight and whimpering with pain, Max made it a few steps down the path before collapsing into a burning heap. They hadn't even bothered to check he was dead before setting the house on fire. Or maybe they just didn't give a crap.

It was too much to bear. Robert reached up and pulled one of the men's gas masks off, then swung it at his other captor.

"*Oh-shit-oh-shit-oh-shit* –" gibbered the first man, fumbling to replace his mask, while Robert wrestled out of the other one's grip. Then he ran.

"Get him!"

The third man shot into the air, careful not to hit their prisoner, powerless to stop him.

Robert made it round the corner, glancing back over his shoulder only once. His house and everything in it was a blazing inferno, like many of the others nearby.

"Goodbye, sweetheart," he whispered to his wife. "Goodbye, son. I love you both very much."

The men would come after him, he knew that, but they wouldn't kill him. Instead they'd take him away somewhere to be prodded and poked, to provide a cure for the men in the masks and their superiors. People he'd once served (*no, not like that... never like that!*). So Robert ran, harder and faster than he ever had in his life. He didn't have a clue where he was going, just that he had to hide – he needed to get away from people: the living and the dead. If only those with O-Neg blood were immune, as the man back at his house had said, then most of the population had already been wiped out. Joanne would probably have been able to give him a more precise estimation... if she'd been alive.

On his journey he came across a small abandoned army surplus store, which had been partially looted, the window smashed and whatever was in the display long since stolen. That wasn't what interested him. Robert climbed through, hoping that there might be at least some of the things he'd need: a change of clothing, for starters. He found a pair of tough khaki combat trousers, a green t-shirt and a hooded top that fitted him, and a long, waxy outdoor coat. All that remained was to find a decent knife, a compass and some twine. Once he'd scrounged them up, he left whatever money he had on him by the till.

In the end it was a logical choice. Head for the woodlands at Rufford, where he'd spent so much time with Max, where he'd taken Joanne and Stevie occasionally at weekends and bank holidays. Robert would let the oak, silver birch and ferns hide him from what was left of society, live out his life until death took him from natural causes; hopefully soon. Maybe he'd just slip and break his neck one day...

Until then, he would get by. Robert would draw on the survival training he'd gone through as part of his job. He'd thought it was daft at the time, all those role-playing exercises, the team building out in the middle of nowhere. But he'd picked up quite a few things on those courses without even realising it. Unlike some of the lads, he'd actually been paying attention when the tutor had explained about things like making shelters and hunting if you were stranded. The first thing he'd done when he got to the woods was construct a simple lean-to between a couple of trees. He'd whittled down branches to make the poles, tying these together with the twine, then he'd covered the framework over with all the foliage he could find in the surrounding area. A new home, designed for one.

For water, to drink and to wash, he visited the huge lake at Rufford or trapped rain – filtering it through material torn from his disused clothing, then boiling it over a fire. The fire Robert made with a bow and drill, spinning the sharpened piece of wood on a fire board until it caught light. Using kindling, he'd build it up and warm himself.

For food, he picked edible mushrooms to begin with, then set simple snares and drag nooses to catch small animals, placed over trails or runs, attached to poles. These were large enough to comfortably pass over the creatures' heads, but then grew tighter as they struggled to get out. In his former life he might have felt some guilt about doing this, but it was a different world now. He was a different person. And he'd eaten meat all his life, hadn't he? Just never thought about where it came from. Now that was his responsibility, because Robert couldn't allow himself to become weak, not when the men might still come after him. He would catch ducks and geese by the water, using a bolas – two stones connected by the twine and thrown, after some degree of practice, around the bird's necks to weigh them down. And he'd hunt small game with a sharpened spear, not throwing it as you might see in the movies, because that was a good way to lose the weapon, but jabbing at his prey. Then he'd cook whatever he could find over a spit beside the lean-to.

But the bow he used to light the fire gave him other ideas as well. Robert selected a hardwood branch – dead and dry – about two metres or so long that was relatively free from knots and limbs. With his knife, he scraped down the largest end so that it had the same pull as the smaller one. The wood had a natural curve to it and he was careful to scrape from the side facing him, so it wouldn't snap the first time he used it. Robert spent ages attaching the twine and getting the pull of the bow just right. Moving on to the arrows, he used the straightest dry sticks he could find, scraping and straightening the shafts. For the arrowheads, he used sharpened stone – then attached feathers from his previous hunts to the shaft, notching the ends. In many respects all this was the easy part, because Robert only had limited experience with a bow and arrow, amounting to the handful of times he'd taken Stevie for archery lessons on holidays.

So he'd practised; for many hours. Drawing back the bow, letting the arrows fly into a target carved on a tree. To begin with Robert had been miles away from the trunk, let alone the target, but gradually his aim improved.

Just like darts... only with bigger arrows, he'd tell himself.

He recalled the day that he hit the bull's eye – he'd been determined to do it before the dark skies emptied their load. The sense of satisfaction was tremendous, and for a split second he'd almost forgotten where he was and how he came to be there, turning and expecting Joanne and Stevie to be behind him, clapping.

"Way to go, Dad, way to go."

"Quite the outdoorsman, now, aren't we?" Joanne's beautiful eyes were filled with love, not terror. Her smiling mouth not stained with blood anymore.

But all was quiet except for the usual sound of birdsong.

As the first spots of rain came down, Robert had hung his head, pulling the hood up. Then he'd returned to camp for the night, walking past the cloth catchments collecting the water.

Once again, the days blurred into each other – and Robert could only go by the fact that the grass on the once neatly-trimmed golf course and the parks was now knee-length, that the beard he'd begun growing was thick and bushy, that he'd had to begin stockpiling meat in the ice houses at Rufford, man-made stone buildings set into mounds of earth that would keep it chilled, and insulated by the soil. He'd busted off the barred doors and used them as his own personal larder.

The meat mainly came from sheep in the fields, in particular the shaggy Hebrideans that had been introduced to the scrubland before the Cull: easy, slow-moving targets. But he'd noticed that deer were running free now too in the woods, and this was a chance to really put his new-found skills with the bow to good use. The first time he'd attempted a kill, he'd completely messed it up, stumbling through the undergrowth like the most uncoordinated of bulls blundering into Ming vases, alerting the startled deer to his presence. Since that day, he'd learnt to be very stealthy, and adept at blending into his surroundings. He'd bagged more deer and sheep than he could remember, ensuring enough to eat through the past two winters at least; and enough skins and wool to keep him warm during the colder months.

But today he was hunting something altogether different. Something that was worth all the waiting, the crouching, the memories that had come flooding back. Because there, in the clearing, was the magnificent sight of a stag: its strong grey and white torso moving fluidly as it paused to sniff at the air.

Robert held his breath. It was the ultimate test of his hunting skills; one false move and he'd tip off his quarry. Through the long grass and ferns, he looked at the animal, and he was so sure it was looking back at him. All hunted creatures were aware of being watched – if only on a subconscious level – he'd observed. It was the same thing he'd seen when he was just about to give chase to a pickpocket or bootlegger. They'd make a break for it just a fraction of a second before spotting Robert. The trick was to be quicker than them.

If he was going to make his move, it had to be right now. Robert rose, breaking cover, the leaves, twigs, and branches he'd used to camouflage himself falling from his body. Though he'd been hunkered down low, unmoving all this time, his legs were far from stiff and his muscles held him steady. Simultaneously, he raised his bow, which could easily have been mistaken for another branch, another piece of camouflage, were it not for the taut twine attached to its length. Robert and the stag exchanged a glance, the merest of heartbeats and yet lasting forever.

Hunter and prey.

It was only during this time that he felt something akin to being alive again, felt a surge of energy that reminded him he wasn't just a shadow, simply a ghost of his former self.

But in this animal, he also recognised a kindred spirit; a once proud creature reduced to a victim by circumstance.

Robert lowered the bow, nodding to himself and to the stag. The animal stood stunned for a second or two, not understanding how it could still be alive – the hunter had him in his sights. But it didn't question for long, running off back into the woods; vanishing from sight.

Robert watched it go, knowing that another kill had never really been the purpose of this exercise. He didn't need any more meat, and didn't hunt just for sport – Robert didn't have a trophy room in the lean-to. They'd shared something in that one brief moment, the stag and him. Both knew what it was like to be on the run, what it was like to escape.

Above all else, both Robert and the stag knew that he could have taken that life, but chose not to.

All of which meant that the hunter, the hooded man, was still the victor.

And so it was his turn to disappear back into the trees.

CHAPTER THREE

How had this happened? How had they gone from being the hunters to the prey?

One minute, they'd been the top dogs around here, now they were facing a serious ultimatum. Granger still couldn't quite believe it, back to being pushed around again, just like when he was growing up. Back to following orders.

In the past it had been his mother's boyfriends issuing them, a succession of no-hopers who seemed to view him as their personal slave half the time. His mother said nothing to them, mainly because she did the same: *fetch me this, fetch me that, make us something to eat, get us something to drink.* And if he didn't comply immediately, he was looking at being beaten around the living room of their tiny council flat in Finchley. Granger might have blamed it on growing up without a father, except that particular 'role model' would probably have made things worse, from what little he'd heard. That's if he could have stayed out of jail long enough.

None of the boyfriends had lasted, not once they'd got what they wanted out of Granger's mum: somewhere to stay rent free for a while and someone who wouldn't complain in the bedroom when they forced her to do the most depraved things. He could hear them at night, no matter how much he pulled the pillows up around his ears – the moans and the screams, and, sometimes, the crying afterwards. That was when he wanted to go to her, when he felt what you were supposed to feel for a mother. The last boyfriend, Jez, had been the worst of the lot. He'd even been dealing from their flat. And, once, when they were alone in the place together, Granger had said something back to Jez so he'd pulled a handgun on him, one of those customised replica imports from abroad.

"You're a smart kid, aren't you? Got a smart mouth... How smart are you now, eh? Eh?" he'd said, turning it on him. Granger closed his eyes, fully expecting the man to shoot. Luckily, his mother had come home at that moment, and Jez had tucked the gun quickly back away in his jeans.

It wasn't even as if school was an escape from what was going on. His teachers barked at him because he hadn't done his homework – especially his old French teacher, Mr Dodds. When did he ever have time? Where was he supposed to work? As for the other kids, he never fitted in with them either. They all had their little gangs and they made it abundantly clear he wasn't welcome in any of them, pounding it into him when he didn't get the message. As for girls, well, who would look at him twice?

When he'd left home at sixteen, bailing as soon as he could to move into a shared digs only one step up from a squat – his mother's cries of "You ungrateful little sod!" still ringing in his ears – it had been the people down the dole office who'd lorded it over him. They sent him to interviews for jobs he so obviously wasn't qualified to do. Until, eventually, he'd been taken pity on. Hired as a labourer: paid peanuts for the privilege of being a dogsbody to the other workers on the building site.

"Hey, streaky bacon," a site manager called Mick always used to call across, after Granger's gangly teenaged frame, "we're parched over here – fetch us another round of tea, will you? Come on, move your skinny arse!" Then, when he brought the tray across, they'd make fun of him again, getting him to pick up tools from the floor, then kicking him over. It was just a bit of fun, they said. That's all.

Granger used to wish they would drop dead; wished every last one of them would just drop dead, in fact.

He'd never expected his wish to come true.

People hacked and coughed in the streets, spraying blood over pavements, falling where they stood in some cases.

And while everyone else got sick from the disease they were calling the AB Virus, Granger finally got a break. Instead of coughing up blood, his actually saved him. Against his better judgement, he'd called round to see his mother while she was still alive... just. Even when she was dying, she'd ordered him to fetch her stuff; bring pills so she could get better.

"There isn't anything that can do that," he'd told her.

"You... *ack*... you fetch me something right now you... *ack*... you fucking –"

"You ain't going to get better, Mum!" he said, finally losing his temper. "There isn't a medicine on this planet that can cure you. How d'you feel about that?"

She coughed and spat blood in his face, though whether it was intentional or not Granger didn't know.

"I'll be seeing you," he told her as he began walking out, knowing full well that he never would again. Then he'd gone to the bathroom and washed his face, drying it on the towel. It was as he was doing so that he noticed a shape behind the shower curtain. Granger jumped, but the thing didn't move. Slowly, he reached out and pulled back the plastic curtain. Jez was lying there in the bath, a needle sticking out of his arm and sticky redness dribbling from his mouth. He'd OD'd rather than face the final stages of the virus. Granger had seen plenty of dead bodies lately, but not up close like this. He shook his head, remembering what a bastard this man had been. Bending down, he cocked his head and whispered, "Who's the smart one now?" Then he lifted the body, checking the back of the man's jeans for the pistol he always kept about his person. Granger had taken the pistol, and turned his back on Jez, his mother, and the place where he'd grown up.

To Granger's mind, he was at last reaping the rewards of years of misery. During the Culling Year, when those in charge had attempted to stop the spread of the plague, there had been rich pickings for the likes of him. Rumours flew around of soldiers trying to take control, even of something big taking shape on Salisbury Plain, but it hadn't affected Granger's plans. He'd moved relatively freely from place to place, taking whatever he liked from the shops, stuffing his pockets with money (it never occurred to him at the time that it would be useless later on) and generally having the time of his life... while everyone else was losing theirs.

And he encountered more like him, young men who saw opportunity in the wake of this new turn of events. Granger befriended a few – like Ennis, who he found working his way through the entire stock of beef burgers in a deserted McDonald's: it was where he'd used to work before it all hit the fan. Others he gently 'persuaded' to join him. Just having the pistol helped in that respect, though later they found all the weapons they needed when the men in yellow suits who were supposed to be cleaning up the streets came down with the virus too. Their numbers grew, all with a common goal – to help themselves to everything they'd been denied before. Granger finally had a gang to call his own and, though he knew there must be more in other parts of London, beyond that even, they ruled the roost in their little corner of the world. They called themselves 'The Jackals' and operated out of Barnet's council offices in Whetstone. Granger liked the irony of that; sticking it to the owners of his former home.

Girls, the ones that were left alive – and the ones who needed protection from other dangers on the streets these days – suddenly found Granger irresistible. Some of them were pretty good looking, as well; the kind he wouldn't have stood even the remotest chance with before.

At last they were the ones on top. None of them, especially Granger, would ever have to take another order or do as they were told ever again.

Or so they'd thought.

Then came the night of the attack. The first Granger knew about what was happening was when he got a garbled message over his walkie-talkie. It was Ennis, on watch outside, screaming that a bunch of men had come out of nowhere and taken down a handful of Jackals at a stroke. Granger, who was in the middle of making paper aeroplanes out of old council records, rushed to the window to see.

Men on bikes were shooting at the building, making passes and picking off the Jackals on guard duty downstairs. They were much better trained than his gang. Older too, nothing like the punks they'd fended off in the past.

"Ennis..." he shouted into the mouthpiece. "Ennis, get back inside and bring the rest of the guys with you! We'll hold them off from up here." But, even as he said it, he heard windows smashing from several different directions at once. The men were entering the building right now, giving them no time to prepare. Looking back, Granger would realise just how amateurish The Jackals had been – how much more they could have fortified the building in readiness for just such an attack. Though even then, he doubted whether they'd have stood a chance against merciless professionals like these.

Granger called to the rest of his 'men' further inside the open-plan office, telling them to group at the stairwell, just by the lift doors. There were hardly any replies.

By the time he got down there it was all over. Those Jackals who hadn't been shot were on their knees in the entranceway to the office itself, hands behind their heads. Yet more were being marched down the stairs, along with some of the girls who'd been keeping them company. Granger raised his pistol, the one he'd taken from Jez so long ago and which he always kept about him – mainly as a reminder that he would never be pushed around again.

Several automatic rifles swivelled in his direction, clacking, ready to fire. Granger's gun hand began to shake.

"Gentlemen... Gentlemen... *Écoutez*!" came a voice from the doorway. There was a distinct accent that Granger recognised from those French lessons with Mr Dodds. "Hold your fire. This is obviously the very person we have come here to speak with." The man the voice belonged to came forward. He had dark eyes, which bored into Granger, making him feel cold inside. He smoothed down his black and grey combats as if he were wearing a Savile Row suit.

"Get out," shouted Granger, his voice wavering. "Get out now or..." But he had nothing to back the threat up with.

The guy facing him, their leader – he could tell by the way he was carrying himself – smiled chillingly. "Oh, I believe we will stay for a while. Won't we?" he said to his men, and the closest half dozen – obviously his elite – nodded. "After all, we have a lot to discuss."

Discuss? Granger couldn't see much room for manoeuvre in that department; it was a pretty clear-cut situation. This man had them by the balls. "What... what do you want?"

"What does any of us want?" answered the man. "Respect, loyalty... Fear."

They both knew he had the latter, and probably commanded the others through it. "I'm... I'm listening," Granger told him.

"Of course you are. All right. My proposition is simple," explained the man, taking off a pair of black leather gloves and revealing the rings on his fingers. "It's one I have put to several little 'operations' like yours, on the way to London and through it. Some listened. Some didn't."

Granger raised an eyebrow. "Proposition?"

"Yes. *Un choix*. You understand? A choice." He walked past one of the girls being held captive, who was only wearing a shirt, and ran a finger down her cheek. She flinched and he gave a small laugh, revealing hideously yellow teeth. Looking back over at Granger, he said, "You and your people can either join us or..."

"Or what?" Granger demanded, albeit half-heartedly, regretting it even as the words were tumbling from his mouth.

"Tanek?" called the leader to one of his men. The crowds parted and a huge, bulky soldier with olive skin and short hair stepped forward. Granger couldn't help thinking that he should drop the 'e' in his name and just go with 'Tank.' He held Ennis by the scruff of the neck, was practically carrying him like that, the boy's feet barely touching the floor.

"Granger... I'm sorry, I –" Tanek threw him down on the ground.

"Now," began the man wearing the smart combats, "show our friend here what the alternative to joining us would be."

Tanek unhooked the crossbow dangling on a strap from his shoulder, and aimed the weapon at Ennis's head.

"No!" shouted Granger, raising his pistol.

There was a nod from their leader, and Tanek turned in Granger's direction. Quicker than anything he'd ever seen in his life, the larger man had fired, the bolt catching Granger's gun hand, sending the pistol flying out of his grasp and pinning his hand to the wall. He shrieked in pain as the bolt drove itself through his palm. Tanek then turned the crossbow – so unusual in its design, not needing to be reloaded, it seemed – back on Ennis. He looked up pleadingly at Granger for a moment before the bolt was shot directly into his head.

Granger howled, the pain in his hand forgotten for a moment. His friend, his 'second in command' was dead. The girl in the shirt was shaking and crying, and the other members of The Jackals – how stupid that name sounded now – gawked at Ennis's body in disbelief.

"You bastard!" Granger spat.

The man in combats pointed to his chest with one finger, like it had nothing to do with him. "You asked. We gave a demonstration. As simple as that." His accent grew thicker with each word. "Now, what you have to ask yourself is, can we get past this and work together?"

Work together? He had to be joking. After what he'd just done to Ennis... But Granger knew what the option was. When this man had said there was a choice, he'd been lying. Really there was no choice at all.

"So, your answer, if you please." The man clasped his hands behind his back, tapping one booted foot. "I am waiting."

Granger, still in agony from the bolt in his palm, hung his head, nodding.

"Excellent, then allow me to introduce myself. My name is De Falaise. My aim is to bring order to this country, *oui*? Like your comrades here, England is on its knees. I intend to offer it the same choice I gave you: a killing blow or the chance to serve."

Granger stared at him; this guy was insane.

"Myself and my men are heading north," De Falaise continued, visibly enjoying his speech. "As my ancestors recognised, the seat of true power is not the capital at all. That, *mon ami*, is just for the tourists. It is from another place entirely that we will expand. We will reach out to every corner of this island, crushing any form of resistance. You are now a part of my army, making history, as it was once made long ago. In years to come, people will look back on this moment as the start of something truly wondrous."

He actually believes what he's saying, thought Granger. *He wants to become like the King of England or something...* But then, stranger things had happened. And wasn't it only what Granger himself had done on a smaller scale? Hadn't this been his kingdom until De Falaise came along? Now, instead, he was one of the subjects in another man's realm – or maybe even the fool?

De Falaise returned Granger's stare. "So, do we understand each other?"

Granger nodded reluctantly again.

"Then answer me."

"Yes," Granger whispered. "We understand each other."

"Louder."

Granger gritted his teeth then raised his voice. "I said we understand each other."

De Falaise grinned. "Good." He reached up and yanked the bolt out of the wall, and Granger's palm. The younger man screamed again as blood flowed freely from the wound. "You may want to bandage that before we set off."

Granger, breath coming in hisses, gasped: "S-set... set off?"

"That is correct. We leave for the army base at Hendon within the next half hour," De Falaise informed Granger, then told the rest of them: "Make yourselves ready."

As his men escorted The Jackals out, Tanek joined De Falaise standing in front of Granger. De Falaise handed the bloody bolt back to its owner, who wiped it with a cloth. "Do you know, I can see this being the start of a beautiful business arrangement, *non*?"

Granger sneered at him and De Falaise laughed.

He laughed long and hard, almost until it was time to leave the council offices at Whetstone.

CHAPTER FOUR

AT FIRST HE thought they had come for him, finally.

Robert was aware of voices before he saw the group of men. They were skirting the edge of the woodland, about seven or eight of them in total. He'd been checking some of his snares when the sound of their talking carried to him. Robert had frozen. He hadn't heard another human voice in as long as he could remember – not since the men in the yellow suits...

"You must be O-Neg... Completely immune, you lucky bastard..."

"He's too valuable..."

"Get him!"

Surely they couldn't have tracked him down after all this time? There would be a certain irony to it if they had. If the hunter was again being hunted.

Leaving the looping trap, and stuffing the last wild rabbit into his skin-pouch, he'd moved swiftly and silently along the edge of the wood, before climbing up a tree to gain a better view. The first time he'd tried this it had been like being a kid again, doing something forbidden, and he heard his late mother's words in his head: *"Come down from there at once, Robert, before you really hurt yourself!"*

There was a part of him that wanted to get hurt this time, wanted to get hurt severely, in fact. Fall down and crack his skull open; wouldn't that be nice? But there was just as big a part of him that really didn't want to break his back and not be able to move, laying there dying slowly. Not a good end.

Better than Joanne's. Better than Stevie's.

It was like the bow and arrow: the more times he'd done it, the better he'd become. Now, Robert was so used to it, he could scale even the largest of oaks. Up through the branches he went; strong hands, roughened by the elements, hauled him higher and higher. The tips of his boots found notches and ridges, like a mountain climber scaling a rock face.

When he was high enough, he looked down at the sceneand saw the men. No yellow plastic suits, no gas masks or flamethrowers. Just blokes dressed in ordinary clothes, if a little the worse for wear: trousers, shirts, some in jumpers. They were carrying bags, had backpacks slung over shoulders. They knew each other well, were chatting and... yes, even laughing once or twice. Robert's eyes scanned the men but he could see no sign of rifles, automatic or otherwise. Which begged the question, who were they and where were they going?

He decided to find out. Call it a policeman's curiosity, which he didn't even know he still had, or an attempt to find out as much as he could about a potential enemy. Whichever way you looked at it, he was on the move.

Robert leaped from one tree to the next, trailing the men at height until they headed out across a field. If he wanted to know where they were going now, Robert had to break cover and follow on foot. But this didn't mean exposing his position. The men would still have no idea he was behind them.

As he crested a small hill, Robert saw where they were making for. In a big field just off the road, folk were gathering in fairly large numbers – large for post-virus times, at any rate. Dozens of them: men, women and children. Some brought sacks, some trunks, some holdalls. From his hiding position behind a hedgerow, Robert saw a couple of cars, a couple of vans, but these were few and far between. He guessed petrol was a rare commodity these days, with nobody to keep refilling pumps, without anyone to bring it over from abroad.

Some had reverted to using horses for transportation. Robert watched as a woman dismounted from her steed, swinging a bag down as she went. Set up here and there were makeshift tables, trays with legs, or blankets laid on the ground. People were getting things out of their bags to place on them, arranging them carefully.

My God! It's a bloody car boot sale. Robert thought to himself. To his surprise, he found the corners of his mouth curling up. *An honest to goodness car boot sale!*

Only there weren't enough 'car boots' to justify the name. It was more like a market, just not as well laid out as those in Mansfield. The purpose was the same, however. Except that here the traders were swapping items rather than paying money for them. In this 'society' what use were coins and bits of paper with the Queen's head on them? This part of England, at least, appeared to have regressed back to the barter system. Having seen nothing of his fellow man in an age, Robert was suddenly engrossed in the unfolding dramas, the flurry of activity as people from miles around gathered to do business. He'd completely forgotten what it was like to be in the proximity of other human beings, to have that contact with them. Was there a part of him now that missed it? No, it was better that he shut himself away, pretended the rest of the world didn't exist. Live out the remainder of his life ignorant of how the human race was getting along. It had no need for him and vice-versa.

But the same twist of fate that had saved him, killing the two most important people to him in the process, had other ideas.

Robert had been so distracted by the ad hoc market, he didn't notice the man behind him until it was too late.

"What ye doin' skulking about there?" said a voice with a thick, Derbyshire accent. "Aye, you there – you with the hood on. Get up and turn yessen around. And don't get any funny ideas about that bow yer carryin'."

Robert rose slowly, trying to stop himself from shaking. Was it fear or just excitement at being addressed after so long, at having someone other than a wild animal acknowledge his existence? He heard the distinctive click-clack of a gun being primed for action. And, sure enough, when he turned around, he was greeted with the sight of a man – early forties, though he might have been younger, it was hard to tell after what he must have gone through in the past couple of years – and he was holding up a double-barrelled shotgun. It was a farmer's weapon, probably wielded by an ex-farmer. There'd certainly been enough of them round these parts. The ruddy complexion had faded somewhat, but Robert could tell that he must still spend a lot of his time outside. The pigeon-chested man wore a checked shirt beneath a tank top with holes in it, his trousers were loose as if he'd lost weight, and his boots had definitely seen better days.

"I'll say it again. What ye doin' spying back here?"

Robert said nothing, not even when the man lifted the shotgun higher, not quite aiming at him, but not pointing it away, either. Robert held up his hands to show he meant him no harm.

"What's a matter, can't ye speak or summat? Bit slow, eh?"

Robert shook his head. There was nothing wrong with his faculties. It had just been so long since he'd spoken, he wasn't even sure if he could anymore. Carefully, he began to reach across into his open coat.

"Keep yer hands where I can see 'em," instructed the man, moving forward.

"I..." began Robert. The sensation of talking felt odd; alien even. The look of shock on his face must have registered, because the man frowned.

"Just what's yer game? We don't want no trouble at the market."

"No game. No trouble," Robert assured him. With each word, his voice grew stronger. "I've just come along to trade."

"That so?"

"It is. If you'll let me...?" Robert reached into his coat again, very slowly, the shotgun trained on him the whole time. "Easy... easy... See, in my pouch."

The man drew nearer to get a better look. "Rabbits?"

"Rabbits," repeated Robert.

Then the 'farmer' began to laugh: long, hard chuckles that caused his frame to shake. "Oh, that's a good un," he said eventually. "Rabbits... Judas Priest! What yer thinking of swappin' for them scrawny devils?"

Robert shrugged, pulling down his hood. "Whatever I can."

Lowering his shotgun, the other man wiped the tears from his eyes. "Aye, I'd be interested to see it an' all. Well, come on. Let's take yer down there, then, before all the best bargains are gone."

For a second, Robert hesitated, the very thought of meeting, of mixing with that number of people was terrifying. What if the men after him should happen by? "Is... is it safe?" asked Robert.

The man frowned. "Safe? What yer talkin' about?"

He didn't have a choice, he had to ask. "The... the men in yellow suits. The ones who set fire to the bodies."

He looked at Robert like he was insane. "Where yer bin, on Mars or somethin'?"

"Something," admitted Robert.

"They haven't bin round for ages, that lot. Not since the early days."

"What happened to them?"

"Dead," said the man, his face stern. "Like everyone else."

"So there was no cure?"

"Cure?" He laughed again, but there was a bitterness to it this time. "There were never any cure. Look, are ye comin' to the market or not? I haven't got all day."

Robert gave a small nod, and they began to walk across the field. The closer they came, the more he wanted to run – even though he knew the fear was irrational.

What if he's wrong – what if they're still out there somewhere, looking for you?

You heard what he said, they're all dead. Only the O-Negs are left. It's the grand total of the human race.

But...

"So, yer a poacher?" the man said, interrupting Robert's argument with himself. He nodded at the bow to emphasise what he meant.

"Can you poach something that doesn't belong to anyone anymore?"

"I meant before, like?"

"Not exactly," Robert said. *And you wouldn't believe me if I told you.*

They were nearly at the market and Robert could feel all eyes turning upon him. He wasn't a regular here, and everyone knew it. It was the same feeling as when he used to enter an unfamiliar neighbourhood to make an arrest.

"Well, 'ere we are then," said the man. "My name's Bill, by the way. Bill Locke." He stuck out his hand and Robert examined it for a moment before looking back up at his face. Such a simple act of humanity, of friendship, and it threw him completely. Then he reached out and shook it. The man's grip was rough and firm, once again emphasising that he'd worked with his hands all his life; Robert couldn't compete with that – too many years of domestic bliss before embracing the wild.

He noticed the man was waiting for something, then realised he hadn't told him his own name. "I'm..." *I was... I used to be a man called Stokes. But what am I now? Who am I now?* "They call me Robert."

"How do then, Rob."

Bill finished pumping his hand, then let him go. Robert noticed that the people in the market seemed to accept him more now that they'd seen the handshake. Whatever Bill did here, whether it was organise the events, provide security, or simply trade, he was well respected.

Robert looked around at what was on offer. On one stall there was hand-made pottery, plates and cups; on another, knitwear. A young woman of about twenty was selling these, but Robert imagined some old lady with O-Neg blood, sat somewhere knitting with whatever wool they could get her. And there were piles of other clothing, manufactured before the Cull: no dresses and skirts for women now, though, only more practical fare like trousers and jackets. One man had axes, knives, hammers – tools of various sizes and shapes – set out in front of him, obviously scavenged from hardware shops. A few batteries caught Robert's eye, mainly because he hadn't seen anything even remotely technological in so long. He found medical supplies on another blanket, antiseptics, pills – some identifiable, some not – plasters and bandages. There were suitcases, haversacks and holdalls, which at first he thought were just what the items had been carried here in, but then he saw people bartering for these, too.

There were tins of food, just like the ones Joanne had stockpiled and on which he'd lived after his family had died, but there was more fresh food to be found than anything else. Fruit and vegetables, which looked more appetising than anything he'd ever seen in a supermarket. Someone had taken their time growing these: ripe tomatoes, apples, runner beans, potatoes, most of them sold by a willowy woman with auburn hair. Very few pieces of fruit from more exotic climes, Robert noted, such as bananas or oranges. Hardly surprising now that there were fewer people to bring them in from overseas (*and just what was happening over there anyway – were they in the same state as this country?*). Everything here smacked of a survival instinct he could relate to, of human beings making do in the face of adversity. The ones that were left behind were obviously slowly forming communities of their own. He could tell that by the handfuls that had been sent to represent them at the market.

The meat – pork, beef and chicken – looked mouth-wateringly good, and now Robert understood why Bill had laughed when he showed him the rabbits. They weren't even skinned or properly prepared. Maybe next time he could bring some tastier treats from the ice houses.

Next time? What the hell was he thinking about...? Robert couldn't come back here again. Couldn't allow himself to get drawn into the world again, to make friends, to talk with other people. Even if it were true and the men in those gas masks were no longer a problem, he still had his waiting to do, was still sworn to live out the rest of his life – however long or short that was – alone.

"Your first time here, huh?" said someone to the left of him. Lost in his thoughts, Robert gave a start. Then he looked over and his mouth dropped open.

Stevie?

He blinked once, twice, then saw the reality of who was in front of him.

The boy was twelve or thirteen, with a scruffy mop of hair that had once been blond – possibly could be again given a proper wash – and deep green eyes. He was wearing a baggy tracksuit, bound by a belt round the middle with numerous pockets attached. He looked like he was playing superhero, but Robert knew full well that every single pocket would be filled with something important. The lad had a rucksack slung over his shoulder, which appeared to be full.

Robert opened his mouth, then closed it again, having completely forgotten what the kid had said.

"I haven't seen you here before," he continued, not put off by Robert's silence. The boy looked him up and down. "Would've remembered you, that's for sure. You have much to trade?"

Robert shook his head.

"That's a pity. It's a good market today, lots on offer. Isn't always that way, you know. Have to make the most of it while you can. I'm Mark, by the way."

Again, Robert just gaped at him. Was there a resemblance, or was it just in his head? True, Mark had a similar hair-tone, but his eyes were a different colour and he was much thinner, the cheekbones less padded with puppy fat.

"Who you here with, Mark?"

"What do you mean?"

"Your parents –" began Robert, then kicked himself when Mark looked down. Of course they were dead. Everyone was dead. "I'm sorry... Look, haven't you got anyone who takes care of you?"

Mark scowled at that one. "I take care of myself," he replied indignantly. "I'm not a kid."

Robert shook his head. "That wasn't what I meant."

"I find stuff myself, bring it here myself, trade it myself. Just like the others."

"There are more like you?" said Robert, barely able to conceal the shock from his voice.

"'Course. We're not professional collectors, mind, just snatch what we need to get by from the towns and cities." He appeared very proud of his profession. "We can get into places other people can't. And we're small enough to hide if there's trouble. I've got plenty of hiding places, me. So we go in, we come back out again. Easy."

"My God," Robert whispered to himself. He'd once seen a documentary about orphans who lived on the streets – or more specifically in the sewers of Bucharest, Romania. As the people had filmed them for the news report, bottles floated past in the dirty water and cockroaches climbed over the pipes where they slept. They were called 'The Forgotten Children.' When Robert looked at Mark he saw the same thing. In the wake of the virus, the Cull, these were England's forgotten children, left to fend for themselves, because if they didn't they would die. What kind of future did they have to look forward to?

"It's no big deal," said Mark, smiling. He reached into his bag and pulled out a chocolate bar with a purple wrapper, then proffered it to Robert. "You want one? I got dozens."

Robert held up a hand to say no, then reconsidered. How long had it been since he'd tasted chocolate? Far longer than he'd been in the woods. It used to be his weakness at Christmas and Easter. Part of him was tempted now, but another part was linking this small pleasure to those times in his life when he'd been happy; seeing Stevie opening his presents, his eggs, Joanne playfully threatening that she'd take the box of Dark Delicious away from Robert as they sat watching the holiday movies. What right did he have to that now? "No," he said to Mark, "thanks, but no."

Mark shrugged and opened the bar, biting off a chunk with the same glee that Stevie always did.

Stevie.

Robert was suddenly aware that he could no longer stay here. That if he did he might just break down and start bawling his eyes out in front of all these people, in front of Mark. The pain was still too real for him, still too close.

"I've got to go," he said, voice shaky.

"Wait..." Mark started, but Robert was already walking away from the boy, from the market.

"I'm sorry," Robert called back over his shoulder, pulling up his hood as he went. He strode past Bill, who was haggling with another man over the 'price' of an onion.

"Off s'soon?" said Bill. "Any joy with them rabbits?" When Robert didn't answer him, he laughed and said: "Thought not. Better luck next time, eh? We're 'ere most Wednesdays, all day..."

But the voice was fading as Robert broke into a run. He sprinted across the field, not daring to look back. He just needed to return to the safety of the woods, the cover the trees and foliage gave him.

Just like Mark, he had his own hiding places.

CHAPTER FIVE

As De Falaise sat back in the seat, he'd pull down his sunglasses occasionally and glance in the wing mirror of the Bedford armoured truck. From this angle it was difficult to see the extent of the line, but he knew it stretched right back along the motorway, zigzagging its way around the stationary cars with skeletons at the wheels. From the air it would have looked like a convoy: one of the wagon trains from the Old West, or even an army during the crusades (as a student of history, these kinds of comparisons amused him). But instead of being on horseback or in wagons, his men were encased in Challenger 2 battle tanks, Warrior Mechanised Combat Vehicles, Hummer muscle jeeps, Land Rover Wolves, open top WIMIKs, and other Bedfords: some capable of carrying up to twenty troops. Keeping them all in line were motorbikes patrolling the length of the convoy, ridden by his trusted elite, brought across the Channel with him.

Like Tanek, driving this truck. The olive-skinned man stared ahead at the road, changing gears every so often, but never taking his eyes off the route ahead. De Falaise admired his single-mindedness. It reminded him of his own. He recalled the first time he'd come across the soldier, in a small provincial town in Turkey. De Falaise had been engaged in a highly illegal gun-running operation when the virus struck, and was quite grateful that people began dropping like flies: he'd been well on his way to getting caught... or killed. He subsequently decided to make his way towards Istanbul, with a plan to somehow travel through Europe and get back home to France. The plan wasn't very clear in his mind, mainly because it was every man for himself in the region at that precise time. What money he had acquired from the deal meant nothing, and De Falaise was beginning to regret handing over the firearms he'd snuck across the borders.

Bullets now seemed to be the only way to get anything, and the only way to stay alive.

He certainly hadn't expected to run into his soon-to-be second-in-command outside a small watering hole there. The bar had been quite full, some of the men inside immune to the disease that was sweeping its way across the world, some of them in the later stages of it and desperate to drink themselves to death. De Falaise had realised long ago that there was no point in attempting to outrun the virus, nor was there any point in trying to avoid the people who were coughing up blood everywhere. If it was his time, then so be it; he'd meet the Devil and shake his hand. Who knows, maybe he'd even get a line of congratulation or two for services rendered. As it turned out, De Falaise was one of those spared, so perhaps his 'good' work hadn't gone unnoticed after all. *The Devil looks after his own,* isn't that what they always said? If so, then he'd also looked after this hulking great brute of a man who'd been taking on all comers in that very bar.

Drawing nearer, the Frenchman watched, increasingly impressed, as the fighter picked up men and swung them over his head, using moves he'd never come across before to floor others (De Falaise had later found out this fighting style was called krav maga, a martial art taught by the Israeli army, which Tanek had adapted to suit his own purposes). Breaking one man's nose, driving his fist so hard into it that there was nothing left of the bridge, Tanek had incapacitated another by arcing his forearm and crushing the man's windpipe with a crack that made De Falaise wince. It was then that De Falaise spotted an attacker creeping up on Tanek, knife drawn and ready to spring. He shouted out to the big man to warn him, but Tanek was already pivoting – with a grace that belied his size – and was unslinging what looked like a rifle. It wasn't until the two bolts had been fired, striking the man squarely in the chest, that De Falaise recognised it as a crossbow; but no ordinary one (modified by Tanek himself based on ancient Chinese *chu-ko-nu* repeater designs, able to fire from a magazine without the need for reloading). The rest of the men fled from the scene after that, leaving Tanek and De Falaise alone.

Tanek had raised the crossbow, inserting another magazine, and for a moment De Falaise thought he might shoot him too. But no. Tanek walked over, kicking fallen chairs and bodies aside, and stood before him. Then, in that hybrid Southern European-Middle Eastern accent of his barely anyone got to hear, Tanek thanked him for the warning.

Taking a couple of bottles of whiskey and two glasses from behind the now deserted bar, De Falaise and Tanek drank and talked, though the larger man would only disclose the least amount of information about himself that he could get away with, all in that monotone voice of his. Information like the fact that he'd once worked as a torturer and knew every single pressure point on the body, especially those that caused the maximum of pain. De Falaise, in turn, told Tanek why he was there, what he was doing, and what he was about to do next.

"I've been in this business for some time, *mon ami*, but have always had a craving to see the guns I sell put to better use. To build up an army of my own." He recalled joyous times as a child, playing with toy soldiers – when he wasn't constructing gallows out of Meccano, much to his parents' dismay – sending his troops into 'battle,' relishing the authority it gave him even at that young age. "It strikes me that we can look upon this little... incident as either a setback or an opportunity," De Falaise had said, knocking back a shot of the whisky. "And I, for one, have always been an opportunist. There is much to gain from being organised where others are not, from being able to take advantage of a certain situation and use it fully. History teaches us that, if nothing else." And to emphasise his point, he quoted the Carpetbaggers at the end of the American Civil War, who had come from the North, exploiting the South's weakened state to gain money and power. He laughed when he saw Tanek's eyes glazing over. "I apologise. The subject has always fascinated me. History goes in cycles, that is what my old teacher once said. Now he was a dying breed of patriot."

The more he talked, about moving up into Europe, about gathering a band of men as he went, about taking their fair share of the glory on offer, the more De Falaise convinced himself that night. Before, he hadn't really had much of a clue what to do, but now, as he explained the basics of his spur of the moment plan, the more it sounded like the one and only course of action.

There was scope here to take control fully. But where to start? Germany? Italy? Or – De Falaise's dream – his homeland of France? But, as they were to discover, it would not prove so easy to achieve. Others, just like De Falaise, had already had the same idea. They were professionals and they'd organised themselves more quickly than he'd had a chance to. It was true that he'd recruited his core group during this sweep of Europe – like Henrik the German with a passion for fine cigars, silver-haired Dutchman Reinhart, an expert marksman, the Lithuanian Rudakas, the broad Italian Savero, and Javier, originally of Mexican descent but now operating out of Spain, who in spite of his belly was a mean fighter. All were former mercenaries, their allegiance given to power and riches, rather than any flag. But together they hardly constituted the army De Falaise had envisaged. And though they'd been lucky in acquiring some weapons and transportation, the group finding bikes easier to manoeuvre in the heat of guerrilla warfare, they'd also been thrashed any number of times and been forced to retreat, losing many good foot soldiers in the process.

All of which meant that by the time De Falaise and his officers entered France, they were in no mood for the resistance they met there either. On the one hand, it made him proud that his people hadn't just rolled over and given in. But on the other, it meant that De Falaise would be denied the role of Governor here as well.

"Merde," he'd muttered to himself as they were driven out of Paris by the most powerful gang in charge there. "It was such a good plan, too."

But there was still hope. Whispers reached them that across the sea, the once 'Great' Britain was but a shadow of its former self. And something about that definitely appealed to De Falaise, as it probably would have done to his old history teacher. Just like in 1066, when William the Conqueror's Norman army had landed at Pevensey beach and then defeated Harold at Hastings, De Falaise would claim the place as his own. William had quashed all the rebellions after he was crowned King, so why shouldn't he do the same? It was also the chance to put right a few wrongs. The outrages of the Hundred Years' War, for example, when repeated attempts to take over France had failed – and then, of course, there was Napoleon's defeat at Waterloo. That still stung. The one-time Emperor's downfall after that had been swift and marked a turning point in the war between Britain and France that straddled the eighteenth and nineteenth Centuries. A war which, at its heart, went back much further.

De Falaise had to know for sure, however, what condition the island was in. Which was why they'd made the effort of staking out the Channel Tunnel. Sooner or later, he realised, someone was bound to come through it from the other side, and then... well, they'd get first hand information about the situation.

"Everything's gone to shit. It's chaos... Fucking chaos. Why do you think we came through the tunnel? It's like being back in the dark ages."

How appropriate, thought De Falaise.

So they'd made the trek to Britain, penetrating the island at Folkestone and working their way up to the Nation's capital. What they'd found en route backed up everything the tortured Englishman had told them. Small groups of thugs roaming the streets, with no imagination, no sense of the 'bigger picture.' Here and there certain areas were 'ruled' by tin-pot dictators, but their troops were few in number and there was no sense of working together for a common goal; at least not on the scale De Falaise was aiming for. In London itself, they found the same thing – nebulous gangs with no one person in charge of all of them. When he came along, all of that soon changed. He'd offered them a simple choice: life, under his leadership and protection, or death – which could either be swift or not, depending on what mood his men were in. Tanek did like to keep his hand in, to practise his skills. Back in the early days, De Falaise had once seen him keep someone alive for a week in constant agony. There was a talent to that, an art.

But this hadn't been their only reason to visit London. De Falaise needed information. He remembered the day they entered Parliament, the ease with which they'd dispatched the mob that had taken it over; its defences already immobilised at some point in the past. Those morons hadn't had the first clue about defending their position. He could have held the building and stayed there, or perhaps staked his claim on Buckingham Palace. But De Falaise was much smarter than that. All he was after was paperwork: not the documents these street thugs had managed to rip to shreds in their boredom, but the really secret stuff hidden in safes that De Falaise cracked with plastic explosives. He found nothing about the AB Virus, but then he wasn't expecting to here. The politicians had probably known just as little as everyone else and the real secret of what had happened – whether it was man-made, natural or whatever – was probably tucked away in some covert location long forgotten about now, in whatever country its origin lay. Anyway, that didn't interest him.

De Falaise was more concerned with finding a list of all military installations – Army, Air Force and Navy, and any American bases – which he eventually did. Especially secret barracks, Special Ops and the like. The defence systems had all been computerised, but when the electricity failed they reverted to multiple key lock systems, which his men got through with explosives. Quite a number of places had already been cleaned out, they found, and when they came across a couple of ex-squaddies still laughably trying to defend one of the installations, they discovered why. Operation Motherland: a botched attempt to round up all military weapons when the dust of the Culling Year had barely settled. Unorganised and misguided, the authorities thankfully hadn't had enough manpower to reach every UK base, particularly further up north. At various sites they found such weaponry as SA-80A2 assault rifles, Enfield L86s, MP5s, M4Comp, Colt Commandos and M203 machine guns, along with Milan Anti-Tank missile systems, LAW 90 anti-armour weaponry, bazookas, grenade launchers and plenty of grenades. At US installations around Northamptonshire, and USAF Molesworth, and the RAF/USAF Alconbury Air Base, they came away with M16s, Remington combat shotguns, Minimi machine guns, Colt, Berretta and Sig Sauer handguns.

And so, on his way to the Midlands, the real seat of power for any invasion, De Falaise not only swelled his ranks, he also built up his arsenal. Clothed in a strange mixture of uniforms and kept going by food supplies and untapped fuel reserves they'd needed to power the vehicles they were driving today (including additional Honda and Suzuki motorbikes loaded onto the trucks) the men he'd picked up along the way didn't seem to regret their decision. Once they were armed to the teeth – though not without a little training 'on site' at the ranges – and had full bellies, they were content enough. Some of the pressure had lifted, they didn't have to think for themselves anymore. They were his to command.

Which brought him back to the present and their last drive up the motorway. He was taking his ever-burgeoning army to set up a headquarters, from which he could spread outwards. But where would they go? That was the question he had thought long and hard about. Buildings like the council offices in Whetstone, like Parliament, were not easy to defend, as they'd proved. What they really needed was something designed to repel attacks. Tailor made to that one specific purpose.

So De Falaise once again looked to the past.

According to guides of the United Kingdom he'd picked up on his jaunt through the capital, there were several castles to choose from in the central area of England that might suit: Castle Howard, for example, North of York; Conisbrough Castle, near the town featured in Sir Walter Scott's novel, *Ivanhoe* – and just to the west of Doncaster; or Bolsover Castle, dating from the seventeenth century. But in the end it was a very easy decision.

The sign on the motorway showed that they were nearing their junction, and Tanek radioed to the rest of the convoy that they would soon be branching off for their target. Their truck led the way into the city itself, down roads that were more densely packed with abandoned cars: so much so that one of the Challengers had to overtake and plough them out of the way, parting the metallic sea like a khaki Moses. It made sense for this behemoth to be in front anyway, now that they were heading into potentially hostile territory again.

The vehicles made their way into the middle of the city, but saw very little in the way of action until they'd almost reached the bus depot, passing red brick buildings, some with square windows, others arched, many with looted shops below. The square grey building, which looked like it housed a multi-storey car park as well, was obviously being used as some sort of HQ. And the people inside, who leaned over and started firing at the vehicles, were also quite well armed.

Bullets pinged off the tanks, the trucks and the APCs, as the motorcycle escorts zipped just ahead of the shots.

De Falaise radioed to Henrik, driving the tank up front. He could imagine the man, still chomping on one of those cigars he loved so much, loading a live shell and then working the tank gun so that it pointed at the depot. The thunderous roar that accompanied the blast was deafening. It took out a chunk of the building's side, and with it most of the people who'd been firing at the vehicles. When the smoked cleared, a blue sign with a white 'P' on it was dangling from the corner of the wounded building.

More gunfire, this time from the ground level. Men and women emerging from the white classical-looking buildings to the left. De Falaise's men returned fire using the range of rifles they'd amassed which, even in their rookie hands, were more than a match for cannibalised handguns and shotguns. Some hostiles were even using air rifles!

The skirmish lasted all of ten minutes. It was obvious that, as elsewhere, no one was anywhere near ready to fight such a potent foe.

That proved to be the case again as they carried on up towards the market square, its fountain long-since dried up. Packs of armed people used the city's buses and trams – some of which had been tipped onto their sides – for cover. More shells from the tanks caused them to calm down and a series of rockets were launched at the square's council house, cracking the grey-green clock tower dome and the pillars that stood out front, while the stone lions guarding the entranceway looked on. Its inhabitants raced from the building, fleeing like mice from a skirting board. They held their hands in the air, not saying a word as De Falaise's men took them prisoner. Each would be offered the same 'opportunity' to serve in his employ.

Onward they went, trampling what little resistance they encountered like a size fourteen boot stamping on an ants' nest. To De Falaise's surprise and delight, he found the main object of their campaign virtually untouched. Not one person appeared to have had the same notion as him, to use this as their base – when it seemed such an obvious candidate. They entered through the black metal side gates round the corner from the main arched gateway, letting their vehicles inside.

Once his men had established that there was nobody in residence, De Falaise and Tanek stepped out of their Bedford to survey the area. The gardens were in turmoil, now that there was nobody to maintain them: in fact they were creeping over onto the path, snaking their way towards his future residence. To his right, De Falaise spotted a war memorial, the names of the dead who'd fallen in action. And he could just see some steps behind all the foliage, beneath which were two archways set into the rocks.

But there would be time to explore both the grounds and the inside later. For now, De Falaise just wanted to drink this all in.

The grand majesty of the square, cream-coloured building – not the original one, by any means – was steeped in history, and had reinvented itself several times over. It was also still here to tell the tale; standing in front of him for a reason.

"So," he finally said to Tanek. "What do you think?"

Tanek grunted, but De Falaise couldn't really tell whether it was in approval or not.

Then, turning to the rest of his men he said with a sense of pride: "Gentlemen, is she not *magnifique*? Our new home. I give to you the famous... Nottingham Castle."

CHAPTER SIX

IT WAS THEIR new home, and they were very proud of it.

Life was good.

Clive Maitland stepped back, took off his glasses, and wiped the sweat from his brow. Although he'd complained before, he'd never worked as hard as he had in the time since the virus. Back then he'd only had paperwork and a handful of unruly children to contend with. Now he was getting this community back on its feet; a new community made up of what was left of many others. He was proud of the fact that he'd drawn them all together, that were it not for his efforts they might have just faded away, not quite sure what had happened to the world, but positive that they wanted nothing whatsoever to do with the new one they'd found themselves in.

They'd lost more than he could ever imagine. Loved ones dying right in front of them, and there was nothing they could do about it. Clive had been single, had never really had a relationship that had gone past the 'let's be friends' stage, and had no surviving family save for an aunt who now lived in Canada. Or at least she had lived in Canada, until the virus caught up with them over there. His Aunty Glenda had been type AB Rhesus Negative, he was pretty sure of that because his Mum used to comment on how rare a group it was.

Much rarer than O-Negative.

In a funny sort of way, though, he'd had the most to lose of all. None of the kids that he'd taught had survived, leastways he didn't think so; he'd certainly never come across any of them in the post-Cull period. Sometimes he saw their faces in his dreams; his nightmares. *Christ*, what a time that had been...

He'd seen registration in the mornings dwindle down to virtually nothing. Then again, there were hardly any teachers reporting for duty either. In the weeks that followed it soon became apparent that the human race was facing its toughest test since the floods of Biblical times. Only instead of drowning in water, people were drowning in their own internal juices. It didn't take a genius to work out what would happen next.

So, when the authorities had tried to round up survivors, burning the dead in the streets or in their houses, Clive had driven away from the towns and cities, his estate car laden with cans of petrol, food, and bottles of water. He'd driven as far north as he could, finding, quite by chance, a tiny little village – if you could even call it that – out in the middle of nowhere. The kind of place they put on picture postcards advertising Britain to tourists. The authorities hadn't touched it, and Clive doubted whether they'd ever get round to it in time. But, like everywhere else, the dead were in the streets, and they were in their homes.

The stench was incredible, but he'd covered his mouth with a scarf and dragged the bodies from the two main streets – all this place boasted – into one of the fields. Then he'd gone into the houses, carrying out men and women, parents, grandparents (one old man had died alone in his cottage, just sitting in his rocking chair, blood staining his light blue shirt), and children. They'd been the worst of all, because again it brought back scenes of the playground, the classroom. But Clive had to be strong. They weren't coming back and there was a definite risk of other diseases if he just left them as they were. Diseases that the survivors could catch if they weren't careful. Wouldn't that beat all, dying from a secondary virus? The dead would have their revenge after all.

Whether there hadn't been anyone with O-Neg blood in this village or they'd simply left, he had no idea. All Clive knew was that there wasn't another living soul here, which suited him fine for the time being.

After burning the bodies, careful to do it in the most secluded spot he could find in case the smoke should draw unwanted attention, he bided his time.

When he'd been a teacher, the most important subjects had always been Maths and English – even the government said so. People who taught stuff like he did were virtually second-class citizens; that's how he'd always felt, anyway. But what good was Shakespeare right now, and why would you ever need to work out a quadratic equation when faced with the end of the world? Clive's subject – Sociology – had suddenly been promoted to one of the most important, along with Woodwork and Metalwork (sorry; Technology, as they called it these days), people who worked with their hands. Not to mention the domestic sciences, and those who also knew how to grow food.

Clive was more than familiar with how the structures of society operated; realised that it would be better to sit out all the violence and mayhem which would follow the collapse of reason and logic. Without law and order, without the police and judicial systems, everything would go to rack and ruin. One day, a dominant force or authority might well take control, hopefully for the better good – but meanwhile it was time to build up smaller communities so that the values of civilisation were not lost for ever. It was time to go back to basics.

First things first, Clive had to gather that community. He travelled round other rural areas, searching for survivors. It was in a medium-sized village just outside Derby that he came upon Gwen, a young woman who had also decided to live rather than just give up. He first saw her sitting at a bus stop as if waiting for a number 22 to come along. Thin, but naturally so, she was dressed in jeans and a jumper, her auburn hair tied back in a ponytail, and she was smoking a cigarette.

"Hi," he'd called from his car. "Are you okay?"

She took a drag on the cigarette, looking over at him. When she stood up, Clive saw the bloodstained carving knife at her hip.

"Look, I don't mean you any harm. I'm searching for other survivors."

There must have been something about the tone of his voice, perhaps the kindness in it – or maybe it was his inoffensive appearance? – that told her she didn't need to defend herself this time. She'd gone over to the car and, after a moment's hesitation, climbed inside. When he'd coughed at the cigarette smoke, she'd thrown it out of the window. "Sorry, I had quit before..."

Clive nodded.

She told him her story, of what it was like in Derby now – exactly how he'd pictured it. Gangs of hooligans were in charge, acting like animals. With no fear of reprisals and after seeing people they cared about die in such a horrific way, the darker side of human nature had emerged. Like him, Gwen had been single, and she'd tried to hide away in her house, down a street not far away from the Metro Theatre. There she pretended everything was okay. It was when a trio of men broke in and tried to attack her that she'd had to defend herself with the knife. She'd got out the back window, and run – away from the house, away from the city. That's how she'd lived since that day, alone, on the run.

As Clive drove, he explained what he was trying to do and asked

a) if she wanted to join him, and b) if she would help in the search. Gwen had thought about this for all of ten seconds before replying yes. All she really wanted now was a chance at normal life, or as close to normality as anyone got these days. Clive could relate to that.

Together they'd scoured the outlying regions of Derby, Mansfield, Sheffield. There had been some frightening moments, like the time Clive had stalled the car just as a nutter brandishing a cricket bat had appeared to start battering the vehicle.

"Six... Six...?" he'd shouted as he hammered the paintwork. "Umpire, he's out, surely?" One look at the man's wide eyes and slavering mouth told them that he'd lost his mind completely. Fumbling with the ignition, Clive had restarted the estate and backed it up away from him.

However, slowly but surely, they grew in number, bringing the sane and willing people they found back to the safe haven Clive had created for them. As he said to each and every one of them, it didn't matter what the place had been called before: now the village was named 'Hope.' They'd even made a sign, which they planted on the main street.

It was a name Reverend Tate definitely approved of. They'd found the very special man one day, on his knees, praying inside a vandalised church. The thugs that had been desecrating the building were strewn around him. Tate had crossed himself and risen, leaning on his thick walking stick, asking what he could do for the newcomers. When they just stared at the felled men, Tate's explanation had been, "The Lord moves in mysterious ways." (Later they learned that the Reverend actually taught self-defence out in the community to the vulnerable. "God helps those who help themselves," he'd explained, patting his stick. "But not that way.")

The small, squat man, who walked with a slight limp and looked like he'd probably been bald since his teens, had hesitated when they'd asked him to come with them, arguing that he couldn't leave his flock. When Clive pointed out there were precious few of those left, and that the new flock he was gathering would need religious guidance, Tate finally agreed.

Clive was pleased he had, because he enjoyed his late night chats with the holy man, who suggested that there was a rhyme and pattern to all of this, that it was part of God's plans for them.

"Everything happens for a reason," Tate often said to him, "even if we can't see what that is right now."

"You really believe that?"

"Don't you?" the Reverend threw back at him. "He spared you, spared all of us for some purpose. And I think you might well have found yours, Clive. Your brains, your leadership qualities have saved these people. Saved us all."

It was true that without him the community of Hope would still be out there, lost. He'd organised them, found out what people's strengths were and put them to practical use. For example, June Taylor was a former midwife, so she had medical knowledge. Graham Leicester used to work in a garden centre, but as well as cultivating flowers he'd also had his own allotment. Clive worked in conjunction with him, at first taking over one of the large greenhouses they found in someone's back garden, but then on more ambitious schemes, planting crops out in the fields. This is where Andy Hobbs, who used to be a gym instructor, and Nathan Brown, who had worked as a farmhand one summer, came into their own: ploughing the fields so that Hope would have a good harvest this year. It was only recently, in the last six months or so, that Clive had got wind of the markets where food and other items could be traded, so every now and again they would visit these with produce or whatever else they had to offer. Already, the 'economy' – however rudimentary – was getting back on its feet, it would seem, society finding a way of rebuilding what had been destroyed. This also proved an opportunity to touch base with other burgeoning communities.

Though they were small in number, maybe thirty people at most (others were much, much smaller), they all got on and were working towards something together. Without Clive's influence and guidance there would have been none of that.

And without his pro-action he would never have met Gwen, who, over the course of time they'd known each other, had become extremely important to him. In the days before the virus, Clive doubted that a woman as good looking and kind – and, let's face it, pretty much perfect – as Gwen would have even looked his way, although she always told him he was wrong. Now, in this bubble, this experiment – a micro community really – he was rapidly becoming her whole world. They'd already 'adopted' a couple of the little ones they'd found on their searches, some no more than five or six, alone and scrabbling about for food or water. But one day, Clive realised, there would come a time when he and Gwen might start a family of their own. They'd even talked about asking Tate to marry them. They weren't the only ones, either. Folk of all ages, were pairing up, whether it was for companionship, or love, or a human instinct to carry on the species.

Which was why he was out here today, working on turning the tiny village hall into an even tinier school. He was fixing up the place with the help of young Darryl Wade. The lad was barely into his twenties, but had been trained well by his handyman father before he'd died – in the hopes Darryl would take over the family business one day. It was this kind of passing down of skills Clive sought to encourage. The world no longer needed IT experts, estate agents or insurance brokers.

Outside in the sunshine, Clive was sanding down the first set of desk tops. He'd been working hard all morning and was looking forward to the communal dinner they would have outside the local pub, with freshly baked bread (that was one of Gwen's talents) and fresh meat picked up just recently from one of the markets: lamb today, if he wasn't very much mistaken. And as he placed the glasses back on his head, bringing a figure walking towards him into focus, Clive smiled a greeting at Gwen. All things considered, life was good in Hope, and much better than the alternative.

"Hello you," said Gwen, carrying a tray of blackcurrant juice across from the house they'd picked out together. She looked over at the desks, then at the work he and Darryl had done on the door to the hall. Gwen nodded, suitably impressed. "Been working hard, I see."

She placed the tray down and Clive gave her a kiss. She was wearing a flowery summer dress, even though they were barely into the spring, her auburn hair loose, flowing over her shoulders, and Clive thought that he'd never seen anything so beautiful in his life. He slipped a hand around her waist and she placed an arm over his shoulder. They both looked at the hall, knowing that in years to come it would probably become the true embodiment of Hope.

"Who's looking after Sally and Luke?" Sally was their little girl's real name, Luke was the one they'd given their boy when they found the poor mite.

"June's got them; they're happy enough playing out in the garden. Where's Darryl?"

"Inside; he's taking a look at the rafters. Apparently there was quite a bit of rot up in the roof. That's something else which'll need sorting out."

"There's time," Gwen told him.

"There is," he agreed, kissing her again. "For all kinds of things. Gwen, I –" There was a noise in the distance that made him pause. "Do you hear that?"

Gwen cocked an ear. "Sounds like an engine."

Clive listened again. "Sounds like *lots* of engines."

"Might just be someone passing by up on the main road," she offered, but her expression told him she was worried. They never had visitors to Hope – not even from the other communities they'd made contact with – and that was the way they preferred it.

The noise was drawing closer.

"Does... does that sound like a motorbike to you?" asked Gwen.

Clive took her hand and ran down the street, rounding the corner. The people of Hope had come out of their houses to see what was happening. Andy and Nathan had heard the racket and ventured down from the upper field. Graham Leicester was approaching from up the street, running towards Clive. "Men..." he spluttered, out of breath.

But then Clive saw for himself. They rode up the small street behind Graham, just as Clive had done all that time ago when he first came upon this place. There were three on bikes, the rest in jeeps. All wore uniforms, but as they got closer Clive could see they were a mishmash of Army, Navy and Air Force, British and US; obviously stolen. As were the weapons they were brandishing, heavy duty rifles and pistols. Some looked uncomfortable handling them, others looked very much at home. One of the soldiers on the bikes stretched out a leg and kicked Graham over into the dirt when he passed.

It was now that Clive realised his fundamental error. In seeking to gather together people who could make this community flourish, leaving behind the violent and the psychopathic, he'd left this place wide open to attack. Hope had no defences whatsoever, and they'd been too reliant on its isolated location to shield them from the outside world. Now that outside world had found them, and they were about to pay the price.

Several men climbed from the jeeps, their boots stomping the street. And their apparent leader, his paunch so big he only just fit inside, got out too. Andy ran at one of the soldiers, swinging a hoe, knocking the man to the ground. For his trouble he was hit in the back of the head with the butt of a rifle. He went down hard and stayed there.

The man with the belly waved his hand, giving the signal to open fire. There was some hesitation, but then muzzles flashed, spitting bullets at the cottages which housed the people of Hope. These men didn't appear to care whether there were folk inside or not. Windows shattered, walls were pock-marked. The sign they'd made came crashing down to the ground. From somewhere Clive heard screaming, but couldn't tell if it came from a man, woman or a child. Gwen held on to him, and he pressed her head into his shoulder, covering her ears.

How could I have been so stupid?

The fat man gave another signal and Clive watched as small objects were tossed at the cottages, and at the pub. Seconds later, the first of the grenades exploded. There followed two or three more, drawing out the rest of the inhabitants of this place. They fell to the ground, covering their heads. Behind Clive and Gwen, Darryl appeared, his mouth gaping open. Then Clive saw June with the kids; she had Luke in her arms, crying, while Sally was holding her hand.

This isn't what I promised them.

Their leader held up a hand for them to cease, simultaneously pulling a pistol from a holster with the other. "That's enough," he shouted. Clive detected a slight Hispanic accent when the man spoke. He walked down the small street, eyes darting left and right, as if daring anyone else to trying something.

"So, people of..." The man looked down at the fallen sign they had made. He chuckled. "People of Hope. My name is Javier. Major Javier. Who here speaks for you?"

Clive made to move forwards, but Gwen tugged at his shirt. She shook her head, but he patted her hand to tell her it was okay. "That would be me," Clive called out.

Javier looked him up and down, perhaps wondering how such a man could have banded together the group; how he could have commanded such respect and loyalty without the threat of fear. "And you are?"

"Clive Maitland," he said, trying to toughen up his voice but failing miserably. "And I demand that you –"

"Demand? You *demand?*" He lifted his pistol and pointed it at Clive, who bit his lip. "Well, let me tell you what I demand, little man. I represent the new power in the region and he has sent me out to meet his... subjects. In fact, he's sent out many more of his men to do the same. His name is De Falaise of Nottingham Castle, so remember that. In the years to come everyone will know it. Cooperate and things will go smoothly for you. Oppose him, and they will not."

"What does this De Falaise want with us?" Clive asked.

"Your fealty, your tribute," came the answer. "You have stocks here of food?"

"They are for trading, for feeding my people."

Javier wagged a finger. "Except they're not your people anymore, are they? Were you not listening, *Señor* Maitland?" He waved a hand around to indicate the community of Hope. "They belong to De Falaise: just as this village is now under his 'protection.'"

So this was what would fill the void. He'd been expecting something one day, but not this. Not a return to the old days that history warned them all about. "He's like a monarch, then," observed Clive. "Or would he prefer Sheriff?"

Javier thought about this for a second. "Sheriff? Yes, I think he would like the sound of that title very much. We will take most of what you have to feed our troops." He rubbed his inflated stomach. "Like me, they are all growing boys."

Clive stepped forward. "But how are we expected to eat? There are children here."

Javier paused before answering. "That is not my concern. But if you keep this up, we might well be tempted to take a few... other things back with us as well." He leered over Clive's shoulder at Gwen. "She's yours, yes?"

"She doesn't belong to anybody!" snapped Clive.

"What did I just say? You all belong to De Falaise. And I think he would be more than happy if I brought her back for him." Javier pushed Clive aside and made for Gwen. Darryl looked like he was going to do something, but the raised pistol dissuaded him. Clive knew that Gwen no longer carried the knife she'd once used to protect herself. If only he'd left her at the bus stop, she might have been safe. Or she might be dead already, he told himself. At least this way they had a fighting chance.

"Wait... wait," said Clive, following Javier. "Look, take the food – you're welcome to it. We'll manage somehow." There were a few gasps from the villagers, but he knew they'd understand. This was one of their own at risk, and any of the women could be next.

Javier turned. "I don't need your permission. And the more I think about it, the more De Falaise will be pleased if I bring back such an elegant lady." He stepped forward, reaching out to touch Gwen's cheek. Her face soured, then she bit the hand he was proffering.

"Ahwww!" screamed Javier, sticking it under his arm. "You'll regret that!" He struck her across the face with the pistol, sending her reeling back.

"Gwen!" shouted Clive and dove at the fat man. He didn't want to join the rest of the survivors in their grieving, couldn't bear to lose the only person he'd ever truly loved – not now, not like this. But sensing the imminent attack, Javier spun and fired a single bullet. It hit Clive in the ribs, tearing into him and out the other side. He dropped to his knees, glasses falling from his head. Clive clutched his side, bringing one hand up and seeing the blood there – his blood, spilling out of him like juice from a punctured carton. The people of Hope gaped, horrified. Gwen lay on the floor, blood and tears pouring down her face.

"I have to ask myself, is it brains?" said Javier as he approached Clive. "Is that why they follow you? Is that why she looks at you that way?"

Clive didn't know how to answer.

"I think it is." Javier leaned over him and snatched the glasses from his head. "You want to see them, *Señor* Maitland? Want to see those brains?"

"No!" shouted a voice. Someone, a blur to Clive, was moving towards them. It was too big and bulky to be Gwen, that was for sure. He squinted and saw the outline of Reverend Tate there. "In God's name, no!" He brought down his walking stick hard across Javier's shoulder blades. The Major let out another cry, then spun on his second attacker. Clive saw Javier raise his gun, but Tate grabbed his arm. The two men wrestled for control of the weapon. Other soldiers were coming across to help, but not quick enough. Javier was struggling to bring the pistol up, Tate attempting to stop him – but it was obvious who was winning.

"Please! This serves no purpose. Can't you see that?" Tate shouted.

The figures were just fuzzy outlines to Clive now. Then there was a sharp bang, followed by a scream from Gwen. Tate fell back, leaving Javier standing above him.

He's killed him, thought Clive, *that bastard's killed the Reverend*. But then he was aware of a cold sensation spreading over him. His sight was no longer fuzzy, it was dim. Fading. There was a pain in his temple, only the briefest of twinges. But there was no time to register anything else.

Clive didn't feel himself toppling over – though in the final few milliseconds of his life, Tate's words echoed all around him. "Everything happens for a reason."

He was at a loss to understand this one, he had to admit. He'd never see Sally or Luke, never see Gwen again: never hold her in his arms, feel her lips brushing against his.

Clive wouldn't feel the loss now, but she would. He knew she'd mourn him, and he was truly sorry.

But none of that mattered anymore. It was all going black, completely black.

And never before had he realised the true significance of what he'd thought earlier.

Life was indeed good.

"You evil... evil thing," the Reverend Tate hissed from the floor, several rifles trained on him. "He was a good man and now..."

Javier walked over and looked down at what he'd done. Clive

Maitland's brains were spilling out onto the sign he'd helped to make, the name he'd given to this place. "There are no good men anymore. And there is no hope." A tight smile played on his lips at the double meaning of his words. Turning back, he said: "It is fortunate for you that you are a man of the cloth; it is bad luck to shoot a holy man."

"May you burn in Hell for what you've done."

Javier snorted. "Look around you," he said, pointing to the fires with his still smoking pistol. "We're already there, together. Now, if you will excuse me." He nodded to the men to pick the catatonic woman up off the ground, her eyes still fixed on the dead man. "Put her in one of the jeeps."

Two of the soldiers grabbed Gwen by the arms, dragging her up and along the street.

"Christ who art in Heaven," said Tate, "how can you allow this?" It wasn't the first time he'd asked since the virus had struck, but the first time his faith had been shaken in such a way.

Though Tate thought he detected Javier flinching when he'd mentioned the Saviour's name, the man ignored his words and made to follow his men.

Tate clenched his fists and repeated his question, looking away from Clive's body as he did so, towards June and the children Gwen and Clive had been looking after – both now in tears. Then he thought about what Javier had said. That there were no good men left, that there was no hope...

And prayed to God that he was wrong.

CHAPTER SEVEN

THE LAKE STRETCHED out ahead, a mirrored surface. He was walking around the edge of it, strolling along without a care in the world. Rich green foliage surrounded him, and across the other side of the lake, trees whispered in the faint breeze. Robert took in the view, breathed in the sweet air.

He looked down at his hand and found something in it. He was clutching a brightly-coloured ball. Robert frowned as he examined it more closely. There was barking to the side of him. Now Robert saw Max, waiting for him to throw the object. Robert pretended to toss the toy for him, laughing when the dog began to scamper after nothing – then he threw it for real.

"Fetch!"

The ball swerved off to the side and landed in the lake, but it didn't matter: Max happily jumped in after it and started to swim. Clamping the ball between his teeth, the dog paddled back to the bank and clambered out. Max shook himself, spraying lake water everywhere. Laughter filled the air. But it wasn't Robert's.

A young blond boy held up his hands to shield himself from the deluge. He was laughing so hard he was almost doubled over. Robert froze.

"Stevie?"

The spray continued, as did the laughter. All Robert wanted to do was join in. He was moving forwards, virtually running towards the boy, who was pulling the ball out of Max's mouth, preparing to toss it into the lake once more. The boy brought back an arm, then let go of the object. It spun in the air, catching the sunlight for a moment, and Max was after the thing before it had time to hit the surface. The blond boy laughed hard again when Max finally splashed into the lake.

Robert was drawing near, only metres away. "Stevie... Stevie, is that really you?"

"Read to me some more, Dad... please..."

But he could see subtle differences now. As the child turned, the cheekbones were slightly less curved, the brow more stooped, shielding green eyes. This boy was a bit older than his Stevie, as well.

Robert's mouth formed the name, but he couldn't say it out loud. *Mark*...

No, it couldn't be. Because if he acknowledged that this was the boy he'd met at the market, then so many things were wrong with this picture. And yes, as soon as he'd thought it, Robert saw Mark pointing out across the lake. Except it wasn't filled with water anymore.

Max was bobbing up and down, ball now in his mouth – but he was swimming in a lake of fire. The flames lapped at the dog, but he didn't seem to be taking any notice.

"Max!" screamed Robert, rushing to the bank. The heat from the rising blaze drove him back. The dog, however, was still swimming towards them through it all – its fur all but burnt away, patches of blistered skin clearly visible.

Robert expected to see the men with the flamethrowers at the edge of the lake – surely they must be the ones doing this? But no. Instead, he saw the vague outline of figures, could hardly make them out, except that they were holding weapons of some kind.

One of them began walking across the surface of the lake, the flames hardly touching him. The man was wearing sunglasses, grinning madly as he approached. He pulled out a pistol, his fingers covered in rings, and aimed it at Max... Except it wasn't the dog anymore, it was something else. Something with antlers...

That didn't seem to matter because the man fired three times without any hesitation, blowing it away.

Now gunfire turned the scene into a war zone. Flashes from across the lake. Robert ducked, turning to see if Mark was okay. The boy was crouching, hands covering his head, tears streaming down his face.

Robert gritted his teeth. "No. No, I can't. I've got to go..." he said.

"Wait... please... please help..."

Robert turned and began walking away, his back to the scene, to Mark. "I've got to go. I've got to go..." he kept on repeating, then finally: "I'm sorry."

"Help us!" The boy's cry followed him, but Robert had to ignore it. Yet could he? Could he just walk away? Robert began to turn.

There was one last loud bang and –

*   *   *

ROBERT JERKED AWAKE, breath coming in short, sharp gasps. He sat up under the shelter of his home, a much improved and portable version of his original lean-to, adjusting back to reality. Robert inhaled more slowly, reaching for the water he kept by the side of his bed of grass and leaves. He drank greedily.

It had been the same dream – or a variation of it – ever since he'd visited the market, seen Mark. Robert never used to be able to remember his dreams, but out here they were so much more vivid, more intense. The boy had looked just enough like Stevie to affect him, like seeing a ghost made flesh. And now this. If he'd thought he might be going insane before, then this was putting the finishing touches to it.

He would have been lying if he'd said he hadn't thought about going back again. It wasn't that far, and it was almost a fortnight since the last market – he'd marked off the days on a fallen branch, the only time he'd ever bothered to keep a track of the time. He'd stayed away the first week, but it was almost Wednesday again, almost time. He could trade some of the meat he had, some of the better meat – there were things he'd seen there that he could use.

Again, he wrestled with his conscience. How could he allow himself such luxuries when his family... If his stay in the woods and the forest was his penance, his time to wait before joining them, why should he make life easier for himself?

He shouldn't. He couldn't.

Yet there was Mark. All Robert could think about was the boy asking for, pleading for his help. It was only a dream, but it felt so real.

Robert put down the water and lay back again. He wouldn't sleep now, he knew that – but dawn wasn't that far away.

He just hoped he could hang on till then.

THE MARKET WAS busy that week, but there was something missing.

Bill Locke knew most of the regulars by sight and one stall was conspicuous in its absence: one that offered fruit and veg, mainly. Sometimes it would be manned by the woman with auburn hair, sometimes the fellow with glasses, sometimes a vicar. Bill didn't know their names because they preferred to keep themselves to themselves, which was fair enough. He wasn't in charge here, after all. Nobody was. This was a free and open market – he just liked to see that things went smoothly, that's all. Keep the peace. It was a little foible of his. Bill guessed that people saw him as the boss because he'd been one of the first to set these markets up, but it seemed pretty logical to him, just an extension of what he'd been doing for years.

It was rare that he'd have to break up any trouble, though. Only minor disagreements about what things were worth. Usually it could be resolved, especially when Bill stepped in, the very sight of his shotgun enough to make people agree on a reasonable settlement.

Apart from the missing stall, everything was relatively normal – the same faces, the same names. Like Mark, the kid who scavenged in the cities and towns for items to trade. He was good at it, too. There was a part of Bill that felt sorry for the lad, left all alone in the world. But Mark was getting by, the only way they knew how. He was the next generation, the ones that would grow up in this world, whatever shape it would eventually take. He was learning early, that was all.

Mark caught him staring, smiled, and offered him a sweet from a bag he was chomping his way through.

"Those things'll rot yer teeth," said Bill, but took one all the same. "Better off eating some o' that beef or pork over there."

Mark pulled a face. "Next you'll be telling me to eat my greens."

Bill laughed softly. "Cheeky bugger."

The boy stiffened, and at first Bill thought it had been what he said. Then he saw that Mark was reacting to something he couldn't yet perceive.

"What is it?" asked Bill, but then he heard the engines himself. The people with the fruit and veg stall, maybe, showing up late? was his first thought. But they tended to arrive in an estate car. This was the sound of more than one engine.

Before anyone knew it, the motorbikes were in the field – at least a dozen of them, churning up the grass. The open-top jeeps followed next, handling the soft terrain with ease, men hanging from the seats, carrying weapons Bill hadn't seen outside of pre-virus news reports about the troubles abroad.

"This is an illegal gathering," came an electronic voice, some kind of megaphone system attached to one of the jeeps. "By order of your new lord and master, High Sheriff De Falaise, all goods here will now be confiscated. Resist, and there will be serious consequences."

"Bloody Sheriff? What's he talkin' about?" Bill looked down. Mark would have taken off at that point, if there had been anywhere to hide. But this wasn't the city, this was open countryside. And there were precious few places to find cover out here. Bill hoisted up his shotgun, not really knowing what good that would do when – not if – this turned ugly.

Without any provocation at all, the men on bikes raced round and round the stalls, shooting into the air. Others were climbing from the jeeps, knocking people to the ground and pointing rifles at them so they wouldn't move. Some of them snatched food. Bill saw one young man grab a hunk of cheese and bite down into it, waving an automatic pistol at the owner, daring him to do something. A pair of people did run, in fact, off across the field to get away. Apparently that counted as resistance, because one of the soldiers threw a grenade at them. It exploded just a few feet away from the couple, blowing them metres into the air. When they landed, they weren't moving.

"Yer bunch o –" began Bill, moving towards the men. Mark got behind him, perhaps reasoning that if he couldn't hide in a building he'd hide there. Bill raised the gun to his shoulder, then let off a round that hit one of the bikers squarely in the chest. The rider slumped over the handlebars, and the machine he was on smacked straight into the side of a Sierra belonging to one of the marketeers. The body was flung over the bonnet to land in a slump on the other side.

Bill let off another blast. This time it only glanced across the front of one of the jeeps. Several rifles turned in his direction, but something made them hold their fire. Bill cracked open the gun and loaded up two more cartridges. "That's it, yer bastards, ye do well to be frightened."

He was aware of Mark tugging on his jumper, trying to get him to turn around. When he did, Bill understood why the men had held off. The noise of the engines had masked the approach of something else: a great beast of a thing, rumbling over the hill. Bill gawped at the tank, blinking as if that might make it go away. He'd never seen one up close like this. But it was real, it was solid, and the cannon on the front was swinging in his direction.

"Judas Priest!" said Bill. Mark tugged at him to run, to get out of its path. But Bill stood there, raising his shotgun again. "All right, then, bloody well come on!"

As Mark fled, Bill shot at the tank twice, having as much effect as a wasp sting trying to penetrate a suit of armour. The tank carried on advancing; it must have looked like some kind of surreal modern twist on George and the Dragon, or even David and Goliath. Only Bill was out of stones for his slingshot.

The tank rumbled up and didn't stop until the cannon was inches away from Bill's head. He looked down that black hole, expecting at any minute to be on the receiving end of a live shell.

* * *

MARK RAN; HE hated leaving Bill but didn't know what he could do if the man wouldn't budge. He'd be dead in seconds if that tank opened fire.

The boy was aware of a bike riding up alongside him. A quick glance to the side told him a boot was kicking out, trying to knock him over. Mark ducked and rolled away, but the bike swerved round, readying itself for another pass. Mark reversed direction, aware that the bike was gaining rapidly on him.

He looked up and saw that another one of the riders had decided to join in the game. That one was coming after him from the front. He was being hemmed in.

On the first pass, he managed to dodge sideways, hoping the two bikes would just slam into each other. It wasn't going to be that simple. Avoiding one another, they rode now in a pair, leaving a gap between to squash Mark. He ran as fast as he could but knew that he wouldn't be able to get away from them this time, that he'd be crushed beneath one set of tyres or another.

Then something odd happened.

Mark heard a whizzing sound, felt the brush of something flying past him. He heard a loud bang as the front wheel of the bike to his left exploded. He risked a look over his shoulder, just in time to see the spokes and mudguard of the bike bite into the field, sending the rider over the handlebars.

But Mark couldn't stop running. The second bike had weaved out of the way, and was still chasing him, unwilling to give up on this cat-and-mouse fun just because his partner's tyre had burst. In fact, the rider had a grenade in his hand and was getting ready to toss it at Mark.

Another couple of whizzes and this time Mark saw the arrows hit the bike and its rider. They went down heavily, leaving Mark to throw himself out of the way, just as the grenade the man had been holding went off.

Mark felt a searing heat, then there was a ringing in his ears.

Shapes passed overhead, arrows flying through the air. Two more soldiers crumpled beside him. Mark finally got to his feet and attempted to track the source of the arrows, but he could see nothing.

Panicking, they began firing every which way, because that's where the threat appeared to be coming from. Now that Mark's hearing was coming back, he caught barked orders, and more than a few scared yelps.

Someone had got these people spooked, even with their guns and their armoured vehicles.

The same someone who had just saved Mark's life with a few bits of wood.

BILL HEARD THE explosion at the same time as the tank crew, it appeared. To begin with he thought it was the soldiers killing more people from the market, but when he looked properly he saw it was one of their own bikes in flames.

The cannon swivelled away from Bill, chasing the person who had done this. It couldn't find anyone – and neither could Bill. To his right, a couple of soldiers holding rifles dropped to their knees. No bangs, no gunshots – nothing. But now Bill could see they were clutching at arrows protruding from their chests.

Farther down the field, a jeep had stopped dead – its two front tyres useless now that they had been punctured. The men inside were climbing out, rifles poised, but already three had gone down.

Bill grinned.

He took this opportunity to get out of the tank's way, rushing back towards the market. One soldier was heading in his direction, but before he could bring his rifle up, Bill had already whacked him in the face with the butt of his own gun.

The top portion of the tank was still swivelling, and Bill observed the hatch opening up on top. A thickset man smoking a cigar emerged. He was trying to get a bead on whoever was firing those arrows. Then he pointed, shouting in a German accent: "There, you idiots, he's over there!"

It was the man Bill had met a fortnight ago, but hadn't forgotten. The 'poacher' with the rabbits.

The man called Robert who'd worn a hood.

HENRIK COULDN'T BELIEVE how incompetent these foot soldiers were. Granted, there were only a handful of properly trained men to spread around the units (hence the fact he was doing the job of three – tank commander, loader and gunner – while his driver, chosen for his previous experience with tracked diggers, sat behind a 10 mm partition up front). The rest of their 'army' was made up of dregs they'd struck the fear of God into on their journey. But surely even they should be able to handle one man using such a primitive form of weaponry?

Yet he was running rings round them; running, ducking and hiding behind bushes. *Bushes, for Heaven's sake!* Henrik couldn't get a shot off fast enough with the cannon, so he dropped back inside and ordered his driver to lead the rest of his squad down towards the figure, or at least where they'd last seen the man firing.

Looking through the viewfinder, Henrik saw the remaining vehicles not only following, but getting ahead of them, taking the hunt to the cretin with the arrows.

And there, yes, Henrik could see the speck running. He wouldn't get far, not on this terrain, not with bikes, a jeep, and a tank in pursuit. He'd picked the wrong people to play tag with. He was outnumbered and outgunned.

They followed him over the next small hill, and it was then that Henrik saw what the man had in mind. He was trying to get back to cover. He was going back to ground.

If he made it there, they might never find him. And he'd never let a kill get away.

Henrik bit down on his cigar, then ordered the Challenger driver to speed up.

RORY WILKES DIDN'T even know what he was doing here.

He'd gone along with all this since the armed men had arrived in his home town of Coventry – let's face it, they hadn't really given any of them an option. But now people were getting hurt; and there was a good chance he might be as well. While he had to admit the feel of the combats, the weight of the M16 in his hands, did feel good (what little boy hadn't wanted to play Action Man at some point, even after he'd grown up?) this was all getting a bit too serious for his liking.

Rory had been impressed by the ease with which they'd taken Nottingham, De Falaise's words as they moved into the castle like something from an old movie. But if one man could now send them into confusion like this...

As the jeep bounced up and down in pursuit, Rory and the other men in the back looked ahead at the bloke they were after. He was running fast, hard, towards the trees. *We should let him reach them, then we won't have to deal with him at all*, thought Rory. But the man was spinning around, not even stopping – running backwards even while he was notching another arrow.

The projectiles bounced off the front of the jeep, and Rory ducked in case any found their way inside. One of the bikes flanking them went down. Rory looked around to see the unfortunate man get crushed under the tracks of the Challenger tank that their 'commander' was operating. *God Almighty, enough was enough, wasn't it?*

Obviously not, because they were still in pursuit.

Then the hooded man was gone. The woodland absorbed him, sucking him inside itself like he was an extension of it. Surely they could give up now?

Rory felt their jeep slowing, the bikes and the tank behind doing the same. All the vehicles stood at the perimeter of the woodland, as if expecting the man to emerge again and give himself up. No such luck.

In the end the silence was broken by their unit leader, who appeared from out of the top of the Challenger. "In there, you lot," ordered the man. "After him on foot!"

If the men with him hadn't known the consequences of disobeying, they would have turned the jeep around and just driven off. But going in there was preferable to having a tank turn on you... just about. And there was no way any of them wanted to mess with Henrik. Not one of them could take him; Rory doubted whether all of them put together could, in fact.

Reluctantly, they climbed out of the jeep, climbed off their bikes and, holding their weapons in front of them, walked up to the edge of the woods. Rory hung back as far as he could.

"I said in!" screamed Henrik from behind them. "Right now!"

The men all looked at each other, not really knowing what to do for the best. Then one of them made the first move into the undergrowth. The next man followed, then the next. Soon there was only Rory left. Swallowing, he stepped forward into the line of trees.

It wasn't as densely packed as some woods that he'd seen – though admittedly, his experience was fairly limited in this respect. It was thick enough, however, to hide the person they were tracking. As the men in front of him walked further in, they automatically fanned out – partly to give themselves some room if anything happened, partly because they didn't want to be standing too close to anyone who might be a target. Rory could feel the beads of sweat trickling down his face.

There was a rustling off to their right and one of his group opened fire, splintering the trees. When the sound died down, there was nothing to see.

"Where'd he go?" Rory heard one guy say.

There was no answer to that, none of them had a clue. Then the one who'd asked the question went silently down, falling over as if fainting. It wasn't until Rory looked more closely that he saw the arrow sticking out of the man's side.

More dropped like him, only a couple getting a chance to let off a round or two. Rory spun, looking for a direction the arrows might be coming from. He saw nothing. It might as well have been the trees themselves.

Then the guy to his left let out a piercing scream, dropping his rifle and clutching his leg. There was a huge knife sticking out of his thigh; the man hissed a swear word before dropping to the ground. The group that had gone in were already half their number and the rest began to open fire randomly – in the hopes that they'd get off a lucky hit, maybe wing their enemy.

Not much chance of that. Even as they were firing, the arrows flew – and one by one the noises died down until the last man was silenced.

That just left Rory. He was no hero, he hadn't signed up for this – hadn't signed up for anything, actually – so it was time to get out of there, whether the mad German was waiting for him or not.

Turning to run back out, he came face-to-face with the man they'd been hunting. Or rather, the man who'd been hunting them. Only he couldn't see much of that face because it was obscured by his hood. There was a strap around his shoulder which held a handmade quiver, with a few arrows left in it – but he'd made every single one of his shots count. There was also one in the bow Rory was looking at, pointing at his head.

He dropped the rifle on the floor, holding up his shaking hands in surrender. "Please... please don't hurt me, I had no choice. He was going to kill me. Kill us all!" Rory was almost in tears.

The man raised his head, looked directly at him. His eyes were narrowed, but whether he was readying to shoot or just didn't believe a word of Rory's excuse was unclear. Then he lowered his bow.

"Who?" asked the hooded man.

"What?"

"Who was going to kill you?"

"Th-the Frenchman. H-his name is De Falaise."

"Get out of here," he said to Rory. "Take the ones who can still walk with you." Then he went over and pulled the knife out of its home in the felled soldier's leg.

Rory gave a quick nod, searching for any survivors. There weren't many: two, three at most. Rory helped the guy whose thigh was pouring with blood, half dragging him along as he seethed in pain.

Rory risked one last glance over his shoulder at the man, who was now bending over some of the fallen soldiers. A single man, but he'd managed to take out most of their group in no time. He had never seen anything like it... and never wanted to again.

Head down, he half-carried the injured man out of the woods.

HENRIK TAPPED HIS seat, keeping his eyes on the panorama ahead of him.

He had never been very good at waiting. Everything had to come to him yesterday. It was one of the reasons he'd thrown in with De Falaise. It was a quick route to the top: to power, to influence over this new world. The man had made such an impassioned speech about his plans that Henrik would have been a fool not to listen. Yes, he could have tried to build up an army of his own, he supposed, but that would have taken longer. De Falaise already had Tanek, Savero, and a handful of other loyal followers – this would be the easier route to success. Then later, maybe...

Things had been going well. They'd been spreading out from Nottingham, tracking down small communities that had set themselves up and obliterating any thoughts of resistance. The local people would serve them or they would die. Which was why these markets had to be stopped; free trade meant independence, and De Falaise could not allow that. The villagers would work for him and him alone, and he would take whatever they had to offer without recompense.

That was why they'd been dispatched to this area. It was why they'd come down on these people so hard: fear equalled respect.

But it had only taken this one spanner in the works to cast doubt on their mission. One survivalist who thought he was pretty handy with a bow and arrow. Henrik grunted. *Amateur*.

He sat up when he saw movement in the woods. Two figures emerged, one dragging the other. His team had done it; they'd killed the primitive and were bringing back the body. No, wait, the body was still moving – not only that but he was dressed in their unique uniform, a combination of colours and styles that De Falaise had chosen himself. He was certainly not hooded. A couple more of his 'men' staggered out behind them. The useless dickheads had failed, and now they were returning with their tails between their legs.

Henrik almost chomped through the cigar he was smoking. He climbed up through the hatch, cursing them in German.

"Incompetents! Where is he?"

"I'm here," came a voice from the woods, strong and loud. In spite of himself, Henrik flinched. But if the man had wanted him dead, then wouldn't he be already – an arrow between the eyes?

"Show yourself, coward. Come out of your hiding place and we will discuss this."

There was a pause before the reply came. "You come out of yours."

Henrik thought about this. Seriously considered hopping down from the Challenger, going to meet this man at the edge of the woods and pounding him into the ground. No weapons other than their fists. They would see who won then.

But why give up the advantage? Pride was something for romantics, not mercenaries. "I give you thirty seconds to come out, or I will come in after you... personally."

"Go back to your Frenchman and tell him this is over," came the reply. It was not the voice of someone easily intimidated.

This man was more infuriating than all of his ex-wives put together! Henrik didn't even give him the thirty seconds. He just slipped back inside and fired off a high explosive shell into the woods, hoping to obliterate the insolent fool, and clearing some space for them to enter. "Forward!" he shouted to the driver, who reluctantly obeyed.

The hulking thing trundled into the woods.

I will teach this man a lesson!

Henrik would knock down or blow up every single tree in this place to get to him if he had to. He swung the 120 mm gun around and was just about to load up another shell when...

Suddenly there he was, the fellow with the hood, standing ahead of him, bow over his shoulder. He was holding something in his hand, something small and round, like a ball. Henrik watched as the man drew back his arm and tossed it at the tank. It hit the front and bounced off, rolling underneath the Challenger. He felt the explosion, though it didn't rupture the shell of the tank. *Damn him, he must have taken grenades from my troops!* "Forward!" Henrik yelled to the driver, but the tank was going nowhere. The explosion had disabled the treads.

When he peered through the smoke, all he could see were trees.

The bastard had left him little choice but to come out now, to kill him the old fashioned way. But Henrik didn't intend on using his fists. Picking up his machine gun, he opened the hatch and stuck his head out, mindful again of the fact that the man could very easily fire off an arrow. He scanned the area. If the hooded man made a move anywhere within sight, he would be dead.

Henrik was aware of something above him in the treetops, something big. A figure. He ducked back down into the hatch, gun poised and ready to fire upwards. An object dropped into the tank, hard and round. He was still about to fire when his mind registered what had just happened. Henrik's eyes grew wide and he let go of the rifle, scrabbling around for the grenade that had just been tossed inside.

"Fetch!" he heard the man shout as he dropped. The hatch slammed shut. Henrik could hear the driver's voice shouting something, but he wasn't listening – he was still looking for the grenade, not caring that he didn't have the pin, nor that he couldn't toss it out of the top anymore...

There it was!

Henrik was actually reaching for the thing when he realised it was too late; he'd taken too long, there was no way he would survive. Just before the explosion came, a phosphorus blast that would set off all the ammo and cook the entire inside of the tank, the cigar fell from Henrik's open mouth, one of the few times he'd ever been without one in his adult life.

And, it was safe to say now, the last.

BILL AND MARK finally made it down the field.

Even from a distance they could see the smoke from inside the woods, curling up into the air. On the outskirts the bikes were left abandoned, one jeep limping off at a snail's pace with maybe three or so people inside it. Of the tank there was no sign, but they could both see where it had pushed its way into the green.

"Judas Priest!" whispered Bill as they drew even closer. "Better wait out here, lad." Mark was having none of this, and Bill had to admit he'd earned the right to see how this thing had played out. They both had.

So, following the trail of the Challenger's tracks, they made their way into the wood. It wasn't long before they came upon the remains of the metal beast. Bill made the mistake of opening the hatch at the top and looking inside.

"Trust me, ye don't want to see in there," he warned Mark before the boy got any ideas.

"It's over," said a voice from behind them, "there's nothing to see here."

Bill and Mark spun around, and spotted Robert.

"Sound like a copper," commented Bill.

"Go home. It's over."

Mark was still looking from the tank to Robert, but the man was trying desperately to avoid his gaze.

"They'll be back," Bill told him. "If this De Falaise thinks he's lord of the manor. And there'll be a lot more folk needin' help, an'all."

"Go home," Robert repeated and began to walk away, into the trees. Mark's next words made him stop.

"What home?"

The man in the hood, with his back to them, hesitated only briefly. Then he blended in with the green.

CHAPTER EIGHT

DE FALAISE STOOD on the balcony, hands on the rail, and surveyed the city below him. There was a glass information plinth – cracked, but still quite readable – which told him exactly what he was looking at, or the major landmarks at least: The view from Castle Rock, south to west, from what had once been the Inland Revenue building, disused now, to Wollaton Hall. Built for Sir Francis Willoughby in 1588 (the year of the Spanish Armada's defeat), the hall was almost as saturated with history as the site on which he stood.

De Falaise's initial explorations of the castle and its grounds had taught him much about this place, all of which had earned his respect and confirmed that it was the best location he could have possibly chosen to mount his takeover.

Surprisingly, the castle had been left relatively untouched by those still alive in the City. As expected, there had been some vandalism – such as spray paint on the side of the castle and various colourful phrases inscribed on the wooden doors of the souvenir shop, as well as defacement of the busts that guarded the door. Lord Byron would definitely not have been happy that they'd turned him into a buffoon with a moustache and a red nose. And the vandals had done some damage inside, too, beginning with the shop – its contents strewn about the place: books about the castle shredded, plastic figures torn from their packaging.

Once it was ascertained that nobody was in residence, De Falaise had insisted on taking his initial tour alone. The ground floor contained the remains of a museum. Glass cabinets housing examples of metalwork, ceramics and woodwork had been smashed, their contents tossed aside. Security grilles over the windows in the shapes of branches and leaves remained intact, sadly useless since the doors had been breached. In one room De Falaise discovered a children's mural depicting an ark, which asked, 'Can you Help Noah Find The Animals?' There were bloodstains smeared over the simplistic paintings of a horse, lion, elephant and toucan.

Similarly, the exhibition called simply 'Threads' had been ravaged, the clothes from various centuries broken out of their cabinets and tried on, then discarded as if in a budget high street shop sale. Dummies were on their sides, some headless, some stamped on till they were flattened.

But it was on this level that De Falaise also found one of his favourite rooms, containing items from the history of the Sherwood Foresters Regiment. The glass cabinets here had been broken into, as well – presumably so that people could reach what they thought were working weapons inside. Upon finding they were either too old, or merely replicas, they'd left them behind. De Falaise was surprised that they'd also left the rather lethal-looking sword bayonets and knives, but then he had no way of knowing how well armed the people who'd broken in here had been. If they'd already had guns, they probably wouldn't have felt the need for close combat weaponry.

He'd noted that the case containing the book of remembrance had also been smashed, the book itself thrown on the ground. De Falaise had stooped to pick up the tome, placing it back where it should be, when his eye caught a pair of dummies wearing full dress uniform: red jackets, white shirts, bow ties and cummerbunds. They were standing in front of a couple of silver cups, worthless now. But if nothing else, this reflected the more civilised side of war. *To the victor, the spoils*, thought De Falaise absently, making a mental note to come back and check what size the uniforms were.

Parts of the wrecked café could be salvaged and used as a mess hall for the men – though as their numbers grew this might have to be reconsidered. In the South Hall he found the long, regal-looking stairs, the white banisters dirty and the grey steps chipped. There were torn posters for an exhibition on the upper floor, which must have still been running when the virus struck Nottingham. De Falaise gazed up at the images showing historical characters who may or may not have existed, but had become legend. The exhibition was all about the latest TV incarnation of these characters, information about each one contained on huge cardboard standees.

It took him through into the long gallery, once a place where the great masters hung: home to Pre-Raphaelites and Andy Warhols alike. The paintings that had run the length of this airy room, its creamy walls smudged with dirt, had now either been slashed or stolen. It upset De Falaise a little, not because he was any great lover of art, but because he loved the *idea* of it. He'd always imagined himself surrounded by the finer things in life. And art was a connection to the past, to history.

Descending into the bowels of the castle, he found one of the most interesting areas – and one remarkably still intact. If there was anything he needed to know about the history of the Castle or the city, it was down here. When the castle had power, a movie theatre had played a twenty-minute film. 'Relive the excitement of battles, intrigues and power struggles,' it announced on the sign, and De Falaise wished that it was still working. Of all the things on this level, De Falaise found three the most fascinating. Firstly, there was a model of the castle as it was in its prime, a natural fortress – at its highest two hundred feet – protected by three sheer rock faces. Many of the same principles of defence still applied, and it would help him considerably when he came to position guards.

Secondly, he found skulls and bones behind glass: 'Evidence from Cemeteries.' He crouched to look at the long-dead, those who had made their mark in history – pledging to do the same. Down another flight of steps, he found the more recently deceased – or pictures of them, anyway, next to a gigantic representation of one of the lion statues from the Council House they'd fired upon. 'Meet You At The Lions,' this display was called, revolving around a focal point in the city where people would get together. Metal rods held plastic squares with photographs of people and messages. Men, women, children: families that were long gone now. De Falaise stared into the faces of the dead citizens, snapshots of a frozen moment in time.

"Rather you than me, *mes amis*," he whispered to them.

A side exit took him back into the open air. He wouldn't stay there long, because he was desperate to check out the famous caves. Man-made, carved out of the rock, he'd had to smash some of the locks that kept out intruders – nobody had bothered before; why should they want to come down here? – and he'd made use of the industrial-strength torches they'd brought with them. Down in the western defensive wall he found a chamber that had been meant for a medieval garrison, and 'David's Dungeon,' where King David II of Scotland had once been held captive. It hadn't been used for this purpose for quite some time, but De Falaise fully intended to put that right. In fact, walking up some steps and outside again, he found a pair of stocks that would also be ideal for his needs.

Down yet more steps, just off from the café, was another man-made structure. De Falaise navigated the sandstone stairs which took him into 'Mortimer's Hole,' a lengthy tunnel named after Roger Mortimer: an Earl of March once taken captive by Edward III (who'd used the passage to enter the castle). The first thing De Falaise would do would be to secure the entrance at the bottom of the tunnel, at Brewhouse Yard, so that nobody could do the same to him. The castle was only vulnerable at points like these – leaving the iron side-gate and the arched Castle Gateway the main causes for concern. As soon as he was satisfied he knew the castle inside out, De Falaise had ordered those defensive positions fortified.

He left the balcony rail now and strolled round the property, along the East Terrace. A glance up to the rooftop revealed the barrel of a sniper rifle, ably handled by Reinhart. Men were positioned at various points along the balcony and armed guards patrolled on a constant basis in shifts. As he made his way along to the steps, De Falaise looked out over the piece of overgrown grass that had once been the site of the Middle Bailey. Now that, and the small car park behind, were home to just a few of the vehicles they'd brought with them – those not out and about, that was.

De Falaise smiled. He thought about the troops already in circulation, making 'contact' with the small communities that had banded together, letting the people know that there was a new force to be reckoned with. They would not just be left alone to get on with things, but would have to bow down to him if they wanted to live. As in Nottingham, as in all of the places over here they'd ploughed through, they'd encountered little resistance. Most saw the wisdom of giving him his tribute, especially with a couple of deaths to illustrate the alternative.

Like the community Javier had reported back on: 'Hope,' its residents had optimistically called it. Their leader had tried to put up a fight, though from what Javier had said, the man hadn't been any kind of threat – which was probably why his people were mourning him right now. Javier had also brought a little unexpected gift back from Hope, the thin, auburn-haired woman who waited inside for him. She'd apparently had a spark in her back at the village, though now she was just like a rag doll which he would use as he pleased; her eyes dull, resigned to the fact she was a possession. It was how he preferred his women to be: malleable. De Falaise took great pleasure in dressing her up in some of the gowns he'd found inside the castle, imagining himself back in the past. He'd tire of her eventually, but for the time being it amused him to have her around. Hands behind his back, he made his way to the nearest doors.

His plans were coming together nicely. And there was nothing and nobody to stand in his way.

THE BOY HAD skirted around and was now standing in his way. This kid had been silent, he'd give him that; and quick.

Robert had been running away – been desperate to get away, in fact – when Mark had appeared in front of him. He hadn't wanted to get involved, wouldn't have done if he hadn't heard the explosions and gunfire coming from the direction of the market. The fact that he'd been hanging about on the edge of the woods, determined not to attend the market, but somehow gravitating towards the place, had nothing to do with it.

Instinct, that's all it had been: a throwback to his years on the force. His curiosity and the fact that people might be at risk was what made him break cover again. Or was it the idea that Mark might be in danger? He dismissed that, because it was dangerous thinking. Whatever the reason, once he'd seen what was going on at the market, he'd had little alternative but to act.

Robert had to admit he'd been shocked. He'd never seen tanks and guns like that outside of visits to museums. And definitely never in action. What did he have to fight these people with? Only the bow and arrows he used for hunting, his knife. They'd cut him to ribbons before he got anywhere near them (a part of him actually found this appealing). But then he got to thinking: it was all a matter of hunting, wasn't it? Maybe he didn't need to get anywhere near them to pick a few off. And if he kept on moving, perhaps they'd miss him initially.

He'd been lucky.

The more adrenalin that pumped through him, the more he used skills he didn't even realise he had: hearing keyed into every bullet fired, every bike or jeep engine; muscles lean and strong, thanks to nothing but exercise and eating from the land; eyes sharp enough to pick a target, enough practice with the bow to hit it faultlessly. It wasn't until now, when he looked back on what he'd just done, that it felt real.

Lucky, that's all. Pure luck.

That and the fact the majority of the 'soldiers' appeared to be novices. Barely a step up from some of the thugs he'd dealt with on a daily basis during his early years on the beat. They knew how to handle their weapons, but that didn't make them fighters. Pin them down and all they really were was scared.

And you killed some – badly injured others...

It wasn't his fault, he reasoned. It was this... what was his name? De Falaise, the Frenchman. And that bastard in the tank, another European. What was this, some kind of invasion?

Not your problem, Robert told himself. *Stay out of it and go back to waiting. Waiting for your death.*

But Mark was preventing him from doing that, barring his path. He pulled off his hood and sighed. "Look, move out of the way, will you?"

Mark shook his head. "I'm not going anywhere."

"Fine," said Robert, stepping to the left in an effort to get around the boy, "then I will."

Like a shadow, Mark sidestepped with him. He could be just as quick as Robert, probably quicker. Robert backed up and tried to go right. Mark was in his way there too,.

"Oh, come on!" Robert shouted, quickly getting fed up with this game. "Let me through or –"

"Or you'll what?" Mark challenged. "Do to me what you did back there to them? I don't think so. You saved us."

"Maybe that was a mistake." He regretted the words as soon as they'd tumbled from his mouth, but couldn't take them back. Mark stuck out his bottom lip – more child than canny adolescent now. "That came out wrong, I didn't mean..."

"S'okay," Mark said, rubbing his nose on his sleeve. "I understand."

"No, you don't," Robert told him. "I meant maybe I should have just left well enough alone. If Bill's right and they do come back, then I could have made things ten times worse for you all."

"They were shooting up the place. They were running me down with motorbikes! They had a tank, for fuck's sake –"

"Watch your mouth," snapped Robert instinctively, chastising himself almost as he did so. He had no right to tell this kid off.

Mark looked at him, confused, then added softly: "How much worse could it be than that?"

Robert considered this for a moment. "More men; more guns; more tanks. People like that always come back stronger than ever."

"Then you agree with Bill?"

That was clever – Robert had walked right into that one. If he agreed that De Falaise's troops would return in larger numbers, then didn't he have an obligation to help out? Hadn't he just admitted his own guilt in the next stage of whatever this was? Robert said nothing, for fear of digging himself a deeper hole.

"It weren't no surprise, anyway," Mark said eventually to break the awkward silence.

"What are you talking about?"

"The men coming. You hear things, touring round, y'know? I knew something was going on, just not what – or that it would reach us here."

"So this is already happening in other areas?"

Mark nodded. "Lots. Food, clothing, all sorts taken. Even people, sometimes."

"Why didn't you tell..." Robert had forgotten himself for a moment and Mark punished him for it.

"Tell someone? What, you mean like the police?" He knew Mark was studying his face for some kind of reaction; what Bill had hinted at just ten minutes ago had obviously stuck with him.

"No. I meant... Isn't there someone..."

"I told you before," Mark said. "There isn't anyone. I haven't got a regular place to stay. Nobody to take care of me..."

"I thought you said you didn't need anyone to do that," said Robert, turning the boy's own words back on him.

"I don't," snapped Mark, puffing up his chest. "But..."

"What?"

"It's hard sometimes. Being on my own." Mark looked down. For all his bluster, this kid missed having a home, having parents. Missed TV, games, holidays.

"Read to me some more, Dad... please..."

Robert shook his head. "I don't know what you want me to say."

Mark nodded at the woodland. "You live out here, don't you? All by yourself."

"Yes."

"Don't you miss... y'know, people? To like, hang out with and stuff?"

Robert thought back to the men in yellow with the gas masks, then pictured the men with machine guns. Nothing had really changed in all that time, had it? The answer had to be no. But how could he write off the rest of the dwindling population when there were still people like Bill out there, the men and women from the market? And Mark. "I... I try not to think about it," was all he could answer.

There was another awkward pause before Mark came right out and said what was on his mind. "Can I come with you?"

So many emotions flooded through Robert at that moment he couldn't really make sense of them. But chief amongst them was fear. He'd felt oddly calm as he'd dodged the bullets and gone up against the German in the tank. Now this simple question petrified him. How could he let Mark come with him, how could he risk spending any time with him at all, when he could be snatched away at any moment like Stevie had been? Robert had come here to wait, not to be an adoptive father.

"Out of the question," he said at last.

"I know people in lots of places, I could keep tabs on what's going on and get back to you with –"

"Didn't you just hear what I said?" Robert's tone was harder now. "I can't... Look, I just can't. Okay?"

Mark frowned. "I'll pull my weight, honest. I'm a hard worker."

"No," Robert told him.

Mark pulled items out of his bag now, as if he was trading at the market. "Please. Here, you can have it all... And I have other stuff, stashed away, really cool stuff that –"

"I said no!" Robert surprised himself with the harshness of his reply.

The boy's face fell sharply, and for a moment Robert felt sure he was going to cry. As he'd suspected, the streetwise attitude was simply a front, and now Mark had let Robert see too much of the real him. Slowly, the lad began to gather the things back into his bag.

"Listen, I'm sorry," began Robert, reaching out a hand as if to place it on Mark's shoulder, then quickly withdrawing it. "It's just that... I can't let you come with me."

Mark stared at him. "Why?"

It was a simple enough question, but the answer was so complicated. "I can't tell you that, either. Go back to Bill, Mark. You'll be safe with him." Robert pulled up his hood and stepped around the boy. This time Mark didn't try to stop him.

What are you doing? said a voice in Robert's head, the small part of him still connected to the past: to his family, to his job. *He needs help... they all do.* But he'd 'helped' enough for one day, caused more trouble than he'd prevented, probably. *So what, you're just going to run away now and let them get on with it?*

Robert tried to force the thoughts out of his head, but they persisted. *Can you do that? Can you really? Have you strayed so far from who you used to be?*

He was tempted to look back over his shoulder at Mark, but gritted his teeth and told himself that the kid would be better off without him; a dysfunctional excuse for a human being. Robert couldn't give him what he so obviously wanted, someone to look up to, someone to admire.

After a few minutes Robert broke into a run. Pretty soon he was swallowed by the wilds he now called home.

DE FALAISE NEVER liked to be interrupted when he was entertaining. Especially with news like this.

The knock on the door of the converted office was light, but curt. It had been followed by a cough, then: "My... my Lord?"

De Falaise answered the door dressed in his robe. He recognised one of the young men they'd recruited on their travels – he didn't remember his name (it began with 'G'... Granville, Grantham possibly?), but he'd been a member of that ridiculous gang that called themselves The Jackals, and De Falaise did remember ordering one of his friend's deaths. Yes, there was the scar on the back of his raised hand, where Tanek's bolt had found its mark. Now the only thing that had stopped De Falaise from grabbing this silly boy by the throat and carving onto his chest 'Do not disturb' was the use of his new title, a mark of respect he was owed.

"Ahem..." said the young man, attempting to keep his eyes dead ahead, and not on De Falaise's lack of clothing, nor what was beyond him in the room. "My Lord, I bring news of an incident involving one of our units."

"What kind of incident?"

"We're... we're not quite sure. Tanek sent me to fetch you, he said it would be better if you talked to one the survivors yourself. He's down in the stables."

De Falaise caught the youth gazing past him, at the woman on the bed. "Tell Tanek I will be with him momentarily, *oui*?" The youth made to leave. "Oh, and next time you see too much, I will take out your eyes. Do you understand?"

Granville or Grantham, or whatever his name was, nodded. There was no hint of disobedience anymore, just terror – pure and simple.

"Run along, run along." De Falaise clapped his hands to get the moron moving, then closed the door and prepared to get ready.

Ten minutes later, after dressing and posting a guard to watch the woman from Hope, he'd joined Tanek and a handful of others in the former stables. He was not at all surprised to see that the big man had already put the stocks there to good use, but he did raise an eyebrow when he saw that the youth occupying them was wearing a uniform.

As De Falaise joined them, Tanek explained that the 'soldier' and a couple of others – currently being held down in the caves – had been caught trying to flee the area by one of their routine patrols.

De Falaise bent slightly and asked the man his name.

"R-rory," he gasped, obviously having trouble breathing in the stocks.

"Was he not in Henrik's unit?" De Falaise asked Tanek. The larger man nodded.

"What happened? Why were you trying to escape?"

At first Rory didn't answer, but then De Falaise gestured to Tanek, who grabbed hold of the captive, yanking his head up by his sweaty hair. "Answer!"

"*Gak*... I was scared... Scared of... of what you'd do to me."

"I see," De Falaise said, "as opposed to what we are doing now, you mean? No one has the option of walking away from my army, my young friend, I thought I had made that abundantly clear?"

Tanek pulled Rory's head back further and he let out a frightened choke.

De Falaise leaned in, his face inches from Rory's. "Tell me what happened. Tell me what was so... frightening that you could not return."

Rory's eyes flitted from Tanek to De Falaise. "Our... our unit... wiped out."

De Falaise raised another eyebrow. "A whole squadron of men, with jeeps, motorbikes and a tank?"

Rory tried to nod, but Tanek's grip held him fast.

"And your commanding officer?" De Falaise enquired.

It was barely a shake of the head, thanks to Tanek, but it was enough.

"Impossible! Henrik was one of my best!" De Falaise searched Rory's features for any hint that he might be lying. "How could this be? A gang, a group of resistance?" Had the people of the region banded together to fight back so quickly? If so, it was serious news indeed, and they would require wiping out. Then another thought occurred to him. "Or did you organise this yourself, perhaps? Kill the rest of the men and then make a run for it?"

Again, Rory attempted to shake his head, his breath coming in quick gasps.

"Then what? I need to know!"

"A... A man."

"What? Just one man? You're lying."

Rory forced out the words. "No. A man... one man did it all. He came from the trees."

"The trees? What on Earth are you talking about?"

"A man wearing a hood. He was like a ghost."

De Falaise frowned. "Where did this skirmish take place?"

It was Tanek who answered him this time. The incident had occurred not far from Rufford. De Falaise stood up and felt the corners of his mouth rise slightly. In spite of himself, and in spite of the fact he'd just lost one of his most capable and trusted fighters in Henrik, De Falaise was smiling. Then that smile turned itself into a chuckle, the chuckle a laugh. Suddenly De Falaise was guffawing like he'd just heard the funniest joke ever. Rory gaped at him, then stared upwards at Tanek, who appeared equally mystified.

"Can none of you besides myself see it?" De Falaise asked as he looked from the captive to Tanek. "Someone else is playing the game." They looked at him blankly. "Do you not understand? A man wearing a hood... A hooded man? Just like the statue outside this very castle!"

He waited for it to dawn on them. This all made sense now, especially when you factored in what Javier had told him about Hope; about the name De Falaise had acquired there. If he was to play the role of the Sheriff of Nottingham, then someone was auditioning for the part of his arch nemesis. Someone who was a little too enamoured with the old legends of this place.

"Gentlemen, history is repeating itself, is it not? But there will be a different outcome this time. History is written by the victors, and it has painted my 'predecessor' in a remarkably bad light. That will not be allowed to happen again. This hooded man must be destroyed at once, before news of what has happened reaches the rest of the towns and villages. Before we really do have rumblings of rebellion."

De Falaise ordered Tanek to extract as much information from Rory as he could about what had happened. "Use any means necessary; and when you are finished with him, work on the rest. Then we will send out as many men as we can spare."

"Where to?" Tanek enquired.

De Falaise grinned once more. "Where else would we send them to hunt for the hooded man, but to Rufford? Rufford, at the heart of Sherwood Forest!"

CHAPTER NINE

IT WASN'T AN easy thing to do, but Robert was putting what had happened behind him. Not the big thing, not the thing that sent him out here in the first place, but the thing that had happened a couple of days ago at the market. He'd returned to his life as 'normal,' busied himself with the everyday, with catching food and living out his time. At night he still dreamt of the men, of his son, of Mark, but on waking he was able to slot them into some hidden compartment of his brain. He'd quietened the voices that told him he was leaving Bill and the others to fend for themselves against overwhelming forces; armed men that he'd brought down on them. It was none of his business – *Oh, so suddenly it's nothing to do with you? Weren't saying that when you were rushing to their defence, were you?* – it didn't matter anymore what happened, he of all people should know that.

He could just keep on running, keep on hiding. It was for the best.

But when you cast a stone into the water it creates ripples. He could no more run from his destiny than he could kill himself.

A FEW DAYS later he spotted an intruder near to his camp.

Or at least he thought it was an intruder – he'd been on edge since his encounter with De Falaise's men, for which no one could really blame him. Robert had been bringing back some of the day's spoils when he spotted movement in the undergrowth not far from his tent. Robert had done his best to camouflage his home, and doubted whether any passers by would see it from a distance. But what if they were looking for it?

Relax, he told himself, *might only be an animal.* Though it hardly ever happened, deer had been known simply to walk into his camp before now. They never stayed long, though, and could count themselves lucky that the times they'd done so had been when he'd had more than enough meat to last him.

But it wasn't an animal. As Robert crouched down he saw the shadow cast across the trees. Leaving the catches where they were, he began to move around, encircling the camp, keeping low and nocking a freshly-made arrow onto his bow at the same time. The approaching figure was stealthy, but over time Robert had become the master. When he was close enough, he rose up out of the woodland, aiming his arrow at the intruder's head. His finger twitched, almost releasing the missile.

What he saw made him ease up, and let the tension of the bow lapse. There, holding his hands in the air, was Mark. "Don't shoot!" he urged, a little too late.

Robert let out a long sigh. "What are you doing here? I could have killed you."

"I..." Mark began, the implications only now sinking in. "You could've as well, couldn't you?"

Robert's gaze never faltered. "I still could," he informed him. "Why have you come here when I specifically told you not to?"

He wasn't expecting Mark's answer. "To warn you."

"What?"

Mark nodded. "They're coming for you, Robert. De Falaise's men."

"How do you know?"

"How do I get to know anything?" Mark said with a smile. "I keep my ear to the ground. And right now I can hear marching feet."

"Let them come."

The boy moved closer. "You don't understand, they're coming in mob-handed. De Falaise got wind of what you did and he's going to take you down before you cause any more trouble for him."

"Is he now?"

"Yes," said Mark. "And they're on their way from Nottingham. You have to get out of here."

Robert gave a hollow laugh. "I'm not going anywhere."

"Don't you understand? They're going to kill you!"

"I understand, and what I said the other day still stands. Get out of here – go where it's safe, Mark."

Mark scowled. "After all that? After risking my neck to come and tell you, you still –"

"Sshh," Robert told him, holding his finger to his lips.

Mark froze; he'd been too busy talking to notice. "What?"

"Gunfire," said Robert. "They're already here."

*   *   *

MAYBE IT WAS being the one to deliver the news that had landed Granger in this mess. Here they all were, entering a forest, looking for someone who had taken on a whole unit of De Falaise's men and won. Granger thought of them as De Falaise's men rather than his own now, though there were a few other former members of the Jackals here today with him. They'd been through too much on the road up north to ever be the same again. If the Cull had changed them once, set them free, then meeting De Falaise had changed them back again, into drones of a new machine.

Every night when he slept – when he could even get to sleep in the crowded makeshift barracks on the upper floor of the castle – he saw the bolt entering Ennis's head. Saw what that git Tanek had done to him on De Falaise's orders. He'd wake, sweating, the scar on his hand throbbing.

And he'd seen many more die at their hands when they'd refused to sign up for this mad army, run by an even madder dictator. Christ alone knew what he was doing to that poor woman in his bedroom.

You can hardly talk, what about the girls that The Jackals took in? That was different, he argued with himself. *They needed protection, they knew what they were doing and got something in return.* The woman brought back from that village by 'Major' Javier – who'd be leading them into the forest today – had been virtually catatonic. He'd seen her eyes when they ushered her into the castle. They were cold and dead. Whatever had been done to her, even before De Falaise entered the picture, must have been enough to bend her mind.

So here he was, serving that lunatic, calling him 'Lord' just so he wouldn't do to him that he'd done to those men they'd caught deserting. One poor sod was still hanging in the stocks after he'd been tortured for information, his screams heard throughout the grounds as Tanek had done things to him Granger didn't even want to think about. The others had been interrogated down in the caves.

It was how they knew what they were up against today: a single bloke who'd shot out the wheels of bikes and jeeps just using arrows. Who'd killed that psychotic cigar-smoking kraut, Henrik, blowing up his toy tank in the process.

Yep, they were looking for bloody Rambo out here.

Given the option, Granger wouldn't have been present at all – he would have been cheering this guy on from the sidelines. This man had the guts to take on De Falaise and obviously had him rattled. So much so that he'd sent along a bunch of heavily armed troops to bring back the man's body. De Falaise was definitely taking no chances.

Something rustled in the undergrowth to their left and, almost in unison, the men turned and fired. The forest came alive with light, the muzzles of machine guns flaring. Even before Granger had a chance to aim, the ceasefire had been given. Javier stepped in front of the men, examining the shredded bushes and trees.

"It's nothing, false alarm. Just a hare or something," he said to his men by way of headsets.

Granger groaned. So they were shooting at Thumper now? What next, Bambi's mother?

"I don't like this," muttered a soldier to Granger's right. He knew what the guy meant; even with their firepower, it felt like they were sitting ducks, felt like they were the ones being targeted. And they'd just told whoever was out there exactly where to find them. Smart.

They moved forwards, following Javier, knowing that they didn't have a choice in the matter. The overweight Mexican was De Falaise's eyes and ears; he might as well *be* him. If they revolted, more men who had no choice would come after them. Granger knew that, they all did.

"Why don't you try picking on someone your own size?" came a voice out of nowhere. It echoed all around them, impossible to trace. "If you can find anyone."

"There!" shouted Javier, "It's him!" He pointed, and the men opened up on the trees once more. Except for Granger. He had his finger on the trigger of his weapon, but something told him he'd be wasting his ammo.

When the gunfire died down, he was proved right. All was quiet and still for a moment or two, then came the voice again. "Nice try."

"*Bastardo*!" spat Javier, red faced.

There was movement again in the foliage – but this time Javier himself was on it. He brought up his M16/Colt Commando, firing an incendiary from the grenade launcher fitted underneath. He laughed crazily as the forest burst into flames, burning everything ahead of him. "How does that suit you, my friend?"

There was no answer this time.

The next movement was sudden, and from a completely different direction. Javier pointed, ordering a handful of his men into the trees, Granger included.

Shit! he thought. *More orders, more trouble.*

Granger held well back as the troops moved in. They crept along as they scanned the area. A guy on his right was the first to go down.

Granger heard a snapping sound and turned, quickly enough to see a snare around his ankle yanking him sideways as the branch it was attached to dragged him away into the foliage.

"Place is booby-trapped. He's led us into a fucking trap!" shouted another man, right before his leg disappeared into a hole covered over with bracken. He cried out in pain, eyes watering. Another ran across to help him, tripping some twine on the floor, which in turn dislodged the stick holding a weighty branch in place. This swung down and hit the man squarely in the chest, sending him reeling backwards, rifle flying out of his grasp.

Granger didn't see how the next soldier set off the trap, but he spotted all too late the spear that was fired from what looked like a huge bow. It hurtled across the green into the man's shoulder, with enough impact to carry him back a few steps before he eventually fell.

More cries came as the rest of his 'comrades' experienced the same. Spears, snares and tripwires caught them out. Set in a concentrated area to catch animals, they were now decimating their number. Another fell when a homemade bolas wrapped itself around his neck.

Granger retreated, slowly, glancing down at the ground as he did so. Nervously, he checked around him in case he set anything off. Too late he heard the cracking sound below, then the next thing he knew he was being yanked upwards, the net closing in around him and pulling him into the air. His gun fell out of his hands, the mike from his head. He felt his stomach roll as he was hoisted up, only stopping when it reached a certain height.

There he was left, dangling. He took deep breaths, calming himself down. *You're still alive, still alive. Just caught in a net, that's all. You can get out of this.*

Even as he thought it, someone passed by beneath him wearing a hood. He paused to look up at Granger, and the youth thought that was it – his time was finally up. Then the hooded man went on his way, disappearing into the undergrowth as if he'd never really existed at all.

JAVIER HAD HEARD all the screams through his headset and scowled.

It was one thing he hadn't anticipated, although he probably should have. Having led men into battle in the jungles of South America, he should have thought more about the possibility of traps. But who would have expected the quiet English countryside to be like those war zones? These were different times, though, weren't they? This was post-Cull

Britain and anything was possible. The man they were dealing with was a hunter, of course he'd know how to lay traps! Now a good part of his squad had been incapacitated, probably killed.

Bastardo!

Javier shook his head. He couldn't let some fucking Englishman with a sense of the theatrical get the better of him. He still had over a dozen well-armed men and –

There was a noise. It sounded like something whistling, travelling fast. "Take cover!" screamed Javier, but the single arrow didn't strike any of the men as he'd expected. Instead it hit the ground, some distance from where they were standing.

What is he doing? thought Javier. *Either he's a very bad aim or...*

"Get up! Get up and get out!" Javier barked, but he was too late.

The explosion was loud, the live grenade attached to the arrow suddenly detonating. The nearest men were thrown into the air, jerking as if performing a circus act on wires. Smoke was everywhere.

Through the smog, he saw a figure. It darted between the trees, entering the arena of battle, taking on those who were still standing, making the most of their confusion. Javier could have warned them, but wanted to observe his enemy in combat, get the measure of him. The hooded figure was trained well in the defensive arts, that much was obvious by the way he handled himself. Deflecting punches with his forearms, kicking, throwing men onto the ground and winding them. One pulled a Browning pistol out of his holster and the hooded man spun around, grabbing the soldier's arm and bringing it down over one raised knee until the gun was relinquished. He fought as if he didn't care what happened to him, and yet at the same time Javier recognised some sort of survival instinct there. It was a curious and very dangerous combination.

By the time the smoke had cleared, Javier had brought his grenade launcher to bear again, letting off another incendiary in the hooded man's general direction. And, just as he hadn't anticipated what had happened with the traps, he didn't see what came next, either.

The hooded man cowered from the spreading fire.

Could it be that... Yes! He was actually afraid of the flames. Javier grinned. The hooded man held up his hand to protect his face, stumbling backwards, his mouth open in fear.

This wasn't any ordinary aversion, Javier could see that. It was as if the fire held some kind of special significance for him – some private terror that only he knew about.

It didn't matter. He'd burn the bastard to a crisp and take his remains back to De Falaise. Javier could imagine what the Frenchman might say: "You have done well, Major. Pick a county and you will rule it as my deputy." It was why all of them were with the man, wasn't it? Power? A chance to rule? Or maybe he should take the hooded man back to De Falaise alive so that he and Tanek could have some of their special brand of fun?

Javier had only let his mind wander for a moment or two, but it was enough for everything to change. Suddenly, out of nowhere, there were other people there. One of the rising soldiers was struck across the face by what Javier thought at first to be a piece of wood, a branch of some kind: another trap the hooded man had set? No... now he could see it was a walking stick, brandished by a squat, bald man, who was even now attacking again. He looked very familiar.

And who was that on the other side? Smaller than the rest, throwing stones at a couple of the other soldiers. A rock caught one man a glancing blow across the temple and he collapsed to his knees.

So he has friends, then? Javier mulled. As he suspected there was no way he'd been able to do all this on his own. *No matter, I'll fry the lot of them.* He brought up his weapon one final time, then felt something hard pressing into his cheek.

Javier's eyes swivelled left and down. They traced the end of the shotgun to another man. "How do," said the ruddy-faced man in the checked shirt and tank top. "I'd be droppin' that about now if I were ye. We don't want no accidents, do we? Nice and slow."

The Mexican lowered his weapon, which the man with the shotgun took off him.

"When De Falaise learns of this, you will all be in big trouble," grumbled Javier. Even to his ears, it sounded lame.

"That so?"

Javier nodded, but the ruddy-face man just laughed. The battle – the hunt – was over and they'd lost. Javier knew it, his enemies knew it. But the next thing he knew was blackness, as the man turned the gun around and hit him hard with the butt.

ONCE THEY'D DEALT with the fires and tied up all prisoners left alive, the trio turned their attentions to Robert.

He had barely said a word; just sat propped up against a tree, eyes staring out from beneath his hood. It had been the incendiary that had done this, but no one knew why. None of them dared to ask. Instead, they discussed what should be done about De Falaise's men.

"I know what I'd like to do to that one," said the Reverend Tate, leaning on his stick. He pointed across at Javier, still spark out and helpless as a baby. A complete reversal of the last time they'd met. "He took a friend of mine away, killed another."

Bill nodded. "Aye. But could ye really do that? A man of God and all?"

"An eye for an eye, the Bible says." But Tate conceded the point. "All right, maybe just a bit of a pummelling, then."

"I'm worried about Robert," interrupted Mark. They both looked at the boy who'd brought them here today, who'd sent word that De Falaise's men were on their way to the forest and that Robert might need their assistance. In spite of the fact the man had turned his back on them earlier on that week, Bill knew that he owed him a debt. And when news reached Tate, even though he hadn't met the man, he came. Maybe it was partly for revenge – a concept he wasn't supposed to believe in – or was it something else? To meet the man who'd taken on De Falaise's troops at the market, the person that people in neighbouring villages and towns were already talking about? The Hooded Man. Someone they might be able rally behind? A figurehead?

A hero?

He didn't look like one at the moment.

"Perhaps I should talk with him?" offered Tate. "I'm used to it, after all. Giving counsel. I can be quite persuasive when I need to be."

Mark and Bill both shrugged, then watched as the holy man walked over to the tree where Robert sat gazing at nothingness. They could just about hear the conversation between the two men, which was woefully one-sided to begin with. Tate introduced himself, explained what had happened in Hope, the things Javier and some of his men had done there, when all the community had really wanted was to start over again.

That had done the trick, woken Robert from his stupor. "Start over? There is no starting over. No forgetting the past."

Tate frowned. "No one's suggesting we should forget what's gone before, my son. It's just that –"

"Don't you understand? There's no going back!"

"And where would you go, if you could?" asked Tate, resting on his stick. "To somewhere before the virus, hmm? To save someone you loved? Is that why you're out here all alone?"

Robert's lips were a straight line.

Tate waved over his shoulder. "And those people back there, Mark and Bill; do you not think they would give everything they have to turn back the clock? Don't you think they lost people they loved as well?"

"It's not the same," Robert said. Then, more quietly: "Not the same."

"How can you say that? For each and every one of us, it's personal. I lost parishioners, people I cared about a great deal," Tate continued. "And for a time, the briefest of times, I almost lost my faith as well."

"Faith," huffed the man in the hood.

"That's right. Don't think I haven't questioned what all this was for, what it was about. But still I have to believe there's a purpose to it. That something good might come out of this yet."

Robert looked up, the shadows disappearing from his eyes. "What purpose, what good?"

Tate shook his head. "I honestly don't know. But I do know one thing, if we stand by and let men like De Falaise have their way, then this world hasn't got a chance."

"What exactly do you expect me to do about it?"

Tate leaned in further. "I saw what you did back there, or at least some of it. And I heard about what you did at the market, the people you helped. In spite of what you might say, I know you care. Now, you have a choice. You can turn your back on them." He looked over at Bill and Mark once more. "Even though they came here today to warn you, to help you. You can turn your back on everything again, in fact, detach yourself from the hurt, from caring about anyone ever again. Or..." Tate paused. "Or you can save them. You can lead them. You can stop De Falaise. Ask yourself what the people you lost would have wanted you to do."

Robert didn't answer Tate, just sat deep in thought. Then he got up. Trying hard not to catch Mark and Bill's eyes, the hooded man strode over to where the prisoners were tied up. He examined their faces one by one, the men he'd attacked, those who'd fallen foul of his traps.

One of them, a soldier Robert had last seen dangling from a net, stared at him. He couldn't have been more than twenty.

"Please don't kill us." The young man spoke with a southern accent.

Robert pulled down his hood. "You want me to let you go, is that it? So you can return to De Falaise?"

The youth thought about this, then shook his head. "Not after what he did to the others. The men you let go last time..."

Robert remembered what another young man had told him in similar circumstances, almost in tears. *"Please... please don't hurt me, I had no choice. He was going to kill me; kill us all."* Then Robert looked across at the other troops, saw that they were terrified of the same thing.

"You did these things, joined De Falaise's army, because you had no choice, right?"

He nodded.

"Okay, now I'm going to give you one," Robert told him.

The youth looked puzzled.

"What's your name?"

There was a moment's hesitation before he replied: "Granger."

"All right, then, Granger. I'm going to offer you, offer all of you, a choice." He looked back over his shoulder at Tate. "You can join me... join us. Help take down De Falaise, provide information so that we can put an end to his operation. Or you can take your chances out there."

Tate limped over to join him. "Hold on, what are you doing? This isn't what I meant. They were sent here to kill you, Robert."

"They're scared."

"They can't be trusted," argued the Reverend. "They've committed terrible acts."

"Many of them because they were forced to. Because De Falaise rules through terror, not trust." Robert undid the bonds that held Granger. "If we're going to do this, that's not how it'll work here." Robert held out his hand. "So, what do you say?"

Granger looked at the outstretched hand, as if not quite sure what to do, as if nobody had ever shown such faith in him before.

Then, finally, he reached out with his own scarred hand and shook Robert's.

CHAPTER TEN

IT HAD BEEN rich pickings that day.

In the front seat of the truck, Savero nursed his rifle and smiled. De Falaise would be more than happy with the hoard his unit were bringing back to the castle. As specified, they'd started up near a place called Worksop a few days ago and wound their way down the map, back towards Nottingham. De Falaise had guessed correctly – as he usually did – that the most productive communities had actually sprung up away from the major towns and cities, in countryside like this. It made sense for people to gather together out in rural areas, away from the attention of the gangs and violence that characterised the larger, urban localities. These were the communities using a network of markets and trading to get by. England had indeed been thrown back to the Middle Ages in some respects, to a time before rail networks and airports. People had to be self-sufficient, which suited De Falaise and his army well... because they weren't. Why bother, when they could just go around creaming off food, clothing and any other useful items they might want from less well organised – and less well armed – factions?

Just outside a place called Sutton-in-Ashfield, in fact, they'd come across a clump of people who'd gone back to their roots. They thought the world had forgotten about them, off the beaten track, but what they didn't know was Savero and his troops were actively searching for such places. They'd steamrollered in, the three jeeps, four bikes and two trucks, enough to put paid to any resistance from the inhabitants. In the face of uniformed men with automatic weaponry, they'd handed over their goods without complaint. Savero had organised the collections, ordering the men to take whatever they could find that might be of use, loading it up into the back of the Bedfords for transportation to the next location, and then finally on to their base.

They used the back roads mainly, as it was easier to spot houses hidden by trees or in the dips of hills. A couple of times they'd come across isolated farm houses, with only a handful of people gathered there. It always amused Savero to see how the 'men' of the villages and households crumpled when confronted with people armed to the gills. Now and again you'd get one who fought back, but usually only with crude weapons like knives. England's pre-Cull gun ban ensured that only criminals and those from large cities had any halfway decent weaponry. Certainly nothing compared with De Falaise's arsenal.

Savero hated using the old cliché, but it really was like taking candy from babies. It was just as De Falaise had promised when he recruited the Italian. The practised speech he'd given when they met in Parma might have come across as so much hot air had anyone else been speaking the words. But the Frenchman's impassioned plea, the way he carried himself, and the way he had already inspired loyalty in the men he'd recruited to his cause, made Savero take him very seriously indeed.

"You have balls, Savero. Come with me, work for me," De Falaise had said, "and I promise you won't regret it."

Savero hadn't in the slightest, not even when they'd been in the heat of battle. Because his life had turned around at that moment. He was no longer on his own, scrabbling for survival, fighting off the nuts stupid enough to approach him, avoiding the gangs that had sewn up pockets of Europe. He felt a part of something special, however small, and look where that decision had taken him, look how it had all grown. Savero was an officer in De Falaise's army, had men under him once more. Just like the old days in the Esercito Italiano – the Italian Army – before the lure of money persuaded him to go AWOL. Granted, they weren't the elite he'd fought with then, but there was strength in numbers. And they were petrified of him, of De Falaise. With good reason. Savero watched his driver for a moment, a man in his late twenties, dressed in the uniform of a soldier but with the uncertain look of a new recruit. Even more uncertain the longer Savero stared at him, uncomfortable under his scrutiny.

No, there was something else. Something his driver had spotted down this country lane they were following towards Nottingham, fields, trees and hedgerows on either side of them. Savero faced front again and saw what the problem was. Up ahead, just as the lane hit a kink, was a car... Wait, a jeep. One of *their* jeeps, a Wolf like those accompanying his unit today. It was blocking off the narrow road, bonnet up, a couple of uniformed men examining the inside as if there was something wrong with the engine.

Savero ordered the truck to slow down – they were going nowhere till this was sorted out. He wound down the passenger window and stuck his head out.

"Hey, you – what's the big hold up?" he called out to the soldiers by the broken down vehicle. One of the men standing by the bonnet came forward, shielding his eyes from the mid-afternoon sun. He shrugged, pointing back to the jeep. Savero sighed deeply, opened the door and clambered out. He was going to leave his rifle on the front seat, but at the last second took it with him. It was habit. A good soldier always kept his weapon with him at all times.

Savero walked towards the young trooper, even more fresh-faced than his driver. "What's wrong with it?"

The man shrugged again, this time adding, "No idea. Don't know much about engines. It just started making this funny noise and..."

Savero wasn't really listening to him anymore. He was listening to his instincts instead. Something wasn't right here. Something didn't add up. "What are you doing out here anyway? This was our designated route back."

"Routine patrol, sir," said the soldier, but there had been a brief hesitation before answering.

"Who's in charge? It can't be you."

Another one of the soldiers, the guy with his head in the engine looked up at the pair of them. Suddenly Savero saw it, the panic in his eyes.

"Er..." began the first lad. "In charge... er..."

"I asked you a question!"

"That would be... him." The soldier nodded behind Savero, and even as he turned, raising his eyes, he saw the shadow dropping down from the overhanging trees to land on the roof of the truck.

He swore, raising his rifle, and the soldier jostled him, spoiling his aim. The man in the hood ducked sideways as the bullets completely missed their target. Savero spotted more men emerging from behind the hedgerow, armed just as they were... because they *were* them: soldiers from De Falaise's ranks. What was happening here, some kind of revolt?

Before his own men could react, the rebels had pulled them from their jeeps, prodded them off their bikes with the ends of their rifles.

Savero spun back around, training his gun on the youth who had knocked his arm. But before he could fire, the man on top of the truck leaped down on him.

Savero was pushed forwards, the rifle knocked from his clutches. It was quickly picked up by the traitor who had led them into this trap.

"*Figlio di puttana*!" cried Savero, wriggling out from under his attacker. He was up in seconds, but then so was the bearded man in the hood. "Who are you?"

The man didn't answer him, which only infuriated Savero further. He went to punch the man in the stomach, but his opponent shifted his weight slightly so the blow landed east of where it should have.

The man brought his own fist down and the Italian moved towards the blow, angling himself so that his forehead took the full force of the punch. But he didn't stop there. Savero continued to bring up his head so that he caught the man's chin from beneath, knocking the hooded man sharply backwards. His enemy stumbled a few feet, shaking his head.

Savero grinned. "You won't win." By now he saw people gathered round, his own men and those who had come out of the hedges. He also spotted a couple of people out of uniform, one who looked like a farmer holding a shotgun, another – unarmed – limping with a stick. They were all fixated on the fight.

This is more than just a brawl, realised Savero. Whoever wins this will have their respect... *But you can take him. He's just some guy who thinks he can play in the big leagues.*

He launched himself at the hooded man again, attempting a roundhouse punch to the ear. The bearded man bent, not allowing the blow to settle, then responded with an uppercut, which snapped Savero's head back. It was his turn to shake himself, his vision slightly blurred. Savero saw the hooded man rolling up his sleeves, ready to go again.

He didn't give him the chance.

Savero ran at him, grabbing him by the middle, shoving him backwards into the truck. The air exploded out of his opponent's body. Savero stepped back again, watching with satisfaction as the hooded man crumpled. Then he took a run up, to kick the winded man. Instead, he found his foot being grabbed, then twisted and pushed back so that he lost his balance completely. Savero fell onto his shoulder blades; hard.

"*Merda*!"

Savero rolled onto his side as the hooded man climbed to his feet. Getting a knee under himself, he rose as well, but not quickly enough. The man was on him, not letting up for a second. Savero was being pummelled with blows from the left and right. He held up his arms to defend himself, swinging blindly. In the end he tried to push the man away, but after a few seconds the punishment continued. Savero reached down to his belt, loosing the knife he kept there. He brought it up in an arc, slashing the hooded man across the chest, though not deep enough to penetrate his clothes.

Now, squatting down, he slashed at his enemy again. But then he saw the hooded man produce his own knife: a hunter's blade with serrated edge. Savero acknowledged it with a tip of the head. They circled each other, two sets of eyes fixed. Savero watched for any sudden movements, as the hooded did the same. At last, it was the Italian who moved first, running at his enemy and bringing down his blade. The hooded man blocked him by raising his forearm, linking the pair together so that neither could strike. They pulled each other around, as if in some kind of crazy dance, until finally the hooded man brought up his knee and levered Savero back. The Italian was not fast enough to avoid the slash that cut open the top of his right arm, and he let out a wounded shout.

Through clenched teeth, Savero cursed the man again. *Why won't you just lie down? Why won't you die?* In all his time he had never encountered an opponent so reluctant to give an inch, so hard to read. It was as though he wasn't bothered about dying; and if he wasn't frightened of death, why should he be scared of Savero?

When the Italian came at him this time, he made a false play, pretending to go in one direction, then dodging back behind the hooded man, snaking an arm around his neck so that it was in the crook of Savero's elbow. The knife point dug into Hood's chest. One false move and he'd drive it downwards into his heart.

"Ah, that's it... " he grunted in the man's ear. "You're mine n –"

Savero was aware of a numbness. Something warm and wet was leaking into the crotch of his trousers, and for a bizarre second he thought he might have somehow wet himself. But a wave of pain was spreading outwards; enough for him to let go of his captive. Savero looked down and saw the knife sticking out of him, right in the 'V' of his legs. The sight, the knowledge of what had happened, multiplied the pain a million fold.

Savero dropped his own knife and his hands went to the other one. He thought about it, but daren't touch the thing, let alone pull it out. He saw the faces in the crowd, the 'thank God that's not me' expressions, and he stared at the hooded man, uncomprehending. It was one thing to kill him, to die in battle – it was quite another to do this to someone.

Savero staggered a couple of feet, but the pain when he moved was tremendous. He knew the blood draining out of him rapidly – the femoral artery sliced. Wincing, he dropped to his knees, then fell over sideways. Tears were streaming from his eyes.

The shape of the man standing over him was indistinct, the pain that had been so sharp a minute or two ago was now dull and throbbing. *So this is what it's like*, Savero thought to himself. In a funny sort of way he welcomed death, for what kind of a shameful life would he be able to lead after what had happened.

Something De Falaise had said that first time they met came back to Savero. "You have balls..."

He would have laughed at the irony, had he been able.

ROBERT TOOK NO great delight in what he'd done.

It had been kill or be killed, and once again his survival instinct hadn't allowed him to give up. Breathing hard, he gazed down at the dead man, curled up on the road in a foetal position, then at the people who'd been watching the fight. Their mouths hung open. They'd never seen anything like it, not even during the Cull. He knew he had to say something – anything – to break the silence.

"Check the back of the trucks, see what we've got... and where we need to return it."

They all continued to gawp at him. He'd said only recently that he didn't want to be like De Falaise, couldn't rule through fear, and yet here they were all so scared of him they could barely move. Thank goodness Mark hadn't been here to see this; Robert was grateful he'd got him to see sense about staying out of harm's way, if only this time. The kid had probably seen worse, out there on the streets, but still...

His opinion of you matters, doesn't it? Go on, admit it.

"Didn't you hear me? Check the truck, I said. We have work to do." This time they snapped out of their reverie, welcoming the chance to leave the scene. Robert nodded at Granger, who'd been the bait in the trap. "You did well," he told him.

The young man blinked and nodded back. "Thanks."

"You're in charge of talking to the men from this unit – finding out whether we can trust them or not, weeding out the bad bets."

Robert had to admit, he still hadn't been a hundred per cent sure about his men until they'd come out from behind their hiding places, until Granger had pushed the commander's arm when the man was firing at him. Now he knew he'd been right to do what he did, freeing them, giving them the option of walking away or teaming up with him. He'd seen wayward kids like Granger before on the beat, who needed to be shown trust before they could trust. Given the right circumstances – and motivation – they could be turned around.

But that hadn't been what changed Robert's mind. Nor that little pep talk Tate had given him, right after he broke down in the face of those flames.

(All he'd been able to see was his house burning, his wife and son being cremated inside, his injured dog crawling out of the door on fire... *Jesus, it was enough to make anyone seize up, wasn't it?*)

Though Robert had to declare that something Tate mentioned sparked the turnaround. He asked him what Robert's family would have thought, what they would have wanted him to do...

"Read to me some more, Dad... please..."

It was then that it all fell into place for him. It was all connected, he saw that now. Even down to how he'd chosen to dress, where he'd picked to hide away from the world.

"Read it to me again, read the part about where he robs from the rich to give to the poor."

Somebody, somewhere, was playing a game with him – providence was having its own little joke. Robert Stokes's life was now a storybook. Only an idiot couldn't spot the parallels, and only an idiot couldn't figure out what he had to do next.

"Read the bit where he defeats the evil Sheriff..."

What would his family have wanted him to do? Joanne would have wanted to keep him safe, of that he was certain, but she was also so very proud of what he did.

"You help people. It's what you do, it's who you are, even without the uniform."

As for Stevie, he'd been trying to tell Robert all along.

"Read to me, Dad, go on."

That's when he'd got up and walked across to the captured men. That's when the decision had been made, not even really by him, but by two people he'd loved so dearly and lost so suddenly. If he was to wait it out, bide his time until he could be with them again, then he might as well do some good while he was at it. But if Robert was going to bring down this new 'Sheriff of Nottingham,' he'd need men. And he was banking on the fact that Granger and his lot could be persuaded to switch sides.

Some had been unsure, of course, and some Granger had marked out as being dangerous; the ones who hadn't needed any threats to throw in with De Falaise. Robert would still let them go, in spite of Bill and Tate's protestations. He was, after all, a man of his word.

The others had told him all they could of De Falaise. What the set-up was like at the castle, what his plans were – which Robert had pretty much guessed anyway – and roughly how many troops he had. The answer to that one was too many, not all of which could be relied on to do what Granger had done, especially in the core group that De Falaise had brought with him or had bribed with promises of power and fortune.

Which brought them to Javier.

"Let me talk to him," Tate had practically begged Robert. "I can get you all the information you need."

He'd hesitated, taking note of Bill's shaking head, before finally relenting and giving the Reverend his time with the man. Tate promised not to hurt him... much, though it was very hard to tell whether the holy man was serious or not. They'd left Tate all alone with the bound Javier, splashing water in his face to wake him up.

Three hours later, Tate had fetched Robert. As good as his word, there hadn't a mark on the prisoner that hadn't been there before. "He's ready to talk now," Tate said. Which the fat man begrudgingly did, detailing De Falaise's operations that he knew of, routes back to the castle, routes the patrols took in the area, villages they were planning on targeting in the near future.

"How did you do that?" Robert asked him later on.

Tate merely smiled. "I can be very persuasive, as you know. I also have God on my side. There were just the three of us there in that forest today."

"Faith again."

"Faith," Tate confirmed. "It can move mountains. Ultimately Javier is more frightened of divine retribution than anything De Falaise might do to him."

Robert shook his head. "Do you ever think that's what all this might be about?"

"Sorry?"

"The virus. Divine retribution, for man's sins? After all, God didn't do much to stop it, did He?"

"Perhaps. All I know is that He is at work here, in you and in me. We have to trust that He knows what he's doing."

Pursing his lips, Robert held his tongue and walked away, unwilling to get into another debate with the holy man. He had too much to do. For starters, he had a trap to set. They'd tackle one of De Falaise's supply lines, striking where it would hurt the most.

"There's something else you should know," Tate called after him.

"My friend, Gwen, who was taken from Hope. She's still alive and in the castle, a plaything of De Falaise."

Robert paused, head turning to the side. "Then you pray for her, Reverend. And while you're at it, pray that we succeed in our endeavours." He'd continued walking. Robert hadn't wished to sound callous, he just didn't see what he could do about the woman right now. One step at a time was how they'd have to take it, and that meant not rushing to attack the castle if it was as heavily fortified as Granger and his men had described.

Once this first step, first attack, had been figured out, he'd ordered that Javier and the ones who wanted out – or Robert didn't want in – to be driven back to the outskirts of Nottingham in their own vehicles, then sent on their way. It amounted to about four or five men in all.

"I reckon you're makin' a mistake there," Bill had informed him when he learnt of the releases. "Why should we let 'em go?"

"What do you suggest?" said Robert. "Hold them prisoner here, feed them and keep a watch on them in case one escapes and kills us all? Or maybe just murder them in cold blood?"

"They're bound to be spotted by patrols, and they know too much about where we are."

"They know we're in the woods, in the forest. De Falaise knew that already. Don't you see that this sends him a clear message?"

"Aye, come and get us."

"Let him come," answered Robert firmly. "We'll be ready."

One of his men interrupted Robert's thoughts, bringing him back to the present. He'd found a list of villages that the unit had passed through on its expedition. Robert had heard of a lot of them and Bill knew the rest. In any event they had a map they could follow, replacing what had been stolen from people in those communities. It would be a long job, but splitting up would make it easier. And at least the people out there wouldn't starve. Then they'd do the same again with any other supply lines to the castle.

"Right, then," Robert said. "Let's get all this stuff back to where it belongs."

In his head he heard that voice again: *"Read it to me again, read the part about where he robs from the rich to give to the poor..."*

IT HADN'T COME as a total shock, of course.

News about the bound men walking through the streets of

Nottingham had been radioed in from look-outs near the train station more than fifteen minutes ago. Orders had come back to leave them be, and so they'd walked past the red brick of the Gresham Hotel, over the bridge, past derelict shops, making their way up towards the centre of the city.

So no, it hadn't come as a complete surprise to De Falaise, who was now standing on the roof of the castle, but it was still an unexpected turn of events. To his left, the Dutchman, Reinhart, was on one knee, leaning over the side. De Falaise had swapped his sunglasses for powerful binoculars and was watching the tiny group of men shuffling along the road towards the Britannia Hotel, wrists tied in front of them: trussed up like Christmas turkeys. All that was left of the assault team he'd sent to dispose of the hooded man.

Right at the very front was his Major, Javier, looking like the sorriest turkey of the bunch. Around his neck was a crudely painted sign. The message read: 'You Missed.' How could the simpleton have let this happen? De Falaise stamped his foot., his ringed fingers tightening around the binoculars. Reinhart watched through the scope of his sniper's rifle.

"He failed me," griped De Falaise. "And I don't like to lose."

"What would you have me do?" asked Reinhart.

De Falaise thought about this for a moment. "Wing Javier somewhere... uncomfortable, but not fatal. Kill the rest." Before the man could fire, De Falaise laid a hand on his shoulder. "No, wait, shoot the others first. I want Javier to see them die."

The Dutchman closed his left eye, centring a soldier's head in the crosshairs. He pulled the trigger as De Falaise observed. The soldier carried on walking for a second, then stumbled and fell, the contents of his skull leaking out onto the road.

The other men only really began to register what was happening when two more of their team went down. They ran, then, not so much turkeys now as soon-to-be-headless chickens. Javier looked around him, screaming as more men were picked off.

"What is he doing?" asked De Falaise, watching as Javier dropped to his knees "Is he praying? I don't believe it, he actually is! How pathetic."

"What should I do?" Reinhart enquired.

"You have your orders.

The Dutchman picked a spot on his target, the side of Javier's head. It would take all of his skill and precision; very delicate shooting indeed. Reinhart blew away the Mexican's right ear. Though neither of the men on the roof could hear his cries from this far away, they almost felt they could. Javier clutched at the red mess the bullet had made, hands shaking.

"No, it is far too late to repent, my friend," De Falaise said in hushed tones, then he radioed the troops he had on the ground, ordering them to bring the injured Javier to him at the castle..

CHAPTER ELEVEN

IT CAME AGAIN, the dream of water and fire.

Of De Falaise and his men.

But something was different this time, something that gave Robert hope. When the soldiers appeared brandishing their weapons, when De Falaise began his walk across the lake, Robert realised he was not alone. Not only was Mark by his side, but Bill was there, as were Tate and Granger, and another man that wasn't so well defined. Behind them all stood a further line of defence, the new recruits who had chosen Robert over their former master. De Falaise's face fell when he saw this united front. He was no longer dealing with just one rebel, but a group.

It came to the point in the dream where the Frenchman was about to shoot Max – but Robert was ready for him this time. Hands tried to stop him, but he ran across the lake of flames – towards De Falaise – the burning liquid somehow solid beneath his feet. Max was morphing into the stag once more, but the stag was also transforming. It was like watching one of those old Universal movies where the wolfman changed in dissolves under the influence of the full moon. The stag was taking on human features. De Falaise appeared totally oblivious to this – still intent on shooting the creature.

"Stop!" shouted Robert, notching an arrow. For some reason he felt sure that if the stag-man died, everything would be lost.

De Falaise laughed. Then pulled the trigger.

Robert could see the bullet leaving the chamber, as though it moved in slow motion, but he was powerless to stop it. The stag had changed into a man, though it still wore its antlers. The creature turned just before the bullet struck.

Robert drew in a sharp breath when he recognised the face. The features were his own.

He recoiled in terror, the bow falling from his grasp as he witnessed his death at De Falaise's hands. But more than that, Robert was now the one facing the bullet, was now in its path, helpless to get out of its way.

Time speeded up and the darkness was deafening.

ROBERT WAS BEING shaken.

"Wake up –"

Robert was awake, and holding his knife blade to someone's throat. He tried to focus on whoever had interrupted his sleep. It was one of his new 'guests,' a member of Granger's old gang. After seeing what Robert had done to their unit, anyone would have thought he'd take more care. Robert asked him what he wanted, lowering his weapon.

"S-s-someone," stuttered the lad, eyes still on the knife. "Mark says he saw someone enter the forest, told me to get you quickly."

Robert let him go, pulling the weapon away. "Tell him I'm coming." He watched the envoy scramble back and out of the tent, glad that he hadn't accidentally hurt him. But he still wasn't used to having people around, even after a week or more and a move deeper into the mature woodland areas of the forest. It would take a while to adjust.

The suggestion had been put forward that they make use of Rufford Abbey or the visitors' centre at Sherwood itself – at least then there would be a roof over their heads. Robert had reminded them that they would be one of the first places De Falaise's troops would search, and would be infinitely harder to escape from.

"You want a siege on your hands, that's the right way to go about it," he told them. "Here you have cover, roughly four hundred and fifty acres of forest, and you have the element of surprise. It was how I got the jump on you lot, remember?"

In truth that centre held too many memories for him. It was one of the occasional bank holiday haunts he and Stevie would visit: going in the shops and buying souvenirs; taking photos; walking the trail to see the Major Oak, its sagging branches held up by poles now. His son would marvel at the history connected with it, would imagine the outlaws hiding their stolen goods there before tackling the Sheriff's men.

Robert never thought that he'd be doing it for real.

He grabbed his bow and arrows. Walking through the camp, he saw Granger and some of the others asleep in the army-issue sleeping bags from the trucks, the blackened remains of the fire from the night before now a charred heap. He'd show them how to build their own shelters at some point, along with a few other things, but for now he had other matters to deal with. Like the figure Mark had spotted. The kid was turning into quite the little lookout.

Seeing Mark, Robert went over to him.

"What is it?"

"A bloke, really big. He came into the forest not long ago."

"Did he see you?"

"Naw, I kept well away. Looked like he meant business by the way he was sneaking through the trees."

"Was he armed?"

"Couldn't really tell," admitted Mark. "What're you thinking?"

"I'm thinking the Frenchman has sent an assassin. He couldn't get me by brute force, so he's switching tactics. All right, take me to the last place you saw him."

"You're going up against him alone?"

"Better that way; only myself to worry about."

"I don't think you understand how big this guy is. I mean, he's fu... well, he's huge."

Robert didn't show that the size bothered him, but he was thinking back to what Granger had said about De Falaise's men – about one man in particular he'd called Tanek. "Just take me there," he said to Mark. The boy nodded, then led him into the undergrowth.

THEY'D BEEN TRAVELLING ten or fifteen minutes, heads down, moving swiftly and silently, when Robert heard the noise. The snap of wood underfoot. A foot far too heavy to be that of a woodland creature. Robert tapped Mark on the shoulder, then signalled for him to stay and keep low.

Robert nimbly climbed the nearest tree, bow slung over his shoulder. From the upper branches, he surveyed the scene, and didn't have to look too far to see the trespasser. Mark had been right, the man was gigantic! If anything, the description he'd given had been an understatement. He wasn't dressed in a uniform like the rest of De Falaise's men, but instead wore clothes pretty similar to Robert's, designed to camouflage him. A cap was pulled down low on his head, obscuring his features.

He couldn't see any weapons, but they could well be concealed about his person. Robert shifted his weight on the branch and nocked an arrow. Best to take this bloke out in one clean shot, he thought.

But before he had time to pull back the string, the man turned and threw something in Robert's direction. A stone came hurtling towards him.

Robert flung himself out of its way, but in the process lost his footing and tumbled from the tree. He forced himself to relax as he fell and managed to land without breaking anything. When Robert looked up, he discovered he'd rolled right into the big man's path. He reached for his bow but he appeared to have lost it in the fall.

The behemoth leaned down and hoisted Robert above his head.

Knife. Go for your knife, he thought to himself, but as he reached for his belt he was thrown through the air.

Robert landed awkwardly this time, the air driven from his body by the impact. He shook his head, dazed, but he was given no chance to recover. Something was falling on him. At first his confused mind thought it was one of the trees toppling over; then he realised his attacker was dropping with all his weight behind him. Robert twisted out of the way at the last moment, as the big man flopped heavily onto the ground.

Robert staggered to his feet and adopted a defensive stance. The man suddenly reached out and grabbed his arm, swinging him around. He crashed up against the nearest tree. The edges of his vision began to blur, but he managed to shake away the haze in time to see the big man charging with his shoulder raised. He was going to ram Robert. If he wasn't careful he'd end up being the filling in a very painful sandwich.

Robert twisted away just as the man rammed the trunk. The goliath cried out in agony and Robert could have sworn he heard the wood creaking as though the tree might collapse.

All I've done is make him angry, Robert thought as he again went for his knife. But even as he was sliding it out, his opponent was slapping it from his hand, leaving Robert with no way to defend himself... unless....

As the man came at him again, Robert ducked sideways and picked up a fallen branch. It was almost as tall as he was, and strong with it. He hefted it like a staff, jabbing at the bigger man who kept trying to wave it away.

Robert slammed the staff forward with both hands, but the man grabbed it and pulled. Bringing a knee up, he shoved it into Robert's stomach and flipped him over, losing his cap but gaining the staff. The man grinned.

It was his turn to jab at Robert, who snaked left and right to avoid the blows. Robert dropped and scrabbled around in the foliage. His fingers brushed another branch, not quite as big as the first, but beggars definitely couldn't be choosers. Robert snatched it up and met the man's blows, the stick almost splintering with the force. Wood smacked against wood and, suddenly, Robert spotted his chance. He lowered his weapon and struck the man's knee, causing it to buckle. Then he hooked the bigger staff with his own, flipping it out of his enemy's hands and catching it. Robert dropped the smaller branch and raised the huge staff. He was about to bring it crashing down on the man's head when –

"Wait! Hold on, I know him."

Mark came rushing out of the undergrowth towards them, hands flailing to stop Robert delivering the final blow.

"I told you to stay hidden back there," Robert said.

"But now I can see his face," Mark continued. "I'd know him anywhere. And those moves."

Robert cocked his head, looking from the boy to the giant. "You know him?"

Mark nodded enthusiastically. The man on the ground, nursing his sore knee, looked just as mystified as Robert.

"Of course. Don't you?"

Robert studied the man's features – the curly hair, the goatee beard – but couldn't recall having ever seen them before.

"That's Jack 'The Hammer' Finlayson," said Mark. "You're Jack 'The Hammer' Finlayson!"

The man looked up at Mark, his eyes warming. "Been a while since anyone called me by that name, kiddo." There was a US accent, but it was blended with English, as if the man had lived on these shores for some time.

"Who?" asked Robert, genuinely confused.

"What do you mean, 'who'? The Jack-Hammer – as in 'he'll hammer all comers into the floor.' Only one of the best wrestlers on the circuit!"

"Wrestler...?" But it made sense. The techniques this Finlayson character had been using were very much in keeping.

"I saw tons of your matches, some on the sports channels, but my Dad used to take me to..." Mark let the sentence fall away, his brow furrowing. It was the first time Robert had heard him mention his parents. For some reason it hurt him just as much as it must have done Mark. The boy caught Robert looking at him and carried on, as if nothing had fazed him. "You should have seen him against Bulldog Bramley at the Sheffield Arena, he tore that guy apart!"

"I always thought that stuff was faked," Robert countered.

The wrestler sneered. "Maybe in some places, but not when I was in the ring. Back then it was about as fake as the little tussle we've just had, fella."

"So you can vouch for him?" Robert asked Mark.

"He signed me an autograph once, on the way back to the dressing rooms. They didn't all do that."

"That doesn't mean a thing these days. Everything's changed." But Robert could see now there was a kindness to Finlayson's face as he smiled at Mark – even though the guy probably didn't remember giving him that signature. Besides which, Robert was starting to get a feeling about him. It was the sort of judgement call he made all the time back when he was a policeman. The kind of instinct that had told him Granger was okay. Realising this, it made him even angrier to think he'd fought Finlayson. "I could have really hurt you – that was a stupid thing to be doing, walking around in here."

"Hey, you started it," Finlayson pointed out. "You were about to ventilate me, pal. Never heard of asking 'friend or foe'?"

Robert had to concede the point.

"I'm sorry," said Robert quietly. He stuck out his hand and the big man took it. Robert almost went down again when Finlayson used it to pull himself up.

"Thanks," the large man said, brushing himself down and picking up his baseball cap. "Hey, you know, you would've made a pretty decent go of it on the circuit yourself. I'm a bit out of shape, granted, but no one's given me a run for my money like that in quite a while."

Robert was more than flattered by the comment. "If Mark here says you're all right, that's good enough for me." He caught Mark's chest swelling when he said this. "Let's hear your story, Finlayson."

FINLAYSON HAD GROWN up on the rural outskirts of upstate New York. "It was too quiet there for me, man. And the winters were harsh." His father would make him chop wood for the fire during those snowbound months, something that gave him a taste for exercise and honing his body. "I began weight training before I hit eleven. Not with real weights, you understand – with anything I could get my hands on: engine parts, rocks, the wood I was choppin'. 'Course, I was also growin' some by then. My old mom, God rest her soul, used to joke that I'd fallen from a beanstalk when I was a baby and her and Pop had adopted me." It had been his father who'd taught him the basics of wrestling, one of the few pastimes they had out in the sticks. "I remember the first time I beat him as well. The look on his face!" Finlayson laughed.

He'd begun to find rural life too stifling and, when he was old enough, Finlayson went in search of the great American dream. He wanted a taste of the bright city lights, so he got a job in a gym, mopping up at first in exchange for the use of their equipment. "All kinds of people would train in there, footballers, boxers, wrestlers. They were the ones who interested me. I got talkin' to some of them and they suggested I should try out for some of the local matches, maybe even get a manager. I did all right over there, but I was a small fish in a very big pond."

It was on a visit to the UK one summer as part of a tour that he fell in love with the country. "Must have seen most of what there is to see of Britain, but I always loved this part especially. So, I decided to stay. Oh, they tried to get me to go back to the States, but over here I could actually be someone – perhaps not on the scale of those WWE big shots, but in my own way I'd be recognised." Finlayson smiled again at Mark, who grinned back. "I carried on doing the circuits for several years, places like Lincoln, York, Leeds, Doncaster, Manchester, and closer to home in Nottingham and Sheffield, which is I guess where you caught up with me, huh, kiddo?"

Mark nodded.

"Quite a few of those matches were televised, as well. I used to send tapes to my pop. I think he was proud of what I was doing. Towards the end, though, I began to think: what am I getting in there, getting myself all banged up for? Counting the bruises at weekends, visiting the doc more and more. That's when I began to pull back from it all a bit."

"So what were you doing when the virus hit?" asked Robert.

"Working in a gym again, believe it or not. I was teaching classes at a Health and Fitness Centre this time – wrestling classes, no less."

Finlayson told them what had happened when the virus had hit. It was the same old story. The people either clogging the doctors' surgeries or hospitals, taking to their homes, or dropping in the streets. Robert listened, trying not to let his mind go back to his own experiences, trying not to think of Stevie and Joanne. After the Cull, Finlayson, like so many others, had taken off for a quieter spot. "Guess I finally saw the wisdom of getting away from it all like my folks had done, all those years ago. Things were gettin' too, I don't know, out of control in the towns and cities."

"Didn't you have anyone... anybody that you left behind?" asked Robert, then immediately said: "Wait, don't answer that. It's none of my business."

Finlayson didn't seem to mind. "You mean a gal, a family and such? No woman's ever been able to pin me down, if you'll pardon the expression. As for family, they were all the way over in the US.

Like I say, my mom died before all this, thank the Lord. My dad... he wouldn't have made it."

"How do you know?"

"Wrong kinda blood."

They sat in silence for a while then, before Finlayson broke the quiet.

"I sometimes get to thinkin' about what happened over there, what it's like back in the States. You know anything?"

Robert shook his head. "I've been a bit out of touch. You never thought about returning, to see for yourself?"

"It's not my home anymore. This is. Which brings me to why I'm in Sherwood Forest. Word's spreadin' about what's gone on here. Stories about a hooded man helping the communities, about how he took on a bunch of men single-handed at a market and won. About how he gave back food and supplies to those who've been robbed by that son of a bitch holed up at the castle, pardon my p's and q's. I figure that you've got a cause I wouldn't mind fighting for."

Mark must have caught the look of shock on Robert's face, because he added, "You can't be that surprised they've heard of you. There aren't too many people, too many communities left."

"Not only have they heard of you," Finlayson chipped in, "some of 'em want to join you. Not many folk care for a bully. Anyway, I thought to myself, hooded man in Nottingham... in Sherwood... hmm. I'm pretty damned big, maybe I ought to be in the runnin' for one of the starring roles in that flick."

Robert quickly glossed over the obvious reference. "We thought you were one of De Falaise's men. We thought you'd come here to kill me."

"Nope," Finlayson confirmed. "I came to offer my services."

"So why the fight, why creep up on us like this?"

"To show you what I could do. And to see just how good the set up was, if the stories were true about you... Like they say, you never really know a man till you fight him."

"What's that, some kind of mystical thing?"

"Actually, it's from one of them *Matrix* movies," chuckled Finlayson. "Man, I really miss films, don't you?"

Robert found himself laughing, too. It felt weird, alien even. But good. He stepped forward and offered his hand again; this time in friendship. Finlayson shook it immediately.

"I won't let you down."

"I know," came Robert's reply. He looked at the staff he was holding. "I think you might be needing this. It's more you than me, anyway." He handed Jack the weapon and the man smiled. Out of the corner of his eye he could see Mark grinning wildly. "Right, well, I think we ought to introduce you to a few people."

Robert ushered the big man into the forest and then waited for Mark to fall in behind. If Finlayson was right, if there were enough people like him willing to fight, then maybe things could go their way after all.

And if the struggle against De Falaise could be turned around, well, maybe a few other things could be too.

CHAPTER TWELVE

AFTER A WHILE you grew accustomed to the screams.

De Falaise had learnt that fairly early on in his career. He was damned sure Tanek had as well. In fact, the huge slab of a man in front of him had probably been born with the capacity to shut out the cries of pain. Or was it more than that? Had he grown to actually *enjoy* hearing them, to find them just as pleasing as a Beethoven symphony?

When it came right down to it, this represented everything De Falaise was about. The strong having control over the weak. And he had all of his troops' lives in the palms of his hands, could send for any of them at any time and just pop a bullet into their skull as an example. But there was something infinitely more satisfying about doing it this way. It was the difference between a nuclear explosion destroying a city, killing millions, and a laser cutting out a tumour. Meticulous work. De Falaise had observed Tanek's technique on many occasions. He'd seen Tanek extract information from the most reluctant of sources, men De Falaise thought would never crack. In the end they all did; it was just a matter of pushing the right buttons.

Which brought him back to the screams. Down here, away from prying eyes, and illuminated by a jury-rigged lighting system, Tanek laboured at his work. The subjects this time: two men and a woman. All were hanging in chains. None of them knew each other, but they did have one thing in common. They'd all been turned in for speaking about The Hooded Man: at markets, gatherings in villages, on street corners. De Falaise had his spies, so scared to put a foot wrong they'd rather turn in those who had befriended them than risk being brought down to these caves themselves.

The reports filtering back were displeasing. Yes, people were frightened of the Frenchman, as well they should be. A legend was forming around De Falaise, of what he did to anyone who opposed him, what he did under the castle with his prisoners. But stories of his men's initial attacks on villages had only dominated talk for a short time. Now other tales were being spread.

These new stories revolved around Henrik and the tank, around Javier's incompetence in the forest (for which he'd not only lost his ear, but his freedom down in these dungeons). The last outrage had made De Falaise so angry that in a fit of rage he'd ordered the statue outside the castle to be torn down...

Word had also spread about the soldiers who'd swapped their allegiance. De Falaise had put paid to any ideas of resistance amongst his own men quickly enough, by stringing the bodies of the soldiers who had returned with Javier up on posts in the courtyard for all to see. He'd even called a gathering to say a few words about their presence. "This is the price of failure," he'd shouted. "Look upon it, and mark that it is not yourself next time!"

But if De Falaise was inspiring dread among not only the populace, but his own army, then this man who was following in the footsteps of an old legend was sending out another message. One of hope, of freedom.

And hardly surprising: in the past weeks since De Falaise had lost Savero – another one of his elite – and the goods he was carrying, there had been more attacks, more losses. It was clear that if something wasn't done soon, the tide could very swiftly turn against him.

"I will not lose everything I've worked so hard for," he'd screamed at Tanek. "Not because of some half-breed savage with a knife and a bow and arrow!"

It was clear that this man – whose real name De Falaise did not even know – had learned a lot about him, and his plans. De Falaise intended to redress the balance.

Hence these three prisoners, cherry picked for shooting their mouths off about the Hooded Man. They'd been bundled into the backs of jeeps under armed guard, brought to the castle, and deposited here in one of the dank chambers De Falaise had requisitioned for his needs. Or, more specifically, for Tanek's.

The girl he'd taken as his plaything would end up in the dungeons soon, too, De Falaise thought to himself. He was growing tired of her. The limp rag doll impression he'd found such a turn on at first was growing wearisome to say the least. While it was true he preferred no resistance, he was not a huge fan of necrophilia, either.

Another scream brought his attention back to the prisoners. Tanek was applying a hot iron to the oldest of the men, rubbing it up and down his thigh. He'd worked his way up the leg and would soon reach a place that would cause the maximum amount of pain. De Falaise had no sympathy for him. It could all end now if the prisoner would only tell them what he knew of the renegade... the renegades, he should say.

For they now knew that the man in the hood was no longer alone, after Javier had spilled his guts about what had happened in the forest. There were at least two trusted aides, it would seem.

"A holy man, you say?" De Falaise had questioned, rubbing his chin.

"The... the one from Hope, my Lord," Javier spluttered, the side of his head a mess of dried blood.

De Falaise struck him. "You no longer have the right to call me that!"

"I'm sorry... I'm so sorry..."

De Falaise had leaned forward. "What was that, I didn't quite catch what you were saying?"

"I said I'm sorry!" Javier hissed, spittle flying from his mouth. "I was scared..."

"More scared of your 'maker' than you are of me?" De Falaise said. "Why?"

Javier couldn't answer. He just stared at De Falaise.

"Do you not understand, is it not apparent to you? Around here *I* am God! Your allegiance is to *me!* It is too late anyway for you to make your peace with whichever deity you choose to believe in. You've travelled too far down another path for that. The holy man lied to you if he was offering you salvation, you stupid turd. But I will keep you alive until you have learned your lesson, Javier. Which starts with telling me more about this Hooded Man's gang."

De Falaise had listened as his former major described a man in a checked shirt who carried a shotgun, someone small he hadn't got much of a look at, and now Granger, the halfwit they'd picked up down in London.

"Ah, yes, him," De Falaise had nodded knowingly. "I thought he might be trouble eventually."

Even including the men he'd commandeered from Savero, the man in the hood couldn't have much of an army... Unless more joined him from the villages.

It was nothing compared to De Falaise's militia, but it was still a worry.

Tanek left the man he was burning and turned his attention to the woman. "Please, I've told you everything I know," she said, sniffing back tears. "He lives in the forest somewhere. I haven't even seen him!"

"No need to cry," De Falaise said softly. "No need at all." A sharp nod of the head and Tanek was reaching for his knife – not the one he usually carried, the soldier's knife. This one was more like a scalpel. He brought the blade up with one hand, cupping the back of the woman's head with the other. His hand was so big it covered almost the whole of her scalp. Then Tanek jammed the blade into her left eye and scooped out the orb. The woman screamed, the cry louder and much more piercing than the man who'd endured the iron.

"You see," commented De Falaise. "No more tears now. Much better."

Tanek flicked the eye from the knife, then made to take out the other one.

"For pity's sake!" shouted the younger man.

"Pity?" asked De Falaise, turning towards him. "*Pity?* Pity is for the feeble and the foolish. You do not know this, which is why you are the one in the shackles, *mon ami*."

Tanek finished up with the woman. When he moved to the side, De Falaise could see the holes in her face where the eyes had once been. Her scream had turned into a low moan. De Falaise gestured for Tanek to tackle the next subject.

"And it is also why, you see..." the Frenchman continued, stepping aside so that Tanek could get past with his next implement of torture, a drill, "you will be next."

The man began screaming even before Tanek drove the drill bit into his kneecap.

THE THREE PRISONERS told De Falaise nothing he hadn't already known. The people feared and hated him, they admired and cheered for the Hooded Man.

"Something has to be done about the situation," De Falaise commented when they exited the chamber, leaving the half-dead bodies behind them, "before it gets out of hand."

"What?" Tanek asked, climbing the steps behind De Falaise.

"I have an idea. You see, it strikes me that if we cannot take him in his native environment, we must smoke him out somehow, *non*? And the way to do that is to eat at his conscience. You do know what that is, don't you?" said De Falaise laughing. Tanek didn't even crack a smile. "Yes, that is it. Tanek, if all goes to plan, then we will soon bring down this 'hero' and his band. We will rewrite history, and I will have his head before the summer is out!"

CHAPTER THIRTEEN

TODAY HAD BEGUN much the same as every other day since the world ended.

Though, to be honest, things hadn't really changed on the farm much anyway; work-wise, at any rate. She still got up at sunrise, still fed the pigs and chickens at the same time, tended to the fields, saw to the bees. Life was pretty much how it had been for as long as she could remember. Apart from the fact that her brother and father were gone.

Mary Louise Foster looked out over the tracts of land that formed the backdrop of her house. It was an inherited property, which strangely enough she never thought would be hers – and certainly didn't want to come by in the way that she had. Her mother left when Mary was only small, unable to cope with the lot of a farmer's wife, and the two kids the farmer had given her. In many ways Mary resented the fact she'd disappeared like that, leaving her father to cope on his own. In some ways, though, she totally understood. At any rate, it had meant that Mary and her sibling, David, had to grow up fast. They'd been set to work on the farm, David taking to it like one of their pigs to muck, while she always felt oddly out of place. And always scrutinised. In their eyes she could never lift as much as David or her father, could never work quite as hard as they did. So the older she became the more she was expected to do what they called the 'woman's work': cleaning the house, making the meals.

Then one day Mary decided enough was enough. She'd told them out and out that they had to do their fair share of work around the home.

"Only if you do your fair share out there, Moo-Moo," David had replied.

"Fair enough, then, Diddy," Mary responded, folding her arms.

So she'd rolled up her sleeves and joined them again out on the farm, resolving to work not just as hard as them, but harder. She hadn't given up, not even when her limbs ached and her feet were sore. Mary lugged bales of hay, learned how to drive the tractor, got stuck in with the pitchfork and, in return, demanded that David and her father get in the kitchen from time to time and learn exactly how a Hoover operated. Her father refused, no matter how hard Mary toiled. Bernhard Donald Foster was stuck in the past, and not just because he liked to collect his precious historical memorabilia. He came from a different generation, who had buried their heads in the sand when it came to treating women the same as men. He had taken his lead from his own father, and his grandfather before that, who thought their wives were put on this Earth just to serve them. Which was probably why Bernhard had spent so many nights alone in that big double bed. Sometimes she'd hear him tossing and turning in the small hours and her heart would go out to him. Then he'd get up the next morning and ask her what was for breakfast, when he could expect it, and all that sympathy would vanish.

David, on the other hand, had admired his little sister's tenacity: so much so that he began to help out with the cooking, did the dusting on a Saturday and even – shock, horror – gave a hand with the washing-up from time to time. Her father looked on with great disdain but said nothing.

Before Bernard died of a massive stroke at the age of fifty-five, David and Mary had developed an extremely close bond. David had just turned twenty, so he took on the legal guardianship of Mary. Both agreed they didn't want to look for their estranged mother – who'd already been written out of the will. They'd be okay, here, together. They didn't need anyone else.

Like David before her, Mary attended the local school, only she excelled in the arts. When the time came to choose, though, between moving away to attend college and remaining on the farm, Mary stayed with David. He hadn't pressured her, but she'd felt it was her duty nonetheless. There was a big part of her that really didn't want to leave him, anyway. Every year that went by, however, it grew tougher and tougher for farmers. For them. She continued to draw and often wondered what it would have been like if she'd made it to college. Would she have had a successful career in graphic design, met the man of her dreams that she'd been saving herself for?

But then, looking back, none of that had mattered in the end. Because of the Cull.

The first they'd heard about the virus, living all the way out here, was when David had returned from trying to sell the pigs at auction.

"They're all talking about it. They're saying maybe it's come from the animals. Like foot and mouth, only worse, spreading to humans.... People are getting real sick, Moo-Moo."

"There's nothing wrong with our animals!" Mary said defensively.

"I know that! I'm just telling you what they said."

But nobody knew where the virus had come from. The television threw back images of cities in chaos, of throngs of people desperate to get somewhere, but not knowing where. Mary and David locked themselves away from the outside world, pretending it didn't exist.

Then, one morning, David began to cough.

"Look, I'm bleeding, Moo-Moo." She could see that for herself. The blood was all over the towels in the bathroom, all over the floor. Mary had cleaned him up as best she could, helping him back to bed. She had no formal training in nursing, but had done a few courses in first aid and learned what she could from books. She was also used to looking after two grown men who insisted they were dying every time they came down with something. The only difference this time being David actually was.

They had all kinds of medicines in the house – the Fosters were very self-sufficient – and she tried him on antibiotics, anti-inflammatories, whatever she thought might help. Nothing did the trick.

The phone lines were all busy, the emergency services non-responsive. Mary thought about running David into the nearest town, but by that time he'd deteriorated rapidly. He probably wouldn't have lasted the journey. All she could do was sit with him and hope he made it through the night.

He did, but only just. Delirious, he kept asking for their father in the final moments, wanted to tell him he was sorry for abandoning the farm. "It's down to you now. There's only you left. You have to promise me, Moo-Moo. As long as it's still... still standing."

"I promise, Diddy," Mary had said, tears streaming down her face.

Then she realised he was already gone.

Mary buried David out by one of his favourite trees, where he used to read on summer days when they'd take picnics into the top field.

It still made her sad that she'd never gone off and started a family somewhere, but Mary had made her peace with the life she'd chosen – wouldn't have missed spending those final few years with her brother for anything. Besides which, in retrospect, what might have happened to that family even if she'd started it? She'd probably have had to say goodbye to a husband she loved, to children. She couldn't even begin to imagine what that must be like; what it could do to you.

Mary never really questioned why she didn't get sick. She just assumed there was something inside her stronger than David. In the end she'd been proved stronger than both him and her father, had been bequeathed the entire farm and its lands.

And today had begun just like any other day: she'd done quite a few of her chores and was now looking forward to a nice bacon sandwich.

No sooner had she put the pan on the range, standing with her long, dark hair tied back in a ponytail, than she heard the sound of approaching engines. Apart from the tractors, which she'd used sparingly since David passed away – conserving the fuel they kept out in the adjourning garage – she hadn't heard a car engine in longer than she could remember. It sounded strange to her; not just the noise, but the connotations of it. That people were, in fact, out there in the world.

That they were heading her way.

Mary rushed to the kitchen window, craning her head to try and see up the dirt track leading to her farm.

They were dots to begin with, no bigger than the bees. But they were growing larger with each metre of road they devoured. Mary hadn't encountered another human being in all this time, and now she was about to meet several, all at once. She counted two jeeps, three or four motorcycles and a truck.

What do I do? she thought to herself, realising her hands were shaking. *Hide? Pretend I'm not here and hope that they'll just go away?* But she'd done enough of that already. It didn't sit right anymore. This was her farm now, and she should see what they wanted. After all, they looked sort of official. Perhaps civilisation was piecing itself back together? Perhaps they were here to help?

It wasn't long before the vehicles were in the yard: the chickens in the run protesting, the pigs in the sty oinking for all they were worth. Mary hung back at the window, crouching and peering out through the netting. The men wore uniforms, but they weren't like any she'd seen before. They looked as if they'd been standing in an Army & Navy store when a hurricane hit: each soldier sporting items from different branches of the forces. The man stepping down from the driver's side of the truck was wearing a peaked cap – obviously the guy in charge.

He reached into the truck and pulled out a megaphone, as more of the soldiers came to join him. Each one was heavily armed, she noted, holding machine guns close to their chests.

"If there is anyone at home here, please come out with your hands where we can see them," the man shouted. His accent betrayed him; definitely not from England, though Mary couldn't place where it had originated.

They don't sound very friendly, Moo-Moo... came the voice of her brother in her head. It didn't freak her out at all, because she knew – hoped – she wasn't crazy, just imagining what he might say if he were here. *No, I definitely don't like the looks of this.*

Neither did she.

"If you don't come out, we will be coming in. We are here under the authority of the new High Sheriff of Nottingham."

The what? said David in her head. *He's got to be kidding, right? Have we just gone through a time warp or something?*

Mary watched as the men spread out, investigating the chicken run, the sty. They reported back to the fellow with the peaked cap. She watched, horrified, as one of the soldiers stepped into the run, grabbing a chicken and snapping its neck. Mary had just about got over that when she heard gunfire coming from the pigsty, a *rat-ta-ta-tat* noise as someone massacred the helpless creatures. Her hand shot to her mouth.

They're going to do that to me, too, aren't they?

Probably, Moo-Moo. I don't think you should hang around to find out, do you?

Mary came away from the window and noticed the smoke; the bacon had burnt to a crisp. Then the smoke alarm went off, proving that even if everything else in this world had gone to crap, then at least one thing could be relied on. The incessant *beep-beep-beep* gave her away, and she knew she didn't have long before they stormed the house.

Mary ran from the kitchen into the hall, passing the crossed broadswords that hung there, on her way to the combined study and living room. She hurried to the desk at the back, her father's antique desk. On her way, something caught her eye through the window – figures rounding the back of the house, ensuring any escape route would be cut off. Mary yanked open the drawer nearest to her. There they were, lying in the bottom, shiny and fully loaded, with packs of bullets next to them. When they'd been little, her father had kept them safely locked away, only bringing them out to admire and clean when they were in bed. As they grew, he'd been less bothered about safety, even letting them hold the pistols when they were unloaded. David had always looked at them like he was handling live snakes, but Mary had felt the weight in her hand comforting. Whereas most farmers might have a shotgun to protect their land, Bernhard Foster had two replica Smith & Wesson Peacemakers, and he knew how to use them. Mary had watched him out in the field sometimes, able to knock nine out of ten tin cans from their perch on top of a wooden crate at thirty paces or more.

She'd watched and she'd remembered.

When the handgun ban had come into effect in the UK, David had wanted to take them in. But she argued against it, saying that it was one of the few things they had left of their father, but really just wanting to keep them around the place. She felt safer with them in the drawer. There was a reason she'd looked after them and kept them loaded ever since David had gone. A reason she'd practised with the tins just like her father had when she was young. This was the reason, she understood that now.

Taking them out, her fingers curled around the handles, and it gave her confidence. Mary felt like she could do anything now, anything at –

There was a banging on the front door – which she had a clear view of from her position. Placing one pistol down on the desk momentarily, she stuffed bullets into the pockets of her jeans, as many as she could cram in there. Skirting back around the desk, she used the living room door jamb for cover and risked a glance out. Heavy boots were stamping against the wood of the front door, but it was holding for now. It wouldn't for long.

Just like Custer, eh? Dad would've been proud, said David.

Great, thanks...

The door was splintering at the lock and Mary knew in seconds they'd be through. She slid down the wall, breathing heavily, waiting to act until she heard the door give completely. She heard it smash open, and turned to fire upwards – assessing the situation quickly before pulling the trigger.

The soldiers burst in and she let them have it. At the awkward angle, her aim was a little wide, ricocheting off the stone wall above the door. Nevertheless it was enough to force a retreat.

She smiled to herself – that wasn't so hard. But then a hail of bullets filled the hallway; Mary only just managed to roll back into the living room and avoid them.

"Tin cans don't do that," she muttered to herself.

Luckily they were aiming high, the soldiers either not that well trained or hampered by the smoke wafting out of the kitchen and filling the hall, masking her from sight.

Mary looked around for an easy exit. The enormous back windows were probably her best option, but even now she saw shadows there as more men ran around the back of the house, trapping her.

She heard the shattering of windows elsewhere too, possibly the dining room on the other side of the hall. The stairs were between there and here, so a dash for the landing or bedrooms was out of the question. Mary shuffled up against the living room wall.

First order of business was to defend the front door – they'd be coming through there again any moment. Mary rose and peered around the jamb. Sure enough she spotted figures there – responding to orders given by their commanding officer outside – and she fired blindly through the smoke. She dived as the muzzles of their machine guns flashed again, rolling as she did to the other side of the jamb.

There was gunfire at the back of the house as well, raking the stone, shattering the glass of the living room window. Mary fired a couple of shots in that direction to try and ward off any soldiers entering that way.

She risked another glance into the hall, and it was at this point she saw something rolling towards her. It was small and black, ball-like but metallic; it rattled along the wooden floor as it went.

Move, Sis! Get out of there, right now!

"Oh, shit!" she cried, scrambling to her feet. Mary was about halfway across the room, already diving for the shelter of the desk, when the grenade exploded in the hallway. The force of it flung her the rest of the way, bouncing her off the top of the desk and pitching her against the far wall, as most of the room appeared to follow behind her.

Mary landed on the other side of the desk, protected from the resultant blast but barely conscious.

Moo-Moo... Wake up! You've got to wake up... Those men are in the house and they're going to hurt you! Please, Moo-Moo!

So, her mind was still working then, still keeping up the imaginary dialogue with her dead brother? She drifted in and out of wakefulness, desperate to keep her eyes open. Mary could hear sounds, men calling out to each other. A creaking from above, someone walking on the floorboards upstairs. They were searching the house from top to bottom.

"All clear," someone called.

She blacked out for a few moments, then another voice not far away was shouting, "In here... Look."

"Careful, she's still alive."

"Call Colonel Rudakas, quickly."

Mary was aware of hands on her, of being lifted up – but she couldn't do a blessed thing about it. Again, a few more seconds of blackness, then she felt her face being slapped.

"Hey! Wake up!"

Another slap, followed by a shake – rough hands holding her

on either side were pushing her backwards and forwards in quick succession. Mary screwed her hazel eyes up tight, then opened them. The figure in front of her was blurry, but she could tell by the peaked cap it was the man in charge, this Rudakas guy.

She was shaken again. "I'm awake," Mary burbled. "Stop shaking me."

"Good." He smiled. "This is quite a place you have here..." He waited for her name, but when Mary didn't offer one, he proceeded. "Hidden away, miles from civilisation. We almost missed you on our spree today."

Mary struggled against the men holding her, but they had a firm grip.

"You're headstrong, I'll give you that – but it will fade soon enough. You're also very beautiful." Rudakas looked her up and down. It made Mary feel sick to her stomach. "My Lord De Falaise grows weary of the companion he has at present. He is in need of some fresh company."

"Who... who are you people?"

"Us? Have you not heard? No, I do not imagine you have. We are the new order, we are your new masters."

"You're not my anything." Mary scowled.

Rudakas toured around the room, approaching the desk that had shielded Mary after the grenade went off. When Rudakas turned back to her, he had both the Peacemakers in his hands.

"Collector's items, I believe. Where did you come by such magnificent pistols?"

"They were my father's," Mary told him reluctantly.

"Ah, a family heirloom, then... Like all of this, I presume." He gestured at the room, the house. "I must apologise for the untidiness, but you left us little choice. Had you made your presence known, surrendered earlier, then...Well, things might have worked out a little differently. I am not an unreasonable man; nor is the Sheriff."

"Sheriff? I don't understand."

"It's quite simple, really. My Lord has taken over these lands and appointed himself their keeper. Which, put simply, means that everything found on said lands belongs to him. These" – he lifted the pistols – "your property, such as it is... Your animals, which we have already begun slaughtering for meat. Your crops and, finally, you, my sweet."

Mary stiffened.

"I take it you do have a name?"

She clamped her mouth shut.

"Tell me, for that too belongs to him."

When Mary defied the man, he stuffed one of the pistols into his belt and then punched her hard in the stomach. The breath exploded from her, but she wasn't allowed the luxury of doubling over – the men holding her on either side saw to that.

"Now, I ask again, what your name might be?"

Tell him, Moo-Moo. Tell him or he might do something worse.

"Ma... Ma..." was all she could manage, but it wasn't just the effort of speaking when winded; it was the principle that was sticking in her throat.

The man grabbed her just under the chin. "We have all the time in the world, but it would go easier on you if you just told me right now."

Mary spat in his face.

Rudakas recoiled. "You fucking bitch! I will teach you some manners before dragging you to the castle." He pulled back his fist again, and was about to strike Mary when there came a noise from outside.

It was the sound of gunfire.

"What is that? Are there more of you here?" When he got no answer, he said to the men, "Hold her until I return." Rudakas strode off up the hallway.

Mary's face stung and her stomach was killing her. But she recognised an opportunity when she saw one. Feigning weakness, she lolled forward, forcing the men holding her to yank her back again. As soon as they did, she made her move. Mary stamped on the foot of the soldier to her right. He was wearing boots, but then so was she, and Mary dug the edge of her heel in hard for maximum effect. The man let go and, as soon as he did, she swung her newly-freed arm around and smashed a fist into the face of her other warder, giving a satisfying grunt as his nose shattered.

Without anyone to hold him, the man did double over – so she punched him again, this time at the temple. He toppled over sideways and didn't get up.

Mary suddenly felt arms around her. The first guard, who'd got over her treading on his toes, had wrapped himself around her, clasping his hands together over her chest. Mary dropped, letting go and turning into a dead weight, slipping out from under his grasp. On her back, and on the floor, she brought up her left leg and swung it over her head, kicking the man squarely in the crotch.

He fell backwards with a loud yelp. Mary ran to the smashed window at the back of the living room. More of Rudakas's people were standing guard there but, as she watched, something very strange happened. Out of nowhere came an object, a spinning thing flying through the air. It hit one man at speed, wrapping itself around his neck, the twine whipping round until the stones attached to each end came together. He reached up for this throat, unable to call out, choking as other newcomers approached.

One of them was a huge bear of a man wearing a baseball cap. He came up behind a soldier and swung what appeared to be a staff, knocking him into a beehive.

What's going on, Diddy?

I'm not sure, but I think they're here to help, Moo-Moo.

Then she heard the second explosion of that day, and the house rocked with its intensity.

RUDAKAS HATED HAVING to leave the girl, especially at such a crucial point.

He knew De Falaise would not want a woman who would spit and fight back – he preferred them to be docile. If he could tame this one, he'd be in his Lord's good books for weeks, or at least until he grew bored of her too. Not that it was always a good thing to be among De Falaise's most favoured, mused Rudakas. Just look at Javier. He'd brought their leader the last girl, and in return had been rewarded with a very 'special task.'

Rudakas wondered absently how well he might have fared in the forest against the Hooded Man. Surely he would have done better? He pushed such thoughts aside, concentrating on the here and now, on the fact that the woman back there was not as alone as she seemed. He looked down at the pistol he held in his hand. "They were my father's," she'd said, and he'd assumed the man was dead, just like most of the population. But what if she'd meant him to think that? What if her father had seen them approach and hid, maybe in one of the barns? Maybe in that rickety old garage joined on to the house? Or perhaps a brother or cousin, if the father was no more? Anything was possible and someone was certainly causing a ruckus outside.

The door had swung to again, so Rudakas pulled on the handle to see what was happening. Once more he heard gunfire. He looked outside and couldn't believe what his eyes were telling him.

His unit was under attack, but not just from one man – or even a couple. Gunfire emanated from the bushes ringing the fields, from behind the barns, even from behind their own vehicles. They were being hit by an organised and motivated group. One of his own soldiers dropped, falling from a shoulder wound. Another was hit by something much cruder – a stone, flung with force.

"Pick your targets," shouted Rudakas. "Watch for muzzle flashes and –"

Something embedded itself in the wood of the door jamb, inches away from his head. He examined the arrow, obviously handmade, but lovingly fashioned and extremely deadly. Then he traced its trajectory back to the person who'd fired it. He was standing on top of their truck, head down, a hood covering much of his face. The bow he was holding – a strong wooden longbow – was still reverberating from the shot.

Be careful what you wish for. You wanted to know how you'd fare against the Hooded Man? Well, now you will find out.

The figure on the truck, set apart from the rest of the battle, and barely seeming to take notice of the bullets flying back and forth, raised his head. From beneath the cowl Rudakas saw two of the most penetrating eyes he'd ever had the misfortune to gaze into. It was as if the man had fixed on him, and him alone, for his prey.

Rudakas was suddenly conscious that the only guns he had on him were the Peacemakers he'd taken from the woman. With one in his hand already, he snatched the other from his belt and raised them, moving forward at the same time.

The Hooded Man smiled, a grin only just visible beneath his beard. And like a blur, he was reaching for another arrow from his quiver, jumping down onto the hood of the truck, hitting the ground running.

Like gunfighters from an old western movie – quite appropriate, considering the weapons Rudakas held – they faced off against each other. The colonel fired, expertly aiming and yet somehow missing the target every time. The Hooded Man let off a couple more arrows, one of which scraped Rudakas's thigh, the other only just missing his head.

"Fuck!"

Rudakas fired again, the Hooded Man mirroring his actions. This time a bullet nicked the latter's shoulder: a flesh wound, but enough to ensure the man's aim was off.

Rudakas grabbed his chance. Raising both the Peacekeepers, he fired directly at his enemy's head. Both pistols clicked empty. He'd become so used to automatic weaponry, easy to reload and discharge, that he'd forgotten he was holding revolvers – and that the woman had already fired off a number of bullets at them as they broke into her home.

The Hooded Man, however, still had one arrow left in his quiver. Rudakas swallowed dryly as he watched the man reach for the projectile. The arrowhead was aimed right between Rudakas's eyes. But he refused to close them; he'd always told himself he would meet death with his eyes wide open and, if need be, his arms too.

The Hooded Man's fingers twitched on the bowstring.

Rudakas waited for the end – and if time had slowed before, then it practically ground to a halt now.

But when it lurched forward again, the colonel was surprised to see the Hooded Man's aim shifting, the bow and arrow pointing several metres to Rudakas's right. He looked over, saw that one of his men had a grenade and was about to toss it into the middle of the fight; not the most sensible thing to do, as that would cause the Colonel just as many problems as the arrow, but in the end it proved a satisfactory diversion.

The arrow caught the soldier just below the collarbone, with such force that it went right through to the other side, pinning him against the wooden doors of the garage. The grenade slipped from his fingers and rolled underneath the gap at the bottom of the garage doors. Both Rudakas and the Hooded Man looked on as the man struggled to free himself, understandably not wanting to be anywhere near the grenade when it went off.

The soldier frantically tugged away at the arrow, an expression of pure horror on his face, then finally he pulled it out of the wood, bringing his shoulder with it. He had little time to celebrate, though, because at that point an inferno was unleashed behind him. The explosion blew the doors off their hinges, lifting the man, and some of the ground, into the sky. He cooked instantly in the blaze.

Rudakas wondered what exactly had been stored in that garage. Explosives? Hardly likely. And it was too strong for just a vehicle's petrol tank. Then what? Reserves of fuel?

There was no more time to think about it, as the wave of heat came their way. The Hooded Man stood planted to the spot, mouth open, as if he'd seen the Devil himself in those flames. Rudakas, saved from certain death by the arrow, wasn't about to waste the gift of life. He dived back into the house, into the hallway, just as the shockwave hit. The house, as he was to discover not long afterwards, wasn't that much safer, connected as it was to the garage, but it would provide temporary shelter. While his enemy out there was still gawping at the mini-Armageddon.

Rudakas covered his head and laughed.

ROBERT COULDN'T MOVE.

He was back again outside his house so long ago, as the men in the yellow suits burnt everything he ever cared about. He screwed up his eyes, waiting for the blast to hit him...

NO!

Maybe before, when he was on his own, hiding away from the rest of the human race. Hiding away from his destiny. But not now. There were people relying on him, just as they had when he was in the police. Whereas before he'd hated his survival instincts for keeping him alive when all he wanted to do was curl up and join Joanne and Stevie, now Robert willed them to kick in – to save him from the explosion that was about to tear through him.

He opened his eyes, turning to run at the same time. It was too late. The blast scooped him up, then slammed him down on the hood of the armoured truck. He rolled over onto the ground at the other side, hitting it hard. If the petrol tank hadn't been shielded, that would have gone up as well, but as it was it at least provided some cover from the explosion.

Robert ached everywhere, drifting in and out of consciousness, his mind replaying the events that had led him here...

The noise of gunfire had attracted them initially, forcing them to break off from the delivery of more stolen goods back to the people.

"Sounds like trouble," Jack Finlayson had said.

"And where there's trouble these days, you can probably count on the Frenchman's involvement," Robert had answered.

They'd ditched the truck and spread out, approaching the farmhouse via the fields: Jack taking a few men round the back, Robert leading the rest in an assault on the soldiers scattered about the yard. There was no way they'd even have known the house was here if they hadn't been attracted by the noise. It was completely cut off, a place where he himself would gladly have lived out his remaining years up until recently.

Robert had been proud of the way his men had fought, doing just as he'd taught them in the short time they'd been with him – using their environment to conceal themselves, never showing their hand too quickly. Some he'd even begun to train with the bow and bolas. For his part, he'd picked off choice targets, hoping to draw a more worthy prize out of its own hiding place.

Then he'd seen him: the man wearing the peaked cap emerging from the farmhouse. Robert delighted in letting him know just who was behind it all.

The first arrow was a message, the next few intended only to slow the man down. Though Robert hadn't had time to study them closely, he saw that the man's firearms were quite unusual: old-fashioned, but still in perfect working order. Enough to wing him and throw his aim, anyway.

Then, when his enemy had run out of bullets and Robert had just one arrow left, he knew it was his lucky day. Except for the fact that out of the corner of his eye he saw the soldier with the grenade. It had been pure instinct to fire at him instead, a case of dealing with the most severe crisis first. That was when his luck had run out.

He tried to raise himself, failed, and slumped back down. Robert could see more of the soldiers – he couldn't tell whether they were De Falaise's or his – lying face down not far away from him. With a shaky hand he reached out and grabbed the dirt, attempting to pull himself along and back round the front of the armoured truck.

He made slow progress, desperate to get a better view of the scene – to find out who was still standing, who had fallen. Who had won the battle.

"Going somewhere?" The voice had a nasal quality, instantly dislikeable, and Robert wasn't at all surprised to see De Falaise's minion standing over him. "You do not look like a legend now, my hooded friend. You look like the worm you are," the man continued. He had his hands behind his back and Robert assumed he was holding the pistols, reloaded and ready to fill him full of holes.

However, when the man brought his hands back round, Robert saw he was hiding a broadsword instead. Different era, different weapon, but no less deadly. Where was he getting this stuff from?

"After all I had been told, I was expecting some kind of indestructible super-being. You are nothing of the kind. It will be my pleasure to put you out of your misery. There's a saying in my country, a curse: Let the earth swallow you!"

The man hefted the sword, preparing to bring it down, to embed it in Robert's cranium.

I can't fight it anymore. Finally I'm going to join them.

The man juddered, then stopped, like a robot that had rusted stiff.

Come on, if you're going to do it just get on with it!

Slowly the man looked down at his chest, where a crimson stain was blooming on the material of his uniform. Then the fabric split as something very sharp, and very long, was pushed through his torso.

That sword fell out of his hands and dropped with a clatter to the ground. Robert flinched as it landed just inches away. The impaled Colonel dropped his weapon, managing only a thick wheeze as his eyes rolled back and he collapsed sideways – the foreign object pulled wetly from him as he dropped.

A woman with dark hair, her cheek bruised but with a determined look on her face, stood looking down at the corpse, a dripping sword in her own hand. She looked at Robert and gave him a brief nod as if to say, 'That's another job done.'

"Are... are you all right?" he managed, then groaned loudly.

"I think I should probably be asking you that question. You look terrible."

With shaky fingers, Robert reached for the sword the man had dropped, wrapping his fingers around the handle, struggling to get it beneath him.

"Here," said the woman coming over to him. "Let me help."

She steadied him as he used the sword as a crutch, and he almost fell again. "This... this is your place?" he asked, every word hurting him.

"It is..." She looked back at the remains of the garage, the fire spreading to the farmhouse, spreading through it, smoke billowing out of shattered windows. The alarm had given up the ghost long ago. "It was," she said sadly.

"I'm sorry." His breathing was uneven, his chest hurt when he spoke. "I know what it's like to lose your home."

She looked at him, and gave the faintest of smiles. "I made a promise a long time ago that I'd stay here, alone, run the place while it was still standing. Something tells me it won't be for much longer."

Behind them Robert's men were coming closer, including Jack Finlayson.

"You came here to help me, didn't you?" she asked, looking at the men clearing up.

Robert could barely nod, all his strength leaving him.

"That's what you do, isn't it, help people? Hey, easy, take it easy," said the woman, bearing more of his weight. "So I guess you know all about this Sheriff? And that would make you –"

"It's all pretty much over," Jack interrupted. "De Falaise's remaining men have been rounded up... Robert?"

"Give me a hand, would you."

"Who're you, little lady?" asked Jack.

She nodded towards the dead man. "I'm the 'little lady' who did that. Now stop asking stupid questions and help me – he's been pretty badly injured."

Jack did as he was told, then said, "We'd better get him back to Sherwood."

"Sherwood, right, of course..." She rolled her eyes. "Oh, hold on, could you take him a second?"

"Sure," said Jack, puzzled, watching as she rushed back into the house. She emerged a couple of seconds later, tucking one of the Peacekeeper pistols into her jeans, and holding the other.

"There might still be some wheat and corn left in the barns if you want to tell your men, and we can load up the animals those scumbags slaughtered. No sense in wasting the meat, we might as well salvage what we can."

"Wait a second," said Jack. "You're coming with us?"

"Yeah, well... you have someone who can look after him?"

"Can you?"

"I've done my fair share of tending to the sick," she answered.

As they began to carry Robert away, he turned to the woman and asked weakly, "What's...what's your name?"

The woman gave him a worried smile. "Mary. My name is Mary."

CHAPTER FOURTEEN

AGAIN, THE DREAM...

Robert somehow knew that he was unconscious rather than sleeping, but that didn't appear to matter. It came anyway, different as always.

This time he could see more faces of the people who stood by him at the lake. The large figure of Jack Finlayson with his staff, for example, more defined than he had been before. Now there was Mary, standing holding those Peacekeepers of hers – with Mark hiding behind her, peeping out.

He looked down into the surface of the lake – while it still was a lake – and saw his reflection, the Stag-Man from the last dream, staring back up at him.

What am I? asked Robert. *Who am I? Why do you keep showing me this?*

The reflection didn't answer, but Robert knew what it would have said. He was tied to this place, connected. Then the reflection vanished, consumed by the fire that accompanied the Frenchman's walk across the lake.

Even before Robert could reach for his bow and arrow, De Falaise was firing into the crowd, randomly hitting Robert's men. There was confusion as his people panicked, each one trying to find cover. He saw them diving to the ground, throwing themselves behind bushes and reeds.

When he looked up again, De Falaise had a hostage.

It was Mark.

The Frenchman laughed as he held the gun to Mark's temple.

No! screamed Robert. He attempted to move forwards, ignoring his fear of the fire, his only concern being to rescue Mark. But Robert found he couldn't shift. Looking down, he saw that he'd caught several bullets when the Sheriff's weapon had discharged. He fell to his knees, tears flooding his eyes. Robert reached out to Mark, his form flitting between Stevie and the boy he now knew.

Robert fell backwards, gazing up at the clear blue sky. He felt pain, but it was an odd sensation: disjointed, like the wounds didn't really belong to him.

A face hovered into view above him, concerned, frightened. Mary. She was asking if he was all right, then telling him to keep still, that she was putting pressure on the bullet-holes, stemming the blood flow. Promising him that he'd be okay.

But even as she uttered these words of comfort, her own appearance was changing. Suddenly the words were being spoken by Joanne. He began to shake, twitching as he lay bleeding to death on the bank of that flaming lake, the heat reaching for him. Joanne was trying to hold him down, pleading with him to keep still. Her face pulled out of his line of sight for only a second, but it was enough for the features to change again.

This time, when she dipped her head again, it was a skull – not white and bleached like you might see in a science lab, but faded and yellowing, with shreds of skin still hanging from it.

Robert struggled to get up again, but the skeleton – a real, honest-to-God skeleton now – was holding him down with more strength than he could muster in his weakened condition.

The skull drew closer to his face, coming in for a kiss. He brought up his hands and tried to fight it off, but as it filled his field of vision, the blackness of the eyes obliterated everything else.

Until there was nothing left...

ROBERT'S EYES SNAPPED open.

It was dark, but only because his vision was still adjusting to the half-light; torchlight under cover. His head was pounding and his body ached. But it was his arm that throbbed the most. He was suddenly aware that he'd been stripped down to his boxers, and covered to the waist with a blanket. The familiar 'ceiling' of the makeshift tent that served as his home slowly greeted his eyes, and he relaxed slightly. Tentatively reaching across he felt the bandage around his arm, where the bullet had grazed him. Only a flesh wound, but sometimes those can hurt the most.

There was something wrong with his face; it felt strangely naked and exposed. Robert touched his chin, his cheeks. His beard was gone.

For some reason this was even worse than being in his underwear. He couldn't believe that had happened while he'd been unconscious, and wondered just who would have had the balls to do it anyway.

He heard a rustle and sat up, seeing the figure at the other end of the tent. He squinted and Mary's face came into focus. She was holding a clipboard and writing on it. Robert pulled up the blanket, trying to hide his semi-nakedness.

"Hello again," said Mary looking up. She gave a little laugh when she saw his actions. "Don't bother on my account. Who do you think it was undressed you? Had to if I was going to wash your clothes. They really stank."

Robert rubbed his chin again, furrowing his brow.

"Oh, yeah, that too. I figured you'd never let me do it while you were conscious. Don't worry, I'm very good at it. Used to have to shave my dad all the time when I was growing up – never used a knife before, though. And that hair could use a bit of a trim at some point as well."

"What... what happened?"

Mary placed the clipboard under her arm and crawled over beside him. He pulled back slightly. She noted his discomfort and increased the distance between them a little. "It's all right, you know. You haven't got anything I haven't seen before... Under that beard, I mean." Mary smiled. "You shouldn't cover it up; your face. You're quite handsome, in a sort of mean and moody way."

"You didn't answer my question," Robert said, feeling the blood rush to his bare cheeks.

"The short answer is, you passed out in the truck. Had a bit of a turn actually – put the wind up that mate of yours, the big guy."

"Jack," clarified Robert.

"Right, Jack. In fact you scared me a bit too. You even stopped breathing at one point."

Robert's frown intensified. "I dreamed I was dying."

"It was no dream. We had to give you the kiss of life."

Robert looked at her.

Mary closed her eyes slowly, then opened them again. "All right, *I* had to give you the kiss of life. Don't worry, I knew what I was doing. I have some medical knowledge; I looked after my brother when he got sick... And the animals, of course... not that I'm comparing you to... oh, you know what I mean."

He continued to stare, saying nothing.

"You're very welcome, by the way," said Mary, her tone hardening.

"Er, thanks," said Robert.

"That's better. Now, how do you feel?"

"Strange. A bit out of it; sluggish."

"That'll be the sedatives. The injections I've been giving you."

"What?" He clutched his arm.

"There was all kinds of good stuff in the medical packs from the trucks. Helped you sleep, helped with the pain... The priest guy –"

"Tate."

"Yeah, Tate – I'm getting there with the names – he showed me where everything was. To be honest, it's a wonder you didn't fry when my garage blew."

"What was in there anyway?"

"Fuel for the tractors. We always made sure we had a good stock in and I've only been using it when necessary. Fields don't plough themselves, you know."

She leaned over to examine his arm and he shuffled backwards, recalling the skull-thing from his nightmare.

"Hey, what's wrong? I've been looking after you for two days now and –"

"Days?" Robert couldn't believe what he was hearing.

"Your body needed time to heal itself," explained Mary. "You took a bit of a tumble."

"That's one way of putting it."

"Not for the first time, by the looks of it. I always say that there's nothing a good long rest won't cure and this is a perfect example. Don't worry about what's been happening out there, your men seem to have everything under control. They're still delivering stolen stuff back to people it was stolen from..." Mary thought about this for a second. "If you see what I mean."

"You talk a lot," said Robert.

"Not really – that is, not usually. Not that there's such a thing as usual in this case. Sorry, I'm rambling again, aren't I? What I mean is, I think I'm making up for not having talked to anyone for so long, not since my brother..." She let her silence say what she couldn't.

"I'm sorry," Robert said.

Mary looked down. "Yeah, well, I'm figuring that it happened to a lot of folk. Especially talking to some of them around the camp."

Robert nodded. "What were you doing when I woke up just then? Looked like you were making notes or something." He gestured to the clipboard under her arm.

"What? Oh, this..." She took it out. "It was the only spare paper I could find; the back of some inventory or other." Mary turned the board around and Robert saw sketches of himself; not lying unconscious as he had been for a couple of days, apparently, but upright head and shoulder views: one of him with the hood, one without. The one without looked just like him... and again the beard was gone. He took it from her and examined it more closely.

"You're very good," he said.

Mary shrugged. "Had to do something to while away the hours." There was a pause before she spoke again, changing the subject. "Tell me something –" she began, then shook her head.

"What?"

"No, it's really none of my business."

Robert moved forwards, letting the blanket drop a little. "What?" he repeated.

"Who're Joanne and Stevie?"

Robert's lips tightened.

"I only ask because you said both their names when you were out of it. Practically screamed them, in fact. I asked round camp but nobody's called Stevie and there are definitely no Joannes. No one seemed to know who –"

"You did what?" Robert's voice rose and he threw down the clipboard.

Mary recoiled. "I'm... I'm sorry, I just –"

"Just what? Thought you'd try and find out about my past? I hardly even know you!" Robert was edging forwards now, his face red with anger. "I want you to leave now."

"No," she snapped back, folding her arms. "No, I won't. One thing you ought to know about me right off is that I will not be bullied – my father and brother found that out. So did that colonel back there at my farm. Now, I know you came to my 'rescue' and I really do appreciate it, but I saved your life. Twice. You of all people don't get to speak to me like that."

Robert rubbed his forehead with his hand. "Please, I just want to you go." His tone had softened and he was trying hard not to let Mary see him cry.

This change of tack seemed to throw her. "I didn't mean to upset you, honestly. I was just curious, that's all. It's really nothing to do with me."

Robert looked at Mary. He did owe her a lot, but did he owe her an explanation? Could he bring himself to tell anyone about what had happened?

Tate's words rang in his ears. "And those people back there, do you not think they would give everything they have to turn back the clock? Don't you think that they lost people they loved as well?"

Mary had lost her family to the virus, and now her home to fire. What made his suffering any worse than hers?

"I should go, like you said," she said softly. "Leave you in peace."

She made to get up, and he suddenly found himself reaching out a hand and placing it on her arm. Mary turned and looked into his eyes.

"Wait," he said. "I –"

"Robbie! Robbie!" Jack's deep voice interrupted him. It was coming from outside the tent at first, then seconds later it was inside, along with Jack himself. He stuck his head through the gap. "Robbie... Oh, I didn't realise I was interrupting something."

"Mary was just..."

"...checking on the patient," she finished for him. They shared a look of complicity.

"I see." Jack seemed far from convinced. "Like the new look, by the way. Very smooth."

"What exactly do you want?" asked Robert.

The big man faced Mary. "Is he up to coming outside, little lady?"

"I'm up to it," Robert cut in before she could answer.

"Good, because I really think you should see this, buddy."

When Mary left, Robert threw on some clothes, which had been washed, wincing as his body protested. He probably shouldn't be going anywhere, still needed to rest, but Jack's tone told him that he was needed urgently.

In the middle of the camp a few of the men had gathered around. Slowly, Robert made his way towards them, waving down both Jack and Mary's offers of assistance. Inside the circle was a man, probably only in his thirties, but he looked much older: he was losing his hair rapidly, there were heavy bags under his eyes, and he had a ripe, purple bruise on his forehead. His hands were shaking as he sat on a log, a blanket covering his shoulders. Tate was filling a bowl with stew from the campfire to feed the man. When he took it, and the spoon, he nodded a thank you to the Reverend. Robert noticed that his hands were still shaking as he took the food and began to eat.

"What's going on here, who is this man?" Robert asked.

"Robert, you're up." Tate turned towards him, concern etched in his face. The rest of the men there did the same, their fascination shifting from this poor wretch to their resurrected leader. It made him uncomfortable, the way they were staring at him: some of them no doubt saying to themselves, *So, he can be hurt after all – he isn't invulnerable.* Others thinking exactly the opposite, that he'd been caught in the explosion and lived to tell the tale.

"Yes, and I asked a question," he replied, trying to deflect the attention away from himself.

"His name's Mills, comes from a community just outside Ravenshead," said Bill, who'd been leaning on a tree at the back. "We just delivered there week before last; De Falaise had left 'em starving."

"He says he's got some very important information," Jack added.

"Okay," said Robert, "I'm listening."

"Allow the man to eat." Tate let his stick take his weight. "He's about ready to pass out."

Mills held up a hand. "It's all right... really... I need to tell you all this..." He looked around at the faces present, then settled on Robert's. "It happened late last night. They... they came without any kind of warning... started... started..."

Robert came closer. "Who came? What did they do?"

"For Heaven's sake, Robert, can't you see the man's distressed?" Tate snapped.

"Yes, I can. And I want to know why."

Mills was choking back a sob. "They took my Elaine. Came into the village and just took her... right out of our house. I'd only just found someone who..." He sniffed back another tear, then said with hatred in his voice: "It was the Sheriff's men."

It still amazed Robert how easily that name had come back into usage, and how rather than some comic strip villain it now stood for everything that was wrong in this world – striking dread into the survivors of the virus. "They've taken people before," Robert commented, not wishing to sound cold but regretting the words as soon as he'd said them.

"Not on this scale." Mills sighed heavily. "They took at least seven people, maybe ten, and they told those who were left behind that they were going to grab more from different villages. Places loyal to you." It might have been Robert's imagination, but had there been a veiled accusation in that sentence? All he'd been trying to do was help them, protect them from this monster that had taken up residence in the castle.

"What do they want them for?" asked Tate, his voice gentle but firm. "Slave labour?"

"They... They said they were going to kill them... unless..."

"Yes?" coaxed the holy man.

"Unless the Hooded Man surrenders himself to the Sheriff."

Robert had been expecting something like this.

"They have only till the weekend to live, then the Sheriff will begin executing them," Mills blurted out. "Publicly, by hanging them in the grounds of the castle. Beginning at daybreak on Saturday."

Jack whistled, and immediately apologised for his tactlessness.

"He can't do that," Mary said. Then, turning to Robert, "Tell me he can't do that."

"Oh, he can," Robert assured her, "and he will. Unless I give myself up to him."

"Now hold on there just a goddamn minute," Jack said, "if you do that, who'll be left to stand up for these people? The Frenchman will just walk all over them again."

"Jack's right." This from Bill. "The whole thing'll start over again. Everything we fought for will have bin for nothin'."

"And," chipped in Granger, who had been standing silently in the crowd till then, "the Frenchman is just going to kill the villagers anyway. The guy's a psycho."

Robert stepped even closer. "You say that they're doing this all over the region?"

Mills nodded.

"How many people do we have out there at the moment, delivering to villages?"

"Not that many, why?" Jack said.

"Why? Because they're in danger. More than they ever were before. The chances of our men and the Sheriff's men running into each other are much higher."

"Oh no," said Bill, standing upright.

Robert hobbled over. "What is it?"

Bill gazed at him, wide-eyed. "We have a team out deliverin' not far from Newstead today. They set off early this mornin'. Tony Saddler's leading it, the ex-TA bloke we recruited from Kersall."

"Newstead? That's only a stone's throw from Ravenshead," Robert said to himself. "We have to radio and warn them."

"Robert..."

"Go on," said Robert.

"Mark's wi' that team."

Robert's mouth fell open. Mark. Snatches of the nightmare came back to him, glimpses of De Falaise clutching the boy, holding the gun to his head. "How could you have let him go off like that?"

"How was I supposed to stop him? Lad's got a mind of his own. 'E wanted to help, an' I figured he'd be safe enough in Saddler's group."

Robert said nothing, just stared at Bill in disbelief.

"Mark's bin lookin' after himsen for years. I thought it'd be all right. I didn't bloody well know about all this lot, did I?"

Robert turned to Jack. "Get on the radio, find out their location. Warn them they might run into some company."

"I didn't know..." Bill called out after him.

But Robert wasn't taking any notice, he was too busy following Jack as the big man took off his cap, placed a set of earphones on his head, and worked the radio he'd cannibalised from one of the stolen vehicles (as a kid shortwave had been one of his hobbies, and a way of keeping in touch with the world outside upstate New York). "Come in Green Five, are you reading me? Over." Jack listened intently, one hand on the left earphone. He repeated the message.

"Anything?" Robert asked after a few moments.

"Not yet. I'm having trouble raising them. It's just static on their wavelength. Could be that they're just in a black spot."

"Or something else. Keep trying."

"Hey, sure. I like the little squirt. He's my biggest fan." Robert patted him on the shoulder and staggered back to the tent. Mary chased after him.

"I hope you're not thinking of doing what I think you're thinking of doing."

Robert stopped, turned, was about to say something, then didn't bother. He reached inside, bringing out his bow and quiver.

"You're crazy," she told him. "Look at you. You can barely stand."

"I can manage," he assured her.

"Like hell!"

He began to walk away from her, but she raced around in front of him and stood in his way.

"Mary, please. I have to go. I have to try and warn them."

She searched his expression, and eventually said, "Right, well, you're going to need a driver then."

"I said I can manage," he told her, then missed a step and almost keeled over. He recovered before Mary could grab him.

"Either you let me drive or I'm going to fetch that sword. Right now. I mean it."

Robert sighed again, then nodded. She fell in alongside him as they made their way out of the forest towards the confiscated jeeps.

MARY WASN'T THE only one who'd insisted on tagging along. Bill, obviously feeling guilty about Mark, caught up with them as they were climbing into the vehicle. Robert didn't say anything. He just gestured for Mary to start the engine. She was well used to driving Land Rovers and the like, she told them, so this was no problem for her. In fact, Robert had to admit he was impressed with the way she guided the jeep over fields while he consulted the map – steering clear of the roads as much as possible in case they were seen.

They covered the distance cross-country quite quickly, keeping in touch with Jack to see if he'd been able to contact Green Five. Robert had personally okay'd their leader after witnessing how he handled himself when defending his own community against the Sheriff's men. Robert and his group had come in on the tail end of the fight, but when it was over and the invaders had decided to take flight, Robert asked Tony Saddler if he would consider joining them. "We can always use someone with your expertise," he'd told him. The chestnut-haired man had needed little persuasion to put his training to good use. He was an experienced soldier, who'd been serving in the Territorial Army when the virus hit. Mark should be in safe hands with Tony.

So why did Robert have such a nagging feeling that something had already gone disastrously wrong? Was it just the dream, or something else? The radio silence? Could be just out of range as Jack said, or even that the equipment at their end was broken. But Robert doubted it.

When they reached Green Five's last known location, Robert's worst fears were confirmed. As they made their way down one last dirt track, they saw the smoke rising above the trees, into the early evening sky. The village Saddler and his team had been delivering to was pretty much like any other in the region, and had no doubt been beautiful in its heyday. Quaint cottages lined the roads even before they got to the main street, but now they were in ruins, the walls dotted with bullet holes.

It was even worse in the centre of the village. A truck had jackknifed, blocking off the road, though Robert couldn't tell if it was one of theirs or De Falaise's – seeing as they'd originally stolen their vehicles from him. Here and there were upturned motorbikes. And bodies, plenty of bodies.

"Judas Priest!" said Bill as they edged closer.

"Bring us in slowly, Mary – and keep your eyes peeled." Robert glanced over and saw her take one hand off the steering wheel to pick up a Peacekeeper. He gripped his bow tightly, though there wasn't enough room to ready it. Mary braked gently when they arrived at the truck, bringing the jeep to a stop but not putting on the handbrake in case they needed to beat a hasty retreat.

"Wait here," Robert said to Mary, "Keep the engine running." He opened the door and hopped down, still wobbly but feeling better for the fact that he could now use his bow. Bill joined him, shotgun at the ready. They advanced together.

It was no longer a peaceful British village in the countryside; now it resembled the streets of some foreign war-torn land.

Some of the bodies Robert recognised, though they were in terrible condition. These were his men, all right: what was left of Green Five. *My God! Mark...* he thought, scanning the ground to see if he could spot him, but hoping against hope he wouldn't.

What he did see was Saddler. The man had made it several metres from the truck, crawling, leaving a streak of blood behind him. He had given up when he came to a grass verge and simply collapsed onto it.

Bill covered him as Robert crouched down to feel Saddler's neck. There was nothing. He shook his head and caught the look in Bill's eye.

They noticed movement across the street and both Robert and Bill swung their weapons in its direction.

The figure coming towards them had its hands in the air and was shouting: "Don't shoot, please don't shoot."

Robert could see now that it was a young girl of about fifteen. Where her face wasn't covered in freckles it was dirty, the pale yellow dress that she was wearing was ripped in places.

"Who are you?" shouted Bill.

"My name's Sophie," she told him. "I live..." She looked around at the devastation. "I live here. He's... he's the Hooded Man, isn't he? Like in the stories..."

There were more people emerging from the damaged houses. They were all ages.

"What happened here?" asked Robert. "What happened to my men?"

"The Sheriff," she said.

"Your people were in the middle of giving us food and blankets," a man with a shock of white hair told them, "when the attack came. They didn't stand a chance."

"How long ago?" Bill asked him.

"Not long. Two, three hours. They took quite a few of our people with them. Kidnapped them, bundled them into the backs of their trucks. They said that unless you surrender yourself to –"

"Yes," Robert broke in. "Yes, I know what they want. What happened to the boy?"

The old man looked confused.

"About this high. Mop of dirty blond hair, wearing a tracksuit. Always carries a backpack."

"Mark!" said Sophie. "You're talking about Mark."

"That's right. You know him?"

"Only a little," Sophie said. "The men were going to take me away, but he gave himself up instead, told them to take him. He protected me, even when they tried to..." Sophie swallowed hard. "We were in the house back there when they came, you see. I was fixing him a glass of fresh apple juice – they grow not far away in the orchard..."

"Hold on, so the Sheriff's blokes didn't know the lad was one of us, then?" said Bill.

"I... I don't think so," Sophie replied. "I didn't tell them, anyway."

Bill turned to Robert. "That's summat at least. If he's just another villager to them, it might keep 'im alive."

"For now," Robert reminded him.

Mary joined them. She went over to check if anybody had wounds, if they needed help. Robert watched her for a moment or two, then limped across to sit on a wooden bench.

Moments later, Sophie followed. She stood in front of him. "I've heard about the things you can do. You're going to save him, now, aren't you? You're going to bring everyone back? Rescue them?"

Mary came up behind and put her hands on Sophie's shoulders. "Come on, let's get you cleaned up," she told the girl, ushering her away before Robert could answer.

Sophie looked back over her shoulder as if still waiting for him to shout his reply. Robert let his head drop, the words still echoing in his ears, tinged with the naivety of youth.

You're going to save him, aren't you?

Aren't you?

CHAPTER FIFTEEN

THEY'D BEEN WAITING in the truck now for about twenty minutes.

Mark especially. Waiting, tensed, picking at the material of his empty backpack.

He looked round at the faces in here, each one the same tangle of anguish. Every prisoner asking the same thing. Were they going to get out of this alive? All of them had been bound at the wrists with plastic ties, so tight they cut into the skin. They'd been bundled in any which way, face down, sitting, on their knees: manhandled by the Sheriff's men on their rounds amassing hostages.

That's why they were standing now, engine idling, as the men with machine guns ravaged yet another village known to have been accepting help from the Hooded Man. Mark shut his eyes, but then the memories of the attack rushed back. He'd been helping unload goods and distribute them. Jacob, one of the guys who'd been shanghaied into the Sheriff's army, and was now glad to be out of it, had nudged Mark and pointed across at a local girl staring at them. She was wearing a yellow dress and had freckles on her cheeks.

"Think she likes you. She's been gaping over all the time we've been here." Jacob grinned.

"Get out of it," Mark had replied.

Jacob had made a kissing gesture then and Mark hit him on the arm. "Hey, I was only playing with you – should count yourself lucky if she does. Pretty girl, that."

She was. Though he still considered himself too young for all that kind of nonsense, Mark had done quite a bit of growing up in the last couple of years. Had been forced to. So while he was still a kid in many respects, he was more mature than many thirteen year olds. And he had begun, finally, to notice the opposite sex. Maybe Jacob had a point in his own clumsy way, and you could never have too many friends. So, he'd nervously met her eye a few times as Tony Saddler continued organising the drop. Mark had been sad when he looked up at the end and found the girl gone.

"Good work, guys," Tony told them, "take a breather."

Mark looked around for the girl again, but it had been her who found him, tapping him on the shoulder and saying hello. She introduced herself as Sophie and asked if he wanted a drink after all that hard work.

Mark nodded shyly, then followed her into the house where he assumed she lived. "It's not mine, of course, but I chose it when I came here." He remembered thinking that maybe he wasn't the only one who'd had to mature quickly; at just fourteen Sophie was running her own little household, by the looks of things. She'd originally come from West Bridgford, she told him, just the other side of Nottingham: a small place that had been taken over by gangs and thugs believing they owned the joint. They had driven her out, and she'd begun the journey further north, hoping to find somewhere quieter; somewhere safer. On the road she'd hooked up with a group of men and women doing the same, and fell in with them. Then they'd settled here.

"It was peaceful for a while," she told Mark as she fixed him his drink. "We got on with our lives, made plans, began to imagine the future might be different. But then the Sheriff's men came."

"Sounds familiar," he told her.

She shrugged. "We got off lightly compared to some I've heard about. They just took things, not people. So," Sophie had said as she offered him a seat, "what's he like?"

"Who?"

She laughed. "The Hooded Man, silly."

"Oh," said Mark, deflating somewhat. "He's... well, he's pretty cool, really."

"Is it true he once took on fifty of the Sheriff's men single-handed?"

Mark stared hard at her. "Erm..."

"That he's seven foot tall with a square chin and broad shoulders?"

Mark squirmed in the chair; he hadn't been expecting to be fielding questions about her crush on Robert. "He's quite old," Mark informed her. "Old enough to be my... well, your dad too, really."

She seemed a little disappointed by that. "Really? I heard he was about nineteen, twenty."

Mark shook his head. "But you do know I'm like his second in command, don't you?"

Sophie seemed to perk up at that. "Really?"

Mark nodded. "He runs everything by me. I'm his official advisor as well, his PR man, the works."

She pulled up a stool and brought it round the side of the table to sit near Mark. Sophie was only a few inches away and, without realising it, he found himself breathing in and out a little too quickly. "Tell me more," she said, bubbling with excitement. "Have you been in many battles with him?"

"Oh, yeah, course. Loads."

Sophie practically jumped up and down with delight. "So, go on, I want to hear about the best one."

Mark thought for a moment. "Well, there was this one time at market when –"

He hadn't got any further before he heard the gunfire. Both he and Sophie rushed to the window and looked out, in time to see Tony Saddler and the other men dropping to defensive positions as bullets whistled around them. They were being picked off one by one, sitting targets in the middle of the road. Someone started up the armoured truck, but before they could pull away, an explosion flipped it onto its side. Mark pulled Sophie from the window just as a hail of gunfire shattered the glass, spraying them with fragments.

"Get back," Mark shouted to her, and she nodded, terrified. What had been just stories before, entertainment and excitement, was suddenly real and happening right now. More bullets ricocheted off the door of the house – and then suddenly there were soldiers, forcing their way inside.

"Get behind me!" Mark shouted to Sophie, his voice cracking, adrenalin pumping through him.

"Hey, what do we have here?" The lead soldier, a youth with a scar running across his jawline, sneered at them both. "Two little muppets playing happy families."

"I dunno, Jace," said the man behind him, "the girl's fit enough."

Jace tramped towards them, grabbing Mark and swinging him out of the way. Mark hit the wall, bouncing off it and into a chair. "Yeah, you're right there, Oaksey. I definitely vote she comes with us." Jace laughed raucously.

He reached out for Sophie and took hold of the top of her dress. He pulled and the fabric tore easily. They appeared to have forgotten about Mark.

He got up, running at the thugs, grabbing the lead one by the waist and sending all three of them sideways – while Sophie fell back onto the floor. "Fuck me!" Jace called out as he toppled over. Mark had seen Jack use that wrestling move more times than he could remember, but never thought he'd have to put it into practice.

Other soldiers came in, and pulled Mark off – though not before he got a few good kicks in.

"Quit goofing around," one of the newcomers told Jace and his mate as they scrabbled back to their feet. "Let's get these two into the truck."

"Just one from this house, remember?" said another soldier.

"Right." Jace turned the rifle on Mark. "Bye-bye, muppet."

"Wait," Mark said, waving his hands. "Listen to me. The Hooded Man, the one you're looking for. I've seen him."

"Here?" asked Jace's friend.

"He was here, yeah. Just before you came."

"Bullshit." Jace jammed his gun in Mark's face.

"Wait, we'll take him anyway. He might come in useful, and kids make good prisoners."

"But what about her?" Jace whined, thumbing back towards Sophie.

"Leave her. There'll be more skirt, and closer to your age."

Jace considered this. "I guess you're right." He grabbed Mark roughly by the collar. "Come on, you little prick."

Mark just had time to look back at Sophie, who mouthed a silent thank you. Then he was being shoved outside, where the fight was all but over. The men remaining from his group were either dead or badly wounded. Mark saw Jacob lying on the concrete, covered in blood. He just about had enough strength to look up at Mark, a pitiful expression on his face, then one of the Sheriff's men came up behind him and emptied a full magazine into the youth.

Mark bit his lip, unable to let himself cry, unable to even show that he'd known the dead man, let alone that they'd been kidding around together not long ago.

"Move it!" Jace pushed Mark hard, almost sending him over. If he was honest, Mark was glad to get away from the scene; the more he saw of it, the more he knew it would stay with him for ever.

When they got to the prisoner truck, out by the road, Jace pulled the bag from Mark's back and began rooting around inside it. "Got anything valuable in here, shithead? Any weapons, maybe? Bet you'd just love to stick me with something, wouldn't ya?"

Mark's eyes narrowed. *You'll get yours, Jace. Don't worry about that.*

Jace emptied out the backpack, tossing it into the rear of the truck. He ate the chocolate bars and cast aside any items he deemed to be rubbish. "Ah, what's this?" he said finally, pulling out a small photo album. He opened it up, flipping through the pages. They showed pictures of Mark when he was younger, during happier times: birthdays, holidays, bonfire nights, Christmas.

"Leave that alone," spat Mark.

"I'll do whatever the fuck I want," Jace snarled back, tearing the clear plastic of one page like he'd pawed at Sophie's dress. He took out a photo, dropping the rest of the album on the ground. Jace spun it around, showing Mark the picture of himself with a man and woman in their late thirties, standing with their hands on his shoulders. They were all dressed in walking gear, wearing backpacks and woolly hats. There were fields behind them, and a couple of mountains. "Who're these boring twats?" Mark didn't reply. "Your folks, right? S'pose they bought it when the virus came, huh? Personally I was glad to see the back of mine, the interfering... Do yourself a favour, muppet. Let it go. They're fucking dust." He began to tear the photo in half and Mark snatched at it. Jace smacked him to the floor, then he threw the photograph over his shoulder before binding Mark with the plastic ties.

As he was thrown into the back of the truck, after his backpack, the vehicle was already filling up with other captives. Mark stared down at the ground, at his belongings there – gathered over the course of his time on the streets – and the photo album being trampled on, kicked around: the picture in two halves ground into the concrete by heavy boots. He fought back the tears. It was like having his childhood taken away from him a second time.

But there was nothing he could do, as the doors of the truck were closed and they trundled away.

Those same doors opened again now, as the waiting was over, and the soldiers directed more people to climb inside. Mark sprang for the exit, attempting to squeeze through and run away. He knew he only had a slim chance, but how many times had he escaped the crazies in the cities, in the towns, on his quest to pick up items for the market, in his quest to stay alive?

He could do it, just this one last time – escape and find Robert, bring him back here so that he could free these people. He only made it as far as the door when the barrel of a rifle appeared.

"Ah-ah-ah," said the soldier – not Jace, but they were all beginning to look the same to Mark. He knew there were good amongst the bad, those who Robert had brought over to his side were testament to that. But there was precious little evidence here today, just men who followed the orders of De Falaise blindly, and to the letter. "Get your scrawny little arse back inside the truck, or I'll fill you so full of metal you'll need a can opener to take a dump."

He pushed Mark backwards, where he landed on someone's legs.

ONCE THE LAST prisoner was on board, the doors were shut again. The truck's engine revved, getting ready to set off again. There couldn't be many more stops on the journey to the castle, Mark realised that. No more chances, if he was being realistic.

Mark wondered what was happening back at the camp, whether they were aware of the massacre yet? Did Robert know – and what would he do when he found out? Contrary to what Sophie, and many others, believed, he wasn't some kind of superman. The state he'd been in the last time Mark had seen him proved that.

Nevertheless, Mark had faith. He'd seen Robert do amazing things since he'd met him.

The Hooded Man, as he'd come to be known, was really and truly their only hope.

And Mark wouldn't – couldn't – give up on that hope.

CHAPTER SIXTEEN

By THE TIME they got back from the village, the rest of Robert's men already knew what had happened. A sombre Bill had radioed and told Jack he could stop trying to raise Green Five. On the return drive, the atmosphere was tense. Bill and Robert only had one brief conversation, which turned into an argument.

"You should never have let Mark go with them," Robert said again.

"I've known the lad longer than you have," Bill had retorted, "and when Mark sets his mind on somethin'... Anyway, ye can talk – never really wanted him around in the first place. Didn't want any of us, if the truth be told."

"Shut your mouth."

"It's true – look at ye, playin' the hero. Didn't want to get involved, though. Not really. Wanted to hide and hope everything would go away."

"I said, shut your mouth or, God help me, I –"

"Boys, boys," broke in Mary, who was trying to concentrate on the dirt track ahead of her. "We're all on the same side, right? I know you're both worried sick about Mark, but how is fighting among yourselves going to help?"

Robert and Bill settled back into their respective seats, sulking.

"We need to keep a level head," advised Mary, not even sure if they were listening to her. "Figure out what to do next."

"Didn't hardly know the lad," Bill took great pleasure in pointing out.

"Maybe not, but I've seen the way things work in that forest; you're a team, and if one of you is in trouble, the rest rally round."

"Reckon you're part a the team, now, eh? Only bin 'ere five minutes, lookin' after lover boy there."

It was Mary's turn to answer him back. "Look, I didn't ask to be dragged into this. But the Sheriff's men destroyed my home, I very nearly ended up like Mark – I think that entitles me to be a member of your little club, don't you?"

Bill said nothing.

Silence reigned then, but what Bill had said played on Mary's mind. What right did she have to interfere? Yes, she'd saved Robert's life – but he'd saved hers as well, just by showing up. And sure, she'd gone with them to look after their leader, but wasn't there a huge part of her that tagged along because she wanted to fit in somewhere again? Because she was tired of being alone, tired of talking to an imaginary dead brother in her head?

Hey, I object to that. I'm as real as you are, Moo-Moo.

Mary ignored the voice, focussing on her driving and getting them all back to the camp before a scrap broke out.

When they returned, Tate was to the first to greet them. "So?"

Robert waited for the rest of the question.

"Are we finally going to do something about this Sheriff, once and for all? Are we finally going to go in there and get those people out?"

"Like your Gwen, you mean?"

"Who's Gwen?" Mary wanted to know.

"Someone I failed," explained Tate. "Someone else the Frenchman took, like Mark – except she's been there much longer. They took her to be with him." His face fell at the thought. Mary's hand went to her mouth and he saw it. "What, child?"

"It's just... just something that Colonel said, the one who came to my home with his soldiers."

Robert and Tate frowned.

"What did he say to you?" Robert asked.

"I was to be her replacement, I think."

"What?" Tate moved forwards.

"He told me that the Sheriff, De Falaise, was growing bored of the woman he has... He called her a 'companion.'"

"I think we all know what's meant by that," said Bill, not helping matters.

"What exactly did he say, Mary?" Robert coaxed. "It might be important."

"Something along the lines of De Falaise needing fresh female company, and he thought he'd found it. I was a little too 'headstrong' though, apparently – maybe he can't handle strong women?"

"This is gettin' us nowhere," Bill said. "What're we goin' to do about Mark?"

Robert rubbed his neck. "I need time to think."

As he walked off, pulling the hood over his head, Bill called out after him, "Time's summat we don't have. You heard what that there Mills said: the weekend. We need a plan, bloody quick."

But Robert was already disappearing into the foliage. Bill looked like he was going to go after him, but Jack stopped him. "Ease up on him, eh, fella? Let the guy do his thinking." Bill didn't argue, just gave him a stern look and tramped off.

Mary watched Robert go. She'd heard Jack's words, too, but something was nagging at her to follow. As the rest of the group went back to the fire, in preparation for the night ahead of them, they left her gazing out into the forest.

Then, once she was alone, she disappeared into it herself.

MARY SOON REGRETTED her decision. The further into the forest she went, and the darker it became, the more her imagination began to play tricks.

There was no sign of Robert. He was like a spirit who'd suddenly decided to leave this plane of existence. Mary blundered onwards, pushing back leaves and banging into tree trunks. Though she'd spent much of her life outdoors, these surroundings were alien to her – nothing like the open fields she was used to.

There was a strange noise off to her left. She looked down and found that she'd instinctively drawn her Peacekeeper.

Another sound, and Mary turned again – her gun hand shaking. She had absolutely no idea where the camp was now, and couldn't find it again even if she tried. The light was waning and the shadows the trees cast in the moonlight made her shiver.

Crack! – off to her right, this time. She cocked the pistol, but stopped herself from firing. What if it was someone from the camp, someone who'd had the same idea? It might even be Robert, for all she knew.

Or someone else, Moo-Moo. Could be one of De Falaise's men.

They wouldn't be that stupid, she told him. Mary had been told about the times they'd been totally humiliated by Robert. Now that he had more men on his side – some of them the very soldiers that were sent in to catch him – they wouldn't dare enter. Especially at night.

But are you sure? Better be sure, sis.

Mary headed in the direction of the noise. David was right. What if it was one of their enemies creeping through the forest, on a mission to kill them all? She couldn't just let them get on with it.

"Reckon you're part a the team, now, eh? Only bin 'ere five

minutes..." Bill's offhand comment came back to her. She barely knew these madmen living out in the back of beyond. Yet she'd felt a kinship with them from very early on; even Bill. They were banding together to fight a common foe, one that she'd had a run-in with herself. She felt a loyalty to them, even if this place was yet to feel like any sort of home.

Mary tried to be as quiet as she could, heading in the direction of a clearing. The trees were parting, offering her a view of something ahead: the thing that had been making all the noise. It looked like something out of a horror movie, dark horns, a snout: demon-like in its appearance.

She let out a gasp, startled by the shape no more than a few metres away. Her gun hand was shaking as she brought it up to aim.

There was someone beside her, at her ear – someone she hadn't heard approaching. Someone raising her gun arm into the air and snatching the Peacekeeper from her in one quick movement. Mary looked sideways, terrified, seeing only another dark shape there.

"Ssshhh. Watch."

The same hand that had taken the pistol from her pointed towards the clearing, at the creature now illuminated by the moonlight. It bathed the animal in its rays, uncovering it as it did so. Another gasp issued from her as she saw the stag in all its wonderful glory.

It looked towards her, fixing Mary with its ebony eyes. Then, as suddenly as it had appeared, it was gone. Still shaken, she looked again at the shadowy figure beside her. A hooded man.

"Robert?" she whispered.

"Yes." He raised the hood and his features caught the moonlight too. "Why did you follow me, Mary?"

She shook her head, at a loss to explain it to herself, let alone him. In the end she decided to just change the subject. "What... what just happened here?"

"Couldn't you feel it?" Robert replied.

She had felt something; the seconds slowing down to match her heartbeat, the fear of the beast and a stranger beside her, giving way to a sense of supreme tranquillity. "It was the most beautiful thing I've ever seen."

"You almost killed it."

"I'm sorry."

"Don't be. I almost killed it myself, once." Robert handed her back the pistol. Then he left her side and walked into the clearing.

She watched him standing there, as he looked up at the moon.

Unlike her, he was totally at home here. This was where he drew his energy from, where he felt at peace. She understood now why he'd come so deep into the forest to think.

"Who are you, Robert?" she said.

"I've asked myself that question a lot recently. I used to know, implicitly, who and what I was. Now…"

Mary walked over.

"Sometimes I…"

"Go on," she encouraged.

Robert let his head fall, shaking it. "It sounds ridiculous when I say it out loud."

"Tell me."

"Sometimes I feel as if the forest is speaking to me. Like just now, and in my dreams." He let out a weary laugh. "Does that make me a lunatic? Lord knows I've been through enough to send me crazy."

Mary laughed herself. "I'm afraid I can't really judge. I hear the voice of my dead brother in times of stress. Now you think I'm crazy."

Robert turned. She could feel his gaze on her and looked away, though only for a moment.

"I guess Tate is right when he says we've all been through our own personal tragedies."

"And what did you go through, Robert? What made you run away?" Mary stepped closer to him. "Joanne and Stevie, right?"

Like the stag, she was expecting him to bolt. She felt him tense, but he didn't move. Finally, he spoke. Opened up to her, told her all about what had happened: having to watch his wife and child die, powerless to help them. Waiting to die alongside them, but being denied even that. Then he told her about the men in yellow suits, what they'd done to the house, to Max. How it had driven him almost over the edge, driven him into the heart of this place so he could wait out his life alone and be with them again. It hadn't quite worked out that way.

Tears tracked down her face as Mary listened to Robert's story – a tale he'd kept from the closest of his men, but which he was now revealing to her.

When he was done, she put an arm around his shoulder, pulled his head down and held him to her. He didn't resist, but she felt him shaking as the tears came.

"It's okay… it's okay," she repeated over and over. The words sounded so hollow. It wasn't okay, nothing about what Robert had been through was. But destiny, or whatever you wanted to call it, had given him a new identity, a new purpose. Where he hadn't been able to protect his family, he could still protect the people of this region from De Falaise. It was what he'd been doing these past few months, and it was what he had to do now as they faced their toughest challenge.

Slowly, Mary eased him back when she felt the sobbing subside. "You didn't come out here to think at all, did you?"

"What do you mean?"

"You know exactly what to do – and your men know it too. We just have to figure out a way of doing it that'll work."

"Mary," he said, wiping his cheeks, "if I didn't think you were crazy before – I do now."

"Then we make a good team, don't we?" she said, quickly adding, "we all make a good team. In fact, no, we're not a team at all..."

"No?" said Robert.

Mary shook her head. "Uh-uh. We're a family. All right, maybe we're a little heavy on the testosterone." She laughed. "But still a family. And a member of that family is missing."

"Then there's only one thing to do," said Robert, pursing his lips, "isn't there?"

She nodded.

"Yes. Mark is..." Robert paused, as if he'd just thought of something. Then, suddenly, he was taking her by the hand. "Come on, let's get back to the camp. I have to talk to the rest of my... family."

Mary grinned. "Lead the way, then; I wouldn't be able to find it if I fell over it."

He began to march off back into the forest, pulling her with him. She thought then how much stronger he looked than earlier on that day. *Invigorated* was the word she was looking for.

"Oh, and Mary," he said, glancing back. "Don't tell any of the men you saw me crying, okay?"

She laughed again, and this time Robert laughed with her.

"Funny kind a thinkin', that," Bill said to no one in particular as Mary and Robert arrived back at the camp together. Robert looked down, realised he still had hold of Mary's hand, and released it.

"What did I say about ridin' Robbie?" Jack warned Bill, stomping up alongside him.

"I'm not the dirty bugger doing the ridin'," he replied.

Mary ignored the comments as Robert called for his men to gather around. "I've reached a decision."

All the men leaned forward so they could hear, with Mills on the front row.

"As you pointed out yourselves, it would be foolish to give in to the Sheriff when all he would do is carry on as he has been doing, taking what he wants from the people, ruling through fear, spreading like a disease through..." Robert stopped when the significance of what he was saying struck him. Mary placed a hand on his back to steady him and he turned to look at her. She stepped back again when she felt he was okay to speak. "The point is," Robert went on, his voice gaining strength again, "he must be stopped. And stopped for good."

"What are you suggesting?" asked one of the group at the back.

"He's talking about a full-frontal assault," Jack answered before waiting to hear what Robert had to say. "Aren't you?"

"Not exactly. Attacking the castle head on would be suicide." There were definite mumbles of agreement from the camp. "It's been attempted in the past and a lot of people have died in the process. That's why De Falaise chose the place, because it can be defended so easily."

"Anyone entering the city would be spotted right away by lookouts," Granger chirped up. "Then there's that sniper on the rooftop."

"Yes," said Robert, "I know. That's why I'm going to give them the one thing they want. Me." He went on to outline his plan.

He finished, "Now, you all have your reasons for wanting De Falaise brought down. But this isn't going to be easy, and it's going to be extremely dangerous. So I wouldn't force anyone to join me. That's not my way, it's the Sheriff's way. But I am going in there to put a stop to this, once and for all, so any help would definitely be appreciated." Robert looked around at his men, the people Mary had called family. He waited for someone, anyone, to say something.

"That's probably one of the craziest, most cockamamie notions I've ever heard in my life." This was Jack, who pushed the cap back on his head as he spoke. "But you can count me in, Robbie. I wouldn't miss it for the world."

"You know my feelings on the matter," Tate then said. "I will be by your side, Robert. And I feel sure God will, too, if that means anything to you."

Bill raised his hand. "I've come this far," he said. "An' there's Mark to think about."

"I'm not mad about the first bit," Mary told him honestly, and in fact she hated it with a passion. Robert was just going to hand himself over to them, with no guarantees of his survival. When she could see he was waiting for her to say something else, she tacked on: "But you know I'll stand by you."

He nodded, satisfied. "Granger, how about you?"

The young man looked unsure at first. "If you'd asked me that question not long ago, I'd have said no. But being here, being a part of this... It has to be a yes, don't it? Besides, I have a score to settle with the Frenchman."

A show of hands was called for, and though some of the men were reluctant at first, all of them supported Robert and his idea. Mary could see the pride in him, the way he'd inspired them, brought them together. He'd set an example, as every good leader should, whether he realised it or not.

"Thank you," he said to them. "Thank you all."

"Mills," asked Jack of their guest, "do you think there might be support in the villages for this?"

"I'm sure there would be. We all want the people we care about back."

It brought it home again to Mary when he said those words that while she'd been hiding herself away from everything in the farmhouse, the world had carried on turning, people had found each other, cultivated new relationships, tried to rebuild what they'd lost – for good or for bad. It was what had happened in the forest thanks to Robert: a small, but determined band who would not bow to dictatorship.

"Then it's settled," Tate said. "We have until the weekend, everyone."

A few days. Not long to properly plan what Robert had in mind.

Are you sure about this, Moo-Moo? Are you sure about him?

Mary couldn't answer, because she didn't know.

But something had brought her here. One thing Mary was certain of was that she still had a part to play in this story.

A very important part.

CHAPTER SEVENTEEN

THE DREAMSCAPE, THE arena – and a challenge now accepted.

Here, Robert and De Falaise faced off against each other. No preamble this time. No symbolic nonsense or veiled meanings, just raw hatred and a sense that this was all building to a climactic head.

Though they had never met in the flesh, they felt like they knew each other inside out. Villain and hero, though each would disagree with those descriptions, they circled each other. Stripped of weapons, they had only their hands to attack with... which they did, De Falaise coming in fast and low, Robert blocking his punches.

They fought, growing closer and closer, arms and hands a tangle, until they were at each other's throats. Each looked into the other's eyes, recognising the fury there, reflected back. Could one exist without the other?

De Falaise tightened his grip on the Hooded Man's throat, and Robert did the same. They were choking the life out of each other at the same time, with the same force. At this rate they would cancel each other out.

Still they continued, both hoping that their opponent would show a chink in their armour, offer up a hint of weakness.

Who would win? Who would lose?

It was a question that would soon be answered...

SHE COULD TELL by his breathing that he was asleep. In the darkness of the small hours she listened to the sound, guttural at times as he began to snore. The very noise caused her stomach to do somersaults. She felt like she was going to be sick, in fact. And not for the first time since she arrived here.

Like all those other times, however, Gwen had fought the sensation. Fought all sensation, all feeling, all awareness. She'd made the decision very early on that if she allowed herself to be conscious of what was happening to her, she might just go stark, staring mad. Like if she thought about what had happened to Clive back in Hope, when that murderer Javier had put a bullet in his head. Gwen felt the nausea rising again, and swallowed to try and halt its progress. It was little comfort to her that the man was now being held down in the caves after failing De Falaise; as far as she was concerned, if he'd been stripped of his skin and then made to roll around in vinegar it wouldn't begin to make up for what he had done.

Javier had handed her over to the disgusting man with yellow teeth lying by her side.

"You had better not try anything like you did with me back there. He likes his women to be seen and not heard. Compliant, if you know what I mean, *señora*," Javier had explained on the drive back to the castle.

Oh, she'd complied all right. Not because she feared what might happen to her if she didn't – though the thought of being handed over to that animal they called Tanek far from appealed to her – but because she was biding her time until she could have her revenge.

That time had almost come, necessitated by De Falaise becoming bored with his possession.

"She is beautiful, that is not in question – it is why I have kept her around for so long, *non*? But it is as though she is not really here at all," she'd heard him tell Tanek one time. "She is somewhere else entirely."

That was true. Gwen had shut herself off, retreating to the darkest corners of her mind when the Frenchman wanted his 'fun.' Switching off as he dressed her up in those ridiculous costumes, while he pretended to be some kind of time traveller, an historical conqueror who'd taken over this land and its women. She'd had to pretend herself while he did this; pretend she was some place safe – with Clive.

"I'll avenge your death," she'd tell him. "I promise."

"I know you will, sweetheart, I know."

Javier would get his in time, but she was closer to the man who'd given the orders right now, the man who'd orchestrated this whole affair. She'd begin at the top and work her way down. To that end she'd waited, patiently and silently – so silent he believed that her spirit was crushed. Little realising that she was lulling him into a false sense of security.

It happened bit by bit, leaving her alone in the room for ten minutes to begin with (possibly testing her at first to see what she would do), with no guard inside or even on the door. She'd done nothing, sometimes not even moved between the time he left and the time he got back. He'd begun to spend the night with her after doing what he needed to, the exhaustion of his efforts causing him to fall asleep. Again, at first he would doze very lightly, then when nothing untoward happened he'd eventually relaxed more fully.

In addition, Gwen had kept her eyes and ears open on her tours round the castle. De Falaise no longer kept her under lock and key, knowing that the place was well guarded and she could never possibly escape. And no one really noticed her anyway, as she drifted through rooms, along corridors; all they saw was De Falaise's broken play thing. No threat to anyone. As long as she was back in the room when De Falaise was in the mood, there wasn't a problem – and she knew his routines well enough by now.

The soldiers who brought her food barely acknowledged her. They just left the plate, picked it up again half an hour later; unless, of course, De Falaise wanted to dine with her – which again involved a change of outfits and a small banquet on a wooden table. Many of the men didn't even want to be here – she'd got that from listening as well – let alone scrutinised what she was doing with her meals.

So, yesterday, she'd decided to take a gamble. Gwen had hidden her knife, hoping against hope that the soldier wouldn't take a blind bit of notice when he came to retrieve her tray.

She held her breath as he picked it up. Gwen tried to act casually as he bent and grabbed it, but she overdid it, and he caught her looking at him as he turned around.

"What?" he asked. "What's wrong with you?"

Gwen didn't reply, hadn't spoken for so long, in fact, she was frightened her vocal chords might have seized up.

"I asked you a question." The soldier didn't look much more than about eighteen, she surmised. Had probably never had a woman, either in the pre-virus world or in this one. Thinking fast, she got up and went over to him, letting the loose robe she was wearing open just a fraction too much. His eyes flicked down to the curve of her breasts, then back up again. Smiling, she'd reached out a hand, brushing his arm with her fingertips. He looked down again, right down inside her robe. Then her hand had reached lower, brushing against his stomach. Before it could move further down, the soldier stepped back. "I... er... that's enough. You go and sit back down again and... er..." His face was crimson, his gait half slouching. "Sit back down or I'll have to report this... I..." He backed up against the door, reaching for the handle and pulling it open, desperate to get out of there. The soldier said nothing more, he just left in a hurry, probably not quite sure what had happened.

But he wouldn't report it. Gwen had bet her life on that. For a start, who would believe him? *The zombie woman came on to you? Piss off!* Even if they did, he wouldn't want it getting back to De Falaise or he might find himself down in those caves.

Flustered, he would return the tray to the kitchens and with a bit of luck the missing knife would go unnoticed. Gwen waited most of the afternoon for someone to come back and accuse her of hiding it, but they didn't. She then began sharpening the implement, using a rock she'd picked up on one of her outings. By the time she was done, the labours focussing her attention in a way nothing had since she'd been dragged here, the blade was rough but sharp.

She'd had to hide it quickly when De Falaise returned, inside a cushion belonging to the couch she was sitting on. Her 'master' had been dressed in the garb of a general or admiral (she wasn't very good with ranks), medals splashed across his chest. It looked like a hybrid of styles, which had become the trademark of De Falaise's army, and was in keeping with his abnormal personality.

He'd looked at her strangely from the doorway, as if trying to read her mind. Then he smirked and threw a dress at her: blue silk. "Put it on. We are going for a little stroll."

At this point any normal man might have turned his back, or exited the room, but De Falaise wasn't an ordinary man. He liked to watch his plaything disrobe and put on new outfits. This was all part of the game.

His eyes traced every contour of her as she climbed into the dress, which should really have been worn with a corset beneath, though that didn't appear to bother De Falaise. "Hurry," he snarled when she was taking too long and she did as she was told. Then she joined him at the doorway, walking that zombie walk she'd perfected. Taking the part of his pet.

Putting on his sunglasses, he led her outside and along the East Terrace. "Did I ever tell you the story about King John and what he did along here?" She didn't say a word. "*Non?* Well, John was the brother of Richard the Lionheart, as you may know. When Richard went away to fight in the Crusades, John tried to take over the country, using this as his base. He'd always had a soft spot for this castle, you understand; in fact, his father had bequeathed it to him before his death. Needless to say, when Richard found out, he was – how you put it – more than a little pissed off with his sibling. Having only reached Italy, he returned to see to his brother himself. That happened here in 1194. Richard got into the Outer Bailey and rounded up all the people he could find – not just soldiers, but families of the garrison, tenant farmers – and he hung them, just strung them up. John's men didn't surrender at this point, not until the archbishop threatened them with excommunication. They then abandoned John and he was put into exile. However..." De Falaise held up a finger at this point in the lecture, halting their walk. "When Richard died, John returned and used the castle as his permanent residence, the only king to do so. Which brings me to the story I originally wished to relate. It was here that John hung twenty-eight Welsh boys over the side of the rocks after inviting them along for dinner. They were the sons of Welsh barons and John did it because of a disagreement with their fathers over the Magna Carta. Ah, those were the days, *non*? If someone disagreed with you, you hung them. If there were traitors in your midst, you simply disposed of them."

Gwen was almost certain that he had found out about the stolen knife. Why else would he be giving her a speech about traitors? Was she to suffer the same fate as those poor people at Richard and John's hands? She considered running, but knew she wouldn't get twelve paces without being gunned down by one of his men. There were a good dozen in sight along this wall of the castle alone.

De Falaise held out his hand for them to begin walking again down the East Terrace, towards the steps guarded by twin lions. As she reached the top she realised her mistake. The recently mowed field below had been practically cleared of vehicles and was now was filled with people, all bound, all standing with heads bowed.

"Behold, the traitors of our time," announced De Falaise. "Those who have accepted aid from our friend, the Hooded Man. Those who have shielded him from me, who conspire against my new regime."

He's insane, thought Gwen, as if only just realising it for the first time. *He's completely lost his mind.* Of course she'd heard about the Hooded Man, the one who had stood up to De Falaise and was rallying support to his cause – in fact, she'd mentally punched the air a few times when she'd heard of his victories over the man standing next to her. But she had no idea the stakes had been raised so high. There were children down there, children just like Luke and Sally who she missed so much. Gwen's eyes settled on a boy near the front. His dirty blond hair was ruffled, the tracksuit he wore tatty and torn, and he was clutching an empty backpack like a security blanket.

Looking at the people before her, she understood that De Falaise was going to kill them all. And he'd think nothing of it. In a way, they were just as much his toys as she was, as they all were.

It was then she knew she had to strike that night. This monster had to be stopped.

So, once he'd had his way with her again, the thrill of the imminent executions obviously arousing him – and she'd blotted it out the same as always, retreating to that place in her head where Clive waited – Gwen lay awake and waited for him to drop off. Then she'd waited some more until he'd drifted further into sleep.

Experimentally, she eased her shoulder away from his. *Gently... Gently...* she told herself, struggling to keep her own breathing even. Now she moved her left foot, the one furthest away from him. If she could only slide it down and feel the floor, she could manoeuvre the rest of herself out of the bed more easily. Her heel reached the end of the mattress and she allowed it to drop slowly, anchoring herself, pulling herself, straining with her calf muscle.

Almost there... almost –

De Falaise rolled over with a snore, arm flailing out and landing on her. It felt like a bolt sliding across a cell door. Gwen lay stock-still. De Falaise murmured something and his right foot kicked out, twitching in his sleep.

Gwen bit her lip hard. How the hell was she going to get off the bed without waking him? And even if she did get the knife and use it, how was she going to get out of the castle, past the guards? And how would she find this Hooded Man?

De Falaise muttered something and rolled onto his back, withdrawing his arm. Gwen let out a long, deep breath. Then she looked across at him. His head was cocked back, neck exposed. A thought suddenly occurred to her...

Why do you even need the knife at all? You could do what you should have done a long, long time ago. You could wrap your hands around that neck and just squeeze.

There'd be less chance of him waking up before she could do the deed. All she had to do was roll over and grab him. But was she strong enough? Could she kill him before he came to his senses and fought back? It was risky, to say the least.

Risky, but oh, so tempting.

Yes, I'm going to do it, she told herself, even as she was turning over, hands reaching out, ready to encircle his neck, thumbs itching to press down on his windpipe with all her might.

* * *

HE FELT THE hands around his neck and immediately snapped awake.

In the darkness a figure was on his chest, looking like some kind of ghastly apparition. But the pressure around his throat was real enough. He felt the hands gripping tight, and shock more than anything prevented him from fighting back.

You're going to die. If you don't do something right now, then you're going to be throttled to death!

The figure above was replaced with patches of deeper darkness that began to cloud his vision as his brain was starved of oxygen.

Do something...

He clamped his hands around his attacker's wrists and tried to pry the grip free. But he couldn't budge them.

"I'm sorry," he heard. "I have to do this."

He brought up his knee, hard. There was a grunt, but the assailant didn't shift. He did it again. This time it worked; he twisted the figure onto its side. He shook his head, clearing his vision. Bringing a knee round, he shoved it into his attacker's side, winding them. They grappled with each other for a moment, both on their sides now. Then suddenly the roles were reversed and the victim was on top. He struck out with a punch that caught his attacker across the jaw, enough to stop their struggling.

The voice came again. "I'm... I'm sorry." A whimper this time. "My Elaine... I... I had to do something."

Robert kept the man's hands pinned down as he heard voices outside the tent. Light filled the space, torches shone in. "What's going on?" asked Jack. Robert turned, though it hurt his neck to do so, and saw Tate there too – plus a couple of his other men – alerted by the sounds of the struggle. He opened his mouth to speak, but found it hard to get the words out. Luckily, the man he was holding down answered their questions quickly enough.

"Dead or alive... that's what they said. The Sheriff doesn't care which," gibbered Mills, the man who'd come into the camp and told them about the raids. Only he'd withheld that one crucial piece of information.

"Jesus," Jack whispered. "You traitorous –"

"I did it for my Elaine," protested Mills. "They're going to kill her. And... and your plan, it's never going to work in a million years."

Jack huffed. "You think so?"

"I know so. They'll be expecting something... De Falaise will murder the hostages."

"Weren't..." croaked Robert, then coughed. He turned to the man again. "Weren't you listening earlier? He'll murder them anyway."

Mills shook his head, not willing to accept the truth. The next stage was lashing out again. "It's your fault they took her in the first place! All this is your fault. It's you he wants! If only you'd left them well enough alone to do what they wanted."

"You'd have been even further up shit creek, pal," argued Jack, then looked over at Tate. "Sorry, Rev."

The holy man wasn't really listening, he was too fixated on the scene before him.

Robert rolled off Mills, and rubbed his windpipe. The man didn't try to get up, didn't even try to escape. Jack and the others came and grabbed hold of him, dragging him away from Robert. "Don't hurt him," their leader managed.

"Hurt him? I know what I'd do, given half a chance," Jack told Robert.

"He was just scared for someone he loves."

Another snort. Then Jack told them to take Mills away and put a guard on him. He knew too much about what they were planning for them to just let him go.

Tate came fully inside, leaning heavily on his stick, and waited for Robert to look up. "If..." Robert coughed. "If that's an... an example of support in the villages, we don't stand a chance."

"You don't believe what he said, do you?"

"Trying to assuage your guilt, Reverend?" Robert said in broken words, massaging his throat.

"Guilt?"

"About persuading me to do this – setting all this in motion." Robert coughed again.

"It wasn't me who persuaded you, Robert."

He fixed Tate with a stare. "People are probably going to die because of me. You do know that, don't you? Maybe even Mark."

"And how many live today because of you, answer me that? How many of the men out there have a purpose now?"

"I'll probably get them killed as well."

"It's their choice to follow you. Their decision. In a broken world like this, you should feel proud of that."

There was someone else at the flap of the tent, a female face, and Robert looked past Tate, locking eyes with Mary. "I just saw that man Mills being taken away and..." She rushed over and knelt down beside Robert. "You're hurt."

He waved a hand to let her know he was okay, aware of the half-smile on Tate's face. "Remember what I said, Robert," said the Reverend, then left.

Mary watched him go. "What's he talking about? What went on here?"

But Robert didn't answer her, because he didn't quite understand it himself.

It was somehow connected to a dream he'd been having before he felt Mills' hands at his throat, that much he did know.

Though whether good or evil had won this particular battle, he couldn't really say.

THE KNOCK ROUSED him from his slumber.

He saw a shape almost on top of him – looming over. Hands were reaching down. It brought back flashes of the dream he'd been having. A struggle of some kind, a fight with the Hooded Man. They'd had each other by the neck, each fighting to squeeze the life out of the other.

But this was no man – it was the woman from Hope. His doll. And she wasn't trying to strangle him, he saw that now. No, she was shaking him, rousing him even further from his sleep. Pointing to the door.

Or was that just a cover for what she'd really been about? It was unlike her to be so animated, certainly in the bedroom.

De Falaise looked at her suspiciously. Then he rose, pushing her to one side.

"*Oui, oui...* I am coming," he shouted, pulling on his gown as he marched over to the door. "This really had better be good."

Tanek was standing there. "It is."

For the briefest of seconds De Falaise noted the bigger man's interest in what was beyond him: the body of the naked woman on the bed. That made him feel good, the fact that even his right hand wanted what he owned. Perhaps he would hold onto her just that little bit longer – especially if she was becoming more... responsive.

"So?"

"A boy," Tanek said simply.

"What?" De Falaise rubbed his tired eyes. "What are you talking about?"

"Javier recognised him when we brought the new prisoners through."

De Falaise frowned. "As who?"

"One of Hood's gang."

The Frenchman beamed from ear to ear. "Really? You are sure? Give me a few minutes to get dressed and I will be with you."

De Falaise closed the door and clapped his hands. "Did you hear that, *mon cherie*? It would appear that we have an added bargaining chip." He began to put on his clothes, looking up only once or twice at the woman. She was leaning against the headrest, knees pulled up close. She regarded him with an odd expression, somewhere between defeated and catatonic.

"I will return," he promised her. Then he exited the room and closed the door behind him.

Gwen clutched her knees, pulling them even tighter to her body.

She'd been so near to grabbing him, a fiery strength rising in her. She could have done it, and done it easily – but the knock at the door had thrown her into panic.

In an instant she had altered her stance, from attacker to concerned 'companion,' rousing him. Had he bought it? There was no way of telling, but the news about the boy had probably chased any immediate thoughts about her from his mind. The very idea that they'd stumbled upon one of the Hooded Man's gang, and completely by accident, was nearly enough to make the Frenchman dance a jig on the spot.

Gwen knew which boy Tanek had been talking about, as well. It had to be the young kid with the tousled blond hair. Good God, what on Earth would that maniac do to try and get information out of him? Let Tanek loose? Would he do that?

Of course he would – the man had no scruples.

It was at that point, as she imagined Luke or Sally in his place, Gwen began to cry. She'd never cried for herself in all the time she'd been at the castle, but she did then.

Because she knew in her heart that she had failed.

CHAPTER EIGHTEEN

THE WEEKEND, THEY'D said.

A couple of days now to turn the men into the finest troops Sherwood had ever seen – able to face a superior enemy, with superior firepower. Could it be done? Possibly, but only if they returned once more to the basics of fighting.

Robert had already been giving some of his men lessons in the use of bow and arrows, even how to make their own. Granger had proved the most proficient, and volunteered to oversee the development of those particular skills. Obviously it would be madness to send the men into battle against machine guns without them being similarly armed... But Robert's own preferred weapon had the added advantage of being quiet and the ability to take out a target from a surprisingly long distance. He'd proved this again and again on strikes against De Falaise's troops.

For his part, Tate was teaching the men hand-to-hand combat. They'd had virtually no training in this while in De Falaise's army, the Sheriff preferring to rely solely on firepower. That was all well and good when your enemy was far enough away, but what about when they were on top of you? Robert couldn't help grinning when he watched a pair of younger men try to take Tate down.

"Come at me, then, let's see what you're made of," the Reverend had said. They were on the floor in seconds, with the minimum of effort, the holy man hardly having to move. "I see... It appears we have quite a lot of work ahead of us, then."

On that first day after the plan had been outlined – and after the attempt on Robert's life – two people came to him for a talk. The first was Bill.

He began in his usual gruff way. "Judas Priest. Sure ye know what you're doin'?"

Robert shook his head and regretted it immediately. He coughed loudly.

"Aye, I heard about the Mills thing. Shoulda been more grateful for what we were tryin' to do. For what you've done for all of 'em... All of us." He looked at Robert then, seeing whether his roundabout way of apologising had worked. Robert nodded to tell him it had, and that he was grateful. Men like Bill very rarely said they were sorry, if ever. This was the closest he was ever going to get.

"He thinks the world of ye," added the farmer, "Mark."

Robert closed his eyes, picturing the boy's face – trying not to imagine what he must be going through at the castle. Hoping he could hold on until they mounted their rescue attempt.

"We're goin' to bring him back," continued Bill, as if reading his thoughts. "Bring 'em all back."

"I hope you're right," said Robert.

"Aye. Listen, I've bin thinkin' – you'll need a way of knockin' out that pillock on the castle roof an' his pop-gun." Robert would hardly have described the high-powered sniper rifle De Falaise's man had as a 'pop-gun,' but then compared to the cannon Bill carried around with him...

"Have any ideas?"

Bill smiled. "As a matter o' fact, I do. Care to go for a little drive?"

Robert was reluctant to leave the forest at such a crucial point, but Bill promised him it would be worthwhile. So they'd taken one of the jeeps out, travelling east. Bill had refused to tell him where they were going, leaving it as a complete mystery. "Just hope no one's got to 'em first or wrecked the place," was all he would say.

"Look, are you going to tell me where we're heading?"

"Towards Newark – that give ye any clues?"

Robert didn't need any, especially when they turned off, following the brown and white signs which eventually led them to a large car park and concrete runways. He stuck his head out to get a better glimpse of the corrugated metal hangars, camouflaged grey and khaki aircraft left abandoned outside to rust. The air museum, once a thriving tourist attraction built on a former World War Two airfield, was now empty and neglected. It was somewhere Robert had always intended to take Stevie but just never got around to it, never found the time. How he would have marvelled at the planes. Robert felt a twinge of guilt as they drove in, because it was way too late and the only reason he was coming here now was because he needed to save another boy.

Bill parked the jeep in the virtually empty car park. Anyone with any sense working here would have returned home to be with loved ones when the plague hit; the owners of the few cars that remained probably left it too late. Whether they'd see any bodies here today depended on if the clean up crews had bothered with this place. Robert just hoped it hadn't appeared on De Falaise's radar.

Thinking along the same lines, Bill took out his shotgun as he climbed from the jeep. "Can never be too careful," he said, as if Robert needed telling. He already had his bow raised.

As they walked over towards one of the hangars, Bill pointed to various aircraft.

"See that, it's a BAC Canberra bomber. In service up until the '70s. There you have a BA Sea Harrier. A Vertical Take Off and Landing aircraft, it was still in service with the UK and US Marines up until... well, y'know. Best all round fighter-bomber in the world. Oh, that there's an Avro Vulcan bomber. Superb British heavy bomber in service until the 1980s, last used against Argentineans in the Falklands Campaign, the nuclear bomber of the UK. An' over there's an Avro Shackleton. Old turbo-prop bomber..."

Robert gaped at him, astonished.

"What?"

"Aeroplanes? I just never..."

"Wouldn't have pegged me as an enthusiast?" Bill tutted. "Have to say, I'm not really. Me uncle was ex-RAF, nuts about these things. Taught me all I'll ever need to know, even took me up on a few flights in his civilian life. This place was like a second home to him, God rest his soul."

"And you know how to fly these things?"

"Aye." He closed his eyes, imagining the cockpit. "Airspeed indicator, heading, altimeter, fuel gauge, landing gear, throttle." With his finger he traced the position of each instrument. He finished with a tap in the air in front of him. "Yoke. Simple."

"So, your plan is to take one of them up... and what? Strafe the castle? Use a few of those relics of missiles they have here?"

"Naw," Bill replied, as if he'd even considered it as a serious suggestion. "This is a museum, lad, not a military installation – leastways it hasn't bin for a good many years."

"Then what? He'd see us coming a mile away in one of those things!"

"Who said I was thinkin' about a plane?" Bill winked.

He directed Robert across to one of the hangers and smashed open the locks. They stepped inside – the light from windows above illuminating the scene. Robert saw more aircraft: one grey, one red and blue, another silver and yellow, all remarkably untouched. He guessed the survivors of the virus had other things on their minds than visiting air museums.

"I did think about an early Gazelle. The Sud Aviation SA 341 Gazelle prototype they have here. But this is more manoeuvrable." He strode over to a helicopter, which had a huge see-through bubble on the front. It was a bit like those Robert had seen in old reruns of *M*A*S*H*. "Westland Sioux Scout/Trainer. Very quick, very small. Somethin' to draw his fire, but hopefully avoid it."

The doors opened wide and Bill undid one, swinging it outwards. He climbed inside it and stuck a thumb up to Robert, who followed him.

"She's not fuelled," Bill called to him, "but I daresay I can scrounge up some aviation fuel from around here somewhere. They used to have demonstrations all the time."

"And how do you intend on getting it out of here?" said Robert, asking the obvious.

"Same way they got her in." Bill pointed down. "She's on wheels, look. Once we clear some space, we can tow her through the hangar doors. Bit of an effort, which is probably why no bugger else's bothered, but it can be done."

"This is insane," said Robert.

"More insane than what you're plannin'?" Bill asked, not expecting a reply. "Look, we've got the element of surprise – that bloody Frenchman 'asn't got anything that flies."

"As far as we know," Robert pointed out. "That doesn't matter – the sniper will shoot you out of the sky before you can get close."

"I may look as rough as a badger's arse, but I'm pretty nifty once I get up there. Besides, while the bastard's shootin' at me, he's not shootin' at anyone else."

Robert had to concede that. At the same time he also had to wonder just why Bill was so eager to launch himself – literally – into this suicide mission... not that he could talk. Was it because he felt bad about what had happened to Mark? Or did he really think he could pull it off? Robert didn't question him, just helped Bill to get the chopper out into the open, using the jeep to tow it from the hangar. It caught on the nose of a plane that was a little too close for comfort, but in the end they managed it.

"We should have brought more men," Robert complained to Bill.

"An' take 'em away from their trainin'? They need all the help they can get. Anyway, it's like I said: a surprise."

After that Bill filled the chopper with fuel they managed to scavenge: enough to get the thing home – and both of them – and stocks for the Nottingham run. Robert stared at the flying machine in front of him. He'd never flown before, apart from three or four holidays abroad with the family. He definitely hadn't been suspended above the ground in a bubble, and didn't relish the prospect now.

"It'll be fine," Bill assured him. "A doddle. Tell ye what, I'll show ye."

And he did, beginning with the main differences between how a plane and helicopter fly: one creating lift by angling the wings, the other by manipulating the rotor blades to change the angle at which they meet the air. He took Robert through the pre-flight checks, explaining briefly what the main controls did – from the collective control stick through to the cyclic control joystick and, finally, the tail rotor pedals on the floor. "So, no accelerator?" enquired Robert, only to get a groan from Bill.

Next he walked Robert through the instruments, stopping when he noted the man stifling a yawn. It was as if Bill needed an outlet for all this information, like he'd been bottling it up inside for years, and it was all coming out now he had a captive audience. "Anyway, ye get the general idea. Time to go."

He made Robert strap himself him in, warning him that it had been a while since he'd done this.

"How much of a while?"

Bill didn't answer, instead he put on the earphones and instructed Robert to do the same. With nothing else to occupy him, and more to take his mind off what was about to happen than anything, Robert watched Bill as he started up the chopper. Bill patted the instrument panel that lay between them. "At-a-girl." When he noticed Robert looking at him, he explained: "They can be very sensitive, needs a light touch. The biggest mistake new pilots make is to 'over control.'"

Robert had to admit, the take-off was incredibly smooth. Even so, he gripped the end of his bow, squeezing tightly until they were up in the air.

It was an odd sensation and Robert wasn't sure whether he loved or hated it. He thought that it would be interesting to fly the length of this land, see what had become of it. See who had survived where – and what had been destroyed.

It was a land worth fighting for, Robert finally realised as he saw it stretching out in front of him in all its beautiful patchwork glory. It was a land worth keeping free. If ever the human race was to get back on it shaky legs again, then men like De Falaise had to be defeated.

"All right?" asked Bill beside him.

"Just drifting."

"Aye," said the ruddy-cheeked man, coaxing more speed from the chopper as they headed back to familiar forest terrain.

ONCE THEY'D LANDED on the outskirts, Robert and Bill made their way back to the camp to find new faces waiting for them. Strangers in their den. Robert's first instinct was to bring up his bow, but Jack raised a hand, jogging over to explain.

The men and women were from communities the Sheriff had terrorised, communities Robert had been trying to help. Though these were new, and small, they represented the first seeds of rebuilding this part of England. The people that made up their number had found each other, in spite of all the odds, and built new friendships, relationships and homes. Now those they cared about were in danger and they wanted to do something about it.

"We found them gathering at the forest's edge," Jack explained. "They're volunteering, Robbie."

"For what? To kill me in my sleep?" Robert said, slowly lowering his bow.

"Mills were just one man," Bill threw in. "Look at 'em, they've had enough of bein' scared. They want to fight."

Jack nodded. "They want to help."

Perhaps they do at that, thought Robert. "Okay, then, start training them up. But first, see if any of them have combat experience. You never know, we might drop lucky again and find another member of the TA or something. Or, who knows, maybe even a Kung Fu clergyman or ex-professional wrestler?"

Jack laughed, clapping Robert on the shoulder. "We might at that." He began to walk back to the crowd, then remembered something. "Oh, I think Mary's been waiting for you to get back. She wants a word."

"What about?"

Jack shrugged. "None of my beeswax, Robbie. None of my beeswax."

"Best not keep the lady waitin', then," Bill told him.

ROBERT DIDN'T HAVE to look far to find Mary – she was just outside of camp, practising with her own bow and arrow, aiming for a target notched on a tree trunk. She was holding the weapon awkwardly, her aim off. Robert came up behind her quietly, so quietly that she started when he reached around and took hold of her arms.

"Robert!" she cried, turning round. "I wish you'd stop doing that, you nearly gave me a heart attack."

He could feel Mary shaking and regretted not announcing himself. He still wasn't quite used to how stealthy he'd become. "Sorry, but the way you're holding the bow... May I?" He could feel her arms relax slightly, the muscles still bunched but more flexible, allowing him to guide her aim. "Don't think about the shot too much, just let yourself *feel* it. Feel the arrow against your fingers, that's how you're going to guide it to the target." Robert brought up her bow arm a touch, bending down to look along her line of sight, squeezing one eye shut to get a better view. "Nice... Nice..." he murmured. "All right, now just pull the string back, feel the tension building. Can you feel it?"

"Y-yes."

"Now just let go." She did. The arrow didn't hit the carved circle dead on, but it was pretty close. "There, you did it."

"Yay me."

Robert let out a small laugh. "Yay you." He realised that even though the arrow was embedded in the tree, he was still holding Mary's arms, his chest pressed up against her back. He moved to step away, but she moved with him. She was quivering again, but this time it wasn't because of the fright.

Robert was trembling too.

"You took off before I could talk to you this morning. About Mills, about what happened," she said. "Tate told me about it."

"What's to talk about? People try to kill me all the time these days. Since I decided to become a recluse, I've never been so popular."

Mary turned. "Don't joke about it, Robert. You could have died last night, and I might never have..."

"Might never have what?"

Mary looked right at him. "Had a chance to tell you how I feel."

"Mary, listen. I think you –"

She dropped the bow and put a finger to his lips.

"You can feel the tension too, can't you?" She placed her hand on his arm. "Now just let go..." Mary kissed him then. Gently and briefly. "There. We did it. Yay us."

Robert shook his head. "I... I can't. You know why."

"I do." Mary's eyes were glistening. "At least I know what my head is telling me... But this..." She placed her hand on her chest. "Well, that's telling me something entirely different. I'm sorry." Mary let her head drop, though Robert wasn't sure if it was because she didn't want him to see her cry, or she was embarrassed.

Robert lifted her chin. "Hey, you have absolutely nothing to be sorry about, Mary. You're wonderful. I've never met another woman like –" He stopped himself short. "In another time, another place, and if things weren't so screwed up..."

"Yeah," she said, sniffing, then pulled back from him.

"Don't be like this. We're friends, Mary. At least I thought we were." Robert made to move towards her, but she stopped him. "No, please."

"Mary –"

She rounded on him, eyes red. "Oh, what does it matter anyway? What you're planning on doing... You're going to get yourself killed, you know that, don't you?"

"Thanks for the vote of confidence."

"You're walking into the lion's den, Robert. What do you expect me to say, 'good luck and goodbye'?"

"It's something I've got to do, don't you see? For Mark, for all the people mixed up in this."

She didn't have an answer to that, probably because she knew he was right. But after a pause Mary came back with: "It's what you've wanted all along, isn't it? To be with them."

"What?"

"You want to die, don't you? You have done all along."

Now Robert kept quiet. He was frightened that anything he might say would give away the truth. That there was a part of him that still desperately wanted to be with his family again. But there was also a part that recognised he had a new family, that people were relying on him. That he had to focus on those who were still alive.

"Well, you're about to get your wish, I think," said Mary, the tears coming more freely. "I hope it makes you happy." She picked up her bow and ran. Robert started after her, then decided to let her go. There was nothing he could say that would make things better. He couldn't tell Mary what she wanted to hear, couldn't back out of what he was going to do. He could only watch her disappear into the forest – *his* forest – and hope that someday she might find it in her heart to forgive him.

CHAPTER NINETEEN

"So, HOW DOES it feel to be in favour again?"

He'd first been asked that question in the small hours of the morning, by the guard who'd come to collect him. Javier, his wrists still bound, had instinctively touched his wounded ear, remembering what it was like to be *out* of favour. He had to admit, it felt good. And all because of his saviour: the boy.

Javier hadn't recognised him to begin with; hardly surprising, seeing as he'd only gained a glimpse of him once. It didn't help that the kid had been thrown into the dim caves along with the rest of the villagers De Falaise's men had captured. The place was packed with them, in fact, hardly any room to move even an elbow or a leg. It reminded Javier of the illustrations he'd seen as a child from Dante's *Divine Comedy* by Gustave Doré. One of the levels of Hell with naked bodies piled on top of each other, the masses suffering for their sins. The only difference was, in Dante's *Inferno* they didn't have men with automatic weapons guarding the exits, ready to shoot you if you made a wrong move – there were no exits.

It was a stark contrast to the early days after the virus. Back then, you'd be lucky if you saw one person a week, let alone dozens all crammed into one tight spot. Javier had been dumped here after De Falaise and Tanek had had their fun with him, most of which he'd tried to blot out, and every day that passed he'd been fully expecting them to return to finish off the job. Nothing they'd done had resulted in any permanent damage, just some flesh gouging, a few broken ribs, plenty of burns, and a scar in a particularly delicate place that he doubted would ever fade. The ear he had lost before he'd been dragged back up to the castle. How could he have feared the wrath of God over that? What possible pain could any deity inflict that would match Tanek's skills? Yet he'd felt he had no option but to talk, back there in the forest. Not only had there been the constant bombardment of scripture – the threat of the Almighty's wrath taking him right back to his formative years when his grandmother would quote from the 'Good Book' – but he'd also felt the weight of the place pressing down on him. It seemed ludicrous now, but it had almost been like the trees themselves were watching him, pressuring him to comply.

But what had made him think De Falaise would be lenient? In his mind's eye, had he pictured a scene where the Frenchman would simply rap him on the knuckles for what he had done and then let him get on with his job – or let him go, free to wander wherever he wished so long as it was out of the Sheriff's sight? The truth was he hadn't really been given a choice. Those fuckers back in the forest had more or less forced him to return with his tail between his legs, an action which was rewarded by seeing his men shot dead in front of his eyes and his ear ruined.

Of all the things he had endured since his fall from grace, though, the waiting had to be the worst. Not knowing when his former leader would return and what things his right hand man would have in store this time. Agonising weeks, with only the scraps of food the guards tossed to him and whatever bugs he could find crawling around on the cave floors to sustain him. Javier's belly had never been so flat as it was right now, not even when he was a youth in the military.

How proud his family had been of him then, as he worked his way up the ranks, before he'd been arrested on suspicion of dealing in black market goods and drummed out. The only reason he hadn't been tossed in jail as well was that his superiors hadn't had any hard evidence. Left with his career in tatters, he'd pursued the only option available to him, becoming a gun for hire. Those had been dangerous times, but Javier fought dirty and always got the job done. The rewards had been great, allowing him a luxurious lifestyle and all the women he could ever desire. Yet something was missing. No matter how much he pretended to be the big shot – growing bigger every day, literally – it was all an illusion. He'd never make Major in any army, because they simply wouldn't have him. And though he'd led men into 'battle,' most notably those skirmishes in South America, they'd showed him no respect. It wasn't an official army, just a bunch of mercenaries doing what they were being paid to do.

With De Falaise, it was different. Javier was feared by the men they'd commandeered, that they'd enlisted to their cause. He'd agreed to follow the Frenchman because there was something about the way he talked, just as persuasive as the Reverend. He had a vision, and he wanted Javier to become a part of that. They would have power, wealth, sex, whatever they wanted. There was just one downfall. If you let him down, there were no second chances. Usually.

Javier had failed him so spectacularly that he didn't think this would ever be a possibility. That is, not until the Mexican had spotted the boy, his eyes now accustomed to the gloom. The tiny figure had been swimming in a sea of people, struggling not to drown. Javier might not even have noticed him if it hadn't been for that backpack he was clutching in his hands: a makeshift float to stop himself going under.

I see you, little man, he thought to himself, smiling at how appropriate that phrase was this time. *I know who you are*. He remembered the battle, the fighters involved. One of them had been smaller than the rest. The more he thought about it, the more he remembered seeing...

A backpack, Javier had spotted a backpack.

Sure, there must have been thousands that looked like the one the kid was gripping. But somehow Javier was sure it was him. There was only one way to prove it, however.

Though he was weak from lack of proper food, Javier had pushed himself forwards, propelling himself through the arms and legs of the prisoners. Some complained, but not for long – he headbutted one and poked another in the eye. Javier had to get over to where the kid was, see his reaction when he caught his gaze. Only then would he be a hundred per cent convinced. Determination drove him onwards.

Sure enough, the boy looked across in his direction. Nothing unusual in that, Javier was causing quite a fuss. But when he stared right at him, Javier saw the fear in his eyes. The boy knew him, all right. Even in this half-light, the look of recognition was unmistakable.

"I see you, little man," he said out loud. The kid with the backpack attempted to scramble away. "Hey, you, come back here. You're my ticket out!" There were more shouts of alarm and protest, the other prisoners unable to fathom exactly what was going on.

Finally, Javier came within snatching distance. He reached out with his bound hands and his fingers snagged the strap of the boy's backpack. Summoning all the strength he had left, Javier tugged the boy towards him.

"No!" he shouted, but it was too late. The kid had no footing to lose, and so fell easily into the Mexican's clutches.

"I have you now, don't I?" Javier whispered in his ear. "Your friends have caused me much pain."

"I... I don't know what you're talking about."

"I think you do. They don't know who you are, do they? De Falaise? Tanek? Otherwise you wouldn't have been dumped in here with the rest of the dregs." This gained him one or two severe looks from the prisoners, but they did nothing to antagonise him.

"I still don't know –"

"Quiet! We will soon see what you know. Guard! Guard!" Javier began shouting, his voice echoing through the caves. It was crazy to think that his whole survival depended on one of the runts he'd once commanded, one of the men they'd picked up on their rampage through Britain. Javier just hoped that the fuckwit had enough sense to listen to what he had to say. "Guard!"

He saw one of De Falaise's men appear at the entranceway. He flashed a torch into the caves. "What's all this shouting about?"

"It is I, Javier."

"Who?"

"I used to be a Major in your army." *I used to command respect, and fear, and wish to again – so listen to me, hear my words...* "I need you to fetch De F... the Sheriff. Fetch him quickly."

"Are you off your fucking head? Do you know what time it is? He'll have my balls for breakfast."

"He will have them anyway if you don't give him my message. I have identified one of Hood's men." The guard passed his torch over the boy Javier was holding and cocked his head. The Mexican rephrased what he'd just said. "One of his gang."

"Fuck off. Him?"

"He was with them when they attacked us. I saw him," Javier explained. "Now go and fetch De Falaise."

The guard looked again at Javier's captive, then seemed to think about the consequences if he was wrong. "I'll... I'll fetch Tanek," he told Javier.

So he did. Javier didn't know what he'd said to the big man – and wouldn't like to have been the one to rouse the brute – but within ten minutes the swarthy giant was down in the caves with them.

"It's true, I tell you," Javier promised. "Why would I lie?"

"To get out," Tanek said, blankly.

"Tell him." Javier shook the boy. "Tell him who you are."

The kid remained silent.

"I recognised him. Please, you have to believe me. What harm would it do to make sure?"

Tanek nodded. "Pass him over."

Javier began to ease the boy across, but he struggled. Some of the people in the cave were aiding him, getting in both Javier and Tanek's way.

They're helping him because he's with the Hooded Man, realised Javier. *My God, are they stupid enough to risk their lives for him?*

Apparently so, because Tanek took out a pistol and began to shoot those closest to him. He put bullets into two people before the crowd began to relent. "Better," said the big man.

He reached over and grabbed the boy by the collar of his tracksuit top, holding him off the ground. Then he put him down and pushed him towards the stairs.

"No... No, wait!" shouted Javier after them. "Where are you going? Tanek... Tanek, don't leave me down here with these people!"

But Tanek was gone.

The prisoners mourned for their dead. Then they looked to Javier for revenge. He lashed out at them, warding them off, but the sheer force of the throng was too much. They pulled him down into their sea, hand upon hand, bodies climbing on top of him until he could barely breathe.

Then, just as he thought it was all over, there came a voice: "Let him go. De Falaise has ordered it." It was the young guard again, Javier saw through a crack in the bodies. He was pointing his rifle at the prisoners and they understood what would happen next if they didn't comply.

Javier was spat out of the mass, thrown onto the cold floor in front of the guard. As he was helped to his feet, Javier spat into the crowd, who bayed for his blood.

The guard led Javier up through a corridor in the cave system. It was then that the question was asked of him: how did it feel to be in favour again?

Javier had answered honestly, after touching his wounded ear. "It is better than being dead."

The guard led Javier up and out, through into another part of the caves. It was a place all too familiar. Tanek's torture chamber.

He saw the boy first. Too small to hang in the chains they'd fixed up, the ones Javier knew intimately, they'd tied him to a wooden chair instead, hands strapped to the arms. He looked up as Javier and the guard entered, eyes already wide with panic.

Then Javier saw the duo of De Falaise and Tanek. Like Victor Frankenstein and his hideous monster, they loitered in their underground lair. The difference was that where the famous doctor sought to bring about life, albeit misguidedly, these two brought only suffering and death.

"Major Javier," De Falaise said in greeting. "How nice to see you again." He gave a chilling smile, lips pulling back over those yellow teeth, black eyes twinkling. "Is it me, or have you lost weight?"

Javier bit his tongue. This kind of goading was De Falaise's speciality. To put a foot wrong now would see him back in the caves with those bloodthirsty villagers.

"Well, do not simply stand there – come inside and make yourself at home. Ah, I forgot, you are already familiar with the surroundings, are you not?"

Javier held his silence.

"What's that?" De Falaise cupped a hand to his ear. "Would you like me to speak louder? Is that it?"

Javier shook his head. "I hear you just fine."

"I am sorry. I do not think I caught that properly." He turned to Tanek. "Did you catch that?"

Tanek admitted that he hadn't.

"I hear you," Javier repeated, but now added, "Sir."

"Sir will suffice, I suppose. But also acceptable would have been 'My Lord,' or even 'My Lord High Sheriff.'"

Javier grimaced, remembering it was he who'd told De Falaise about that name on his return from Hope. Absently, he wondered what had happened to the woman he'd brought back from there, and whether the Frenchman had dispatched her yet after having his pleasure.

"And how is your relationship with your God, these days? Do you still fear his retribution more than mine?" De Falaise laughed. "Look at you, *mon ami*. How you have changed. But then, you know what they say: easy come, easy go." De Falaise approached Javier. "I do have one thing to thank you for, however, and that is giving me this important bargaining chip. If it does turn out that the boy belongs to 'Hood,' then you will have done well."

"N-no..." stuttered the blond-haired lad.

De Falaise spun around. "So, it speaks, *oui*? Are you begging for your life already? Come now, the night... or rather the *day* is young."

The boy was shaking but he got the words out. "No... Nobody belongs to him. P-people aren't property."

That's exactly what the woman's boyfriend had said back in Hope, thought Javier, and look what happened to him.

"Quite right," snapped De Falaise. "They are pawns. Pawns in my game!" His eyes narrowed. "But the way you jump to Hood's defence like that, it makes me think Javier was not just trying to save his own skin after all. That you may well be in collaboration with my enemy."

"It is as I told you," Javier insisted.

"You are not vindicated yet, Major." De Falaise strolled over to the prisoner. "He still has to admit that he is one of Hood's gang, that he has been plaguing my efforts over these past months. Are you ready to do that yet, boy?"

"Mark... my name is Mark."

De Falaise nodded. "I see. But don't think that a name makes you any more of a person to us. You are a handy tool. You serve a purpose. Right now that purpose is information."

"I don't know anything. I was taken from my village by your men..."

"And is it not correct that you told them that you'd seen the Hooded Man?" De Falaise turned to Tanek. "A fact that has only just come to light, although the soldiers in question have been reprimanded for their forgetfulness."

"He was with the troops bringing us food and supplies."

"So what happened to him when my men got there? He wasn't killed with the rest of the scum, that much I am certain of. My soldiers would not forget to tell me that or they'd swing with the rest of your kind at the weekend."

Mark gulped. "He took off."

De Falaise grabbed the boy by his collar and pressed his face up close. "Liar! If there's one thing I do know about my nemesis, it's that he wouldn't abandon his people to their fate. It is something I am very much counting on at the moment. Unlike myself, he has principles. But then you'd know that, being so close to him."

"I-I've never met him..."

That was enough to set De Falaise off. He back-handed Mark across the face, his rings opening up cuts on the boy's cheek. As Mark began to cry, the Sheriff said: "This will not go well for you if you insist on withholding the truth."

De Falaise threw a look back over at Javier who was standing uneasily, watching.

"What is the matter, *mon ami*? You gave us this child, did you not, to do with as we will? Or is that another sin in the eyes of your God?"

Javier didn't know what else to do but shrug. Inside, though, he was beginning to doubt himself again.

"If so, then what we are about to do to the boy will really piss Him off." De Falaise called for Tanek to approach. "I suggest you answer my question truthfully this time," the Sheriff told Mark, "or I will instruct Tanek to do something thoroughly unpleasant."

Mark looked from Tanek to De Falaise, then finally across at Javier. His eyes were wet, pleading for help, but Javier kept his mouth shut.

As did Mark – an act for which he paid dearly. Tanek got down on his knees in front of him and held up his leg. Removing the boy's shoes and socks, he placed the heel in one hand and then took out a small needle, barely big enough to sew a button back onto a shirt. Without further ado, he shoved this into a chosen spot on Mark's sole. The boy let out a scream.

Javier cringed.

"You see, Tanek has been trained in both reflexology and acupuncture. Techniques which, in the right hands, can heal or harm. He knows just where to inflict the maximum of pain with the minimum of effort," De Falaise explained to Mark. "All the other nonsense with chains and knives and red hot pokers... well, he mainly does that just for kicks." The Sheriff glanced down at Tanek holding Mark's quivering leg. "If you'll pardon the pun. So, I ask again – are you a member of Hood's gang?"

Gritting his teeth, Mark shook his head violently. De Falaise nodded at Tanek, who repeated his procedure. Another yelp came, less piercing than the last, but no less disturbing.

It took several jabs with the needle, on both feet, before Mark would admit to De Falaise's accusation, and then all the Frenchman got was a slight tip of the head that could just have been the exhausted boy drifting into unconsciousness. Not that De Falaise would allow that, of course. He was there, all the time, slapping Mark on the cheek to wake him – just in time for another fresh bout of agony.

They continued like this for a good few hours, De Falaise asking questions, Mark refusing to answer at first, then finally giving in when he couldn't hold out any longer. Tanek appeared to be able to reach every single part of Mark's body from that one spot, as Javier noticed arms, shoulders, torso and neck all spasming in turn. Mark eventually told the Sheriff how many men Hood had, what their capabilities were, and about the main members of his team – complete with descriptions of Bill, Tate and newcomer Jack. When it came to the exact location of the camp, however, Mark kept shaking his head.

In the end they called a break. "My, is it afternoon already?" De Falaise exclaimed, looking at his watch. "Time flies when you are having such fun, does it not?" He directed this at Javier. "Are you pleased with our progress, Major?"

Javier, who had witnessed so many shocking things in his time, but nothing quite like the last half a day – a torture that left no physical scars, but had obviously taken its toll on the boy – responded with a weak: "Y-yes."

"Good."

Food was brought down and they ate in front of a starving Mark, De Falaise biting into chicken legs, wiping the grease from his chin. Tanek tucked into a practically raw steak, dribbling blood as he shoved each forkful into his mouth. A plate of eggs and bacon was placed in front of Javier, and though his bonds were cut, for the first time since he'd come back to the castle – for the first time in his entire life – he found his appetite gone. He should have been wolfing down the meal, but every time he looked at it, then at Mark, he felt his stomach give a lurch. *It's just because you haven't eaten in so long,* Javier told himself. But was it? He thought back to the way Tate had gotten information out of him, a hardened soldier. The holy man had needed no needles, no pain – just the right combination of words, the right things to play on the guilt Javier had buried. Though the Reverend had wanted to do more – and who could blame him? – he hadn't. He'd shown the kind of compassion that was lacking here today. The torture of a boy... a fucking boy!

What had you expected them to do with him? Give him an ice cream? It was with that same stupidity that he'd hoped De Falaise would forgive him for failing to kill the Hooded Man. For singing like a bird about their operations. He'd seen an opportunity for getting back in their good books and selfishly taken it, relished a bit of revenge on one of the people who'd put him here in the first place.

But Mark wasn't much older than his little brother had been when Javier left for the army. A little brother who was now dead and gone. No matter how tough he acted, Mark was scared and vulnerable.

The image from Dante's *Inferno* flashed through Javier's mind once more, bodies writhing. He imagined what it would be like to experience what those prisoners were going through for all eternity.

"You want some, eh?" De Falaise called across to Mark. The boy regarded him with disdain.

The Sheriff tossed across the bone from the leg, which hit the boy in the chest and dropped into his lap. Even if he hadn't been bound, there was no meat left on the thing. De Falaise had picked the drumstick clean. "He'll come for me, you know," Mark promised them. "Then you'll be sorry."

"You don't seem to understand. I *want* him to come," chuckled De

Falaise. "But he will be the sorry one." He turned to Javier. "What is the matter? Eat, Major. We have a long session ahead of us and must keep our strength up."

A long session? With his leader watching, he forked some of the egg into his mouth. It tasted like ashes.

De Falaise left them alone for a while – Javier suspected he needed to work off other appetites, though he had no way of proving this and wasn't about to ask – but when he came back, the questioning began again.

"Where is Hood's camp located in Sherwood? Is it central, on the outskirts, where?"

Javier knew the information would do them no good anyway; even if they were to send a whole battalion in there, the men would come back defeated. It was Hood's turf, and his alone. There were traps, lookouts, probably guards. He was as safe there as De Falaise was in his castle.

Mark held out for a long time and, by the end of it all, he could do nothing but mumble. "We will get no more from him," said Tanek. Javier wasn't sure whether the man meant today or ever.

"That is a pity. But we have one last thing we must attend to. I wish to send the Hooded Man a gift; a souvenir, if you will. Something belonging to the boy that he may remember him by." De Falaise went over to where Tanek kept his instruments of torture. He picked up a set of bolt cutters. "Major, would you care to do the honours?"

Javier touched his chest. "Me?"

De Falaise nodded forcefully, as if he wouldn't take no for an answer. Javier walked across to him, his movements slow. In the end, De Falaise grew impatient and covered the rest of the distance between them, slapping the cutters into his hand. "There. Now, which do you think? Finger or toe?"

Javier's mouth dropped open. He could not be serious, surely?

He was. "I think a finger. We have done enough with his feet already, *non*?" De Falaise chortled. "So, which one? Little finger, index? How about a thumb?"

Javier was rooted to the spot.

"No suggestions? Then I will decide for you. Hmmm... little finger it is, I think." He took Javier by the wrist and curled his fingers around the handles of the cutters. Then he got hold of Mark's little finger and placed that between the blades. The boy woke up then, realising what was about to happen. He shook his head, mumbling something that sounded like: "Please."

"I know how weak you must be, but it will take only the slightest of pressure – the mechanism is spring-loaded. Do it, Javier," ordered De Falaise. "Do it and prove that you are one of us again."

Javier saw the bodies in his mind's eye, saw flames this time accompanying them. Saw Tate, heard his words about damnation. *"God will punish you for all you have done wrong. Repent, repent!"* He felt the throbbing in his ruined ear.

His hands shook, causing the blades to scrape against the sides of Mark's finger.

"Do it!" De Falaise screamed. "Do it or I will blow your brains out all over the wall." The Sheriff had snatched Tanek's pistol and was aiming at Javier. This was no bluff. He would shoot if Javier defied him.

Clenching his teeth, Javier snapped the blades together. The little finger fell to the ground. If Mark had howled before, then that had been nothing compared to what he did now. Bucking in the chair, his head rocked backwards, the intense pain causing him finally to black out.

Javier dropped the cutters. He took a step back.

De Falaise clapped, then began to laugh. Tanek came over and stemmed the bleeding. They didn't want Mark to die quite yet.

"Good work, my dear Javier. You overcame your fears. He was only a boy, when all was said and done."

No, not just a boy – a man today ("Your friends have caused me much pain, little man."). *More man than you'll ever be... My... My God, what have we... what have I done?*

It was then that he was asked the question again, now by De Falaise. "So, how does it feel to be back in favour once more, Major?"

Javier stared at De Falaise. If he was honest, he felt damned. More damned than he ever had before.

"He'll come for me," Mark had said. "And then you'll be sorry..."

Right now Javier didn't fear De Falaise with all his men and firepower, didn't fear God with all of His angels and the ability to cast Javier down into the pits of Hell.

He feared the Hooded Man.

And what would happen when he finally did reach the castle...

CHAPTER TWENTY

THE TRAINING CONTINUED on into the next day, though by noon Robert and his men had things on their mind other than the battle to come.

One of the lookouts reported that a uniformed man on a motorbike had skimmed the border of the forest at about 11.30, acting strangely. The rider kept making passes at the perimeter but never actually came in. He then took his rifle and fired into the air. The lookout almost fired back, but then saw him sling off a backpack and toss it into the forest, riding in the other direction as fast as he could. The lookout assumed it must be explosives of some kind and raised the alarm.

Robert was called and, along with Jack, came to investigate. They got close, but not close enough to get caught in a blast if there was one. Both men recognised the backpack, and knew who it belonged to.

"Doesn't mean it isn't going to blow," Jack reminded him. "Haven't you ever seen those spy films with the briefcases?"

Robert gave a shake of the head. "It's not a bomb." He began walking towards it.

"For Pete's sake, be careful," Jack called after him.

He watched as Robert paused by the backpack, then as he toed it with his foot. "There's something inside," Robert reported back. "Square but remarkably light. Doesn't feel heavy enough to be an explosive device."

Robert opened up the bag, taking out the cardboard box inside.

"Don't you go opening it, now, Robbie," warned the big man. "I don't want to be scraping you off the trees."

Robert ignored him, pulling open the lid. He gazed at the object inside, then blinked once, twice, as if making sure what he was seeing was correct.

"What is it?" Jack shouted, curiosity now getting the better of him.

When Robert didn't reply, he came over – but soon wished that he hadn't. Inside the box was a severed finger packed in cotton wool. The stump end was caked in dried blood, and the whole thing had a rubbery quality to it, like one of those joke fingers people once bought to scare their friends. But this was real; it smelt bad, like it had been detached for a while. Jack honestly thought he was going to throw up. *It's Se7en all over again*, his mind kept saying, but he shouted it down – this was no time for stupid movie references.

There was a note next to the finger. It read: *See you soon. D.F.*

"The sick... You don't think that's really –"

"It's his," Robert stated.

"So they know about Mark. That poor kid. Holy shit, Robbie! How do we fight people like that?"

Robert rubbed his forehead, and for a moment Jack thought he was going to run off and punch a tree, or do something to vent the feelings building up inside him. Instead, he put the lid back on the box, replaced it inside the pack, and began to walk off into the forest. Jack didn't question him, didn't ask if he was okay – Hell, *he* wasn't okay and he hadn't known the kid half as long as Robert.

Your biggest fan, eh, Hammer? Went to your matches... Now he's at the castle and they're cutting bits off him. Jack shook his head as he followed Robert. He just couldn't believe anyone could do that to a child, just to send a message.

Not a message: A warning.

It was designed to put Robert and his men on the back foot, to make them think twice about trying anything stupid. Now the more Jack considered the plan, the more unwise it seemed. He had come up against some vicious opponents in the ring, some of them bigger and stronger than him – hard as that was to imagine – but even the mightiest crumbled if they showed even a hint of self-doubt. If, psychologically, you could trick them into thinking you were playing for keeps, they'd slip up somewhere down the line. That's what De Falaise was hoping with Robert, that he'd think twice. That he'd see the Frenchman was playing for keeps.

When they arrived back at the camp, Robert wouldn't – couldn't – answer any of their questions. He left Jack to handle all that and retreated into his tent. Jack thought it best to just let people see for themselves.

Tate crossed himself and Bill swore. If De Falaise had been around right then, Bill would have blown his head clean off with that shotgun he carried around. Granger wasn't surprised at all by the sight.

"He's even more twisted now than when I was at the castle," was his reply. "We should think about moving the camp – the kid may have told the Frenchman where to find us."

"No," Jack said with confidence. "He wouldn't have done that, no matter what. Besides, they'd be mad to come in here and risk being picked off. Not when they're banking on Robbie coming directly to them."

"Should someone go and see how Robert is?" Tate asked.

"Best to just let him gather his thoughts, I reckon," Jack told him. "Unless... has anyone seen Mary around today?" She'd be the only one who might be able to comfort him right now. Jack had noticed the way they'd been together lately, the body language. They seemed closer to each other than anyone else in camp, that was for sure.

"She was training with a bow and arrow last time I saw her," offered Granger. "But that was last night sometime."

"Fair enough," said Jack.

"I still can't get over that poor mite back at the castle," lamented Tate, who'd been left holding Mark's bag.

"The best thing you can do is pray for him, just like you've been doing for that gal the Sheriff took." Jack straightened his cap. "And the best thing we can do is prepare for what's to come. You all know what you have to do."

They did, and they got on with it – more so now because of what they'd seen, throwing themselves into training to take their mind off it. Jack got on with the task of teaching some of the men wrestling moves.

But all the time his mind kept flashing back to that box, to the finger – and he couldn't help wondering how Robert was.

And how it would affect them all come the morning.

BY EVENING, JACK wasn't the only one worried.

At various moments other members of his gang had gone to the tent and asked Robert if he would like something to eat, if he wanted to see how the training was going. They'd received no response. Finally, Bill had said: "To buggery with this..." and gone inside. He emerged a minute or so later with a confused expression on his face.

"What is it?" Tate asked, limping over.

"The man's gone."

"What?" Jack came to join them now. "How can he be gone? We all saw him go in there."

More of the group stopped what they were doing and came over, desperate to find out what had happened to Robert.

"Disappeared," reiterated Bill. "Bloody well vanished."

Tate looked for himself, not doubting Bill but needing to see it with his own eyes. "He's right," said the Reverend when he came out again.

"But... but where?" Jack said.

"How the hell should I know?" said Bill. "Judas Priest! That's just effing great, that is. Eve of the big day and he's gone walkabout."

"He wouldn't do that," argued Jack.

"Wouldn't he? Perhaps what happened to Mark affected him more than we realised..." Tate clicked his fingers. "Or he's gone off to try and rescue him alone. I do know he was having misgivings about dragging the rest of you into this."

"Is he off his head?" Granger said.

"It's been said before..." came a voice from somewhere. It was difficult to pinpoint, seeming to originate first from the left, then the right. "And to be honest, right now I'm not even sure myself."

Jack gave a grin. "Robbie."

"Where are you?" Tate shouted.

"I'm over here..." That definitely came from behind them. "Or am I here?" That was in front. The men looked first one way, then another.

When they turned back to the middle of the camp, though, there was Robert, leaning on his bow. They gazed at him, then at each other, unsure how to respond. Should they clap, as they would after a magician's trick? In the end Robert spoke up and saved them the trouble of deciding.

"Misdirection. It's the one thing we have on our side, the one thing that might help us to pull this off. While you were all busy training, not one of you noticed me slipping out, did you?"

There were mumblings, shakes of the head.

"When people are busy, they take their eye off the ball. I'm banking on that tomorrow. But I'm giving you one last chance to back out. I have to do this, now, especially after..." He couldn't finish. Under his hood, they all knew the sadness that must be reflected on his face. "If anyone has cold feet, I wouldn't blame them."

No one said a thing, there weren't even any murmurs from the crowd.

"You're good men. You've restored my faith in human nature, something I never thought would happen. You give me a sense of hope, and I thank you for that."

Just then there was movement at the rear of the crowd. Everyone turned to see Mary standing there.

After a beat, Robert continued. "You all know the plan. You all know your roles. I know you won't let me down. If I should fall, you have to get the villagers... get Mark out. That is imperative above all else. I may not see you again, but you'll all remember what we did here in our time together, what we are about to do. And know that you have right on your side. Good hunting."

They did clap and cheer then – none of them caring whether the noise could be heard from outside the camp, possibly even outside the forest. It reminded Jack of soldiers from olden times before heading off to fight. We're about to do our *Lord of the Rings* thing, he thought.

Eventually the crowd broke up. The Hooded Man cast just one look back as he returned to his tent, over at Mary who was still watching him.

Then he disappeared inside.

HE WAITED FOR some time, almost gave up on her – but in the end she came, as he knew she would.

Robert was sitting cross-legged on the floor, head down, hood covering his features. When Mary entered he didn't even look up, just said: "You came back, then?"

"Yes. I promised I would stand by you – that I would help in whatever way I could. I don't break my promises." There was a steely quality to her voice tonight that hadn't been there when they'd spoken yesterday. He recognised it, because he'd used it himself before.

"Actually, I'm not so sure you should have."

"You know, for a hero you really can be a wanker sometimes," she snapped.

Robert raised his head at that. "Is that what you came to tell me?"

"No." Mary dawdled at the entrance, not wanting to come too far in, but not wanting to be outside either. "I came back to wish you luck."

"Thanks..." He looked up at her properly now. "Mary, listen, when I said I'm not sure you should have come back I meant... I know you can take care of yourself and everything, I just wouldn't like to see something... I wouldn't want anything to happen to you."

"Like it has with Mark, you mean?"

He didn't answer.

"That's sweet, but I make my own decisions in life. You're about to go and get yourself captured or killed. Why shouldn't the rest of us? Why shouldn't I? Give me a reason, Robert."

"*Because* –" He started too forcefully, too hastily, then took an age to finish the sentence. "Because... I care about you."

"Yes. I know. We're friends, right?" Mary sighed. "That was quite some speech you gave out there, you know? You certainly have a way of rallying the troops."

"I just wanted them to know how... how much I've come to think of them."

"As for that little trick with the voice throwing; pretty nifty. Then appearing in the middle of them –"

"You were watching?"

"A-huh," she admitted. "I've been watching all day, saw you set the rope up – just like you've been teaching them. When you asked if anyone had seen you leave the tent; I did. I saw you Robert. I wasn't preoccupied."

Robert got to his feet.

"One day you'll be a legend, Robert Stokes. One day stories will be written about you, just like they wrote about him."

"Him?"

"You know who I mean. Your... predecessor."

"Oh."

Read to me, Dad... Read some more...

Mary came a little more into the tent, hands behind her back. "I didn't just come here to wish you luck," she admitted at last.

"No?" He got up and moved forwards.

"No. I came to give you this..." She brought her hands out where he could see them, and she was holding one of the broadswords from her home. "You may as well look the part."

"I... I can't take that," said Robert.

"Yes you can. They might not let you keep it, but you never know. They might not even see it as a threat."

"One hell of a hunting knife, though," Robert said, with a lightness of tone that had been absent during the rest of the conversation. "Thank you."

"No need. Just take that stupid hood off and let me see you."

Robert pulled it back. "I meant what I said, you know. About another time and place..."

"I know." Mary smiled weakly. "But this is the only one we have."

He opened his arms and she walked into them. They held each other and both knew that this might be the last time they saw one another alive. Mary kissed him on the cheek. It felt like the end of everything, and in a very real sense it was. By that time tomorrow everything would have changed.

"I'm sorry," he whispered.

Mary whispered it back.

CHAPTER TWENTY-ONE

THE TWO MEN remained like that for some time...

Hands at each other's throats, neither one willing to give ground. This was the final fight, their only real fight in fact, and both men were desperate to win. The Hooded Man because he saw it as his mission to rid the world of this new infection; the Frenchman because he needed to pluck this thorn from his side before he could rule completely.

Tighter and tighter they grasped each other, spinning in the dreamscape – the fire on the water raging higher all around them.

Then one of them removed a hand. It was the Frenchman, reaching down, grabbing a hidden knife and bringing it up. It was too quick for the Hooded Man to block and he looked down, eyes wide, as the blade slid into him. It pierced his stomach, slipping through flesh and into him almost up to the hilt. He gave a cry and coughed up blood, his grip on his opponent's throat weakening.

Neither of them said a word; they didn't have to. It was obvious what had happened. The darkness had triumphed, winning out overall.

The time of the hero had almost passed.

And the Hooded Man would pass just as quickly into the arms of death.

DE FALAISE HAD woken with a smile on his face.

He couldn't remember all of the dream but he recalled the ending, recalled sliding the knife into Hood's gut and killing him.

Au revoir, he said to himself, *you've proved a worthy adversary, but it is time for this whole affair to draw to a close.*

The Frenchman looked over and saw the woman from Hope lying there, asleep. He contemplated waking her so that he could begin the morning by celebrating, but he had so much – too much – to do. There would be time later, when he'd dealt with his enemy. All the time in the world, in fact; perhaps even time for a change. When she'd been getting dressed the last time, he'd noticed his plaything was putting on weight. He was obviously feeding her too well.

He'd got to bed late last night, after overseeing the last few hours of construction himself: the culmination of two days' labour. The men had worked hard, but then so they should have; they were doing it for their Sheriff. The platform and gallows were crude but sturdy. Six in a row, so they could get through the executions as fast as possible, regardless of whether Hood showed up – though De Falaise was positive he would come. The platform, located out on the grass where Middle Bailey had once been, was high, punctuated by trap doors that could be released by a single lever. That idea had been his, and he'd explained in great detail how it could be achieved, muttering afterwards about the shortcomings of the British school system when it came to carpentry and woodwork.

What a sight it all was when it was finished, much better than simply hanging bodies over the sides of the rocks. This had style, flair – *panache*, as his people would say. It would be a spectacle; just one of the things that he would be remembered for. De Falaise had even appointed an official photographer, a soldier named Jennings who had an interest in such things and could develop film as well as take the actual photographs.

His inspiration had been the photos down in the basement of the castle, depicting all those different eras. One day, he realised, people would look back and remember what he had done here and applaud him for having the vision and bravery to pull it off. They would cheer his achievements, bringing Britain together again – perhaps even under a different name? Yes, something more fitting like... like Falaisia. That had a certain ring to it.

But he was taking small steps: towards a much larger goal. The only thing standing in his way was Hood and his malcontents. Once they were out of the way he could rule this region however he wanted. Build his army up even more, spread out and conquer from this one, fortified base.

It was his right, and his destiny.

One day, those who came after him would look to his lead in governing their own lands. Just as he'd drawn from the past to establish his empire.

He'd left the woman and gotten into the outfit he'd handpicked for the day's proceedings – the red dress uniform adorned with medals and topped off with a ceremonial sword. Ignoring the new guard on duty outside his room, De Falaise made his way down into the basement one last time. He had examined the history of this castle and its surrounding areas frequently, but only today did he feel like he was making a contribution to the museum. He would have his men erect some kind of memorial to his achievements before too long, continuing on the story of Nottingham and its castle.

De Falaise paused to examine the model of the place he now called home. He bent and placed both hands on the glass cabinet.

"You are not just living history, De Falaise, you are making it," he said to himself.

Next he made his way upwards through the castle and onto the roof, putting on his sunglasses as he went. He walked across to where Reinhart was camped out. He'd been up there for two days straight, watching the city – if not with his sniper's scope, then with the binoculars De Falaise had left him. The Dutchman was like a machine, never complaining, never faltering. Just watching, ever vigilant.

"Anything to report?" De Falaise asked.

Reinhart shook his head. "No unusual activity at all."

"And our scouts in the city?"

"Checking in as usual – once every half-hour."

"Good, good. We will begin the executions within the hour. If you see any sign of the Hooded Man..."

"I will let you know, my Lord," Reinhart promised, holding up his walkie-talkie.

So that was that. It only remained for them to ready the prisoners, roust them and get the first batch onto the platform. De Falaise would allow most of his men to watch; those who were not busy patrolling the walls, that was. It would serve as both example and, he hoped, entertainment. There was so little on TV these days.

As for the Hooded Man...

De Falaise would await his presence with eager anticipation.

GWEN FELT DE Falaise shift about in bed first thing, then heard him laughing as he woke. His dreams had obviously amused him. He'd been restless prior to that, though, just like he had been the night she missed her opportunity to kill him. She hadn't been able to find the right moment since.

She'd feigned sleep in the hopes that he would leave her alone, knowing that nine times out of ten he'd do whatever he damned well pleased, not giving a toss whether Gwen was awake or not. This was the tenth time, obviously, because he got up and got dressed, barely making a sound. If he had tried something then she might well have reached for the knife now under her pillow, ramming it into his throat as he groped her. He was clearly waiting until after the day's events for that particular 'delight.'

Not that she had any intentions of still being here then.

Not that she had any intentions of still being alive. Her plan was simple. Free the prisoners, kill De Falaise. Yes, she was aware she was just one woman. Yes, the odds were impossibly against her, but still she had to try.

She couldn't leave that young boy to his fate. Hopefully, he could lead them all back to his hideout where they'd be safe (*if you can get them past that nutjob on the roof with the sniper's rifle – don't forget about him, Gwen*).

They had to make a run for it, at least. They'd be dead anyway if they stayed here.

She was surprised, given his heritage, De Falaise hadn't insisted on a guillotine. But then, they'd executed the nobility that way, hadn't they? And that's what De Falaise aspired to be. Hanging was for peasants and criminals. Today, it would be used to put an end to the lives of people like she'd known in Hope, who just wanted to get on with their existence from day to day; just wanted to forget about the horrors that had befallen them during the Cull.

You're thinking too far ahead, Gwen, she told herself. *First things first... the guard.*

She got up off the bed, grabbing her robe. She didn't have too long before she'd be expected to join De Falaise at the ceremony, wearing yet another ornate dress he'd picked out. Gwen had other ideas. She slipped on the silk, hastily fastening the dressing gown with the belt around the middle, and made her way to the door. Controlling her breathing again, she took hold of the handle and turned it, opening the door a crack.

There was the guard, sitting opposite and to the right: a yobbish-looking youth today with a scar across his jawline. He didn't appear to notice the door opening – obviously the perfect choice for a guard – so she had to cough to get his attention. Now he looked up, then stood, raising his rifle as he did so.

"E-excuse me..." she said in a low voice.

"What are you doing out? It's not time for you to come out yet. The boss will go spare."

"I-I don't want to come out. I want you to come in." Gwen let the door open a bit further, hoping she'd read this one as well as the shy boy. The thug in front of her was a different kettle of fish – no virgin, and probably cut from the same cloth as De Falaise.

Well then, let's give him what he wants, shall we?

"You what?"

She crooked her finger. "I said I want you to come in, pass the time a little."

He licked his lips. "I-I can't. The boss would kill me. He was bad enough when I forgot to tell him about..." The soldier realised he'd said too much and shut up.

"About?"

"Doesn't matter."

"Is that why you pulled guard duty?" A blink of the eyes told her it was. "Can't be much fun, playing nursemaid."

"Isn't."

"Bet you'd rather be out there getting ready for the executions." He nodded, grinning.

Oh, you're a piece of work. I might enjoy this after all.

"De Falaise has left me all alone, he's too distracted with the preparations. Didn't even have time to see to my needs. A woman has needs, you know." As before, she let her gown fall open a little way and she saw his eyes flash downwards. Unlike the other guard, though, they stayed there. It made her feel sick, but she knew it was just a means to an end. "What's your name?"

"Jace," he told her, eyes still cast downwards.

"That's a nice name, I like it. Why don't you come inside for a minute or two, so we can talk properly? Doesn't have to be long. No one will know. You can keep an eye on me much better from in here."

Jace looked left and right. "All right," he finally said.

She allowed him in and his eyes lit up when he saw the unmade bed. "I've heard what they say about you," he told her.

Gwen smiled, getting more and more into the part with each passing second. "And what do they say?"

"That you let him do things. All kinds of things to you."

She closed her eyes slowly and opened them again. "What would you like to do to me, Jace?"

His cheeks were glowing bright red, but there was none of the hesitation of the other soldier. Jace planted a kiss on her; rough, without any feeling. Gwen tolerated it, putting her arms around him, more in an effort to lead him to the bed than anything else. They inched their way across with her guiding him, until the backs of his legs hit the mattress. Gwen pushed him onto it, climbing on top.

Jace lay back, rifle still in his grip, so she bent down to kiss him again. Her robe fell open even more and his eyes were glued to her breasts. "That's right," she said seductively. "You get a good look..." Gwen bent further down, and while he was distracted she snaked her hand under the pillow and brought out the knife. She held it against his neck and, for a second or two, he didn't even realise what was going on. "Move and I'll slit your throat. I mean it!"

With her other hand she reached down and relieved him of the rifle.

She rose from the bed, putting the knife in her pocket and training the weapon on Jace. "Now, stand up and get undressed."

Jace still seemed bewildered, as if he couldn't quite understand how the situation had gone from one thing to the other.

"Fucking well get undressed!" she hissed, jabbing the barrel of the rifle in his direction. "Lose the sidearm first." Jace scrambled to his feet. With fumbling hands he undid the belt of his holster. "Slowly," Gwen warned him. He dropped it to the floor with a *clunk*, then began to take off his clothes. "All of them..." Gwen ordered, then laughed as he took off his boxers. "I don't know how you were expecting to do anything with that maggot."

"You fucking bitch!"

Gwen hefted the rifle and hit Jace squarely in the face with its butt, and with enough force to knock the beret from his head. He collapsed onto the bed, unconscious.

Quickly, Gwen took off her robe and began to get dressed in the uniform. It was loose in places, but would disguise her well enough to get to the caves. She tucked her auburn hair up into the beret, strapped on the holster – hiding the sharpened knife away in a front pocket of the combat trousers. Then she left Jace behind, opened the door a crack again to check that nobody was around, and slipped out.

Gwen was already on the ground level, so only had to make a bolt for the exit to get outside. Rifle over her shoulder, she skirted the building, keeping her head down and praying that nobody would notice her. Thankfully everyone was busy today, men dashing to and fro, and hardly anyone gave her a second glance. Once she was on the other side of the castle, she saw she was too late.

The prisoners were already being led out from the caves under heavy guard – up the steps and into the light, hands shackled in front of them, shielding their eyes from the brightness. Gwen scanned the line as the soldiers forced them up at gunpoint, but she saw no sign of the boy.

Dammit, I waited too long...

What she did see, however, at the end of the line, was Javier. A thinner, more defeated-looking version of the Mexican, with a large plaster over one ear. But it was him. She'd never forget that face. What was he doing out of his makeshift cell? He was in uniform, too, but didn't look to be giving orders. If anything, he was just milling around observing what was going on. He didn't even appear to be armed.

Gwen ground her teeth. There was no way she could take on all the guards and free the prisoners, much to her regret – it would just get them killed all the quicker – but the temptation of taking some kind of revenge on Javier was simply too much to resist. Head down again, she made her way across to the far end of the line, striding confidently as if she belonged there.

Coming up behind Javier, she took the pistol out of its holster.

"Hello, Major," she whispered, jamming her weapon into his ribs.

"Who –"

"Quiet..." she growled. "Let the soldiers go on ahead, you're coming with me. We have unfinished business."

As the string of people and soldiers headed off in front, she steered Javier to the side and then marched him back down into the caves.

"AND HOW IS our prize this morning?"

Mark grimaced at the man who'd entered the upstairs room; the Sheriff, as he called himself. He'd ordered Mark to be kept inside the castle for the last day or so, too valuable to be lumped in with the rest of the bunch. Tanek had kept a watchful eye on the pale boy, now strapped to another chair, to keep him from falling into unconsciousness, perhaps even dying. De Falaise couldn't have that... Not before his time, at any rate.

"Are you ready to be our star attraction?"

"G... get stuffed," Mark managed, croaking out the words.

Tanek pulled his head back by the hair. "Show some respect."

De Falaise waved his hand. "It is all right, I understand totally. The boy is upset. But do not worry, you will soon see your beloved Hood again. If he doesn't just leave you here to hang."

Mark scowled.

"Bring him," De Falaise said to Tanek. "It will soon be time."

Tanek undid the bonds tying Mark to the chair and the prisoner almost collapsed. Picking up his crossbow, the big man dragged Mark to his feet and half carried him out of the room by the scruff of his neck, following the Sheriff to the landing. They made their way down the stairs, and out onto the eastern side of the castle. De Falaise led them towards the stone steps, overlooking where Mark and the other prisoners had been examined when they first arrived.

Now that area was looking very different. The platform for the gallows took up much of the space, with men still making final adjustments to the structure.

"What do you think? I may even leave it there for future occasions." De Falaise mused out loud.

Mark was quiet.

"I think our star attraction is lost for words, Tanek."

The big man nodded.

"In awe, I'd say," De Falaise went on. He bent, smiling. "How would you like to be the first to try it?" The man talked as if he'd just unveiled a new theme park ride.

Mark attempted to break free of Tanek's grasp, but even with all his strength present he wouldn't have stood a chance.

"Better hope the Hooded Man comes for you, then," said De Falaise, chuckling, "but I'll let you into a little secret, shall I? It doesn't matter anyway. You are still going to die. You all will. Now come along, do not dawdle. We both have a date with the inevitable."

GWEN FORCED JAVIER back down the steps and into the now-abandoned cave system. There were no soldiers or guards down here, as there were no prisoners left. It was just the two of them.

"Am I at least allowed to see who my executioner is?" he asked as Gwen ushered him onwards.

She stepped down and spun him around. "There – remember me now?"

He screwed up his eyes in the half-light. "Yes, I remember you."

"Then you remember what you did, to Clive... to me, back in Hope." Javier's eyes brushed the floor.

"He... he was the one good thing that's ever happened in my life," Gwen said, raw emotion in her voice. "He never mistreated me, never used me. He just wanted to give me the life I'd always dreamed about. But then you came along, you and the Sheriff."

"The Sheriff is totally insane," Javier replied. "I once believed in him, but I was wrong. I was frightened."

"So you did it to save your own skin, is that it?" Gwen raised the gun higher, hand trembling. "Just like you turned the boy over to him."

Javier appeared shocked she knew about that, but he nodded a third time. "What can I say? I am a weak man. A selfish man."

"You enjoyed the power, though, anyone could see that. And you enjoyed killing Clive."

"No. That was an accident. If the holy man hadn't –"

"He was trying to stop you."

Javier shook his head. "If your friend hadn't argued in the first place..."

"He was protecting me, you idiot! He was killed because he was protecting the woman he loved, the place he loved. And now..." Her hand grew steadier, her aim true as she pointed the gun at his head. "Now you're going to feel what it's like to have your own brains blown out, Major."

Javier winced. "That is the second time I've heard such words in as many days, *señora*."

"And what, you're scared? Good!"

He shook his head once more. "I am not scared of you. But I am scared of what waits for me when I die."

"Judged by a higher power, is that it?"

"Yes. That is why I say to you, put down the weapon. If you kill me like this you will be damned just as surely as I am." He held out his hand for the weapon.

Gwen's laugh was harsh. "You've got to be kidding me!"

"No. I wish to save you this."

Her gun arm began shaking again, and it lowered a fraction. Only a fraction. *Maybe he's right; are you really a killer?* she asked herself. *Won't that make you just as bad as him, as De Falaise? Isn't that why after all this time you still couldn't murder the Frenchman? Couldn't stick the knife in him and twist it? Not even to rid the world of his sickness?*

Gwen shook her head. No, she had to do this. Do it to avenge Clive, for her own satisfaction – even if the man in front of her in no way resembled the bloated slug who'd driven into Hope. First Javier, then De Falaise.

She made her mind up.

Closing one eye, Gwen took aim.

THE PEOPLE FROM the villages were being herded onto the field by De Falaise's men.

One man looked over at the gallows and made a run for it. He didn't make it as far as the pathway before being gunned down. De

Falaise clapped at the action, nodding curtly to the men who'd opened fire. Then he motioned for Tanek to bring Mark up to the platform.

Jennings, who had been taking shots of the crowd and capturing a general sense of the occasion, began to snap De Falaise.

"Where is that woman?" De Falaise said under his breath, hardly breaking his camera smile. "I told her to be here for the pictures."

"Shall I send someone for her?" asked Jennings before Tanek got a chance, earning a hateful look from the Frenchman's second.

"No, no, no. It is high time we started. It is her own fault if she misses it. I will think of a suitable punishment later." De Falaise called for five 'volunteers' from the crowd. The soldiers pushed forward the handful of people, at gunpoint. They were forced to climb the steps to the raised area, where a couple more soldiers placed their heads in the nooses. Tanek brought down the rope so that he could shove Mark's head into the gap.

The first six were ready.

"This is an historic occasion," De Falaise said, walking along in front of them, looking down at the faces of those who would be next and the soldiers he had allowed to watch. He resembled a game show host in front of an audience. "The first hangings in your country for over forty years. And not a moment too soon, I say. Stop jostling down there! If you are well behaved, I might still let some of you live to tell of what transpired here today." De Falaise turned to the poor unfortunates about to be executed. "If any of you have anything to declare, it is too late now anyway." He tittered to himself. "I suppose I am not alone in my disappointment that the man you put so much stock in has not even bothered to show up. At least it tells you all that your faith was misguided. He is both a coward and a murderer, responsible for all your deaths."

De Falaise looked across at the soldier holding the lever. He held his hand up, ready to give the signal.

When his radio crackled into life.

"My Lord..." came a voice over the airwaves. De Falaise raised an eyebrow, looking down at the walkie-talkie hanging from his belt. "My Lord, the Hooded Man is here. Repeat: the Hooded Man is here!"

CHAPTER TWENTY-TWO

REINHART COULDN'T FIGURE it out.

He'd had his scope trained on the city below, moving left and right, taking in as far as a mile ahead of him. None of the teams had reported anything suspicious, all checking in on their half-hourly rota as per normal. Then, suddenly, there he was. The Hooded Man. As large as life, walking up Friar Lane towards the main entrance to the castle. Reinhart blinked several times. He couldn't believe what his eyes were telling him. It was as if the man had just appeared out of nowhere.

In reality, he knew Hood must have come out of one of the buildings nearby when he wasn't looking. But how had he come this far into the city without any of them knowing?

Reinhart watched as the man proceeded slowly up the road, bow and arrows on his back, that trademark hood of his pulled down over his face. There was something dangling at his hip as well, which glinted in the morning sunlight: a sword. So this was the person who had caused them so much trouble? Hardly looked like a threat at all. Why, with one bullet Reinhart could just end his life right there and then. No more problems. De Falaise would probably thank him for it.

Or would he?

The Dutchman knew his superior wanted to do that job personally. Had arranged all this just for that purpose, in fact. Quickly, he snatched up the radio and called it in.

Within seconds De Falaise had answered him. "You are quite sure?"

"I am," confirmed Reinhart.

"Very well. Keep your eye out for anything else suspicious." Reinhart heard De Falaise switch to the other channel, ordering his men at the gates not to open fire on pain of death. He was glad now he hadn't acted so rashly.

By this time Hood had reached the entranceway, passing beneath a tree briefly, then vanishing out of Reinhart's sight at the gatehouse.

But he heard the knock as the Hooded Man demanded entrance.

DE FALAISE GAZED down the incline, towards the gatehouse.

They all heard the banging on the old doors, a fist smacking the wood.

He was aware that his free arm was still in the air, frozen at the moment of ending the six prisoners' lives. Slowly, he withdrew that arm – staying the execution for now. He had other, more pressing things to deal with first.

Even if he hadn't just aborted the hangings, De Falaise doubted whether the order would have been obeyed. The soldier at the lever was staring down at the gate as well, along with the assembled crowd.

The banging came again.

"Sir..." A crackle over the radio reminded him he still had it in his grasp. "Sir, should we let him in?" This was a soldier at the gate.

The Sheriff brought the radio to his lips. "Yes, of course, you imbecile. Open the gate. This is what I have been waiting for. He is just one man, alone. He is not to be interfered with."

De Falaise walked to the very edge of the platform, Tanek joining him.

Several men ran out of the buildings at the gatehouse, clambering to undo the huge doors.

"Come on, come on!" De Falaise said under his breath.

The doors opened wide and the Hooded Man stood there, a dark figure in the shadows. He took one step forward, then another. The men at the gate watched him pass.

In spite of the fact the Hooded Man had his bow slung over his back and a sword at his hip, the men there did nothing to take them. They'd been told not to interfere with the visitor, so they didn't. It wasn't as if the man could do anything with such antiquated weapons anyway, not before being gunned down.

The Hooded Man strode up the pathway, his gait confident, his head bowed so that they still couldn't make out much of his features.

He began up the incline, and as he did so De Falaise's men at the rear of the crowd ran to the edge and trained their guns on him. The Hooded Man gave the war memorial on his right a glance, then continued up the snaking path, until finally he reached the summit – steps led up to the East Terrace on his left, the crowd and the platform on his right.

"So," shouted De Falaise, holstering his radio, "you finally came."

The Hooded Man moved forwards, still with dozens of guns trained on him. One false move and he'd be torn to pieces, with no forest to cover him or swallow him up this time. Now he was on De Falaise's home turf.

A strange thing happened as he walked towards the crowd. To begin with, the nearest few people moved aside – they didn't really have much of a choice, as the man was coming no matter what. It caused a ripple effect, and soon another path had been created for him up towards the platform. Like a human Red Sea, the people – soldiers and prisoners alike – parted almost as one, creating a safe passageway for him.

The Hooded Man walked through them, looking neither left nor right. But the people stared. If there was to be anything worthy of record today, then it was this – something Jennings also recognised as he snapped off several pictures of the event. De Falaise glared across at him and he lowered the camera slowly.

"Sorry."

"Take as many as you like when I kill him," said the Sheriff.

The Hooded Man was almost at the steps to the platform. He paused there, looking up slightly at the wooden construction. At Mark, slumping in his noose; it was the only thing keeping the boy on his feet.

"Do you like my new little toy?" De Falaise asked.

In a low voice, the Hooded Man replied: "Every pantomime villain needs a stage."

De Falaise pouted. "Why do you not come up onto my stage, then, and participate in the production?"

The Hooded Man accepted this invitation, but drew out the act, taking one step at a time. For De Falaise, the wait was agonising, and he nearly ordered Tanek to put a bolt through the man's head immediately. But he wasn't quite finished with Hood yet – not after everything he'd put him through. For one thing, he needed to see his face; needed to look into his eyes. If he was to let some of these peasants go today to tell the tale, he wanted them to spread the word about the death of Hood. How the Sheriff of Nottingham – *of Britain, by Christ!* – humiliated him first, then shot him... no, wait, slit his throat... no, perhaps strangled him? De Falaise realised he'd given absolutely no thought whatsoever as to how he would actually finish this. How he would see an end to the Hooded Man, who was still wearing that damned piece of clothing even now: his trademark, his mask. Then he remembered the sabre hanging from his hip. It mirrored Hood's own sword, one which he would never get to use. That was a good way – with Jennings documenting proceedings for posterity.

De Falaise realised that up until now the Hooded Man had stolen most of his thunder. Walking through the streets of Nottingham, only letting himself be seen when he wanted to, that business at the gates, even the crack about pantomime villains. But he would have the last laugh. He would win, just like he always won.

"Good. And now, I think it is time," De Falaise began. "Time that we all saw what the Hooded Man looked like. Time to see that he is not a legend at all, far from it. He is just a man. Just a man."

The two faced each other on the platform, just metres apart. De Falaise stepped forwards, hands raised. His enemy had been covered, not only by the men near the platform, but also Tanek with his crossbow and Reinhart above, since Hood had come into the grounds. He felt safe enough approaching his enemy. But before De Falaise could get close enough to do the deed himself, his rival reached up and grasped the sides of the hood.

It fell back, revealing more delicate features than De Falaise had been expecting. Much more delicate – beautiful, in fact. Full lips, chiselled cheekbones, and the deepest hazel eyes he'd ever seen. As the hood dropped a length of long, dark hair fell with it, trailing down the back.

De Falaise removed his sunglasses slowly and dropped them on the platform.

The girl stared at him and said: "I hear you have a problem with strong women?"

The Sheriff looked at Tanek, as if expecting answers from him. "What is this?"

But before anyone could reply, and just as he was turning back to face the woman who had pretended to be Hood – who surely couldn't be Hood? – the first gunshots were already being fired.

IT HAD BEEN their signal to move.

Seeing Robert through the binoculars, approaching the gates, knocking on them – knowing most of the eyes at the castle would be on the Hooded Man at the other end of the wall, it was their opportunity to make a break for it. Though Granger had serious doubts about whether Tate would be able to make the short sprint across the street to the Trip to Jerusalem pub; then, skirting the sides of the buildings through the Brewhouse Yard, before breaking cover so that they could gain entrance at the barred door of the caves. It was fortified now, Granger knew, men posted on guard round the clock. But they had the element of surprise on their side.

That had been part of the plan Robert outlined, inspired by Mark's hidden incursions into the towns and cities. To use the buildings of Nottingham to hide their own journey – going through them rather than around them. "The quickest way between two points has always been a straight line," Robert had told them. "Like an arrowhead passing through a target."

The teams had entered during the night, silently picking off or capturing the lookouts placed around the city and leaving some of their men behind to answer the radio check-ins. They'd reported no activity, every half-hour, while the rest of them had made their way through the buildings that hid them. It was just like being back in the forest, except it was concrete and stone now masking their presence rather than wood and foliage. The same principles applied, though. And that psychotic on the roof of the castle, who would definitely be on the case today, wouldn't see them coming – hopefully – until it was too late.

For his part, Robert had entered the city alone. He would wait until it was time and then make his appearance, at which point they would make their move.

It was risky, crossing the street and heading towards Brewhouse Yard, but worth it if they could get into the castle that way.

Tate had surprised them all, moving pretty sprightly for a man with a stick. Now that would be used as a weapon, the only weapon he would carry, in fact. It was his choice.

Granger wondered if he would have felt better using a rifle at this stage of the operation, but understood the reasons why Robert suggested bows and arrows – so as not to tip off the rest of the soldiers inside the castle too early.

The barred door usually had about three guards on it, but when his group reached the edge of the rock and Granger grabbed a quick look around the corner, he saw that number had tripled today. De Falaise was obviously taking no chances with security – and who could blame him? Granger held up his fingers to show how many guards there were.

The only thing they had in their favour was that to all intents and purposes, none of Robert's men had joined him on his lonely walk up to the castle. As far as anyone knew, he was all alone.

"When we do this," Granger whispered, "we have to do it quickly. We can't afford to have any gunfire alerting the rest of them."

The men nodded. He felt like he was finally in charge again, at least of his squadron. It was payback time for Ennis and the other Jackals. "Ready?"

More nods.

"Wait a moment," Tate said, gripping his arm. Granger thought there was something wrong, or someone had seen them, but then the Reverend closed his eyes and said a prayer. He finished it by crossing himself.

"Nice to know we have the big guns on our side," said Granger, smiling.

"Always, my son," Tate told him. "Always."

Granger slipped an arrow into his bow. "Right, let's do it." He came out from hiding, loosing the arrow as he ran. It hit the first of the guards, a man he actually recognised now as he approached, as Oaksey – a nasty piece of work. It caught him in the shoulder, though Granger had been aiming lower, and he went spinning back into another guard. Meanwhile, the men behind Granger were all letting off their arrows as well, with varying degrees of success. Some found their homes in legs or sides, others in upper arms. Only one guard fell right away, an arrow in his throat.

None of them had a chance to fire back. They didn't even have the opportunity to raise their rifles. Now those who were wounded were too preoccupied to think about their guns, crying out in pain at the wounds the arrows had inflicted.

Well, that was a piece of cake, thought Granger, but the extra guards weren't the only security measure De Falaise had added. There was a flash of a muzzle from inside the barred door. The bullets howled past Granger, taking down a man to his right, killing him outright.

"Get down!" Granger called back, but they were sitting ducks out in the open. Lying down, they couldn't shoot back with their bows and arrows. Not that they had to anymore. Shots had been fired, the cat was out of the bag, and his men drew their pistols, primed their own rifles – firing back at the door in the cave. Their own bullets sparked off the rocks protecting the men inside, none of them hitting their targets.

Shit! Granger tried to wriggle backwards, but enemy fire chipped away at the floor around him. *We're going to die out here.*

So much for having the Big Guy on their side. Just like before, there was nobody who would help Granger except himself.

Even here at the end, when he was a part of this, whatever it was, miles away from his home, he was going to die alone.

* * *

JACK PEERED OUT of the window.

He'd been looking out long before Robbie broke cover, mainly because there was nothing else to do while he was stuck here. They'd entered the building from the rear, as it was directly opposite the metal gates at the side of the castle, and afforded a view of what was happening in the grounds too. Jack had seen the preparations for the hangings, seen the prisoners being led out on the grass, followed by De Falaise and the man he knew as Tanek, dragging Mark up onto the platform. The kid looked as white as milk, hardly surprising after what he'd been through. But, as if that wasn't enough, they were now fixing to put his neck in a noose.

Jack had almost charged out there with his team right then. Even if he hadn't had the handful of fighters with him, he probably would have done it anyway. He felt like he could just rip down those metal side gates and take on the whole of De Falaise's army single-handed at that moment.

But he had to wait for Robbie, had to do this the way they'd discussed. The kid meant more to him than any of them – and vice versa, Jack suspected. He had to give Robbie the chance to act. So what was keeping him?

Finally, just as the six people – including Mark – were about to be executed, Robert appeared. Hood drawn as usual, he'd made his way coolly to the main castle gates. Jack had watched, anxiously, as De Falaise countered the order to hang them, and he breathed a deep sigh of relief.

"Here's where all the fun begins, guys," Jack said over his shoulder to his team. But as he kept watching, waiting for his cue, he could tell something wasn't quite right. It was to do with Robbie's walk, his height. In fact, the more closely Jack looked, the more convinced he became that it wasn't his leader down there after all, but an impostor.

The question was: *Who?*

The mystery was cleared up when the person in the hood stepped up onto the platform and revealed her face.

Jack let out a sharp breath. "Mary? What the blazes is she doing in there?" As far as he knew she was with one of the other strike teams about to hit the front wall of the castle, or at least that had been the strategy. When had that changed, and how come Robbie hadn't informed the rest of them?

Where the devil was he, anyway?

The sound of gunfire broke into his thoughts. Mary or Robbie, it made little difference to the plan – it was still a distraction. What could mess it up completely would be if their men were already being shot at, as appeared to be happening somewhere.

"Time to kick the bad guys' butts," he shouted and opened the door. The men behind Jack covered him with a hail of bullets and arrows, as he ran and tossed two grenades at the barricade. The explosion blew the metal inwards, buckling it and causing the side gates to swing back on their hinges. Jack ran towards them, staff in hand. Two soldiers with rifles were firing at him through the smoke, but he dropped to the ground, rolled, and came up sharply – jabbing with his staff to catch one in the face, then swinging it around and knocking the legs out from under the other.

"You've just been Jack-Hammered!" he said to the felled soldiers. Then he rose and led his team into the grounds of the castle.

AT THE SAME time as all this was going on, three more teams were making their assault on the castle from the front, springing from buildings adjacent to the wall.

Reinhart could see them, but couldn't take them all out at once – especially when he had his rifle trained on the site of the old Middle Bailey. He was only one man. Then there was the explosion, and more of the Hooded Man's – woman's? – men were pouring in from the side entrance. It was impossible to keep up with what was happening in so many different locations at once.

You should not be here – any of you! Reinhart shouted inside his own head. He was used to one, two, maybe even three or four targets at once, not so many, from from so many different angles. Luckily there were men on the walls that were shooting at the other assault teams; they could hold them off for a little while.

Just then he heard something – a faint sound in the distance. He turned to see the dot on the horizon... which was reducing the distance between them fast.

And there was the distinctive sound of helicopter blades cutting through the air. *They must have been keeping low, out of my range, waiting, hiding, before rising up to let themselves be seen, Reinhart thought to himself. Clever. Very clever.*

But it did mean that his targeting options were now more simple. He had to focus on the helicopter, which was obviously intended to give support to the men on the ground. They didn't have anything they could put in the air to meet it and no one else was ready to fire on it. He couldn't take the chance that it wasn't armed, either.

The choice had been made for him.

Reinhart swung his rifle around. He looked through the scope to see a man in a checked shirt, with a tatty tank top pulled over it, piloting the chopper. The scope was so good that he could even see the man's ruddy features; he'd spent a lot of time outdoors – a lot of time at Sherwood. But he wasn't alone. In the passenger seat was another man, younger, wearing the cobbled-together uniform of De Falaise's men, albeit slightly bloodstained. Another traitor to the cause? Something told him different. It wasn't just the fact he had a bow and arrow with him, because many of Hood's men were carrying those ridiculous weapons: it was something about the way he held it, something about the steely look of determination in his eyes.

This was Hood, the real one. Reinhart had never been so sure of anything in his life. He aimed at the man, then remembered De Falaise's orders about wanting to take out his enemy himself. Were they still relevant now that chaos reigned down there?

And what about afterwards, when they're all dead and you have to explain to De Falaise how you killed his prize? What will he do to you then? Reinhart thought. Take down the chopper, but don't kill them. Cause them to make an emergency landing and then radio De Falaise to let him know.

It was a plan indeed. After all, what harm could they do from this distance? Put an arrow in him? Hardly.

Reinhart smiled and closed one eye, aiming for the side of the helicopter. "Time to bring you down to earth now, birdy."

He squeezed the trigger.

A COUPLE MORE shots rang out in the cave entrance. Granger saw the muzzle flash and ducked, but nothing flew past him. Raising his head slightly, he heard more bangs – saw the cave light up – and it was then that he realised the shots were on the inside.

Then there was silence.

Nothing moved in the cave entrance, no rifles poked out and took pot shots at the men spreadeagled on the ground.

"What's happening?" shouted one of the men behind him.

"Not sure," Granger called back. "Stay down." He got up, keeping his bow raised in case a sudden volley was let loose – and wondering what good it would do him anyway. Then a figure appeared at the gate, a woman with auburn hair that he recognised.

"Hold your fire," he called out.

"Gwen!" This was Tate, who was already getting up, albeit with a little difficulty, using his stick for support.

"Reverend?" came the reply.

Granger watched as the woman who had been De Falaise's love slave worked to open the door with keys she'd taken from the felled soldiers. He motioned his men to move forwards, but still keep low.

When Tate reached the gate, Gwen had it open already. She fell into the holy man's arms.

"My God, I can hardly believe it. Are you all right?" he asked her, but she didn't answer. Instead she shouldered the still smoking rifle she'd used to dispatch the men laying on the floor, and pointed up the sandstone steps.

"You can get into the grounds this way – it's pretty clear. I got rid of any soldiers you might run into between here and there, but can't say there won't be more once you leave the caves. They're bound to have heard the shooting." When Granger and the other men looked at her blankly, she said. "Look, follow me. But promise me one thing when we get there."

"What's that?" asked Granger before Tate could.

She looked at him. "I know you, don't I?"

"I used to be here at the castle before –"

"Yes, I thought so." Gwen unslung her rifle, as if to shoot him.

"Wait, wait..." Tate put himself between them. "Things have changed since Granger was in the Frenchman's army. Unlike the Sheriff, Robert – the Hooded Man – gave him a choice. A real choice," Tate explained to her. "Granger's here of his own free will. He's here to fight De Falaise. So are all these men who once served him."

"He killed the best friend I ever had," Granger told her. "I'm sorry I couldn't do anything to help you when you were here, but I'd have been killed on the spot. You know yourself that he never needs much of an excuse. But..." He shrugged. "Well, I'm here now."

"I could have... should have been dead by now," she said, but Granger saw her eyes soften, and the rifle lowered. "We'll discuss this later. We're wasting time." Gwen turned to lead them up the steps.

"Hold on," said Tate. "You didn't finish what you were saying, Gwen. What did you want us to promise?"

The auburn-haired woman cast a glance over her shoulder. "To leave the Sheriff alive," she said in a serious tone. "At least until I get to him. He's mine!"

*   *   *

DE FALAISE HAD flinched when he heard the first round of gunshots. But that was nothing compared to the explosions down below at the castle's side gates.

The woman in front of him had used the distraction to nock an arrow and aim her bow – shooting at the soldiers closest before they could do a thing. He thought he heard her say something that sounded very much like, "Yay me." Though some went wide, as if she hadn't quite got the hang of it yet, most of the arrows found their mark, diminishing the numbers around the platform.

A much smaller arrow whistled past her, and when De Falaise looked he saw that Tanek had taken the shot with his crossbow. But what should have gone into her cranium missed because of the boy. Perhaps spurred on by what was happening, Mark had somehow found the strength to raise his hands, lift his head out of the noose, and then swing over to where Tanek was standing, letting go when he reached the right spot.

The lad flopped onto the larger man rather than landing gracefully, and although he spoilt Tanek's aim, he couldn't hang on to him. Mark slid down the length of his body – helped by a shrug from the giant himself.

Just as Tanek was about to stamp on the boy, a second man – who matched Tanek in height – leapt up onto the platform. He was carrying what appeared to be a staff in one hand.

"I'd advise against that, buddy," said the guy in an American accent. Then he smacked Tanek across the face with a balled fist. Tanek took the blow, his face shunted to the side, though not by much. Then he hit the man wearing the cap, squarely in the chest – and he went back by a couple of steps. It was like watching a colossal clash of the titans.

Tanek raised his crossbow to take a shot at the other giant, but before he could shoot another bolt, the man lashed out with his staff, knocking the weapon to the floor. Tanek ran at him, nimble for a man of his size, and swatted the staff aside. Both fell backwards heavily onto the already creaking platform.

The other villagers waiting to be hanged, seeing now that there was a chance of escape, and a possibility that the soldier with the lever might accidentally get knocked and pull it anyway, followed Mark's lead. Unhooking themselves with their bound hands, they leapt from their places, fleeing the scene as quickly as they could. The soldier in charge of the lever – seeing no further use for his services – hopped off the back of the platform, swiftly followed by Jennings and his camera.

Which left De Falaise facing the woman, the impostor who had started all this. In the absence of Hood, he decided to take it out on her. Afraid of strong women, indeed! She had simply thrown him momentarily...

He drew his sabre and slashed it through the air, catching her bow and sending it flying out into the panicked crowd. It was difficult to see now who was guard and who was prisoner, mixed up as they were, but every now and again there was a hint of uniform, a rifle barrel to show allegiance.

The woman, unperturbed at losing one weapon, drew her broadsword. She met De Falaise's strike with not inconsiderable strength. The two of them came together, hilts of their respective blades sliding upwards, and he only just managed to back away before she kicked out – hoping to catch him between the legs.

De Falaise's face soured.

"Not used to fighting a woman, are you?" she goaded him. "Used to them playing nicely, eh?"

He came at her again, the sabre swishing as it narrowly missed her. She leaned first one way, then another, countering his next swing with one of her own, before hefting the sword and almost opening up his belly.

There was a sound from above, heard even over the rage of gunfire. The *thrump-thrump-thrump* of a helicopter. It had been so long since De Falaise had heard the noise of rotor blades that he stopped what he was doing and looked. Shots rang out from the rooftop of the castle, hitting the side of the machine, but as De Falaise kept his eyes trained on the scene, someone leaned out of the side of the chopper and attempted to shoot a bow and arrow.

When he looked down again, he saw that the woman was also gazing upwards – mouth wide in surprise. He took his opportunity, to make her as 'compliant' as the others females he had known, to knock the fight out of her as someone should have done long ago. De Falaise gripped the handle of the sabre and punched her with the hilt, splitting her lip open with the guard of the blade.

Her cry was music to his ears. She toppled backwards, losing her grasp on her sword. De Falaise grinned wildly. Whatever else was happening around them, he was at least winning this fight...

"How's the head?" Bill asked as they'd manoeuvred in and out of buildings, keeping low to avoid detection.

Robert let out a soft moan by way of a reply. Whatever Mary had stuck him with had left one stinker of a headache behind. The last thing he'd remembered was them hugging goodbye, then something in his shoulder – the prick of a needle.

"I'm sorry," she'd said, as he slumped forward into her arms. But all he could think was: *Why are you doing this? Had she been a spy of De Falaise's all along? Impossible. The Sheriff's men had been attacking her when they arrived at the farmhouse.*

Then there were no more thoughts, just dreams. The same one he'd had many times before, where he'd faced De Falaise. This time the balance was shifting, the darkness was winning.

He'd come to at some point in the early hours of that morning. Sitting up in the tent, he felt his head spin and nausea rise. What had she injected him with, that same stuff from when he'd been shot? Or something else, something stronger she'd found in the supplies?

"There was all kinds of stuff in the medical packs..."

Whatever it was, it packed more of a punch than any fist.

Robert looked down and realised that his clothes were gone again, stolen. He glanced to his right and saw the clipboard with the sketch on Mary had drawn. Him with and without his hood. It was then that he'd had the first inklings of what she was intending to do. "No... Mary, what were you thinking?"

Snatching up his bow and arrows, and the sword she'd given him, he'd staggered from the tent wearing virtually nothing. It didn't matter, because there was nobody in the camp apart from a sleeping Mills, tied to a tree. All Robert's men had left to put the plan – *his* plan – in motion. But they'd left without him!

He looked up at the sky and saw the first hints of light there. Whatever Mary had used had put him out for most of the night. But there was still a slim chance. Robert raced round, grabbing clothing where he could find it – spare bits of uniforms, mainly. Then, though his head was pounding fit to burst, he ran through the forest he knew so well, taking a short cut to try and reach Bill. With a bit of luck he wouldn't have set off yet.

Robert just about made it, propelling himself from the trees just as Bill was preparing to take off. He'd waved his hands to attract the man's attention, but when that hadn't worked, Robert had fired an arrow across the front of the helicopter's nose bubble. Bill had looked over, mouthing the words 'Judas Priest!' when he saw Robert.

"Yer supposed to be in the city," he said as Robert climbed inside and put on the headset. "Left ages ago."

"That was Mary," explained Robert. "I'll tell you about it when we get in the air." And he had, waiting until they were well on their way.

Bill tutted. "What's she playin' at? Lass'll get herself killed."

Robert knew exactly what she was doing, and why, but he didn't say anything. He just instructed Bill to follow the plan as if nothing had happened. They'd assess the situation when they reached Nottingham.

They came in low over the city. If all had gone well, then De Falaise's spotters on the ground had now been replaced by theirs, but they couldn't risk using the radios to check in case frequencies were being monitored.

"We 'aven't been shot down yet. That's a good sign," Bill commented. He kept low until dawn had broken completely, then he lifted the helicopter up above the rooftops and began their run.

By the time they reached the castle, everything was kicking off. "Looks like the party's already started." Bill pushed the chopper forward, dipping the nose to gain more speed.

Robert had his face pressed against the glass, looking down at his men attacking on several fronts – Jack from the north; Granger and Tate from the south; the rest from the east. It was the latter who were encountering the most resistance from the soldiers on the walls firing at them. Robert also saw the crowd and the gallows, making out the figures of De Falaise, a huge man who had to be Tanek, a smaller figure who was undoubtedly Mark – and someone dressed in his clothes. "Mary," he said.

Even as he watched, he saw Jack tackle Tanek – quite possibly the only man who could stand a chance against him at close quarters – then De Falaise and Mary's duel begin.

There was a heavy ping as a bullet ricocheted off the side of the Sioux. "That were too close for comfort!" Bill exclaimed. "Looks like we got our man there's attention."

Robert took his eyes off the scene below and refocused on the castle rooftop. There was the sniper Granger and the others had told him about, and he had his weapon trained on them.

"Think you can keep us alive long enough for me to take him out?" Robert asked Bill.

"Aye."

Bill zigzagged the chopper and Robert saw now what the man meant about manoeuvrability. If they'd attempted this in any one of the planes from the museum, they'd have crash-landed.

Robert opened the door of the helicopter, wrapping one thigh around the safety belt and using it to hold him while he leaned out. He didn't dare look down, and kept his mind totally on the job at hand. This was a tricky shot, especially while the chopper was moving, and with the sniper still firing at them, but Robert shut everything else out apart from the gunman and the threat he posed. Time slowed down; he was back in the woods, in the forest, hunter versus prey. Robert slipped an arrow into his bow, drawing it back as far as he could.

Bill helped him by bringing the chopper sideways on, though he couldn't hold the position for long. It would be a case of who fired first, and who was the most accurate shot.

"Now! Y'have to take it now!" Bill shouted.

Robert let out the breath he'd been holding, then let go of the arrow. At the same time, the sniper fired off another shot.

The sniper's round grazed the back end of the Sioux as Robert's arrow rocketed through the sniper's scope and straight into his eye. The man let out a howl that could be heard above everything else. Flailing around, his hip caught the edge of the roof's wall and he went over.

"Shot!" Bill clapped Robert on the shoulder as he eased himself back inside.

The helicopter made a strange noise that sounded like a cough. That cough turned into a splutter and Bill wrestled with the controls.

"What's happening?"

"Must've nicked somethin'," Bill told him.

"Can you get us in lower, I need to help Mary and put those soldiers on the wall out of commission."

"We'll be goin' in lower, all right," said Bill as the chopper took a turn downwards.

It was the speed they were coming in at that Robert didn't care for. He glanced at Bill, who threw a look back, and they both focussed their attention on the ground that was coming towards them fast.

THEY SAW NO more soldiers on their way up through the caves. Only when they reached the exit did some of De Falaise's men begin shooting.

Granger and his group returned fire, picking them off with bullets and arrows alike. It was Tate who pointed out that the men on the walls needed to be incapacitated first. "Try just to wound or injure if you can. The fewer deaths the better," advised the Reverend.

"Tell that to them," replied Granger, nodding at the soldiers with machine guns. "They're not holding back on our men outside." But they took it on board and, where possible, fired to debilitate rather than kill.

Gwen ran off ahead on her own, desperate to reach the Middle Bailey and find De Falaise. Tate limped after her, knocking one soldier out with his stick and taking another one down with a series of simple judo moves.

"Gwen, wait! God will provide his own revenge," promised the Reverend. But just then he got caught in a crossfire of bullets and was hit in the shoulder. Gwen turned and doubled back to check on him. She pressed his own hand against the shoulder and told him to keep pressure on it.

"I have to go," she told him firmly.

"Gwen..." mumbled Tate, but she was already on her way to meet De Falaise.

CHAPTER TWENTY-THREE

GWEN STRODE THROUGH the grounds of the castle, spraying bullets from her rifle as if she was dealing with a bug infestation.

She was out of ammo by the time she reached the Middle Bailey where the bulk of the action was taking place. So she cast the rifle aside and took out her pistol – the one she'd used to murder Javier.

No, she hadn't simply killed him outright in the end, had she? Appropriately, it had been more by accident than intent. Just as she'd been wrestling with what to do, gunfire had echoed through the caves: Granger and Tate attacking the south side entrance. It had proved enough of an interruption for Javier to make a play for the gun, spluttering that he mustn't die, couldn't risk what would happen to him if he did.

Javier had grabbed the weapon and they'd wrestled with it. He'd almost turned it around on her when she summoned strength from somewhere, jostling him back against the wall. His hands had closed around the pistol, forcing her finger on the trigger, and the sudden bang had made them both jump. Her because of the noise; Javier because the bullet had entered his chest.

She backed away from him as he clutched at the wound – tried to stem the blood pouring from it – then he reached out with one of his shaky hands. "You... You must forgive me, *señora*... please... before it's too late."

Gwen shook her head firmly. "Damn you."

He smiled, though it was more of a grimace. "I... I am already damned..." The light went out in his eyes, and he slumped to the floor.

Gwen stepped over the body. "For you, Clive," she whispered. Then the sound of gunfire came again, snapping her out of her daze. The castle was under attack. It had to be Hood's men, an attempt to stop the executions. She had to go and help.

Holstering the pistol, she'd unslung her rifle and followed the sound to the fight. Before long Gwen came upon the soldiers defending the lower cave entrance. They'd turned in her direction, but before they could fire she'd pulled the trigger of her own rifle, filling the cave with light and sound.

It had paved the way for Granger and his men to enter, for them to begin taking down De Falaise's regime. Whether or not Granger could be trusted still remained to be seen – he hadn't lifted a finger to help her when she was being held captive – but she'd deal with that later. Right now, she had a mission... a promise to keep.

And absolutely nothing was going to stand in her way.

JACK WRESTLED WITH Tanek on the platform. He tried using some of his moves on him, but the olive-skinned man had a few of his own.

A swift elbow in Jack's stomach saw him releasing his grip, and Tanek was up and had a dagger drawn. He was just about to plunge it into Jack when he paused, his eyebrows twitching. Then he looked down.

Jack's eyes followed and discovered what had made him hesitate. There was a bolt from a crossbow sticking out of his calf. Tanek scowled, but before he could do anything, another bolt hit him – this one in the side. Jack traced its trajectory to Mark lying on the floor. Resting on his stomach, the boy had the crossbow propped up and was shooting at Tanek.

Jack took the opportunity to rise and land an uppercut – not a legal move in wrestling, but something that came in handy when the referee wasn't looking. Tanek reeled backwards, but didn't fall. Instead, he cleared his head, then threw the dagger in Mark's direction. It missed the boy by inches as he rolled over, letting go of the crossbow in the process. Jack came at Tanek again, but this time the giant sidestepped him, bringing down his own fist on the base of Jack's neck – sending him crashing into one of the wooden gallows.

Tanek stalked over towards Mark, snatching up the crossbow where it had fallen. Jack attempted to get up, but failed. All he could do was watch as Tanek picked out the bolts like splinters, still not showing the slightest sign of pain.

Tanek looked down at Mark and pulled a strange face – halfway between a smirk and a scowl – then he turned the crossbow on the boy who'd caused him so much trouble.

*   *   *

NOW THAT THE gunmen on the walls were falling, Granger saw that their own men had begun climbing up the other side using grappling hooks and ropes. They were swinging over the tops and taking out more of the guards.

In the grounds, confusion reigned supreme. Gunshots were ringing out and nobody really knew who was firing at who. De Falaise's army was bigger, but they were panicking.

Granger spotted Tate as he was making his way towards the Middle Bailey. The Reverend assured Granger he was okay, and begged him to go after Gwen, so he left one of his squad to look after him.

She didn't take much finding. The auburn-haired woman was striding through the mayhem, shooting at anything that moved until her rifle was spent. Granger ran off after her just as she was pulling out her pistol.

But there was a soldier behind her, off to her right, aiming his gun at her head. Quickly, Granger loaded an arrow and pulled back the twine. He let the projectile go and it embedded itself in the soldier's side, causing him to fire up into the air. Gwen heard the noise and turned, saw the arrow and mouthed a thanks to him.

Then she turned back to get on with her task.

Granger began after her again, but before he'd got three steps an arc of bullets patterned the sky above him – then lower, hitting him in several places all at once. He seemed to go down in slow motion, holding the bow close, feeling the red-hot blood leaking out of him.

He toppled to the floor, vision blurring.

Granger could just see the figure of the woman heading off towards the platform, off to do what he'd been trying to stop her from doing – though would have done himself given half a chance.

"Go... on, girl... do it for E-Ennis..." he managed. "Do... it for m –"

Granger closed his eyes and lay still, while all around him the battle raged on.

SHE SAW HIM – there he was.

The man who'd left her in bed that morning, the man who'd done all those things to her. The man who'd given the orders for Javier to follow. Gwen approached the platform. A soldier came up on her right and she shot him in the leg without even blinking.

"I've heard what they say about you... That you let him... do things. All kinds of things to you."

Not anymore. Now it was payback time.

De Falaise was terrorising some other woman now, she saw; a

dark haired girl dressed in green and khaki. They were looking up at something, and though Gwen registered the sound of the helicopter, she didn't take any notice. Then the Sheriff punched the woman in the face with the hilt of his sabre.

That did it.

Gwen rushed up towards the platform, pistol drawn. *"FRENCHMAN!"* she screamed, mounting the steps.

De Falaise looked over and puckered his brow. Perhaps he didn't quite realise what was happening, how she could be here in uniform, brandishing a gun – instead of in a nice dress by his side. "My dear..." he began.

"Don't!" she warned him. "I'm going to kill you now, just like I killed Javier." Gwen pointed the gun at his head.

"Then by all means get on with it," he said snidely.

Gwen's hand shook. She remembered what Javier had said about sparing her from what he was to go through, about saving her soul.

"You cannot do it, can you?" De Falaise grinned that smug grin of his. "You cannot just kill me like this, defenceless."

Gwen pulled the trigger.

The gun clicked empty.

De Falaise's eyes widened, then he began to laugh.

Gwen saw red. She threw the useless pistol at him and took out the knife from her pocket, the one she'd originally intended on using.

"I am afraid that mine is much bigger than yours." He held up the sabre to illustrate.

Gwen didn't care. She ran at him anyway, shouting at the top of her voice.

She was stopped in mid-lunge by something hard plunging into her shoulder, sending her spinning. It was De Falaise's second in command, shooting one of his crossbow bolts at her, a young boy hanging on to his leg and skewing his aim.

Gwen toppled sideways, falling away from the laughing Sheriff. He was slipping out of her reach. But before she fell off the side of the platform completely, she threw the knife with her one good arm.

It landed in De Falaise's thigh.

As she dropped, uncertain of where she would land, she at least had the satisfaction of hearing the Frenchman let out a shrill yelp.

Then she was tumbling away, falling and hitting her head. Before she lost her grip on consciousness, she looked up, and it was then that she saw the helicopter flying overhead, much closer than it should be to the ground.

* * *

THE SIOUX CAME in to land with a bump, not far from the war memorial.

Robert and Bill jolted forwards, but both chopper doors were wide open within seconds, the blades still turning. Bill took up his shotgun, Robert had bow and arrow ready again.

On their sprint up the incline, Robert bagged a couple of soldiers and Bill opened fire over the heads of two more, causing them to drop their rifles and run off in alarm.

They ran up the path – back up towards the platform and the scene they'd just passed over. "I'll take the left, you take the right," Robert told him.

On the right, there was Tanek, reaching down to grab Mark again – to shoot him, finally, with a bolt to the head. On the left were De Falaise and Mary.

Bill aimed his shotgun at the bigger man and ordered him to let Mark go. The olive-skinned giant looked at him like he was speaking gibberish. Then he pointed the crossbow in Bill's direction. He shot, but at the same time Mark produced Tanek's own discarded dagger and rammed it with all the strength he had left, through the man's foot.

Tanek did make a noise this time, more a growl than a scream.

The bolt hadn't flown straight, though it had found Bill – lodging itself into his pelvis. As he dropped, though, the farmer squeezed his own trigger. The blast hit Tanek in the middle of his chest, sending him reeling backwards with a grunt. The whole platform shook when he fell, but he didn't get up again.

Robert, meanwhile, had an arrow trained on De Falaise's head. But the Frenchman already had a dazed Mary pulled close to him, and he took this opportunity to bring the sabre up to her throat.

"The real Hooded Man, I presume." said the Sheriff.

Robert's eyes narrowed. "You know who I am. And I know you."

"Indeed." De Falaise kept Mary between him and the line of arrow fire. "You care for this woman, I can see that. I can use that." He looked all around him at the devastation, looked back over his shoulder to see Tanek lying on the deck, then he added: "And much as it pains me to leave before we have had a chance to get properly acquainted, there is a saying that seems appropriate: *Prudence est mère de sûreté.* Discretion is the better part of valour. And so I will live to fight another day, *non?*" He began to drag Mary backwards with him, limping – a knife still in his leg. Robert kept his arrow on him the whole time, but couldn't risk a shot.

He dragged Mary down the rear steps, disappearing from sight. Robert skirted around the side of the platform, missing only a few moments, but by the time he rounded it, De Falaise and Mary were almost at the farthest end of the lawn. Almost at a truck parked there.

"You've got to let her go to climb inside, you bastard," said Robert under his breath.

But De Falaise managed to keep Mary in front of him as he got into the cab of the truck, sitting her on his knee. The engine started up, the vehicle shuddering.

"Damn it! Jack... Jack, get Mark off the platform – right now!" Robert kept a bead on the vehicle as it powered towards them, but also kept an eye on what was happening on the gallows. Jack had managed to drag Mark to the edge and then over it, both of them tumbling off the right hand side of the platform. The truck clipped the left hand side, ramming through it, just missing Bill and a prone auburn-haired woman. Robert barely had time to dive out of the way, rolling as the truck tipped over the incline and drove down past the helicopter, scattering people as it went.

Robert raised his head in time to see the truck power through the devastated side gate and out onto the street.

His eyes flicked back to the helicopter, its rotor still turning. "Bill..." he called out on his way over to the man. "Are you in a fit state to fly?"

"Does it bloody well look like it?" Bill replied, nursing his wound. "Judas fucking Priest, I can't even get up!" He thumbed back towards the helicopter. "And I doubt if she will, either."

Robert ground his teeth. The truck could be heading in any direction, even if he could get to a jeep or truck in time to follow. The helicopter was the only option if he was to find De Falaise and stop him.

Bow in hand, he began down the path, ignoring the calls from Bill and Jack.

What are you doing? What exactly are you doing, Robert? he asked himself. He couldn't fly, not even with a chopper that was in any fit state to get off the ground. Robert knew all this and still he had to try.

It was Mary's only hope. God alone knew what would happen to her once she no longer served her purpose as a hostage. That lunatic De Falaise...

He tried not to think about it as he threw the bow into the cockpit, then climbed in himself. Closing his eyes, he visualised what Bill had done before take off, remembered what he'd said about lightness of touch.

With one hand on the collective and one hand on the cyclic, he attempted his first ever take off.

For long moments nothing happened, and Robert wondered if this was because of the state of the battered machine. But then, all of a sudden, and with a lot of mental encouragement from its pilot, the Sioux rose a few feet off the ground.

"Attagirl," said Robert, coaxing more height from her. Once he was high enough to make it over the castle entrance, he pushed the chopper forward, practically kangarooing it, bouncing onto the other side. It would never get up to the height it had before, but Robert was hoping he could get at least high enough to see where the truck was going.

As he lifted away, he saw the devastation of the battle he was leaving behind. His men were pretty much mopping up, and those soldiers who were left were surrendering in droves now De Falaise had cut and run. There would be time for sorting all that out later – time to find out how Mark was later. Right now, all he could think about was getting Mary safely back.

CHAPTER TWENTY-FOUR

Wake up, Moo-Moo – you're in serious trouble. Even worse than the last time.

She heard David's voice rousing her, but it seemed so far away.

Moo-Moo, please wake up. The Sheriff has you as a hostage. You're driving through the streets of Nottingham in an army truck and when you get far enough away he's just going to kill you and dump you. Moo-Moo, are you listening to me! Mary! MARY!

That did it. David very rarely called her by her proper name, only when he was angry with her about something. Right now, that would appear to be because she was going to die. Mary opened her eyes a fraction, looking to the side. She saw De Falaise in his dress uniform, hunched over the wheel of the truck. A knife was buried in his leg, but he didn't seem in any rush to take it out. Beyond him she saw buildings going by. He took a right at speed, almost causing the truck to tip over. It was all Mary could do to keep quiet.

Good, said David. *He still thinks you're out of it, so there's no reason for him to question otherwise, is there? He also thinks you're unarmed. Oh, God, Moo-Moo, however did you get yourself into this mess? Because you thought you felt something for someone you hardly even know? Because you always said to yourself even though you were hiding away that one day the perfect man would come along and you'd know it instantly?*

She told him to shut up. Mary needed to concentrate, which wasn't easy when you were pretty sure your nose was broken and your head was splitting. She waited, watching De Falaise through the slits of her barely open eyes. Waited for him to turn the wheel again, so that she could use it as a cover to flop a hand below the seat. Then, with his attention still on the road, she reached that hand up behind her, reaching under the bottom of Robert's hooded top, reaching for the Peacemaker she had tucked away there, hidden in the folds.

She wasn't expecting to still have the gun by this late stage in the game – just how stupid were the soldiers under the Frenchman's command? – but then she wasn't expecting to fight De Falaise, get knocked senseless, and get dragged along for the ride in his mad dash for freedom.

And he was mad, no mistake about that. As Mary and the others had suspected all along, this guy was a total loon, playing out his fantasies of being a dictator in a world where he thought nobody could stop him.

He was wrong.

Mary had her fingers curled around the handle of the gun, her thumb ready to cock it. She wasn't thinking about what would happen once she'd shot him, whether he'd crash the truck and kill them both, she just wanted to end this right here and right now.

"*Merde!*" She flinched at De Falaise's raised voice, thinking that he must have noticed what she was up to. But he had caught sight of something out of the corner of his eye in the wing mirror. Something following them. Mary could just about make out the shape of the vehicle from her angle – but it didn't look like any car or jeep or truck she'd ever come across. "The cretin does not know when to give in. But I will show him."

"Robert," she whispered, too quietly to be heard.

Yes, said David. *He's come for you, Moo-Moo. He's come for you. Perhaps you were right after all.*

De Falaise stamped on the brakes, sending her back into her seat as the low-flying helicopter crashed into their rear.

ROBERT GRAPPLED WITH the controls. It was taking all his effort and concentration just to keep the Sioux off the ground, but it had done its job – got him high enough to pinpoint where De Falaise was going, heading blindly towards the market square. Then, having little choice in the matter, he brought the damaged chopper back down to hover as near to the ground as he could. The landing gear scraped the road, causing sparks.

Knowing De Falaise's direction helped Robert to take a short cut, emerging from one street just in time to see the truck go by. He was then in full pursuit.

Robert kept just a little way back, trying to hide behind the vehicle and hoping that the Sheriff wouldn't see him. But it had to happen eventually, and so Robert found himself having to pull on the collective control quickly, as the truck braked and the helicopter slammed into it. Then the chopper rose, groaning in protest, and just about made it above the height of the truck, settling down on top of it as it accelerated again.

The truck wove this way and that, trying to shake the chopper. Robert fought to keep her level with the vehicle below him. They were driving down a road heading along the tram tracks when De Falaise pulled his braking stunt again.

This time, the helicopter shot forward and over the front of the truck, and suddenly both vehicles clipped the side of a building. They crashed through overgrown foliage onto what had once been the fountain of the square. Robert attempted to disentangle the chopper, but that only made matters worse, and soon they were heading towards the Council building.

Grabbing his bow, Robert opened the door of the chopper. He was just about to jump clear when he remembered something else he'd brought with him, and leaned across quickly to retrieve it. He dove out just as the truck rammed into one of the once majestic stone lions, a match for those back at the castle. Whether De Falaise had been deliberately trying to crush the chopper was unclear, but Robert hit the concrete and rolled, feeling something pop in his shoulder as he did so.

From his position on the floor, Robert raised his head and looked up at the mess of twisted metal. The truck and the helicopter were fused together like a piece of modern art. A river of diesel ran all the way across the market square like a slug's slime trail. And it was spreading into a lake...

"Mary..." groaned Robert. He had to get her out of the truck.

Hauling himself to his feet, he slipped the broadsword he'd grabbed into his belt, and staggered across to the wreck. He'd only got a few feet when two figures came into view around the side. It was the Sheriff and Mary, the former holding his sabre to her throat again, the latter still dazed.

Robert slotted an arrow into his bow and raised it, wincing at the pain from his shoulder. The pair moved sideways like a crab, De Falaise dragging Mary away from the truck as if he still thought escape was an option. Robert moved with them, keeping his arrow on the pair, but not being given the opportunity to take a shot.

"Let her go!" ordered Robert as they hobbled away, though his voice lacked any kind of authority.

"I think not," replied De Falaise.

"Look around you, it's over. You're done."

"*Non*. It is only just beginning, *mon ami*. We are –" De Falaise's face crinkled up, then he let out a piercing cry.

Robert glanced down and saw Mary's hand, twisting the knife still embedded in the Frenchman's leg. She seemed fully awake, intent on causing De Falaise the maximum amount of torment.

He threw her roughly to the side and she hit the ground, rolling over twice. It was as she came to a stop that Robert saw what she had in her hand. Her Peacekeeper, trained on the Sheriff.

"Mary, no...!" But she didn't hear him in time. Mary fired at the Frenchman, missing him, but hitting the truck some way behind them, igniting the leaking fuel tank.

De Falaise looked behind him, looked down at the trail of diesel, and began to limp quickly away. Robert ran for Mary, but the resultant blast as the truck and helicopter exploded knocked him off his feet – pitching him backwards into the middle of the square. A streak of heat whooshed between the two enemies as the diesel caught fire, then fanned outwards.

Robert slipped in and out of consciousness. He was back in the dreamworld suddenly, back at the lake of fire – then he was here, at the market square. There seemed little difference. The Sheriff came at him, but he couldn't tell whether it was real or an illusion. The man appeared out of the flames, burnt, his clothes smouldering, but he wasn't stopping.

It was only when his sabre descended that Robert realised this was no dream. He rolled over and the blade connected with the concrete, clinking loudly. Robert struggled with his own sword, but couldn't disentangle it from his belt at this angle.

De Falaise struck again. "I will kill you," he said, his face wild.

Robert kicked out, knocking his attacker backwards and reversing the descent of the sabre. While De Falaise wobbled back, Robert clambered to his feet, and finally pulled the broadsword from his belt. When the Sheriff attacked this time, metal clashed against metal. The strokes were clumsy – both men were inexperienced with a sword – but any one could have ended the fight, skewering through flesh.

Neither man had the strength to really fight anymore, so in that respect they were evenly matched. After several slashes at each other with the swords, they grabbed one another's wrists at the same time. Robert squeezed as hard as he could, forcing De Falaise to let go of his sabre, while his opposite number followed suit, wrenching

Robert's arm forward and aggravating his shoulder. Robert let go of the broadsword, and it landed with a clatter.

They locked eyes, set against a backdrop of flames. It was clear that they recognised this scene, and knew what came next. Letting go of each other's wrists, they went for each other's throats. Both men found reserves of energy, just enough to try and choke the life out of each other. Robert had a slight edge, and could feel De Falaise's grip on him weakening.

Too late, he remembered the dream – and what the Frenchman had done in it. Robert let go of De Falaise's throat, just in time to move back and see the knife as it was shoved into him. The crazed Sheriff had torn the weapon – a sharpened table knife – from his own leg and had been aiming for Robert's gut. It embedded itself in his side instead, but was no less painful.

Their faces centimetres apart, the Sheriff snarled. "And so it ends, English."

"Everything ends eventually." Robert headbutted De Falaise, causing him to let go of the knife and stagger backwards.

At the same time, Robert reached into his quiver, taking out an arrow. He held it as he would have done a dagger, then shoved it into De Falaise's open mouth, ramming it home.

The Sheriff's eyes widened and he clawed at his throat, choking as he might have done on a fishbone.

"That was for Mark. This is for Gwen and Mary."

Robert took out another couple of arrows, and this time shoved them into those eye sockets, snapping off the ends as he did so.

De Falaise couldn't scream, so he just gargled in agony, toppling to the floor, where he writhed about.

Robert stood above him, holding his side. "And this," he said, pulling out a final arrow. "This is for the rest of us."

De Falaise held up a quivering hand, but Robert ignored it, bent down, and plunged the arrowhead into the man's heart, hard and deep. The Sheriff twitched for a few more moments, then lay still.

Breathing heavily, Robert rolled off the corpse, still holding his side. He lay beside the Frenchman, not able to move any more – and to the casual observer there might have seemed hardly anything to choose between them. Two dead men, covered in blood.

But one was alive. Even after everything he'd been through – even after willing it to happen – Robert was still alive. The difference was, today he was glad of the fact.

He felt something, someone at the side of him. If he'd had the energy he would have brought up the knife still in his side, defended himself in case it was another attacker. But he didn't. So he was glad when the face that appeared above him was a familiar, friendly one.

"Yay you..." said Mary half croaking out the words. She wasn't in a much better state, her face all banged up, dried blood at her nostrils – yet it was still beautiful in spite of all that.

Robert laughed at her words, coughing, and when he did his shoulder and side felt like they were on fire, while the actual fire on the square was seemingly burning itself out. "Yay... Yay us," he managed.

Mary smiled and kissed his forehead, her hand reaching down and helping to stem the blood flow at his side.

"You... you finished with my clothes now?" he asked her.

"Why, you going to need this old hood again, Robin?" she asked him.

He smiled weakly, the sound of vehicles in the distance reaching his ears. Maybe it was De Falaise's men fleeing? he thought. But when he saw Mary waving he knew it had to be his own men, drawn to the place by the smoke from the crashed vehicles.

It could mean only one thing. The battle for the castle, for Nottingham and the region, was finally over. Certainly the villain of the tale was dead...

But what of the war?

What of the future?

Those were questions for another time, another day, he told himself as he closed his eyes.

Yes, those were questions for another day entirely...

CHAPTER TWENTY-FIVE

IF HE HADN'T wanted to be found, he wouldn't have let her.

But Robert was getting better at allowing Mary to track him down these days – getting better at letting her in. It would still take time, and she knew that. This wasn't some magical fairy story, and he couldn't simply erase the past. She wouldn't expect him to. Though the past seemed more distant, the more time he spent with her.

"They said you'd come to the forest." Mary joined him in the clearing. It was the same one she'd followed him to that night, when they'd both seen the stag – except now the leaves were turning autumn gold. He knew that once, she would have said it all looked the same, but now she actually recognised the place... he could tell from her expression.

"They were right," he said.

"You're waiting for it to come back again, aren't you?"

Robert sighed. "It won't, I know that."

Mary closed the gap between them. "You miss this place..."

He nodded. It had been two months since they'd taken over the castle, but he'd come back here often. He just couldn't settle. Bill, Jack, Tate; they had things running pretty smoothly now they were all fully recovered – thanks in no small part to Mary's attentions and a few other medical people who'd stepped forward. The soldiers who hadn't fled had been either placed under arrest until they worked out what to do with them, or offered a minor post in their ranks... under supervision, of course. The dead, like Granger, had been buried – not cremated, Robert hadn't allowed that – and words had been said by their graves in the grounds, near to the war memorial. They'd done this for their men and for those who'd sided with De Falaise. After all, many of them hadn't had a choice. Some had, of course – some wanted the power that came with serving their demented master. Men like Tanek, whose body could not be found anywhere after the battle ("There's no way he was getting up after what I did t'him," Bill said, but still there was no sign of the man...). At any rate, word had gone out to the villages, and through the markets, that there was a new force in Nottingham, a force that wouldn't tolerate violence or stealing or attacks on the communities it sheltered. If the region was to stand again on its own two feet, it would need policing; it would need defending. And they were the ones to do it.

Still, he'd been thinking about coming back, even though he hadn't said anything aloud. But every time he stepped foot inside the forest, he felt it. Something was missing; something had changed.

"You don't belong here anymore, you know," Mary said, her little finger brushing his. "What you came here to run away from..."

"Mary, don't," he said, but she pressed on anyway.

"What you wound up doing here... It's over. You have a different life now, a chance at a new beginning."

(Robert had a sudden flash of De Falaise in his head then. "*It is only just beginning, mon ami...*")

"There's no need to run anymore. And they need you back there," Mary went on. "Mark needs you." Now Robert saw a picture of the boy... the man who'd had to grow up so fast. He remembered the first time he got a chance to speak to him after the battle, once they'd both rested up and gained their strength back. Mark's hand was bandaged; so was Robert's side. A right pair they'd made. Robert told him how very proud he was of him, how brave he'd been holding out under torture. Mark looked at him, fighting back the tears, then he'd hugged Robert – so hard he had to suck in a breath from the pain, but he'd endured it gladly. For a little while the child in Mark had returned; it was nice to see.

"They all need you. And... and I do too."

Robert nodded slowly. "How's Gwen?" he asked, changing the subject.

"The Reverend's looking after her. She's really starting to show now; late bloomer, I guess. She's still convinced it's Clive's, though. A legacy of their love."

"Better for her if she carries on thinking that." Gwen's would be the first baby born in the castle, but the more time his men spent out there in the villages, the more relationships were blossoming. It wouldn't be long before other children came along. Each one would give them all new hope.

"And how's your side today?" she asked him.

"Better. Still twinges, especially now it's turning cold, but it's okay." Mary had seen to that too. A proper little medico she'd become, whether she intended to or not.

"You'll live, eh?" She smiled. "That's my Robert... So, are we going back to the castle, or do I have to stick a needle in you again?"

"I still haven't forgiven you for the last time." He laughed softly and took hold of her hand.

Mary looked down and squeezed it. "Come on, there's still lots to do – and it looks like it might rain anytime. Let's go home." Now she tugged on the hand, and for a moment or two he held fast. Then he relented, turning, walking with her out of the clearing, back towards their jeeps on the outskirts of Sherwood.

There was a noise behind them, something in the undergrowth. Robert looked over his shoulder quickly and caught a glimpse – or was it his imagination? A flash of antlers against the green. Then it was gone.

"What is it?" Mary said craning her neck to see.

"Nothing," he told her. "Nothing at all."

As they walked, Mary chatted, but he wasn't really listening to her. He was taking in the trees, remembering the first time he came here. The reason why he'd hidden away...

Suddenly he recalled what Stevie had said the first time he'd finished reading him his favourite storybook.

"Is that it? Is that the end of the adventure, Dad? What happens to them all afterwards?"

Robert couldn't answer him, nor the many times after that he'd asked, because he didn't know. Robert still didn't know. What did come after the end? Peace? Love? Or would they find themselves having to deal with another threat one day? What came afterwards?

What came next?

With his free hand, Robert reached up and pulled his hood over his head.

Then, falling in step with Mary, he walked to the edge of the forest without looking back.

Knowing that there was one – and only one – sure way to find out...

THE END

ACKNOWLEDGEMENTS

A BIG THANK you to Trevor Preston for all the sound military and weapons help, and for answering all my niggling little questions; you're a complete star. Thanks to the staff at Nottingham Castle for the tour around the caves and especially to Pete Barnsdale who took us round the castle early in the morning before the crowds arrived. Ditto to the people at Sherwood Forest Visitors Centre and Rufford Abbey Country Park, plus thanks to Nottingham County Council for the use of the quote at the beginning of this book. Thank you to David Bamford for the help with checking historical details. Thanks to my friends and family for all their support not just while writing this, but during the last twelve years as I've been making my way in the writing biz. A special thanks to John B. Ford who gave me that all important first break and has been encouraging me ever since. A huge thank you to Jonathan Oliver who saw the potential of the idea, and Mark Harrison for bringing my protagonist to life. Thanks to Simon Spurrier for letting me play in his sandpit, and to Scott Andrews and Jaspre Bark for the opportunity of being part of something bigger than the whole. Thanks to Richard Carpenter for creating what will always be, for me, the definitive Hood, in the '80s; without him my version would not exist. And lastly a 'words are not enough' thank you, as always, to my wife Marie. The first person to read this and offer such excellent advice. Love ya, sweetheart.

BROKEN ARROW

Original cover art by Mark Harrison

For Simon Clark. Mentor, master of post apocalyptic fiction, and friend.

"Nothing's forgotten.
Nothing's ever forgotten."

Robin of Sherwood,
by Richard Carpenter

CHAPTER ONE

It was a blood moon. A hunter's moon.

And she was most definitely being hunted. As she ran down the road, almost slipping on the icy surface, she looked over her shoulder. She couldn't see her pursuer, but she knew he was there – and he was close.

The light from above gave the snow-covered streets a crimson tinge. She pushed on, dodging the rusted carcasses of vehicles that hadn't been used in an age. Not since before the world went to Hell – and you could actually believe you were there tonight. Once, this road would have been jam-packed with motorists making their way through the city. Now it was simply full of memories and ghosts.

It was a different place, and it wasn't safe anymore to be out at this time of night. She knew that, yet she'd ventured out anyway. Clutching a bag holding a half-dozen cans she'd managed to scavenge from various shop storerooms, she was beginning to wonder if it had been worthwhile. After all this time, most of it had already been picked over by the starving survivors of the virus. There weren't that many, granted, but they'd been living on their wits and whatever they could find for a long while.

Folk had raided houses first, homes on the outskirts – rather than head into the towns and cities; where gangs of thugs had banded together, hoarding the lion's share of food and other items. Only those stealthy enough to creep in and out could get away with it.

Or at least that had been the case before...

Word had reached people far and wide that the gangs were no longer in control. That they were being driven out. Whether it was true or not, nobody could confirm, but when people are hungry enough, they'll believe anything. She'd believed it. And she'd risked her life because of it.

Now she was paying the price.

She ran as fast as she could, skidding as she turned a corner, legs everywhere. Looking up, she saw it: a dark shape on top of a hill, the edges defined by the glowing red sphere overhead. A castle; the very heart of the city. For a moment she considered making for it, but she knew she'd find no refuge there. Whoever was following just out of sight would surely follow her there, too. She'd be trapped.

Might be help up there? Might be someone who could –

She shook her head. There was no-one living there, no lights, not a sign of life at all. No, her best bet was to try and lose her persuer in the narrow streets.

She heard footfalls behind her – boots crunching the snow. She had to keep moving, didn't have long before they caught up with her. Pulling the bag in close to her chest, like a mother cradling her baby, she ran into the labyrinth: a warren of houses that seemed to be leaning in to watch her progress. It shouldn't be too hard to get lost in here, to hide until the hunters had passed by.

Another quick glance over her shoulder told her it would be harder than she thought. Now she saw him, and if he was revealing himself, the hunt was almost at an end.

The man was wearing a hooded robe, which prevented her from getting a good look at his face. She caught something glinting, something the man was raising up.

A knife, twenty inches or more long. She'd seen their like before in old horror movies back when she was in her teens, usually wielded by masked killers. One slice could cleave someone in half.

If he had been alone, she might have reasoned that this was just some nut, using the apocalypse as an excuse to live out his fantasies. But there were more where he came from. Many more.

They emerged from the shadows, all hooded, all wielding those deadly weapons. She froze. Her situation was so much worse than she'd imagined. The lead figure came closer, reaching a hand up to pull down his hood.

She let out a gasp when she saw his face – or what there was of it.

Perhaps this place wasn't only populated by ghosts, but by the living dead as well? The skull was white – or at least would have been were it not for the moon's glare. The eyes were sunken and black, merely sockets from which this thing stared out. In the middle of the forehead was a symbol she couldn't quite discern, etched into the bone.

I'm going mad. I must be.

When she finally found she could move again, the apparition gave her feet wings. Head down, she sprinted faster than ever: up one street, down another. The ground beneath her was still treacherous, but somehow that didn't matter anymore. She lost her footing a couple of times, but ignored it, desperately trying to get away from the nightmare behind her.

Rounding a final corner, she let out gasp. It was a dead end. The houses seemed to lean in closer.

Looking to the left and the right, she thought about trying a few doors, bobbing inside the buildings now mocking her. But she'd be just as trapped inside as she would have been back at the castle.

Instead, she headed back up the street, in the hopes she might find a way out before the dead men arrived. She'd taken only a few steps before her exit was cut off.

A figure appeared at the mouth of the street, seemingly materialising out of nowhere. Then, seconds later, others joined him. She counted ten at least. The leader, slightly taller than the rest, began to walk towards her. She backed away, knowing that she didn't have much street left before she hit a wall, but in no rush to meet her fate.

"P-please... Please, just leave me alone..."

He took no notice – they took no notice – approaching now as one, swinging their machetes.

"What do you want from me?"

The dead man at the front paused, contemplating this question. Then he answered in a hollow voice: "Sacrifice."

They didn't want her physically, as so many had before. Didn't want to paw and molest her – why would dead men want that? They wanted her to join them; to become one of them. To give up her life so that she could exist forever walking these streets, preying on the warm blooded. Maybe living forever wouldn't be so bad?

But what if, when they killed her, she stayed dead? Or, even worse, went to a place that made this look like Heaven – as impossible as that might seem? She looked again, searching for a way out, a way up perhaps?

Then she saw another hooded figure on the rooftops. The bastards were up there as well! She was well and truly finished. The hunt was over. Bowing her head, she sobbed, accepting the inevitable.

One of the walking dead fell. At first she thought he might have slipped on the wintry ground. Blinking tears from her eyes, though, she spotted something sticking out of his shoulder. Something long and thin and feathered.

She traced the shot back to the figure above her. Even as she looked up, he was falling, legs bent to take the strain of the landing. The shape rose, standing between her and the dead men... except she knew now they weren't dead at all, not if an arrow from this man's bow could fell them. This man who wore a hood just like her enemies.

He waved her back, then plucked another arrow from his quiver. He'd nocked it and fired quicker than she had time to register, already reaching for another.

Two more of the 'dead' men dropped. But that didn't stop others taking their place, charging at her rescuer. He had time for just one more shot, but it went wide – his aim spoiled as he avoided a blow from one of the swinging machetes. Too close to rely on his bow, the hooded figure let go of it and pulled a sword out of his belt. He first blocked one machete swipe on his left, then another to his right. Metal clanked against metal, but the man seemed as quick with the sword as he had been with his arrows.

As she watched, he pushed one of the robed men back, headbutting a second – dropping the man like a stone. A roundhouse kick sent a third into the wall, and she heard a definite crunch of bone. But he couldn't be everywhere at once, in spite of how it seemed. A couple broke through, machetes high, ready to be planted in her.

The hooded man punched one attacker in front and elbowed another, before swinging around and chasing after the ones making for her. He leapt and landed on them, taking them both down just inches away. She fell backwards, landing on the snow, bag falling from her grasp.

The three men struggled to their feet, and the hooded figure narrowly avoided a machete swipe to the stomach, arcing his body and bringing his sword down to meet the challenge. No sooner had he thrown off one man than he had to meet the other's blow. The force knocked him back, hard, into the wall. A flash of gritted teeth, and he slid the hilt up to the man's hand as they struggled to force the weapons out of each other's grip. The stalemate was ended when the first assailant, now recovered, swung again; but the hooded man dragged the figure he was locked onto around, creating a human shield, and the sword buried itself in him instead. The injured man fell to the ground, but her hero wasn't quick enough to avoid a punch that caught him a glancing blow on the chin. Shaking his head, he brought his sword up and into that first attacker, the point emerging from his back.

Breathing heavily, each puff turning to steam in the night air, he looked across at the woman and she caught just a glimpse of the intense eyes under the cowl, searching her face. Then she saw one last glint of metal just behind him, a machete whipping through the air. She didn't have time to scream or point, but he heard the sound anyway... just not in time to do anything about it.

The machete halted in mid-air and the blade quivered. As she lifted her head she saw what had stopped it. A large wooden staff, held by an equally large man. He was wearing a cap and sported a goatee beard.

"Whoa there, fella," said the big man, with a trace of an American accent. "That's enough of that." Taking one hand off the staff, he punched the robed man in the face, knocking him clean out. The machete clanged to the floor.

Beyond the giant she saw others: his men. The hooded man's. They were armed as he was, with bows and arrows, with swords. They were grabbing hold of her attackers, pinning them against the wall. Two or three of her assailants who'd been taken down by the stranger seized their chance to get up and barged past the newcomers, shouldering them out of the way.

"Don't just stand there," the large man barked, "get after 'em!" Then he held out his hand, helping her saviour to his feet. "Don't worry, they won't get far."

"They'd better not," said the man in the hood – a hood she realised was not attached to a robe, but part of a winter huntsman's jacket (sliced across the front where the machete blade had almost cut him).

"If you'd waited for the rest of us, we'd probably have got them all," replied the man in the cap.

"This woman was in serious trouble."

"Yeah, and so were you, Robbie."

"What's that supposed to mean, Jack?"

"You've... Well, you've been out of the game for a little while, boss. You're rusty. That psycho almost had you."

Robbie grunted, ignoring his friend. Then he turned to her, pulling down his hood as he did so. She saw him for the first time, in the glow of the moon – a glow that gave his features a strange kind of warmth. He was clean-shaven and handsome, just like folk said. Oh, she'd heard the stories all right. Who hadn't? It was why she figured it might be safe to come into York tonight. The Hooded Man and his forces were cleaning up the area, or so went the rumour.

Finally, she found her voice. "Y-you... You're him, aren't you? The Hooded Man?"

"What gave it away?" Jack answered before the man could say a thing.

Though it was hard to tell in this light, she could swear Hood's cheeks were flushing. He nodded shyly, like he was embarrassed to admit the fact.

"Are you going to help the lady up then, Robbie, or should I offer my services? Which, I might add, I'd be happy to do..."

The Hooded Man held out his hand and she took it, feeling its strength. Her heart was pounding, not because of the skirmish, not because she'd been seconds away from dying, but because she was this close to him. Could he feel it too? Their connection?

As she rose, she stumbled slightly, unsteady on her feet. She fell into him and he held her there for a second... before the embarrassment crept back and he righted her, letting go. She felt somehow bereft, but still managed: "Thank you... Robbie."

"It's Robert," he corrected, stooping to pick up her bag and handing it to her, "or Rob."

"Or sometimes even Robin," added Jack, grinning.

Robert sighed. "Only this big lug calls me Robbie, I suspect because he knows how much I hate it."

The big man feigned offence, then grinned again, resting his staff on his shoulder. "And I'm Jack. Always a pleasure to help out a damsel in distress... 'specially one as pretty as you are, ma'am." Once he'd got a smile from her, Jack turned to address his superior. "Looks like all those hours of stake-out actually paid off. We got most of 'em."

"I wanted all of them," said Robert.

"Who are they?" she asked as they walked towards the men having their hands bound behind their backs.

"We're not entirely sure; some kind of cult," Robert informed her. "We've had reports of them cropping up in various locations. It never ends well for their victims."

Sacrifice...

She could see now that they were merely wearing make-up. Their faces and shaved heads had been painted white, the eye sockets black in contrast. Mimicking the deceased to intimidate the living. She peered closer at one of them, trying to make out the tattoo on his forehead. The robed figure bared his teeth, snapping like an animal before the young man holding him could pull him away.

"You might want to get back a bit, miss," he told her.

Jack clapped him on the shoulder. "You did good work tonight, Dale. I'm proud of you."

The youth beamed, clearly delighted by the praise. "Are we taking these back to Nottingham?"

"I believe that's the plan."

"You're going back to the castle? To Nottingham Castle?" the woman asked Robert.

He nodded.

"Then please... take me with you." Robert was silent and she looked at him pleadingly. "I'm begging you. I have nowhere else to go. I've got no-one... not since my mum... my family..." She didn't need to finish that sentence; they'd all been there, it was reflected in their eyes. His especially. The hurt, the pain he'd tried to bury but which still lurked there, slumbering in his mind – and only took a prod like this to wake.

"Come on, Robbie," said Jack. "The lady's been through a lot tonight; what harm can it do?"

"All right, all right," said Robert. "You can come along."

She flung herself at him, giving him a big hug. "Oh, thank you, thank you." Jack coughed and she felt Robert tensing up. This was obviously too public a display of affection. Pulling back, she then gave Jack a hug as well. "Thank you. Thank you both."

"Er... Jack, when the others get back, ready the horses."

"Sure thing," said a happy Jack, walking away, out of the alley, and taking the men and prisoners with him.

"So," Robert continued, turning to her; he'd looked more comfortable facing death than he did right now. "What's your name?"

"Me?" She hesitated for a second or two. "Do you know it's been so long since anyone asked me that? It's Adele."

Robert stuck out his hand. "Well then, Adele. Pleased to meet you."

She smiled. "And I'm so very pleased to meet you, Robert... the Hooded Man."

CHAPTER TWO

So much had changed, and yet so much remained the same.

Take this place they now called home, for example. The castle itself still looked the same, on the outside at any rate. But inside things were definitely different. Instead of a barracks for an army, this was now a headquarters for the fledgling constabulary they'd built up over the past year and a half. Ever since they'd kicked that Frenchmen's arse; just a handful of them against his entire militia. Robert had killed the self-styled Sheriff of Nottingham himself, while the rest of the men had mounted a covert attack on the castle.

The castle doubled as a home for Robert and those closest to him. Like Mary, the woman who'd coaxed him out of the forest, who'd taught him to love again after his own wife and son had died from the virus. Like his second-in-command, Jack, a former wrestler from the US who had come to Sherwood to join Robert's fight against injustice.

And it served as a home to him, Mark, a boy who'd had to grow up way too quickly: a former scavenger on the streets who finally found a new family. He'd first met Robert at one of the makeshift markets on the outskirts of Sherwood, and soon afterwards the man had saved his life – just like he had so many others. He and Mary had taken on the mantle of adoptive parents, loving and protective. But like all good parents, they also set the rules – some of which Mark completely disagreed with.

Like the one about his training. He was ready, but Robert kept putting him off.

"You need to face your fears properly first."

As Mark walked down the East Terrace, towards the Middle Bailey, memories flooded back to him of the first time he came to this place. Bundled into a truck, hands tied, then deposited down in the caves beneath the castle – which now held all of De Falaise's modern weapons (as Robert often said, "His way is not our way."). There he'd been tortured, used to lure Robert from Sherwood. Mark looked down at the stump of a finger, all that was left of the digit the evil psychopath Tanek had cut off and sent to Robert. The stump ached sometimes, especially in winter, and he even felt it there wiggling occasionally. *Phantom pains*, they called it. The mind not letting go of the past.

Mark shook his head and walked towards the Bailey where Robert's men – his 'Sherwood Rangers' – were being put through their paces. Swordplay (techniques mainly gleaned from books: "You can find out everything about anything from books," Mary had said); archery; hand-to-hand combat. It was all going on down there. In lighter moments, Mark couldn't help comparing their training ground to something out of an old James Bond movie.

Jack would just love that, he thought to himself.

Mark watched as arrows smacked into painted targets; as men tackled each other with wrestling moves Jack had imparted, and martial arts skills either taught by Robert or passed down from Reverend Tate's time. The holy man had returned to the village of Hope, along with Gwen, who he'd known from before his time in Sherwood. They'd left right after Gwen had given birth, in spite of Mary's concerns about letting them go. Gwen had wanted to put the failed community of Hope back together, in memory of her beloved Clive – who the Sheriff's men had so brutally killed. Tate had gone with her, arguing that the people out there needed spiritual guidance much more than they all did. Mark wondered, though, how much it had to do with Robert's personal thoughts about faith.

Not that Tate had been the only member of their family they'd said goodbye to. Bill had also gone off to start again after constantly butting heads with Robert. The outspoken local hadn't agreed about the gun situation at all, especially when it came time for him to relinquish his canon of a shotgun. "He's daft as a brush," Bill had told Mary. "Judas Priest! With them weapons rusting away down in the caves, we can really make a difference, an' what's Robert want to use? Bloody swords and sticks!" Last Mark heard Bill was back running markets, up the coast this time. He was doing all right, too, by the sounds of things. Oh, Robert kept tabs on him all right – just in case he needed help. He was still very fond of the man who'd once been his second, even if he was too proud to admit it.

Arriving at the top of the steps, Mark suddenly had a flashback to when the Bailey had been used as a staging ground for De Falaise's executions. The men below were clattering swords together – swords which, along with other ancient weapons, had either been gathered from various museums or made on the grounds by their budding blacksmith, Faraday (who also shoed horses and gave the men riding lessons). Robert and his Rangers shunned the jeeps, tanks and motorbikes left behind, not only because fuel was becoming a rare commodity, but, again, because they represented a different time. They'd rely on other defences to protect the castle, like the projects some of the men skilled in woodwork had been drafted into. Robert promised they'd be as effective as anything modern weaponry could offer.

Now in Mark's mind, the training session was replaced by the gallows that mad Frenchman had made.

Of all the times Mark had come close to death, that had been the worst. The feel of the rope cutting into his neck, the agonising wait for De Falaise to give the signal for them to be dropped; how helpless he'd felt...

The Hooded Man had intervened, of course. Or more accurately, Mary dressed as the Hooded Man, walking in through the gates down there. That had taken some guts, switching places with Robert to prevent him being killed. It had proved distraction enough for the rest of Robert's forces to attack, but it could all have ended so differently.

Phantom pains... Just phantom pains...

Robert told him once what De Falaise had said right before he'd killed the man, ramming arrows into his throat and eyes, breaking them off. *"It is only just beginning,* mon ami.*"* What he'd meant was anyone's guess, but in a sense he'd been right. As they'd begun their policing of the region, Robert had discovered just how hard it was to keep the peace. Even though people came every day to join his ranks, volunteers like the new recruits below, he still had too few men – and now they were widening their protection to surrounding cities like Sheffield, Doncaster, Leeds, Manchester... things were even tighter.

Which was one of the reasons Mark couldn't understand Robert's decision.

"You're just not ready yet," he'd told him when he asked again.

"I'm almost fifteen, not that much younger than Lee and his friends." Lee Keegan was a student from St Mark's School down south, who'd showed up a while back asking Robert for help in defeating some guys they called the Snatchers. He'd eventually loaned them some Rangers, in spite of being stretched so thinly. "I'm not a kid anymore... I haven't been for a long time."

"That's not what I'm talking about. You're simply not prepared, Mark."

"After everything I've been through? You're joking."

"It's *because* of everything you've been through. You need time, son."

"You mean like you're taking?"

Robert had flinched and Mark regretted it as soon as the words had tumbled out of his mouth. It had never been Robert's intention to run this operation; he'd never imagined he'd have to organise patrols on this scale when he gathered together his band of men in Sherwood. Hell, he'd taken enough convincing to get involved, even after saving Mark's and Bill's hides. By doing so, Mark knew he'd exorcised some of the demons from his past. But once that had been done, he'd spent more time in his office than he had on the streets. When it came right down to it, the responsibility rested on Robert's shoulders alone. And it wasn't fair to criticise him for that.

Nevertheless, the man had seen little action since undertaking his work at the castle. The legend of the Hooded Man might have spread, but the reality of the situation was very different. Which was probably why he'd started to brush up on his basics again, why he'd begun going out on missions in spite of Mary's opposition. She said there was no reason to risk his life anymore, but every reason to stay safe. Mark felt guilty about that; like maybe he was the one who'd started Robert thinking about it again. But he was only saying what all the men thought. If they felt like he was hiding away behind a wall, while they tackled who knows what, then their respect for him wouldn't last.

As Mark made his way down the steps, he spotted something that cheered him up. Coming down the main path was Mary, and she wasn't alone. Walking with her, on this crisp February morning, was a girl he'd recognise anywhere. He remembered the first time he'd seen her, in a small village, standing across the way in that yellow summer dress, freckles dotting her cheeks.

Sophie. Lovely Sophie. A couple of years older than him, she'd fixed Mark a drink and then quizzed him about his time with the Hooded Man, flashing that gorgeous smile of hers.

But even that memory was tinged with sadness. The Sheriff's men bursting in, attempting to take her with them... until Mark intervened; until he'd taken her place as a hostage. Then outside, the guys he'd travelled there with to return stolen food: all dead. Massacred in cold blood.

When things had died down, when he'd recovered from his ordeal at the castle, he'd been surprised to get a visit from her. Mary had knocked on his door and told him there was someone to see him. "She came looking for you."

"Who is it?"

It had been so unexpected, but he was delighted to see her. So delighted he'd almost tripped over on the way to give her a hug.

"Sophie! What are you doing here?"

"That's nice."

"No, no... That's not what I meant... I just..."

"Relax," she said, grinning impishly and hitting him on the arm playfully. "I'm just messing with you. I came to bring you this." Sophie reached into a bag and brought out a battered photo album. "Here you go. I found it after the soldiers left."

Mark's mouth dropped open. He thought he'd never see it again. It had been taken off him as he was bundled into the back of one of the Sheriff's armoured trucks. He turned the pages, and they transported him back to a time not just before the castle, but before the whole world went crazy.

"Oh, and here," said Sophie, handing him a single photograph. It was the one of Mark with his real parents that the scarred soldier, Jace, tore up. Sophie had picked up the trampled pieces and taped them together again.

Mark didn't know what to say, so he hugged her again.

"Easy, tiger," she'd said, laughing.

"I'm... I'm sorry," Mark said when he let go. "It's just this is the nicest thing anyone's ever done for me. You came all this way."

Sophie looked him in the eye. "You're forgetting; I owe you, mister. If it hadn't been for you I'd have been driven off in that truck, and God knows what would have happened to me. I certainly know what those men wanted to do."

"It was my pleasure."

"Hardly," said Sophie, taking his hand. "Mary told me about what happened. Thank you." Then she kissed him gently on the cheek. As Mary had taken her away to get some food, Mark rubbed the spot on his face where her lips had just been, and couldn't help imagining what they would feel like brushing against his own.

He'd asked Robert immediately if Sophie could stay and he'd said of course. He remembered her, too, from the village – after they'd gone there looking for Mark. He also recognised a certain look in Mark's eye. One that told him exactly how Mark felt about the girl.

Even now, after months of her being here, his heart felt like it would break out of his chest whenever he saw Sophie. Hormones, his head told him. That's all. But he couldn't help the way he felt. What he didn't know was whether Sophie felt the same. They'd spent a lot of time together, but he still had no idea whether she just wanted to be friends or something more. And now things were even more complicated.

Mark made his way past the trainees and down the path. Sophie was dressed in a thick parka, trousers and boots. It was a million miles away from what she'd worn the day they met, but she still looked beautiful.

He was about to shout across to them when he heard a bellow come from one of the gatehouse crew. "Green Leader is back!"

Both Mary and Sophie turned at the same time, to see the gates open wide. A number of men on horseback rode through, Robert – hood drawn – leading the way, with Jack not far behind. It was good to see them again, and in one piece; they'd been after some very dangerous men in York. There were no prisoners with them, however, which meant that they'd either been unsuccessful or they'd already dropped them off at one of the nearby hotels they used as jails – a step up from the caves De Falaise had favoured, and more than some of the prisoners warranted.

Mark watched the rest of the men ride in, spotting another figure he knew all too well.

Dale.

The twenty-three-year-old had joined them the previous summer, breezing in like something out of a US soap opera. His cropped hair and model looks belied the skill with which he fought. Many of the women under their protection had gone nuts over this guy – he would be the pin-up hunk of the castle, if such a thing existed any more. It didn't help that he'd once sung lead vocal for a band called One Simple Truth, and insisted, even now, on writing songs and strumming them out on that guitar of his to pass the time.

Mark knew it was only jealousy; not only was Dale older than him, he was also much cooler. In fact, he was everything Mark should be, including the first choice for missions like this one. And here he was, not even on the long list for training sessions yet. It just wasn't fair.

Watch those hormones, Mark...

But his jaw set firm when he saw Sophie run over to the men on horseback. Over to Dale's horse. Mark carried on down the path, noticing how Mary hurried over to Robert, who was climbing down off his horse, wincing as he did so.

"Robert! Oh, my God, are you all right?" Mark heard her ask.

Robert gave one of his trademark silent nods.

"He's just a little sore, aren't you, Robbie?" Jack swung down from his own mount, handing over the reins to a lad who'd come down from the castle's stables. "We saw a bit of action, y'see."

"Action?" Mary looked from Jack to Robert, her forehead crinkling; then, carefully, she pulled down his hood. "Oh, no, look at you." There was indeed a nasty purple bruise on his chin. "Are you hurt anywhere else?" She was examining him now for any other wounds, and stopped dead when she saw the cut across the front of his jacket.

Robert pulled away. "Mary, don't fuss... please. I'm fine."

"But you might not have been. I asked you not to go, but you went anyway and –"

"If he hadn't, I might not still be alive." Mark looked up to see a woman riding behind one of the Rangers. She had short, black hair and a striking face; high cheekbones and perfectly plump lips. The Ranger helped her down from the horse and she walked over to Robert and Mary, then stood between them. "He saved my life."

Mary looked the woman up and down. "And who are you?"

"Her... her name's Adele. I said she could come with us to the castle."

Adele smiled and held out her hand to Mary, who took it after some hesitation, and only held onto it for one shake. "I see," said Mary.

Looks like I'm not the only one feeling jealous, thought Mark, eyes darting across to Dale and Sophie again. She was giggling at something he'd just whispered.

"She has nowhere else to go, Mary," explained Robert, drawing Mark's gaze back. "So I said she could stay here for a while."

"I see," repeated Mary and gave him a look that said: *We'll talk about this when we don't have an audience.*

"I'm really grateful for everything he did."

Mark raised an eyebrow. *I'll bet you are.*

"You should have seen him in action."

Mary gave a tight smile, then replied: "I've seen it, thanks."

"He took on all those men on his own." Adele was gazing up at Robert with what could only be described as adulation. "I don't know how I can ever repay him." She placed a hand on Robert's arm, completely ignoring the look of disdain from Mary. Robert saw it, though, and shifted awkwardly around, closer to the woman who'd been at home worrying about him, wondering if he was alive or dead.

"Jack," he said, "would you mind taking Adele up to the castle, showing her what's what, getting her some food? She must be starving."

"My absolute pleasure." Jack offered the woman his arm. "Come on, little lady."

Before she took it, Adele leaned in and gave Robert a peck on the cheek. "Thank you again for everything."

When the pair were gone, Robert turned to Mary, who had now folded her arms. "What could I do? She has no one. Just like you when we first met."

It was absolutely the wrong thing to say. "Lining up a replacement, are we?"

"Don't be silly, Mary. It's just –"

"Silly? *Silly!*" Mary breathed in and out slowly a few times. She looked like she was about to say something else when Mark decided he'd better cut in.

"The men you fought, they were the ones you'd been tracking? The cultists?"

Robert appeared grateful for the reprieve. "Yes. We took several of them into custody. They're at the Britannia right now." Their main penitentiary, a hotel not far from the castle, was guarded by Robert's men. "We're in way over our heads with them, though. They're fanatics, religious nutters. I think I'm going to need Tate's help to figure out their game plan."

Mark nodded, glancing over briefly to see Dale and Sophie still laughing and joking. He looked back at Robert, a serious expression on his face. "So they're potentially a serious threat?"

"Potentially," Robert conceded.

"Then you're going to need all the men you can spare to tackle them."

"I suppose I..." Robert suddenly realised where this was heading. "Look, Mark, we've talked about this before."

"I know, and it never gets any further. I'm ready; you know it and I know it."

Robert sighed, looking from Mark to Mary, then back again. "What is this, some kind of ambush? I've only just got back, I'm tired and hungry, and you two are on me as soon as I get through the gate. We'll discuss this some other time."

Mark wasn't sure whether he meant his problem, or Mary's, but persisted. "I want to talk about it now." Robert began to walk away from both of them. "Please!"

The man stopped, hung his head, then said simply. "I'll have a word with Jack about beginning your training." With that, he carried on up the path towards the castle.

Mark smiled, then saw Mary still frowning. He put an arm around her shoulder. "Hey, you don't have to worry about him. He really loves you, you know."

She shook her head. "I just wish sometimes he'd show it more."

"Yeah, I know what you mean."

Mary followed his gaze across to Sophie. "They're friends. That's all."

Mark shrugged. "I can understand it. He's older than me, gets to go out, play the hero..."

"Is that what all this is about? The thing with the training?" Mary asked him. "Because if it is —"

"No," he replied, but didn't sound very convincing. "Not really... Mary, do you ever think about the past, about what we all went through? About what happened here?"

"You mean, do I miss it? Being in the thick of things, even though we were all nearly killed?"

That wasn't quite what he meant, but he nodded anyway.

"Sometimes. But not as much as he does." She gestured towards the figure heading towards the castle. "I just don't know what I'd do now if I lost him."

Mark pulled her in closer and she put her arm around his shoulder. He thought about saying "you won't," but they both knew he couldn't make that kind of promise.

"Come on," Mark said to her, more to get away from Sophie and Dale than to follow Robert.

So much had changed, thought Mark again. Yet it was true: so much was still the same. But there were so many questions left unanswered. Questions he was trying not to think about as they walked towards the castle.

Questions like what exactly had happened to Tanek's body during that final battle? Mark had seen him go down, seen him die. So why did the man who'd tortured him haunt his thoughts? Another phantom pain that refused to go away? Or something more?

It was then those words of De Falaise's came back to him and he gave a shiver that had nothing whatsoever to do with the cold.

"It is only just beginning, mon ami. *It is only just beginning..."*

CHAPTER THREE

IT WAS COLD, the snow was falling.

But then, wasn't it most of the time, here? And he liked that; it reflected how he felt inside. He'd grown up in this environment, learned to block out the freezing temperatures. No, not block them out – welcome and embrace them. Let them influence who he was, who he would become. Let the cold touch his very heart.

To be fair, the temperature wasn't the only thing that had frozen that particular muscle. The death of his parents in one of the 'postwar' Gulags – they were among the last to still be held after Khrushchev began his de-Stalinisation of the homeland – saw to that. Though officially their camp should not have even existed in the '60s, somehow it had slipped through the net – probably because it was in such a remote region, but also it paid to keep just a few of them operating. It contained some very dangerous prisoners, though in his mother and father's case it had just been an excuse to keep those with certain political or religious views out of circulation. He was too young to remember much of his infancy; just his mother's eyes, so full of love for him...

He found out later that the men who ran the camp treated prisoners like dogs. His father had been tortured regularly, his mother raped and beaten (the thought sometimes occurred to him that the man he thought of as his father might not been at all; but in the end, did it really matter?).

When the camp's activities had finally come to light – or rather whoever had been sheltering and subsidising it finally decided to tie up a few loose ends – it was too late for his parents. He'd been shipped off to an orphanage in southern Siberia, to allow the weather to finish the job the Gulag had started.

In charge of that place was one Leonty Kabulov, a sour-faced man who believed in discipline to the nth degree. The slightest step out of line was met with severe punishment. Kabulov's role models were the Emperors of old, and he ran the place as one – delegating power to his underlings, including a brutish physical education teacher called Nikolin, who would run the children ragged on treks through the snow. But even Kabulov saw the necessity of letting his 'subjects' blow off steam every now and again. Which was why he often turned a blind eye if a fight broke out in the orphanage's playground. Many children had been badly injured that way, though the crowds that gathered round were thoroughly entertained.

He himself had been picked on by one lad called Yuri. It had ended in a fight. Yuri had pummelled him with his fists, breaking a couple of ribs and putting him in the infirmary, tended by a nurse who looked like something Dr Frankenstein had created in his spare time. He never complained; as bad as it was there, it was nothing compared to what his parents had endured.

When he was old enough, he was conscripted into the army. If he'd thought tolerating the orphanage was hard, then training in the military taught him how easy he'd actually had it. They taught him how to kill, and it wasn't long before he'd had to use the skill fighting in the Soviet War against Afghanistan. It wasn't his natural environment – dealing with the heat to begin with had been difficult; it made the mercifully short summers back home seem chilly in comparison – but he'd soon proved himself one of the best fighters in his squad, eventually gaining the rank of Commander. During the '80s, and fuelled by the aid the USA was giving the enemy, his hatred for the West – and especially America – grew. Nuking would have been too good for them, in his opinion. It was just a pity that plans to invade Western Europe, which were only uncovered much later, never came to fruition. By the time the Cold War ended, he was back in the motherland and, though he was grateful for the cooler air, he was not enamoured with the way things were suddenly changing; spitting every time he saw a McDonalds. He fell victim to the army cutbacks Gorbachev initiated, and witnessed, with disdain, the eventual collapse of the Soviet Army.

But there were still jobs to be had for a man of his talents. He began working for the mafia, operating out of central Moscow during the '90s, with a hand in everything from extortion and porn to caviar smuggling. The opening up of trade routes with other countries helped build up organised crime, with the mafia itself taking on more of a Westernised, business-orientated approach. On the other side of the law now, it left him just as much scope to get his hands dirty; a bullet in the head here, a snapped neck there. Little wonder he rose in the ranks, from general muscle and bodyguard, to getting involved behind the scenes. Before long he was in charge of one of the largest criminal networks in the country, soon gaining the name he still went by today: hiring others to do the dangerous stuff for him. While his former comrades struggled to earn a pittance, he was better off than he had ever been. And he liked the feeling of being in control. One day soon, he knew, he would be running more than just this operation. In fact he already had plans to expand further abroad.

Then it happened; the whole world froze.

He could remember seeing reports on television about the epidemic, and in his mind there was no doubt whatsoever that it was of Western origin. Probably from the US – an attack on his country! He took every precaution against catching it, including wearing a gas mask. But when people in his organisation started dropping like flies – one of his closest aids, Gerasim, virtually exploded right in front of him, blood jetting from every orifice – he figured it was already too late. It was in his system already, so he might as well face his inevitable demise.

Except it didn't come. The more he waited, the more he found out about this thing they were calling the AB Virus. It wasn't just affecting his nation, it was killing people all around the globe. Whether it had started out as a weapon in the West was still unclear, but if it had, then the plan completely backfired. The only ones safe were those with a certain blood type: his type. At least here they were spared the secondary infections from the dead littering the streets. Such was the climate during those long winter months that the corpses were preserved and, yes, they were still out there – rotting more slowly than in other parts of the world: a reminder of what had happened. Icy, once-living statues.

At first he had been frustrated. Just when he was getting somewhere, he suddenly found himself right back at the bottom.

In time, survivors began to emerge. He saw them flitting between the buildings in Moscow, chased some of the first few down, armed with his custom-made machine gun and Gursa self-charge pistol. Most had already heard of him and surrendered gladly, welcoming someone to show them the way. Others had been less easy to persuade, so he'd put a bullet in them.

It wasn't long before he'd gathered a decent force, just like the one he'd commanded in Afghanistan – and he soon had a protective ring around himself once more. What worked in their favour was the number of survivors here; this had been the largest country on the planet. Of course, that also meant that there were pockets of resistance dotted all across the land, in towns, villages and, especially, in the cities. There were some even now who were not a part of his new Empire, but given enough time...

For that's what he was building, he'd decided. An Empire. If Kabulov and the Cold War had taught him anything, it was that the old ways were the best. He would rule with an iron fist; ensure that, once again, they would be the force to be reckoned with, even in this post-apocalyptic world. In fact, hadn't the virus done them a favour – weeding out the influence of the West so they could start again as something purer?

How much more fitting his mafia name was now: the Tsar. A monarch whose influence had steadily spread as far East as Magadan, using Moscow as his base. Loyalty was rewarded with protection, treachery with death. Once he had enough troops to spare, he would think about branching out further, reaching into other territories. That day was coming soon and he knew it. A day when he'd have enough power to tackle America itself. Stories had reached him of what was going on there, of factions taking charge and organising themselves, just as he was doing. It was simply a question of who would assemble a big enough army and how quickly. He already had access to all the military equipment and weapons he'd ever need.

The Tsar was pleased when he realised his reputation was already stretching beyond borders. Indeed, his most trusted allies were from China and the Ukraine. The Liu twins, Xue and Ying – never far from his side – had come to him and offered their services, mistakenly playing the Communist card. As if he gave a shit about that. He was more interested in their ability to carve up half a dozen of his guards without breaking a sweat, using those deadly hook swords of theirs, before surrendering and kneeling before him. Their oriental beauty was captivating, and so he kept them around not only as his personal bodyguards, but also his lovers.

Bohuslav was a different matter altogether. In him, the Tsar had recognised a kindred spirit: a soul as cold as his. It was there in those steely eyes. His methods were different from all the others in the Tsar's service, coming as he did from a background of serial killing. He had murdered more than fifty people even before the virus swept Russia, using his favoured weapons – small hand-held sickles – but had never come close to getting caught. No-one should ever trust Bohuslav, yet oddly the Tsar did. He trusted him with his life, which he knew Bohuslav could take at any moment if he chose to. He also trusted him with authority over the day-to-day running of his realm.

All three were with him today, riding in his bulletproof limousine. Bohuslav was driving, with the twins in the back, flanking the Tsar. As they travelled the distance between the Mariott Grand Hotel to one of the warehouses that had once stored goods for his business, the Tsar looked out at the falling snow. Where others might have seen nature's magnificence at work, he was comforted by the proof of the bitter cold outside. The white spots fell on those human statues outside, like Pompeii's ash. His face showed no reaction, no emotion. He'd seen them many, many times, at any rate; but truth be told, there wasn't any emotion to show. On the road ahead of them were two guards on motorbikes, and the same number behind. They pulled in at the rear entrance of the warehouse, and Bohuslav followed, bringing the limo to a halt by the pavement.

His second, dressed in his usual sharp suit, got out first and opened the car's back door; there was the merest glint from the sickle hanging at his belt. Xue hopped out next to check that it was safe for their passenger. He watched the tight black leather of her outfit mould itself to her body as she did so, sword up and ready almost before she cleared the car. Her head appeared then, nodding for him to come out. The Tsar's own red leather outfit – more military in feel than hers – creaked as he stood up, and he pulled his greatcoat around him. Then he placed the peaked cap on his head, tugging it firmly down. Ying wasn't far behind, as elegant as her sister, and just as dangerous. With the specially trained guards now in tow, the group entered the building, striding down a succession of corridors and climbing steps to reach a converted office with an open front, a good fifteen feet or more above ground level. It had once been used to oversee production at this facility, but now it was his official box. The noise drifted up to meet them even before they stepped out: raised voices, whistling and whooping.

Once they were sure it was safe to do so, Bohuslav and Xue parted, allowing the Tsar to stand at the front, viewing his subjects below.

Crammed into the warehouse were dozens on dozens of people, and in the centre itself was a raised, cordoned-off ring. Inside were two men, each armed with axes and shields. One was taller and bulkier than the other, his vest showing off his well-developed biceps. His dyed-blond hair was spiky, and his fair eyebrows made it look like he had none at all – giving him a slightly alien appearance. In spite of his size, he moved like a cat, dodging a blow from the other man, whose clothes were virtually rags. His tattered shirt and trousers, and his untidy beard, made him look like a tramp. He was certainly no athlete like his opponent, and that was also clear from the way they both moved. One of them had done this before... and it wasn't him.

The man in the vest avoided yet another clumsy blow, much to the crowd's delight. They cheered again for their favourite, for the Tsar's favourite: Glazkov.

He was pleased they hadn't missed the first kill of the evening. Sitting down on what could only be called a throne, the Tsar watched the match. It was another idea he'd taken from Kabulov and the orphanage; a way for his subjects to let off steam. It was just like the fights in the playground, except this was organised. It gave his people something to look forward to and indulged their bloodlust, turning it away from any thoughts of rebellion which might arise. He could control them more easily, and it made his iron rule much more palatable. It was also a good way to get rid of the dregs of humanity who didn't fit into his vision for Russia.

Sometimes the men would fight with their fists alone, sometimes – like tonight – they would be given weapons like the gladiators of old. At any rate, it provided much needed entertainment, for both the crowds and the Tsar. Nobody had even noticed he was here yet, and he would have been well within his rights to draw their attention to himself; to the fact they should all be saluting. But he was loath to stop the proceedings at this critical juncture. After all, he'd granted permission for them to start without him while he oversaw pressing issues of state.

Glazkov was obviously having fun with this one, dancing round, tiring him out before having his turn.

Which came now, as the tramp swung his axe again, and missed. Glazkov pivoted, hitting the man on the back with the flat of the blade – sending him sprawling across the ring onto his hands and knees. Glazkov smirked at the audience's bellows and claps. His opponent picked himself up, and came running back for more. He growled as he swung his axe again and Glazkov easily blocked it with his shield. This time, though, Glazkov struck with the sharpened edge of his axe, plunging it into the tramp's thigh. It buried itself deep; when Glazkov yanked it out, a warm redness came jetting out with it. The man let out a cry, immediately dropping his own shield to clutch at his wound. He hobbled back out of Glazkov's reach.

At the sight of the blood the crowd went wild, chanting Glazkov's name over and over. He held up his bloodied axe triumphantly, and they cheered even more.

The Tsar leaned forward in his throne, hand on his chin.

Tossing his shield aside, Glazkov was on the offensive. He ran at the wounded man, twirling his axe like Fred Astaire with a cane. The tramp's survival instinct kicked in, urging him to meet the next blow with his own axe. They clashed together, but it only succeeded in pushing the weaker man back once more. He barely avoided the blow that followed, aimed at his chest, the blade whistling as it swiped through the air.

Glazkov was all for a good show, but it was time to finish this and get on with the next fight. Perhaps it would offer him more of a challenge. Springing forward, he swung the axe twice again, this time almost severing his opponent's arm below the elbow, causing him to drop his weapon. The tramp shrieked in pain, looking from the damaged appendage – hanging by threads of tendons – to Glazkov's face in disbelief.

Before there was any more time to react, Glazkov spun around, planting the blade of the axe in the tramp's stomach, causing him to double over. Glazkov supported his weight for a moment or two, then dragged the axe backwards and forwards in a sawing motion. When he let the injured man go and pulled out his axe, the tramp's guts came with it.

Rolling around on the floor, the man was still alive and – given enough time in a working operating theatre, and with the right doctors (an extremely slim hope in these times) – might yet pull through. But that wasn't an option. Glazkov held the axe high above his head, ready to bring it down on his felled adversary. The throng around the ring were whipped into a frenzy.

"*GLAZKOV!*" came a voice, cutting through the atmosphere like the axe had through the tramp. The crowd, who had been baying for blood only seconds before, were instantly quiet. Glazkov stayed his hand, breathing deeply, the sweat pouring over his face and arms. Even the tramp on the floor dampened down his cries. For they all knew who the voice belonged to. And with whose authority he spoke.

Bohuslav was at the railing of the office. He didn't have to say any more, because everyone below him could now see that the Tsar was in residence. Their Lord and Master had arrived. And when he was present, it was his say who lived and who died. Glazkov waited patiently for the outcome. Did the Tsar want him to finish this specimen off, put him out of his misery, or leave him alive for some reason – possibly so he could die more slowly? Glazkov wouldn't be surprised by that one, although it would leave a sour taste in his mouth after working up an appetite for killing.

The Tsar stood, approaching the rail. All eyes were now on him, everybody wanting to know what he would decide. He was not so pretentious that he would use the old symbol of a thumb up or down. No, the Tsar would simply shake his head or nod: life or death, as if there was really a choice. Today he felt lenient. He ordered the swift execution of the injured man. The crowd roared with delight.

Glazkov smiled and finally brought down the axe, cleaving the tramp's head from his body. It rolled across the ring, coming to a standstill near a little boy in the crowd, its eyes staring wildly into his. (And did it blink a couple of times, or was that the child's imagination?).

The Tsar took his seat again as Glazkov was relieved of his weapon and given a towel to dry himself. The victor risked a glance up as he rubbed his face, but not at his master – rather at the twins that flanked him, appraising first one, then the other. The Tsar noted this, and the looks of admiration Xue and Ying returned: whether they just admired his fighting ability or his physique, he couldn't be certain, but he would watch what developed with interest from now on. The twins were his and his alone.

There was a brief pause in the proceedings, during which Glazkov took a seat on the stool in his corner of the ring – sipping from a water bottle – and the body of the tramp was gathered up. The respite didn't last long, however; by his yawns, it was clear the Tsar was eager for more action. He saw very little himself, these days, instead getting his fill of killing vicariously. But he missed it; oh, God how he missed it. Maybe if Glazkov kept looking at his bodyguards that way, he would find himself facing the Tsar in the ring? The thought both excited and troubled him.

But that wouldn't be tonight. Because the next participant was already being forced to the ring, the crowds parting so that he could be brought through. The man wore what looked to be sacking or a large blanket, and appeared to be in even worse condition than the previous fighter. Obviously picked up off the streets, like the majority of them; his long, greasy hair was straggly and he was having trouble standing, limping into the centre of the ring.

In fact, it looked like this newcomer was about to collapse.

Glazkov rose from his stool, spitting out a mouthful of water. He wandered over to the man, looking down on him in disdain. Rubbing his hands together, Glazkov got started, much to the audience's satisfaction. He threw a punch that landed squarely in the man's kidneys.

Then Glazkov clasped his hands together, leaping up and bringing them down hard on the man's back. The figure toppled onto the floor.

The Tsar yawned again. This fight was barely going to be worth watching; it would be over in seconds at this rate.

The people's champion kicked the beggar creature in the side, rolling him over once, twice, so that again he faced the floor. Then Glazkov raised his booted foot to bring it stomping down on the man's head.

Only it stopped in mid-trample. Glazkov looked down the length of his leg, realising that this man, this frail example of street scum, had actually caught his foot and was holding it fast.

Pushing, the man toppled Glazkov over. He landed on his back, the air forced out of him. The spiky-haired gladiator scrambled about, clambering to get up quickly; he wasn't used to being the one on the floor. And it wasn't good for the crowd to see him that way.

As he was rising, so was his new foe. Only he kept rising, and rising... and rising. Letting go of the sacks and blankets he'd wrapped around him, Glazkov's opposite number revealed his true size for the first time.

He stood a good few feet above the champion, and his muscles, visible beneath the khaki T-shirt he wore, were easily bigger than Glazkov's – as impressive as those were. The crowd, who'd been cheering, though not quite as loudly as they had in the previous match, suddenly took notice of what had happened. There was deathly silence.

The Tsar frowned and inched forward in his seat. Bohuslav placed both hands on the rail and peered down while the twins looked on. It was like they were all watching the miracle of birth, and in a sense they were. A transformation akin to a butterfly emerging from a cocoon. Only this insect was olive-skinned and, as he swept back his greasy black hair, he sneered first at the people in the royal box, then at Glazkov.

The champion swallowed. The roles had suddenly been reversed, and Glazkov now found himself being towered over.

It was small comfort, but he was tossed a mace as spiky as his hair, while his opponent had to make do with receiving a length of chain. As Glazkov hunched down, circling the larger man and trying to weigh up his options, the olive-skinned colossus moved to follow him, obviously still having trouble with one leg... or was it his foot? Yes, the Tsar noted. He wasn't putting as much weight on one side, as if an old injury was bothering him.

Glazkov struck and the blow glanced off the bigger man's forearm, cutting him, but not badly. At the same time, the bigger man unfurled his chain, throwing it out like a whip and snaking it around Glazkov's neck. Tugging, he yanked the champion towards him, then punched him hard in the face.

Glazkov unfurled along the chain, spinning away. His legs gave out. He ended up on the floor again with a thud, shaking his head.

The giant, seemingly in no rush at all, gave Glazkov time to recover and get to his feet as he wrapped the chain around his fist. This time when Glazkov took a swing with the mace, the newcomer batted it out of his hand, then punched the champion again, using the chain as a knuckle duster. Teeth and blood flew from Glazkov's mouth, as his head rocked to one side. Regardless that their hero was getting thrashed out there, the crowd cheered louder than ever.

"Who is this?" Bohuslav muttered to himself, loudly enough for the Tsar to hear.

Glazkov was crawling around, spitting out more blood and teeth. When he looked up, his jaw was a mess. But he wasn't defeated just yet. Someone, probably one of the Tsar's guards, threw him a metal fighting pike.

He used it to help himself up, then turned it on his enemy, running at him – trying to skewer him on the end. In spite of his bad foot, the large man evaded the ungainly attack, whipping out the chain and lashing Glazkov across the back of the neck.

"*Mudak!*" growled the spiky-haired Russian. Livid, he tried again, but the giant used his chain to snag the pike, spoiling Glazkov's aim. Try as he might, the champion just wasn't strong enough to bring the weapon back towards his target. Then suddenly it was snatched from his grasp.

Before Glazkov could do anything, the pike had been turned on him and thrust through the Russian's shoulder until it came out the other side. Then, holding onto the pike, the man brought up a boot and kicked Glazkov off. He staggered, not quite grasping what had just happened. Then the pain registered and he howled.

The giant didn't give him long for self pity. Hefting the pike like a staff, the man struck Glazkov first in the stomach, then under his chin; with such force that Glazkov was lifted into the air, before landing heavily on the floor.

Glazkov didn't have a clue what was coming next – and that was probably for the best. The stranger bent and aimed the pike at Glazkov's head, forcing it in just behind the right temple. With his considerable bulk behind the strike, the man was able to push the sharpened end right through Glazkov's skull. Like the last time, the giant kicked Glazkov off the spear and the former champion's now lifeless body hit the ground.

The audience was speechless. They'd seen Glazkov in some challenging fights, but never known him get more than a few cuts or bruises. What were they supposed to do now? They couldn't chant the new champion's name; they didn't know it. Besides, he didn't look like the kind of man you applauded, but trembled before.

The Tsar was equally shocked, not least when the bear of a man holding the pike and chain looked up and pointed at him. Bohuslav immediately nodded to the guards at the ring, who entered, raising their AK-47's and demanding that he put down his weapons.

"Call them off!" shouted the stranger in perfect Russian. His voice was deep, his words to the point. When the men remained where they were, and then actually moved closer, the man cocked his head as if to say, *that was a big mistake.*

Seconds later, the chain was unfurled and the pike was flicked to the side. The Kalashnikovs all fired at the same time, but were quickly knocked out of the guards' hands, completely missing the man in the middle. Having disarmed them, the giant set to work on the men themselves, taking out the closest by simply charging into them like a juggernaut – or flinging the chain at their faces. The others he dispatched with kicks and pike-blows.

Then, limping towards the edge of the ring, he used the weapon like a pole-vault to clear the cordon. At the same time Bohuslav was ordering the guards with him to open fire into the ring. By the time they'd got their act together, the giant was already part of the crowd, crouching, moving from side to side so they couldn't track him.

"There!" shouted Bohuslav when he saw the tip of the pike above the mass of heads. The guards looked at each other, then at the Tsar, obviously troubled about firing into the throng. The Tsar nodded firmly and they did just that, picking off the people around the troublemaker, but not touching him. It only made the confusion worse. Those who remained panicked, slamming into each other, pushing each other out of the way. At one stage, when the giant saw he was close to being shot, he grabbed a woman and pulled her in front of him.

"Enough!" shouted the Tsar. This was only losing him subjects; it was obvious it had to be handled at closer range. "Xue, Ying." His bodyguards nodded, and ran to the viewing rail, leaping over it, into the crowd. Pockets of clear floor were opening up and in one to their left rose the olive-skinned man.

The twins drew their hook swords, circling him. He grimaced.

They attacked in a flurry of gleaming metal – and he blocked each and every swipe with the pike. The Tsar had never seen anything like it, never seen fighters move so fast. The space cleared much quicker and, were it not for the twins, the Tsar might have ordered his guards to start shooting again.

Swish, clack! Swish, clack! The three of them fought all the way to the base of the viewing platform. The Tsar got up and walked towards the rail, ignoring Bohuslav's gestures to remain out of harm's way.

He saw Xue duck as a pike blow whipped over her head; Ying almost ended up with the sharp end in her thigh. As confident as he was in them, he could also see that this interloper was highly trained. And people this skilled always wanted something... But what? Did he want the Tsar dead?

The giant took his eyes off the twins long enough to find his mark standing at the rail. "Call... them... off," he said, still blocking attacks, then added, "I would speak with you."

The Tsar rubbed his chin, still unsure.

Snarling, the giant elbowed one of the twins out of the way, kicked back the other – and lifted his pike like a javelin, aiming at the Tsar. Bohuslav's sickle was already out and he was about to throw it when the Tsar held up his hand.

"Wait... wait!" Both men halted, staring into each other's eyes. The twins were about to attack again, but the Tsar ordered them to stand down. "Bohuslav, put that away. You men, lower your guns."

When the attacker saw this, he lowered the pike, placing it by his side – though his body was still tense, ready for any surprises. "I came here seeking an audience," he said in those clipped tones.

"You... you came here? You were brought here."

"I let them bring me."

Bohuslav's eyes narrowed.

The Tsar nodded; it did seem unlikely that he would have been captured on the streets if he hadn't wanted to be. "Who are you?"

"I am Tanek."

The name was familiar, but the Tsar couldn't remember why. It would no doubt come to him. In the meantime he asked: "What do you want?"

"As I said, I would speak with you."

The Tsar frowned. "What about? What is so important that you would risk your life like this?"

The olive-skinned man brushed the long, greasy hair out of his eyes and said: "I have a proposition for you."

CHAPTER FOUR

ROBERT MISSED THE dreams.

He'd never mentioned it to anyone, because he doubted whether they'd understand – not even Mary. But God, did he miss them. Those vivid – sometimes nightmarish – visions he'd experienced during his time in Sherwood had saved his life. He'd seen his friends in those dreams, before he'd even met them, and he'd seen what the Sheriff, De Falaise, had planned during their final confrontation – allowing him to twist as he plunged the knife into Robert, avoiding a fatal belly wound and taking the blade in his side instead. It had taken him a while to recover, but he would surely have been dead if it hadn't been for the tip-off.

Since moving into the castle, though, he hadn't been able to remember a single dream. Of course, you needed to sleep to dream – and that was something Robert had been doing very little of lately. The mattress he lay on seemed far too... luxurious. He'd slept much more soundly on a blanket of grass and moss, in his handmade lean-to or outside, looking up at the stars. All he saw these days was the ceiling.

But it was more than simply missing the dreams. They were part and parcel of a way of life. Of a place where he'd felt completely at ease.

Yeah, except when intruders were coming in after you with guns, or firing grenades off into the trees.

No, before. The time when he'd been alone in the forest, just him and nature – with only the birds, animals and foliage for company. He'd been happy –

Happy? You went there to escape, have you forgotten that? You went there because you didn't have anyone else in the world, not after... Now you have. People who love you, people who care about what happens to you.

People who counted on him, every minute of every day. Responsibilities the likes of which he never could have imagined; not even when he was after those promotions on the force. Everything seemed to have snowballed since they came here. He'd turned around and suddenly he was this mythical figure in charge of his very own policing network. How exactly had that happened?

Because you made it happen. You wanted people to be safe, for there to be some kind of law, some justice after the Sheriff's rule. You did a good thing, Robert.

But at what cost? Leaning up against the headboard, he sighed. If he'd had a dream about this when he'd been back in Sherwood, he might not have got involved. Who was he kidding? He wouldn't have done a thing differently. He'd still have saved Mark and Bill; been persuaded by Tate to fight, to build an army that could take on De Falaise; taken in Granger – rest his soul – and Jack.

And Mary...

He looked down at the sleeping figure, her dark hair splayed on the pillow. If anyone had told him, even a year ago, that he could fall in love again – even if he'd dreamt about it – he would have thought it madness. But then, wasn't love a kind of insanity, or so the old pop and rock songs said? Songs like Dale used to sing... still sang on some occasions, when the residents of the castle needed their spirits lifting.

Robert remembered how awkward it had been at first with Mary. He'd pushed her away. The thought of being with anyone again after Joanne was just... But somehow she had broken down his defences, or slipped past them, just as his troops had done when they took the castle. When he remembered what had almost happened to her at the hands of De Falaise, it tore him up inside.

So why was she giving him such a hard time? Why had she barely spoken to him all evening, turning her back on him when they got into bed? She had to know that there was nothing going on with him and Adele – he'd only known her five minutes! How could Mary possibly believe he was trying to replace her?

But wasn't it partly down to Mary that he was stuck in this castle, when he should be out there doing more of what he'd done in York? Was it really the fact that he'd saved Adele that bothered her, that the woman was so grateful, or was it because he'd gone there regardless of Mary's wishes?

"You've been out of the game for a little while, boss. You're rusty. That psycho almost had you."

He'd dismissed Jack's words, but the man had been right. If he hadn't been there, Robert wouldn't be alive right now. Out of the game. Too much time stuck behind a desk. Now where had he heard that before?

Sitting in the dark, a face from the past floated into his mind. Now he flashed back to his very first days as a rookie, to his old station house in Nottingham, just south of this very castle in fact – before Joanne had made him move away from the city. To Constable Eric Meadows, who'd puppy-walked him through his first weeks, pounding the beat alongside him.

Robert watched as the scene played in his head, of them chasing a thief who'd just snatched a woman's purse in broad daylight before disappearing up a side street.

"You go after him," Meadows had instructed. "I'll go this way, try and head him off." Holding onto his cap, Robert raced after the man.

The felon, checking back over his shoulder, saw that there was only one young copper chasing him – and he'd slowed down, fancying his chances. Robert skidded to a stop only metres behind. "N-now don't try anything funny," he said, with absolutely no confidence. "Come along quietly and it'll be better for everyone."

"I'm not going back to jail," the scruffy-looking man had warned him, then approached, balling his hands into fists.

Robert knew how he should tackle a situation like this; he'd been trained, after all. But reality was completely different. Here was a real criminal, a desperate criminal, and only one thing stood between him and his freedom: Robert.

The thief ran at him, readying to punch. But before his blow could land, the man was falling over sideways. A puzzled Robert lowered his gaze and saw Meadows there, rugby tackling the fellow to the ground. His plan had worked, going round the houses to take the villain by surprise while Robert distracted him. It was a good strategy; one Robert would later use on a much larger scale.

The thief tried to fight, knocking off Meadows' cap to reveal his salt and pepper hair. "Well, don't just stand there gaping," Meadows shouted, struggling to hold the scruffy man down. "Get your arse over here and help me cuff him!"

Snapping awake, Robert had gone over and assisted, listening while the veteran officer read the thief his rights. Then they'd escorted him back to the station, putting him in a cell.

"Nothing quite like it, is there?" Meadows said to Robert as they'd come away again, the job done.

"What's that, sir?"

"That adrenalin rush when it's you or them." Meadows' eyes were twinkling. "Facing your fear, lad. Did you feel it?"

Robert nodded, but all he'd really felt was scared. He suspected he wouldn't actually know what Meadows was talking about until he arrested someone himself, until it was just him and the other guy... or guys. In the years since that day, he'd felt that rush many, many times.

"Never let them put you behind one of those," Meadows told him, gesturing to the officer behind the duty desk. "You stay out there, young Stokes. Stay where you can make a difference and leave all that to the paper pushers."

Sadly, they'd all become paper pushers by the time the virus struck, with more and more government bullshit tying them up. But before that, Robert had learned a lot from his old mentor: not least of which was that guns were not the real answer to tackling gun crime. "It all escalates, you see," Meadows had warned him. "And then where's it all going to end?"

Another memory crept in now; Meadows, the last time he'd seen him, before Robert moved to the outskirts of Mansfield. A combination of injury – sustained on football match duty when one crazed supporter had broken Eric's leg – and old age had landed in the last place he wanted to be. Oh, there'd been a promotion that came with the office, to sergeant no less, but the fact remained that Meadows was trapped, drowning in responsibilities. When Robert shook his hand and thanked him for everything, he could see the spark had almost completely gone from those eyes.

"You're awake." The voice made him jump. Robert hadn't even noticed Mary had stirred; he'd been so wrapped up in his recollections. "What are you thinking about?"

In the half-light, Robert stared down at her face and shrugged. "Nothing."

"Liar." It wasn't said in a nasty way, but it stung nonetheless.

"Am I not allowed to just sit here peacefully now?"

"That's not what I said. I asked you what you were thinking about?"

"The past."

Mary sat up, resting against the headboard beside him. "You were thinking about Joanne and Stevie again, then?"

Robert sighed. "No... why does it always have to come back to that? Why can't you let it go?"

"Why can't you?"

"This isn't even about... If you must know, I was remembering an old friend of mine from the force. And before you ask, no, he wasn't a woman." Mary's turn to be stung. "I've been thinking about what's been happening, what I'm doing here."

"With me?"

Robert sighed again. "No, you're twisting it all... What I'm doing here at the castle, Mary. How I've become rooted to this place, been hiding behind its walls for too long. It's not where I belong."

"And where should you be? Sherwood? Alone?"

"No..." Robert shook his head, but there was no conviction in it, only confusion. "I don't know... Anywhere but stuck here, organising the men, sending them out on missions."

"I help you as much as I can, you don't have to shoulder it all on your own."

"No, that's not what I'm talking about. I'm not the man you met anymore, Mary. Staying here's done that. I'm... rusty."

"So this is about York? I said it was a bad idea to –"

"Mary, you're not listening. That's not the issue. The men we saw out there, the cult. They're dangerous."

"More dangerous than the Frenchman?"

"They have the capacity to be. And they're not interested in wealth or power like he was. They'll fight until every last one of them is dead."

Mary was silent for a few moments. "We have men, loyal men," she said eventually.

"And what if they fall? What if the fight is brought here again? How am I supposed to defend the people I care about, how am I supposed to lead men into battle, when I've lost my edge? When I've become..."

"What? A family man? A leader?"

"You just don't see it, do you? I'm no better than De Falaise."

Mary pulled a face. "How can you say that?"

"Because it's true. He stayed here in his ivory tower with Gwen while he sent his men off to their deaths, to do his dirty work for him."

"To do his killing. And he wasn't exactly the dutiful partner when it came to Gwen, was he? She was his plaything, Robert. His toy. You care about your men. You care about me... don't you?"

"You really need to ask that?"

Mary gave a little shrug which he could barely see in the dark. "When girls like Adele –"

"Adele again?" Robert snorted. "What the bloody hell's she got to do with this?"

"It's another consequence of going out there. You're a living legend, Robert; women fall at your feet."

"That's your paranoia again."

"Is it? I saw the way she looked at you. You can't have missed it; and you invited her back here, of all the things, to –"

He pulled the covers aside, climbing out of bed.

"Where are you going?"

"For a drink of water." Robert pulled on his robe, making for the door.

"Robert, I –"

"They don't mean anything to me, Mary. None of them. You'd know that if you really knew me." He took one last look at her, then he opened the door and slid out, whispering under his breath, "I love you." Robert wasn't sure whether she'd heard him or not, but he'd said it and as far as he was concerned that was enough. As he shut the door he thought he heard a faint sob, and almost went back in. But he was in no mood to keep talking about it.

Robert crept down the darkened corridor, careful not to wake the others sleeping in this part of the castle. He padded down the stairs, heading for what had once been the castle café. He struck a match on the counter and lit a couple of candles, then took a glass, opened a cupboard and took out a bottle of water his men had found out on their travels. He looked at it. There weren't many still around, but even this was somehow mocking him – reminding him he'd returned to a life he'd once turned his back on. When he'd been in Sherwood, he'd trapped his own water and filtered it. Now, it was like that had never happened. Hanging his head, he unscrewed the lid and poured.

He felt a hand on his shoulder and dropped the glass, spinning round, simultaneously grabbing whoever was behind him by the throat and shoving them against the wall.

Robert was breathing hard. He blinked, and realised the figure he was holding was a woman with short hair.

"I... I'm sorry..." croaked Adele. "I..."

Horrified, Robert let her go. "No, I'm... you shouldn't creep up on me like that."

She rubbed her throat and said hoarsely: "I... I wasn't creeping, Robert. Honestly. I had to go to the loo and got lost finding my way back. This place is so huge, and I'm still figuring it all out."

Robert's breathing slowed. God, he really was losing his touch; there was a time he would have heard... felt someone come up behind him. If it had been an assassin, they'd have plunged a knife into him before he could even turn.

"I saw the light and, well, if I'd realised you wanted to be alone..." Adele said sadly.

"It's not that. I just..." Robert shook his head. "Did I hurt you?"

Adele coughed and smiled. "Nothing a glass of water won't fix."

Robert walked back to the counter, then stooped to pick up the bits of broken glass. He looked across when Adele followed him, noticing what she was wearing for the first time. A man's shirt – probably Jack's, by the size – with the sleeves rolled up... and nothing else. Her long legs looked pale in the light from the candle, and he chastised himself for letting his eyes linger on them before getting back to his task.

"You're very fast, you know."

"Hmm? Not nearly as fast as I used to be."

Adele leaned on the counter, watching him pick up the final pieces of glass. "You're joking? You really had me back there. And the way you tackled those hooligans back in York!"

Robert put the glass in a bin. "It was nothing." That sounded better in his head than it did out loud. Why didn't you go the whole way and add, *aw shucks*? "It's what I do. Well, what I did."

"Did?"

Robert joined her at the counter, then rounded the other side – partly to fetch another couple of glasses, partly to put a physical barrier between them. He poured her some water and she sipped it gladly. But she wasn't going to be distracted. "You said *did*, past tense?"

Robert took a swig of his own water. "It's just that lately I've felt like I'm not doing any good anymore."

"I don't understand."

"I'm stuck here all the time. Organising."

"Then if it makes you feel like this, perhaps you shouldn't be." Adele put the glass down and absently ran her finger around the rim. "I've always been a big believer in following your heart." She looked up at him. "What's it telling you?"

"That's the thing: it's not telling me anything. Or at least nothing I can trust." Robert let out a breath. "I don't know why I'm dumping all this on you. I barely even know you."

Adele smiled again. "Sometimes it's easier to talk to a stranger than someone... Well, you know."

Robert nodded. "I guess it is."

"This Mary you're with," said Adele after a pause. "She seems really nice."

"She is," Robert said without hesitation, then took another drink.

"It's really late. I should be at least trying to get some rest, I suppose. Not that it's easy in a new place."

"If it helps, you're safe now."

"That why you're so on edge, jumping at shadows?"

Robert laughed softly. "You have a point."

"And you should try and get some sleep as w –" She let out a yelp, sucking in air through her teeth as she hobbled backwards.

"What? What is it?" Robert had rounded the counter in seconds.

Adele was hopping towards a chair, clutching her foot. "I don't think you got all the glass."

"Oh, no, hold on..." He brought one of the candles from the counter, placing it on the floor as he crouched down and took hold of her heel. "Let me have a look. I can't see anyth... wait, there it is." Holding Adele's foot steady, Robert squeezed the area and drew out the splinter. "It needs washing. We don't want it to get infected."

Adele looked down at him. "You really are sweet, you know, Hooded Man or not. I hope Mary knows how lucky she is."

ONCE MARY HAD begun to cry, she couldn't stop.

All the tension, the stress, the worry flooded out of her – not just from tonight's argument, but from the days preceding it. Waiting to see whether the man she loved more than life itself would come back to her.

And when he did, what had she done? She hadn't even given him a kiss, she was too busy firing off questions, checking for injuries (she hadn't seen the worst of them till he'd undressed, his back a mass of bruises), giving him a hard time about bringing the woman he'd saved back to their home. What was she, some kind of jealous teenager?

But then, she'd never done the whole teen in love thing. Hers had been a small locality and, apart from break times at school, she hadn't really mixed with boys. She certainly hadn't been able to go out in the evenings; her brother, who'd looked after her when their father had died of a stroke, would have gone mad.

Damn right I would, Moo-Moo, said the voice of that dead sibling in her head; the one she still heard occasionally, even though David had died from the virus long ago. And who still called her by that ridiculous childhood name. *So would Dad, if he'd still been alive.*

In some ways it had been a drawback, living with two men, all that way out on the farm. But it had made her the woman she was today; taught her to fight and stand up for herself.

But in fighting for Robert, maybe she was also pushing him away. If you love something, you have to let it go – isn't that what people always said? But you run the risk of them never coming back.

To her mind, the jealousy was justified anyway. It hadn't been easy for her, competing initially with the ghost of Robert's late wife – the one he'd loved so much he cut himself off from civilisation – and then with this *character* people thought he was; this symbol of hope. It was tough being in love with an icon.

Though probably not as tough as actually being one, Moo-Moo. You should cut him a little slack every now and again.

"What are you talking about?" Mary caught herself saying out loud.

Remember when I asked you if you were sure about him?

Mary nodded.

Well, you were right. He risked everything to save you when you pulled that stunt impersonating him.

"He'd have done the same for anyone. He just did for that woman he brought back."

It's not the same thing, and you know it. He came after you because of how he feels. Not out of any sense of duty. But you're in danger of losing him, unless you're careful.

"I don't need relationship advice from someone who never had a date in his life."

Suit yourself, Moo-Moo. Just trying to help.

He was right, of course. Robert had come after her that day because he loved her. She'd seen the way he'd fought when De Falaise took her captive.

And even though the months after that had been hard, Robert moving from Sherwood to the castle, them trying to build something up out of the aftermath of the Sheriff's rule – both in the Rangers, and between themselves – there had still been moments to cherish.

Like the first night they spent together, after last year's summer fête. Jack had the notion that it would be good to give the men and their new family a party, and though Robert had been resistant at first he'd finally been persuaded by Mary.

"We could all use a bit of... what was it Jack said? 'Down Time,'" she'd told him.

The grounds of the castle had been open to all that day, with food and drink and music; some provided by a battery-powered stereo, some by Dale and his guitar. People from New Hope and other villages under Robert's protection had visited Nottingham, and said afterwards it had been well worth the trip. It showed that not everything in this post-virus world had gone sour. They were still alive after all, and still human. Even Robert, who'd been on tenterhooks waiting for one emergency or other, had loosened up after a couple of drinks.

"Come on," Mary had said, after some Dutch courage herself. "Dance with me."

Robert shook his head, so she'd leaned in then, whispering in his ear. "Please."

He'd allowed himself to be pulled up, and when he held her he relaxed. Several dances, and several beers later, they'd found themselves walking through the grounds of the castle, alone in the moonlight. She'd pointed up at the stars and when he looked down again she'd kissed him. Not the kisses they'd shared since first meeting, the awkward, tentative brushes they were used to – but a long, lingering kiss. Mary had felt her body turn to jelly as Robert responded: his hands on her back, hers clutching his shoulders.

When both their hands started to explore further, they'd pulled apart – and it had been Robert, surprisingly, who'd suggested they find somewhere a little more private. "Maybe there's a room where people have left their coats," he suggested, and she'd laughed, feeling truly happy for the first time in a long while. Though she should have been scared at her first time, Mary was far from it. Even if things had felt uncomfortable before, nothing on that special night did. It felt right, so right.

Sure, she could put it down to the alcohol, the atmosphere of the party. But to her it just felt like they were finally on the same page. That now he wanted her as much as she'd always wanted him. And it had been amazing, truly amazing. She'd placed herself in Robert's hands and he hadn't failed to live up to her imagination.

Then, waking up that morning with Robert lying next to her, she'd experienced a horrible sinking feeling. *What if he regrets what we did? What if he rejects me?* She'd kept quiet, frozen, just watching – waiting for him to rouse, but at the same time hoping he'd sleep forever so she wouldn't have to face the disappointment.

What a relief, then, when he'd woken up and smiled.

"Hello, sweetheart," she said.

His smile had widened.

Yay me, she'd said to herself.

It was a million miles away from sitting here in that same bed and crying her heart out. When she thought back to those first couple of months of being together, properly together, it just made her feel worse. They'd spent as much time as they possibly could in each other's company, working around schedules, finding private moments. Most of the castle – and most of Robert's men – knew. Had to, by the daft grins on both their faces.

Lately, though, they'd spent less and less time together... especially in that way. Admittedly, Robert had been worrying about this cult – and who could blame him? She had been busy too, dealing with the day-to-day running of the castle, tending to injured men coming back from patrols with nursing skills she'd built on since Robert had found her at her farm; studying from text books she and the men brought back, teaching those same skills to others. They were both tired and, more often than not, would just go to sleep at night.

She'd read about this in women's magazines and glossies delivered with the weekend papers, back before the world changed. The problem pages were full of stuff about 'honeymoon periods' and what happens afterwards when real life intrudes. And although Mary knew this was meant to signal them being more comfortable with each other – solid couples didn't have to show affection like that all the time – she couldn't help feeling more than a little unwanted.

At the same time he was growing increasingly distant. It came to a head when he'd begun training again, working out to try and get fit; exercising muscles that had grown flabby from lack of use.

Then one day he announced he was going out with the patrol again, going out to assess the threat of the cult personally. They hadn't even discussed it, and it had thrown her completely.

"Why, Robert? Why you? And why now? Jack can –"

"I'm going, Mary. And that's that."

They'd rowed, he'd stormed off, and he'd left without even saying goodbye. Maybe she should have been more laid back – after all, he'd been leading a band of men when she first met him, fighting De Falaise's troops. But he'd also got himself blown up that day, would probably have died if she hadn't been there to tend to his wounds. She couldn't shake that image from her mind – of him unconscious in the back of the truck, on his way to Sherwood...

He'd recovered, of course, faster really than he should have. But what if he didn't next time? What if she had to cradle his head as he died? What if she didn't even get the chance to say goodbye?

It was why she'd pulled that 'stunt,' as her brother called it: drugging Robert and taking his place for the final battle with the Sheriff. She'd wanted to keep him safe, that's all. Wanted to protect the man she loved.

He can look after himself, David had told her, and she knew deep down he was right.

That didn't stop her worrying. And none of this would help them get back to how they'd been during those summer and autumn months.

Mary dried her eyes with the bed sheets, then got out and wrapped her robe around her. She'd go down and drag him back to bed if she had to, talk to him, maybe do more than that. Show him how much she'd missed him, how much she still loved him.

He'd said he was going for a drink of water, which he often did when he couldn't sleep. She knew she'd find him in the café, probably looking out through those big windows.

Mary stopped dead in her tracks when she heard voices from inside. Two voices: one Robert's, the other a woman's. As she drew closer, keeping quiet, she saw them inside. Lit by candles, they were sitting at one of the tables. Mary realised she could have marched past with a brass band and they wouldn't have noticed, they were so wrapped up in conversation. Though try as she might, she couldn't hear what was being said.

The woman with Robert – *her* Robert – had her back to Mary. But she knew who it was, even without the short hair.

Right, that does it... I'm going to...

Do what, Moo-Moo, storm in there and make a fool of yourself? They're only talking.

I know, but –

But nothing. Leave it, sis.

David was right. Again. There was no way she could make her presence known that didn't look like she was spying on them. Checking up on Robert. Dammit, right now that's exactly what she *was* doing.

Mary watched them for a little while longer, but had to turn away when she heard Adele laughing at something Robert had just said. So happy. Just like Mary had been the night of the fête.

Feeling the tears coming again, she retreated to their bedroom, where she waited. Not for Robert to come back from patrol this time, but for him to return to her. If he ever would.

Mary tried to stay awake, but eventually sheer exhaustion and all that crying took their toll. Sleep claimed her, and she never heard Robert come in, or felt him climb into bed with her.

If she had she might also have heard him tell her again softly, as he kissed her shoulder, how very much he loved her.

CHAPTER FIVE

THE VILLAGE HAD been named Hope.

But that Hope had died along with its founder. Clive Maitland had been killed defending this place against De Falaise's men, murdered by the fat Mexican, Major Javier. The Reverend Tate knew that Gwen had taken her revenge on Javier for that, shooting him just like he'd put a bullet in Clive. Although Tate could forgive her for that – many terrible things had happened in the heat of that final battle – he wasn't altogether sure the Lord would be able to without repentance. It hadn't been her place to take that life, and more than likely there would be a punishment, one way or another.

Gwen probably thought she'd served her time in purgatory, held prisoner at the castle and made to do unspeakable things at the behest of that mad Frenchman. Tate had to admire her for not going completely mad over those months. But she would have killed De Falaise as well, given the opportunity, and was on her way to do so when Tate had been hit in the shoulder by a stray bullet.

"God will provide his own revenge."

Tate had shouted it after her, but she'd taken no notice, headstrong as she was. She hadn't succeeded anyway, apart from stabbing De Falaise in the leg and managing to get shot herself by one of Tanek's crossbow bolts. It had been left to Robert Stokes, their leader, to end the Frenchman's reign. Tate had often wondered if the Hooded Man had actually been an unwitting part of the Almighty's plan for revenge, but almost always dismissed these thoughts. Robert was a law unto himself and still continued to be so. That man no more believed in God's overarching design than Tate believed he was the reincarnation of St Francis of Assisi.

Not that you had to believe in God to be a part of his plans. But you did have to have faith, something Robert was sorely lacking. It was one of the reasons why had Tate left the castle in the first place; the two of them were never going to see eye-to-eye on that. The holy man knew he could do more good out in the fledgling communities, as Clive had told Tate when he'd found him. The man had a vision of what Hope and other villages could be like, how the survivors of the human race might all rise again, phoenix-like, from the ashes of the Cull. He'd had the necessary leadership qualities to draw together his own community, and if it hadn't been for Javier wrecking it that fateful day – riding in and casually shooting up the place – Clive might just have succeeded.

Of course, he might yet: through Gwen. She'd inherited a lot of Clive's determination, seemingly channelling his ability to make people listen. (It was a quality, coincidentally, Clive had also shared with Robert.) She was dead set on pursuing his dream, putting Hope back together, making a place to fit to raise their child, Clive Jr.

"I want him to grow up in a loving atmosphere, away from the city and out of the shadow of that castle," she informed Tate, not long after the birth. The first part was fair enough, what parent doesn't want such an environment for their child? Yet Tate had to question whether the second part had more to do with the question mark hanging over the baby's origins. Did she really want to get away from the castle because some part of her recognised it was where Clive Jr had been conceived?

Robert, Mary, Jack, even Tate himself. They all suspected the truth of the matter, even if Gwen steadfastly refused to. She didn't want to hear it through the pregnancy and certainly didn't want to talk about it after her son was born. Regardless of the fact there was only a slim chance Clive was the father, Gwen was adamant he be listed as such in the new records system being initiated in Nottingham ("If we start with our own people," Mary had suggested, "then we can add others we find out about as and when."). Tate couldn't blame Gwen for wanting to believe the boy was Clive's. Who would want to think that their offspring was the product of rape? Especially by a man whose genes, Tate suspected, had been given to him by Satan himself. He'd certainly been put on this Earth to do the Fallen Angel's bidding.

Tate always felt more than a little responsible for what had happened to Gwen. Perhaps there had been something more the holy man could have done to prevent Javier from taking her back to Nottingham. Or maybe if he hadn't tackled Javier in the first place, struggling with the man as he held the pistol... Was it as much his fault the gun had gone off and shot Clive? No, Javier was about to shoot him anyway, Tate was sure of it, that's why he'd felt compelled to intervene.

Then later, when he'd joined Robert's band, Tate should have tried harder to convince the man to mount a rescue. There again, they both knew it would have been suicide. And there was no way of knowing for sure Gwen was even alive.

Robert did it for Mark, though, didn't he? Tate would say to himself, then feel guilty for such thoughts. Mark was just a child, being held and tortured, then sentenced to execution. There had been other villagers that were going to die as well. It had been that which had forced Robert to move against De Falaise. In any event, Gwen had remained at the castle, subject to the Frenchman's sadistic whims.

For all these reasons, Tate decided to go with her when she left. It had been a tearful goodbye, but he knew he'd see everyone again. Nottingham wasn't that far from where they were heading, and he'd made the trip a few times, like when the castle had hosted a fête last summer.

He recalled now the day they left, though, and what each of his friends had said.

"Thank you for everything," had been Mary's words, giving the Reverend a kiss on the cheek.

"Gonna miss your words of wisdom. Take it easy," Jack had told him, clasping his hand and shaking it firmly.

"Are you sure you have to go?" Mark had asked. And when Tate nodded, he saw the boy's eyes moistening. Tate had rubbed his tousled blond hair and Mark had laughed.

"See you around, I s'pose," Bill had said next – and it wasn't long after that he had made tracks himself, after some disagreement or other with Robert.

Then came the man himself. The Hooded Man, who Tate had talked into leading these people. They might have had their differences, and Tate might not have agreed on some of his methods, but he knew fundamentally that Robert was a good man. And he knew he was going to miss him.

"If you ever need anything, even if it's just to talk, my son –"

"I know where you are," Robert said, fixing him with those intense eyes of his. "You look after yourself, Reverend."

"You too." He'd leaned in close so the others couldn't hear and added: "Look after them all." It was Robert's turn to nod. "You did a good job, you know," Tate said finally. And he thought then that he'd detected the slightest of smiles playing on Robert's lips.

They'd driven off in one of the jeeps De Falaise had left behind, packed with enough food and water to last them the journey, in addition to whatever items Robert's men had been able to find for the baby: nappies, bottles, jars of baby food (there were actually plenty of these kinds of stocks still left in shops and warehouses; Tate didn't like to think about why). Neither of them had known what to expect when they finally arrived, having heard nothing of the village since they'd left. When Tate had gone in search of the Hooded Man, there had only been a handful of the original members of Hope still living there. Young Darryl Wade, for example, who'd been helping Clive fix up the village hall the day Javier arrived – turning it into a school for future generations. Graham Leicester, who'd been attempting to grow food in gardens and fields. But most had fled the village, fled the region, once the new Sheriff's stranglehold on the area had taken effect. Tate knew for a fact that former midwife June Taylor had done so with Gwen and Clive's adopted kids, Sally and Luke.

"They've seen enough of fighting and death," June said to Tate as she was packing up their things. She was referring, of course, to Clive's brutal demise – something they'd probably never get over as long as they lived. "After everything they've been through, even before Hope, they need some kind of stability." He'd tried to talk her out of it, saying that one day Gwen would return, he felt it in his bones, but it was a half-hearted protest at best. Deep down, Tate realised June was right: Sally and Luke should be away from this place. He hoped they were living a peaceful life somewhere.

Strangely, Gwen had not asked about them when they'd both recovered after the battle. And when he'd told her anyway, she'd nodded as if taking the information in, but had been more concerned about the baby she was carrying inside her. Tate liked to think she felt the same way as him, that she wished them happiness wherever they were. It was what Clive would have wanted. But there was always that niggling feeling – and again, he hated himself for it – that she was okay with them being somewhere else, because now she had a real child she believed belonged to Clive. Sally and Luke must have seemed like something from another lifetime, after her trials at the castle.

They'd driven into the village and it seemed like a ghost town. Nothing much had changed since Tate had been there last. The cottages still had pock-marks on the walls where the bullets had struck, and there were charred sections of road where grenades had gone off.

Gwen had parked the jeep and climbed out. Unlike Tate, this had been the first time she'd returned since Clive's death. Leaving the Reverend behind for a moment, to look after Clive Jr, she'd wandered down the street as if in a daze. When she reached the place in the road where Clive had fallen, she'd knelt.

Maybe this wasn't such a good idea after all, thought Tate. Like the castle, there were too many memories here. They should have sought out another village to start again, dedicated it to Clive – somewhere his ghost wasn't on every street corner.

There was a clacking sound, and Tate leaned forward in the jeep's front seat. Gwen had heard it too and was rising, pulling something out from under her jumper; something she'd tucked in her jeans without telling Tate. It was an automatic pistol, another parting gift from the previous tenant of Nottingham Castle. Gwen held the weapon like a professional, just like she had the machine gun she'd used during that last battle in the city.

"Come out, whoever you are," shouted the thin, auburn-haired woman. "I'm not messing around." The more Tate saw of Gwen like this, the more he realised how she'd changed – or rather how circumstances had changed her – and how much he didn't care for it.

Behind him, Clive Jr began to cry.

Then, at the side of one cottage, Tate spotted a figure. It was Andy Hobbs, another resident of the old Hope, standing with a hunting rifle – aiming it at Gwen's head. She'd turned on him in a heartbeat, bringing her pistol to bear.

"Gwen, no!" called Tate. But she'd already spotted who it was... and so had Andy.

"It can't be," said the man, lowering his gun. "Gwen? Is that really you?"

She began lowering her pistol, though not letting her guard down quite as quickly as Andy. Gwen approached him, eyes darting left and right. "How have you been, Andy?" Tate heard her ask.

"Never mind about that, come here." Andy went to give her a big hug, but Gwen pulled back before he could get anywhere near her. This was Andy, who'd once tended the fields, who'd sat and laughed and joked outside the local pub with Clive and Gwen on balmy summer evenings. She recognised him; she'd even said his name. But the trust was gone – maybe Gwen's trust in all men except Tate. It would take time, but she'd need people like Andy if she was really going to fulfil Clive's dream.

"Andy!" Tate called, in an effort to take the embarrassment out of the situation.

"Reverend? I can't believe it. I never thought... Well, I didn't think I'd see either of you again, to be honest."

Clive Jr. was crying louder and Gwen returned to the jeep. Andy called the all-clear, and other familiar faces appeared: Graham and

Darryl, along with a few others Tate had never seen before. They gathered round, old friends swapping hellos, introductions being made.

"I still can't believe you're really here," Andy said again to Tate. "It's so good to see you."

"You too, my son," Tate replied, leaning on his stick.

"We heard snatches about what happened in Nottingham, but nothing concrete."

"Something about a big fight?" Darryl added.

"We figured something big must have happened when no more men came to take our food."

"We were ready for them anyway, even if they did," Andy said, holding up the rifle.

Tate grimaced. "I wouldn't have thought that was your style."

"Neither is being hit in the back of the head with a rifle butt."

"Granted," said Tate.

"So, you went off to join Hood's men?"

"Not intentionally," Tate pointed out. "But I suppose I did end up getting dragged along for the ride. That's a story for another time, though."

Gwen was standing by the jeep, cradling Clive Jr, feeding him a bottle of milk. Darryl came over and smiled at the little one. "So who's this then? He's really cute."

"This is Clive's son."

"Clive's..." Darryl frowned. "But I thought –"

"Darryl, Darryl." Tate interrupted, limping round the side of the jeep. "Enough of your questions. We've been on the road a while and there's still food and drink in the back of the jeep. Enough for a celebratory dinner, I'd suspect."

So that's how they'd spent their first night back; inside The Red Lion, filling their bellies and swapping stories about what had happened in the time since they'd all last seen each other. The remaining members of what had once been Hope had carried on with their lives, but lived in fear that the soldiers might return. That was one of the reasons why they hadn't cleaned up the place much.

"It was a reminder of what could happen again," Graham told them. "A reminder not to get taken unawares again."

"That's why when we heard your jeep... well, you know," said Andy, now feeling slightly foolish.

"De Falaise is no more," Tate assured them, nursing a brandy. "His men have been defeated, his legacy replaced by a new law in the land."

Gwen pulled a face at this and Tate caught it out of the corner of his eye. As far as she was concerned, she'd got herself out of the mess at the castle. Robert Stokes had been far too late to save her, in every sense of the word.

"Do you really think he can protect us?" asked Darryl, also seeing Gwen's expression.

Tate nodded. "I think he'll try his best."

"So what now?" asked Graham, putting his feet up on one of the tables.

It was Gwen who answered, rocking the baby in her arms. "We start again. We turn this back into the place Clive always wanted it to be. With one or two exceptions."

Graham frowned. "What do you mean?"

"It's like you said." Gwen held Clive Jr in the nook of one arm and picked up the pistol resting on the table in front of her. Tate raised an eyebrow, which she completely ignored. "We're never going to be taken unawares again. This time, we make sure we can defend ourselves. There are more in the jeep; rifles and pistols, and ammo."

"What? Gwen, you stole –"

"I borrowed them from the caves," she said, cutting Tate off. "Besides, from the sound of things, they won't be using them any time soon."

Many of Clive's ideas had been sound, she went on to explain, but in attempting to start again with a bunch of people skilled in various areas – Graham's knowledge of agriculture, for example; Darryl's handyman ability – he'd left out the very people who could fight off an attack like the one they'd encountered. Now, every single person in New Hope, as Gwen suggested renaming the village, would know how to fight as well. With guns, with their hands. This met with nods of approval from the folk in The Red Lion.

All except Tate.

He'd talked to her about it later, asking her if a community based on violence was what Clive would really have wanted. It certainly wasn't the 'loving atmosphere' she'd said she was looking for when they'd left the castle.

"We also need to be safe, Reverend. I don't want to be reliant on Stokes and his people."

"You'd rather create a small army of your own, is that it?"

She shook her head. "We'll leave the outside world alone, if they'll do the same with us."

While Tate conceded that she had a point about defending themselves, he still wasn't mad on the idea of these ordinary men and women being on a state of constant alert, trained in using firearms and hand-to-hand combat. "How is it any different to what you did for Robert?" Gwen had said after she'd asked Tate to teach his self defence tactics.

"That was a war," Tate replied. "Desperate times..."

"These are still desperate times, in case you hadn't noticed. What happens if another threat comes, if another De Falaise decides to try and take over?"

He didn't have an answer. But nor would he willingly teach these people how to fight in what he saw as a time of peace. While it was true he'd taught classes before the Cull, Tate was only trying to keep people safe. So what was the difference here? He couldn't explain it; he just knew that it was wrong and it wasn't what he'd come here to do. These people needed spiritual guidance, not advice on how to disable a person using the flat of your hand. Gwen might not have any faith in Robert to police the area, but Tate at least had that.

"Suit yourself," Gwen said in the end, realising she wasn't going to talk him round.

Thankfully, the task of revitalising Hope had kept a lot of them busy, including Gwen. The first order of business had been to clean up the streets, the cottages – to make it look as good as, if not better than, it had been before. Darryl was put in charge of that operation, while Graham and Andy headed up the task of planting crops in time for the coming harvest (and it had been a good one, Tate had to admit). Meanwhile, some of the newer people had been sent out to look for more skilled workers who might want to boost their numbers. Gwen had gone on a number of these missions, just as Clive had done before her. Tate found out later that she'd even poached people from other villages: like their doctor Ken Jeffreys, who they'd discovered in a community near Worksop. Somehow Gwen had managed to persuade Ken to join them, leaving behind the people he'd tended to up there. "I told him we needed him more," was all Gwen would tell Tate. "It was his choice." But something told Tate that the woman hadn't taken no for an answer.

When she went away on these head-hunting trips (which invariably were getting shorter and shorter), Gwen would leave Clive Jr with Tate. It showed how much she trusted the holy man, as she wouldn't let anyone else within a mile of the little one, but for Tate it always proved a difficult undertaking. Many a time he'd look down on the boy and those dark eyes would stare back. He'd shiver then, but couldn't explain why. It was only a child, after all.

But hadn't their very own Jesus Christ once been a baby just like this one? And look how he'd changed the world.

Tate shook his head; these were ridiculous thoughts. The whole next generation of infants had the capacity to change the world: for better or for worse. What made Clive Jr so special?

Yet he couldn't help thinking...

When she returned, Gwen would always go to the child and make a fuss of him. As she'd rest him on her shoulder, whispering to him, the baby would look over and find Tate again. The Reverend would smile when he saw Gwen looking, but it was pasted on. Was that one of the reasons why he'd stayed so close to New Hope? So he could keep an eye, not only on the welfare of this community, but also on Clive Jr?

Before they knew it, spring and summer were a distant memory, Autumn had come and gone, and winter had set in. They'd celebrated Christmas, this burgeoning group of people, and Tate had led them all in carols in the renovated chapel. All except Gwen and her son.

"I won't be coming," she'd told Tate long before the celebration. "I don't feel it would be right. I don't... I'm just not that religious, especially after..." Gwen's sentence tailed off and he didn't push it.

But her actions, her attitude, troubled Tate more and more as the months crawled by.

That morning, Tate had called round to see Gwen, only to be told she was visiting Clive's grave again; a burial Tate himself had presided over, in the small graveyard behind the chapel, after Gwen had been taken to the castle. Now he returned to see Gwen and her baby, wrapped up warm against the icy chill which also bit into his leg. Clive Jr was in a pushchair, a bobble hat covering his head and thick woollen blankets tucking him in.

Gwen didn't notice Tate's approach until he was almost at the grave – not a stone one, like most of those here, or even marble, but a simple wooden cross made by Darryl. It was all anyone had been able to manage in these times, and it was more than some poor people had been granted. He heard Gwen talking to her baby, then to the grave, before waiting – as if expecting an answer from the man buried there. It was only when she heard the crunch of snow under Tate's feet that she stopped.

"You shouldn't be out here, Reverend," she told him when she did finally look round. He wasn't quite sure what to make of that statement. Was she telling him he wasn't welcome? "It's treacherous underfoot." Gwen nodded at his stick.

"I'm not an invalid," he pointed out. Far from it; even with his disability, Tate could put an able-bodied man through his paces. "I'll be all right. I'm more concerned about your welfare."

"Me?" She looked mystified. "I don't know what you're talking about."

Tate let out a sigh. "This isn't healthy, Gwen. It never has been."

"What, visiting the man I loved? Clive Jr's father?"

"That's not what I'm saying and you know it. You're not facing... certain facts."

Again, she gave him a confused look.

"Facts like –" Tate was interrupted by someone shouting from the gate. Andy, holding one of the automatic rifles Gwen had taken from the castle.

"Someone's coming," he yelled.

Tate and Gwen exchanged glances, then set off down the path. The holy man had nearly stumbled, but only in his haste to reach the street. He saw Gwen take out her pistol, ready to protect her child, and it didn't even seem strange this time – that's how much she'd altered. Gwen with a gun seemed like a natural thing.

They joined Andy out on New Hope's main road and he pointed. "There."

Tate squinted. There was a lone figure heading up the street on horseback. The hood pulled down over the figure's face betrayed his identity, and the bow and quiver on his back confirmed it. And though you couldn't tell for sure just by that – look how Mary had fooled everybody on the day of the attack – something told Tate that this was indeed the man he'd first encountered in Sherwood Forest some time ago.

"You can put those weapons away," he told Andy and Gwen, then he hobbled up the street towards the horse.

The rider brought his steed to a halt, then climbed down. As Tate drew near, the man pulled down his hood. Robert Stokes looked older, more tired than he had the last time the Reverend had seen him.

"Hello, my son. What brings you to New Hope?"

"Trouble."

"Yes, I can see that by the bruise on your face."

"Could someone fetch my horse water and hay?"

"Andy," Tate said, waving his hand for the man to approach. Robert handed over the reins. "Much appreciated."

"I'm surprised to see you travelling alone," Gwen said by way of greeting. As she pushed the buggy towards Robert, she tucked the gun back in her jeans. "Someone of your importance, I'd have thought you'd have two or three men with you."

"I don't need any protection. I never have." There was something in his tone which said she'd hit a nerve.

"You say there's trouble, Robert," Tate said. "What kind?"

"Can we talk inside, Reverend? Somewhere a bit more private?"

"This isn't the castle," Gwen informed him. Tate balked at her rudeness. "It's my village. You can talk in my house if you're talking anywhere."

Robert nodded. "Understood. So lead the way, we've got a lot to discuss."

ROBERT SAT DOWN at the kitchen table while Tate put a kettle on the range.

Their visitor had taken off his bow and quiver but kept them close – and he kept the sword he always wore now at his hip, even though it stuck out behind his chair. Looking at the scene, Tate mused what a curious blend of ancient and modern it was; perhaps that was the way of the future after all?

Gwen, having placed Clive Jr in his playpen, leaned against the edge of the work surface, her arms folded. The silence was deafening, and in the end it was Gwen that broke it. "So, how are things back up at the castle?"

"Ticking over," Robert replied.

"You managing to keep on top of everything, keeping the area safe?"

"I'm working on it."

"Quite a task you've set yourself, though. And quite an ego to think you can right the wrongs of the whole world."

"Gwen, that's not fair," Tate said.

"Let her speak, Reverend. She's obviously got something on her mind."

Gwen's smile was tight. "I'm just making idle conversation."

"Those heavy duty guns you and your friend were waving around, they looked awfully familiar."

"How's Mary?" Gwen said quickly, changing the subject. "I liked Mary. She was good to me when I had Clive Jr."

"Ah, yes," said Robert, glancing over at the baby. "Clive Jr."

The whistling of the kettle broke in, and moments later Tate was announcing that tea was ready.

"No cucumber sandwiches for our guest?" Gwen tutted. "I'm surprised at you."

"Look, what exactly is your problem?" Robert said.

"What's my problem? I'll tell you what my problem is –" Tate interrupted her, calling her to fetch the tea, his voice firm. When she placed the tray down on the table, the china rattled.

"You two knock yourself out," said Gwen, then she picked up Clive Jr and left the room.

Tate eased himself down on the chair opposite Robert, rubbing his temple where he felt the beginnings of a headache. "I'm sorry about that. She's been through a lot."

"We all have. It's no excuse."

"I know. I know. But, well, seeing the man you love get shot right in front of you and then... Well, I don't need to refresh your memory about what that creature did to her."

Robert shook his head. "She blames me for not coming sooner, doesn't she?"

"I think that's part of it, yes."

Tate suddenly recalled the moment Mary told them Gwen might still be alive.

"Are we finally going to do something about this Sheriff now, once and for all? Are we finally going to go in there and get those people out?"

"Like your Gwen, you mean?"

Yes, like Gwen, who he'd failed so spectacularly. Who Robert had failed, too.

"So," said Tate, drinking his tea and feeling the headache waning slightly, "are you going to tell me what this is about?"

Robert explained that they'd been tracking members of a cult, how they painted their faces like skulls and were growing in numbers. How he and his men had caught a few of them. "They're dangerous, intent on killing whoever they come across. I really need you to come back with me and –"

"Robert, I'm afraid my fighting days are over. I never really wanted them to begin in the first place. If circumstances hadn't forced me to..." Tate didn't feel like he could continue that line of argument.

But Robert was shaking his head. "You misunderstand me, Reverend. I need your help figuring out the religious side of all this, maybe to sit in while I question the prisoners. I'm afraid I'm in over my head where all that stuff is concerned."

Tate could feel the headache building again, this time with a vengeance.

"Take this..." Robert reached into his jacket and pulled out a folded piece of paper. "I got Mary to draw it, based on our descriptions of the tattoos the men have on their foreheads. I didn't want her getting too close to any of those lunatics."

Tate put down his cup and took the paper, casting his eyes over the symbol. It was an inverted pentangle within a circle. There were markings around the outside of the ring, and at the tips of the cross: some kind of lettering. Inside the pentangle was an inverted cross. "These people are Satanists, Robert."

"Yeah, I kind of got that."

Tate tapped the paper. "This is a variation on the Sigil of Baphomet, which used to be used by the Official Church of Satan back before the Cull. The symbol of Baphomet was also used by the Knights Templar to represent Satan. It was known as the Black Goat, the Goat of Mendes, the Judas Goat, the Goat of a Thousand Young and the Scapegoat. That sign had a picture of a horned goat in the middle of the pentangle, whereas this has an inverted cross – which is actually the Cross of St Peter, a common mistake made by those practising this kind of thing. St Peter was crucified upside down, you see..."

"I see I've come to the right person."

"They've done something else to the symbol, though," Tate continued. "Usually there are two circles around the pentangle, and between those, at the edge of each point, there's a letter in Hebrew which, when brought together, spell LVTHN anticlockwise."

"I don't follow," said Robert, his brow furrowing.

"Leviathan, my son. The Horned One. The Devil. Here, though, the letters are reversed Latin."

"What do they spell?"

"Well, the outer five spell MRNIG."

"What the Hell is that supposed to mean?"

"Probably exactly that. Because if you look at it in conjunction with the letters around the cross as well..."

"Go on."

"Those spell STAR."

Robert shrugged. "Still not getting it."

"Morningstar? Lucifer. The Fallen Angel."

"Oh, God..."

"Quite the opposite." Tate let out a long, slow breath. The headache was worsening by the second. He was about to pick up his tea again, but his hand wavered as if something had suddenly struck him. "Did you say these men were killing people?"

Robert nodded, then rubbed his bruised jaw. "It's how I got this. They were after a young woman in York, and if we hadn't been there..."

"Then it's even more serious than I thought."

"Isn't it serious enough?"

Tate gripped the side of the table with one hand, and pointed at Robert with the other. "If they're killing, sacrificing, then there can only be one reason."

"They enjoy it?"

"They're attempting to raise him."

Robert looked at Tate sideways. "Come on! Satan? You're telling me they're trying to conjure him up or something? That's ridiculous."

"No more ridiculous than our Lord Jesus Christ coming back from the dead. They want him to appear in the flesh, Robert. After all, hasn't this world been called by many a Hell on Earth? Wouldn't he be right at home here?"

"You don't seriously believe that."

Tate held up his hand. "What I believe is irrelevant, they believe it. And they will carry on executing people until he appears."

"Then what will they do?"

"Anything he tells them to. He's their master."

There was silence for a few minutes, during which Robert looked down at the table. "They have to be stopped. Regardless of what they think is going to happen, I can't just let them carry on."

"I know," replied Tate.

He studied the Reverend. "Will you come back with me to the castle? I could really use your insight."

Tate breathed out wearily before answering. "When God calls me, I must answer."

Robert thanked him and got up, leaving the cottage to fetch his horse. They would set off immediately for Nottingham. Gwen came back into the room when she heard the door slam. She was still cradling Clive Jr in her arms.

"Don't bother to explain. I heard everything."

"You were listening?" Tate was more than a little surprised.

"Of course. I can't stand to be around that man, but I wanted to know what was going on. Seems I was right all along, about another threat coming." Gwen fixed Tate with a stare. "Still think Robert and his men can protect us?"

"As I said before, my child, I know he will try."

"And you will help him?"

"I will."

"Then I wish you all the luck in the world," Gwen said, before walking out again.

"And I," whispered Tate, his eyes trailing her as she disappeared, "pray that God might deliver you from this darkness." Whether he meant the darkness of the conflicts to come, the Morningstar cult and whatever waited for him at the Castle, or the darkness inside Gwen's own soul, not even Tate knew for sure.

CHAPTER SIX

THE BLADE SWISHED as it whipped past his ear, narrowly missing his head.

He rolled out of the way, then leapt up to avoid another stroke, beneath him this time. Landing badly, he toppled to one side – recovering just quickly enough to fall backwards when he saw the blade about to run him through. He hit the ground hard, emptying his lungs. Laying there, sucking in a deep breath, he saw a shadow fall over him.

Then the blade was at his throat.

If it had been a real sword, he'd be dead by now. As it was, all he'd suffered were a couple of splinters in his neck.

A hand reached down and he took it, felt himself being hauled to his feet. The man standing opposite Mark said nothing, merely gestured that he was ready to go again if the boy was. Mark nodded to the dark-skinned soldier, his sparring partner today. Mark didn't know Azhar all that well, but the man wielded a sword like he'd been born with it in his hand. Jack had left Mark to do battle with him over an hour ago, and as he now watched the man spin the sword, Mark wished his tutor had at least given him a weapon to fight back with.

Azhar swung again, the wood clipping Mark's left shoulder. He let out a yelp, hopping back out of its way. He didn't stay there for long though, because his opponent was already moving forward, jabbing for his ribs. "Hey, watchit!" Mark cried when the tip poked him hard in the side. He had to react fast, as the wood flashed past his face. That one really would have hurt...

Azhar's feet were a blur as he positioned himself in front of Mark, preparing to swing the sword again. Mark dived beneath the next sweep, running at Azhar to try and shove him off balance. The man easily sidestepped the boy's attack, causing Mark to dive head-first at the ground. He came skidding to a stop on the slushy snow of the Middle Bailey field, where a pair of size-fifteen boots were waiting.

"Very impressive, kid. The old sliding on the snow manoeuvre." Mark cast his eyes up to see Jack standing there, leaning on his staff and chuckling. He helped him to his feet, then brushed the snow roughly from the front of his jacket.

"It's not funny," said Mark. "And it's not fair, either. How come he gets a sword and I don't?"

"You think you're always going to have a weapon to hand?" Jack shook his head. "Uh-uh. Nope. But your opponent might."

"What if my opponent has a semi-automatic?"

"Then you learn how to dodge bullets as well as swords."

"This is pointless."

"If it helps, think about it like Jedi training."

Mark moaned. "It doesn't. I was never a big movie fan, Jack, remember? I was more into sports – which is how I ended up following your career."

Jack smiled. "Still my number one fan, eh?"

"Depends."

"On what?"

"On how long I have to keep doing this shit for."

Jack clipped him around the ear. "That's 'cause Robert's not here, or he'd have done the same. It's not grown up to cuss like that."

Mark let his shoulders sag.

"Look, tell you what: Azhar, toss Mark your sword a second."

The soldier threw his wooden sword over to the boy, who almost dropped it.

"Okay, now you're armed. He's not. Think you can take him?"

Mark grinned, swinging the sword to test its weight. It was payback time. He stepped into the area of combat, while Jack watched from the sidelines. Azhar hunched down low and matched Mark's circling movements, eyes flitting from his enemy's face to his hands. Mark swung the sword experimentally. He'd practised before with one of these, sneaked away when no one was looking to get the feel of what it was like. He'd taken on trees and fences, fancied himself as pretty good too – not in Azhar's league, of course, but given enough time... Except Azhar didn't have the sword anymore, did he? Now the advantage was all Mark's.

He came at Azhar, swinging left and right. The darker-skinned man moved like a cat, making sure the sword never came within three feet of his body. Mark gripped the weapon with both hands, bringing it up in an arc which would ordinarily have caught his opponent beneath the chin – but Azhar had already leaned back. The difference between his move and the one Mark attempted earlier was that Azhar was soon upright again.

Mark showed his teeth, in an effort to put Azhar off, but there was absolutely no reaction. This made him even angrier. He swung the blade this way and that, as he figured he was bound to strike something sooner or later – an arm, a leg... a whack in the head might be nice in return for all the pokes and prods.

He hit nothing.

Mark was on his final swipe – Azhar right in front of him – when suddenly the man wasn't there anymore. He was at Mark's side, having dropped and slid around, and was relieving Mark of the sword, grabbing his wrists and wrenching the weapon free. In seconds Mark was again on the wrong end of the tip, which was hovering between his eyes.

There was laughter coming from somewhere. At first Mark thought it was Jack again, but it wasn't deep enough. When Azhar stepped back Mark turned and saw Dale sitting on the steps to the East Terrace. He had his guitar with him, and was shaking his head, clapping his thigh at the sight of Mark's defeat.

"Nice one, Marky. You had him right where he wanted you," Dale brought his guitar around and started to play a melody, making up words on the spot.

> *"You try your best, put to the test,*
> *But let's face it now, you need a rest.*
> *Can't be easy, ohhh, it can't be easy...*

> *"Give it your all, but when you're small,*
> *You find out life just ain't no ball,*
> *Can't be easy, ohhh, it just can't be that easy..."*

"Shut up!" shouted Mark, but Dale continued playing. Mark turned and saw that some of the other men training had stopped to listen.

> *"He's just a child playing at bein' a man,*
> *It's hard and he don't know if he can.*
> *Oh, it ain't easy... It simply ain't that easy..."*

Mark's eyes narrowed and he marched towards Dale. "I said shut up!" Azhar came up behind to try and stop him, but Jack put a hand on his arm. This had been a while coming and the last thing Mark needed was anyone interfering.

"What's the problem, Marky-boy?" answered Dale, resting his guitar against the wall and standing to meet him. "It was just a joke. What's the matter, can't you take a –"

Mark grabbed him by the collar, swinging him around and onto the pavement between the steps and the field. He pulled back his fist, then struck Dale squarely in the face, making his nose bleed. Dale brought a couple of fingers up, touched the nostrils, and when they came away red he glared at Mark. "You little sod, look what you did."

"Want some more?"

Dale ran forwards, dragging Mark back onto the field. They slipped, then rolled over on the snow.

"Let them work it out," Mark heard Jack saying as they rolled past him and Azhar. "Bit of old fashioned wrestling never hurt anyone."

On the final roll, Dale landed on top of Mark, pinning him down. He brought his fist back, ready to retaliate, when there was a cry to their left.

"Dale... Mark..." It was a female voice, too young to be Mary's. Mark recognised it instantly. So did Dale.

"What's going on?" asked Sophie, making her way down the steps.

"Some other time," Dale said to Mark, tapping him on the cheek.

Mark wrenched his head away and spat back: "Any time."

"Jack, what's happening here? Why didn't you break the training up when it was getting too rough?" Sophie said.

The big man held up a hand in mock surrender. "Hey there, little lady, it was nothing to do with me."

"Wait till Mary hears about this," she told him.

Dale was up and walking over towards her, wiping his bloody nose. Already, Sophie was pulling a tissue out of her winter coat to dab at it. "Look at you... You should know better. He's only just starting out."

"Yeah," Dale replied, looking back at Mark. "I'm sorry, mate." He grinned as he let Sophie clean up his face.

"You should go easy on him. Come on inside, let's get you cleaned up properly."

Mark stared in disbelief as Dale grabbed his guitar and trotted off back up the steps with Sophie. Go easy on me! Go easy? I nearly bloody well broke his nose! He got up just in time to watch the pair disappear from view.

Jack placed a hand on his shoulder. "All's fair in love and war." He said the words as if distracted.

Mark followed his gaze to the far end of the Bailey, where a woman with short, dark hair was walking past. It was the woman who'd arrived with Jack and Robert the other day, Adele. She'd gone off with Jack then to have a tour of the castle and its grounds, but it was Robert she'd had eyes for – much to Mary's chagrin.

"I'll remind you of that sometime," Mark said bitterly.

"Hmm... What?"

"Nothing," sighed Mark. Adele disappeared from view and Jack brought his attention back to his pupil.

"You up to carrying on with your training, or do you need to take a time out?" Even before Mark could open his mouth, Jack said: "Good, that's good, kid. Azhar, he's all yours again."

With that, Jack was off up the walkway, heading in the direction he'd seen Adele going. "I'm... I'm not a kid," Mark whispered.

But no-one was listening, least of all Azhar, who was urging him to get back on the spot they'd occupied before. The dark-skinned man picked up the sword and started spinning it around again.

Mark hunkered down, trying to recall what Azhar had just done in his position.

"HEY... HEY THERE, hold up."

Jack called out to Adele. The woman had certainly made tracks since he'd spied her, and was now past what had once been the main entrance to the museum. She appeared to be looking for something, when she heard his cries.

"Hey there, Adele. Wait up!"

She waved to Jack then waited for him to reach her. When he got closer he saw that, like Sophie, she was wearing a winter coat – only Adele's clung to her, pulled tight in all the right places. He recognised it as one of the long coats Mary sometimes wore. The kind-hearted woman must have lent it to Adele to keep her warm.

"Jack," she said, smiling warmly. "How are you today?"

"Well, I'm just fine. All the better for spotting you up here. Haven't seen you much since you arrived."

Adele's smiled broadened. "I've been... busy."

"Have you now? Doing what?"

"Trying to get my bearings, mostly. One whiz around the block wasn't quite enough to familiarise myself with this place."

Jack looked up at the castle. "Yeah, I know what you mean. I used to come here sometimes, y'know? Visit in the week. It was always free to get in."

"I wouldn't have thought you were the type to wander round stately homes and castles."

"I'm a man of hidden depths," Jack announced proudly. "Do you mind if I walk with you for a spell?"

Adele hesitated for a second, then gave him another smile. "No, of course not."

"Forgive me for asking this, ma'am, but I figure I don't really know much about you and, well, I'd like to. It's kind of what we do around here when we bring someone into the fold."

"What would you like to know?"

Jack laughed. "Wanna hear somethin' funny? Put on the spot like that... I haven't a blessed clue."

Adele laughed too. "There's not that much to tell, really. I was an only child, my mother brought me up alone because my dad died when I was very little. Average kind of education, did okay at school. Left school, did some travelling, you know how it is?"

"Indeed I do," said Jack, whose own wanderlust had taken him from his native upstate New York, into the lights of the big city, then finally to England where he'd made his home.

"Drifted from one job to the next, never really settling on anything. Never really had something I wanted to do, a life purpose like some people have." She paused to take in the stunning view of Nottingham. "Not like you; I heard you were a pretty good sportsman. A wrestler, wasn't it?"

Jack nodded.

"I'm envious. Not of the wrestling, obviously." She laughed again and touched him on the arm. "But that fact you always knew who you were."

"Oh, I'm not so sure I always knew. But yeah, I guess you could say I was lucky. In more ways than one, when the virus hit." Adele pulled up sharply and her smile suddenly faded. "Hey, I'm sorry... I... That was real thoughtless of me. What you said back there in York, about having no-one. You lost your family, didn't you?"

"Can we change the subject, please?" Adele said, bristling.

"Sure. Hey, no problem."

She began walking again, without waiting for him to catch up. All it took for Jack was a couple of strides. "Do you know where Robert took off to in such a hurry?" she asked then.

"Robbie? Why do you ask?" Jack fought to keep the jealousy out of his voice.

"Oh, no reason. It's just that he left without saying goodbye or anything."

"You get used to that," Jack told her, resting his staff on his shoulder as they walked. "You should have seen him in Sherwood. One minute he was there, the next..."

Adele looked wistfully out at the view. "I really wish I could have seen that. It all sounds so... I don't know, romantic. Living in the forest, with the Hooded Man."

Jack shrugged. "I don't know if *romantic*'s the right word. It was dangerous, I know that. Especially when we came up against the Frenchman's men."

She stopped again. "De Falaise?"

"You've heard of him."

Adele nodded. "You hear things. Rumours of what happened."

"It was a tough time."

"I can imagine."

Jack looked at her, searching her eyes. "Adele, you –"

"You never answered my question about where Robert went."

"To... To get help. We need to know more about the cult, the people who were chasing you."

"Right," said Adele, nodding. "When's he due back, do you know?"

"Any time, I guess. But –"

"Jack," said Adele, pulling him towards a set of steps with a locked gate across it. "You never did tell me what was down there."

"Oh, that's just the caves. You wouldn't like it down there."

"Is it where prisoners are kept?" she asked, biting her lip.

"Not anymore. Not since we took over. It's just where we keep the stuff De Falaise left behind. Y'know, weapons and such."

Adele looked puzzled. "Robert doesn't use them?"

"You've seen what Robert uses," replied Jack, a little more impatiently than he'd meant to. Here he was, trying to get to know this beautiful woman, and all she wanted to talk about was Robert.

"I'm sorry," Adele told him, sensing the mood. "I don't mean to ask so many questions. I'm just curious about what happens here." She took his hand. "Forgive me?"

"Er... Yeah, of course." Jack could feel the colour rushing to his cheeks.

"Listen, how about you give me a bit of time to freshen up – then maybe we could grab a bite to eat? God, that sounds so normal, doesn't it? Sounds like what people used to do."

"It does."

"Okay, then. Meet you in the dining area in about an hour?"

Jack nodded.

"And listen, thank you, Jack. You've been really sweet to me." She leaned in and kissed him, before running off to the nearest entrance.

Jack beamed from ear to ear. "You're very welcome, little lady. Very welcome indeed."

It was a good few minutes before his thoughts returned to Robert. And Jack wondered how he'd got on himself, and whether his trip had been worthwhile.

CHAPTER SEVEN

THE GUARDS WEREN'T that surprised to see the horse come trotting up St James Street. Robert had already checked in with Rangers positioned at the city's edge, telling them not to inform the castle yet, just his people at the Britannia.

"They'll only want to join us, and I'd rather this was just you and me, Reverend," he'd told Tate. "I don't want Mary being placed needlessly in danger here." He'd registered the holy man's look of fear when he said that, possibly the only real time he'd ever seen Tate scared.

Robert tried to tell himself that these were just men whose minds had broken, probably during or after the Cull. It would have been an easy thing to slip into madness back then; he'd come close himself. But Tate's words about the Devil, about worship and sacrifice, had spooked him. Any kind of organised religion bothered Robert, but one which called for the death of innocents... He'd hidden it, but when Tate had been talking about Hell, Robert suddenly had a mental image of flames, of fire licking up around him.

His house burning to the ground, torched by the people in power trying to contain the virus. Robert's family, dead inside.

The lake he'd dreamed of at Rufford, ablaze and then –

The market square where he'd confronted De Falaise finally, their crashed vehicles catching light; the fire spreading out across their battlefield.

In spite of what Tate might think, Robert did like him. More than that, he respected him. They might never agree about their chosen professions – Tate would say callings – but the man talked a lot of sense. Depending on how you looked at it, Robert either owed him for making him face up to his responsibilities, or was the catalyst for everything that had happened since: leaving Sherwood, being put in charge of the Rangers, becoming a figurehead for something much greater than he could ever be.

Robert pushed all this to the back of his mind as they approached the hotel entrance, its glass doors cracked but still in place – the steps stained a faded red with blood that had long since dried.

The guard there – Robert searched for his name, it was getting much harder these days, the more his team grew... Kershaw, that was it – stood to attention. Robert thought he was going to salute and he'd have to go through that whole business of reminding them they weren't in the army. He wasn't their general.

"You just don't see it, do you? I'm no better than De Falaise."

Robert swung down off his mount, then helped Tate from the saddle. The holy man was stiff, and it took him a moment to regain the feeling in his legs. Robert tethered his horse to a nearby handrail.

"I'm here to see the prisoners, Kershaw," he told the guard, pulling down his hood at the same time.

The guard swallowed hard. "We... we thought it best to tell you when you got here. There's been a problem."

"Problem?"

"The men watching them tried to stop it, but... Well, I think it's probably best you see for yourself, sir." Kershaw waved a hand for Robert and Tate to enter. They were met inside by another of Robert's men – and this one he did recognise. Geoff Baker, the man he'd left in charge of this improvised jail, having been a warder in a real prison for years until the virus struck.

Geoff ran a hand through his thinning hair before offering his apologies. "It all happened so quickly, there was very little we could do."

"What did?"

"Go easy," Tate said. "Give the man a chance to explain."

"They did it all at once. We managed to get to one of them, but..."

"Geoff, talk to me."

Instead of saying anything else, Geoff took them to a storage room just to the right of the lobby, past a huge wall-length mirror, and unlocked the door. Inside were several bodies, stacked on top of each other, all wearing the robes of the Morningstar cult. Robert looked at Geoff, confused. "They committed suicide, Rob."

"What? How? You had them secured, right?"

"Two or three swallowed their own tongues, another one managed to get one hand free of the ropes and tear his own throat out."

"Dear Lord," whispered Tate.

"One tipped the chair over that he was tied to, angling it so he struck his temple on the side of a nearby table. Another actually lifted up the chair and ran at a wall, hard enough to smash his own skull in."

Robert was having difficulty understanding. He'd never had to deal with these kinds of prisoners before, people who would gladly end their own lives rather than divulge any information.

"But why weren't you lot keeping an eye on them?" There was more frustration than anger in his voice, but Geoff reacted as if chastised.

"We were doing our best. I don't exactly have a full staff here," Geoff reminded him, his tone hardening. "And when a crisis crops up out there, a few of my men always seem to be called away even though they're vital for guarding this place."

Robert nodded. "Point taken. You say you managed to get to one of them, though?"

"Yeah. We've been keeping him dosed up to try and stop him from doing anything similar." Geoff gestured for them to follow him.

"Just one moment," Reverend Tate said. He made the sign of the cross at the door and closed his eyes.

"Why are you wasting your time with that?" said Robert. "They don't want your help, and they definitely don't want to go to your Heaven."

"We're all God's children, whether we've strayed from the path or not. They deserve the chance of forgiveness. Of mercy."

Robert could see he wouldn't be argued with.

They left the room behind and headed for the stairs. Tate had trouble with these, but refused both Geoff and Robert's help, intent on climbing the two flights himself. Finally, they made it to what had been the bar area, an expanse of carpeted floor that once contained comfy chairs for residents, but now only boasted tables running into the restaurant section. On either side was a long glass window – the left one cracked in places – and the bar at the back was smashed to pieces, graffiti sprayed across the walls, probably during or after the Cull by someone looking for booze.

At each corner of the room stood a Ranger with a bow and arrow primed, keeping an eye on what was taking place. It was lunchtime, Geoff explained, and as they didn't have the time and resources to feed each prisoner individually, they had to do it en masse, bringing out vats of stew from the reclaimed kitchens beyond the restaurant. Robert had to admit, it didn't look very appetising, but it was all they could manage under the circumstances.

There was a shout as one of the inmates spotted Robert and Tate. Then a figure broke away from the rest of the prisoners, making a dash for Robert. Immediately, bows and arrows were raised and the man stopped before he could reach his target. They needn't have worried, as Robert had his bow readied too, an arrow snatched from his quiver the second he sensed trouble.

"This is bullshit. I keep telling 'em, I shouldn't be here!" shouted the prisoner.

"Really?" said Robert, approaching, his weapon trained on the man. "How so?" The man's face looked familiar, but he couldn't quite place it. It was certainly distinctive, the way that scar ran the length of his jaw-line.

"You let some of the others that worked for him go. Fucking 'ell, some of 'em are even working for you, while I'm stuck in this bastard place with them lot."

"Come on, Jason – back in line," said Geoff, moving forwards and signalling to a couple of the guards.

"Fuck off, screw. I'm talking to the organ grinder now."

That was it. Jason... Jace. When it had come time to sort out who might be retrained from the remnants of De Falaise's army, several of Robert's people had warned him about Jace. Mark, Sophie and Gwen especially, detailing how he'd all kidnapped Hood's ward, and how he behaved when Gwen 'seduced' him so she could knock him out and steal his uniform. A nasty piece of work, by all accounts.

"You're talking to the wrong person," Robert told Jace. "He's the one who deals in forgiveness for scum like you." He nodded at Tate, who pursed his lips. "How about it, Reverend? Think we should let him go? Is there a place for him in God's plan? How would Gwen or Sophie feel about that? He would have raped them both, given half a chance."

"That Gwen was up for it," sneered Jace. "She enjoyed being with De Falaise – told me as much."

It was the holy man who moved this time, whacking the youth in the stomach with his stick. He would have done more had Robert not pulled him back. Then the guards were dragging Jace across the room.

"Put him in solitary for a day," Geoff ordered. "That should cool him down a bit." Solitary was a locked storage room with no windows. It might seem barbaric, but for Jace and his kind it was better than some of the justice that was being meted out in other parts of the country. At least here, Robert was more or less sticking to the legal system of old. It was the only way they could build the tentative beginnings of a new civilisation.

When Tate had calmed down, Robert looked at him, perhaps expecting some kind of apology or explanation. Tate gave him neither.

He might represent a higher power, but he's still a man – with a man's emotions, Robert reminded himself. And in spite of everything he's said, Tate's still a fighter.

They were taken up to the next floor – to conference rooms that had once hosted presentations and lectures, but were now being used as holding bays for the more dangerous prisoners. In one of the smaller ones, they found a table with a woman and another guard standing next to it. There was a mirror to their left as they walked in. Strapped down with what looked like belts, buckled across the chest, stomach and legs – and ropes tied around the wrists – was the member of the Morningstar cult Geoff had referred to. It took Robert a second or so, but he placed the Ranger as a man called Lewis, the woman with features that looked too small for her face as a nurse Mary had trained called Lucy Hill. Lucy had her scrubs on, her hair tied back in a pony tail. She was flitting about around the prisoner, around the patient.

"How's it going?" asked Geoff.

"He's stable. Still pretty out of it, mind," Lucy replied. "I gave him some Chlorpromazine to calm him down."

"Is he up to us asking some questions?" Robert inquired.

"You can ask, but I can't vouch for any of the answers you'll get."

Robert approached the table. Tate hesitated, and only when Robert looked back over his shoulder did the Reverend join him. Robert could see the cultist much more clearly now. It was the one who'd snapped at Adele, attempting to bite her like the animal he surely was. The white paint he'd used to mask his identity had rubbed off in places, run in others, giving him – if anything – a more nightmarish appearance than before. The only thing that remained was the tattoo on his forehead. The man's eyes – a steely blue – stared up at Robert, and he had no idea whether his presence had registered. He looked completely stoned, like so many of the druggies Robert had come across in his former life, but he had the feeling this guy's eyes had looked like that even before Lucy had come near him with a needle.

"Can you hear me?" asked Robert.

"Mmmnnnfff," was the reply he got.

Robert looked up at Lucy. "At least he's not trying to top himself," she offered.

"Let me try," said Tate, tapping Robert on the shoulder for him to move aside.

Robert watched as the bald man studied the cult member's features. "I know you're in there," said Tate. The words seemed normal, but

Robert had seen the Reverend do this before, draw things out of a person, force them to answer, force them to think. He'd done it with him once, persuaded Robert to communicate. "Speak, my son."

The cult member's eyes locked on Tate's. Robert found himself holding his breath as the man spoke again. "I... I hear you," mumbled the prisoner, the words barely audible.

"What is your name?"

He continued to stare, as if he didn't understand the question – either that or didn't know how to answer. Tate repeated it and the man simply whispered: "Servitor. I serve."

"No, not your purpose. Your name. Your Christian name." The man shook his head slowly. "Who were you before?"

"No before," the man breathed. "We have always been here."

"Since before the virus, you mean?"

There was the slightest hint of a nod.

"All right then, tell me why your fellow... Servitors all killed themselves."

"S s sacrifice."

So it wasn't just other people they were out to kill; when they were taken captive, they were happy enough to kill themselves.

"A sacrifice? To whom?"

"Our master. The one true Lord."

"I beg to differ. You worship a false deity, can't you see that?" From the man's blank expression it was pretty obvious he didn't.

"He will come. It is written."

"Through your sacrifices?" Tate asked, and the man nodded.

"Looks like you were right," Robert chipped in, but Tate took no notice.

"You believe you will find him here, in this world?"

"He will... he will rise again..."

Geoff whistled. "See? What a loon."

Tate whirled around and shot the warder a look that would have given Medusa a run for her money. Geoff kept quiet.

"You will see him," the Servitor promised. "Feel... feel his power..." Tate's face was almost as white at the make-up the cult member wore. The holy man was clearly terrified. "You know, don't you? You feel it."

This was going horribly wrong. Instead of Tate's words having an impact on the Servitor, the reverse was happening. And his voice was growing stronger by the second.

"He's coming... He who is... who is... blood red... from head to...."

to toe..." The man's mouth was foaming, and he was straining against his bonds.

Robert went over to hold him down. "Lucy," he called out. She already had the needle prepared, and was attempting to stick it into a bottle to draw more Chlorpromazine. Her hands were shaking; she almost dropped the bottle twice.

Then everything happened at once. Robert looked down to see that the Servitor had snatched the knife he always kept at his hip. With another wrench, the man broke free of the ropes holding that wrist, and was in the process of cutting through the leather strap across his chest. Robert made a grab for the forearm, but the man tugged it free. His strength was incredible, as if he was channelling something.

"Lucy, stick him – right now!" shouted Robert.

The nurse brought the syringe across, but when she bent to administer the drug, the Servitor brought the knife up and sideways, slashing her across the arm. She stepped back, mouth wide, dropping the needle and clutching at the gash.

"Tate, I could use some help," Robert growled over his shoulder, struggling with the man. The Reverend was standing there, gaping.

Geoff and Lewis were racing to assist, but somehow the Servitor had managed to worm one leg free. He kicked the Ranger in the face, sending Lewis crashing backwards into the wall.

Robert took one hand off the prisoner to punch him, but the man took the blow without even flinching. Absently, he wondered what Eric Meadows would have done in this situation: would even he have been able to secure this charge? The next thing Robert knew, the strap across the Servitor's chest was in two halves and he was rising, yanking free to attack the other bonds with the knife. When Geoff tried to stop him, he broke off to plant the knife in him up to the hilt, then pull it out again. Geoff looked down to see a bloom of crimson stain his top, then his feet buckled and he fell.

Robert was on his own.

This shouldn't be so difficult. I took a handful of them down back in York. But something was different. Whether it was the confines of the room, or the Servitor's inexhaustible strength, he couldn't decide. *One thing was for sure, if the cultist got free of the table –*

And then it was done. The Servitor was standing. He was still staring at Tate, however, still had him in that hypnotic trance. Lewis was spark out, Lucy had retreated to the corner of the room – what Robert wouldn't have given for it to be Mary here instead now, or even Gwen! – and he didn't even know if Geoff was still alive.

Robert kept the table between them. It was too small a space to use the bow and arrow, and the same went for his sword – one swing and he might end up hurting one of his own. No, this fight was going to be a nasty one: scrappy, clumsy. He hated that.

"I can't let you leave," Robert told him. "You know that."

The Servitor cocked his head, turning finally to face Robert – but in the process caught sight of himself in the mirror just beyond. He paused, frozen just as Tate had been moments before. Then he took the knife and drew it over his own throat. The blood sprayed across the table, across the room, and Robert held up his arm to shield his eyes. Remarkably, when he took it down again, Robert saw the man was still standing, thick gouts of red spurting from the wound at his throat, those cold, dead eyes now fixed on him.

Then he dropped face forward onto the table, almost upending it. Robert gaped at the scene. His mind couldn't quite take in what had happened. Why had this man struggled so hard to get free, only to take his own life? He remembered the other bodies down in the room on the ground floor, remembered what the Servitor had said about sacrificing themselves to their master.

Robert looked over at Tate, who seemed to be snapping out of his daze. "Evil faced itself," the Reverend whispered.

There was a groan from the floor. Geoff! Robert skirted round the table to see him laying there, blood welling from the wound in his chest. He applied pressure to it, then shouted again for Lucy. This time she came, tentatively and still holding her own arm, one eye on the man sprawled across the table, as if expecting him to rise at any moment. "Lucy, for Christ's sake!" snapped Robert. Blinking at the wounded man on the floor, she too snapped out of her daze, immediately crouching to help stem the flow of blood.

Robert shouted at Lewis to go fetch help – other personnel who had medical training. "And Mary..." he said. "Send for Mary. Quickly!"

MARY COULDN'T QUITE believe what she was seeing.

That cow was wearing her coat! It was such a small thing, and there were admittedly few items of female clothing in the castle so it made sense that she should have borrowed it – but it was precisely because of this that Mary was angry. There were precious few things that were hers, only hers. Worst of all, Adele had taken it without even asking.

Though she hated herself for it, Mary wondered what else the woman was intent on taking from her.

What do you want her to do, Moo-Moo, freeze to death out there?
She was tempted to come back with: "Do you really want me to answer that?"

Now, that's really not nice... her brother told her. She'd completely forgotten that whatever she thought, he instantly knew as well. Because he was her, wasn't he? The voice of her conscience, her reason.

I'm bloody well not, you know. I'm me. I'm your brother.

"Oh, shut up," Mary said, drawing Adele's attention.

The woman, standing at the bottom of the steps, about to ascend, waved at her. Mary let her head droop, then lifted it again. She didn't want to give her the satisfaction of knowing she was upset.

"Mary, hi!" the woman called out, coming over. Reluctantly, she met her halfway.

"Adele."

"I was hoping to run into you. I wanted to say thanks." The woman's eyes sparkled when she spoke. Mary looked puzzled, so she continued: "For this, the coat."

"Oh, yes... That's..." Mary didn't know how to complete that sentence because, until a few moments ago, she had no idea Adele was even wearing it.

"Rob said it would be okay to borrow some of your gear."

My gear? "Did he?"

"Er... yeah. Hope that was okay? You've got a really nice room, you know. Love what you've done with it. Considering. I guess anything's a step up from the forest." Adele smiled, but there was no warmth in it.

"You've been in my... in our room?" What she was really asking was, had Adele been in there alone? Not because she thought her and Robert had snuck off there – apart from the fact he hadn't had time before leaving, Mary did know the man well enough that he wouldn't be able to hide that one. (What about the other night, what about the cosy little drink in the café? He still hadn't mentioned that to her.) No, it was the thought of a complete stranger going through her stuff, poking around, maybe laying down in the bed she shared with –

"I... I wasn't in there very long," Adele promised, as if that made it all right.

Mary said nothing, but found herself clenching and unclenching her fists.

"Look," Adele went on, "you've all been really nice to me, and I'm so grateful. But, well, there aren't very many women around here, are there? Bit heavy on the testosterone. I suppose I was hoping you and me could be... well, I had hoped we could be friends. You know?"

"You're thinking of staying a while, then," was all Mary could muster.

Adele smiled again. "Thinking about it, yeah, if you guys will have me. Sure beats being out there on the streets, being chased by murderers and rapists."

"Right."

"I hope it isn't going to be a problem or anything?"

"I hope not as well."

Adele frowned. "Forgive me for saying this, Mary, but you seem to have a... I don't know. Have I done something wrong? Something to you?"

Mary felt like saying, *"Cut the crap, you know exactly what you've done. And it's what you're going to do when Robert gets back I'm interested in."* Instead she said: "No, not exactly."

"Only I'm getting some really weird vibes from you."

Mary shook her head, this wasn't the time or the place. "No, everything's fine. Really."

"Ah, okay." Adele's smile widened, but seemed even less genuine. "Right, well I suppose I'd better go and get ready."

"Ready?"

"I'm having something to eat with Jack."

Now it was Mary's turn to frown. First this woman had been flirting openly with Robert, then she'd caught them having a little late night rendezvous. (*It was hardly that, Moo-Moo. Might've been completely innocent.*) now she was making a play for Robert's best friend.

Don't do it, warned David. *Seriously, keep your mouth shut.*

She couldn't help herself. "What exactly is your game, Adele? What are you up to?"

The smile faded fast. "Excuse me?"

"I saw you with Robert the other night."

Adele looked horrified. "What?"

"Don't act all innocent," Mary said, pointing her finger. "I could see what was going on. What you were trying to do."

Adele stepped back. "There was nothing going on. Robert dropped a glass and I got some in my foot."

Mary pursued her, moving forward, still pointing. "You're after him. And now you're leading Jack up the garden path."

"You're insane."

"Am I?" Mary let the words settle and neither of them spoke for a second or two. Then Adele turned to leave, and Mary grabbed her wrist.

"Let go of me!" she spat.

"I've got my eye on you, Adele."

Adele grinned. "You'd be better off putting your energies into hanging onto your man. There's obviously something lacking in your relationship, if you're this insecure. Maybe you don't know Robert as well as you think you do."

Mary was about to bring up her hand to slap the woman, when she heard someone shouting her name. It sounded urgent.

"Mary... Mary!" She let Adele go and whirled around. One of Robert's men was racing down the corridor. "You have to come quickly – bring your medical stuff. Someone's been injured at the Britannia."

"Injured?" asked Mary.

"Stabbed. You have to come quick, Robert said –"

"Hold on, Robert?" Mary looked at him, then back at Adele, who was still smirking in spite of the news. "He's back? But –"

The man pleaded with her to come with him, saying that there wasn't time, so Mary did. But before she'd got out of earshot, she heard Adele reiterate: "No, maybe you don't really know him at all."

CHAPTER EIGHT

HE FELT LIKE Jonah in the belly of the beast.

Tanek sat in one of the cargo bays, working away on his secret project; he'd been labouring on it since they set off across the Baltic. It was important that he got it right. The various parts were all laid out in front of him on the table, which at the moment was vibrating slightly. Tanek reached for one of the pieces of wood and his sandpaper, running it smoothly across the face. Every curve, every inch would be lovingly crafted, just like the last one.

He recalled the man who'd taught him how to build this weapon – a man skilled in the ancient arts of combat and defence. His name had been Liao and he'd been good to Tanek, offered him a place to stay when he'd had none, a stranger in their land. Liao had been an expert in all kinds of weapons, though the modern ones didn't interest him as much as those from the past.

"You can learn much from studying history, my friend," he'd told Tanek in one of their late night drinking sessions. They were words that another man would echo years later. Both were dead now. The Frenchman, De Falaise, who Tanek followed without question, had been killed by the Hooded Man. Tanek had not been present at his execution, but he'd felt the man's passing.

Liao, who had looked so similar to the Tsar's twins he could have been their father, had died at Tanek's hands long before that. Once he'd learnt everything he could from the man, and it had been time to move on, Tanek had simply snapped his neck, leaving Liao for his wife and children to find. He'd had no qualms about doing it, the man had been of no more use to him. And to Tanek, a quick death was kindness – better that than to be tortured at his hands.

Oddly enough, he'd never foreseen a time when he would have

done something like that to De Falaise. He felt the Frenchman would always have something to teach him, only disclosing his nuggets of genius tantalisingly slowly. Before they met, in that Turkish tavern where De Falaise had saved his life – something that didn't always guarantee the same in return from Tanek – he thought he knew everything about warfare, about killing. Listening to De Falaise, he realised he knew nothing at all. Not really. He also knew nothing about ambition. De Falaise's plans saw him one day stretching his hand out to rule the entire world.

With Tanek by his side.

So much for that plan. But the Tsar; oh, the Tsar... Now he'd done what De Falaise had only dreamed about. Become the ruler of his country, with a force under his command that made their army look like the bunch of disorganised yobs they'd been. Apart from some of the more seasoned veterans, like him, they'd been kids with toy guns and tanks. When it came right down to it, they were no match for Hood's sheer deviousness. While De Falaise and his men had been up front about their business in Nottingham, their enemies had chosen to sneak in and attack.

And it had worked. And one thing Tanek knew about De Falaise was that if something worked, you adopted it yourself. It was the tactic he'd used to get to the Tsar: hide in plain sight. If you want to reach the very heart of your opponent's camp, let them think they've captured you, let them escort you into the belly of the beast.

The tipping of the floor reminded Tanek that, right now, he was in the belly of a Zubr class military hovercraft: one of a fleet the Tsar had dispatched for the trek across the sea. Tanek finished sanding and placed the part down on the table, picking up a rectangular box.

Anyway, just like Hood, he'd been delivered unto his target. The only difference was that he'd come to talk, not kill. Luckily, his reputation preceded him.

"The giant Tanek, De Falaise's right hand man. I heard you were both dead," the Tsar said to him after they'd retreated to a more private place, his luxury suite at the Marriott Grand. And after Tanek had been offered use of the facilities, including a working shower – something he hadn't seen since well before the virus struck.

Tanek had sat in a plush chair, eyeing up the twins that flanked the Tsar, swords resting on their arms. But, more importantly, the Tsar's second: Bohuslav. He was potentially trouble. "De Falaise is. I was," he replied, his face stern.

He remembered the final moments on those gallows, fighting the man with the staff; the infuriating child Mark (oh, how he savoured the memories of torturing the boy, wishing he had the opportunity again, wishing he could go further this time... payback for ramming that knife into Tanek's foot); and the man with the shotgun who'd blasted him and sent him toppling. In the confusion that had followed, as De Falaise had escaped in the armoured truck – driving into the platform and unwittingly giving Tanek the opportunity to crawl away once he was on the ground – he'd made good his own escape.

Tanek had staggered to his feet, stumbling towards the buckled side gates as best he could. The chest wound from the shotgun was stinging, but not instantly fatal, and with a painful summoning of strength, he'd made it out into the street. One of Hood's men spotted him and tried to take him down, but Tanek – as weak as he was – still managed to knock him to the ground and stamp on his skull.

He'd lurched from the scene, making for one of the narrow adjoining streets, flinging himself forward; ever onwards, away from the castle. How he'd made it to the outlying regions of Nottingham, he still wasn't sure. Exhaustion and blood loss took their toll. Tanek had passed out by the side of a country lane, in a ditch in the middle of nowhere. The world around him started to fade. Then all he knew was darkness. He was surely dead – had been from the moment the man shot him. He was just too stubborn to lie down and let nature take its course.

But somehow he wasn't in that ditch anymore. He was in a forest. All the colour had bleached out of the scene. Greens and browns replaced by greys and blacks. Tanek approached one of the trees – apparently able to move quite freely now, his wounds gone. He touched the bark, and where it came away the wood was bleeding, red and moist. In the clearing beyond he saw an indistinct figure – the more he concentrated the more it came into focus. It was his superior, the Sheriff, except he had no eyes and didn't appear to be able to speak, though his mouth was opening and closing. Tanek walked towards him, and as he did so the forest caught on fire. The blind De Falaise held out a hand as if pleading for help. Tanek's pace picked up, running through the flames towards him. The injured Frenchman was mouthing the words, "Help me." Tanek ran and ran, towards the figure, fighting back the fire until –

He woke up panting. For long seconds he blinked, looking up at the ceiling. How, he wondered? How could he be awake when he'd died back there in the ditch? It didn't make any sense. And how could he be here? Tanek was in bed, covers pulled over him. When he moved, the pain in his chest and foot returned, proving that this was no longer a dream. That he actually was still alive. Lifting the covers, he was suddenly aware of his nakedness – save for the bandages around his chest. And, yes, when he wiggled his foot there was one around that too.

All became clear when an overweight, middle-aged woman with a tight home perm – wearing a hideous floral dress – came into the room to check on him. "Ah, you're awake at last," she said, "that's a good sign. I thought you were going to sleep away the rest of the year."

Tanek sat up slowly, looking at the woman sideways.

"Don't try moving just yet, your body's still recovering," she told him, sitting down on the end of the bed. "It's just lucky that William found you when he did. If we hadn't got you back to the cottage, Heaven knows what might have happened."

William? A husband? A son, or maybe a brother? A threat!

"How...?" Tanek asked, then realised that talking hurt.

"Brought the car back for you. Only an old Morris, but... It was too far to drag you, and you're very, well, very big." The woman smiled coyly, looking down. "I'm sorry, where are my manners? It's just been so long since we've had company." She rose and went to the door. "I'll fix you something to eat, you must be starved."

She disappeared, leaving a puzzled Tanek to take in his surroundings: the hideous floral wallpaper, the wooden dresser and wardrobe. From the window sill leered down photos from the woman's life. Her with several children, then at the seaside with a tall man much older than her, who had grey hair.

The woman returned about fifteen minutes later with a tray of scrambled eggs. "From the chickens," she explained, kicking the bedroom door shut. "They've been a godsend." Tanek devoured the meal in minutes. "My..." said the woman, touching her hand to her throat, "you were hungry, weren't you?"

Tanek gave a single, curt nod.

The woman sat down on the edge of the bed again. "I'm Cynthia. Cynthia Reynolds." She looked like she was waiting for his name, but he didn't oblige. "It... It doesn't matter to me, you know."

Tanek cocked his head

"Your wounds. I don't care where you got them. I just wanted you to know that." She was playing with her obviously fake pearl necklace. "You don't have to tell me anything. I know what it's like, out there." It was painfully obvious she didn't have the first clue what it was like. She reached out to touch his arm. "And don't feel you have to repay me or anything."

He didn't. Tanek pulled away sharply.

"I'm... I'm sorry." Cynthia looked like she was about to cry. "It's just that, like I said, I haven't had much company these past few years. Only William. But, well, you know, a woman has certain needs that he can't fulfil."

Tanek looked again at the man with grey hair in the photo.

"Others have come, but they've never stayed. Then, when we came across you while we were out walking..."

"I need clothes," he snapped suddenly. "And your car."

"You're not going?" It was phrased like a question, but it was also a statement. "You're not well yet."

Tanek was well enough. Better than he had been when he'd staggered away from the castle... how long ago? Days? Surely not weeks? He got up, letting the covers drop and not caring about Cynthia seeing his body. It must have been her who'd undressed him, anyway. But she seemed coy again, as if she hadn't just been suggesting he stay for more than his health.

Ignoring Cynthia, he checked the wardrobe first – finding a mixture of men's and women's clothes. The trousers, shirt and jumper obviously belonged to the man in the picture; large enough to fit him, but tight where Tanek was broader across the chest, shoulders and legs.

"Please," said Cynthia as he was getting dressed, "stay with me. I've looked after you, haven't I?"

Tanek grunted, tugging on a pair of shoes he'd found in the bottom of the wardrobe. He made his way over to the door, once again disregarding Cynthia's pleas. Then she grabbed him by the arm. He'd had enough; the woman should have known when to leave well enough alone. Tanek took hold of Cynthia by the shoulders and pushed her up against the wall.

It was then that he heard the growling.

Tanek turned to see the door had been nosed open by a large Doberman pinscher.

"William," he said.

Cynthia nodded. "I had hoped you might be different; William really liked you. I hoped you'd join us here, stay and be our guest for much longer. But, well, as you insist on being so rude."

Tanek never saw the command if there was one, but the dog leaped straight for him, teeth bared. His reactions were dulled from being flat on his back for so long, but the sight of that mutt coming for him soon sharpened them. Tanek let go of Cynthia, whirled around, and punched the dog in the side of the head. It fell across the bed.

Little wonder no one had stayed for very long when this was Cynthia's protector. Leaving the woman, Tanek ran across to the bedroom door, slipping through and slamming it shut just as the hound had recovered sufficiently to leap again. He held onto the door handle for a few moments, grimacing at the snarling and clawing on the other side, and taking in what was around him: a small landing, a steep staircase that led to the front door.

Tanek let go of the handle and pelted down the stairs, almost tripping on the final few. He scrambled to open the front door, only to find it locked. Meanwhile, Cynthia had flung open the bedroom door and was ordering William to attack. Bracing himself, Tanek rammed the door, causing it to loosen at its hinges. There was a growling from behind, very close behind, and he slammed into the door again – this time knocking it flat.

Ahead of him, parked next to the cottage, was the Morris car Cynthia had mentioned. Tanek lumbered towards it, aware the dog was only seconds behind. The car was locked as well, so he elbowed in a window, pulled up the knob and climbed into the driver's seat, barely fitting.

William jumped at the side of the car, desperate to climb inside and bite Tanek. He leaned over just enough to stay out of the reach of those vicious teeth, as he broke open the ignition housing and hotwired the engine. Shoving the gear stick into first, Tanek drove off, and William lost his grip. Through the rear-view mirror he saw the dog chasing after him, Cynthia at the front door watching the pursuit. Tanek sped up and pretty soon he'd left the woman, the animal, and the cottage behind.

With no real strategy in mind, except to get out of the region where Hood's men might be searching for him, Tanek headed east. There was nothing for him on this island anymore and his best bet was to retrace his steps, head back over to Europe. Maybe even head back towards Turkey.

The Morris had an almost full tank of petrol – Tanek doubted whether Cynthia had driven more than a few miles since the time of the Cull – and it was enough to get him to the coast. In a small seaside village, Tanek appropriated a sailing boat and made his way back across the ocean. It wasn't as easy as their bike ride through the Channel Tunnel, but he'd finally made it to the Netherlands.

On nights when he'd let the boat drift and slept down below, Tanek had been surprised to find himself dreaming. He hadn't been able to remember his dreams before. Now they were so vivid, always set in the burning forest and always featuring De Falaise. Somehow he knew, without it having to be explained, that the link his leader shared with the Hooded Man now extended to him. In each dream Tanek had got closer and closer to the man, and in one a stag had trotted up beside De Falaise, seemingly oblivious to the flames licking around it. The Frenchman had pointed to the animal.

"I do not understand," Tanek had told him.

The flames turned to snow, falling on cold, bare branches. De Falaise looked at him with those black, empty eye sockets. "Help me," he mouthed again.

"How?"

The dreams always ended at that point, leaving him none the wiser. Until a few months ago. He'd been sleeping rough on the streets of Warsaw when he'd had his most vivid dream yet. This time it all fell into place: what De Falaise was telling him to do, where he was telling him to go. The stag, the snow... He wanted Tanek to avenge him, kill the Hooded Man – something that had crossed the big man's mind on more than one occasion, but he'd had no idea how to go about it. Now he knew. The trail was taking him to a person they'd often talked about – someone De Falaise had both hated and admired, because he'd succeeded where the Frenchman had failed.

It was how he'd ended up fighting in the Tsar's arena, then sitting in his hotel room. His fighting skills, built up slowly again after suffering his injuries, had impressed. And his statement about having a proposition had intrigued Russia's new monarch.

"So, what is it that brings you to our country?" the Tsar asked eventually, pouring a measure of vodka for himself and another for his guest.

"You obviously know what happened in Nottingham," Tanek said to him, at the same time accepting the drink with a nod.

"I've always kept my ear to the ground."

"Then you know the threat Hood poses."

The Tsar started laughing, almost choking on his alcohol. "Threat? Threat? What possible threat could that woodsman and his followers pose to me?"

Tanek scowled. "That is exactly what De Falaise thought."

"But your dead master was a lot nearer, wasn't he? The world's a much bigger place these days, my friend."

"Hood is already expanding." Tanek knocked back the vodka. "He has appointed himself protector of the region. Next it will be his country. Then he will look to Europe." It was the most Tanek had said in years, probably ever. But he felt he wasn't just speaking on his own behalf anymore.

The Tsar had leaned back, the leather of his suit competing with the squeak of the chair. "Let him come. He will have to deal with others before he reaches me." Other warlords had taken over France, Germany and Italy. They'd driven De Falaise to England in the first place.

Tanek held up the glass, ready for another drink. "But your goal is to rule the whole of Europe, eventually, is it not?" The Tsar was silent, which he took as a *yes*. "Then sooner or later you will meet in battle. Why not now, when his forces are small and yours are great?"

"I've heard enough," snapped Bohuslav. "He just wants revenge, sire."

"True," Tanek agreed, before the Tsar could say anything. "But as I understand it, we could be of some use to each other."

The talks had continued, well into the night, fuelled by liquor. Tanek could feel Bohuslav's eyes boring into him as he appealed to the Tsar's ego, assuring him that it wouldn't take much to stamp out Hood, thereby also gaining a foothold in Britain from which to mount attacks on his enemies in Europe, coming at them from both sides.

"I have to admit," the Tsar slurred, well into his second bottle of Smirnoff, "that the thought of conquering America's biggest ally does appeal."

Tanek nodded. "Once you have control of England and Europe, what is to stop you going after them, too?" The picture he'd painted was one of global sovereignty, with the Tsar well and truly on the throne. The man had lapped it up, as Tanek knew he would.

Placing Bohuslav in charge of the invasion, the Tsar had ordered preparations for the fleet of Zubrs to set sail, with a pit-stop at Denmark before the final leg across the North Sea. It was then that Tanek truly saw the scale of the Tsar's power, the size of his army compared with the one that had been commanded by De Falaise. He also saw that the old-fashioned weaponry he'd used to fight Glaskov was thankfully limited to the gladiatorial arena.

Each craft carried either three T-90 MTB battle tanks or a mixture of APCs, BTR 60 or 90 Armoured Fighting Vehicles, IMZ-Ural motorbikes and UAZ-3159 jeeps, plus around 50 troops (Tanek was told that pre-virus this number would have been at least double). The men were equipped with the standard AK-47s, but also Saiga-12 semi-automatics, 9A-91 shortened assault rifles, PP-19 Bizon submachine guns, compact SR-3 Vikhrs and, for real stopping power, NSV-12.7 large calibre machine guns, RGS-50M modernized special grenade launchers and AGS-17 automatic mounted grenade launchers. The list went on and on, virtually making Tanek salivate.

As he glanced up from his labours, Tanek saw the impressive array of military vehicles and equipment in the Zubr's bay. But in spite of being given full use of a selection of rifles and pistols, there was still something comforting about fashioning his own distinctive weapon. The sight of a crossbow bolt entering someone was so much more satisfying than a messy bullet hole.

He was alone at present, the troops having gone off to eat, so Tanek had taken full advantage of the silence. Just the thrum of the engines and creaking of the hull as the hovercraft made its way across the water, taking him back again to the place he'd departed just over a year ago, where he hoped to use his new repeater crossbow on the people who'd cost him the old one.

There was a noise off to his left, at the back of the bay – someone behind one of the T-90s. Tanek licked his lips and began to assemble his chu-ko-nu, hands flying over the wood, pieces slotting together around the stock, sliding the fully loaded magazine on top last, and pointing it in the direction of the intruder.

"Impressive," said a voice. Somehow the man had appeared at Tanek's back, and there was a cold sensation at his throat. Tanek risked a look downwards and saw the curving blade of a hand sickle.

Bohuslav.

"Now that we're alone, I thought we could have a little chat. I don't know exactly what you're up to, but you're hiding something. And you should know this: If you cross me, or if your actions in any way interfere with the Tsar's designs, I will kill you. And I will enjoy it."

Tanek snorted. As he'd thought: trouble.

"You may have been able to talk him around, but I am altogether a different animal."

"Look down," said Tanek.

He couldn't see the man cast his eyes downward, but he heard the sharp intake of breath when Bohuslav saw that the knife Tanek held in his other hand was hovering inches away from his side.

"Now let me go."

Bohuslav reluctantly eased the pressure on Tanek's throat. The larger man stood, turning to face the serial killer. They each held their respective weapons high: Bohuslav's two sickles; Tanek's knife and crossbow.

"This isn't finished," Bohuslav told him.

"I know."

Then Bohuslav lowered the blades and left, moving soundlessly – which confirmed to Tanek that he'd made the noise up front purely as a distraction.

Tanek sat back down and let out a long sigh. He looked up again at the machines of war, at the hull around him. He was in the belly of a much greater beast than this one, when it came right down to it. So much had happened to him since the castle, and there was still so much at stake. More than Bohuslav or even the Tsar realised. Especially them.

He cast his mind back to the last of his dreams before entering Moscow. The last thing De Falaise – or the dream version of him – had said. "Help me..." the blind ex-Sheriff had attempted to say again. Then:

"Help me and help my child."

CHAPTER NINE

HE'D NEVER WANTED to be in charge.

Not even when he'd helped to set up the floating markets in Nottinghamshire. He'd been content to be the person who guided everyone along, without actually being the focal point. People assumed he was organising things even then, though; had always come to him for advice about trading, to settle arguments and disputes. Mainly because he liked things to run smoothly. Even when he'd worked on the proper markets back before the big bloody hiccup that was the AB virus, folk had done the same. He'd only have to point out the best use of space, where the fruit and veg stalls would work better, or make a few observations on buying and selling, and everyone would think he was running the whole damned thing, instead of just being another trader.

The fact that he'd wandered around the post-Cull markets with a shotgun tucked under his arm hadn't exactly helped in this respect, he had to admit. Good behaviour was a lot more likely when someone was standing a few feet away with a twelve bore. He hadn't really thought anything of it. He'd always gone out shooting with it, even when he was a lad. And when things went wrong with the world, it was a no-brainer for him to keep it close by. It was one of the reasons he'd been so reluctant to relinquish it to Robert at the castle.

Stupid idiot had been glad of the thing when they'd gone into fights together, and he would put it up against that man's bow and arrow any day of the week. He didn't have the time or the inclination to start training with those, or take up the staff like Jack, or swing a sword around. It wasn't the Middle Ages. There were people still out there, dangerous people. People like that mad bastard De Falaise, who had no such qualms about carrying a gun. And Bill Locke was damned if he was going to get caught with his pants down trying to string a bow when someone was shooting bullets at him. He much preferred to be shooting them back, thank you very much.

Which was why the gun had stayed with him, and was with him today – by his side as he flew over the countryside in his Sud Aviation SA 341 Gazelle helicopter – 'borrowed' from the same place as his last one: Newark Air Museum. The Sioux had been smashed to pieces by Robert when he chased down the sheriff and rescued Mary, but flying that had given Bill a taste for it again. So he'd requisitioned the more heavy-duty Gazelle for his trip north-east, away from Nottingham and all the memories it held, good and bad.

Bill had really thought things would turn out differently after the fight for the castle had been won. He and Jack began taking care of things while Robert recovered – again, Bill hadn't been the one in charge, merely gave that impression to old and new recruits alike. For a while everything was okay, until the Hooded Man was back on his feet, dishing out the orders. And for some reason – Bill couldn't for the life of him work out why – Robert had decided to just lock up all the weapons that they'd confiscated from De Falaise's troops. Now they sat in the caves, rusting away, when Robert's men could be using them to really make a difference: to keep the peace, just as Bill had done with his shotgun at those markets. It stood to reason, didn't it? At least it did to Bill. But could he get Robert to see it? Could he bollocks.

There was no way he was staying after their last bust up – too many things had been said in the heat of the moment, including Robert still laying the blame for Mark's capture at Bill's feet. How long was he supposed to go on punishing himself for that? Okay, he'd cocked up – but he'd thought the boy would be safe enough with a whole group of armed men looking after him. How was Bill supposed to know that the Frenchman would begin rounding up people to execute unless Robert turned himself in? Mark had forgiven him, hadn't seen anything to forgive, really. So why couldn't Robert?

"One of these days ye goin' to come a right old cropper," Bill had shouted at Robert. "An' I hope I'm there to see it." He'd stormed out of the castle and – bar saying his brief goodbyes – hadn't hung around much longer.

He'd determined to start afresh, maybe see if he could encourage more market networks to start up, where they hadn't already. It had been hard at first, relocating to another area, but he'd soon found out who was who, and what was what. So fast, in fact, it had amazed him. Yes, there were some markets operating, but they were nowhere near as organised or well-run as the ones he'd known. Bill recalled visiting one, drawing strange looks from some of the stall-holders (little more than goods scattered randomly on the floor). They thought he might be there to cause trouble, especially when they spotted his weapon, but he'd soon assured them he meant no harm. "There's quite a bit o' potential here, if everyone pulls together," he'd told them.

Word spread, and soon Bill had found himself in exactly the position he hadn't wanted to be: running things. He had a team of personal helpers – no, more than that, they were his friends. Ken Mayberry, for example – a former social worker who now handled timeslots for the markets; chipper Sally Lane, who along with her boyfriend Tim Pearson (he hadn't been her boyfriend before the plague – in fact, Bill remembered her telling him she'd been married – but that was happening more and more, people pairing off), they were in charge of location scouting. It was still sensible to steer clear of big towns and cities, just as they'd done back in Nottingham, so venues now included village community centres, playing fields and even some car parks if they were in relatively isolated places.

Bill and his team had set up shop not far from Pickering and had a radio network of marketeers – as Sally called them, though that always made Bill think of pencil moustaches and swashbuckling – that took in a good chunk of the upper east coast. He was managing to keep the chopper fuelled and thus kept an eye on what was happening. They'd branched out recently into ferrying goods up and down the coast, using rowing boats or whatever else they could get their hands on. Bill had even seen one ingenious soul using a RNLI boat; well, it might as well be put to good use.

Bill had heard rumours of things going on in Europe, men who made De Falaise look like a novice. There were actually a number in France, apparently. Just as long as none of them came over to these shores again...

But that was always a possible threat. And when Bill got a call like the one he was answering this morning, he had to wonder. A lookout at Whitby lighthouse had spotted something coming in across the ocean. Several things, in fact, which looked to be separating out. "Can ye give me any more to go on?" Bill had asked over the crackling static. What came back was unintelligible – had he heard the word *ships*? – and they'd lost the signal not long after. It was still not a great way of communicating, but at the moment it was all they had, short of smoke signals or semaphore.

Bill had been en route within the hour, though it would take him a lot longer to reach his destination from where he'd been on the other side of the North York Moors. It wasn't necessarily bad news. Perhaps someone was trying to make contact to trade with them? That would open things up even more, make life easier for a lot of people. If supplies in the UK were dwindling, apart from those people were growing or farming themselves, then there was sure to be more abroad, wasn't there?

He had to hold on to that hope, because the alternative was too terrible to think about.

Large things...

Tankers, freighters, ferries?

Or warships?

Inside the cockpit, Bill shook his head. He'd been conditioned to think like that, was letting his past experiences influence him.

(But didn't he still wake up in a cold sweat some nights after looking down the cannon of a tank? Standing there pointing his shotgun at the metal monstrosity which, in his nightmares, had features – pointed teeth and glaring eyes?)

You couldn't go through something like that without it affecting you. Nor could you look on the aftermath of a battle, see the bodies on either side, and not have it haunt you.

(The pain bit into his pelvis now. It felt like that olive-skinned bastard's crossbow bolt was still lodged in there sometimes.)

Wait and see... wait and see.

He did, but as he flew closer to the coast, coming in low as he had done through the city on the day of the castle run, he saw the smoke rising from one location. It was a community he knew, had traded with, and the irony of its name wasn't lost on him either.

In terms of line of sight, Bill had the advantage over them at the moment – as the angle down to the bay meant those at the bottom couldn't really see him. Landing quite a way from the upper entrance, the buildings at the top giving him some cover, he powered down the chopper and grabbed his shotgun, tucking it under his long winter coat as he got out to investigate.

He worked his way down the sloping, winding King Street. The picturesque quaintness of the buildings should have been a thing of beauty, especially with the light dusting of snow they had on them at the moment. But Bill was just filled with dread. It was a steep trek downwards – though not nearly as hard as it would be to get back up again – and when he was close enough, Bill saw where the smoke was coming from. Down by the dock of the bay itself. The buildings there – including the white Bay Hotel – had taken heavy weapons fire, scarred black where shells had hit them.

And then he saw the bodies.

Judas Priest, not again!

Who had done this to such a small, inoffensive place? More importantly, why? What had they ever done to anyone, either before or after the Cull?

Bill saw a handful of figures. People still alive. His heart sank when he spotted they were wearing uniforms, grey in colour with fur hats that covered their ears. And they were carrying machine guns. A patrol left behind to guard this spot after... after what? It was obvious from the track marks in the snow leading from the dock, up towards the wider New Road, that military vehicles had barged their way through this village. An army. Another fucking army! Before he could wonder how they'd offloaded the vehicles and men from the sea, then simply disappeared, there was a voice shouting from behind him.

Bill didn't need to turn to know it was another one of the soldiers. And he was drawing the others' attention with his bellowing.

Both the tone of voice and language was distinctive. *Russkies,* Bill said to himself. *What in the name of fuck's sake are they doing here?*

"Turn around!" demanded the voice again, this time in broken English.

Slowly, Bill did as he was told, but at the same time he brought his gun up from under his coat, finger squeezing the trigger even before he was fully around. The loud *bang* coincided with his first glimpse of the soldier, barely out of his twenties, but hefting a deadly AK-47 that would have cut Bill in half given the chance. The shotgun blast hit the man in the chest, knocking him clean off his feet. Bullets from the machine gun pinged off a wall to Bill's left, the soldier's finger automatically pulling back, but his aim completely thrown.

As the first soldier fell, Bill risked a look over his shoulder at the others below, rushing up the incline to take him out. He fired another cartridge at them, causing the group to scatter.

Then he ran towards the felled soldier as fast as he could. Ignoring the blood being coughed up by the wounded trooper, he reached down and grabbed the Kalashnikov, swinging it around at the others.

"Welcome to England, comrades!" he shouted before crouching and spraying them with bullets. They hadn't been expecting that, apparently, because they all went down fast, barely getting a shot off. "Like t'see a bow an' arrow do that," he muttered under his breath.

Bill reloaded his shotgun, then rose, holding both weapons out in front as he traversed the slippery road down to where the soldiers lay. He was well aware there could be more in hiding – it was what he and Robert would have done, once upon a time – but felt the risk was worth it for information. He'd killed some of the men, he could see, on approach; others he'd only injured. When he reached one of the soldiers who had multiple leg wounds, he picked up his booted foot and brought it down on the man's thigh.

Then he pointed the twin barrels of his shotgun in his face.

"What are ye doing here, Red? What d'ye want?" he asked him through clenched teeth. The man shook his head, so Bill leaned more heavily on the thigh. There was a howl of pain. "I'm not a patient bloke. Tell me!"

"*Poshyol ty*!" Bill had no idea what it meant, but the way the man spat this out told him he was getting nothing.

"Fair enough," said Bill, taking his boot off the wound long enough to kick the man across the face.

He made his way a little further down the slope, to the dead locals. The women and children among them eased his conscience somewhat about the killing he'd done that day.

Then he heard the groaning. One of the 'dead' was trying to speak. Bill whirled around and immediately went over, getting down on the ground beside him. The man was in his thirties, with a kind face. His thick woollen jumper was stained crimson where the soldiers' bullets had eaten into him.

"Easy lad," said Bill, and though it would leave himself vulnerable to attack he placed the man's head on his knee. "What happened 'ere?"

The man's eyes were glassy, but Bill knew he could still see him. He winced when he tried to talk, but forced the words out anyway. "H... huh... hit us hard... without warning... jeeps and....bikes...and..." The man attempted to shake his head. "We made a stand... but we were no m-match for 'em..."

"Judas Priest," Bill said under his breath. "I don't understand this." The man groaned again, in terrible pain from the bullet wounds. And something else. As Bill's eyes were drawn down the man's body, he saw an object sticking out of his side. It had snapped off almost completely when he fell to the ground – after being raked with bullets – but there was no mistaking the crossbow bolt that was wedged in there. Bill would recognise one of those anywhere.

Quickly, he cast his eyes across the rest of the bodies. Sure enough, he saw it at least a half dozen times. More of the bolts sticking out of people, a way of slowing them down for the infantrymen to pick them off.

"Who did this?" Bill asked the man.

He looked annoyed and answered, "Soldiers," as if he resented the waste of his dying breaths.

Bill shook his head and pointed to the broken bolt. "No, who did this to you? T' the rest of those people. I seen it before, y'see."

The man appeared confused, then it dawned on him what Bill meant. "The... the giant..."

"What?"

"B-big man... olive skin..."

"Shooting people wi' a crossbow," Bill finished for him. The man nodded, then hissed in agony.

It couldn't be. I killed him.

Bill had definitely shot him, square in the chest as far as he could tell – though it had been pretty hard to concentrate on anything when that bolt had punched into him. They'd never found a body, though, had they? In spite of searching, when everything had calmed down. Nothing in the wreckage from the platform; neither Jack nor Mark had seen anything. But still... How could it be? And what was he doing with Russians?

Well, he'd been with the Frenchman, hadn't he? He'd been with the German, the Italian and Mexican. Used them. Race meant nothing to Tanek, only the need to destroy and take what he could for himself.

Bill was brought back to the here and now when the man began to convulse. "Easy," said Bill again. But the man couldn't hear him anymore. Bill held him tightly by the shoulders. When the convulsions ended and the man went limp, Bill closed the dead man's eyes.

He stood, feeling numb: none of his original questions answered, and a whole lot more lumped on the pile. If Tanek really had returned, bringing with him another army, then there was only one place they could be heading. As he was righting himself, though, at least one of the mysteries was solved. Across the sea, and almost obscured from view by an outcropping, he could see some kind of ship. Bill took a pair of binoculars out of his pocket and looked through them. Maybe it was just the light, but it looked slightly silvery, and it had three big fans on its back. It resembled a grey slab of concrete on the water, resting above the waves on a black skirt.

"A bloody hovercraft!" said Bill.

But only one of them, and now he remembered what that lookout at Whitby had said: "Several things." Bill had no clue what one of those brutes could carry in terms of equipment, men and vehicles, but he was guessing it wasn't to be sniffed at. Imagine what had come across in a handful, splitting up and branching out to land at different points along the coast so they could take out observers before a flag could be raised. Bill was betting the army would rendezvous somewhere inland before heading on for their final destination. "Shit," he added for good measure.

Time he wasn't here. Jamming the other rifles under his arm and stuffing anything else he could find of use into a backpack one of the soldiers had been wearing (grenades, knives and spare ammo), Bill began the task of climbing back up towards his chopper. Hopefully before anyone over at the hovercraft realised something was amiss.

What he was going to do first, he didn't have a clue. Deep down he knew not only was the region in danger again, but probably his friends as well.

And he realised they'd only been in the middle of the calm before the next storm. A lull which had made them complacent.

All of this and more was buzzing round Bill's mind as fast as the rotor blades on his helicopter when he started her engine.

Everything being mulled over, especially Tanek, always Tanek, as he made his way upwards and eventually away from Robin Hood's Bay.

CHAPTER TEN

"ARE YOU SURE this is such a good idea?"

If he'd been asked that once today, he'd been asked it a million times. By Mary – of course – by Jack, and now the one person he'd thought would be guaranteed to be on his side: Mark. This was for *his* benefit, after all.

Wasn't it?

Mostly. Robert was finally beginning to concede that the boy was getting older, that maybe it was time he started his training in earnest – and that didn't just mean messing about on the Bailey with Jack and the other men. It meant taking him out to where he himself had learnt his skills.

Where Robert had become the Hooded Man.

"Sherwood? Are you serious?" That had been Mary. "You can't go off again now, with everything that's happening."

Jack had broached similar concerns. They were only just starting to figure out the cult, with Tate's help, and for their leader to keep vanishing like this...

"I'm not vanishing. You know where I'll be if you need me," he argued. The first trip to Hope had been essential. This one they really didn't understand, and his flimsy explanation about Mark hadn't cut it. Especially after he'd been the one who kept knocking the boy back, telling him he wasn't ready.

Robert couldn't blame them for being freaked out, not after the incident at the Britannia. Mary had only just been able to save Geoff Baker's life. She'd set to work straight away after getting there, apparently taking the corpse slumped across the table in her stride. Then she'd had Geoff moved somewhere they could treat him properly. Mary hadn't even acknowledged Robert or Tate's presence.

Though that was understandable with her hands full, Robert still had a niggling feeling she was punishing him.

Later, when Geoff was stable – though there was still a good chance he wouldn't see the next dawn – Mary had demanded to see Robert and Tate alone in one of the small conference rooms at the hotel. That was when she'd asked them what they thought they were playing at, interrogating a prisoner without her present, with only Lucy on hand to deal with the medical side of things. "What were you thinking?" she'd asked, pacing up and down in front of them.

"There wasn't time, Mary," Robert told her.

"No time to let me know you were back, either," commented Mary with a sour face. "But time to send for me when Geoff had been attacked?"

"Lucy had given the Servitor –"

"The what?"

"It's what they call themselves. Anyway, Lucy had given him something to calm him down. He was secured. We didn't think –"

"No, you didn't, did you?" Mary sighed. "Look, some people's reactions to any drugs can be totally unexpected. Obviously the Chlorpromazine had the opposite effect of that intended."

Tate was seated on one of the chairs, tapping his stick with a finger. "Can I just ask, Mary – and by the way, it's nice to see you again." His smile was weak, but sincere. "Could it also have made him stronger?"

"It's possible, yes," Mary admitted. "And it's nice to see you again, too, Reverend. I wish it was under better circumstances."

When they'd finished going over what had taken place, possible causes and reasons, and coming to no definitive conclusions, Tate had left to go and get settled back at the castle, he'd be staying there until this mess with the cult was sorted out. Robert and Mary had hung back in the room, at first hardly able to even look at each other. It was Robert who broke the silence first.

"I'm sorry."

"For what? For leaving so suddenly, or not saying a thing when you got back?"

"For whatever it is I'm supposed to be apologising about this time." It hadn't been the wisest thing he'd ever said.

"How about for giving Adele the run of our bedroom?" Mary had said, hands on hips.

"What?"

"You heard me."

Robert wracked his brains. Had he done that? He didn't remember it... maybe something about borrowing anything if she needed it, but he just assumed she'd ask first. Robert shook his head. This wasn't really about privacy, no more than it had been the other day. This was about him and Mary. About how strong they were together – or, right now, not.

"You've got to stop this, Mary. Adele is –"

"I know exactly what she is – and what she's after," Mary stated emphatically. "What I *don't* know is whether she's being encouraged."

"It's been another long day, I've just been wrestling with a maniac and almost seen one of my friends die right in front of me. I haven't got time for this nonsense."

"I understand," she'd told him; he could feel the chill in her words.

Robert followed Tate's lead, leaving Mary alone in the room. He hadn't seen her again until that night, when he'd felt her climb into bed. Part of him just wanted to reach out and put an arm around her, snuggle up tight and forget everything else. But his stubborn pride got in the way: wait and see if she does it first. She didn't. In fact, she edged as far away from him as possible.

It was as he was lying there awake again that he'd thought of a solution. Things were falling apart rapidly, not only in his personal life, but in every other department. He didn't know how to fight monsters like the one who'd broken free at the Britannia – it was so far removed from his experience. He knew his men were being spread too thinly, both on patrol and looking after the prisoners they'd captured. Robert not only needed to get away from the chaos and confusion for a while, to rediscover who exactly he was, he needed some kind of guidance.

He needed to be back in his one, true home.

So yes, Mark had been an excuse if he was honest – but Robert saw no harm in that. If the youth was one day to take all this over, which was Robert's hope, then he needed to begin where Robert had. Needed to experience what he'd experienced out in the wilderness, or at least start his journey there.

It hadn't gone down well. Mary believed it was just another excuse to get away (from her, though she only implied the last bit). "Go, then. It's obviously where you'd prefer to be right now," she'd sniped.

Meanwhile Jack was worried about the new threat they were facing. "I thought you were, too, Robbie. The kid's training's going okay on the castle grounds."

"There are things I can show him at Sherwood that no-one can show him here. Things I never taught any of the troops when we were living there."

Jack had accepted it, but didn't like it.

Tate, on the other hand, never said a word. It was almost like he knew why Robert was making this pilgrimage, and why he wasn't going alone. He'd merely blessed him and said he would pray for his speedy return. "Bring wisdom back with you," Tate had said.

"I'll try, Reverend."

Mark had been all for it initially. But now, on their way to the forest on horseback, he asked Robert if he knew what he was doing. "I don't want to take you away from important things at the castle," he said, riding at a trot alongside.

"This is important, Mark. What we're doing here. But you're not the only reason we're heading back to Sherwood."

"I'm not?"

Robert leaned across and clapped him on the shoulder. "No. This trip's for me as well. I need to reconnect with something I've lost."

"Oh, okay." They rode for a moment more in silence. "Talking of which," broached Mark hesitantly, "you and Mary."

"Not you as well!" Robert gave him a stern look. It was the face he'd pulled when Mark had first followed him into the forest, first begun pestering him to help them against De Falaise. He'd eventually accepted his other role as well, his relationship with the boy growing, each of them replacing something – someone – they'd lost during the virus. But that didn't mean he could be as cheeky as he liked. "There's nothing to discuss, Mark. Drop it."

"But you need to reconnect with something back there as well, don't you see?"

"Since when did you become the fount of all knowledge?"

Mark laughed. "I always have been, didn't you notice? You two are good together."

"You think I don't know that?"

"I do, and that's the pity. You've lost your way a bit, that's all. What is it you say to me, face your fear?"

"And how about you and Sophie? How's it going there, bigshot?" Robert knew it wasn't really fair to turn this around on Mark, but the boy had asked for it. God, teenagers thought they knew it all, didn't they? But Robert had to stop and remind himself that this wasn't any ordinary teen, not like those he used to see on street corners with their mates during his time on the beat. Mark had already seen more than he should have of life's horrors, and perhaps that afforded him some leeway. Only not to discuss Robert's private life, and not this, frankly.

Mark reacted as if slapped. "There is no me and Sophie. That's the trouble. If we had what you and Mary had... still have, then..."

Robert held up his hand. "I told you, let that drop." But then he couldn't help digging himself deeper. "Jack told me about the fight, you know. You're a brave guy, taking on Dale. He's one of the best fighters I've got."

Mark grunted. "He's not so tough."

"Heard you gave him a bloody nose." Robert smiled. "That makes you pretty good, too, in my book." Mark joined him in the smile. "Mind if I ask what he did to deserve it? Jack told me about the song. He was just pulling your leg, the men do it all the time with each other."

"The *men*," said Mark, heavily.

"Ah, I see. You're fed up of being treated like a younger brother or something."

"Brother?" Mark let out a long, mournful breath. "Yeah, I guess that's how Sophie sees me."

"I meant Dale and the blokes. But now I see what's at the bottom of all this. She doesn't treat *him* like a brother, does she? Dale, I mean?" Mark shook his head.

"Women, eh?" said Robert, then waited for the smile to broaden; and for it to become another laugh. "They operate on a whole other level, Mark. Out here it's simple. Even in a fight, it's simple. But relationships..."

The horses made their way up one final road. Robert saw the faded brown signs saying 'Sherwood Forest National Nature Reserve,' and indicated they should turn in there. Normally, he would have entered the less obvious way, but he wanted to show Mark something before they got to all the survival stuff.

"Come on," he said to the boy, urging his horse to speed up a little and taking them through the first and biggest of the car parks. He looked around, admiring the way the forest had taken back what belonged to it, punching through concrete and bitumen in many places, overrunning the dividing posts and benches where families would have had their picnics in summer months. Where he'd once brought Stevie and Joanna to do the same.

Swinging down from their steeds, the pair walked them down an overgrown trail, marked out by fences, and left them with plenty of hay inside the abandoned and rundown 'Forest Table' – once a thriving eating place for visitors to Sherwood. They walked on into the middle of the Visitor's Centre, with its focal point: the peeling statue of two legendary figures battling it out with staffs. "Reminds me of the night we met Jack. Remember?" said Mark.

Robert did. He'd assumed – wrongly, as it turned out – that Jack had been sent into the woods to assassinate him. He was actually auditioning, as he called it (Jack and his movies!) for the role of the man in front of them. One of the old Hood's most faithful companions. It had worked out similarly this time around as well, Robert had to agree. He didn't know now what he'd do without the hulking American by his side.

Robert lit a couple of torches, then led Mark inside a big building off to their left, forcing open a stiff door. As they stepped inside, Mark could see through into a deserted shop on his right. It looked like a cave filled with ancient treasure. Cobwebs covered everything: from toy bows and swords to hats with feathers in them; from mugs and plates to pens, badges and notebooks. Ahead of them, though, was an exhibition – which, via winding corridors, told the history of the original Hooded Man. Robert took them past another statue of that man, in a more familiar pose, about to loose an arrow. This, too, was covered in cobwebs. As they ventured further inside, there were more representations, including one of the Sheriff of Nottingham in full panto villain mode, rubbing his chin.

"What are we doing here?" asked Mark. "It's all a bit creepy."

Robert knew what he meant: the parallels were too close for comfort. But there was a purpose, as he showed him soon enough. Behind the wooden walls of the displays, Robert had hidden an entire arsenal of weapons. Dotted throughout the exhibition were dozens of real bows and swords, bolas made from twine and rocks, and quivers bristling with arrows, even spare clothes. It was his own private stash.

"The stock room we passed on the way in was far too obvious, and at any rate, I didn't want them all in one place," he explained. "I came back a while ago. Thought I'd leave all this in case of an emergency."

"What kind of emergency?"

Robert shrugged. "It wouldn't be an emergency if I knew."

The boy was studying his features in the light from the burning torches. "You've never really considered that castle your home, have you?" Once again, he had to hand it to him – the fount of all knowledge. "Is that why you left this lot, because you thought you'd be back one day?"

Robert didn't answer that. "I just wanted to show someone. Not even Mary knows."

Mark gave Robert a hand concealing the weapons again, then they made their way up and through the final winding corridor. Before they came to the exit, both of them paused. In a display on their right, behind cracked and smeared glass, an arrow was embedded in some earth. "'And where this arrow is taken up,'" read Mark, "'There shall my grave be.'"

Robert pushed him out by the shoulder. "Not yet, you don't."

THE PAIR HEADED deep into the forest, with Robert preferring to make a new camp rather than seeking out an old one.

He'd noticed a change in himself almost as soon as he'd entered the place. His body had relaxed, but was still coiled and ready to attack if provoked; just like it had been when he'd first moved here. His mind was more balanced than it had been in a long time. Robert had seen Sherwood in all seasons, so the bare trees were not a shock to him – they only added to the beauty of the place on this winter's day, especially with the sprinkling of snow on them.

When they'd found the right spot – somewhere that was hard to locate if an intruder might be looking for it, but gave them a clear 360° view of the area – they set up their camp. "Your base camp should be the safest location in your territory," Robert said.

"This is all so cool," Mark told him. "Do you know how often I wished you'd teach me all this stuff when we were here before?"

Robert gave a half smile. "Well now I am, so pay attention."

He went through how to make a lean-to, using branches for poles and whatever foliage they could find – not easy at this time of year – then how to make a bed out of moss.

"Okay, time to go hunting," announced Robert. Nothing big at first; a couple of hares, which they staked out near a warren. "Rabbits and hares don't hibernate in the winter," Robert explained in hushed tones, "but fortunately for us they become slower and less active to conserve energy. So they're easier to catch when they're rattled. Now keep well out of sight. Always let them come out into the open – then deliver your surprise."

Mark had grumbled a little about preying on such easy targets but, as Robert informed him, when you lived out here, sometimes meat was in short supply. You took what you could find. Besides which, hare was tasty.

When they returned to camp, Robert taught him how to make a fire, tucking away the lighter and forcing Mark to use the traditional method, rubbing sticks together. When the boy had built up a sweat, Robert chuckled and finally showed him how to use a bow.

That night they cooked the animals over a spit and talked more about their time together here before. Most of the stories started, "Do you remember..." and Robert was surprised by how many ended with them both laughing. It had been a trying period, out here waiting to be discovered or killed by De Falaise's troops, but it was also, in some ways, a happy time. With each moment that passed that evening, Robert was more convinced he'd done the right thing by bringing Mark here.

As the fire died down a little, Robert caught Mark resting against his backpack and looking at his missing finger, lost in thought. "You still think about what happened back then, don't you?"

"Don't you?" Mark said, tossing aside a piece of bone he'd picked clean and taking a swig of the water they'd boiled down from snow.

Robert nodded. "It takes a while to come to terms with our demons, whatever shape they take."

"Is this about facing your fear again?"

"Sort of. Only sometimes we get to face it in the flesh." Robert poked the fire, then jabbed a finger at it. "That was one of mine."

"Yeah, I remember what happened when the Mexican used those incendiary grenades. It sent you almost to pieces."

Robert stared directly at him. "It made me weak, that fear."

"Some folk might say it made you human," Mark countered.

"Being human can get you killed."

"Or save you. Are you ever going to tell me why it frightens you so much?"

His house on fire, the men in yellow suits cooking his wife and son, dead upstairs in the bedroom. His dog, Max, limping out, fur alight...

Robert ignored the question, and rolled onto his back, looking up into the night sky. "The stars seem so much clearer out here. Everything's clear, in fact. No distractions."

"You're going to have to open up someday," he heard Mark comment. "To me, Mary. Maybe even Reverend Tate."

"What I'm doing now," Robert broke in, totally off topic, "with you, I mean. Someone else did the same with me. His name was Eric Meadows. He showed me the ropes."

"I don't underst –"

"And do you know the most important thing, the first thing I learned from him?" Robert couldn't see Mark shaking his head, but he supposed he was. "To keep my mouth shut and listen." He rolled back onto his side, resting his head against his hand and looking past the fire at Mark. "He was older than me, more experienced. So I listened."

Mark looked down into the fire. "And was there ever a time when you were able to help him?"

Like most of Mark's questions, this caught him off guard, but his mind supplied an answer. Another memory, not buried, just forgotten until now. Of Robert and Eric being called to a fight in a bar, where two twenty-somethings had decided to kick off over a girl who looked like she wanted nothing to do with either of them. By the time they'd arrived, the men were smashing bottles and throwing punches, so Eric had been the first to wade in. What he hadn't spotted was that one of the guys had mates in the corner, who came at Eric and were about to glass him when Robert stepped in. Several years down the line from the first collar he'd made, and he was a different officer. Confident, though not a risk-taker (because he had a wife to return to and they were planning on starting a family soon), but able to assess a situation like this and turn it to his advantage.

Robert had kicked the glass out of the attacker's hand, then followed up with a punch that sent him to the floor. Technically not the done thing, but Robert wasn't about to play nice in this situation. He'd been ready to tackle the others as well, but when the fighters heard sirens outside – Eric and Robert's backup – they'd fled the pub. Eric had cuffed the two original trouble-makers, leaving Robert to handle his. So he had no idea whether his mentor knew he'd probably saved his skin that night. Neither of them said anything to each other – it was all in a day's work for Her Majesty's Constabulary – though Robert often wondered if he realised the favour had been returned.

But that wasn't what Mark had asked, was it? Had Robert been able to help him? Truly *help* him? Where was he when Eric had been injured at that football match? Robert couldn't even remember now. On holiday? Seconded to one of the CID units? He hadn't been able to help Eric when it came to the real crunch, had he? Only postponed the inevitable.

"Never let them put you behind one of those. You stay out there, young Stokes. Stay where you can make a difference and leave all that to the paper pushers."

Was that what this was all about? Did he need to get back out there for Eric, do something for the man even though he was probably dead by now? Robert had absolutely no idea what his blood group was, but he had to be pushing seventy even if he had survived.

Robert realised that long minutes had passed and he hadn't said a word in reply to Mark. "I'm... I'm sorry. Just remembering something."

"About when you were able to help this Eric guy?" asked Mark, looking up at him.

"I think in my own way I'm helping him right now," Robert replied, not even attempting to explain. He wasn't sure he understood himself.

The fire was really dropping now, so they said their goodnights and retreated to their lean-tos. Robert faster than Mark, if anything. Not to get out of the cold, but to do what he'd come here to do all along: sleep.

And hope that the forest would find it in its heart to speak to him.

CHAPTER ELEVEN

AT FIRST HE thought one of the sparks from the fire must have caused it.

Set this whole portion of the forest alight. Robert felt dreadful; how could he have done this to his beloved home? The bark was on fire, the branches and twigs. It was a good thing there were no leaves; they would only have added to the conflagration. He looked around, frantically trying to find something to douse the flames with. If they'd been closer to the lake at Rufford, then –

But they weren't. Robert had chosen this spot intentionally to be away from the locations he'd lived in alone, when he'd first come here. The locations he'd been drawn to so he could while away the rest of his time and die; be with his late wife and child. To run away from...

From the blaze.

But he was wasting time now, thinking about all that. He should be waking Mark, getting him to help put out this fire. Robert couldn't see the boy's lean-to anywhere – couldn't see his own, for that matter. Perhaps they'd both been burnt away? If that was the case, was Mark all right?

A sudden wave of heat forced Robert to shield his face. He tottered backwards. Then, through the shimmering air, he saw a figure caught in the midst of the licking flames. Blinking, he tried to make out the features, but they were unclear. Once, he would have held back, no matter what – not even attempted to go into the heart of this inferno. Now Robert braced himself and, head down, rushed in to get closer to the figure. It was about Mark's height, could easily be him. Robert hoped not, because even now whoever it was was catching light, going up like the forest around them.

"Hold on," Robert shouted. "I'm coming." He was aware that he must be cooking as well, but had to push through, had to save Mark. He'd lost too much to the fire already, he wasn't about to lose the closest thing he had to a son as well.

Robert broke through into a clearing, the flames raging around him but not touching this section of the forest. In fact the only thing on fire was the figure directly ahead of him. Robert sucked in air, coughing, then refocused. He soon realised his mistake. This wasn't Mark at all; nothing like him. There, not ten feet away from him, was his old enemy: De Falaise.

Yes, he was on fire – the yellow and red rippling over him, but apparently not eating him up. Robert was shocked. The last time he'd seen this man, he'd killed him, and a blaze had played around them that day too. There was evidence of Robert's attack: De Falaise no longer had eyes – and even though he was opening and closing his mouth, the Frenchman couldn't speak (Robert having shoved an arrow as far down his throat as he could ram it). The arrow that had penetrated his heart – like a stake finishing off a vampire – was missing, but the hole was plainly there. De Falaise was saying something, but it was so faint Robert couldn't make it out.

It sounded like one word over and over.

Vengeance.

De Falaise smiled, those broken teeth even more yellow in the flames. The Frenchman opened his arms wide and let the full force of the fire take him, and this time it did crisp his skin, blackening his face and exposed hands. His dress suit – the one he'd worn for the executions at the castle – melted onto him, then that too turned black. Robert stood watching, knowing he couldn't do a thing. Not really wanting to. This was a replay of past events – slightly different, but still a replay. What he wanted to know about was the future, about his new enemies.

As if to answer him directly, the figure burnt brighter... and redder. It took a step towards him, and when it did, some of the black crust fell away. What was beneath was red, and it merged with the fire: creating a figure that was crimson from the feet upwards. Robert's mouth dropped open as he witnessed this transformation. That's the only way he could describe it, a fiery phoenix rising from the ashes. Dressed head to toe in red leather.

The build of the two men was similar, but Robert could see they were very different. This person was stockier, looked like he could really handle himself. Looked like he had seen some action in the past, not just ordered people to their deaths. And he looked... somehow regal. Like the campfire from the night before, the flames died down, and when they did, the man pulled on his greatcoat. Then he placed a peaked cap on his head.

He smirked at Robert. There was no denying the intent was the same. He was here to destroy the Hooded Man, just as the Sheriff had set out to do. Was this the distant future; some kind of reincarnation, perhaps? Robert had no idea, and no more time to ponder, because the fire surrounding them was also changing.

Robert looked to his left and right. There were faces there; faces painted white and black like skulls, with tattoos on their foreheads. *Yes, them! I came here to learn about them*, Robert told the dreamscape, told the forest. *I need to know how to defeat them*. If I *can defeat them!*

Except behind the figures were more people, faces without make-up. The faces of soldiers, carrying automatic weapons. The ground was shaking – Robert felt the vibrations up through his legs, into his guts. To his left, breaking through the ground and knocking charred trees aside, a huge tank shot upwards and righted itself with a metallic *clang*. To Robert's left, an armoured vehicle did the same, followed by a couple of jeeps. In the centre of the burning scene was suddenly an army of two factions. Impossible to fight alone.

Where were his people? Where were his troops?

There were shadows behind the man in red, stepping out. Two Asian women, Robert saw, and a man in a sharp suit. Each was holding a body by the scruff of its neck, which they threw to the ground in front of Robert. The first belonged to Tate, lifeless and limp. Then came Sophie, piled on top. Followed by Mary. Robert's entire body stiffened when he saw her tossed there, like a Guy on a funeral pyre. Her beautiful eyes looked up at him in death.

"*No!*" he screamed. "You can't do this!"

A larger shadow emerged, carrying two bodies – one in each hand. But he could manage them well enough, the size that he was. Robert's jaw dropped again when he saw Tanek, the Frenchman's second, assumed dead but very much alive here. (Though hadn't De Falaise been standing there only moments before? Living or deceased, it didn't mean a thing in this place.)

The two last bodies were thrown over towards Robert, Tanek grunting – more with satisfaction than effort. Robert recognised who they were as they landed: Jack, defeated and deflated... and Mark. Finally Mark. Beaten to a pulp and with more than his finger missing.

Robert sank to his knees, tears flowing freely. He knew it wasn't a good idea to show weakness in front of his enemies, but couldn't help it. When he reached up to wipe the salt water away, he found his face altered. There were antlers on the side of his head. He had a snout too. As he looked up again, Tanek was approaching with that crossbow of his raised, a bolt in the chamber pointing at him. The shot was fired and, though it entered Robert's temple, he could somehow still hear and see everything around him: the flames, the assembled war machine. Tanek crouching, letting go of the crossbow and taking out a knife with a serrated edge.

Robert's vision went black for a second then red, like a filter had been placed over a camera lens. Tanek finished his cutting, sawing, stood again with something in his free hand. Robert's... the stag's head.

He handed the gory thing to the man in leather, who took off his peaked cap and replaced it with the antlers.

In spite of the fire's warmth, Robert felt cold. It spread quickly throughout his body. If this was a vision of the future, as he'd wanted, then he was sorry he'd asked for it. Better to be ignorant than live with the knowledge that they would all soon die.

"Vengeance," said a voice close to his ear, a figure he couldn't see whispering to him. It sounded... familiar. De Falaise, but not him; the voice softer.

Then he felt hands on him, moving him.

Moving his corpse.

IT WAS A revelation when he found he could move – grabbing the hands shaking him. "N-not dead," Robert mumbled. "Not dead!"

"Sshh. Keep it down," another voice whispered, a different voice. "We're not alone."

Robert shook his head, clearing it. It had been a while since he'd slept so heavily, had a dream as intense. He'd forgotten how disorientating it could be. Mark was the person by his side – not the dead, mutilated Mark, but the living Mark who he could still do something to save if he got his act together. Mark, who had been trying to wake him for some time.

"People, circling the camp," he told Robert. "I caught a glimpse when I got up to pee. I managed to crawl across to your lean-to without them seeing, I think."

"How many?" asked Robert in hushed tones.

Mark shrugged. "A couple, maybe."

"That's the next lesson, then. Counting." Mark scowled, then

Robert tapped him on his arm. "Come on, let's see what we're dealing with."

Grabbing his bow, arrows and sword, Robert emerged from the back of the lean-to with Mark beside him, using it to shield them both. Robert slipped the quiver and bow around his torso. It wasn't quite light, but the sun was close to the horizon, giving everything a strange sepia look. There was an early morning mist covering the ground, thin enough to see through close up, but out in the distance it could hide anything. Robert trusted the boy's instincts; after years of living on his wits, the lad had developed a sense about these things. He'd been the first to warn Bill about the attack on the market, and told Robert when Jack first entered Sherwood. Now he was telling him there was a potential threat in the woods, and Robert took that very seriously.

This was real hunting.

Mark nudged him and gestured towards a nearby tree on his right. He saw an elbow sticking out from behind the trunk. Robert nodded, then pointed across at another tree. Mark evidently couldn't see it, but there was bark missing from one side where someone had scraped by it. Robert turned when he heard a noise behind him. Mark may well have dismissed it as a woodland animal, but he knew better. Although it had been a while since he'd lived here, Robert still felt the rhythms of this place – could tell when there was something out of sync. He was surrounded, as in his dream. Robert just hoped the tanks and jeeps weren't about to shoot up from out of the ground.

He made a fanning-out gesture to Mark, who nodded. He hated having to split them up – especially when he could still picture the boy's dead face – but he knew Mark needed to do this as much as he did. Robert pulled up his hood and began to stalk his prey, vanishing into the undergrowth.

Keeping low to the ground, he backtracked round to where he'd heard the noise. Robert closed his eyes and breathed deeply, attempting to sense where the intruder was. Where the disturbance in his forest was rooted. It didn't prove difficult, not when the attacker suddenly showed himself and charged at Robert. He opened his eyes in time to see a flash of machete blade, a painted face leering down at him. A Servitor!

Robert took hold of the rushing figure, at the same time dodging the man's weapon, then used his own momentum against him, flinging him into a nearby birch. "Damned Halloween freak," he snarled. The tree leaned slightly and the robed man fell over it, landing on the other side. Robert was round it in seconds, bringing up a swift knee and clipping the cultist under the chin.

He was suddenly aware of two more attackers on either side of him. They appeared from behind trees and lunged at Robert, machete blades cutting through the morning air. He dodged one, then turned swiftly and ducked another. But as he came up again, he brought his clenched fist with him, practically lifting the Servitor off his feet with the punch. The next swing, Robert met with his own sword: metal striking metal. Gritting his teeth, he pushed the robed man backwards into a tree, winding him. Robert turned his back on the man, turned his sword around and thrust it backwards so that it slid into his attacker's side and out again very quickly, incapacitating him.

By this time the first attacker had recovered and was getting to his feet. Robert had time to quickly glance over and see how Mark was doing, now their cover was well and truly blown. He saw the boy facing at least three of the freaks himself, and he'd already been relieved of his sword.

Holding the sword by the flat of the blade, Robert brought the hilt down heavily on the approaching cultist's head. It struck him dead centre and he fell to his knees. Then Robert swung the sword like a baseball bat and hit the man in the face, sending his head rocking back and a few of his teeth flying.

Unslinging his bow as he went, Robert pulled out an arrow and aimed across to where Mark was fighting, kicking the first Servitor who'd attacked to keep him down. Just as he was about to shoot, though, a half dozen more of the men rose up from the mist or stepped out from behind trees.

"Crap," said Robert under his breath. Mark was on his own, at least for now. He turned the bow on the nearest of the approaching cult members.

WHAT HAD BEEN his first mistake?

Mark was asking himself this even as he realised it was probably the worst time to be doing so. It was only what Jack would ask him later, if there was a later, but this clearly wasn't the time for analysis. He'd blundered in, hadn't he? Gone for the guy with his elbow sticking out, thinking he was an easy target. But then he'd realised, when the figure stepped out and confronted him, that the Servitor had been expecting the strike all along. What the hell was the matter with him? Mark had been so quiet and nimble as a boy, slipping in and out of cities and towns for supplies, scavenging them and stuffing them into his knapsack. But creeping up on people? Not so great at that.

The noise had brought another one out of the trees, and now Mark understood what Robert had been pointing at. Another hiding behind an oak, the bark worn off. He should have taken one out at a distance with a rock, then –

Swish!

Mark was suddenly stumbling backwards. This wasn't a training sword anymore, but the real thing, held by someone who really did want to do him some harm. He reached for his own blade, but had only got it part of the way free before he felt it being lifted out by a third cultist who had appeared seemingly from nowhere. The sword was snatched away and thrown into the snowy grassland beyond the trees.

Swish!

Again Mark only just had time to dodge the blow, as it whistled past his right ear. Stepping back did, however, have the added benefit of knocking the man behind him off-balance, so that Mark could topple him fully over.

Now there were only two to deal with. And where was Robert? Having fun with his own playmates; Mark saw more and more – rising out of the ground itself, it seemed.

"You think you're always going to have a weapon to hand? Uh-uh. Nope. But your opponent might."

That's what Jack had said, and he'd been right. Mark didn't have his sword, and they each had one. Well, really big knives that you could probably call swords, but that was splitting hairs. *Think, Mark, think...* how had Azhar done it again?

Mark recalled the way that man had ducked and slid sideways to take the weapon from him. He had just seconds to react, to copy the move he'd witnessed. Now it wasn't a game, Mark found his body co-operating, his movements less clumsy. Mark grabbed his opponent's wrist and yanked, but the weapon wouldn't tug free. The cultist pulled back and readied himself for another thrust. Thinking fast, Mark let his backpack – only hanging over one shoulder – slide down his arm; then, as the blade came into range, he wrapped the thing in the material, yanking down until the machete fell out of the man's hands. As Mark bent forward to retrieve it, the first attacker fell over him and he instinctively followed through: standing and flipping him, letting his attacker's momentum do all the work.

Snatching up the machete, Mark met the second attacker's swing; the clash made his teeth rattle. The third joined in and suddenly Mark had to block his blows as well. That was one of the major differences between real combat and practising on your own: trees and fences didn't fight back. These people did, and by all accounts they didn't stop till one of you had stopped for good.

Mark batted away the attacks, using sheer desperation rather than finesse to carry him through. It was keeping him alive... so far. What he didn't know was how he was going to keep this going indefinitely, especially as the remaining cultist was rising from the floor. Rising, and searching around for Mark's sword.

What would Robert do in this situation? he wondered. What was he doing right now, in fact?

That wasn't the right thing to ask, to get him out of this – so he asked himself quickly instead: *What would Dale do?*

What would Dale do if Sophie was watching?

And what would you *do, Mark? What would you do to show her you can cut it?*

Cut... cut... Mark grinned. He'd had an idea. Letting the pair he was dealing with get a little closer, though not too close, he pretended to trip.

"Mark!" He heard the anguished cry from across camp, Robert thinking he was injured. Mark didn't have time to answer him. Instead, he lashed out at the men's legs, catching calf muscles and shins beneath the material of the robes. One spun around and Mark took the opportunity of hamstringing him, drawing the blade across where he judged the back of the heel to be.

It had the desired effect. Both men dropped, screaming.

Mark clambered to his feet, the smile spreading across his face.

"Mark!" came the cry again, and he couldn't understand why Robert was still calling. He'd taken down the two –

He remembered too late about the third, the one who'd been reaching for his sword. Mark pivoted, but at pretty much the same time the arrow flew past and into the fellow about to embed the sword in his head. The projectile's tip found the tattoo on the cultist's forehead, as if it were a bull's eye target, and he fell backwards.

When Mark looked across he saw the base camp littered with robed figures, arrows sticking out of various parts of their bodies. Robert was running over and waving something to Mark.

"...let them commit suicide..." the Hooded Man was saying. Mark didn't understand. Then he looked down at one of the men he'd crippled, saw him take his own machete with both hands, then ram it into his stomach. Mark felt his lip curling. The other one was doing similarly, except he was letting gravity do the work for him, lifting himself up as high as he could on his knees and just letting himself drop onto the blade.

Mark joined Robert, checking around to make sure no more were laying in wait. When he reached him, Mark saw he was crouching down next to one of the last cultists alive; the first proper rays of sunlight streaking through the trees onto the scene.

"And... and... he was cast... down," hissed the white-faced man, an arrow sticking out of his side, "on... onto the Earth... and his angels... were cast.... cast down also..." Then he took hold of his head and snapped it sideways, breaking his own neck.

Robert removed his hood and looked at Mark. "Are you alright, son?" Mark never tired of hearing Robert call him that. He nodded. "I didn't know there would be quite so many, or I never would've suggested... But, you did well today. I'm proud of you. Jack would be, too."

"How did they find us here?" Mark asked when he'd finally got his breath back.

Robert stared down at the corpse. "I think we've made an enemy of these guys. They're keeping tabs on us now, just like we've been doing with them. They're worried I'm going to stop their master from making his grand appearance."

"Master?"

"The Devil."

"Oh... What was he talking about just then, before..."

"Tate'll be able to tell us more about that. They seem to think they're fallen angels or something. Explains why they're not scared of dying. They probably believe they come right back again, fighting fit."

"That's scary."

"Fanatics usually are. But that's not what scares me the most." He looked at Mark's puzzled expression. "I think there could be something else coming. Something much more frightening."

Mark didn't ask him how he knew that, because he'd heard some of the mutterings before he'd woken Robert from his sleep.

Besides, Robert hadn't been the only one who'd had dreams last night.

ONE MORE SET of eyes had been watching the camp from close by that morning, had been watching most of the night.

They'd seen the Servitors make their way through the forest, taking their positions outside where Robert and the boy were spending the night. Had seen the boy get up to go to the toilet, spot something and then rush back to Robert's tent to warn him.

Had watched the fight with interest. More than interest: excitement. A tingling that had spread through the body until the last cultist had been defeated. It had almost been as good as being in the middle of it all, back in York.

From behind the oak, Adele let out the breath she'd been holding. And smiled. She'd enjoyed this little episode, but she knew there were tastier treats to come. And she'd be right there in the middle of those, definitely. There with the man she was after.

Right there with the Hooded Man.

CHAPTER TWELVE

HE'D BEEN HEARING the rumblings of discontent for some time.

Dale had debated about saying something to someone, but was faced with a dilemma. He was 'one of the guys,' a member of the Sherwood Rangers who fought on the streets with his friends. Buddies that he'd made since coming to the castle last year. But he was also very close to Jack and Robert. If it wasn't for them, he might still be wandering around the country, looking for a place to fit in. A former lead singer and guitarist in a band, whose life had fallen to bits after the virus struck, and who'd drifted from town to town, city to city, with a guitar in one hand and his other hand folded into a fist.

He often thought back to those days before everyone got sick: to the gigs he'd played with the other guys – Abbott on bass, Lockley on drums and Paige on keyboards. Only she hadn't just been one of the guys, had she?

Paige and he had formed One Simple Truth together while they were studying music in college. They'd been good mates throughout the course, and it just seemed like a sensible progression, especially as they'd just started going out. Paige had a real natural beauty, and she'd come along at a time when he'd just started to notice the opposite sex. She could be a bit serious sometimes, though, which is why, initially, he left a lot of the songwriting to her. It wasn't that he couldn't do it – Dale could make up stuff on the spot if he had to – but she came up with the most soulful tunes.

When they advertised on the bulletin board for more band members, they'd had all kinds of responses – some genuine, some time-wasters. But they'd really gelled with the long-haired Lockley and bearded Abbott, especially in the jamming session the first time they all got together. Jesus, how he missed them!

The first few live shows at local pubs had been the pits; Dale had almost called it a day at one point. Paige persuaded him to go on, and to his surprise they started to develop a fan base – particularly amongst the college and uni crowd.

Then came bigger and better gigs, and soon the money they were getting made attending classes seem moot. They were making it anyway, practising what their tutors only preached. It wasn't long before a talent scout with an eye for the next big thing spotted them. They were signed to a small indie label, but that automatically meant bigger gigs, and supporting turns for artists much higher up the ladder. Local stations played a couple of their releases and they even found themselves being aired on BBC Radio.

By this time One Simple Truth – and specifically Dale – had attracted another following entirely. Girls would hang out at the stage doors after gigs just to try and get an autograph. Or a kiss. Paige said nothing because she knew, at the end of the day, he was still hers. But during the course of their journey, Dale discovered his own simple truth: he found it impossible to be tied down to just the one girl. He loved the adoration his – granted – limited fame brought him. And, girl by girl, tour by tour, he gave in to temptation.

Paige had confronted him, of course, and he hadn't even bothered to deny it. "What can I say? I have a weakness," he'd told her. When she'd threatened to walk from the band, he'd tried to talk her out of it, telling her she'd be slitting her own throat as well. "You're going to hold this against me, when we could be as big as Oasis or U2?"

The decision was taken out of her hands, because that's when the virus had struck. Dale watched his fellow band members die from that terrible disease, while he remained healthy.

Paige had been the first to fall ill, collapsing after a gig one night. She'd been rushed to hospital for tests – back before anyone fully realised what they were dealing with. "Tell me," Paige had said to him from her bed as they'd waited for her parents to get there from miles away. "Tell me you still love me."

He clasped her hand, but said nothing.

"Please," she whispered.

Dale had been about to lie to her when suddenly she'd had a seizure, coughing up blood onto the bed sheets. The doctors and nurses rushed in, flitting around. There was nothing they could do. They whisked Dale outside, but he'd already seen the worst – and when they came and told him half an hour later that she was dead, he couldn't believe what he was hearing.

He got drunk that night, asking himself what the hell was wrong with him. Why couldn't he have felt for Paige what she felt for him? Why couldn't he have committed to her when she'd been instrumental in getting them where they were?

His answer was to spend the night with some blonde girl he picked up in a hotel bar, someone who'd recognised him and he'd taken full advantage of the fact. He left early and hadn't seen her again. For all he knew she'd come down with the virus too, not long afterwards. Dale hadn't really paid it much mind.

He'd always been able to handle himself, a consequence of getting called a sissy for being interested in music growing up. The number of fights he'd been in to show them that no, he wasn't actually a sissy at all and would happily rearrange their faces... It had served him well, after everything went to rack and ruin, and he'd had to defend himself from all kinds of dangers. He'd even stood up to gangs when he came across them, though sometimes came off the worst and crawled away to lick his wounds.

When he'd heard about what they were doing at Nottingham Castle, something seemed to click. It was a chance to be a part of a group again, something that was being talked about. A major part of him knew he could do some good here, but how much of him wanted to join so he could be applauded again? So that he'd be sought after, not for his music this time, but because he could save the damsels in distress? If he could work his way up through the ranks, perhaps he would actually be a star once more?

Which brought him back to his dichotomy. Would keeping quiet about this hamper his relationship with Jack and Robert? Should he tell them about what he'd heard?

Not that Robert was here at the moment. He'd gone off with Mark, that little git who'd given him a bloody nose a couple of days ago. Dale realised that Mark would always be Robert's favourite – he'd heard the tales from the others about how the kid had been taken to the castle and tortured, then nearly hanged by the former sheriff. He was like a son to Robert, Dale got that. He also got that he himself was kind of a replacement for someone called Granger who'd been part of the final battle. Jack and Tate often remarked how much Dale reminded them of the guy, who'd given his life so that they could take the Castle. It was more than a bit annoying at times.

From his usual perch on the steps, Dale spotted Sophie walking through the grounds with Mary. Sophie. Now *she* was a prize worth possessing, a girl he thought he might be able to love. If he could figure out what love was. She'd shown more than an interest in him, that much was certain – but when push came to shove she'd turned him away. "Dale, don't," she'd said when he'd tried to kiss her the last time.

What was the reason? Was it Mark? The kid had feelings for Sophie, any fool could see that. But Dale had always assumed she wanted a real man, or at least someone old enough to vote and drink – or could have in the old world.

Sophie giving him the run around when all he wanted was... to show her how much she meant to him, suggested that she must have feelings for someone else. What right did he have to interfere with that? If he hadn't been able to love Paige, then perhaps he couldn't love anyone, even Sophie.

Dale shook his head. This wasn't what he should be thinking about at the moment. The discontentment and the griping of the men; and whether he should talk to –

"Jack!" he was shouting to the large man before he realised he was doing it. "Hey Jack!" Now he was getting up and waving, grabbing his guitar and dashing down the steps to catch Jack as he came out of a side door of the castle.

"Hey Dale," replied his superior. As always, he had his staff resting over his shoulder. "You haven't seen Adele on your travels, have you?"

Dale hadn't. And though he couldn't help it, a picture of the woman now flashed into his mind: her short black hair, her full lips. How he wished he'd been the one to save her that night in York rather than Robert.

Stop it, can't you see Jack fancies her? You just can't help yourself, can you?

"Not to worry," Jack said. Dale could tell he had more on his mind than where Adele was.

"Is everything okay?" he asked.

"Hmmm? Yeah. Well, no, not really. Did you want something?"

Dale thought about whether this was the right time, about whether he should even be speaking to Jack rather than Robert, but the words were escaping before he could contain them. "It's the men."

Jack turned to him. "What about them?"

"They're... I don't know how to say this."

"Just spit it out."

"They're overstretched, tired. They're beginning to moan about the workload, about patrols, about the last time they had any time off."

"Time off?" Jack said it like the concept was completely alien. "This isn't a damned holiday camp."

Dale held up his hands, his guitar flying out sideways. "I know that, and they do too. But, look, with this new thing – the cult – they've been run ragged trying to fight them. They're only human."

Jack gave a reluctant nod. "I understand. I just don't know what we can do about it. Maybe when we've got on top of this –"

"I don't know if you've got that long."

Jack sighed. "If you only knew." His face betrayed him. He knew something else he wasn't passing on... to Dale *or* the troops.

"What? Tell me." He didn't really have the right to demand any kind of information, but was hoping Jack might tell him anyway.

"I'd rather wait until... Robert!"

Dale followed Jack's gaze down to the gate, where Robert and Mark had appeared on horseback, returning from their visit to Sherwood.

Jack made his way briskly down to the riders, Dale not far behind. He ignored the glare from Mark, using Robert's second as a justification to be there.

"Robbie, I'm so glad that you're back," shouted the big man.

"So am I. In some ways," Robert said, then looked over at Mark. Dale realised that more than training had occurred in Sherwood. More secrets he wasn't yet privy to.

"I've got something to tell you," Jack said, walking up to the horse and stroking it. "Maybe someplace more private, y'know?"

"Could I just say something first?" Dale cut in.

"No," answered Mark without hesitation.

Robert gave the boy a severe look, then turned to Dale: "What is it?"

He studied them each in turn. "I know something's kicking off here. I just thought you ought to be aware that you could have some walkouts on your hands if you're not careful."

"Dale was just telling me that the men aren't too happy."

"Is that so?" Robert said as he dismounted.

"I don't want to go behind anyone's back or anything, just thought you needed to know the score." Dale told him.

"To be fair, they are being stretched a bit thin, Robbie. Possibly even thinner soon."

That was another slip, and now Dale was desperate to know what Jack had discovered. If they were about to face something else on top of the Morningstars, then he and the others had a right to know. They were the ones putting their lives on the line.

"Okay, Dale," said Robert finally, "we'll sort this out later." Dale was about to say something else, but he continued, "I promise. Right now I need to speak with Jack, probably as much as he does with me." Robert turned to his right hand man. "Fetch Tate and Mary, too. If you're about to tell me what I think you are, they should hear this as well."

Dale watched as Mark got off his horse, and the three of them made their way back up the path. Things hadn't quite gone as he'd expected them to. He'd jeopardised his standing in the ranks by telling Jack and Robert about the unrest, but still wasn't part of the inner circle. He'd been noticed by the talent-spotters, but not signed to a label yet. What made it worse was that Mark was turning as the group led the horses away, looking over his shoulder and glaring at Dale again. He was automatically included in the talks, as one of the core band that had come here. Could Dale's hard work all fall apart again because of a girl? Because of his messing about with Sophie, and Mark's feelings about that?

But Robert had promised to talk to him later, so he'd no doubt find out what was going on then. Better late than not at all.

Dale sat down on a bench and began to strum his guitar. One day when stories were written and songs sung about their exploits, Dale still intended to feature prominently.

THEY GATHERED IN one of the rooms inside the castle: Robert, Mark, Tate, Mary and Jack. All the original members of Robert's team, barring one, but it wasn't long before he was mentioned.

"This afternoon we received a radio message from Bill," Jack told them. He'd kept up with his CB interests after moving to the castle, as a way of keeping in touch with places beyond Nottingham. "Actually, it wasn't from Bill himself, it was from one of his... I dunno what you'd call 'em, staff?"

Robert shrugged his shoulders. Bill was a bit of a sore point.

"Anyhow, turns out there's a force that's hit the coastline up near Whitby, Scarborough, Bridlington. They used hovercraft to get their vehicles ashore: tanks, jeeps, the whole deal. And they've been striking villages and towns as they make their way inland. Bill's been monitoring the situation through his network of markets, getting to places that have been struck and offering help. Otherwise I think he would have come here in person to warn us."

"I know," said Robert simply, and Jack, Tate and Mary all looked at him. "About the army, I mean."

"Me too," added Mark, and they switched their focus to him.

"How?" asked Jack. "I only got the call a couple of hours ago, and you've been off in the forest."

Robert looked at Tate, who blinked his understanding. "You've just answered your own question, Jack," the Reverend said, though the American looked none the wiser. "They were in Sherwood."

"The man in charge is Russian, I think," continued Robert.

"I'll be goddamned," Jack said, blowing out a breath. "The radio message mentioned Russian troops."

"There's another thing." Robert walked around the room; Mark was biting his lip in anticipation of what was about to be said. "Tanek's with them."

"What?" said Tate, having to rest on his stick.

"It's true, Reverend. Robbie's three for three. That was also part of the warning."

All the colour had drained from Tate's face. "Dear Lord. And they're making their way here... this force?"

"Seems like," said Jack.

"If Tanek's involved, he'll probably be out for revenge," Robert said.

"I need to warn Gwen," Tate suddenly announced. "He'll be coming for her, without a doubt. She should be brought to the castle, don't you think? Her and Clive Jr?"

"If she'll come." Robert said.

"This is all we need on top of the cult," Jack said. "And if the men really are thinking about quitting –"

"What?" Tate virtually shrieked this. "They... they can't. We need them, now more than ever."

"Let's hope it doesn't come to that," Robert said. "We can't afford to lose a single fighter at the moment."

"Give 'em one of your patented speeches. Do the whole *Braveheart* bit," Jack suggested with a half smile, but there was little humour in his voice.

"The other thing is, we were attacked by members of the cult while we were in Sherwood. It was co-ordinated, intended to put me out of the picture." His eyes flitted across, searching for some kind of reaction from Mary, but there was none. She hadn't spoken, had barely been able to look at him since they'd all entered the room.

"You've rattled their cage," Tate said.

Robert ignored this and dwelt on Mary. "You've been very quiet, don't you have anything to say to all this?"

Mary looked him in the eye then, before speaking. "What's the point? You were in danger again in Sherwood. I know what you're going to do now about the army heading our way. It doesn't matter what I have to say, does it? You'll do what you have to do."

"Of course it matters, Mary," said Mark after a few moments, speaking for Robert because it didn't look like he was going to.

"I hate to say it, but the little lady's right – we are going to have to do what's necessary," Jack said.

"We're going to have to meet the army before it gets here," Robert stated. "We have to protect the people."

Mary nodded, then left the room.

Mark looked from the open door to Robert, his eyes begging the man to go after her, to fix this somehow. But both of them knew there was nothing Robert could say. Just as he'd been willing to sacrifice himself to save the villagers De Falaise was going to hang, now he was going to have to place himself between these new invaders and those who counted on him to protect them.

"Jack, call Dale. I need to sound him out about what's happening with the troops. I can't afford for them to turn tail."

"But Robert," Mark began. "Dale is –"

"Your personal feelings about him don't come into this," Robert interrupted, and Tate and Jack both stared. "I'm sorry," Robert said more softly. "He's one of our best, and he's very popular. If they won't listen to me, they might to him."

"He's popular all right," Mark said.

The meeting broke up, everyone leaving except Robert. He walked over to the far wall and banged his fist against it in frustration.

What's the matter? You got what you wanted, didn't you? To be out there again, in action, in combat.

But even he wasn't sure whether he could win this time against such odds.

And he was frightened that even if he did, he might have already lost the one thing that meant more to him than any of that.

Robert left the room and searched the corridor for any sign of Mary. He caught a flash of a female figure and got his hopes up, decided that he would go and talk to her – try and explain himself.

Except as the woman moved into view, he saw it was Adele. She smiled at him, but he didn't smile back.

Robert continued on his way to the stairs. A man with a mission.

No, more than that. As he was constantly being reminded, he was a man with a destiny. One he could no more control than he could his love life.

CHAPTER THIRTEEN

IT HAD BEEN much quicker this time.

They'd cut a swathe through this country again crushing resistance where they found it, making their presence known. It was all part of the plan. Tanek wanted Hood to know he was on his way, while Bohuslav and the Tsar didn't care about stealth; they were confident in their victory.

It was the kind of arrogance which often led to a fall, but not this time.

They'd also become aware of another faction operating in their area. Tanek had extracted information from various people since returning to these shores, taking up his old hobbies with the burning hot pokers and pressure points. It wasn't quite the same, torturing people in houses rather than caves – or dungeons, as he liked to think of the cave system below Nottingham Castle. It lacked the proper atmosphere. But, he reminded himself, he'd been torturing people most of his life and enjoyed it wherever he happened to be. He'd just been spoilt, that's all.

He remembered one man in his forties, whose belly had hung down when stripped – and Tanek had taken great delight in snipping bits of excess flesh off with a pair of scissors to make him talk.

Bohuslav had walked in during one of the sessions; it had made even his face turn green. "I thought *I* was a sick bastard," he'd said, observing Tanek at work with a block of glasspaper: rubbing one woman's fingers until they were almost down to the bone. They'd probably have told him anyway, what did they have to hide? But there was no fun in that.

As to the information: it seemed that a cult had sprung up in Britain. Or, depending on who you talked to, had resurfaced. They were sacrificing people in order to call forth their Lord from Hell, it seemed. What mattered was there were quite a number of them, and they were methodical.

"They might prove an obstacle," Tanek had said to Bohuslav. He still hated dealing with the toad, but in the Tsar's absence he had little choice.

"Doubtful," said Bohuslav. This was one of those times when his arrogance might stand in the way of preparing against a potential enemy. Tanek had found out what he could about their activities anyway: their preferred methods of hunting, their weapons, their skill at hiding when they didn't want to be seen (this last could certainly trip up their forces – how do you fire at something invisible?).

A good job, then, that Tanek had been with the first division to make contact. They were working their way through somewhere called Thirsk, in the fading light, when they were suddenly attacked. Tanek saw several scouts fall as they were walking up just ahead of the tanks and jeeps. The soldiers were dragged off the streets by men in crimson robes, and by the time the rest of the division reached them, they were already dead – their throats slit.

Gunfire opened up behind Tanek; men shooting at shadows. They'd gone down as well, killed by men who looked like the walking dead. Tanks and jeeps were useless against them at this close proximity, and they knew it.

There was movement off to the side, and Tanek had aimed and shot his crossbow in seconds. He nodded when he heard a muffled yelp, knowing his bolt had struck home. Then he was aware of a swish on his other side, something sharp cutting the air – about to cut into him. The clank of metal against metal followed and Tanek looked round to see that Bohuslav's hand scythe had met the machete blow intended for him.

The serial killer would later explain that, should Tanek turn out to be the traitor Bohuslav thought, he wanted the pleasure of killing the giant himself. For now, though, Tanek was grateful Bohuslav had blocked the attack, forcing the cult member back again with a thrust of his own blade. Before the robed figure could do anything else, Tanek had put a crossbow bolt in his head.

Confusion reigned, as their men fired into alleys, at houses, almost at each other. It was exactly what the cult wanted – exactly what guerrilla fighters would do. Tanek tried to get Bohuslav to order a ceasefire, but they were having difficulty making themselves heard. Soldiers were going down one by one. Tanek noted a guy not far away suddenly clutching at his neck as a powerful geyser of wet redness jetted out, a machete blow slicing neatly across his jugular, almost slicing his neck in two. Bullets riddled the robed figures whenever they appeared, but it didn't seem to deter them. It was as if they weren't bothered about dying at all. That, if nothing else, made them extremely dangerous adversaries. In spite of himself, Tanek found that he quite admired these people.

Then, as quickly as it had started, the fighting stopped.

Someone had appeared in the street, lit by floodlights from the armoured vehicles behind – like a magician materializing on stage. A man, flanked by two smaller women. The man wore a coat that flapped about in the chill breeze, and the leather of his uniform beneath creaked. He adjusted the peaked cap he was wearing, before standing with his hands behind his back and gazing around. The women held their swords level, protecting the man between them.

Tanek traded glances with Bohuslav, who appeared just as surprised as he was that the Tsar was present.

The time for asking questions would come later. Right now, what interested Tanek was the stillness this man inspired. He had some balls to walk out there in the first place – he appeared to have pulled up in his own private jeep – but what was causing the cult to stay their hand? His own men, Tanek could understand. They would rather shoot themselves than risk hitting their glorious leader with a stray bullet. But why were these strangers holding off? It was quite a thing to witness.

Tanek's answer came when one robed figure emerged from a side street, and began to walk up the road. Bohuslav nervously shifted from foot to foot, and Tanek was half expecting him to give an order to shoot. But the Tsar was gesturing with his hand that his forces should hold their fire for now.

When the Tsar began talking, it was in Russian. He soon realised his mistake and switched to broken English. "You speak for your people, yes?" The twins were ready to spring on the figure should he put so much as a foot out of place. They needn't have worried.

"We are Servitor. When one speaks, we all speak." The robed figure dropped to his knees before he was anywhere near the Tsar. If the Russian was surprised, then he didn't show it. "My Lord." The man kept his head bowed, then added: "You are finally here."

Tanek saw the Tsar's eyebrows raise just a fraction. "Yes." Whether he thought the man was simply referring to his title – after all, Tanek had heard the people under the Tsar call him Lord all the time – or he actually knew what the man was referring to was unclear. But the effect was the same. "Now call your men forth."

The robed figure did as he was told, rising and calling to the other members of his order. There were at least twenty of them, and they came tentatively out of hiding. It was only now that Tanek, and probably Bohuslav too, realised that they could have gone on fighting for hours and not got them all, so skilled were they at concealment.

What the Tsar was proposing was preferable to the conflict. A truce and a joining of forces. "We can... help each other," the Tsar explained to the spokesman.

"Whatever you say," he replied. He still wasn't able to look the Tsar in the face.

Later on, Tanek had the chance to ask the Tsar about all this – and discover why he'd made the trip personally across the sea. ("Like Richard the Lionheart in the Holy Land, I wished to see the 'conversion' of this country myself. And bring some additional firepower with me.") He understood that the man hadn't quite anticipated that reaction from the cult leader.

"I was never in any danger. Apart from the twins, I had ample soldiers covering me. So I thought I might offer a proposition. I never knew they would mistake me for..."

For Satan? thought Tanek, finishing off what the Tsar couldn't bring himself to say. *In your red uniform, bringing fire and destruction with you?* It wasn't much of a stretch. But it did do them a favour.

It also meant that progress would be even quicker than they had anticipated. Soon they would be at Nottingham, at the castle's doors in fact. Tanek had persuaded the Tsar that the location was ideal for striking out at the rest of the country. It was what De Falaise once had in mind.

Soon, Hood and all those who followed him would be dead, and Tanek would be back where he belonged.

Perhaps, then, his former leader's ghost would be able to rest in peace.

CHAPTER FOURTEEN

ROBERT HAD TALKED to Dale, who in turn had talked to the men, laying the groundwork.

Then, as Jack had suggested, Robert spoke to them all. He'd requested that as many Rangers as could be spared gather in the castle grounds first thing that morning. A transcript would be circulated for those who couldn't be there, and Jack was even recording it on the battery-powered tape player. Those present who could remember when he'd given the speech the night before the battle for this place felt a certain amount of nostalgia. Tate knew their leader had been reluctant to say anything on that occasion too but, as now, he recognised that it was time to motivate.

Time to lay everything on the line.

He stood in front of the crowd of fighters, and it was obvious that looking over the swell of heads made him uncomfortable. They could see it was having another effect on him, too. The way his chest was puffing up, his eyes glassy; it could only be pride he was feeling when he looked at his loyal brigade. It made some of them, those who'd been complaining about how much work they were doing, feel more than a little ashamed.

Robert was casting his eyes down the rows, looking for someone. All those closest to him were there: Jack, Mark, Tate. All except Mary.

He began anyway, his voice cracking as he said his first few words: "Th-thank you all for listening to me today, I do appreciate it. In fact, and I don't say this as often as I should, I appreciate everything you do, and have done, not only for this... well, I suppose this peacekeeping force... but also for the people of this area and beyond. Many of you probably know already that I didn't want this command, and don't even really see myself as your chief – or whatever you want to call it. Everyone's equal here, everyone's got something unique to offer. Some of us may be more inexperienced than others." Robert made a point of looking at Mark when he said this. "Some of us want to make an impression." Now he found Dale out in the audience. "But that's fine. As someone once said to me: we're a family. And I like to sort out any problems within that family.

"Now, I know that you're tired, that some of you are doing the jobs of three or four people. A consequence of this new world we've found ourselves in, sadly, is that it takes time to build something. To find the people we need or for them to find us. And, believe it or not, we are building something truly special here. Something that's already being talked about throughout the country, and maybe even further afield. We're keeping ordinary folk safe from the likes of the Morningstars, from thugs and murderers and rapists. I don't know about you, but I'm quite proud of that."

There was a rumble of agreement from the crowd.

"The problem with gaining a reputation," Robert continued, catching Adele's eyes briefly where she stood not far from Jack, "is that from time to time people are going to come and challenge us. People like the Frenchman we took this castle from; people who would destroy our homes, kill our loved ones. I'm standing up here today to tell those of you who don't already know – because I realise the rumour mill must be going into overdrive – that there's one such mobilisation heading our way. They landed about a week ago on the coast, and I'm not going to sugar coat this for you: we have it on good authority that they're well armed and in great numbers."

The rumbles turned into mumbles of shock and fear, as the troops turned to one another – some nodding in confirmation of what they'd already suspected, some hearing it for the first time.

"They will reach us sooner or later, and countless innocents will die – are already dying, as they make their way to Nottingham. The question is, do we meet them head on, attempt to stop them before they can slaughter anyone else, and before they reach the places and people we care about?" Robert paused to take in not only the faces of the crowd, but also the people who'd brought him out of Sherwood in the first place. As he did so, he saw Mary standing right at the very back. Their eyes met and from that moment on he was really only talking to her. "Do we do the right thing? Or hope that someone, somewhere will do it for us? Personally, I believe we are the only ones who stand a chance of stopping them, of kicking them back to where they came from and making sure they never try anything like it again." He nodded. "Yes, I know how thinly stretched we are – mainly due to the threat the Morningstars have become. But if we wait, this could escalate further."

"The best defence is a good offence," Jack called out from the crowd. "That's what they always say back where I come from."

There were more murmurs from the crowd. Nobody wanted to face an enemy of this kind, but if they hid away behind the castle walls, then they would have to at some point anyway. Was it better to pre-empt them?

"None of you are here because you have to be," Robert said, once the crowd had quietened a little. "My way is not the way it was with the Frenchman, as some of you who served under him have discovered over the time you've been with me. I said this once before, but I've made my decision and I have to stick by it. I'm riding out to meet the convoy. How many of you choose to join me on this mission, I'm leaving in your hands. I've said this before, too. It'll be dangerous, and there are no guarantees that anyone will be coming back." Robert could see the tears welling in Mary's eyes, and his began to mist up in response. "So I wouldn't blame anyone for not coming. In fact some of you I want to stay behind to defend the castle, just in case we fail. But if you really wanted to leave us altogether, the door – well, gate – is over there."

For a good few moments there was silence. No mutterings from the crowd at all, as they made up their minds what to do. Divided between their loyalty to a man who'd given them refuge, given them a home, and their terror at facing what was to come.

It was Dale who broke this silence. "I'm with you, Robert. Where you go, I'll be there." Azhar, at his side, put a hand across his chest and bowed. Then Dale turned and looked at the other fighters, in the hopes of shaming them into saying something. It seemed to work: they began to nod their heads, and a buzz of positive noises filtered through. That buzz became a wave, which washed over the heads of those present. It wasn't long before some of the Rangers were holding up their swords and waving them in the air. Some might change their minds later, or opt to stay at the castle, but for now it seemed like the majority of Robert's men were on his side.

He thanked them and stood down, relief etched on his face – because he had the support he needed, or because he'd finished speaking in public.

Whatever the case, Robert knew that the hard work was only just beginning. If they were to halt the progress of this new army, they had to leave soon. And he had more than a few loose ends to tie up first.

He scanned the crowd for Mary as it broke up, but she'd vanished again. Before he could go and look for her, he was being pulled in several different directions at once. Being asked a million questions about the mission.

THOUGH THEY WEREN'T too happy about it, Robert insisted that Jack and Mark stay behind at the castle. "I need someone I can leave in charge here," Robert told Jack. "Someone I can trust." The fact that he'd seen them both dead in his dream also had something to do with it.

"I should be out there with you, Robbie," Jack complained, but when Robert asked again, with a firm 'please,' the larger man relented.

Mark was more of a hard sell. "You're still not ready for that kind of combat," Robert pointed out, which wasn't the smartest thing to say.

"But you're taking Dale?"

"Yes."

"Because 'where you go, he goes'?" said Mark.

"Because I want you to stay and look after Mary and Sophie."

"Mary can look after herself. You know that."

That was true. "And Sophie?"

Mark thought about this for a moment. "I think she'd prefer to have Dale looking after her."

"You might be surprised." Robert looked him directly in the eye. "If anything happens to me, and the troops break in here, get Sophie and Mary out. Do you understand? You'll know where to go. That's the most important thing you can do, son." He gave Mark a tight hug, and when he pulled away again he could see the boy was fighting back tears.

Robert asked the same of Reverend Tate when he spoke to him: help to keep Mary, Sophie and Mark safe. "And Gwen and the little one," Tate added. He'd sent word to the woman at New Hope, letting her know about the army that was heading towards them, promising supplies if she would come to the castle to collect them. Word had it she was on her way with Clive Jr, and when she got to the castle Robert knew Tate was going to try and get her to remain there until the danger had passed.

"She won't stay, you know," Robert told him. "She'll want to be with her people. I have to say I can understand that."

Tate agreed. "All I can do is try."

"You do know I can't let her have any weapons?"

"I wasn't specific about what the supplies were."

"But that's what you've let her think."

The Reverend heaved a weary sigh. "You do what you must, and I'll do likewise. You know, I wouldn't normally be the one to say this, but are you sure you shouldn't take some of those things along yourself when you meet this army of yours?"

Robert tutted. "You're advocating the use of firearms now, Reverend? You sound like Bill."

"They were used in the battle for the castle," Tate reminded him.

"We'll do okay without them. Isn't that what you're always telling me, to have faith?"

"There's a difference between that and suicide."

"We'll be armed. Just not in the way they'll be expecting. The men have been trained well, and we'll have a few surprises for our friends."

Tate gave a tip of the head, then said finally: "Remember the story of David and Goliath, Robert."

That just left Mary.

Robert tried to find her, but he knew that if he chose a quiet spot, she would eventually come to him... if she wanted to talk. He went down to the stables, to feed his horse. They'd been through quite a bit together, and he'd be asking quite a bit more of the animal in the days to come.

When he heard the footsteps behind him, he turned and saw Adele, and couldn't hide the disappointment on his face.

"You were expecting her, weren't you?" said the woman. "I'm sorry."

"That's okay."

Adele came a little closer. "It's just that, well, I figured I might never see you again. And I didn't want you to go before... That is, I really need to tell you something, Robert."

He pressed his face up against his horse, closing his eyes. "Adele, look –"

"No, let me finish. Please."

He heard the woman come closer, now only a couple of feet away from him. When he opened his eyes he saw a figure just over her shoulder, cheeks red from the cold, hair tied back; Mary. He was frightened that she would run off again, get the wrong impression. Instead, she coughed politely, causing Adele to start.

"Jack's looking for you," Mary said when she turned around.

"But I was just... I needed to talk to Robert for a moment," she said, turning to him for support.

"You should go and find Jack," Robert advised her.

Adele looked like she was going to say something, but gave an almost imperceptible nod and left the stables. Mary watched her go, a mixture of concern and resentment in her expression. Then she focused on Robert.

"I..." he began, but realised he didn't know what to say. He didn't really need to. Mary walked over, quickening her pace as she came. Then their arms were open, and they held each other; grabbing on as if they felt they might just float away if they weren't anchored down. Robert thought about making a nervous joke, something along the lines of: 'You're not going to drug me this time, are you?' but thought better of it.

The time for jokes, the time for talking, the time for arguing and recriminations, was long over. They knew they may not be together again.

As they kissed, the world fell away. Both Robert and Mary wished that this moment would never end. She took his hand, and led him up to the entrance of the castle; then finally up the stairs to their room, where they would try and make the next couple of hours last an lifetime.

CHAPTER FIFTEEN

THE ARMY WAS using open ground to travel between urban locations. That much they'd been able to ascertain from radio messages. And they had a rough idea of where they were, too: somewhere between Doncaster and Gainsborough.

Robert had sent out advance scouts to get a proper sense of the route the war machine was taking now that they'd regrouped and were heading for Nottingham. It had allowed him and his men to lay in wait, to prepare for the confrontation to come. But, as dawn broke and they watched from behind a scattering of trees, it would have been easy to mistake this for a normal winter's morning in the English countryside.

Holding up the binoculars, Robert scanned the horizon. Nothing to see yet. He glanced over his shoulder at the division of men with him, some sitting on horseback, others standing leaning on their bows. There were more ringing these fields, spread out to cause the maximum confusion when the Russian troops arrived. Robert was just about to put the binoculars up to his eyes again when he heard Dale on the left of him say: "Listen... Do you hear that?"

Robert could hear it, even feel the vibrations coming up through the ground. Something was coming, something big. No, as he brought the binoculars up and focused on the spot he'd been watching, Robert realised that many big things were coming.

The jeeps were first, cresting the hill, bringing with them men swarming like ants – each wearing a grey uniform and carrying a machine gun. Then came the back-up: tanks. More than De Falaise had dreamed of. More than Robert had ever seen, and there'd been a fair few in the Frenchman's command. But that wasn't all. Armoured personnel carriers and other armoured vehicles. Then there were the motorbikes, their drone almost drowned out by their larger companions. They nipped in between, churning up the grass beneath.

"Jesus," said one of the men behind Robert. "How are we supposed to fight *that*?"

Robert had to admit, although he didn't show it, he'd expected something slightly smaller; more in keeping with what they'd dealt with before. A part of him was now wondering if he'd made the right decision, bringing these men – some of them only boys, like Dale – out here to face such odds. And Tate's words came back to him:

"I wouldn't be the first one to say this, but are you sure you shouldn't take some of those things along yourself when you meet this army of yours?"

Those things, those reminders of De Falaise and his rule... But when you were fighting men like De Falaise, shouldn't you meet them on a level playing field – even the odds as much as you could? Robert shook his head. That wasn't the way – he was sure of it. Old Eric Meadows had been sure of it... He just had to have faith that his plan would work, that they could catch bigger prey with the same methods he'd used back in the forest.

"We'll fight them," Robert said in answer to the man's question. "And as long as we stick together, we'll win. They won't be expecting an attack like this one."

"Too right!" said another Ranger. "Who'd be crazy enough to do it?"

Robert looked over his shoulder once more and grinned. "We would. Now ready yourself."

"Time to get up on stage and do our thing," Dale said, though all the usual cockiness was gone from his voice.

"That's right," said Robert. "Time to do our thing."

IF IT WAS going to happen, it would happen here. Bohuslav was counting on it.

As he rode in the lead jeep, he surveyed the ground in front of him. They were out there somewhere, he was certain. Did they not think that their little attack would be anticipated? Far from being herded into this stretch of countryside, he and his men were actually hoping to bring Hood's forces out into the open, let them do their worst, then wipe them from the face of the Earth. They'd allowed themselves to be seen, allowed the radio messages to get through without interference, purely for this purpose. Hood's scouts had even been spotted trying to determine which direction their army was heading.

Oh, was he in for a shock.

Yet Bohuslav didn't really want to be here. As much as he loved the thrill of slaughter – though it would never replace the kick he got from capturing and killing people one to one – he was uncomfortable about this whole operation. He was proud the Tsar had left him in charge, but couldn't help wishing he was with his superior right now; the thought of that bastard Tanek whispering in his master's ear was almost too much to bear. Bohuslav knew the swarthy giant was trying to worm his way in, and there was only room for one second, for one murdering psychopath on the team. Once this was all over, Tanek might well find his throat being slit in the night... if Bohuslav was quick enough to take him. He remembered back to the hovercraft. Not much scared Bohuslav, but the thought of killing Tanek was terrifying and exhilarating at the same time.

But that was for the future. Right now, there was one small thing to do and he needed to stay sharp to accomplish it. Bohuslav must rid the world of this new Robin Hood.

No sooner had Bohuslav thought this than he saw something down below, not much bigger than his thumb from this distance. A man on horseback – who had appeared, quite literally, out of nowhere. His head was bowed, and he had a cowl pulled over his features.

He had a bow slung over his shoulder, and a quiver on his back. He also had a sword by his side, dangling near the horse's flank. He looked like he'd stepped out of a time warp. In no way, shape or form a match for any of Bohuslav's soldiers or their weapons.

Nevertheless, the sight of that lone figure gave Bohuslav pause for thought. He didn't fear him, at least not in the same way he did Tanek (though he would never admit it). But it made the serial killer at least think twice about giving the order to attack.

Is the man insane? he wondered – which was rich, coming from someone who used to have imaginary conversations with his gagged and bound victims. *Or,* Bohuslav thought, *does he know something we don't? Does he have something up his sleeve?*

When all was said and done, this was the person who'd defeated De Falaise's army. A different fight, a different place, but Bohuslav couldn't help thinking: what if...

Then he smiled. If Hood wanted to play, he would oblige.

So Bohuslav ordered one of the T-90 battle tanks to target the man and blow him to kingdom come.

*   *   *

ROBERT HELD HIS position.

They'd be firing any second, but this was more than a matter of drawing a line in the sand, showing both sides what they were up against. It wasn't about weapons, either, or about who was right and wrong. It was about courage, standing up for something you believed in.

Even just as an image.

Robert patted his horse's neck, holding her steady. Then, right at the very last moment, he pulled the steed around and rode her away, back out of range. He heard the shot from behind, the whizzing sound as the shell flew through the air.

It exploded in the spot where he'd stood only moments before. The animal protested, but was used to this type of noise. Robert urged her back round and they stood there again.

This time, though, Robert held up his hand – and dropped it again. Giving his order, as the commander of these troops must have done.

Like snowflakes they fell from the sky. Huge rocks, raining down on the vehicles from strategic, hidden positions on either side. From catapults they'd brought with them, made over the last few months to defend the castle, but wheeled and easily transportable. The rocks landed heavily on the tanks, jeeps and other armoured vehicles, not doing a vast amount of damage, but proving that they weren't as toothlesss as they'd seemed.

It also had the effect of provoking the army into rushing them. Now the jeeps, bikes, tanks and armoured vehicles were moving forward into position. They began firing at the trees, but Robert's men were well-camouflaged. There was nobody apart from Robert on the battlefield for the vehicles to engage yet.

That's how it would stay for a little while, until they'd finished sending their message.

From the trees now came hails of flaming arrows. They hit the vehicles, exploding on impact – their tips filled with a special sulphur brew. The flames spread across the metal, engulfing some vehicles almost entirely. Mini paint bombs broke against windscreens and viewing slats, obscuring vision. One driver rammed his jeep into the side of a tank, scraping along until it got in front and the bonnet of the smaller vehicle was crushed under the tracks of the other.

Meanwhile, the bikes, jeeps and other vehicles with tyres were discovering the presents Robert and his men had left in the field. Clusters of barbed wire burst tyres and tangled up around them. Bikes wobbled and keeled over, jeeps ground to a halt, armoured vehicles could do nothing but sit there and offer covering fire.

Others were introduced to holes the men had dug and covered over: not deep, just enough for the vehicles to dip forward into and be brought to a standstill.

Now came the second wave from the catapults: large gas canisters that hit the vehicles, to be struck by more flaming arrows, igniting the gas. The landscape turned into a field of red and yellow mushrooms. Black smoke was laid down in front of Robert.

He took hold of his bow, grabbed an arrow out of his quiver and nocked it, feeling the familiar tension of the string. Welcoming it like an old friend.

Armed men broke through the smoke. He shot the first one in the knee, the second in the shoulder. Given a choice and when not backed into a corner, he would always choose to incapacitate rather than kill.

Robert nodded and his men broke free of their cover, some on horseback, some on foot. The firing started moments later, the Russians letting rip with their machine guns.

Robert's men raised their shields; specially made by their blacksmith Faraday, steel plate more than 16 mm thick: bullets would make a significant dent in them, but not penetrate. Sparks flew as the bullets pinged off them. Several of the horses were hit and went down, taking their riders with them. Robert saw some of his men get hit and drop to the ground... only to wait until a Russian soldier was near enough and get up again, to take him down in hand to hand.

He grinned again: each man had the extra protection of specially adapted vests – hard metal-plates fitted into ordinary bullet-proof vests like the ones armed response units wore, found in old police facilities. It would give added protection against machine guns and shrapnel. Robert himself was wearing one, and was glad of it.

The smoke was clearing, making this a fight of bullets against bows. Arrows struck the Russian troops, hitting them in arms, legs, necks and taking them down. Flaming arrows set them alight and took them out of the battle altogether. Robert looked down and caught sight of Azhar engaging a couple of foot-soldiers, dodging bullets and slicing them with his sword.

Suddenly an AFV charged through, its tyres ripped to shreds but ploughing forwards anyway.

"Dale," shouted Robert, "with me!"

Leaning forwards, they urged their steeds on through the combat. An explosion off to their right almost caused Dale's horse to rear up, but he kept control. The cannon on top of the AFV was spitting out shells one after the other. Robert nodded for Dale to give him covering fire, taking out the armed men on the ground now flanking the vehicle. The AFV turned and started ploughing diagonally through the fighting.

Robert pulled on the reins, then rode his horse up alongside the armoured vehicle. When he judged it was close enough, he jumped from the saddle onto the side of the thing, landing near the back, and his horse rode off without him, away from danger. He almost slipped down and under the wheels, but his hands found purchase on the rails bolted to the metal. A stray bullet *twanged* off the plating near his head – whoever had fired it obviously reckoning that they couldn't do the AFV any harm but might be able to dislodge the Hooded Man. Robert risked a quick glance over his shoulder and saw Dale take out the shooter with an arrow to the back.

Shot! he thought, then concentrated on getting himself stable. Robert clambered around on the side of the vehicle, looking for a way in, but the hatches seemed to be sealed tight. The cannon on the top swung round in his direction, until he was staring down the black hole of the stubby barrel. Robert dropped down again just as it fired, almost slipping under the grinding remains of the tyres, but somehow swinging himself back along the side so that he was closer to the front. He kept himself low, avoiding the cannon, and climbed round to the front of the vehicle, left hand gripping a rail.

Two metal flaps were open at the front, obviously so the driver could see. The AFV went over a bump, jolting Robert upwards. His shoulder took the brunt of the impact. He let out a grunt, but it just made him more determined to put an end to the vehicle's run.

With his free hand, he pulled out his sword – then, wincing as he did so, swung round and shoved the weapon into one of the viewing slats. He had no idea whether he'd hit anything, until he felt the end of the sword slide into something soft. When he pulled it out, there was blood on the tip.

The AFV veered wildly to one side, away from the battlefield, heading towards some trees. Robert didn't have the luxury of waiting this time; he launched himself off the vehicle, hoping he'd roll far enough out of its way that he wouldn't be crushed. The hatches opened as the men inside scrabbled to flee the vehicle. The first tree it hit didn't stop it, but the second tree was too much for it, and the AFV shuddered to a halt.

Robert rose, barely having time to recover before he felt a presence at his side. He ducked and turned as gunfire passed overhead, then brought his sword round and struck the man on the calf, digging the blade in and sending him toppling over.

Sheathing his weapon, Robert had his bow out again and was shooting quickly: left, right and centre, putting as many of the armed men out of action as he could.

He noted, with some satisfaction, that his troops were all doing the same: picking targets off with the bow or, in close combat, their swords or knives. He also saw something that gave him pause – bodies of Rangers, laying on the field. One's head had been blown almost totally apart, another had been practically cut in half by enemy fire. Robert dwelled on them for a second longer than he should have, but then ground his teeth, setting his jaw firm and raising his bow, felling another three Russian soldiers.

More jeeps and armoured vehicles – including tanks – were skirting the traps, wise to the barbed wire and trenches now. A group of Robert's men, about eight in total, charged the side of one tank carrying a tree-trunk like a battering ram. They rammed the wood into the tracks of the tank, jamming its progress. Another team did the same at the other side. A further team threw Molotov cocktails against the vehicles.

Robert fired at a jeep heading in his direction, just as he had done the first time he'd engaged in combat like this, back when the market near Sherwood had been under attack. Then he hadn't been able to believe what he was doing, going up against a squad of the Sheriff's men on his own. Now, it seemed like second nature. They were fending off an army, but he wasn't alone any more. That made all the difference.

That might make the difference between winning and losing.

WERE THEY WINNING or losing? Bohuslav couldn't even tell.

What should have been a cut and dried thing had suddenly turned sour. Their enemies were using tactics the men had never come across before, but he certainly had. They were the methods of trappers, of hunters. What should have worked in his side's favour – the wealth of armament at their disposal, the sheer number of vehicles – was actually turning out to be their Achilles Heel. Hood's men were more manoeuvrable, running or riding – on fucking horses, for sanity's sake! – between the behemoths, bullets bouncing off what looked like home-made shields. And body-armour! Tanek had conveniently left that detail out of the preparations... unless he hadn't known? It made them harder to kill, or harder to kill quickly, at any rate.

Hood's men were also able to handle close-combat fighting much better than his, probably because they'd never had to do it before.

When the Tsar's troops entered an area, they usually obliterated everything in their path long before it got to that stage.

Bohuslav cursed under his breath in his native tongue, as another explosion went off outside the jeep.

He looked through the windscreen at what was going on ahead of him, and the certainty he'd had when he arrived began to wane. But there was something Hood and his men didn't know – apart from their plan, of course, apart from what was going on while they were all here. Bohuslav had hoped to settle this without having to fall back on them, but the Tsar had brought some special little toys over with him just in case.

Four Kamov Ka-50 single-seat attack helicopters, also known to those in the trade as 'Black Sharks.' Each boasted laser-guided anti-tank missiles located under the stub wings, and 30mm cannons fixed semi-rigidly on the helicopter's side. One of the most lethal pieces of military hardware known to man. Granted, they weren't being piloted by the most highly trained individuals – at least not as highly trained as they would have been pre-virus – but they knew enough to get the job done.

The time had come to finish this, and if his ground forces weren't capable... Bohuslav reached for the radio, knowing now with complete certainty who would be the ultimate victors here today.

CHAPTER SIXTEEN

In the heat of the battle, even above the noise of gunfire and explosions, another sound could be heard. The distinctive sound of rotor blades in the distance.

Robert looked over the horizon to see four dark shapes advancing, like flying Horsemen of the Apocalypse. Helicopters unlike anything he was familiar with – certainly nothing like the Sioux he'd used to chase De Falaise through the streets of Nottingham. They had double rotors, affording them a manoeuvrability most pilots could only dream of.

The two helicopters on the edges broke off, heading for the tree-line. Robert could see what was about to happen, but had no way of preventing it – apart from anything else, he was being attacked by two of the Tsar's men, who he'd relieved of their machine guns.

Missiles were away seconds later, streaming into the trees. The height these monstrosities were flying at gave them a unique view of where the catapults lay. Robert dispatched the soldiers he was dealing with, then closed his eyes as the missiles hit home, killing men he'd posted.

Those Rangers closer by had – like him – paused very briefly to witness the lethal onslaught of these newcomers. As they did so, however, they also saw more heavy rocks being launched at the chopper closest to the trees. It may not have been quite as accurate as whatever those pilots were using, but it was good enough to give the thing a bloody nose – a heavy projectile glancing across the bridge of the lowered craft, knocking it momentarily sideways and off balance. Two more hit it in quick succession before another chopper came to its aid, firing off two missiles and putting paid to that particular catapult. But it had already done enough damage to the first helicopter to make it beat a hasty retreat.

"That'll show 'em!" called out one of Robert's lads, a man called Harris who immediately drew back his bow and shot a Russian soldier in the thigh.

But there were still three helicopters left, more than enough to take out the rest of the catapults. Calling on anyone who was free to do so, Robert began to make his way forward, up the field, past the corpses of vehicles – loosing arrows as he went.

One of the helicopters had bowed its front, sweeping forwards. Robert ordered his men to duck, shouting that anyone who still had a shield should crouch behind it. He himself dived behind the cover of an upended jeep, dragging a couple of his men with him – just as the chopper's machinegun began spraying the area. It seemed not to care whether its own troops were in the way, so long as it got Robert's men. Several were thrown back by the blast, losing their shields. Then, vulnerable, they were torn to shreds by the second sweep – their vests no protection from this kind of intense firepower.

"Damn it all!" growled Robert. "Stay under cover!"

Before his men could say anything, Robert had run out from behind the jeep, sprinting towards a tank that was still on fire. Bullets peppered the earth behind him, but he flung himself forward and, taking cover behind the metal hulk, he readied his bow, igniting one of the special payload arrows from his quiver.

Stepping out, he took a second to aim, which was all he needed.

The arrow was flying even as he took cover behind the tank again. The helicopter had no time to get out of its way, the pilot so overconfident that the arrow could do no damage to his craft that he stayed and waited for the thing to hit. Then it struck its target, glancing off one of its remaining missiles, but in the process smearing the cocktail of heated chemicals across the casing. The missile exploded, taking the entire helicopter with it.

Robert strode out from behind the tank in time to see the blazing ball go down, striking the earth nose-first. He heard cheering from behind him, his actions prompting others to break cover, attacking the two helicopters as they had done the tanks, jeeps and motorcycles.

One of them was hit with a paint bomb across the windshield, obscuring the pilot's vision, forcing him to pull back. A tree trunk hurled by what was probably the one remaining catapult then struck the side of the chopper. The pilot seemed to be trying to land, then attempted to rise again. A couple of petrol bombs to the undercarriage were enough to persuade him to set down, and Robert saw him leap from the cockpit. Two arrows from Dale's bow – the lad still riding

his horse into the action – were waiting for him, pinning him to the ground.

That left one last attack helicopter.

Robert broke cover again, hunting the thing before it got a chance to hunt him. He hadn't gone far through this nightmare of war – explosions going off everywhere; armoured vehicles still ahead; not to mention a good number of Russian troops – when the black beast spotted him. It hovered close into view before him. On the side of this one, somebody had painted a shark. *Not a bad description for that thing in the right hands,* thought Robert. But where the shark was a thing of nature, this wasn't. It had no instinct, no cunning or guile: that was left to whoever was in control. There was nothing organic about its methods of killing at all, hiding behind all those guns and rockets and metal.

The Hooded Man was another story entirely. He was living on instinct and adrenalin. A true force of nature.

He stood, all Hell breaking loose around him. Then he raised his head, still under the hood. Bow slung over his shoulder, he coaxed the chopper to come closer with a crook of his finger.

The pilot was hesitating, probably because of what had just happened to the other chopper. Then suddenly the helicopter advanced, nose down, all its weapons trained on Robert.

Faith, he thought to himself. *If I just have enough faith.*

They seemed to stand frozen like that, an iconic scene from one of Jack's old action movies, everything happening in slow motion around them. Like two gunslingers from a western, each waiting for the other to draw.

Robert reached around the back of his belt first, but as he did he could've sworn he heard the clicking of the machine gun, saw it moving and training on him. He waited for a blast that never came – whether the guns jammed or the pilot hesitated again, he had no way of knowing – but he took advantage of the seconds it gave him. Pulling out a bolas of metal chain, he tossed it at the base of the helicopter's lowest rotor. It got tangled up quickly, the small spiked balls – taken from two maces – sparking as they whipped up into the blades.

The helicopter pulled its nose up and veered to one side, firing its gun now but hitting nothing. Robert watched from under the brow of his hood, as it drifted across the sky, then piled into a bunch of trees at the edge of the field, becoming tangled in the branches.

May not have been a slingshot, Reverend, thought Robert, *but it did the trick.*

He didn't have much more time to think about it, because something hit him. Something big and hard that came out of nowhere, sending him spinning.

Robert felt the pain in his side as he flipped, connected with the ground and continued to roll, his sword flattening against his side. He felt his vest catch on something and rip apart at the front, the metal plate slipping out; heard something round the back of him crack and hoped it was only his bow.

When he came to a halt, he was looking up at the blue sky, the clouds passing overhead. Then it was going dark... He was beginning to black out. *Not now, Robert. Fight it!*

He held on to the image of that blue sky, and for a few moments it felt like an ordinary day in the English countryside.

Then whatever had hit him drew up not far away.

And he heard someone climb out, approaching his battered and bruised body.

BOHUSLAV HAD WATCHED the defeat of the helicopters and had to pinch himself in case he was dreaming. Not that he ever had dreams like this, his were much darker affairs. More personal.

It had all started off so well. The destruction of whatever was flinging those crude missiles was countered with more modern missiles, guided in on target and blowing them to bits. It was when the Black Sharks had got closer to the fighting that the problems started.

And him! *Govno!* That irritating little man with his hood and his arrows and his sword. He'd actually taken down two – count them, two! – of the craft himself. Small wonder his reputation had spread. His men would blindly, and bravely it had to be said, follow him into the very depths of Hades itself if he asked them to. Perhaps Tanek had been right to broach his concerns that Hood might come for them one day. Definitely better to take him out of the equation now. Except they weren't doing such a great job, were they?

Bohuslav's fingers itched. The only way they were still going to pull this around would be for him to put the Hooded Man down personally. Cut off the head and the rest of the body withers – he had learned that at a very early age in his experimentations with animals.

Bohuslav ordered his driver to double back, come at the battlefield from the side. "Ram him," he commanded, pointing ahead to the lone figure who had just defeated one of the most sophisticated pieces of military hardware known to man, as if he was teaching a school bully a lesson. It would definitely be a challenge to fight this individual one-on-one, but there was no harm in stacking the odds in his favour. Bohuslav had no qualms about this, he preferred to pounce on his victims when they least expected it, so the fight would be brief.

This one would be too, he'd make sure. As the jeep slammed into Hood, sending him reeling, Bohuslav smirked. Then he got out of the vehicle, producing his handheld sickles as he strode over towards the leader of the rag-tag team that had held fast against their might.

THROUGH WATERY EYES attempting to close, Robert saw him.

It was a blur at first; he blinked and, as the form took on more shape, Robert made out the man's attire. He looked so out of place here, in that sharp black suit, white shirt and black tie. But, looking beyond that, looking into the hawk-like eyes, Robert recognised what he really was: another hunter, a predator. Not the main man himself, but one of the minions he'd seen in his dream.

The predator was holding in his hands two sharp weapons, like the Grim Reaper's scythe, only smaller and more curved. More deadly. It had been his vehicle that had run Robert over, wounding the prey. This monster liked his meat to be softened up before coming in for the kill. And he'd killed before, enjoyed it.

"Wake up, *mudak*!" shouted the man. He was using one of the sickle points to push Robert's Hood back, exposing his face and head. "Yes, rouse yourself. It is time for you to die."

Robert tried to move, but every inch of him was protesting.

"Your performance was impressive, I will give you that," continued the suited man looming over him, "but ultimately you must have known you'd fail."

"F-fail?" Robert half coughed, half laughed. "You... You must have been at a different battle from me."

"Ah, but this war is being fought on two fronts, my friend." There was a searing pain in his thigh as the man buried one of the sickle points into Robert's leg. "That's it, shout out. Let your men know all about it."

Robert clamped his teeth shut, hissing out the rest of his howl. The man twisted his blade and Robert had trouble keeping his agony to himself. But the man was leaning in, close.

Close enough to...

Even though he couldn't get up, Robert could still swing his fist – and he did just that. He couldn't get as much leverage behind the punch as he would have liked, but it had the desired effect, knocking the Russian back. The sickle blade slid out of Robert's thigh as the stranger reeled.

Robert struggled to get up onto an elbow, his torso and thigh in competition to see which could cause him more pain. With his free hand, he unsheathed his sword, just in time to hold it before him to meet a blow from the enraged Russian.

"That won't save you," promised the man, his piercing eyes flashing. "Nothing will." He struck again. Robert's blade clashed with two sickles this time, but he wasn't strong enough to hold them at bay. The man was leaning hard on the blades, the sickles inching down. "And nothing will save your friends at the castle, either."

Robert's elbow gave out, but he was quick enough to grab the other end of his sword. The sickles were millimetres from his chest. The suited man suddenly put more weight on one side than the other, the left blade dropping – though not before Robert shifted slightly so that it entered his shoulder rather than his chest. Again, an excruciating white hot agony, and Robert let go of his grip on the sword.

Leaving the point in Robert's shoulder, the stranger raised the other sickle high. He wasn't going for the chest any more. Now he was going to bring the sickle round in an arc, slit open Robert's throat, maybe even cut off his head.

There was a swish of air and Robert closed his eyes, steeling himself for the sickle to slice his flesh. Instead he felt something wet on his face and chest. Then came a cry.

When Robert opened his eyes he saw what had happened. Dale was standing off to one side, his sword covered in blood. The suited man was rising and backing off, clutching his hand... no, not his hand. That lay on the ground, still holding the sickle.

Blood was spurting from the suited man's stump and Dale was still on him. He lashed out with another stroke of the blade, which the man had to duck to avoid. Robert heard him scream out something in his native tongue, cursing the man who'd dismembered him. Dale took no notice, waiting for the suited man to right himself before crouching and slashing crosswise. The man arched his body and it looked like Dale's attack had fallen short. Then more redness stained the white shirt, the bottom half of his tie falling to the ground as a slash in the fabric appeared. The man looked up at Dale, shocked, then down at this new wound.

The man scrabbled back and held his stomach, his face growing paler by the second. Then he fell over, curling up in the foetal position.

Dale looked like he was about do some more damage when Robert let out a load groan, the first sickle still embedded in him.

"Hold on," said Dale. He put down his sword and took hold of the handle of the sickle. "Brace yourself, Robert, this is going to really hurt." He pulled out the blade, but it felt like the metal was still inside. Then Dale took Robert's hand and got him to apply pressure to the wound, while he saw to the leg. Robert heard, rather than saw – his vision was swimming – Dale rip a piece off his sleeve, tying a tourniquet around the wounded thigh.

"Son of a... I don't believe it," said Dale, getting up. Robert blinked and saw the blurry, suited man crawling back to the vehicle that had rammed into him. The Russian could just about move, reaching up to drag himself back into the passenger seat. Hands pulled him in, the driver setting off even before the suited man's legs were properly inside. Robert grabbed Dale with his free hand and shook his head.

"L... leave him," he moaned.

Dale looked at Robert, as if about to disagree with him, then nodded. "He's half dead anyway," said the youth. "Let's see to you." He began ripping more material to tie around the shoulder wound.

"How... how are..." began Robert.

Dale frowned, then nodded. "It's pretty much over. The ones that are left seem to be scattering. We did it, we held them back."

Robert let out a breath, and his grip on the young man's arm tightened. "You... You have to gather the men..."

"I don't understand."

"Get... get them together... There's... there's another..." Robert forced the words out. "Another army heading for the castle... Tanek must be with them..."

"Fuck," Dale said quietly. "Okay, we can deal. Let's just get you sorted out first."

Another squeeze of Dale's arm, with all the strength Robert could muster. "Leave me."

"I... we can't do that, Robert."

"Leave me... Get to the castle... Mary... promise me... Mary..." Then his grip relaxed and Dale's features disappeared completely, fading from view. He'd been here before, when he'd been caught in an explosion, fighting De Falaise's men at Mary's farm.

Mary again.

He'd been saved by her that time. But now she was the one in trouble.

In the blackness, Robert heard Dale arguing with someone, with several voices, telling them they had to go.

Dale was following orders, just as he always did. Doing what Robert asked of him. "We'll send back help," were the last words Robert heard him say.

Then there was nothing but stillness – that and the smell of the English countryside – as he lost his grasp on consciousness completely.

CHAPTER SEVENTEEN

THE FIRST SIGN that something was wrong came when they lost contact with the sentries on the outskirts of the city.

"Could just be a fault in the radio equipment," Jack said to Mary when he visited her room, but the look on his face told her he didn't believe that for a second. When Robert's teams had originally infiltrated Nottingham, they'd kept up the pretence that the guards were still on duty, to retain the element of surprise. If the lookouts really were gone, then whoever was on their way didn't care whether they knew or not. "But I've already begun spreading the word among the men, just in case," Jack continued.

"We'd better gather people together," Mary told him. "Just give me a second." She grabbed a coat and fish out her father's precious old Peacekeeper revolvers, along with the bullets she had left. Robert hadn't even bothered asking her to give them up; he'd known what the answer would be. "Okay," she said, and they walked out together along the corridor.

Tate and Gwen hadn't been hard to find, they were still arguing down below.

"The fact remains, you got me here under false pretences. I thought better of you, Reverend." The auburn-haired woman was holding her baby in one arm, and jabbing a free finger in Tate's face.

"I never said anything about sending more weapons back to Hope."

"New Hope," she reminded him. "We have all the food we need, what else was I expected to think?

"You know Robert's feelings as well as I."

"Screw Robert. He's leaving my people out there defenceless!" snapped the woman, then caught sight of Mary and Jack from the corner of her eye. She stopped her rant, but didn't apologise.

Tate shook his head. "I only did this out of the best of intentions. Robert has gone to tackle this new threat, and I thought you'd be safest here."

"You may have underestimated exactly how safe we are," Mary told the holy man.

Jack explained about the lookouts.

"Then we need to break out those weapons right away!" Gwen said. "Start handing them out to your men and –"

"The men are capable of defending themselves as they are," said Mary.

Gwen rounded on her. "I thought you out of all of them had some sense, Mary."

"I do," she replied.

"And what's that tucked away there, a peashooter?" Gwen aimed her finger at Mary's belt, where one gun was stuffed in the front, the other out of sight round the back.

"That's different, it belonged to..." Mary didn't have time for this. "Look, have you seen Mark? We all need to stick together, keep inside the castle."

"And Adele," Jack said. "Have you seen her?"

Mary wasn't actually that bothered where she was.

"Last time I saw Mark, he was with Sophie outside," Tate informed them.

"Right," Mary said, making for the nearest exit and shrugging on her coat.

"Mary, let me –" Jack began, but she was gone before he had time to finish.

Outside, Mary looked for Mark and Sophie. She made her way around the castle, coming up with nothing. She was about to make another pass, but stopped. Something was amiss. You didn't live somewhere for over a year – especially somewhere they'd originally taken over – without noticing subtle differences in your surroundings. This one, however small, was serious.

The lock had been broken on one of the gates leading to the caves, the gate itself slightly ajar.

"Gwen..." Mary muttered to herself. She'd noticed a real difference in the woman since she'd returned to the castle, since she'd set herself up as a leader in her own right at New Hope. Mary had got to know her a little during the later stages of her pregnancy, during and after the birth, but the woman who'd driven in here late yesterday had been barely recognisable. She made some allowance for the fact that Gwen was being forced to return to the place where she had once been held captive, but it was more than that. It was in her eyes. They were colder; the determination she'd exhibited when she left had intensified a hundredfold.

Now she'd taken not a blind bit of notice of Mary, gone down to retrieve the weapons anyway. At first Mary hadn't really understood Robert's instructions herself; surely it made sense – as Bill had repeatedly argued – to use the weapons they'd been handed on a plate? But the more she got to know Robert, the more she saw what kind of man he was and the more she loved him for his convictions. This wasn't an obsession with the past, as her own father had, but rather a revolt against the trappings of a world that spawned the virus in the first place. It had taken everything away from Robert, and left people like De Falaise free to use those kinds of weapons (weapons, she justified to herself, of a different era from her Peacekeepers). If they took up the same kind of arms, Robert had maintained, how long before they were back in the position of country vs. country, with the threat of mass destruction hanging over their heads again?

That was why he'd gone off to face this Tsar character, apparently completely mismatched. But that would be underestimating him, and Mary knew in her heart that Robert was anything but crazy. He believed it was something worth fighting for, a principle worth dying for. She just hoped he was okay.

It was also why she had to go down to the caves and have a word with Gwen, stop her from bringing up more of those weapons. They'd fight whatever was coming in the same spirit as Robert, not as the mad Frenchman would have done. Because he'd lost, hadn't he? And they'd won.

Mary began down the narrow, sheer steps that led into the cave system. The stone was slippery and it was dark. As she descended, though, she saw a flickering light. Someone had turned on the jury-rigged lamps De Falaise had set up down here. For some reason she couldn't quite understand, Mary was as quiet as possible, loath to give away her presence.

She turned a corner and saw it: the arsenal that had been carried down here not long after their victory, Robert's men disarming the Sheriff's troops and locking their toys away where they couldn't hurt anyone anymore. Until, perhaps, now...

Because Mary saw the female figure there in the shadows, hunched down, rooting through the weaponry like a dealer at a scrap metal yard. It was time to announce herself.

"And exactly what do you think you're doing, Gwe –" Mary

cut short her sentence when she realised her mistake. As the figure righted herself, she saw that this woman had short hair, and it was much darker than Gwen's. Slowly, the woman faced her.

"Hello, Mary."

"Adele." For a second or two, Mary's mind couldn't quite process this turn of events. "What are you doing down here?"

Adele just smiled that false smile of hers. "I... I heard about what was happening. And Jack told me about the weapons down here, so..."

"So you just thought you'd come and help yourself?"

"I was scared." But there was something in that voice that told Mary that Adele was anything but scared. This hadn't been a snap decision in the slightest; she knew exactly what she was doing. "Robert's not here and..." Robert again? "I'm glad you and he have patched things up," she tacked on, quickly. "Do you think he'll be all right?"

Mary frowned. What was she doing? Trying to change the subject, attempting to steer it away from why she was down in the caves with these weapons? Mary swept away all the confusion and let her instincts take over.

Don't trust her, Moo-Moo, said her brother's voice, so suddenly it almost made her start. *She doesn't care about Robert. Not really. She doesn't care about any of you.*

Nodding to herself, Mary asked the most obvious question of all, one she should have asked long ago. "Who exactly are you, Adele?"

"What are you talking about?" she said, a bit too hastily.

"Who are you? It's a simple enough question."

Now it was her who frowned. "I'm Adele," she confirmed, as if it answered everything. There was no response from Mary, so Adele began with: "I was born in Durham, moved away when I was old enough, travelled around... What more do you need to know?"

She's lying.

When Mary remained silent, Adele continued, like she was reading from a prepared speech. "Okay, I'm an only child, my mother brought me up on her own. It was... hard. My father... well, he left when I was very young. I never really knew him."

The woman was all caring and sharing now – why? So Mary would have sympathy for her? Another tactic? Were these more lies? Mary couldn't tell for sure, but Adele's eyes appeared to be welling up.

"I never really knew who he was until the end. Until my mother..."

Mary thought about David, about caring for him when he died.

Don't get suckered in Moo-Moo. Don't make this about me, concentrate on what she's saying. Listen, really listen.

"I found some stuff in an old trunk in the attic of the house," Adele went on, as if she needed to get this out, share it with someone after so long. "Papers, old photographs. I knew my father had been a soldier, but nothing more. I didn't even know his real name until then. Can you imagine?"

Was it Mary's imagination, or did Adele's voice sound different, as she was becoming more emotional?

"She told me he died in an accident while serving abroad. Why lie? Why would anyone do that?" Now the tears did roll down her face. "Everyone has a right to know where they came from, don't you think?"

The more Adele talked, the more her accent was slipping.

Born and brought up in Durham my arse... said David.

"Everyone has a right to know their father, Mary! I'd lay odds that you knew yours," Adele almost snarled. "So I set off to look for him. I had nothing but a name. I did not even know if he was still alive. I mean, my blood was his blood, but then we live in such dangerous times. I must have toured the breadth of Europe in those couple of years. But on the streets you hear rumours, and it only took one person to tell me they'd heard that name. One person who'd come across my father. Apparently he had been travelling too. Making friends all over the place. Enemies, as well."

Mary began to move her hand slowly, down and sideways.

"Then he headed across to England. I suppose he thought he could start again. I can understand him wanting to come, I spent some time here myself in my teens. Mastered the lingo pretty well, too, don't you think?" For this last bit Adele's accent jolted back to British, but when she spoke again she didn't bother hiding her true voice, her native accent. "So I followed his trail. All I wanted to do was meet him, get to know him, *non*? But by the time I got over here it was already too late. He really was dead this time. He'd been murdered."

Mary's trembling fingers made their way slowly towards the Peacemaker sticking out of the front of her jeans.

"Strange thing was, he'd been killed by someone wearing a hood, carrying a bow and arrow. A legend. And why was he killed?"

"Because he was a sadistic scumbag," Mary said seriously. "Because he took delight in other people's pain."

Adele shook her head. "Spin, created by those who slaughtered him in cold blood. He had power; he was the Sheriff!"

"He was going to hang people, Adele – if that's really your name."

"It is."

"He kidnapped me and put a sabre to my throat."

"Having spent time with you, I can certainly understand that." Adele's false smile now looked even more wrong. "My mother kept me from getting to know my father –"

"Wise woman," Mary broke in.

Adele scowled. "Then you people kept him from me forever. Well, I decided it was time you paid."

"So you thought you'd worm your way in here, have us all at each other's throats? Was that the plan?" Mary's fingers inched a little nearer to the handle.

"Sort of," admitted Adele. "I believe my father used to use the same methods of infiltration, to get inside his enemies' lairs. But it was always going to come to this in the end."

"It was no coincidence that Robert picked you up in York, was it?"

Adele shook her head. "Hardly. I've been studying the cult's movements, and Robert's, for longer than any of you realise. It wasn't hard to put myself in harm's way, to orchestrate a little... *rendezvous*."

Her fingers were almost there, just a fraction more. *Careful, Mary,* said her brother, which made her even more on edge. He only called her by her real name when he was angry with her or feared for her safety. *She's crazier than her old man was.*

"I must say, I can see why you're attracted to him," Adele stared at her, the tears all but dried up. "Under different circumstances, and if I didn't hate his guts, maybe... Wouldn't be exactly difficult to come between you two, not with all the problems you've both got."

"You didn't come between anyone," Mary said defiantly.

"Right," Adele's tone made Mary want to punch her in the face.

"Look, we don't have much time. The Tsar –"

"Ah yes. An interesting twist," Adele said, stepping forward. "Even I had not foreseen him. I thought I would have to do this alone, but now... Maybe he might want to join forces, do you think?"

Hearing her talk like this, and now seeing her face – her true face – for the first time, Mary couldn't believe she'd been so blind. But then, how could anyone have known about Adele's real origins? In a post-apocalyptic world, what did anyone really know about anyone?

"Especially if I give him a little inside help. It was only what I was going to do anyway, now that a good portion of your compliment are absent... or dead." She said this last bit with such hope, Mary made a grab for her gun – pulling out the Peacekeeper, cocking it, and pointing it at Adele's head. Adele didn't seem surprised; in fact, she smiled again. That same crooked smile. De Falaise's smile. Mary was hardly likely to forget it.

"I wouldn't do that if I were you," Adele told her, then brought up her hands, turning around and showing what she was holding. A live grenade. "The pin's already pulled, in case you were wondering. All I have to do is let go of the trigger. I go, you go with me."

Damn it, said David in her head. Mary didn't have a clue what to do. She couldn't even tell Adele to drop her weapon.

"So, I suggest you let me walk out of here with these." Adele shifted to one side, nodding down at a bag on the floor. Open, because Mary had disturbed her in the act, it contained a rifle, handgun, some more grenades, and what looked to be a mini-bazooka.

"You're not coming past me," Mary said. God knows what kind of damage she'd do with those, and at a time when they might be under attack from the outside as well.

"I don't have to," Adele said. "There are other ways out of here." She grabbed the bag and walked backwards, picking her way through the the weaponry.

Mary's gun arm wavered. "Don't."

"You are not in any position to give me orders."

Mary hated to admit it, but Adele was right. All she could do was watch her as she retreated. When she was a good way off, Adele smiled again.

"I would like to say it has been nice knowing you, but..." Adele let the sentence tail off, then tossed the grenade at Mary.

Mary took a shot, but the woman was already gone. Then her eyes dropped to the grenade bouncing into the middle of the arsenal.

"Nuts," said Mary under her breath.

Run, Mary, run! shouted her brother, but her legs were already in motion. She pelted out the way she had come, making it to the steps and almost all the way up them when the explosion came.

The blast rocked the cave, blowing dust, sandstone, and Mary out with it, causing a section near the exit to fall in just behind her. She felt something heavy land on her leg, pinning her to the steps, pain.

Mary could see the light above, the open gate, but couldn't move. She reached out her hand, yet in spite of the efforts of her brother to keep her awake, Mary found herself blacking out. It sounded like another explosion went off then, but that one was distant. She let it go, able only to focus on one thing.

Her final thoughts were of Robert, Adele's words echoing in her mind.

Absent... or dead.

Absent...

Or dead.

CHAPTER EIGHTEEN

THEY WERE ALL dead.

Piled up, in front of the Tsar. And he was looking down on them with such a satisfied smile on his face. Mary, Tate, Sophie, Mark. And finally Jack, thrown down there by the giant Tanek, while the two Asian women looked on, swords drawn, ready to protect their lord with their lives if necessary.

At the Tsar's feet was the suited man, crawling, half dead; one of his hands missing and blood staining his shirt from the belly wound Dale had given him. All around them the forest was on fire. It was being attacked by the troops they'd found on the battlefield, trees mowed aside by armoured vehicles. The sound of chopper-blades could be heard overhead.

On his knees, Robert made an effort to get up and rush forward, to take revenge for the deaths of the people he loved. But he found he couldn't move. It was like he was stuck, his limbs unable to respond to his commands. His eyes were about the only things that could, and when he dipped them, he saw a light coating of fur on his chest, on his entire body (though he couldn't reach up this time – Robert didn't even think he had hands – he knew there would be antlers on his head). His shoulder was bleeding profusely, and so was his thigh.

But there was something else. A figure behind the Tsar. A woman. He recognised her short black hair, the pretty features, instantly.

It was the woman he'd saved from the cultists. Adele. Indeed, the more he looked at the soldiers flanking them, the more he saw their number amongst the troops: the robed men with machetes here and there, blending in with the Tsar's fighters.

Robert's attention was snapped back to Adele, though, as she draped herself over the Tsar, hands on his shoulders, lips to his ear.

The Russian's grin widened, but his twin bodyguards looked like they wanted to run their swords right through her.

Then she came around the front, stroking Tanek's bicep as he joined them. There was something about the way she looked now, something that rang a warning bell. It was as if the layers were being peeled away, revealing the real face of this woman beneath the façade. There it was in the eyes, in the crooked smile. He'd seen those features before, he'd looked into them as he'd been locked in a deathgrip. A relation? A cousin? A sister?

No. A daughter.

If only he had known earlier.

"Vengeance," whispered Adele in a French accent, now to the side of him. Now at his ear.

The *thrup-thrup* of an attack helicopter drowned her out, about to fire its payload as it had during the battle. The battle which he'd just fought and ended up –

Tanek, in front of him, was raising his crossbow – preparing to shoot and then cut the antlers from Robert's crown. But those damned rotor blades, they were making such a row.

So close, so close.

Tanek raised his crossbow and shot...

...Robert's eyelids cracked open, then immediately closed again.

The noise of the rotor blades from his dream carried on. He must still be there, must still be in the dreamscape. But now he felt pain – real pain. The kind you could never feel in a dream. The kind that reminded him what he'd been through in the battle and the fight with the suited man.

Which meant that the sound of the chopper was real, too.

Robert forced open one eye. Yes, there was the outline of a helicopter. His lid snapped shut again. They'd taken out three of those things, but only incapacitated the first. It had to be that one returning to finish the job, the pilot intent on revenge, about to spray the field with bullets.

Robert kept as still as he could, feeling the shadow of the thing above him. But then his injured leg betrayed him, the pain jabbing into him until the thigh moved of its own accord. That was just great; first he couldn't move at all, then his body was moving independently of his mind, giving him away.

He prised open both eyes, taking in the sight of the chopper directly overhead. If he was going out, finally, then he was going to meet death with his eyes wide open. Strangely, he realised he would miss seeing Mary's face much more than he was looking forward to seeing Joanna. It was a horrible, horrible thing, but true.

"I'm... I'm sorry," he muttered, but he wasn't sure which one of them he was apologising to.

Then Robert braced himself for those bullets.

HE KEPT THE helicopter level, coming in low and sweeping over the battleground.

What the hell had happened here?

Hell actually did look like it had happened to this place. This sleepy, wintry English meadow had been the site of some kind of rift, a portal connecting our world with –

He shook his head. That was cobblers. What had happened here was man's work, not the Devil's. Two warring sides ripping each other to shreds.

The blackened and charred remains of tanks, jeeps, motorcycles and armoured vehicles littered the landscape. As did bodies, dozens of them. If he'd thought it was bad last time then...

"Judas bloody Priest."

When Bill had found out that something big was going down here, from a variety of his sources, he had climbed straight into his chopper and into the air.

He'd spent much of the time since the fracas at the Bay keeping tabs on the army that had landed, and what he was hearing made him sick to his stomach. These people made the Frenchman look like an amateur. They'd crash through cities, towns and villages like a juggernaut, treating those who could defend themselves and those who could not the same, killing both in equal measures.

Somebody needed to stop them, just like they'd stopped the Sheriff. But with guns, tanks, jeeps and armoured vehicles of their own. Fighting fire with fire. It was the only way. Not like this, not with rocks, with arrows and swords. Not on horseback! It was the same old argument, one that had seen him leave these ranks in the first place and, looking around today, he was glad he'd got out in time.

Yet, as much as he believed that, Bill had to admit they'd fared damned well. Robert had again pulled something together out of nothing, led his men in an attack that any modern army would have been proud of. Seen off greater numbers and firepower with what looked like sheer force of will. There were more – many, many more – uniformed bodies down there than Rangers; which wasn't to say they hadn't taken heavy casualties as well. Bill spotted two or three corpses next to a small crater that looked as if they'd been melted down like plastic. Others had been raked with machine gun fire, their bows, arrows and swords laying uselessly by their sides. Robert couldn't have done all this with so few men, surely? Which begged the question, if there were survivors, where the blazes were they?

As he swept across the devastation, Bill saw something else. Someone he recognised down there, hood back and sprawled out on the ground. He was injured, that much Bill could tell – hasty field dressings covered his thigh and shoulder. But whether it was more serious than that, whether he was... Bill shook his head. He couldn't be, not Robert. Ever since Bill had first seen him in action, he'd seemed indestructible. But he wasn't some kind of superhero. He was flesh and blood like the rest of them.

Which meant he could die. There, it was in Bill's head before he could shake it. But he wouldn't find out by staying up in the air like this. Quickly, Bill searched for a place to set the Gazelle down. Everywhere he looked there were the carcasses of fighting machines or the ground was too churned up for a stable landing, but eventually he managed to find a small area of flat ground.

"Back in a sec, girl," he told the chopper, grabbing both his shotgun and one of his newly acquired AK-47s. He had no idea whether there were any Russian soldiers in hiding, waiting for someone to come along, so he wasn't taking any chances.

Cautiously, Bill picked his way across the field, hurrying when he got closer to Robert's position. Taking one last look around him, pointing the guns in every direction, he crouched on the floor beside Robert. Putting the machine gun on the ground, though still ready with his trusty double-barrelled shotgun if he needed it, Bill checked the side of Robert's neck for a pulse. For a second he couldn't find one, then he realised he was panicking, feeling in the wrong place. He calmed down and brought his fingers up higher, to the crevice between the chin and neck. There it was, a faint beat. Robert was still alive.

Bill let out the breath he'd been holding. They'd had their moments in the past, but this was still the man who'd saved his life. The man he'd gone into battle with at the castle. "Rob," he said, slapping the man's cheek. "Rob, can ye hear me?"

There was a flicker under Robert's eyelids.

"Rob?"

Robert opened his eyes, though they were still practically slits. "Not... not dead..." he whispered and Bill almost missed what he said. The man sounded surprised, like he'd been expecting to wake up at the Pearly Gates.

"Naw, but ye doin' a good impression of a dead man. Look at the state of ye, lad."

"B-Bill?" Robert managed, as if he'd only just realised who was talking to him. "Is that you?"

"Aye."

"W-what are you – ?"

"Later," Bill promised him. "Along wi' the *I-told-ye-sos*." He felt bad saying it, but if Robert had only listened to him... "Right now I reckon ye need them wounds lookin' at. Get ye back to Mary."

"No," said Robert, louder than he'd said anything since Bill found him.

"No?" Bill couldn't understand that. Surely Mary would be the first person he'd want to see? They'd been as thick as thieves since they met. And she had all that medical knowledge.

"S-Sherwood," Robert said.

"Eh? What d'you want to go back there for? Ye really have lost it." Robert wouldn't – or couldn't – explain. He just said: "Please."

"But –"

"Please," Robert repeated more emphatically, and placed a trembling hand on Bill's arm.

"All right, but let's get yer wounds dressed properly first. I've got a medical kit in the helicopter."

Robert nodded, then winced in pain.

"Ye know," said Bill, standing. "Yer one stubborn man, Robert Stokes."

"Look... look who's talking," wheezed Robert, a slight smile playing on his lips.

Bill shook his head and went off back to the chopper.

CHAPTER NINETEEN

MARK HAD BEEN having the most serious conversation of his life when it all hit the fan.

Stupidly, he'd figured now was the perfect time to talk to Sophie. Dale was out of the way – though it still smarted that Robert had chosen to take him along and not Mark – and the place was more peaceful than it had been in weeks. Plucking up the courage had proved to be more difficult. He would rather have faced another dozen of the men in robes than come out and tell Sophie how he really felt. Fighting was much simpler than dealing with all these emotions.

Eventually, he decided he couldn't put it off any longer. They were facing all kinds of threats; he might not get the chance to say anything later on. What was the worst that could happen?

She could shoot him down in flames, that's what. Bullets to the heart doing more damage than real ones ever could.

Mark had thought about Sophie a lot, even before she came to the castle. He'd even wondered whether it was worth going out and finding her himself, to see how she was after he'd been dragged off by De Falaise's men. But then she'd followed him here. It had to be a sign, didn't it? Some kind of omen?

But Dale had come along before Mark had a chance to say anything. Dale with the good looks and stories about gigging; Dale with his guitar, making up songs to impress her. How could Mark hope to compete with that? For starters, Dale was older and much more experienced. He knew what to say to girls.

Whereas you'll probably make a balls up of this, he told himself as he went in search of Sophie. *Just like you do with everything.*

Then she'd found him again. Coming round a corner, he'd bumped right into her, almost knocking them both over. "Sophie!"

"Hey, it's all right. No harm done. Although if you do it again I might just have to retaliate, soldier boy."

Soldier boy, thought Mark. *There's that word again. That's all I am to her really, a boy.* When we first met, all she'd talked about was the Hooded Man, though she didn't know then how old he was. Imagined him closer to Dale's age.

"So," she continued. "Whatcha doing?"

"Oh, er..." Mark scratched the back of his head, losing his hand in his tangle of dark-blonde hair. "Nothing, I was just... Sophie?"

"Yeah."

"Can I talk to you?"

"I thought that's what you were doing," she said and gave another little chuckle. "No, I'm sorry, I'm in a daft mood today: go on."

"Somewhere a bit more, I don't know, private?"

Sophie looked around, there was nobody in sight. "Sure. Inside?"

Mark shook his head, then gestured for her to follow him. They walked down the steps to the overgrown grounds, formerly a recreational park with a Victorian bandstand. That was still there, and it was where Mark chose to make his confession.

Sophie sat on a bench, then watched as Mark paced in front of her. "Sophie... I..."

"Mark, what is it? You can tell me." He looked at her freckled face, the most beautiful thing he'd ever seen. How could he upset her?

"No. It doesn't matter."

"Obviously it does, or you wouldn't have brought us down here." He stopped pacing. "Sophie..."

"Come on, Mark, just tell me."

He swallowed hard. "Okay. We're friends, right?"

She laughed again, only this time it was a kind of *I don't believe you just said that* laugh. "Of course, silly. You're like my best friend, Mark."

His smile came out wonky. *Best friend is good. But is that all we'll ever be? And if I say this, will it ruin that friendship forever?*

"What's all this about, Mark?"

He decided to risk it.

"Sophie, I really love you." There, it was out.

"Well, I love you too."

Now that he hadn't been expecting. "What?"

"'Course I do. We've been through a lot together, Mark." He couldn't believe what he was hearing. "We'll always be friends and I'll always love you to bits."

Now he could.

"Sophie, what I meant was... When I said I love you, I meant..."

She looked blank, then the penny dropped. "Ooh. I see."

Mark stared down at his boots. "God, this is awkward."

"Listen," she began, getting up to join him. "I don't want you to take this the wrong way. You're incredibly sweet, but..."

Don't say it, please don't say it. You're loading up the gun, about to shoot. Soon there'll be flames everywhere. Crash and burn, Mark, crash and burn.

"...but I'm not looking for anything like that right now."

Mark looked up. "You mean with me?"

"I mean with anyone."

"Does that include Dale?"

Sophie laughed again, then she saw he was serious. "Dale?"

"He's older, you spend a lot of time together."

"Mark, there's nothing going on between me and Dale, I promise you. I'm just happy to be alive right now, happy to be here. I need to be around people who make me feel safe."

"But Dale –"

"Oh, my God – Dale's a laugh, Mark. I like his company, that doesn't mean I'm going to jump into bed with him!"

"I didn't mean..."

"My sister went out with plenty of men like him, before..." She looked sad for a moment, remembering. "Trust me, I'm not looking for a guy like that."

"Then there's still a chance?"

Why can't you keep your big mouth shut, Mark? If you push it, she'll tell you – and this way you can live in hope.

"No... I don't know. Not right now, anyway. Look, this is starting to make me feel uncomfortable."

"I just wanted to –"

"Mark, just drop it. Please." She made to leave.

Mark stood in her way. "Sophie, just let me explain."

"Mark, I said drop it!" Something in her eyes told him to do as she asked. This had gone from talking to arguing and Mark couldn't see the join. He got out of her way.

Almost immediately Mark changed his mind and went after her, but she had a lead on him and was heading for the steps. In fact she was racing up them; he'd really upset her.

His head was telling him to leave this alone, yet his legs were still carrying him forwards. Perhaps that was his immaturity. In the same situation, Dale might let her calm down, talk to her later. But he wouldn't have created this situation in the first place! All Mark knew was that he wanted to make this right again.

He was part of the way up the steps when he heard the explosion, felt the earth tremble beneath his feet.

Sophie! was his one and only thought.

His legs worked harder, getting him to the top. His eyes scanned the area quickly, as he shouted Sophie's name. Then he saw her. She was on the ground, had been blown over by the blast. He raced across and checked her for wounds. She didn't seem hurt, just extremely shaken up. He couldn't help thinking about her words not ten minutes ago:

"I'm just happy to be alive right now, happy to be here... I need to be around people who make me feel safe."

"Sophie, are you okay?"

Eyes wide, she nodded. "Mary," she said, pointing. He followed her finger and saw the gate to the caves wide open, smoke coming from beneath. "I saw her. She was trying to get out."

Mark left Sophie and ran over. He had time to glimpse a figure on the stairs, with long dark hair, partly buried under the rubble. There was blood on the walls. His hands went to his mouth, but before he could do anything about it, there were more explosions – this time coming from near the castle entrance.

THE FIRST VOLLEY of shells hit the side of the castle wall, fired by tanks and armoured vehicles coming from two directions.

Mortars were also fired into the grounds, to send the enemy into turmoil, taking some out in the process. The guards positioned on the walls and at the castle's front gate did their best to fight back, but they were unprepared for an attack of this scale. Robert was supposed to have slowed the army's progress at least. That they could have split into two, that they had enough weapons, vehicles and men to do that, hadn't been regarded as a serious possibility.

Until now.

It wasn't long before the side gates were breached, an AFV smashing through them, busting them wide, allowing smaller vehicles to follow; jeeps and motorbikes. The assembled Rangers in the grounds shot at the vehicles with flaming arrows, the concoctions attached exploding on impact. Returning machine gun fire from the mounted guns dropped the Rangers in turn. Men entered the grounds, overrunning the place – not just soldiers, but men in robes. Members of the cult.

Robert's troops stood more of a chance against them, swords

clashing with machetes, but again there were just too many. One by one, those defending the castle fell, and a path up towards the castle keep itself was cleared.

A rocket blast hit the side of the castle, but oddly it didn't seem to come from the outside. It appeared to have been fired by someone in the grounds, its tail winding down towards the Middle Bailey. Masonry dropped on people below, taking out more fighters.

From an AFV near the back of the convoy, they watched all this with satisfaction: Tanek, the Tsar and the twins. Tanek was itching to get out there, to take his place with the men on the ground. To, as he put it, 'crack some skulls.' The Tsar insisted he wait a little while, at least until they'd put down the first wave of resistance.

Tanek huffed at that, and watched for his opportunity to leave the vehicle.

TATE, JACK AND Gwen were still inside when the first explosions came.

Tate told Gwen to go to one of the rooms while they checked on the situation. Ordinarily, she'd have argued, but having Clive Jr with her, she did as he suggested. She could protect him better inside.

When the Reverend and Jack stepped out of the castle, they could scarcely believe what they were seeing. Already the grounds were flooded with enemy foot-soldiers. "Where are they all coming from?"

Jack shook his head and clutched his staff.

It wasn't long before they encountered the first couple of men, running towards them. Luckily they were cult members, not soldiers. Jack and Tate looked at each other. Since when was the Tsar in league with the Morningstars?

Then they were on them. Jack met a machete blow with his staff. Tate dodged his opponent, but seemed reluctant to fight. He only just got out of the way of the second swing, his face a rictus of fear.

"Rev, look out!" shouted Jack, striking his man in the stomach, crumpling him up, and then slamming the staff down on the back of his head. Without drawing breath, Jack swung the staff around and smacked the cultist attacking Tate in the face. He went down backwards, dropping the machete. "Are you okay?" Jack asked Tate, who looked dazed. These guys really freaked the holy man out.

"I... I don't understand," the Reverend said finally.

"Me either. But let's figure it out later. Right now we've got to –" He dragged Tate down as a hail of gunfire tore into the wall behind them. The soldiers hadn't been that far behind, as it turned out.

Leaving Tate, Jack ducked and rolled, coming up and striking one of the Tsar's men across the legs, sending him toppling over. Another he whacked in the side, then brought the staff around again to catch a third across the chest. Not seeing another way to tackle those coming up the steps, Jack grabbed a Kalashnikov belonging to one of the incapacitated soldiers and shot over the heads of the approaching troops. They backed off.

He returned to Tate, taking him by the arm. "Come on, we have to fall back!" It wasn't easy getting away with the Reverend's limp, and when they turned the next corner, Jack saw Mark and Sophie running to meet them.

"Jack, what's happening?" asked Mark.

"We're under attack, kiddo. And not just from those Russians – from the cult as well."

"What?"

"We don't have much time. Have you seen Mary? Adele?"

"Adele, no."

"But you've seen Mary?" said Tate. "She went looking for you."

"Oh, no, did she?" Sophie was choking back tears.

"What is it?"

"There was an explosion," Mark told them. "In the caves. Maybe the soldiers got down there, I don't know. But... I think she might be..."

Jack shook his head. "No way, not Mary!"

"I didn't get a chance to check, there were men coming up the steps," Mark told him.

"There are men everywhere," Sophie added, with a worried frown.

Jack gave Mark the rifle, then placed his hand on the lad's shoulder, squeezing firmly. "Anyone can see which way this is heading. It's *Assault on Precinct 13*, and you've gotta get out of here. Remember what Robert said if things went south."

"But –"

Jack looked at him sternly. "That's an order, Mark. Get Sophie out, get Tate out. I'll follow when I've checked on Mary and found Adele."

Tate's hand went to his mouth. "Gwen! She's still inside." As soon as he said it, the castle took a hit. The shell punched out the top corner of the building, across from where they were standing. Mark shielded Sophie from the dust, as Jack and Tate turned their backs on it.

Coughing, Jack spluttered, "I'll find her too, now go!"

"I can't leave her alone, not again."

"Go!" repeated Jack, taking off himself.

Sophie and Mark took an arm each and tugged, but the Reverend was still reluctant to leave. Then more soldiers found them, bullets spraying the floor. Mark lifted the rifle, but he'd never fired a gun in his life – hadn't even trained for it. But he had no bow and arrow with him, no sword or staff. He had no option other than to use the weapon he'd been handed. He tried to fire it, but all he got was a *click* as he pressed the trigger.

Mark looked up and saw several soldiers all aiming their weapons in his and Sophie's direction. This was it. They were dead.

Then, suddenly, he was being relieved of the rifle, and bullets were fired from it. Tate aimed for the men's legs, wounding but not killing them. Mark's jaw dropped, but he didn't have time to ask where the Reverend had learned to use one of those things, nor how his aim was so good. There was another wave of attackers coming, a mixture of Russians and cult members.

Pushing Sophie behind him, Mark laid into the first one, a robed figure who ran at him a machete raised. Mark used his momentum against him, grabbing that arm and breaking it at the elbow. He relieved the screaming cultist of his weapon, just in time to meet a blow from another blade heading for Sophie.

Tate, for his part, was still firing at the soldiers, slowing their progress towards the castle. When the rifle ran out of ammo, he picked up his stick again and tackled the closest of the soldiers. When it came to fighting the cultists, though, Tate was still wavering; dangerously so, as Mark had to hack at one of their arms to stop a machete swipe from finding the Reverend's neck.

While he was doing this, his attention divided, Mark felt someone at the side of him. When he turned, a fist glanced across his chin. He stumbled, shocked, snapping out of it just in time to see a bayonet about to be rammed into his chest.

Then the attacking soldier was being struck, with almost as much force as the blow which had taken Mark by surprise. When the soldier looked to see who'd done this, he got a kick in the groin as well. Sophie nodded in satisfaction. Mark smiled at her, and she smiled back.

"We've got to get out of here," he called over to Tate. "Before the castle's riddled with them. Jack said he would follow. Reverend? Reverend, we need you!"

Tate still looked like he was going to disagree, then at last relented, and the trio made their way towards the path that seemed to have the least amount of troops flooding it.

CHAPTER TWENTY

HIS PLACE WAS with the men.

But his mind was also on the women in danger: Mary (who wasn't dead, no matter what Sophie and Mark had seen), Gwen and Adele.

Her especially.

Since she'd come to the castle, Jack had felt a certain connection with Adele. They'd talked and spent time together. She'd reminded him what it was like to be in the company of an attractive woman. Reminded him there were more things in this world than fighting the bad guys. Just as Mark was protecting Sophie, and Gwen was in Tate's thoughts, Adele was all he could think about. Where she was, if she was all right, how he could get her out of here. She'd said that she'd at last found a home after all that travelling, and now it was being torn down around her. Jesus, she must be terrified.

Jack paused to dispatch a couple of Russians, dropping and rolling along the floor so that he knocked the feet out from under them; one of his favourite wrestling moves back when he'd been on the circuit. This was usually the place where he'd say, "You've just been Jack-Hammered, pal!" but it wasn't the time for glib remarks. His newfound family was being attacked, being threatened. Being destroyed.

Suddenly, there she was. Adele. Down on the Middle Bailey, soldiers crowding in on her. It looked like she was trying to surrender, but they kept on coming. Jack made to get down there as quickly as possible, but in the end he didn't need to. Somehow, from somewhere, Adele had acquired a rifle of her own. She swung it around, shooting the Russians dead.

As Jack watched, he saw two of his men come to her aid – he recognised Wilkes and Ferguson – and she spun fast, about to blow them away as well. "Adele, no!" he shouted. "Friendlies!"

She turned to see who was calling, saw it was Jack, then saw the men were there to help. As he hurried to join her, however, his attention shifted to an armoured vehicle that had crested the incline and was now on the bailey itself.

As Jack stood there, he saw the hatch on top open, and a very familiar figure clamber out. If his size hadn't given him away, then his olive skin certainly did. They'd met once before, over a year ago now. Back then the man had been shot by Bill after Jack had taken a beating from him. He'd often wondered what would have happened in a rematch, and it looked like he was about to find out. Tanek was staring straight at him, and for a second or two it seemed like he'd only ventured out because of Jack. Then Tanek produced his crossbow and shot a couple of Rangers for sheer sport.

Grinding his teeth, Jack made it the rest of the way to the Bailey, hollering as he went: "Come on down, you big ape. We got unfinished business!"

Tanek grinned, aiming the crossbow at Jack. Then he placed it on top of the AFV and reached inside the vehicle. He pulled out what looked like a large metal spear, about the same size as Jack's staff.

The olive-skinned man hopped down, and swatted away another one of the castle's fighters with the pike. Jack spun his own staff. There was no way this sadistic sonofabitch was going to get his hands on Adele or the others – he'd personally see to that.

"Come on, then. Let's see what you got."

"You. Talk. Too. Much," was Tanek's staggered reply, and he rushed Jack, hefting the metal lance high.

Jack blocked the move, his arms juddering with the vibrations of the blow. Christ, the man was strong; his 'death' had done little to change that. He was also as quick as ever, in spite of the limp – given to him, Jack remembered, by Mark.

Nevertheless, Jack pushed him backwards, getting in a strike to the stomach with the end of his heavy staff. He might as well have been hitting concrete, because Tanek hardly even flinched.

Okay, thought Jack, *try this.*

He cut to the left and brought the staff up to strike the back of Tanek's neck: the same spot he'd punched Jack the last time they met – signalling the end of the fight. Tanek's pike was up in a flash, catching Jack's blow and retaliating with one of his own – which caused Jack to roll forward. He came up poised to fight, narrowly avoiding the sharp end of the spear.

Tanek tried again to impale Jack. As he shifted sideways, Jack noticed more people emerging from the armoured vehicle. First up were two oriental women in skin-tight black leather outfits, carrying lethal-looking swords. They climbed down like spiders navigating a wall. A couple of Jack's men had a go at them with their own swords and soon found out how outclassed they were, the women spinning and twisting as they slashed open necks, arms and thighs. One move from the girl on the right practically sliced some poor fighter's head – a young Ranger called Mundy – clean off.

The women stood ready to protect the next person getting out of the AFV, whopulled on a peaked cap before dropping down. In his long coat and maroon military outfit, it could only be the Tsar himself. Here to oversee the fall of the castle, of the Hooded Man's empire.

If Jack could take him out, then –

But he had more pressing issues to deal will. Literally, as Tanek and he clashed weapons, each pushing against the other, neither willing to give ground. Jack's feet slipped a little on the slushy grass, but he dug his heels in, unwilling to let Tanek take an inch.

Although his identical bodyguards were there to protect him, the Tsar was not averse to getting his hands dirty, it seemed. Jack saw him take out his own long, curved sword: Jack had seen its like in movies, but had never seen one being used for real.

The Tsar ran one of the wounded soldiers through, pulling out the blade and admiring the blood dripping from it.

He's just as sadistic as De Falaise... as Tanek, Jack thought. *Possibly a fighter in the past, but now prefers the sure-fire kill. I might be able to use that, if I can get close enough.*

Then the Tsar's attention was drawn to Adele and the men flanking her: Jack's men. With the oriental sisters – twins? – in tow, the Tsar glided forward across the Bailey towards them.

Jack had to finish this right now. Had to get across to Adele before she ended up like Mundy.

That was easier said than done; Tanek wasn't in the mood for quitting. The olive-skinned man flashed his teeth and gave one last shove, but Jack realised what he was doing and decided to give him the inch he wanted. In fact, he could take the whole middle bailey if he liked. Without warning, Jack took the pressure off his staff and stepped aside, causing Tanek to lunge forward, struggling to keep upright. As he passed by, Jack gave him a whack across the shoulder blades to help him on his way. Pitching him almost into the side of the steps.

He wasn't completely out of the game, but it would do for now.

Jack sprinted across the field, holding the staff horizontally to take out two more Russian soldiers, each end smacking into a face. He was going to be too late to reach Adele; the twins were already closing in, and although she had a rifle, they'd still make mincemeat of her. Wilkes and Ferguson lunged forward, their intention to stop the women, but in reality all they could really do was try not to get themselves killed.

To begin with they did pretty well, holding their own against the two bodyguards, as fast as they were. And Jack was almost there when Wilkes received a savage slash to the side, biting into him to a depth of about four or five inches. He looked over at Jack, his eyes pleading as blood poured from the wound.

"You bitches are gonna to pay for that," Jack promised, holding his staff by the end and swinging it so that it caught one of the bodyguards across the forearm. The shock bought him enough time to kick her over onto the ground.

Her sister looked across, and paid the price – as Ferguson got close enough to aim a punch at her head. The Tsar, instead of coming to their aid, pulled back slightly, raising his sword in a defensive stance.

The sister closest to Jack was recovering quickly, getting to her feet and taking a swing at him with her sword, then skirting past and making for Adele. "Where do you think you're goin', huh?" shouted Jack, grabbing her hair and yanking her back.

Ferguson had the drop on the second, raising his sword to bring it down on her. But she'd only been feigning weakness from his punch, and lifted her sword up to meet his, before kicking high and knocking him out of the way. Her path to Adele was now clear. Adele held the rifle up, then cast it to the side, attempting to surrender once more.

Dropping his staff, Jack dragged the first sister back and wrapped his free arm around her neck in a wrestler's chin lock, forcing her to her knees. "Back away from the little lady, sweetheart, or I'll crush your sister's windpipe." He hoped she could tell from the look on his face that he meant business.

The other bodyguard did as he asked, slowly backing away from the defenceless Adele. "Th-thank you, Jack," the woman called over to him. The look of sheer relief on her face was thanks enough. They weren't out of this yet, though. He glanced over and saw Adele take a handgun out of her coat.

Attagirl, thought Jack.

She pointed it at the other oriental woman, covering her. Then a weird expression passed over Adele's face, a sort of calmness... as she pulled the trigger. Jack was stunned; he didn't think she had it in her. Then again, life on the streets post-virus could do a lot to a person. He expected to see the bodyguard fold up and hit the ground. Instead, she stood there – apparently as surprised as everyone else that she was still alive.

Then he saw it. Behind the woman, just to the left of her, was Ferguson, who'd been coming up behind to restrain her. Adele's bullet had put paid to that. Jack's head was spinning. She'd missed and shot Ferguson by accident, clearly not as used to a gun as she appeared. But the wound was slap-bang in the centre of Ferguson's forehead, a million-to-one shot for a mistake. She'd been aiming for him, and she'd hit her target.

Adele turned the gun on Jack. "Now let her go," she told him.

He couldn't take any of this in. "What are you doing, you can't –"

"I said let her go, Jack. Don't make this any more difficult."

Difficult? What was she talking about? Jack looked at the other twin, then at the Tsar. If they hadn't appeared as puzzled as him, he might – just might – have leapt to the conclusion that she was working for their side. An infiltrator. No, that was impossible. Not Adele. She'd just seen the way the wind was blowing, that was all. Had chosen to try and switch sides to save her life. All that time surviving out there alone, you put yourself first. But it didn't have to be that way, he'd show her.

"We can still get out of here, you and me. Don't –"

"Shut up," Adele snapped. "I'm not going anywhere with you."

"You're scared, I understand that, but –"

"You understand nothing!" she screamed, and this time it wasn't her voice. Not the one she'd spoken with before, anyway. Not the voice of the Adele who'd toured the castle with him, eaten with him as they'd gotten to know each other. This was the voice of a ghost. A voice he knew all too well. "I say again, Jack. Let her go."

For a second he almost did it, purely because he was so astonished. But Jack instinctively held on to his hostage. If he was walking out of here, it was with the Chinese woman as his captive. Not with Adele – or whoever she was – arm in arm, like in some stupid chick flick. Jack should have known better, he'd never had the greatest luck with women. But for her to turn out to be...

There was a sudden pain in his back. He was forced to let go of the woman then, to reach round to his back to understand...

The Chinese bodyguard stumbled forward out of his grasp, towards her twin, rubbing her throat. Jack looked over his shoulder and saw Tanek standing there, pike held like a very long club, having just returned the favour for Jack knocking him on his ass.

Another blow and Jack was on his knees, his staff on the floor, kicked out of reach. Adcle still had the gun trained on him and he couldn't decide which way would be better to go, a shot to the head – like Ferguson – or having Tanek ram that pointed piece of metal through him.

Through his broken heart.

The twins were edging their way towards Adele, and she was watching them out of the corner of her eye. Jack had no doubt that she'd turn the gun on them in a heartbeat if she thought she was in danger.

"Leave her be," Jack heard Tanek say to them. He'd recognised her as well, or at least a part of her. The part that must have come from *him*; the psycho who'd started all this in the first place. The reason they were all here today. As Adele came closer, still holding the gun out straight, Jack could see the same look in her eye now: an insane look. The look of a daughter out for revenge.

Jack gave a sad laugh. "I thought we had something there, for a while."

"Oh, please," she said, then spat at him. "You were one of the men who murdered my father! How could I ever have feelings for you other than loathing?"

Jeez, do I have lousy taste in broads or what? Well, it's cost you this time, hasn't it, numbskull?

"Father?" asked the Tsar, now deeming it safe to come closer, though not before his bodyguards joined him again. "You don't mean that –"

Tanek nodded. "She is De Falaise's child." He exchanged a long look with Adele, who smiled. "The person I came here to find."

CHAPTER TWENTY-ONE

THEY'D BEEN LIES, pure and simple.

No two ways about it. Tate had lured her here under false pretences, as she'd told him repeatedly. When the message had reached her about the approaching army, one that apparently made De Falaise's look like a joke, she'd leaped at the opportunity to come to the castle for more weapons. If the soldiers passed through New Hope, then her people would need all the help they could get. It wasn't as if Robert was using them, was it? Gwen had to admit she'd been puzzled as to why they were suddenly going to give them to her, after denying them for so long, but she wasn't about to look a gift horse in the mouth. Telling Andy, Darryl, Graham and the others that she'd be back soon, she'd headed off for Nottingham with Clive Jr.

When she'd driven back through the gates and found the Reverend, he'd stalled her to begin with by offering her food and drink after her journey, then insisted that they should stay at the castle overnight as it was growing late. It was then that she discovered Robert and a good chunk of his men had gone off to meet the Tsar's forces, taking with them only rudimentary weapons.

"He's completely crackers, you do know that?" Gwen told Tate.

The Reverend said nothing, no doubt thinking God would be on the man's side. Oh, well, it was his funeral – and it meant that there would be more real weapons for her to take back with her (and they'd damned well need them after Robert had finished agitating the Tsar). When she discovered that would not be the case, Gwen went ballistic.

She argued with Tate until she was blue in the face, but he refused to see reason.

"Is this about what happened before?" Gwen asked him. "About how you left me here?"

"I didn't..." Tate faltered. "I wanted to come sooner, but –"

"But you didn't because of Robert, right? Meanwhile that lunatic Frenchman was..." Gwen's eyes hardened, the memories too painful. "You want to help me, salve your conscience? You give me those weapons and let me return right now."

That hadn't happened, of course, and they'd been discussing it yet again when Mary and Jack had joined them. Apparently the army was coming to the castle. Robert's men had hardly slowed them at all. Tate had screwed up again, and he knew it. Now she and her baby had been placed right in the firing line, when she'd probably have been much safer back home.

There was a part of her that recognised Tate had only been doing what he thought best, that he genuinely did care about her. But he'd deliberately misled her, and for that she would never forgive him. If only to protect Clive Jr, she'd done as he'd asked when he'd told her to go and wait in one of the bedrooms, while outside she could hear explosions and gunfire.

Gwen had sat there holding her child, telling him everything was going to be alright, but knowing that it really wasn't. *He's placed you in so much danger, little Clive,* Gwen said to herself, looking down at her son. *What in Heaven's name was he thinking?*

She peeked out of the window, and it was then that something hit the side of the castle. The whole room shook and she grabbed Clive Jr, dashing out as quickly as she could. She ran back up along the corridor, desperate to find somewhere safe. She'd brought a machine gun with her in case she'd been attacked on the journey, but that was in her jeep. Luckily, she'd kept her pistol about her person, in spite of the 'rules,' which she didn't give a shit about. If Mary could break them just because of some sentimental rubbish, so could she.

Gwen reached around and pulled the gun out, tucked away in the back of her jeans, under her baggy jumper. No sooner had she done so than she heard voices below her, heading up the stairs. Russian voices.

She backed away, but Clive chose that particular moment to start crying. Gwen shushed him, but he cried all the more. She turned to run, only to crash into a figure that appeared in front of her.

The man was wearing dark red robes, a hood pulled up over his head. In his hand he held a lethal-looking blade.

He was not alone. There were two more dressed just like him. Gwen knew who they were. Members of the cult Robert had told Tate about. What they were doing here was another matter. She'd been expecting to see soldiers, not religious fanatics.

It wasn't important. All that mattered was they meant her and her son harm. Gwen raised the handgun. None of them even twitched.

"Don't move!" Gwen warned them.

The closest raised his hand.

"I said don't you fucking move! I'm not afraid to use this thing." She meant every word. It wasn't like the first time she'd held it, when she'd made her first kill: shooting the bastard who'd murdered her beloved Clive. She'd hesitated then, but she wouldn't now.

It didn't stop the cultist from continuing to raise his hand, peeling back the hood to show her his face, painted to look like a skull, a tattoo on his forehead, the one Robert had described. That fazed her momentarily.

But then the cultist on the right rushed forward, raising his machete. Gwen fired twice, hitting him in the chest. He dropped to the floor, blood pooling around him.

The taller one, Skullface, looked down slowly at his fallen comrade. If he was angry or upset by the man's demise, he hid it well.

Gwen heard noises behind her. The soldiers! She'd forgotten all about them. As she pivoted, she saw uniformed men holding automatics, training them in her direction. Holding Clive Jr in the crook of her arm, she fired the gun with her other hand, causing the little one to cry out even louder. Gwen hit the first soldier in the neck and a red spray jetted out of the wound.

Gwen spun round again, aware that she'd taken her eye off the cultists, and saw the man rushing forward, brandishing his machete. It connected with the end of her pistol and sent it flying out of her hand, over the rail of the stairs to fall somewhere below.

Now she was defenceless.

Gwen saw the machete blade rise again. "No, please," she implored. "Spare my son."

The robed figure didn't answer, but Skullface stepped forward, looking down at the crying child she was holding. He cocked his head.

Yes, that's it. That's right. See Clive Jr as a person. See him as a person who could grow up and have so much potential, who could do so many things in this shitty world we've found ourselves in. So much good. Yes, that's it. See him. Really see him.

It might be the only thing that saved her child.

The lead cultist was staring at Clive Jr, dark eyes fixed on him. But other one was about to finish her off. If Gwen didn't do something now, it would be too late. "No, please!" she screamed.

"Wait!" ordered Skullface. "Look."

The machete hung in the air above her like the sword of Damocles. But then, slowly, it began to drop.

Gwen didn't have time to relax. There were more Russian troops suddenly at the top of the stairs.

The cultist pulled Gwen and Clive Jr around, putting himself between them and the guns. Seconds later, she heard the *rat-ta-tat* of automatic weapons, and the man who'd protected them was toppling over, his body riddled with bullets.

Skullface rushed forward, waving his arms for them to stop – which they did, too late for the Morningstar who'd given his life to save them. Gwen looked down at the man, unable to figure out what had just happened. It was one thing for them not to be able to take a mother and child's life – though that still didn't tally with what Robert had said – but it was quite another to protect them from the Russians.

Why would they do that? she asked herself, and would keep asking herself, even as she was taken away.

Taken prisoner again in this castle.

THE TSAR SURVEYED the devastation and laughed.

The battle, if you could call it that, was over. They had crushed what was left of Hood's men in less than twenty minutes. It was what they were best at, crashing in and stamping out all resistance. He stooped to pick up one of the arrows that had been used against them, turning it over in his hands. Now this place was his, and – he had to admit – it felt good. He was glad he'd listened to Tanek, even to the point of coming over here himself to be involved in the final stages. Back in Russia, his empire was being run by underlings who knew that if they put a foot wrong, they could kiss their private parts goodbye once he returned victorious from English soil, leaving similarly loyal subjects to rule here in his name.

Which he would, as soon as he had confirmation that Bohuslav had done the same thing to the rest of Hood's forces. Once he knew that the Hooded Man himself was dead. Maybe they'd put his head on a spike outside the castle walls, as a reminder to others that the Tsar was now the great power in this region. And, in time, the greatest power in this country.

Then, perhaps, once he had more soldiers drafted in from England, and even Europe, they could think about turning their attentions to the US. Their real enemy.

The Tsar waited while his troops brought him progress reports on the mopping up operation, which included disabling Hood's people at the hotel prisons and assessing which of the prisoners might be of use. The twins were, as ever, by his side as he looked down on the grounds below. He'd feared he might lose them during the confrontation with the man with the staff – one of Hood's lackeys named Jack, he was reliably informed (who'd been taken away for Tanek to have his fun with a little later). But they'd been saved by an unexpected new ally.

De Falaise's daughter, who had gone off with Tanek to look for the other members of Hood's inner circle. The Tsar had to admit she was as deadly as she was desirable. When this was all over, he would seal their newfound alliance in the bedroom – however much that might pain Xue and Ying. Yes, she definitely looked like a woman who would respond well to his particular appetites.

It wasn't long before the pair returned, descending the steps to the Middle Bailey with a prisoner in tow. A woman being held up by a couple of his soldiers.

"There is no sign of the holy man, Tate. Nor of Hood's adopted son Mark and his little girlfriend," Adele said in that accent the Tsar found so sexy. "But your men did manage to dig out this whore from the rubble." She looked at the woman being held up and spat on her. "I thought I'd killed the cow when I blew up the caves."

"Who is she?"

"Hood's woman," Tanek replied.

Hood's woman did not look very well. She was unconscious for a start, her face and arms battered and bruised, blood pouring from several wounds. One of her legs looked severely twisted. If she was still alive, she wouldn't remain that way for long.

"She needs medical attention," Tanek said, "if she is to survive."

"And why would we want her alive?" the Tsar said. "I thought the intention was to kill all those close to Hood, including the ones that you have clearly let escape."

"She might yet prove useful," Tanek retaliated.

"The big man will tell you where the others have fled, will he not?"

"Possibly."

"If your skills are lacking, my friend, then I'm sure Bohuslav will oblige upon his return."

Tanek shot him a contemptuous look. "I was thinking more in terms of leverage... against Hood."

The Tsar laughed. "Hood? I would not worry about him. He will soon be dead, if he isn't already."

"Don't underestimate the man."

"He's right," Adele said, siding with the brute who had once been her father's second. "Not that I want to save her, but I've seen the man fight, my lord."

The Tsar smiled. He liked the way that sounded coming from Adele's lips: *my lord.*

"Nonsense," he said. He gazed down and saw people being herded in through the castle's entrance, the first batch of prisoners from the nearby hotel, under armed guard. "We let her die. Look at her, she is well on her way already. She might even have died as we stood here talking about it."

Tanek looked her up and down, and the Tsar was satisfied he'd made his point. Apart from anything else, there weren't many men with medical knowledge amongst his troops. If one of his men was injured, then he was of no use anymore and would either be left to die or shot right there and then. And the Tsar himself relied on Bohuslav to see to his personal health needs. With his detailed knowledge of anatomy, he was better than any doctor. But Bohuslav wasn't here, and even if he was, the Tsar wouldn't waste his talents on this whore.

"Sire, sire!" This came from behind and the Tsar whirled around. It was the radio operator from the AFV they'd travelled in. "I have news of the other skirmish."

"Ah, excellent." The Tsar's smile intensified.

"Our... our forces have been..." – the Tsar smiled expectantly – "...defeated."

"What?" The Tsar grabbed the messenger by his collar. "Repeat that, man."

"I... They have been defeated, sire."

"You lie!"

The man shook his head. "One of the remaining vehicles just checked in. Commander Bohuslav's."

Remaining vehicles? What the fuck was this cretin talking about? The Tsar had sent enough firepower to lay waste to an entire city. And what did Hood's men have? Sticks and stones! How was this possible? Bohuslav. He was to blame. Oh, when he got his sorry hide back here the Tsar would personally punish him.

"He himself is reported to be extremely badly injured," the man blurted out, still petrified. "Near to death, in fact."

"Bohuslav?"

The Tsar looked across at Tanek, who was nodding and grinning, probably at the thought of Bohuslav's fatal wounds. "Impressive," said the giant, "even for Hood."

The Tsar shook his man again, tightening his grip.

"They... the enemy suffered heavy losses as well, majesty," he blurted, probably hoping to be spared the Tsar's wrath, "including the Hooded Man himself."

At this news, the Tsar did let him go. The messenger fell to the ground, landing on his backside. Without even bothering to get up, he crawled away in case the Tsar should change his mind.

"Not so impressive, after all," the Tsar countered, and forced a smile – though he couldn't help thinking it had taken all those tanks, armoured vehicles and men to bring down that one man.

"Can we be certain he's dead?" This came from Adele.

The Tsar glowered. "What is the matter? You seem disappointed."

She shook her head. "It's just that I hoped I might be the one to kill him."

The Tsar nodded. He could understand that. He'd never met the man and he wished he could have done the deed personally. Now they'd both have to settle for recovering the body and putting the head on a pike.

"Those still alive will return to the castle," Tanek said, not reacting to the news about Hood at all. Perhaps he didn't really believe it.

"But they will not be expecting us to be here. They will return, battered and exhausted, leaderless, demoralised, expecting a warm welcome... only to find guns jammed in their faces instead. We have more than enough men to stand against them, taking into account our new comrades from the cult and these prisoners."

As he waved a hand at the folk from the hotel, there was a sudden cry from one of them, a short woman dressed in scrubs, with a Ranger's jacket on top. "Mary!" She'd broken ranks and was attempting to get to them, in spite of several automatic weapons now trained on her. But she was unarmed, and the Tsar was curious about who she was. He held up a hand to signal the men to hold their fire. She couldn't do much harm with the twins and Tanek standing so close by.

"Mary," cried the woman again, tears in her eyes. "Mary, what have they done to you?"

"And who might you be?" the Tsar asked.

She glared at him before answering. "Lucy Hill."

The Tsar looked across at Adele, who shrugged. She'd obviously not had much contact with this woman who'd been lumped in with the prisoners. Lucy took another step towards Mary, but it was one of the twins – Ying – who stood in her way this time, arms folded.

"Please," said Lucy, the tone of her voice changing from defiant to pathetic, "let me go to her. She's been training me as a nurse and –"

"Oh, dear. If only you'd been here ten minutes ago," the Tsar cut in. "We have just learned that we have no further use for her. You see, Hood is dead."

"Robert?" Now the tears ran freely down Lucy's cheeks. "I don't believe you."

"Believe what you like. It is the truth."

Tanek placed a hand on Ying's shoulder, and was lucky the bodyguard didn't cut it clean off. "Let her go to the woman," he said, making it sound more like a command.

"But why?" asked the Tsar. "What purpose would it serve?"

He didn't answer, but that just backed up what the Tsar suspected. Tanek didn't believe Hood was dead either. He sighed and nodded for Ying to let the nurse through. What did it matter to him if Hood's woman was fixed up, only to be executed later? It was their time and energy they were wasting, not his.

Ying moved aside and Lucy went to Mary, immediately checking her over. Tanek moved to join her, but the Tsar was not quite finished with him yet. "I want to know where Hood's closest companions are," he told the giant. "That is your priority."

Tanek tipped his head, then continued on his path. Lucy said something to him the Tsar didn't quite catch, but the next thing he knew Hood's woman was being taken back up to the castle with the nurse. Tanek and Adele followed on behind, but took a different route when they reached the steps, heading down instead of up.

"As useful as he has been, I think Bohuslav may have been correct about Tanek. The time is fast approaching when he will have outlived his usefulness. Do you not agree?" the Tsar said to Ying and Xue. The women concurred with silent nods. "And when that time comes, I will call on one of you to do the honours."

They smiled, no doubt remembering the embarrassment of not being able to best Tanek back in Russia.

The Tsar would have smiled himself, were it not that he might have to give the same instruction about Adele, depending on where her loyalties lay. He hoped she would be sensible and see the benefits of life with him. Who knew, if she behaved herself and lived up to his expectations – in all departments – he might even give her this castle as a present. Call it her inheritance.

In the meantime, they at least had something to celebrate.

The Hooded Man was dead. The Tsar was sure of it, even if Tanek wasn't.

CHAPTER TWENTY-TWO

THE MAN SHOULD be dead.

But instead of getting him back to Mary so she could treat his injuries, Bill had done as Robert requested. Once he'd cleaned up his wounds – stitching up the deep cuts in the shoulder and thigh before applying proper bandages and antiseptic – Bill had taken his former leader to Sherwood, bringing the Gazelle down in the car park of the old visitor's centre.

All the way here, Bill kept glancing over at him, as Robert drifted in and out of consciousness. *One o' these times I'm going to look and 'e won't wake up,* Bill thought. Robert was that bad. It wasn't like he hadn't seen Robert this way before, after the explosion at Mary's farm. But even then he hadn't looked this ill, this close to the end.

Bill remembered them bringing Robert to camp – Jack carrying the man into his tent, Mary by his side, as she'd been ever since. Days later, Bill was flying him into Nottingham for the final battle, where Robert took on the Sheriff alone. He shouldn't have been fit enough then, either. Shouldn't have recovered nearly as quickly as he did, even with Mary's attentions.

They'd been in Sherwood, though, hadn't they? Robert had been in Sherwood. So maybe he did have a point after –

Bill dismissed the notion. But he couldn't ignore the fact that as they flew to the forest, Robert seemed to rouse from his stupor. He was muttering something, half dreaming, calling out Mary's name.

"Right, we're here," Bill informed him when the helicopter was down.

Robert lolled to one side. Then he opened his eyes wide and Bill saw him take a good look at the trees, before his eyelids began to flicker again and then close. Bill shook his shoulder gently.

"Let me take you back home, lad."

Robert coughed, then mumbled: "I am home." He was clawing at the door, fingers uselessly slipping off the handle.

Bill climbed out, rounded the chopper and opened the door. He had to catch Robert as he fell out. "Judas Priest, yer in no fit state t'be goin' anywhere!"

Almost as soon as he'd said the words, he felt Robert stiffening, summoning strength from somewhere, forcing his legs to support him. Robert lifted his arm, pointing in the direction of the forest.

Bill had to half carry him down the path that led to the Major Oak. When they reached the ancient tree, Robert craned his head.

Then, nodding, he shooed away Bill's hands and leaned on the fence surrounding it.

"Robert, come on. Enough's enough."

"Don't... don't try to... Bill, promise me you'll... stay here... The others... They'll... they'll be arriving soon..."

"What others?" Bill said, fearing he'd lost his mind completely.

"This... this is where it's going to happen... They'll die unless..."

"Yer not makin' any sense, Robert."

"Promise me!" repeated Robert, his voice strengthening.

"Aye, all right. Bugger off, then!"

Robert was already pulling up his hood and stumbling away, using the fence and the trees for support as he made his way into the forest. Bill nearly went after him, but something held him back. Something told him to go and wait with the Gazelle, even though he was almost certainly leaving the Hooded Man to die amongst the trees.

And his legend along with him.

THEY WERE PUSHING the horses too hard, even Dale could see that.

But he'd made a promise – and even as he was riding his mount across the next hillside, Dale wondered how Robert was. Robert, who he'd left in that field, bleeding to death but insisting that they go because the castle was – or very soon would be – under attack. Mary was in danger, that was the man's one and only thought, but how exactly was Dale going to explain to her that he'd abandoned the man she loved?

"We'll send back help..."

He'd shouted that as they'd left and he'd meant it. As soon as they'd assessed the situation at the castle, tackled the threat – and *just how exactly are you planning on doing that? Take on another army with your own numbers depleted and no Robert to lead the charge?* – Dale would do it, he'd send medical aid and –

But Lord knows how long all that would take. Robert might be – *would* be – dead by then. He'd lost a lot of blood from the sickle wounds, had been crippled by that jeep.

Dale squeezed his eyes shut, then opened them again, willing himself not to think about it. But when he closed his eyes, all he could see was Robert's mangled body.

Quit it! He's relying on you to get to Mary, Dale. Now, I know you've never cared enough about a woman to sacrifice yourself like that, but it's what Robert's doing. His life for hers. So get on with it, get going, get to the castle!

Azhar was pulling up alongside him, having broken away from the pack behind, and was pointing to the horse he himself was riding; telling Dale what he already knew. Dale stabbed his own finger ahead. They were not stopping. The horses could rest when they arrived.

They had to reach the castle before it was too late.

EVEN DURING HIS days sneaking in and out of towns and cities to gather supplies, Mark had never pulled off a getaway like this one. He still wasn't quite sure how they'd made it out of the castle grounds, let alone Nottingham.

They'd surfaced from the caves out by the Brewhouse Yard, a reversal of what Reverend Tate had done to gain access when De Falaise had been in residence. Tate had a fun time negotiating the steps, but with Mark and Sophie's help he'd got down them okay. Of course, there had been men stationed in the Yard, who'd killed the Ranger guards, but Mark managed to creep up on them and took both out with blows to the head, hitting them with a fallen half-brick he'd picked up on the way.

The jeep had proved trickier, but while Tate and Sophie waited by the gate, he managed to creep up on the driver. Most of the vehicles had already entered the grounds, with some congregating up top or waiting down side streets because they couldn't get in. They'd been lucky to find this one, very lucky.

Once he'd taken care of the driver, reaching in through the window and landing a well-aimed punch, Mark had climbed in and backed the jeep down to where his companions were hiding.

Sophie pulled the unconscious Russian out of the passenger side, and they'd climbed in, Tate having terrible difficulty getting in until Sophie helped out. That's why they'd had to steal something with wheels; the Reverend wouldn't have made it half a mile on foot.

Mark had kept the engine idling a good few minutes, however, at the Brewhouse gate, expecting to see Jack come bounding down those steps, Gwen, Adele and Mary with him.

No, not Mary. Mark had seen her, seen what the cave in had done. If she wasn't dead already, she would be when the Tsar's men or the cultists got their hands on her. He gripped the wheel until his knuckles were white.

He'd wiped the tears away, but not before Sophie saw them. She reached across and put a hand on his forearm. "We have to go, Mark."

"Just a couple more minutes."

"Jack's resourceful. He'll find a way to get out, to meet up with us. He wouldn't want us to get captured. Would he, Reverend?"

Tate said nothing, but she was right. They should get away, wait for Jack at the rendezvous point.

They had to head for Sherwood.

Mark's driving left something to be desired – he'd been too young to drive pre-virus, and Robert and his men went everywhere on horseback. Luckily, Bill had given him a few lessons before leaving. "Never know when it's goin' to come in handy," he'd said, tapping his nose.

Mark hadn't thought about Bill in months, and it was strange that he should do so now; as they pulled in to the car park at Sherwood Forest, who should they see but the man himself, standing next to his helicopter, holding his shotgun as if he'd never been away. He was pointing it at their vehicle, squinting as he tried to make out who was inside.

For a second Mark thought he was actually going to shoot, so he stuck a hand out of the window. Bill kept his gun raised, but when Mark braked and shoved his head out, he smiled, lowering the weapon.

Mark hopped out and ran towards him. "Bill? Is it really you?"

"Aye."

They gave each other a hug as Sophie helped Tate out of the jeep. When the pair came over, Bill greeted them both. "How do?"

"What are you doing at Sherwood?" Mark asked him.

"Long story. Yerself?"

Like Bill, Mark didn't know where to start. He told him about the attack on the castle, and how they'd only managed to get out by the skin of their teeth. They were still hoping that Jack would make it, with Gwen and Adele.

"Well I'll be," said Bill when he'd finished. "It's a good job I didn't take him there, then."

"Who?" asked Mark.

"I'm not goin' to lie to you. The bloke's in a pretty bad way, Mark."

"Who? Who's in a bad way?"

"Robert."

"You're here with Robert?" Tate rubbed his head. "I don't understand."

"Makes four of us, then, I reckon," Bill said. Then he went on to explain how he'd found Robert after the battle, badly injured and not making much sense. "Just kept on insisting we come 'ere."

"Where were the rest of the men?" asked Sophie, and Mark guessed she probably meant Dale. "They weren't...?"

"Reckon you lost a fair few – bloody insanity goin' up against them things in the first place." He scratched his stubbled chin. "Tho' I will say this much, you lot gave them Russkies a good hidin'. Not sure what happened to the rest. Like I say, Rob wasn't makin' much sense by the time I showed up."

"How long's he been in there?" asked Tate.

"Good few hours. Wanted to fly 'im back to Mary, but... Do y'think she'll get out with Jack, then?"

Marked opened his mouth, then closed it again. He shook his head.

"What? Is the lass all right?"

Sophie suddenly burst into tears and turned to Mark, pressing her face into his shoulder. Mark hesitated, then wrapped a comforting arm around her. He was having trouble holding back the tears himself. "Bill, we think Mary might be..."

"What?"

"I was the last one to see her. She was... crushed in a cave-in. Happened when the Tsar attacked. I think we've..." Mark sniffed. "I think we've lost her."

"Judas..."

"No," said a voice, so quietly it might have drifted in on the wind. The three of them turned, Bill automatically raising his gun.

There, in front of them, was Robert. Or rather, the Hooded Man: features still obscured by the cowl he wore. He was standing straight, in spite of the bandage on his leg, but when he took another step towards them he was hobbling. Even so, it was nothing like the figure Bill had described.

"Robert?" gasped Mark. He'd come up on them silently, making all of them start. But then, he was good at that; self-trained in this very place.

"No," Robert continued in those hushed tones, ignoring everything but what had been said about Mary. "She can't be."

Bill was staring at Robert in disbelief. Slowly his gun dropped again, but he didn't say anything.

Mark nodded. "I think so. I'm really sorry. Everything happened too fast for me to..." He saw Robert's body stiffen, his back straighten. Then he saw the man's fists clench.

"We have to prepare ourselves," Robert said, his voice strong.

"For what?" Tate asked, but didn't get a reply. Robert had already turned and was walking back towards the visitor's centre. He knew what was about to happen, of that Mark was certain – just as certain as he was that the forest had somehow healed Robert (though later Bill would argue that maybe he'd looked worse than he actually was). The forest had shown Robert what would happen, or at least what might happen without their intervention.

Mark looked at Sophie, then at Tate and Bill. Their confused faces said it all, but he knew exactly what had to be done.

They'd follow Robert, just like always.

So, as the sky began to grow dark and as a light mist started to roll in from the surrounding fields, they did just that.

Followed the lonely figure into Sherwood.

CHAPTER TWENTY-THREE

SHERWOOD FOREST.

It was the most obvious choice, after all. Deep down, Adele knew that's where they would go, because she'd followed them there once before. She knew that's where Robert belonged – if he was still alive (no-one seemed to be able to confirm it either way). So it was where Mark, Tate and Sophie would go, too.

They hadn't really needed the torture session with Jack at all: conducted in the smithy, in one of the archways adjoining the stables.

But it had been fun.

Adele – the... what was it Jack had called her just before his interrogation? Oh yes, the *femme fatale*. The pain Jack had experienced at the hands of this master craftsman, this *artiste*, had sent tingles through her entire body. He hadn't had time to do a complete number on the man – the Tsar was demanding results – but it had been enough.

In lieu of his usual equipment, Tanek had made full use of the blacksmith's furnace (after all, he wouldn't be needing it, now he was over in the corner riddled with bullets): the tongs, the poker, the red-hot coals spitting in the open-sided tray. He hadn't even asked any questions to begin with, just inflicted his agonies on Jack – the screams of the big man so piercing they could be heard throughout the grounds.

Tied to a chair, naked apart from a pair of boxers, Jack had looked up at Adele and the betrayal on his slick face was incredible. It was like a physical thing. Adele knew that he had been starting to fall in love with her, in spite of everything she'd done to show her 'affections' lay elsewhere – or at least her obsession. With Robert. With his downfall. With his death.

Tanek had even let her have a turn with the irons, sweet man that he was. Her father's second, and now her protector. They'd hardly had a chance to talk since meeting earlier that day, but they hadn't really needed to. Tanek recognised her almost immediately, knew she was from the great man's stock. And that allegiance continued even after Daddy was gone. Murdered by Robert and his followers; including Jack. It brought her great satisfaction to torture him, chasing any last doubts from his mind that she might be talked around or turned.

Or be his.

"Y-you... traitorous s-slut," Jack spat through clenched teeth, love turning to hatred.

She studied his face again, then she kissed him – it would cause more pain than she ever could with the irons. Adele bit his lip as she pulled away, laughing as the blood dribbled down Jack's chin. "Poor, deluded idiot," she said in her true accent, the one she'd been so careful to conceal during her time playing the helpless heroine.

"Where are the others going?" Tanek asked. Maybe he was uncomfortable with the way the session was going. Maybe he was just jealous. Was he hers for the taking as well? Adele had already observed the way the Tsar had been looking at her. But his time would come soon enough, she understood that. At some point she and Tanek would rule this army, or rather she would – with Tanek by her side. Whether that was as her willing slave, bodyguard or lover – or all three – remained to be seen.

"I saw how this went in *Reservoir Dogs*. Go screw yourself, pal," Jack breathed. That earned him a slap in the face. Adele could still taste the copper in her mouth as she watched Tanek at work; now picking precise spots on Jack's body and hammering in horseshoe nails. It wouldn't kill him, but would deliver lasting pain. Tanek hammered them home until Jack passed out. Then he threw a bucket of cold water over him.

But they were getting nowhere. "He'll never talk in the time we've got left," Adele said, and Tanek could see that she was right. Given a couple of days, he could get anyone to talk, even someone as loyal as Jack. But the Tsar was breathing down their necks and, like it or not, he called the shots.

"Let me try a different tack." She brushed a finger over one of the nails. "If you'll pardon the pun."

When Jack was awake, Adele ran a sharp fingernail down his cheek. "If you don't tell us where your little friends have gone, we will execute Mary."

Looking at her through a haze of anguish, Jack spluttered, "Don't have her... Mark said..."

"Oh, in spite of my best efforts she's still alive. Just. But how long she stays that way depends on you, my dearest Jack."

"How do I know you're telling the truth?"

She couldn't help but smile at that. "You don't, *mon chéri*. But you have my word as a De Falaise that she will die if you do not co-operate. And that really *does* mean something. That is important to me."

He thought about it for a second or two, weighing everything up and concluding that if she'd done all this to avenge her father, then she would never take his name in vain.

"Tell us what we need to know," she'd pressed.

So, hanging his head in shame, he did.

SHE REMEMBERED THE shame.

The nights lying awake as he snored beside her. Spent, after he'd done whatever he pleased with her. Of all the places the soldiers could have stuck her.

Focus on Clive Jr, not the room. Not the bedroom where De Falaise kept you locked up, where they are keeping you locked up right now.

Gwen screwed her eyes shut, then opened them. It was just a room, just a room in the castle. At least it was on the ground floor, with no chance of rockets hitting the wall. Not that there was any fighting going on anymore. The Tsar's forces had won, swiftly and confidently.

Perhaps he'll be like the Frenchman, her mind whispered. *Do you think he'll want to play games, as well? Dress you up and pretend, while you lay there, catatonic?*

Gwen felt sick to her stomach. If Tate was here right now, she might just put her hands around his neck and squeezed. Reverend or not.

But it could be worse. She was still alive, and so was her son – her one connection to home, to New Hope, to Clive.

Could be in the same state as Mary, she said to herself. Gwen had seen her being carried in, helped by Lucy, the woman who'd assisted when Clive Jr was born. She'd been training as a nurse. And Mary looked like she needed one, looked like she was barely hanging on to life. Gwen had exchanged a brief look with Lucy as they'd passed, and could see pure terror in the woman's eyes. Like she knew it, too. Like she wasn't sure she could pull Mary through.

Gwen had been bundled into the room then, the door locked behind her. As far as she could tell there weren't many other survivors, unless they were being held in different parts of the castle? Perhaps the Tsar had shot them all?

She wondered what might have happened to Jack, Mark, Sophie... and, yes, Tate. She did still care about him, in spite of herself. Were they all dead, or in the same state as Mary?

But the room. Oh, God, this room.

It looked different; had no bed in it, for a start, and had been turned back into some sort of office. Probably where Robert organised his little missions. Just who did he think he was, appointing himself the guardian of this land, withholding vital things like weapons from people who just wanted to protect themselves? Leading suicide squads of young men to their doom? He was lucky they'd go with him, though she had to admit he had a way of sucking people in. Didn't work on her, of course. Too bloody-minded.

Gwen rocked Clive Jr on her knee. "I won't let anything happen to you, sweetheart. Not while there's still breath in my body."

The door lock clicked and Gwen jumped. She watched as the handle slowly turned. When the door opened, she felt a lump rise in her throat.

"Remember me?" said the man standing there.

Gwen said nothing.

"I had to see if it was true, that you were back." He grinned, but it came out more like a leer. A leer that stretched the scar across his jawline tight.

"Jace," she said.

"That's right," he chuckled. "You haven't forgotten me, then?"

How could she? He'd been her means of escape, the guard posted to keep an eye on her. She'd lured him inside, then stolen his clothes and knocked him unconscious with the butt of his own gun.

"But you were –"

"A prisoner? Just like you were back then? Fucking locked away when I hadn't even done nothin'."

Is that what you really believe? Yes, I think it is.

"Well, the new boss around here's letting all of the prisoners free who want to work for him. Good old Tanek vouched for me."

Shit, he's here as well? One big, happy family reunion.

"Hey, it'll be just like the old days, 'cept for the fact you've got a sprog now, eh?"

Gwen stood, holding Clive Jr close to her. "If you go near him, I'll –"

Jace pulled out a pistol and levelled it at her. "You'll what, Duchess?"

Her eyes were fixed on the gun. He'd pull the trigger in a heartbeat. He had a grudge not only against her, but this whole place.

"Now, take it easy and everything will be fine." Jace's eyes were crawling downwards, over the front of her jumper, just as they had the day she'd enticed him into the room. He'd been distracted then, the horny little shit, and she'd been able to get the better of him. How was she supposed to do that now, holding Clive Jr and with a handgun pointed at her?

"I seem to recall that you got me to strip off the last time we met. So, how's about we start by you returning the favour?"

"Please... My son."

"What about him?"

"You can't, not in front of him."

"Listen, I've been banged up in that fucking hotel jail the best part of a year, bitch. I haven't had any in all that time, so I'm going to make up for it. Just a happy coincidence that it's you, so I can kill two birds with one stone. Now, put him down and get on with it."

Gwen closed her eyes out of resignation. It was all happening again, wasn't it? It would happen in this room, just as it had before. But instead of the Sheriff it would be some wet-behind-the-ears young thug. Only she'd changed so much, been forced to change. She'd do what he wanted, just until she could get that piece off him. Then she'd fucking well blow his brains out.

"I said put him down!" shouted Jace.

Gwen placed Clive Jr in the corner, telling him everything was going to be okay. Then she turned to Jace.

"Make it nice and slow. I don't want to miss nothing," he said.

Swallowing dryly, Gwen took hold of the bottom of her jumper and began to raise it. She took her time, like he said, but was apparently taking too long, because Jace jabbed the gun in her direction and told her to get the jumper off. "Now! I want to see."

Gwen pushed her elbow into the hem of the jumper and peeled it off. It wasn't particularly cold, but she shivered anyway, and thanked God she'd worn a bra today. It was the last thing standing between Jace's beady little pig-eyes and her nakedness.

"That too," Jace ordered, indicating the bra. He licked his lips, eyes glued to her chest. With his free hand he began to undo his belt, his trousers swelling where he was growing excited.

Gwen began to walk towards him. "Wouldn't you like to get a closer look, Jace? Maybe touch them?"

He straightened his gun arm and pushed her back. "I'm not falling for that twice. I'm not a moron."

Are you sure about that? thought Gwen. Quick as a flash, she flung the jumper at him, knocking the gun sideways and allowing her a clear shot with her foot, to kick him between the legs. Jace managed to twist around, though, and the kick caught him on the thigh.

Angrily, he pushed her back, shrugging the jumper off his gun and pointing it at her again. "Gonna regret that."

Gwen tensed herself, but the shot didn't come. He didn't want to kill his plaything. Instead, he turned the weapon in the direction of Clive Jr.

"No, please. Not my son. I'll do anything."

"You will anyway," Jace reminded her. "Remember what you said to me last time, how was I going to do anything with my 'maggot'? Heh. When I've shut the kid up, I'm going to show you exactly what I can do."

Everything seemed to happen in slow motion. As she flung herself across the room – throwing her body between the bullet and Clive Jr – Gwen noticed every tiny detail. The slight pressure on the trigger of the pistol; Jace's forehead crinkling as he aimed at her boy; the scar along his chin stretched tighter than ever. And the exact moment Jace's expression changed, his face creasing up in pain rather than concentration. At the exact same time a trickle of blood sprang from the corner of his mouth and began its downward journey.

Then there was the flash of metal and Jace was pitching forward, the gun falling from his grasp. He caught her eye as he followed it, dropping first to his knees, before coughing up blood. Even now he seemed to be thinking: Why is this happening to me? I'm not a bad guy.

Gwen felt nothing as he collapsed onto the carpet, but she could now see the vicious blow that had caused his death. A long cut across his back, so deep it had probably severed his spinal column. And behind Jace, his attacker. A man she hadn't even seen or heard come in.

He stood there, blade dripping with Jace's blood, the hood he wore obscuring his features. But Gwen knew what he looked like. Knew it was him.

Knew that under that hood there was a painted face, a skull . Lifting the machete, he wiped the blood off on the edge of his dark robes.

Frozen in the process of running to Clive Jr, Gwen gaped at him, not comprehending. Skullface had just saved her, and her child.

Clive Jr! Gwen found she could move again and went to her son, gathering him up into her arms. She didn't once take her eyes off the cultist, though.

He had something in his other hand, his free hand. He tossed it over, and when she held it up she saw it was one of their robes. "Put it on," he said. His voice was flat, robotic, but was she imaging things or was there a hint of humanity in there? At first Gwen thought he might be telling her this to cover up her dignity – as she was still standing in only her bra and jeans. Then she realised he had other plans.

"They will be coming for you soon," he stated. "You must leave the castle."

"Who will? The soldiers? Are they going to kill us?" Gwen placed Clive Jr down by her feet a moment while she slipped into the robes.

Skullface, who still hadn't removed his hood, answered: "They are taking you and the other women to the forest."

"What?" Gwen was more confused than ever. Why would they take them to the forest to kill them? And why just the women?

"You are to be bait."

Bait? She still didn't understand... unless Robert had returned to Sherwood? But then surely they'd take just Mary? Gwen cast her mind back to the hostages that had been on the gallows when De Falaise had been at the castle – Robert had been willing to come into the castle grounds alone to save them. Perhaps they were banking on him coming out because they had some of his closest friends? Closest female friends? The sexist shits.

It still didn't explain why this guy was helping her escape, why he'd stopped Jace from attacking them. From attacking Clive Jr...

"Why?" she asked as she scooped up Clive Jr again, joining the cultist at the door. "Why are you doing this for us? For him?"

"He must be kept safe," said the man in that monotone voice, tinged with the slightest hint of compassion. "Hide him under your robes."

Gwen did as she was told, covering Clive Jr as much as she could, before pulling up the hood to conceal her features. Their saviour led them out of the office and into the castle, where other robed figures were waiting.

She didn't have much option but to go with them, especially as they were able to move freely. Where they were taking her, she had no idea, but Gwen began to hope again.

For her there was always New Hope.

CHAPTER TWENTY-FOUR

IT WAS ALREADY dark by the time they arrived, and they hit the mist about a mile outside Sherwood. The moon was on the horizon, tinged with red. A hunter's moon, they called it. Tanek smirked, grimly.

Fog lamps kicked in and allowed the drivers of the armoured vehicles to see roughly a car's distance ahead of them. They'd brought three AFVs – a couple of armoured personnel carriers, and their cannon-wielding BTR-90 – and a couple of jeeps. All they'd need to tackle a few fugitives.

Tanek rode with the Tsar and the twins. The Tsar had insisted on coming along personally, he'd said because he didn't want Hood and his men escaping this time. Tanek suspected it was more to do with keeping an eye on him. They were coming to a parting of the ways, anyone could see that, but it was fine. The Tsar and his men had played their part. Tanek was based back in Nottingham again. And, by a twist of fate, even that dolt Bohuslav was out of the picture. Which meant, if Tanek was to take control of this operation, he would only have to deal with the twins.

Only.

He remembered how adept they were. How skilled with those swords. One at a time, maybe. But when they worked as a pair, they were lethal.

Actually, everyone being in the same place, at the same time, might work to his advantage. If they were killed, he could blame the renegades – after killing them as well, and any witnesses among the Tsar's men. Wouldn't be easy, but he'd pulled trickier things off.

Then he and Adele would have a little chat about how to move forwards. He could see her mind ticking over about what would happen once the Tsar was no longer in command. Ultimately Tanek thought she'd make a fine leader. Eventually. He'd already seen shades of his old master in her, especially the cruelty she'd displayed when torturing that scum, Jack. But she needed guidance. De Falaise had asked him to look after her, and he would. She'd take the reins only when he deemed she was ready.

She caught his eye as he was thinking this and smiled. Adele had come along as well because, "None of them know the truth about me. I can be another hostage." Along with a virtually unconscious Mary and the nurse, who'd managed to stabilise Hood's woman and splint her leg. The Tsar had at least told him he was right to keep her alive, because in spite of Hood being dead – and Tanek still wasn't entirely convinced about that – the others would still surrender if their leader's woman was threatened.

Tanek had also been told that Gwen had been captured, and he'd ordered someone to go fetch her because she had a link to the holy man. Worryingly, they'd only found the body of ex-prisoner Jace in the room where she was being held. The grounds had quickly been searched, but there was no sign of her. Tanek wasn't surprised, not after the way she'd behaved on the day of the hangings. It really wasn't that much of an issue – just another loose end to tie up at a later point, like finishing off Jack – but it irked Tanek all the same. She had been De Falaise's woman, so it was a matter of principle.

"How long until we are there?" Tanek heard the Tsar shout to the driver.

"We are almost at Sherwood, sire," came the reply.

The Tsar nodded, satisfied. "You see? Russian efficiency. We have made excellent time."

"We should have waited until the morning," Tanek replied. Night had fallen and now there was this mist. If the trees didn't provide cover enough, either of those would. Except the plan was not to go into the forest – which would be suicide even at the best of times – but to force them to come out.

"And allow them to move on? We suspect they are here, right now. Why give them the opportunity to slip through our fingers again?" The last was another dig at Tanek, even though he'd been busy dealing with Jack at the time of their escape.

"They won't leave Sherwood. It is where Hood will come when –"

"Hood? Hood again. Tanek, the man is dead. Will you not get that through your thick skull?"

One more crack like that and I will reach over and crush your windpipe, thought Tanek.

"Then we should have waited for Hood's men. They will almost certainly try to regain the castle."

The Tsar waved a hand. "And do what? Shoot their little bows and arrows at my men?"

"It's what they did to Bohuslav's troops," Tanek retorted. It didn't do to underestimate Hood or his men, as they'd found out to their cost in the past. Tanek had a grudging admiration for the man, which he knew De Falaise would understand. It wouldn't stop him obliterating all of his followers, or indeed the Hooded Man himself if he still existed. Tanek had made a promise to avenge the man he had followed, not because of his lures of power, but because he had a vision. A vision that might yet become a reality.

Before the Tsar had a chance to say anything more, the driver informed them that they were pulling into the visitor centre's car park. It was empty, which Tanek knew didn't prove a thing. Any transportation the fugitives might have used would have been moved by now; that's if they'd even entered the forest from here in the first place. Sherwood was a big area, but Adele seemed to think this would be the best spot, having followed Hood before.

"Turn the spotlights on," ordered the Tsar. The vehicles formed a rough semi-circle and trained their beams on the area ahead of them, breaking through the mist. "This will get their attention, yes?"

Armed men were already filling up the lit area, standing guard by the vehicles, and a rap on their AFV told them they were ready for Adele. Tanek opened up the hatch and climbed out, dragging Adele with him; the crossbow he was carrying pointing at her temple. They had to make this look realistic.

From another AFV came the small nurse and Mary. The latter was carried by two soldiers, still pretty much out of it. The left leg of her jeans was ripped, the broken limb beneath straightened between two pieces of wood. Her face was a mess, right eye swelled and black from bruising, but the nurse had managed to clean her up somewhat. There were plasters covering the wounds on her cheek and forehead, the edges of stitches poking out from beneath. She lolled between the two men as they dragged her along, then dumped her on the ground in the middle of the spotlights. When the nurse shouted something at them, she got a backhanded slap for her trouble.

"I am addressing the deserters who fled like cowards from Nottingham Castle," came the Tsar's address through the loud-speaker attached to his vehicle. "We are holding three of your friends in the entrance to Sherwood, and will kill them one by one unless you surrender yourselves to us. You have one quarter-hour to comply and then the first is dead."

Anyone on this side of the forest should have heard that; it had certainly been loud enough. Depending on where they were, it should also give them enough time to reach the car park, unless they were deep into the trees. If they couldn't get there in time? Well, too bad. They'd execute the nurse.

Tanek scanned the edge of the mist for any movement. There was nothing. So they waited.

When they'd been there almost ten minutes, the Tsar repeated his demands. Tanek looked at his watch. They were running out of time.

"We need to get Mary back inside!" said the nurse. "She's freezing out here."

"No one is going anywhere," Tanek told her, turning the crossbow on the woman.

She glowered, but stayed put.

Come on, Tanek said to himself. *Where are you? Make your move.*

Then someone stepped out of the mist. A figure wearing a hood, carrying a bow. On the ground, he saw Mary stir.

Tanek grinned to himself, not just because he could picture the Tsar's face in the AFV – and imagine him having to swallow his words – but because he would now get the opportunity to kill Hood himself.

The Tsar's voice came over the speaker. "So, you are still alive after all? Then I will have your head for what you did this morning!"

Shots rang out, and before Tanek could tell them that the Hooded Man was his kill, bullets from one of the soldiers guarding Mary and the nurse peppered Hood's torso. He sank heavily to the ground. If he hadn't been dead before, then he certainly was now. Tanek swore under his breath and, turning, shot the offending guard with his crossbow. "He was mine!"

As he was turning back to the scene, though, Tanek's mouth fell open. Hood had climbed to his feet, bow and arrow readied. Adele stared in amazement too. What was he, indestructible? A ghost? He certainly looked the part, with the mist swirling around him.

They'd hardly had time to recover from this when another figure stepped out of the fog on their right, also wearing a hood and carrying the same weapons.

Seconds later, there was another on their left. It was almost as if the man had cloned himself.

Tanek frowned. One of these had to be the real Hood – he'd just kill them all! With his bare hands if necessary.

Before he could do anything, arrows were shot into the circle from somewhere beyond the trio. They took out the spotlights on the lead vehicle, then the others.

"Shoot!" Tanek ordered. But, glancing around, he saw that a good number of the soldiers were already on the floor, unconscious. They'd been silently put out of commission by someone else while their attention had been focused elsewhere.

Then he saw the culprit. Yet another hooded figure jumped from the top of an AFV, down into the small group guarding the hostages. He was dispatching soldiers with a sword, incapacitating them before they could get a shot off – slashing two across the face, then burying the point in another's shoulder before Tanek could blink. Tanek collected himself, raised his crossbow and shot.

The man stepped sideways, letting the bolt bounce off the AFV. He took out a knife and threw it at Tanek, embedded it in his right arm. Tanek immediately lost his grip on the crossbow.

More lights were put out. Everything was taking on a crimson shade from the light of the baleful moon.

The remainder of the Tsar's soldiers were climbing out of their vehicles, but were being picked off by the three Hoods who'd come out of the mist, moving forward and firing all the time. One was not using a bow and arrow, but a shotgun.

Meanwhile, the Hood with the sword was helping the nurse get Mary to her feet, the gentle way he was holding the injured woman speaking volumes.

"Robert," said Adele.

Tanek indicated that the women should move off into the mist, where another figure had appeared; a fat, bald man. The mystery arrow firer, Tate.

Tanek pulled the knife out of his arm, wincing only slightly. He felt pain, just didn't show it; he never did. As the Hood who'd thrown it – the original, of that he was certain – came towards him, he grabbed Adele and put the knife against her throat.

"Tell them to put down their weapons. Or I'll put it to use."

Hood paused. "Go ahead."

Adele looked from Tanek to Hood. "How can you say that?"

"Because you're his daughter! The Sheriff's!" growled Robert. "Because you deserve the same as he got."

"Take cover," Tanek said to Adele, letting her go. There was no point pretending any more. The only two hostages worth anything were getting away. But perhaps he could do something about that.

Turning the knife around, he threw it at the escaping women. He had been aiming for Hood's pet, to put her out of her misery, but the nurse saw what was about to happen over her shoulder and positioned herself in the way. The blade slid easily into her back and she slumped forwards, falling on top of Mary.

Good enough, thought Tanek.

All around them the Tsar's men were falling, none able to get off more than a round or two. The replica Hoods had revealed themselves now, hunting coats flapping open to show bullet-proof vests beneath. The first was the boy Mark, the other a girl Tanek had never seen before. Next, the farmer who'd shot him over a year ago.

So many here who needed to be taught a lesson.

But first: Hood. He was coming towards him – was that a limp? – sword high, enraged at the attack on the nurse. Tanek braced himself to grab the man's forearm when he made his first swing. As it turned out, he didn't need to.

Hood's blow was blocked by another sword. One of the twins had left her sister behind to guard the Tsar. Hood seemed taken aback, but not as much as when she kicked him squarely in the chest. He flopped against the AFV, then slid down it.

Maybe I won't kill her so quickly after all, thought Tanek, although he knew she hadn't done it for him. *She can keep him busy while I see to other matters.*

An arrow whizzed past him and he remembered there were still four of Hood's people out there. Picking up his crossbow and switching it to the other hand, he fired at the girl. It didn't matter if he killed her quickly; it was the other two he really wanted to savour.

The boy dived across and pushed her out of the way, taking the bolt in the thigh. At first Tanek was mad, but it was poetic justice. Payback for the bolt the boy had shot into his calf the last time they'd met.

"Oi!" came a call just off to his right. "Remember me?" It was the other one. The fucking farmer.

"Oh, yes," said Tanek.

"Then you remember this, dontcha," the farmer raised his shotgun and let off a blast.

Not this time, my friend. Tanek ducked sideways to escape the shell's bite. "And you will remember this," he said, loosing a bolt at his enemy and nicking the man's gun hand. He dropped his weapon.

Tanek was up and running towards him moments later, issuing a terrifying, bloodcurdling roar. He put his head down and rammed the farmer, lifting him up into the air and launching him backwards.

*   *   *

ROBERT MOVED JUST in time to avoid the blade, which clanked off the side of the AFV. Dammit, she was fast.

Here was he thinking that the difficult part had been creeping up and fixing the Tsar's men while Mark, Sophie and Bill created their little diversion. Or getting Mary to safety... except she wasn't yet, was she?

Mary.

Words couldn't describe how he'd felt seeing her alive. He thought the dream was coming true (it might still, he reminded himself, all of them dead; Jack probably dead already). He wasn't going to let that happen, even if he wasn't quite back to full strength – and how he'd recovered so quickly was still something Robert didn't want to question.

He recognised the woman fighting him from the dream. One of the Tsar's bodyguards. But only one, which begged the question, where was the other? Would she attack when he least expected it?

Robert silenced the thoughts – he needed to concentrate, to keep dodging this twin's swipes. Over her shoulder he saw Tanek shoot Mark and go after Bill. If he could get rid of the bodyguard, he might be able to help them.

This time he met her sword with his, sending shockwaves up his arm, across his chest and into his bad shoulder – strapped up under his coat and bullet-proof vest. He groaned, which seemed to spur the woman on. She beat at his sword, hacking it like a woodsman chopping at a tree. Each time the pain was tremendous.

Robert waited for her to do it again, then pushed forwards, hooking their hilts together and headbutting her. He tried to wrench the sword from her grasp while she was dazed, but it took her seconds to recover and she disentangled the swords with practised ease. He was woefully outclassed. Here was someone who'd spent years studying with this weapon, while Robert – although this came naturally to him – had only been using his a little over a year. Good enough to tackle machete-wielding cultists, but out of his depth with a true professional. He had to get that thing away from her before she –

Another swipe, this one slashing his combat trousers, almost cutting into his good leg. He was just about managing on it, but if she wounded that one as well...

Spinning round, she came at him again. No respite, no pause for breath. Robert found himself being forced backwards, losing ground. He couldn't hold her off much longer.

Suddenly, she drooped. Something had struck her from behind; as she fell to the side, Robert saw Tate wielding his walking stick, the hard wood still wet with her blood.

"Now Robert!" For a moment he thought the Reverend was advocating murder, but Tate quickly clarified: "Disarm her, now!"

Robert brought down the hilt of his sword on her clenched fist, which opened like a sprung trap.

A thought struck him. If the Reverend was here, then who was watching Mary? Robert searched for her, zeroing in on the spot where Lucy had been murdered, brought down on top of Mary. Tate had at least managed to pull Mary out from under the dead woman, but now Robert saw Adele approaching her. And she had a gun; one of Mary's Peacekeepers, in fact.

Shit! He began to go after De Falaise's daughter, but before he could move, he felt a presence behind him – vaguely heard Tate's "Look out!" The other twin was there, had come to save her sister. Was bringing down her blade on his blind spot.

About to cut into the side of his neck and deliver her master the Hooded Man's head.

MARY!

She heard the voice but it was dull, muffled.

Mary, you're in big trouble again. Even worse than before! Mary, you have to wake up. Have to get up! She's coming for you!

She would have asked her brother who, but Mary didn't care. Her whole body was numb, from the cold or because of the last thing she really remembered: things, heavy things, falling on her.

Adele, David told her, *the harpy who did that to you. She's on her way over here with Dad's pistol – your pistol! – and she's going to finish the job. Mary! Mary, PLEASE!*

She told him to leave her alone. The blackness was calling again, regardless of the fact she thought she'd seen a glimpse of Robert.

David wouldn't leave her alone.

Mary, Mary, Mary, Mary. On and on like a stuck record, telling her that she was in danger, telling her that she was going to die. (Funny, she thought she had already.) Telling her that Adele was coming.

Adele.

That's right. The one who was all over Robert, who led Jack on. Who tricked you all, Moo-Moo. Lucy's already dead, she died trying to save you.

Lucy? No...

Finally, an answer. Hallelujah! Now look, Adele's coming, so you have to do something or Lucy will have died for nothing!

But I can't move, David. I was blown up!

You can move, it's just that you're telling yourself you can't. You're giving up Moo-Moo, and if there's one thing I never thought you were it's a quitter.

It's so hard. Too hard.

Bull. Get up Mary. Get up, or you'll just prove Dad right. He always said that you could never do a man's job, that you were weak.

Mary felt her hand twitch.

Do you think that's what Robert thinks, as well? Does he think you're weak, not up to being by his side?

Mary's fingers began to curl.

He thinks you're a –

"– useless wretch. Look at you. This will almost be a mercy killing." Suddenly Mary was listening to Adele. The woman was close – close enough to fire at any moment – but she obviously wanted to vent first. "You were there, weren't you? When my father's life was cut short. You were partly responsible. You and that bastard who sleeps with dogs. Flea-ridden dogs like you!"

Mary's fingers balled into a fist.

"But both will die. First you, and how fitting it should be by your own weapon. Then him. If there is anything left after the Tsar's bodyguard has finished."

"Robert..." Mary gargled.

"What was that? Are you trying to speak? Are you begging me for your life, Mary? Is that it?"

Mary said something unintelligible.

"I did not catch that. You will have to beg louder." The voice was close now. Very close.

Mary lashed out with her fist, connecting with Adele's cheek. She heard a surprised shriek, then a *bang* close to her ear as the Peacekeeper went off. There was a ringing in her head, but she said the words again, louder, not knowing or caring whether they were heard: "I said, shut your filthy mouth or... or I'll shut it for you!"

Then she opened her eyes.

IT HURT LIKE nothing he'd ever felt before. Not even having his little finger cut off compared.

Because that was quick, over in a flash, and although the pain lingered, it dulled to a throb eventually. This? This was different. Every time he moved his leg it felt like someone sticking a knife into it. Not a knife. A giant splinter. Mark hissed through his teeth as he shifted position and the bolt in his thigh moved again.

"Oh, my God, Mark. Shall I pull it out?" asked Sophie, squatting next to him.

Mark didn't know. Were you supposed to pull them out? Would he bleed to death if she did that? Mary would know, but... Mary was out of it at the moment. Better than dead, he reminded himself, as he'd told Robert she was. Imagine, thinking the woman you loved was –

That's why Mark acted when he saw Tanek pointing his crossbow at her. The same reason he'd protected Sophie back at the castle, and even when they'd first met. At least he'd had a chance to tell her. At least if they bought it, she knew. He looked into her eyes. Now she was really looking at him, and all the panic, the fear he saw in her eyes was gone. He saw only one thing. One thing that made him want to fight. That made him want to survive this and keep Sophie safe.

"Aaauughh!" he cried out, the moment broken.

The bolt was being pulled, and he thought, to begin with, it was Sophie going ahead with the makeshift operation regardless. When Mark looked down, he realised his mistake.

There was Tanek, pulling and twisting the bolt, then shoving it back in. "How does it feel, boy? What you did to me?"

It felt bad, really bad. Not because of the pain, or because he'd shot Tanek back on that platform. Mark was actually regretting not being a better aim, not having another chance.

Tanek didn't look like he was going to give it to him. The big man had finishing playing with the bolt, and had slung his crossbow over his shoulder. He grabbed Mark by the scruff of the neck, dragging him round and hoisting him up.

Tanek whirled him around like he weighed nothing. He lashed out, his fist catching the side of Tanek's head, but Mark suspected it probably hurt him more than it did the giant. Where was Jack when you needed him?

As if reading his mind, Tanek suddenly said: "First you, then the farmer... Nostalgic. Pity your tall friend is not here, but I think I broke him during our torture session."

Having been on the receiving end of one of those, Mark could well understand how. Now, on top of everything else, he was worried about what this sadist had done to Jack.

"Now, boy, I break you."

Tanek lifted Mark up sideways, facing the sky. Although he couldn't see it, he imagined Tanek had raised his knee, in preparation for dropping Mark across it. A thigh wound, he might be able to get over, but a broken back? No chance.

"Yah!" Tanek let out, and Mark thought it was a cry of victory before dropping him. He fell, sharply, and Mark braced himself for the impact... which never came. Instead, his whole body fell and smacked flat against the concrete of the car park. It winded him, but at least he could still move.

For some reason Tanek had let him go. As Mark raised his eyes he saw the figure of Sophie on the giant's back, riding him like he was giving her a piggy-back.

She was clawed the sides of his head, raking his eyes with her nails. Tanek shouted again: "Gah!" Mark bet it was the closest they'd ever get to hearing him scream.

He was reaching up to grab Sophie's wrists, to prevent her from doing any more damage, but she was holding on like a rodeo rider. Desperate to keep Tanek away from Mark.

Saving him.

THOUGH IT WAS agony, Robert hefted his sword aloft, threatening to tear the rough stitches in his shoulder wound.

But he caught the other twin's blade just in time. Robert twirled, still locked with her blade, but she did the same and disconnected them. Then she took a swipe at his midriff, which Robert only just stepped away from. She was definitely pissed at their treatment of her sister. So much so that she'd left her master's side to come to her aid, probably fearing Robert would kill her twin. Which would be no more than she deserved, but only as a last resort.

Probably should have, though, he thought when he saw the first twin getting up again. She retrieved the sword and turned it on Tate. He blocked it with his stick, which was just about thick enough to take it – but splintered nevertheless.

They had to end this, and quickly, before either he or Tate wound up being skewered.

Meeting the blows of the second twin's sword – which, if anything, were harder than her sister's – Robert tried to manoeuvre her around. He hoped Tate could see what he was trying to do, but didn't have time to make sure. He was too busy trying to keep himself alive.

Clang, clang. Robert blocked another swing. *Clang!* And another. He couldn't keep it up for much longer.

He felt something press against his back. "Reverend, time for evil to face itself again."

"Agreed," panted Tate.

"On three... one..." Robert lashed out at the twin in front of him, expecting Tate to do the same on his side. "Two..."

"Three!" shouted Tate.

Robert dived to the left – he had no idea whether Tate was going that way or the other. It didn't really matter. The result was the same. Both twins had gone in for the kill, lunging in retaliation to Robert and Tate's swipes. Their blades entered each other at the same time – the one Robert was fighting taking hers slightly higher than her sister, just beneath the ribcage. They remained like that for a moment or two, eyes wide, staring at each other. Perhaps they couldn't believe they'd been caught out by such a simple trick. Or perhaps they were relieved they'd die together?

Simultaneously, both pulled their swords out. And, simultaneously, they fell.

Robert looked over to where Tate lay. The Reverend nodded that he was all right. Switching his attention to what was happening in front of him, Robert spotted that Mark and Sophie needed help. But his main priority was Mary.

He gestured for Tate to help with Tanek, while he made for Mary and Adele... even as he heard the Peacekeeper go off.

Robert feared he might already be too late.

CHAPTER TWENTY-FIVE

FROM HIS POSITION inside the AFV, the Tsar had witnessed everything.

The death of his men; his precious Xue and Ying, killed by their own hands. He'd warned Xue not to follow her sister. Now they were both dead, and who would protect him?

You've spent too long letting people do that anyway, he told himself. Why, even now he was hiding inside this hulking metal beast while others fought. What had happened to the warrior who'd fought in Afghanistan? Who'd been one of the Mafia's most dangerous men? Who'd gone onto the streets armed only with a pistol and machine gun (all right, a huge PK machine gun) and built his own kingdom from the ground up? Was he hiding inside the Tsar?

If so, he wasn't coming out right at that moment. Ordering his driver to put the AFV into reverse, the Tsar set about giving the players in this little drama a leaving present. There was nobody left out there he cared about. Even the woman Adele was a delight he would have to do without savouring. She would probably have remained loyal to Tanek anyway.

The Tsar could still remember how to load up a shell.

He would blast them all to high heaven, then return to the castle where the rest of his army was waiting.

It was a grand plan, sure to succeed.

BILL SHOOK HIMSELF.

It felt like a rhino had hit him at full speed, throwing him up and over into the trees. For a few seconds he'd flown without the aid of his helicopter. Might even have broken some ribs, if it wasn't for one of those vests Robert had given him. That Tanek was as strong as he was fast, and he was mad as hell. Hardly surprising, seeing as they were responsible for almost killing him.

Bill tottered to his feet. He felt like he was still in the air, unable to feel the ground beneath him. His hand was killing him, but he bit back the pain. Thank God the bolt had grazed it rather than going through. He started walking in the direction he'd come from, picking up his pace when he reached the edge of the mist and saw what was going on with Mark and Sophie. Tate looked like he was coming to help, but it'd probably take all of them to bring down Tanek, and even then it wouldn't be a walkover.

He spotted his discarded shotgun and snatched it up, then raised it, hoping to get a clear shot at Tanek. But the big man kept dancing round, desperate to dislodge Sophie from his back. Bill couldn't chance hitting her by mistake.

By the time he reached them, Tate was already there – and had delivered a blow to Tanek's stomach with his stick that should have doubled him over.

Tate nodded a welcome to Bill as he joined him, and they both set about attacking Tanek; Tate with the stick, Bill with the butt of his rifle. He jabbed the man in the places he thought might hurt the most – including a wound on his upper arm that was still bleeding.

At last, Tanek managed to get a grip on Sophie, bending forwards and throwing her over his head to land in a heap on the floor. He was about to stamp on her when Mark crawled between them and caught Tanek's foot.

Grimacing, he pushed and, with the help of Tate and Bill's battering, toppled the giant. Bill struck him in the face with the butt of his shotgun. "Ram me, would ye?"

Tanek took the beating and more, holding up his huge forearms to protect himself. Then he reached up to swat away the annoyances. He grabbed Tate's stick and shoved, knocking the holy man over backwards. Then he rose and took hold of Bill by the throat, squeezing hard as he got first one knee beneath him, then both legs.

"Now, I finish this," he said, his face only inches from Bill's. So near he could smell the big man's fetid breath.

It was then they both heard the whistling sound.

ROBERT WAS ON his way to help Mary.

Not that she needed it. Somehow she'd come to, and was grappling with Adele. Mary was trying to wrestle the Peacekeeper out of the

short-haired woman's grasp. And, as Robert watched, Mary punched
her in the face, hard. He recognised that look; Mary was furious.
Enough to spur her on, tackling the woman who'd been a thorn in
her side since day one.

Then came the noise. The sound of one of the armoured vehicles
backing up, its eight wheels spinning, creating smoke that was soon
lost in the mist.

Someone is still inside one of those things. Has to be the Tsar...

Robert saw the cannon on top swinging in their direction. The mad
Russian was going to fire; obliterate him and his core group in one decisive
stroke. Robert guessed Tanek and Adele didn't mean a thing compared
with a win like that. Anxiously, he looked from Mary to the AFV.

He started after the vehicle, running as best he could with a leg that
was far from healed. The AFV was reversing, backing into the mist.
But it drove into the hidden wooden posts on the left-hand side of the
entrance, where it juddered to a halt.

At the moment of collision the cannon spat its load, and Robert
dropped to the ground. All he could do was watch as the shell flew
overhead, whistling as it went. But the cannon's aim had been spoiled
by the prang, and it flew over the top of the group. It cut through
the mist and exploded somewhere off in the trees beyond. But it was
enough to blow those who weren't already on the ground off their
feet, dust mixing with the mist coming in from the forest.

He had no time to check whether Mary, or indeed any of the
others, were okay, because the hatch of the AFV was opening. A
soldier – probably the driver – was climbing out. Or rather, was
pushed out. He was armed with a pistol, and began shooting in
Robert's direction. Robert rolled over, bringing his sword close to
his body. The bullets pinged off the concrete. Robert glanced up and
saw another figure climbing after the first: the Tsar, using the driver
to cover his own escape.

Robert swore loudly, then got up on one knee. The bullets came
again and he rolled, sideways this time, so that he would end up
underneath the AFV – out of the driver's range.

He waited under there, knowing the man would come down
eventually, knowing that he would have been issued with precise orders
to finish off the Hooded Man. Robert was only one guy, after all, and
he had no gun. Sure enough, he saw two boots drop to the ground and
the driver crouched, shoving his pistol underneath the machine.

Robert prodded his sword through the gap in the tyres, feeling the
now familiar resistance of flesh. There was a grunt. The gun went off,

but it was already falling from the man's hands. He fell to the ground, clutching at his wound.

Robert scrambled back out, catching sight of a shadow disappearing into the mist off to his left.

He got up and immediately gave chase.

THE BLAST FROM the shell caught them all off guard.

Tanek let Bill go as they were both blown over, black smoke from the flames covering them. Judging from the far-off hint of yellow and red, the forest was on fire, or at least part of it. Tanek coughed, then surveyed the area. Hood's people were already stirring, as was Mary. Adele was laying motionless a little way from Hood's woman.

It was time to retreat.

The whole thing had gone to shit, and he needed to get De Falaise's daughter to safety. He'd promised. Tanek got up, kicking the farmer across the face and grabbing his crossbow as he made his way to Adele.

"Time to leave," he told her, taking her by the arm and lifting her to her feet. She didn't complain, a ripe bruise flowering on her chin and eye. It seemed that Hood's woman still had some fight in her after all.

Tanek pulled Adele towards a jeep with one working headlight. Just as they were about to climb in, the sound of gunfire came from somewhere across the way – from the direction the shell had originated. Somebody was being shot at; Tanek hoped it was Hood.

Adele slumped forward, hanging heavily in his arms. She was staring up at him, as if shocked. When Tanek shifted his position to help her into the vehicle, he felt the wetness at her back.

More shots – closer, in tandem with the others. Tanek traced them back to Mary, who was sitting upright, holding one arm with her other hand and shooting the Peacekeeper. Once the gun was empty, she slumped, spent.

Adele was bleeding heavily from her back wound. Tanek lifted her into the vehicle and ran round to the driver's side, gunning the engine, he pulled the jeep round and retreated, urging Adele to stay awake, telling her he'd get her back to the castle, get her fixed up.

"Hold on," he kept repeating as he drove past the stuck AFV and back onto the main road, cutting a swathe through the fog. He knew once he got far enough away from Sherwood, the mist would clear.

"Everything will be okay. Just hold on!"

* * *

As HE STUMBLED through the undergrowth, the mist thickening, the Tsar couldn't help thinking that this was just like one of the old folktales, something parents tell their children to stop them running off. *Don't go into the forest, especially after sunset, because something might just come for you. Something might just be hunting you.*

Well, something was definitely hunting him.

The Hooded Man, on his own turf. He knew every single one of these trees, where the Tsar was completely and utterly lost. They might be within spitting distance of the road, but he couldn't see a thing. He ventured on, stumbling through the fog, his great coat flapping behind him, waving his blade ahead of him.

The Tsar tripped and crashed into a fence, breaking through the wood. He rose, tumbling forwards, the ground less grassy here. He smacked into another fence and when he looked up, he gasped. The figure of the Hooded Man was towering above him. He was about to swing his sword when he realised it was just a statue, that the representation was holding a staff and was fighting with another, much larger figure. That the hood was thrown back.

Must be in the old tourist section of Sherwood, he thought, *the place where they honoured the first of his kind.*

The original, not this... *copycat* who'd come along centuries later.

Even so, that mimic had managed to cripple his forces. Now had him on the run. The Tsar was searching for the warrior within himself, the man who'd fought so valiantly in the 'eighties, who'd beaten people up for protection money, taken assassination jobs.

You have grown soft, so used to luxury in your hotel back in Moscow, shielded from everything. Now you must fend for yourself because there is no-one else.

No-one else here to face him, Andrei, but you.

It was the first time in years he'd heard that name, his true name. Not Lord, or Sire, or the Tsar. The name he'd had as a child, an orphan. The name he'd used in the Russian army.

He remembered all those battles now, the bloodlust that had been in him, and the way he'd deal with those enemies of the mafia during peacetime. Actually doing the damage himself instead of just watching others in a ring beating the hell out of each other.

The Tsar gnashed his teeth and trudged on, feeling his way along the sides of buildings, then up along an overgrown path. Suddenly, ahead of him, he saw the fire. *His* fire. The one he'd created with the explosion. He'd got turned around somehow and gone in a circle.

The fire was spreading through the trees, from branch to branch.

"I'm coming for you, Tsar!" shouted a voice that echoed all around, full of fury. He'd invaded Hood's country, his city, killed his men and taken his women hostage. Now this: the Tsar had set fire to his beloved Sherwood.

But an angry man makes mistakes. *If I can just keep calm, keep my cool.* The Tsar let out a small laugh at the ridiculousness of that, while all around the fire raged.

Find the warrior inside, find that same fire in your own belly!

He stood up straighter, then called back: "Then come. I am read –"

The shape leaped out of nowhere, out of the flames. It dove headlong into the Tsar, shoving him sideways into a tree. His shoulder stung as it connected with the wood and he let out a cry. Swearing, he shrugged off his greatcoat.

"What's the matter? Too warm for you? I used to be afraid of the fire," said a gruff voice from under the hood. "Afraid of the memories."

The Tsar stood again, swiping sideways with his curved sword and hitting thin air. "You should be afraid of me!"

"I don't think so." Hood lashed out now with his weapon, and the Tsar met the thrust. They exchanged blows against a background of mist, smoke and crackling flames. Then Hood rammed him up against a tree, crossing their blades so that they were either side of the Tsar's neck. Even as the man was doing this, the Tsar couldn't help noticing a wince of pain when Hood raised his arm. Some wound at his shoulder? A weakness?

The Tsar pressed the man back, then twisted the crossed swords so he could angle them sideways. He gave another push and the hilts smacked into Hood's wounded shoulder. He let out a howl, fell back, and dropped his sword. Then he dropped to his hands and knees, gasping.

That *is where you should be!*

The Tsar kicked him in the side, rolling him over. As Hood clutched at the shoulder wound, the Tsar spotted blood staining the leg of his trousers. He trod on the second wound, and again Hood let out a wail.

"So, you can be hurt. Not as invincible as you would have people believe, eh?" Hood lay on the ground, with the Tsar above – sword at his throat. "All this will have been worth it just to kill you, comrade. Tanek was right; one day it would have come to this. Better that it should be settled here and now."

Hood didn't move, apparently helpless, the Tsar victorious over him. He finally felt like that warrior again. He, who had defeated Hood after the Frenchman failed; when tanks, guns and men had failed.

Then Hood grabbed the blade with his good hand. He levered it back, though it cost him – the sharp edges cutting into his skin, slipping and causing even the Tsar to cringe.

"I agree," said the man, wrenching his head to the side and letting go of the sword. It dug into the soil behind, holding it there fast. Hood slid from beneath the Tsar, kicking the legs out from under him at the same time.

There was nothing he could do. He was falling, knowing what was going to happen but powerless to prevent it. The spiked hilt of the sword, as smooth as it was, went into him – helped by his own bodyweight and forward impetus. The Tsar grunted as he dropped down over the hilt, and onto the blade itself. Impaled.

He was still alive, just, when Hood picked up his own sword and walked round to his head.

"You should have stayed where you were, comrade," he told the Tsar, spitting out the final word.

Then there was a final swish and the Tsar had to concede, in the end, that the Hooded Man had a point.

CHAPTER TWENTY-SIX

HEAT. FIRE. PAIN.

It was all he could remember of the torture session. Naturally, Tanek had left Jack a few reminders: scalding burns, and several nails still digging into his body that hurt whenever he twitched. Though not even they hurt as much as the thought he'd let down Mark, Tate and the others. Not to mention Robbie. He'd given them up – granted, because they were threatening Mary's life, but she would have been the first to tell Tanek and Adele to take a hike. Even Mark probably lasted longer. And Jack had fallen for Adele; just how stupid was he? The daughter of their greatest enemy. Greatest till now, anyway. Not even De Falaise could have pulled off the stunts this Tsar character was responsible for.

Jack had passed out again a couple of times since the pair left, and night had fallen in the meantime. He'd also been left unguarded. They probably thought he didn't warrant watching any more. That he'd be going nowhere considering what Tanek had put him through.

They obviously didn't know Jack very well. He'd screwed up, big time, and he aimed to put things right. How, he didn't know, but he'd start with getting free of this fucking chair! Easier said than done, when you were tied to the arms and legs.

He should have been freezing, stripped to his underwear. But they'd also been making use of Faraday's furnace. Jack recalled seeing the body of their blacksmith in the corner. How many more would be counted amongst his number by the time the day was out?

During the torture, the furnace had been an instrument of terror; now, though it had died down, it was probably keeping him alive. And might just be the answer to freeing him.

Mustering what little energy he could, Jack stretched his toes – the rope tying his ankles to the chair legs prevented him from placing his feet properly on the floor. As he strained, the cords in his neck tightened, and the nails that had been banged so methodically into his torso, arms and legs sent more ripples of torment through him. Never, not even after all those rounds in the wrestling ring, had his body felt so battered and abused.

His toes brushed the cold floor, but he was going to have to do better than that. He stretched again, and this time they connected. He pushed down, enough to raise the chair slightly. Breathing heavily, Jack did it again, only this time he tried his best to lean to the side as well, angling towards the furnace. Just when he thought it wasn't going to go, the chair tipped, pitching him on his side. It knocked the square furnace over, sending a slew of coals and ash across the floor. The nail in his shoulder was driven even further in by the fall, and he bit back a cry of anguish.

Ignore the pain. You're not done yet, and someone might have heard all the racket you've just made!

Jack looked down and found a handful of coals had rolled near to his bound wrists. They were no longer as hot as they had been when Tanek made use of them, but they might be hot enough for his purposes. If he could just inch a little closer...

Jack wrenched his body sideways, lifting the chair off the floor, then threw his weight in the other direction. The chair moved a fraction across the floor. Dismissing the pain as best he could, Jack lifted the chair again, bringing it down closer to the coals. He was centimetres away, so he did it again. This time he landed virtually on the coals, and he yelped, but kept still – the rope was also on them. Slowly, they were burning through it. It took a few minutes, but he at last began to smell smoke. Jack held on a little longer, but eventually lost patience. The ropes were now loose enough for him to break free.

Making a fist, he tugged on the bonds, and was surprised when they gave first time. Quickly, he reached over, untying his other hand – then did the same with his ankles. Jack collapsed on the floor, and crawled away from the sea of coals and ash.

Before he had a chance to pull out the nails still sticking in him, a Russian soldier appeared at the arched entranceway, barking something in his native tongue. He raised his machinegun. Part of Jack just wanted to lay there, let him shoot and get it over with. But people were relying on him. "T-take it easy, buddy," he said, his voice hoarse. "We can work this out."

Just when Jack thought he was going to open fire, the soldier shouted something else, motioning with his rifle for Jack to come out.

Jack held up a hand, rising slowly and wincing. "All right, all right. I'm coming." The man shouted again, and it was now that Jack revealed his other hand – flinging coals at the soldier, hitting him in the centre of his forehead. Before the soldier could fire, Jack had reached him and followed through with a punch in the face, knocking him spark out.

"Yeah, you sleep it off, pal," Jack muttered as the man slid to the floor. He dragged him inside and began pulling off the soldier's uniform. Jack braced himself as he pulled out the nails, so he could slip on the clothes: biting on his bottom lip to keep from screaming again. There were half a dozen or so, positioned like acupuncture needles across his body. When he eased them out, they didn't bleed as much as he'd thought they would, but even after they were gone it still felt like the nails were there.

The jacket was a tight fit, but at least it was long, and though the trouser legs didn't go all the way down, anything was better than freezing his butt off. Grabbing the rifle, Jack poked his head out of the stables and couldn't see any more soldiers, but just as he was venturing out, a squadron of men came up through the sloping tunnel, where the horses usually made their way to the nearby stables. He ducked back inside, opting to hide until they'd gone past.

Too late he realised he'd left the bare foot of the Russian soldier sticking out near the entranceway. All it would take would be for one of them to look sideways and they'd see it. Jack listened as boots stomped by, and breathed a huge sigh of relief when he couldn't hear them anymore.

He stepped out from behind the wall where he was hiding...

Only to see several more rifles trained in his direction, another smattering of Russian coming from the soldier in charge.

"Hi, fellas," said Jack. "Don't suppose we could talk about this, could we?"

THEY'D ENTERED THE city under cover of darkness.

It was obvious when they found the dead men at the look-out points that the Tsar's army had arrived ahead of them. But he hadn't left any of his own men on watch. Which meant he either hadn't had time yet, or he'd already taken the castle and was supremely confident his forces could defend it.

Dale was hoping for the former, but if it did turn out to be the other option... Well, they'd already fought and won one battle that day against the very same forces. Okay, that also meant the men who'd come with him – who'd made that tiring journey, with no rest and not even a pit stop for something to eat – were not exactly at their best. Robert had already asked a lot of them, and now they were expected to fight another army, this time entrenched behind the castle's walls.

Dale was no good at making speeches. That was Robert's forte. *Could try singing to them, I suppose,* he thought. In the end he managed to persuade the men to come with him and do a recce, scope out exactly what was happening. They left the horses behind and made their way up through the city, keeping to the shadows and conscious that the Tsar could well have posted armed men anywhere.

When they got close enough, they entered a building offering a direct line-of-sight up Friar Lane, towards the castle. From one of the upstairs windows they observed through binoculars. They saw the devastation the Tsar's men had caused, illuminated by lights from the armoured vehicles parked inside the castle grounds and beyond. The castle itself had taken a hit, too, a corner chipped away by a rocket or shell blast.

Once each member of the squad had taken a turn, Dale hadn't needed to give any speeches. This was their home – the only one a lot of them had known since virus times. They'd headed the Tsar's forces off because they'd been trying to prevent this. But the sneaky bastard had divided his troops and hit the castle anyway. Now, each and every one of the fighters with him wanted it back.

And they didn't care what it took.

"So Robert has somewhere to return to," Dale said to them, and they all agreed.

There had been no sign of any of those closest to the Hooded Man, though: Mark, Mary, Jack and Reverend Tate especially.

Or Sophie. Where was Sophie?

Dale had to assume they were being held somewhere inside the castle, because the alternative was just too horrifying.

All they needed now was a plan of action, and they were looking at him to provide one. He thought about what Robert would say if he were here.

"Okay, we'll divide into three teams," said Dale when they regrouped. "Hit them from the front and sides at the same time. We have our ropes, our arrows. We can scale the cliffside, the walls, and get inside. They haven't fixed up the mess they've made of the gate yet, so we don't even have to break in there. We've trained for this, guys. We know that place inside out. They don't." He split the numbers, giving the cliff job to Azhar and his band, detailing how he wanted covering fire laid down for the frontal assault, and explaining how he would lead the third team in through those busted gates. "None of us are gettin' any younger. Let's do this."

Dale had played some gigs in his time, but this one had to take the cake. *One day,* he said to himself, *songs actually will be sung about what we've done... what we're going to do today.*

He just hoped he would be the one singing them.

"BEFORE YOU START, you should know: I've had a really, really bad day."

Jack ducked back inside the stables a fraction of a second before he heard the first *bang*.

His reactions were definitely slower than usual; a bullet nicked his arm. Compared with everything else he'd been through, it felt like a gnat bite. And it made him angrier than ever.

"Right," he said, taking hold of his machine gun. Reaching across himself, he poked the end out and treated the soldiers to a blast. After the first burst, the weapon clicked – either empty or jammed. "Goddamn!" shouted Jack, tossing the gun away.

He looked around desperately for something, *anything* to use in its place. Then he saw it: an old broom over in the corner. He edged sideways and grabbed it – pulling off the head and testing its weight. It was a far cry from his staff, but it would have to do.

Jack crouched and rounded the corner, this time holding his makeshift staff out in front of him – charging at the soldiers still standing and slamming it against their knees, bowling them over.

He stabbed the handle left and right, hitting one soldier in the temple and smashing another's front teeth in. Jack let adrenalin take over, just like he used to in the ring.

One soldier attempted to get up, and Jack jumped on him. Another was running back down the slope towards the tunnel. Jack struggled to his feet, hefting the stick like a javelin, and threw it. The end of the wooden pole struck the fleeing man in the back of the head and he went down.

Jack moaned, only now feeling the mounting pain. He made his way down to the tunnel himself, willing his exhausted body onwards.

Picking up the staff, he checked the tunnel for the approach of any more soldiers – knowing that somebody must surely have heard the gunfire. But if they had, they'd be coming down the steps above him, not up the path, and so he was shielded for the moment.

Jack made his way down through the tunnel, pressing himself against the side when he got to the other end, seeing the armoured vehicles still on the castle grounds near the gatehouse. There were also clumps of troops – not as many as he'd been expecting (not as many as when they took the castle from De Falaise), but enough to cause him to groan in frustration. Not all were in uniform; some he recognised from the hotel prison. Heck, some he'd even apprehended himself! They'd been given weapons as well, it seemed, drafted into the Tsar's employ. What he didn't see this time, strangely, were any of the cultists.

Suddenly there was shouting and Jack saw one of the troopers point up the slope in his direction. Then a squadron was heading his way, hefting their rifles.

They hadn't got halfway up the drive before they opened fire. Jack squashed himself flat against the wall, expecting bullets to spark off the stone. They didn't. And he could hear more gunfire, coming from another part of the castle, up and over to his right, over near the cliffside.

Jack looked again, and the group he thought were coming after him had veered off to the left, towards the gate. Then one of them was suddenly on fire. It was like he had spontaneously combusted, the flames spreading outwards from his chest to consume him. When he turned sideways, just before falling over in a blazing ball of orange, Jack saw the arrow sticking out of him.

Robbie! It had to be. The very thought that the Hooded Man had returned from fighting the Tsar's forces filled him with new energy.

More flaming arrows struck home, the soldiers they were hitting running this way and that, firing indiscriminately at shadows. His men were following their training, sticking to the darkness where they wouldn't be seen; hitting their opponents hard and then retreating.

It was time Jack joined them.

He came out of the tunnel, just as a Russian soldier was running past him. Jack swung his staff, connecting with the man's face, knocking him flat on his back. Jack trod on him to get to the next soldier, hitting that one in the stomach as he swung his rifle in Jack's direction. Jack struck the soldier's temple and he fell on top of his companion.

As he cleared the tunnel, Jack looked up and saw other soldiers running from the castle, jumping down from the middle bailey, joining their comrades in the struggle. This time they were on the receiving end, but it was a stealth attack – not a show of force. And they'd been caught on the back foot.

Nevertheless, it was still machine guns against bows and arrows. And if they brought some of that other heavy weaponry into play... Jack had no idea how many allies he had out there – it was difficult to tell, with a flash here, a flash there – but they had to cripple as many of the Tsar's men as they could, or this would be over as quickly as it had been the first time around.

More flaming arrows whizzed by ahead of him, but as he watched Jack saw them exploding in the grounds, flinging bunches of soldiers into the air as effectively as if someone had just tossed a grenade into their midst.

Soldiers ran around the grounds, confused. Nobody seemed to be in charge, and no-one apparently wanted the job. Jack guessed Tanek and Adele must have gone after Mark, Tate and Sophie at Sherwood. But where was the Tsar himself? Where were his bodyguards? Surely he wasn't so stupid – or overly confident – that he'd leave his castle with just his foot soldiers looking after it?

Somehow, over the top of all the gunfire, Jack heard the clack of a rifle being cocked behind him. He turned, expecting to have his head blown off. What he saw when he made it round was one of the men he'd imprisoned in the hotel. Jack couldn't remember his name, but recognised him from his patchy beard. He'd caught him a few months ago picking on a group of teenagers who'd banded together, threatening them with a pickaxe if they didn't hand over their food. Now the man was out for revenge.

"Just wanted you to see who it was who offed you," said the man, venom in every word. He put the rifle to his shoulder.

"If you're going to do it, get on with it. Won't be the worst thing that's happened today, fella."

"Fair enough."

Jack waited for the bullets to hit home – with no archway to duck into, what choice did he have? But they didn't. Instead, the man's body jerked, his whole frame dancing like he was being electrocuted. His eyes went wide and he let go of his weapon, following it to the ground moments later.

Behind him stood a young man, his sword dripping with the bearded man's blood – which looked oddly black in this light. The youth beamed when he saw him. "Jack! You're alive."

Jack laughed, rushing up to Dale and clapping him on the arms. They didn't have time for a proper reunion though, as more soldiers happened across them.

Dale was on one of them in a flash, his blade slicing left and right. Jack handled another with the makeshift staff, forcing himself to ignore the tremendous pain he was still in.

More explosions nearby, and more gunfire. Jack's eyes flicked up to the castle again and saw troops being hit by arrows up there. "Your doing?" he asked quickly.

"Azhar," was all Dale needed to say.

As Jack's gaze was drawn towards the wall in front of him, he saw the black shapes of more Rangers clambering over. Some were immediately sprayed with bullets, tumbling over onto the top of the wall: dangling like lifeless marionettes. Others managed to get a foothold at the top, targeting the shooters with yet more arrows.

The grounds had seen better days, but there wasn't an end in sight. Another wave of soldiers were coming from above, leaping down and firing into the dark recesses, covering any inch of ground their enemies might be hiding in. This lot seemed more together, and had obviously hung back to get a handle on the situation before rushing in.

"They're picking off my... Robert's men," Dale said.

Jack could easily see this kid leading his own division of the Rangers someday. He wanted glory, the adulation that came with bravery. But that was in the future. In Robert's apparent absence, Jack was in charge. "We need to round up as many of our lot as we can, bring them together and make a stand against the Tsar's remaining forces," Jack said, coughing and wondering how much longer he could hold out. This wasn't his first battle of the day, and he'd been tortured by a maniac in the meantime.

Dale nodded, then whistled: a signal for the rest of the Rangers to converge, to make their way into the centre of the grounds. They did so, fending off the soldiers in their way with swords and arrows, fighting more valiantly than Jack had ever seen in his life – in reality or on the silver screen. It made him feel very proud.

They were still outnumbered and outgunned, but none gave up. It was quite a thing to see.

The remaining Rangers were gathering in the spot where Dale and Jack stood, forming a ring. They were being surrrounded by soldiers and prisoners still swarming from every part of the castle and grounds.

Backs to each other, the Rangers loosed arrow after arrow, stuck the Tsar's men with knives, struck them down with swords. But it was obvious who was winning. As Jack feared it would, the tide had turned, and not even the appearance of Azhar, swords in both hands, cutting and slicing his way through the mayhem, did any good.

"Always wondered what I'd choose for my final number," Dale shouted to Jack.

"What?"

But the youth wasn't listening. He was singing. Lines from a song Jack hadn't heard before, probably one from Dale's old band, or maybe something he was improvising – he was good like that. The words were beautiful and poignant, though, and spoke of kinship, loyalty and of trust.

> *"So we stand here on the brink,*
> *Hardly able to even think.*
> *Who'd have thought we could make it here,*
> *Together.*
>
> *What's waiting? Who can say...*
> *But we'll face it anyway.*
> *You can –"*

He never got any further before the first of the explosions came. Their heads whipped sideways; it was from outside the grounds.

As Jack and Dale looked on, astonished, one of the armoured vehicles at the wall blew up. The Tsar's troops turned to watch as well.

"Is someone still outside?" Jack asked.

Dale shook his head. "We needed everyone for the assault."

Another explosion, another vehicle going up in flames. Now the Tsar's men were worried. They'd concentrated so much effort on the attack from Dale and his men that they'd taken their eye off the ball where the castle's defences were concerned. The result: somebody was having a merry old time blasting their toys to pieces.

The explosions died down and there was silence for a moment or two. Then:

"*Invaders of Nottingham Castle. This is Robert... the Hooded Man. Your beloved Tsar is dead.*"

"Robbie? Well, I'll be," said Jack. "Looks like you were only the warm-up guys, Dale."

The youth frowned and for a second Jack thought it was because of the crack. Surely he can't be mad at Robbie for stealing his thunder, can he? When Dale spoke again, it all became clear.

"I-I left him, on the battlefield. Jack, he was really hurt bad."

"Aren't we all?" Jack pointed out.

"No, I mean... bad."

Jack frowned. It did beg the question how in God's name he'd got from there to here, let alone what he was doing talking to the Tsar's men on a speaker system.

The Russians surrounding them were all exchanging blank looks, those who spoke English translating for the rest. It was clear none of them believed what this Hood character was saying.

"Unless you surrender, you will suffer the same fate." With that there was another noise. Not an explosion, but something overhead. The sound of a chopper's blades as it hopped over the buildings next to the castle to hover just above the grounds.

Jack peered up, hand covering his brow. "Is that... Holy smoke, it's Bill!"

The door of the Gazelle helicopter opened and something was dropped into the grounds. The Russians attempted to scatter, thinking it was some kind of grenade. But it was big, more like the size of those old bombs from cartoons. In any event it had landed before they could get very far.

It dropped with a dull thud and rolled into an open part of the grounds the soldiers had vacated.

Jack heard the first of the cries a moment later.

The Russians were backing away, as fast as if it actually was a bomb. However, when Jack, Dale and the others came closer, they saw it was white in colour, with features: eyes, a nose, a mouth.

The head of the Tsar.

"Now... get the HELL OUT OF MY HOME!" came a thunderous roar over the speaker. Some of the Russians dropped their weapons right there and then, holding their hands up in surrender. Others made a dash for whatever exits they could find. The prisoners who had been released, while not overly concerned about whether the Tsar was alive or dead, recognised that the tide had turned. They fled, prepared to shoot their way out if necessary.

Dale and the Rangers began rounding up as many of the Russians as possible, but they were too few in number to go after both the soldiers and the escaping prisoners.

It wasn't long before an armoured vehicle came in through the already smashed gates, following closely by a jeep.

Surfing the AFV was Robert, bow in one hand and mike in the other, the cable stretching into the vehicle. He called for help and two Rangers came over. Soon they were carrying a half-conscious Mary from the vehicle. Sophie, who was driving the jeep, needed assistance as well, and a Ranger put an arm around Mark, helping the lad hobble out. Tate was also helped from the jeep, but waved the Rangers away once he was on his feet again. Up on the middle bailey, Bill's helicopter was setting down.

Jack and Dale went over, and the first thing Jack did was hold out his hand, which Robert shook gladly. "It's good to see you, boss," he told him. Jack watched Mary going past, saw Mark and Sophie's injuries, and he struggled to fight back the tears. "I'm sorry. This is my fault. I told them where you'd be... I mean, I didn't know you'd be there, but they were threatening Mary and –"

"Don't, Jack. It's okay." Robert placed a comforting hand on Jack's shoulder; a hand wrapped in a bloodied bandage. "Really."

"How did you..." Dale began, then: "The last time I saw you, you were..."

Robert held up a finger. "Later, eh? I'll tell you guys everything then. Let's make sure the grounds and castle are clear first, then tend to our wounded."

"Like you?" Jack pointed at the bloodstains at Robert's leg and shoulder.

"We've all been in the wars," Robert said quietly, nodding at the state of Jack.

"Aye, that's one way o' putting it." This was Bill, joining them, and Jack hugged the member of their family he hadn't seen in so long.

Jack felt Dale moving away from his side, going off towards Sophie, asking how she was. Jack also saw the look Mark gave the lad. Even after everything that had happened, there were some things that still needed settling. Lots of things, in fact.

But it would take a while, Jack knew that. They'd been here before. Yet that victory had felt so much cleaner, much more final. When they'd ousted the Sheriff it was after a lengthy campaign of terror on his part. The Tsar had managed to achieve more than he did in much less time. And they almost hadn't regained what was theirs. The price had been high: so many injured, including those closest to them. So many dead.

Everything felt broken.

Jack also knew what Robert would say to that. What was broken could be mended... usually. He just couldn't help thinking that the scars from today would remain long after the battles were just a memory. That the ramifications might prove tremendous.

Jack exhaled. He didn't have the energy to think about it. His body was crying out for rest, reminding him of every little thing he'd gone through. Like Mary, Mark, Robert and the others – even the castle itself – they needed to heal the physical before anything else.

Then, and only then, could they begin to find their way.

CHAPTER TWENTY-SEVEN

THEY'D ALL LOST their way to some extent.

It wasn't until he took a step back from everything that he saw. It had taken so much to go wrong, before it could start to go right again. But then, spring was here and it was the time for new beginnings.

Robert looked out over the flowers blooming near the war memorial. The place they'd buried the dead from the battle with De Falaise, and those who'd died when the Tsar's forces had – briefly – taken the castle. Those who had fallen in the skirmish with the suited man's legions (Robert had since learned his name was Bohuslav) were buried where they'd made their stand against them, once all the detritus had been cleared. Tate had performed moving services at both sites.

They were still counting the cost, not just in terms of numbers but also morale. Those who were fit enough had been given the task of repairing the worst-hit parts of the castle. It had kept them focused on something other than training and fighting, given them a common goal of restoring their home.

Because that's what this place was to them. He'd said it himself over the speaker when they'd arrived back here, commandeering the Tsar's own vehicle to take the place back (he'd used it reluctantly, conceding that Bill was right and they had no choice on this occasion; they needed to get Mary back to the castle quickly and safely).

For the first time, he'd actually meant it. This was where he belonged, at least for now.

That didn't mean he was abandoning Sherwood – his other home. For one thing, he was continuing Mark's training there. The young man had certainly faced his fears: faced Tanek, and taken his first steps towards becoming the person he was destined to be. And Robert would always need to return, in spite of what Mary had said about not belonging there. She understood a little more now, had seen more of the place – after experiencing its strange effects herself, when she was close to death. And Robert would always carry a little bit of the wilderness inside him; he couldn't escape it. Now he knew that the dreams would come wherever he was. He just had to let them.

Relationships were being renewed, re-forged. From here, Robert spotted Mark walking with Sophie, holding hands. Things had definitely changed between them since returning. It looked liked they'd finally worked things out with Dale, who seemed to have backed off to give them space. Mark had told Robert there'd been a conversation or two – between Dale and Sophie, Sophie and Mark – but he hadn't asked for details. He'd just been pleased that his adopted son was happy. Meanwhile, Sophie herself had turned out to be a pretty good nurse, with Mary's instruction and hours of dipping into text books on the subject. She'd definitely helped to patch them all back together when things had calmed down. Sophie said she'd always had an interest in medicine, and now that Lucy was gone...

Poor Lucy. It hurt Robert to even think about her, with the others near that memorial.

Bill, though he had things to attend to first with his market network, had agreed to come back and help with the general day-to-day running of the Rangers. He claimed Robert needed someone to "keep a bloody eye on him." It would allow the Hooded Man to go on more patrols, to be out there where he should be. "I still think ye should be armin' them lads properly," he'd said, Bill being Bill. But for now he seemed to have dropped the subject. For one thing he was busy fixing up one of the Black Shark attack helicopters they'd retrieved near Doncaster. "Look at that beauty," he'd practically drooled. "It'll be protection for the castle while you get your other defences up and running again..." Robert was too tired and too preoccupied to argue with him this time.

Bill would be helped by Tate, who'd moved back permanently. Robert felt the most sorry for him. They'd both gone out to New Hope, after hearing that Gwen and Clive Jr were alive and safe, that they'd somehow escaped on their own. But Robert and Tate had been prevented from entering the village by the armed guards at the entrance. After Tate told them they weren't moving until they saw Gwen, the woman had reluctantly appeared. At first she wouldn't even look at the Reverend, even after he apologised. Then, when she did, she told him:

"I never want to see you again. Don't come here any more."

Robert saw how much the words upset Tate – he'd only been doing what he thought best. The Reverend never spoke all the way home.

But even he hadn't moped as much as Jack. Robert's second had taken both Adele's betrayal and his own – he called it that no matter what Robert said – to heart. Or maybe it had been the torture; sometimes he woke the whole castle up at night with his bad dreams. Perhaps Robert's forthcoming wedding would take his mind off things. Who knows, maybe Jack would even meet someone from the neighbouring villages at that; like last year's summer fête, they'd invited all the people under the Hooded Man's protection.

Robert recalled now those agonising days waiting by Mary's bedside, with Sophie telling him he should still be recuperating himself.

"I need to be here," he insisted, and she'd left it at that.

Robert held Mary's hand and was there when her eyelids finally fluttered open, a smile breaking on her bruised, lovely face. "Hey..." she'd croaked.

"Hey yourself."

"Did... did we make it? Back, I mean. What happened... with..."

"Sshh, shh." He stroked her hair, then kissed her forehead. "Everything's okay. We're at the castle. The Tsar's dead. Mark, Sophie, Jack, the Reverend, Bill, they're all..." He paused, but said it anyway. "They're all fine."

Mary nodded, then winced. "I feel dreadful."

"Well, you look beautiful."

"Liar," she said, laughing, then wincing again. "How about Tanek... and Adele?"

Robert shrugged. "Tanek I don't know. Adele you shot."

"Good old Dad; all those hours hitting tin cans were definitely not wasted. Yay me. Did you find the other Peacekeeper, by the way? In the caves?"

Robert nodded. "I know how much they mean to you, even though I don't technically approve. But yes, you have a pair again, now." He was skirting round what he really wanted to say, so he just got on with it. "Look, this probably isn't the right time or place, but, well, I've been thinking."

"That's dangerous," she said.

She must be feeling better. "I almost lost you, and I'm not sure if I could go through something like that..." Robert let the end of that sentence float away. "Mary, I guess what I'm trying to say is –"

"The answer's yes, you know. It always was." She smiled back at him. "You looked like you needed helping out."

And that had been that. They'd set a date over the summer, a special one that marked the anniversary of becoming a proper couple, and asked Tate if he'd perform the ceremony. His answer had been: "Nothing would give me greater pleasure." Now, if this quiet period would just hold out till then.

They'd had no more reports of invasions, nothing about the Morningstars – it was as if they'd vanished, just as they did from the castle – no trouble yet from the prisoners that had got away, and that was how Robert hoped it would remain, for the time being.

As Mary joined him on that sunny, but slightly chilly morning – still using a stick to get about – he thought about what he'd said, about almost losing her. Not even the castle had been safe; they both realised that now.

"When you're feeling up to it," he told her, slipping an arm around her waist, "how about we go out on a few patrols together? I know Dale would welcome the back-up. So would I."

"You old romantic," she said to him, slapping his shoulder. He gritted his teeth, feigning pain at the wound he'd received at the hands of Bohuslav. "Oh, I'm sorry, love."

"Maybe you should kiss it better."

Mary grinned. "I think that can be arranged. I wonder if the stables are free..." She took him by the hand and led him down the path.

As she did so, Robert realised that he didn't feel lost anymore. He been found, in more ways than one. He was both Robert Stokes – the man – and the Hooded Man, the legend.

There were worse things in life he could be, and this woman had rescued him from that.

In a broken world, he said to himself, what more could anyone ask for?

THE COUNTRY HAD welcomed him back into her arms like a concerned mother.

One that also admonished him for ever wanting to leave. He comforted himself with the knowledge that none of this had been his idea. It had all been the Tsar's, the old Tsar's. Now that man was dead, along with Xue and Ying. Just as he had almost been.

As he stepped out into the cold, flanked by soldiers to the left and right, on his way to the combat arena from the Marriott, Bohuslav's wrist throbbed again, at the stump he'd cauterised himself, almost passing out from the pain.

He felt the pull of the stitches at his stomach, the wound which would have seen his intestines spill out on the floor had it been a couple of millimetres deeper. As it was, he'd had to sew up the flesh with his one good hand – his driver useless at anything medical, it seemed – dosing himself with antibiotics against infection.

By the time he was fit enough to travel, news had reached them of the failure of their troops to retain the castle. Bohuslav had been numbed by the realisation that their entire operation had been a spectacular catastrophe.

There had been only one thing to do at that point. Waiting for them just off the coast were the fleet of empty hovercrafts, including the Tsar's. He'd told his driver to radio that he would be returning, and that he would now be taking charge of the fleet – and indeed of the Tsar's entire army. They would return home to Russia to bide their time and replenish their forces.

It had been enough of a pasting to make him think twice about trying it again for a good while. Or at least without any major allies. One day, however, one day...

Because, as much as he loved his motherland, Bohuslav was also thirsty for vengeance. Not just on those who had done this to him, but also on the man who had lured the Tsar and his men across to that fated isle in the first place.

Tanek.

Even the name caused him to clench his fist as he climbed into the limo. He couldn't clench the other, as that position was now occupied by a sickle, attached directly to the stump.

Yes, one day he would meet both Hood and Tanek again. And when he did...

Bohuslav wondered where that cowardly giant had run off to after leaving his leader in the lurch. Reports were sketchy, but he'd apparently abandoned him at Sherwood after a confrontation with their enemies.

"Drive," he instructed the man in front, once his personal bodyguards were seated on either side. (They were no oriental beauties, but they would give their lives for him.)

As the car pulled out into the snow-covered road, Bohuslav cursed Tanek, hoping that wherever he was, he was suffering.

For weeks now, he'd sat there, beside her, watching her suffer.

Quite how he'd managed to keep her alive was beyond him, not with the wound she'd suffered. He could put so much of it down to his skill with the blade, his knowledge of anatomy allowing him to perform the operation and remove the bullet – which had come so very close to penetrating her heart.

After leaving Sherwood, Tanek's plan to return to the castle had been waylaid by Adele, who had finally passed out from the loss of blood, in spite of the field dressing he'd applied. He needed to get her to an old hospital, anywhere he might be able to find replacement blood quickly. Tanek already knew her type: O-Neg. He consulted the map he found in the jeep they'd taken, and decided to head for King's Mill in Sutton-in-Ashfield because it seemed to be closest to their current position.

As he'd expected, the place was run down. People had picked over the stocks of drugs, but some of the medical equipment remained and the emergency operating theatre was still relatively intact – if woefully unhygienic after years of disrepair. They weren't in a position to be choosy, though.

Placing Adele on the table, Tanek went off and gathered what he could find – including tubes and needles for a transfusion, seeing as there were no stocks of blood that he could find. Running out of time, he'd hooked himself up and conducted the transfusion at the same time he began to operate. Not ideal, but necessary. There was alcohol in the medical kit from the jeep, so he'd been able to sterilise the bullet wound that way. He hadn't needed to knock Adele out with anything as she was totally unresponsive.

Tanek had cut into her with a scalpel that had survived the scavenger hunts, searching for the bullet that was causing all the bleeding. Little wonder, because it had glanced off the ribs and come close to puncturing her heart. Tanek had managed to remove it, stemming the blood flow; stitching her up and treating her with antibiotics, also from the jeep. But he knew they couldn't stay there for ever.

He was too woozy to drive that night, but once he'd recovered enough, Tanek carried her to the jeep and prepared to make the trip back to the castle in Nottingham.

He hadn't got to the city limits when he saw that Hood's men back on point. Tanek knew what that meant – they'd taken back the castle. He was tempted to go there anyway, gun them all down, but realistically he wouldn't get very far. And he had to look after Adele.

The dreams, the promise... they were never far from his mind.

He needed somewhere quiet, out of the way, somewhere he could care for her. So he'd retraced his steps from over a year ago, returning to Cynthia's little house out in the middle of nowhere.

The door had been wide open this time when he arrived. Stepping cautiously inside with his crossbow raised, Tanek had searched the place for any signs of the woman or her fucking demon dog. There were none, just evidence of some kind of struggle. Obviously someone had stumbled upon this place and they'd either fled, or been taken away and killed. There were no corpses to indicate it had happened in the house. He neither knew nor cared.

Tanek had carried De Falaise's daughter up to the bedroom, placing her on the comfortable, still-untouched bed. Then he'd looked after her, continuing to give her the antibiotics until they ran out, mopping her brow as she sweated out the pain, and willing her to wake.

She opened her eyes only twice. The first time she asked for water, which he gave her. Tanek had been feeding her intravenously with a drip he'd found back at King's Mill, while he'd been surviving on what he could hunt in the nearby meadows: small animals mainly, some birds he killed with crossbow bolts. He'd lived on less.

Adele told him she'd seen her father, that he'd talked to her.

Tanek nodded. She'd had the dream as well.

"He said I had to get better, had to... because..." She began to cough, and he gave her another sip of water.

"Take it slow."

"No, I must... must tell you... We have to... have to save..." That was all she could manage before losing her tenuous grip on consciousness. There was something wrong with her, any idiot could see that. Even in sleep, her face was a rictus of agony. Maybe he'd missed something internally, some fragment from the bullet that he hadn't spotted? Although he knew about the human body, he was no doctor and hadn't had the best of facilities in which to work.

Whatever the case, it was too late to do anything but sit and wait.

The second time she woke, three days later, was the last. Tanek sat up when he saw her stir, especially when she'd grabbed his hand, gripping it tight. Adele looked at him, eyes wide, with an expression that only came when you knew you were close to the end.

"He made me promise," she spluttered. "My father."

"Promise what?" Tanek leaned in. Maybe if he hadn't been able to keep his own pledge to De Falaise, he could fulfil Adele's. Would that make up for his mistakes?

"Save –"

"You said that before. Save who?"

The grip tightened again. "His child."

Tanek shook his head. He'd tried, he'd really tried.

Then Adele said her final words: "My brother. My little brother..."

She fell back on the pillow, letting Tanek's hand go. Tanek felt her neck; she was gone. It had taken this long, but Mary had finally killed Adele with that bullet. He shed no tears, though. Not because it wasn't in his nature – he was just too preoccupied with what she'd imparted.

A brother, a younger sibling. But where? In France, over here? A sudden thought struck Tanek. Perhaps the child De Falaise had been talking about in his dreams hadn't been Adele at all. What if it never had been?

Perhaps he was meant to save someone else? Meant to keep someone else safe?

It was a thought that would plague him even as he buried Adele in an unmarked grave. Even as he left Cynthia's house and drove on up the road again.

It was a thought that would continue to plague him for some time to come.

GWEN FINISHED FEEDING Clive Jr, spooning the food into his mouth and wiping it.

She sat back and looked at her son, and not for the first time she wondered just how and why they'd been spared.

He must be kept safe...

That's what the cultist had said. A man she'd been led to believe was evil – who painted a skull on his face and had the mark of a sinner on him – and yet had actually saved her from Jace, smuggled her out of the castle when she was about to be used as bait, when Christ alone knew what was going to happen to her son.

What had he meant? She didn't have a clue, and hadn't had a chance to ask again. Because after they'd dropped her off near to New Hope, they'd all disappeared: Skullface and the rest.

Gwen had ditched the robes before walking into the village, Andy and Graham rushing over when they saw her. They'd bombarded her with a flurry of questions she either couldn't or didn't want to answer. But once she was safe again inside her own home, once she was sure she wouldn't be spotted or followed, she took Clive Jr and headed out to retrieve those robes.

They hung, even now, in her wardrobe upstairs. Gwen didn't know why she was keeping them. A souvenir of her escape? She doubted it, she wasn't the sentimental type anymore. Not since Clive...

Then why?

That wasn't all. Ever since she'd got back, every time she left the house to visit Clive's grave, or walk through New Hope, or attend meetings about the best way forward for the village – by which she and the others meant the best way to get hold of more weapons – she'd had the uneasy feeling she was being watched. Gwen would turn around quickly in the hopes of catching a glimpse of what was in the periphery of her vision. But it would always be gone.

Now, as she rose and walked to the window, hugging herself in spite of the fire that she'd made in the hearth, keeping out the dying breaths of winter, she thought she saw something out there in the dark. Just a quick flash, a figure perhaps, amongst the trees, wearing a hood. But not *him*: not the person she'd sent away when he'd brought Tate back to plead forgiveness.

No.

This was a different kind of Hooded Man altogether...

His presence heralding a different kind of future.

THE END

ACKNOWLEDGEMENTS

ONCE AGAIN, A huge thank you to Trevor Preston for all his help with the weapons and military stuff – and for even knowing what thickness the metal should be for the Ranger shields! Cheers, mate. A big thank you to Sue Pacey for the medical and drugs advice, who didn't bat an eyelid at my strange questions. My thanks once more to the staff at Nottingham Castle for that trip around the caves, and to Pete Barnsdale who gave us a private tour of the Castle itself. A thank you to Sherwood Forest Visitors Centre, and especially Mark for the archery lesson. To the staff at The Britannia – where Marie and I hosted our first FantasyCon as co-chairs, and the seeds were planted. Thank you to Simon Clark and Lee Harris for looking over the Robin Hood's Bay and York sections. A massive thank you to Richard Carpenter, one of my heroes, who let me use the quote from Robin of Sherwood at the front (for my money the best adaptation of Hood there's ever been). Thanks to Scott Andrews for the conflabs about where we're taking this future vision of Britain, and how we can cross over our characters. Thanks to my support mechanism of fantastic friends and loving family. To Jon Oliver for his great edits, Mark Harrison for the excellent cover artwork (I was a fan even before he started bringing Robert to life), and to my darling wife Marie, who was – as always – the first to read this and give me such insightful feedback. Love you more than words can say, sweetheart; you're the best.

ARROWLAND

Original cover art by Mark Harrison

*For Richard Carpenter, as much of an inspiration
now as he was back then.*

"Then Robin Hood bent a very good bow,
To shoot, and that he would fain;
The stranger he bent a very good bow,
To shoot at bold Robin again.

"'O hold thy hand, hold thy hand,' quoth Robin Hood,
'To shoot it would be in vain;
For if we should shoot the one at the other,
The one of us may be slain.'"

– *Robin Hood Newly Revived*
(Traditional Ballad)

CHAPTER ONE

THE FIRST SIGN they were in trouble was when a crater the size of a garden pond appeared ahead of them.

There had been very little sound until that moment – then an almighty *bang* which hurt the ears. The vehicles they were directing up the road rocked with the noise.

Mick Jamison, in charge of the lead truck – or, as he called her, 'Stacey' – pulled on the steering wheel to avoid the smoking hole, then glanced in his mirrors to see his companions doing the same. Those using horses and carts, however, had to calm their animals first – not an easy task when none of the animals were used to loud noises. A couple reared, kicking back at the carts and riders.

Mick snatched up his radio, but it hissed static. "Jesus," he said, looking through the windscreen and spotting the tail of another mortar winding its way down to earth. This one struck the side of the road, but had just as much impact. Even with all his years of experience – before and after the nightmare known as the Cull – he struggled to control the tons of metal and cargo.

This hadn't been part of the deal. Actually, there hadn't even *been* a deal. Unlike his jobs before the virus, when he'd been employed by large haulage companies to transport goods, there was no paperwork for this gig. Back then it had been a nice, relatively safe job – the only danger being from other, less careful drivers on the motorways. People who took chances, nipping in and out of traffic at ridiculous speeds, driving all night without taking stops when they felt tired. But in all his years in the delivery trade, Mick himself had never been in a single accident. He'd certainly never been fired upon.

These were different times.

He'd realised that when the people in his neighbourhood had

started dropping in the streets, bleeding from every orifice, coughing their guts up onto the pavement. He'd realised it when he'd reached his girlfriend's house and found her –

That seemed such a long time ago now, years beginning to feel like decades.

If he'd been left in any doubt that things were different, the gangs and cults roaming the streets had soon changed that. At first only disorganised handfuls, then in greater numbers as they'd banded together for a common cause: mayhem and destruction, making the most of the lack of authorities.

Some had even come from overseas to wreak havoc, like that insane Frenchman they'd heard about – De Falaise. In pre-virus times, he would have been locked up for doing what he did, attempting to take on the mantle of Sheriff of Nottingham. As if that hadn't been bad enough, there had been that Russian, the self-styled Tsar, a year or so later. Mick had lost friends to him and his forces when they invaded Britain, cutting a swathe through towns and villages.

Yes, he had friends – even in these bleak times. *Especially* in these times. Because just as there were those who gathered together to cause chaos, there were others intent on bringing some semblance of normality back to these shores. It was how the markets had started, how he'd become involved in them – stumbling on one outfit not far from Wickham. He was impressed that communities had pulled themselves together enough to produce their own food, replacing what had been taken for granted before. Impressed that they were cultivating links with their neighbours, bartering now that money was obsolete.

The markets and trading system had been steadily growing, so when Mick got wind of the fact that folk were also delivering these goods, picking up the traded items in the process, he offered his services – and his truck. He'd felt like a bit of a spare part all this time, on the road, hiding out in Stacey's cab and living on whatever he could find in out of the way places, scavenging whatever fuel he could from abandoned vehicles; some days even wishing he'd caught that virus along with the rest of 'em. At least now he could make himself useful, doing the only thing he'd ever really been good at. He was working for – and with – good people; helping to make a difference, perhaps even helping turn things around.

Then came reports of convoys being attacked by armed raiders. These weren't like earlier encounters, small parties chancing their arm in the hopes of coming away with a vanload of fresh beef or eggs;

easily driven off by the weapons they carried to protect themselves. No, these guys were well organised and extremely well armed.

Up until now, they'd been lucky. Mick and his mates hadn't come face-to-face with them. He could fool himself into thinking it was just like old times on the open road again. If you ignored the fact that, thanks to the scarcity of diesel, some of the transportation had to be of the old fashioned live variety.

That luck had just run out. On their way up through Corbridge, towards the Scottish border, they'd suddenly become the target of one of the raiding parties. He remembered the reported pattern: first creating confusion from a distance, an attempt to cut off the route ahead; next cutting off radio communications, probably with some kind of jamming equipment.

Then they would attack.

And if the stories were to be believed, not many of Mick's group would survive.

Another mortar fell to the right of Mick's truck and he grappled with the wheel again, almost tipping the vehicle over – clipping the edge of the second crater but not falling into it. Some of the others were not as fortunate, or as skilled. One truck, being driven by a guy Mick had known only a few months called Jed Elliott, tipped into the first of the holes head-on. It was now stuck there, looking like a mole burrowing into the ground. Mick thought about stopping, but saw something in his mirrors which made him press down on his accelerator instead.

Jeeps and motorcycles – quite obviously military issue, from their colour – had joined the party, skidding down hillocks on either side of the road. A couple of the jeeps had no roofs; mounted on top were huge machine-guns, spitting out bullets as the raiders opened fire. They raked the road ahead of one cart, and the two horses pulling it broke free of their reins, running for freedom, leaving both driver and cart at the mercy of the raiders.

If they had any.

Already the lead bikes had caught up with the truck behind Mick's. Riding on the bikes were pairs of raiders, one handling the steering, the other clinging to the back. Both were dressed similarly, though: goggles over their eyes, breathing masks over their mouths, wearing thick, leather gloves and boots. Some kind of dark tartan Mick wasn't familiar with flapped in the breeze, overlaying the combats beneath. And at their hips hung what appeared to be claymores, with rounded guards over the handles.

As he watched, one bike pulled alongside the truck and its passenger fired some kind of hand-held harpoon, like he was hunting a landlocked metal whale. A length of rope unfurled with it and the next thing Mick knew, the raider had leapt from the bike and onto the truck, swinging from its side. The raider launched himself forward, level with the driver's door, then grabbed hold with his free hand before letting go of the rope. He produced a handgun and shot out the window. The driver, a woman called Kimberly Johns, looked terrified when the glass shattered, but at least she was still alive. Mick saw her reach over and bring up the rifle she always carried in her cab, but before she could use it the raider had tossed something inside. Within seconds, the cab filled with smoke, and the truck began weaving. That explained the breathing masks. Through the smoke, Mick saw Kim's outline slump against the big wheel, and gradually the truck ground to a halt.

Again, he knew he should stop – but Mick had problems of his own. More bikes catching up, two flanking him, both carrying raiders with similar harpoons. They were going to pull the same stunt on him. "Shit!"

He sped up, but his vehicle wasn't meant for racing. They could outrun and outmanoeuvre him easily. That didn't mean he should just give up, though. There were alternatives to running, and he wasn't going to let them take Stacey without a fight.

Mick lined up one of the bikes in his mirror, making sure it was directly behind him. Then he stamped on the brakes: not enough to tip the truck, but enough to cause the bike to slam hard into the back of his trailer. With a certain amount of satisfaction, he noted the dislodged raiders sprawled across the road, their bike laying a few feet away from them.

Another two bikes joined the remaining one on his tail. Mick accelerated again, but already they were firing their harpoons – up and into the top of his trailer. At least two of them swung over. Mick heard them trying to break into the back – then their footsteps across the top of his truck, heading for his cab.

Unlike Kim, he didn't carry a gun, had never used one in his life and didn't intend to start now. But he was far from unarmed. Even back in his early days, he'd kept his trusty baseball bat – a holiday present from a cousin, now long dead – down the side of the seat. His fingers curled around the handle. Mick didn't know how much use it'd be against bullets or gas canisters, but if even one of those raider bastards stuck their head in here, they'd get one hell of a shock.

Mick flinched when he heard the gunfire, however – waiting for the bullets to pierce Stacey's cab.

Then him.

CEALLACH HELD HIS bike straight, but off to the side of the truck in front of him.

He'd seen what the driver had just done to Ròidh and Machar back there, braking so that they'd run slap bang into the truck. Ceallach glanced across at Garbhan, on the bike running parallel, and Flannagan riding his just a little behind. They'd deposited their kinsmen onto the truck: Neas and Osgar were hanging by their harpoon ropes, while his partner, Torradan, had climbed on top to see if he could take out the driver.

Neas had smashed the lock and Osgar pulled up the shutter. Ceallach watched as the pair peered inside. It was a fine haul today: sacks of potatoes, crates of cabbages, carrots, tomatoes and cucumbers. If an army marched on its stomach, then they would be going far.

Just as *she* had promised.

Towards the back of the truck were more sacks. But as Osgar swung in and approached them, he seemed to stop, cock his head, then stumble backwards. Neas, directly behind him, moved towards his companion – then caught him as he fell.

Ceallach frowned. What the fuck was happening in there?

Neas fell back as well; it looked for a second like he'd lost his footing and both men were about to tumble out of the truck. Ceallach angled his bike slightly, just in case – signalling the others not to get in the way. Then Neas straightened up, letting Osgar go. He reached for his pistol, but even before his hand was at the holster, he was spinning as if he'd been punched. Ceallach inched his bike closer to see what was going on.

It was then that he saw what was sticking out of Neas. Thin feathered wooden shafts, embedded in his shoulder and midriff. Neas had fallen to one side, revealing who'd done this. There, rising from under some covers, hidden amongst the sacks, was a man.

Not just any man. This one wore a hood and held a bow in his hand – and Ceallach knew immediately who he was. The man whose legend had spread across this entire island over the past couple of years; the man who had dispatched the Frenchman at Nottingham Castle; who'd led his troops into battle against the might of the Tsar's forces, armed with only arrows and swords. Some of it was made up – had to be!

Christ, how could one man take down attack helicopters using that kind of weaponry? To hear people talk, you'd think he was bullet-proof or something. Rubbish. Yet Ceallach felt a twinge of fear when he looked at him, especially when he saw the man's eyes under that cowl. It felt as if he should be ordering a withdrawal before it was too late.

Osgar, who had also been wounded, clambered to his feet again, clutching the parts of his body now punctured by the Hooded Man's arrows. It was a clumsy attack by an already defeated opponent, and Hood dodged it easily enough. But then he did something else, something he probably wouldn't have if Osgar had stayed down.

Hood shouldered Osgar, almost giving him a fireman's lift, then bent slightly before throwing him out of the back of the truck. His aim was as true with the man's body as it had been true with the arrows, striking Garbhan's bike full on, knocking the rider off and dragging the bike itself into Flannagan's path. Ceallach swallowed hard as he saw Flannagan hit the obstacle, the bike tipping up and pitching its rider over the handlebars.

The result, which Ceallach left behind him, was a tangled mess of bodies and machinery. Hood stepped forward, standing on the edge of the truck, taking aim at the final rider and his bike.

Ceallach manoeuvred sideways, avoiding the arrow by inches, and drew his pistol to fire a couple of rounds. Hood took cover behind a crate, while more of Ceallach's bullets bounced off the shutters.

Another close call with an arrow convinced Ceallach to veer off, hopefully out of the Hooded Man's line of fire. He accelerated, gesturing wildly to Torradan, who was still on the roof.

"Inside!" shouted Ceallach, but knew the man couldn't hear him through the mask. He pointed his own gun downwards and pretended to fire, hoping Torradan would get the message. The man shook his head in bemusement. Ceallach couldn't blame him – who would have expected there to be a man with a bow and arrow in the back of the truck they were hijacking?

"Shoot!"

Torradan pointed downwards.

"Yes, for fuck's sake! Through the roof!" shouted Ceallach, though the words were again lost. An arrow whipped past the side of Ceallach's head and he struggled to keep balanced. He swore into the mask. But at least it got through to Torradan, who now began shooting down at the roof of the truck.

"Now," whispered Ceallach, "let's see if you really are bullet-proof, Hooded Man."

*   *   *

ROBERT STOKES LOOKED out from the back of the truck.

The biker who'd been firing at him had skirted round the side, trying to get away from his arrows. He'd keep for a moment or two, while Robert scanned the horizon, searching the vehicles that they'd left behind in their wake. Looking for –

There!

The raiders checking the backs of the trucks and carts were getting just as much of a shock as the two who'd broken into this one. Because there were his Rangers – trained men and women – waiting, hidden, unbeknownst even to the drivers of this convoy, and now jumping up to tackle the armed men.

At the same time, the jeeps accompanying the bikers were being set upon by Rangers on horseback – horses that *were* used to the noise – led by one of his best men: Azhar. They were springing their own sneak attack, jumping over onto the jeeps to fight the gunners.

Satisfied his men were handling the situation, Robert risked a peek around the edge of the truck. He spied the remaining biker, making hand gestures to the raider on the roof. Confident the rider was distracted, Robert leaned around and shot off an arrow. His aim was thrown by the movement of the truck, though, and the projectile went wide. But only just.

More frantic hand gesturing followed, then the first shot through the ceiling. Robert retreated just in time to avoid it, pressing himself up against the wall as three more came in quick succession.

He readied his bow and shot upwards. There was little chance of an arrow going through that metal, especially at this range, but thanks to the idiot above him, there were now several holes in the trailer's roof. Robert's knack with the bow and arrow had always been good, but since he'd stepped out from behind his desk back at Nottingham Castle – to fight the Tsar and the Morningstar cult – it had improved beyond measure. So it was no problem now to guide his arrows through those holes, returning the favour to the man above him.

For a second or two everything was still, and Robert thought he might have incapacitated him. That theory was shattered when more bullets raked the ceiling. Fruit and vegetables exploded in all directions, crates splintered.

He had to leave that confined space, take out the guy on the roof. Thinking quickly, he looked towards the back door. Robert grinned, then shouldered his bow and ran at the open space.

At the last moment, he grabbed one of the harpoon ropes still dangling there, attached to the roof. Robert swung out of the trailer just as another shower of bullets was pumped into it, arched his body around and twisted, so that his booted feet slammed against the top edge of the door. The rope taut, Robert pulled himself upright, then onto the roof of the truck, crouching on one knee.

The raider looked across at him, his jaw falling open. The man's combats were torn at the knee, a wound bleeding there.

A bullet whizzed past Robert, but not from the raider on the roof. His companion on the bike, riding alongside, was providing covering fire. But before Robert could do anything about that, the truck veered sideways, causing the raider on the bike to swerve to avoid a collision. Robert made a mental note to thank the driver of the truck when this was all over. Both Robert and the raider on the roof had staggered sideways, but Robert was the one who recovered first, leaping at his enemy before he could raise his pistol.

Robert grabbed his arm, trying to keep the gun down. A shot almost went through Robert's left foot, forcing him to step back a little. It gave the raider a chance to bring the gun up sideways, though Robert still had a firm grip on his wrist.

Robert let go with one hand and punched the man in the stomach. The raider bent, allowing Robert to wrestle the pistol from him. It clattered onto the roof and disappeared over the side.

The raider retaliated by bringing up a fist, striking Robert's cheek and causing him to reel. Then he drew his claymore and attempted to run his opponent through – but Robert met the blow with his own sword. Metal struck metal, the vibrations going up Robert's arm. The raider wasn't exactly a novice with this weapon; Robert met a couple of crafty swipes that almost opened up his throat and belly.

Pushing the raider back, Robert suddenly had the advantage – slashing across the man's blade and kicking out at him at the same time. He was about to deal the winning blow when bullets raked the side of the truck. More heavy duty than the biker's pistol, they could only have come from one of the mounted machine-guns on the jeeps. As Robert was pitched sideways by an erratic swerve from the driver – there'd be no thanks for that one! – he saw that one of the raider jeeps had broken through his Rangers and was attacking.

Another lurch, and Robert found himself going head over heels, losing his sword in the process and slipping over the side of the truck.

He held on to the edge by his fingertips, while the raider above him climbed to his feet. The man started to laugh. He held his sword aloft, then brought it down on Robert's fingers, forcing him to shift his weight from hand to hand as he dodged the swings.

He couldn't do this indefinitely – either he'd end up with no fingers or he'd fall off the truck. Then there was the alternative of being riddled with bullets from the jeep's gun.

But there was nothing he could do. His enemy was giving no ground. Perhaps this was it, perhaps he *was* about to die.

The raider lifted his sword one last time, about to bring it down on Robert's head and cleave his hood in two; destroying both the man and the legend with a single blow.

Then there was another blast of gunfire, but not from the jeep or the biker. Robert recognised the sound immediately. There was a spark as the bullet stuck the raider's claymore, forcing him to drop the weapon.

Robert traced the line of fire back to a woman riding a horse. She was just behind the jeep, her dark hair flowing in the wind.

"Mary," breathed Robert, still struggling to hold on to the truck.

She fired again at the raider, the barrel of her dead father's Peacekeeper still smoking from the last shot. Like Robert, she'd been a decent aim even before this past year, but had become even sharper – able to use either hand and either of the two pistols with equal precision. The raider ducked, but in his confusion stepped too close to the edge. Quick as a flash, Robert reached up and grabbed his ankle, tipping him off balance and pitching him over.

Robert climbed back up, and both the jeep and Mary swerved to avoid the felled raider as he rolled over and over on the concrete below.

The gun on the jeep swivelled in Mary's direction, but before the raider could do anything, Mary had urged her mount forward, pulling alongside the jeep, then jumped onto it, pistol tucked back in her belt. Robert watched proudly as she gave the gunner a right hook that looked like it would have floored a gorilla, then turned and backhanded the raider climbing through from the front of the jeep – so hard that his breathing mask and goggles came off. It gave her time to pull her Peacekeeper out again and 'encourage' them to surrender.

Robert smiled, but it faded fast when he saw the biker from the other side of the truck pull back, his pistol drawn and trained on Mary.

Snatching up his sword, Robert ran back along the length of the trailer's roof and leapt, grabbing another harpoon rope, swinging round like a pirate in the rigging.

As he passed the bike, he drew back the sword and slashed at the rider; the bike wobbled as the raider dodged. He got the bike back under control as Robert swung back in the other direction, and this time he hefted the sword like a javelin and threw it at the front wheel.

It jammed in the spokes and held the wheel fast. The rider was flung from his bike, landing awkwardly on his shoulder.

Robert was dangling from the rope, banging against the side of the truck, but he felt the vehicle slowing. The driver had obviously seen him in his side-mirrors. Mary was forcing the jeep to slow, as well. Soon both had stopped and Robert was able to let go, dropping gracefully to his feet. He peeled back his hood.

He looked over to see Mary kicking men off the jeep. "That's it; down you go, boys." She mouthed a silent 'Are you alright?' to Robert, who nodded.

Overhead there was the sound of chopper blades. Robert looked up to see a Gazelle helicopter coming in to land between them and the Rangers cleaning up further down the road. The familiar figure of Bill hopped out even before the blades had stopped turning, holding up a hand. He'd been monitoring the situation from above, keeping well enough back that the raiders didn't see him, but close enough to let Azhar and the cavalry know exactly when they were needed. Of course, if he'd had his way he would have brought his brute of an attack helicopter instead; the one that the Tsar's men had left behind.

Robert could hear that rough Derbyshire accent in his head right now: *"It'd all have been over in seconds if ye'd just let me blow 'em up."* But what would that have achieved? These men were no good to anyone dead. Apart from the fact he and his Rangers weren't cold-blooded killers, Robert wanted to question them, find out for sure who'd been behind the raid. Not to mention the many others along the border and inside Scotland itself.

Robert waved back. In fact, it had been Bill who'd brought them all here, drawing their attention to the attacks on trade routes interfering with Bill's markets, causing people to go hungry. It smacked just a little bit too much of what De Falaise and his army had been doing in Nottingham all that time ago, reminding Robert too much of those days to simply ignore it.

As Robert watched Bill make his way towards him, carrying that beloved shotgun of his, he suddenly became aware of Mary screaming, "Look out!"

The expression on her face was pure shock, but she was looking past him, over his shoulder. Robert turned in time to glimpse the remaining raider from the back of the truck – the one he thought he'd put down – leaping with his sword raised.

As Robert was tensing to avoid the blow, the raider was dropping to his knees, claymore falling from his hand. Behind him stood a man holding a baseball bat. The cab door of the truck was open.

"That's for what you lot have done to Stacey," said the driver, hitting the raider again just to make sure he stayed down.

Robert nodded a thanks to the man.

There was an engine gunning off to his right. *God, what now?* He looked over to see the raider who'd been trailing them all this time, who he'd forced off his bike. The guy looked half dead, practically slumping over the handlebars, but was able to get the bike upright, gun it, and get it going in spite of the damaged front wheel.

Bill was bringing his cannon of a gun to bear, but Robert motioned for him to lower the weapon.

"But he's getting away," complained Bill.

"Let him." Robert's eyes trailed the lone, injured biker as he made his way up the road, attempting to mount the verge. "We need someone to go back and tell whoever's running the show. Tell them what happened here. Tell them they can't get away with what they're doing anymore."

Bill shook his head. Shoot first and ask questions later, that was his philosophy. The number of arguments they still had about the use of modern weapons... Robert went over and retrieved his sword from where the biker had left it, after plucking it from the wheel. This was the weaponry of the future; he'd tried to get Bill to see that. Someday, all the bullets and missiles would run out and this is what they'd be left with: swords, bows, arrows. Robert and his Rangers were just getting a head start.

You only had to look at this convoy to see the way things were going: horses and carts mixed in with the trucks. Of course, not everyone wanted to accept that.

"Bill? Was this your idea?" asked the driver of the truck, slapping the baseball bat into the palm of his hand.

"Aye, Mick," he admitted. "Had to draw them bastards out."

"So we were bait?"

Bill looked down for a moment, then back up. "I was keeping an eye on things, making sure ye were all safe."

"You call *that* safe?" Mick pointed down the road at the truck that had ended up in the crater, the Rangers digging its driver out "Explosions were going off all over the place!"

"Look," said Robert, cutting in. "Those raiders would have attacked anyway, whether we were here or not."

"That's right." Mary had joined in now, Peacekeeper still trained on her captives. "You'd probably all be dead right now if it wasn't for us, so maybe a little more gratitude would be nice."

Robert suppressed a grin. When his wife had the bit between her teeth, there was no stopping her. It was one of the many reasons he loved her so much.

Mick thought about this for a moment. "I suppose when you put it like that... You still could have warned us you suspected an ambush today. And that bloody Rangers were hiding in our cargo."

"We needed you all to act as naturally as possible," Robert explained.

"Running scared, you mean?"

"To keep them lot on the back foot," Bill told him.

Azhar joined them to report – or rather to whisper his report to Bill. The dark-skinned young man didn't say much, and when he did it wasn't to an audience. "Ta, lad."

Robert inclined his head, waiting for the information to be relayed.

"He says the raiders are rounded up – didn't put up much o' a fight. Weren't expectin' this kind of resistance."

"Excellent," said Robert. "And do we have confirmation about who runs their operation? Is it who we suspected?"

Bill said nothing.

"Then let's find out, shall we?" Mary said. She pushed the barrel of her Peacekeeper into the face of the closest raider, tearing the goggles and breathing mask off. "Who do you work for? C'mon, talk."

The man shook his head. Mary smiled, then grabbed his privates with her free hand, squeezing. "If I don't get a name, I'll just keep twisting until they come off. Understand?"

The raider nodded vigorously.

"So?"

"Th-the Widow." the raider gasped. Mary let go and the man breathed a sigh of relief.

"I knew it," said Robert.

"Widow?" asked Mick.

"Someone we'd heard rumours about, but couldn't confirm the existence of until now," Robert said. "She's been gathering troops in Scotland, and by all accounts generally making a nuisance of herself with the local population. That tartan they're wearing must be her personal calling card."

"Seems like it's time the Rangers looked into this Widow character more closely." Mary said.

"Agreed, especially if we're to cultivate better links with the Scots, and recruit more local Rangers to help police those territories."

It was something they were already experimenting with in places like Wales, and even down south. Robert realised he was running the risk of being seen as just as much of a dictator as the men he'd fought against in the past, which was far from the truth. All he wanted was to extend the protection he was offering people in and around Nottingham outwards, across the land. He envisaged local Ranger stations being run by locals. It was the only way to stop people like this Widow from rising to power. And it was the only way to keep invading forces out. If they saw a more unified territory that could fight back, they'd definitely think twice before coming here.

It wasn't going to be easy, Robert understood that as well, but then it hadn't been easy getting the Rangers off the ground in the first place. Hadn't been easy rebuilding what they'd lost when the Tsar had almost brought them to their knees over a year ago. But then, what worthwhile thing was ever easy?

Robert noticed Bill frowning, rubbing his chin. "What is it?"

"Hmmm." He was looking at the jeep next to them, then at the bikes that had fallen by the wayside during the attack. Bill bent and picked up one of the raider's pistols.

"Bill?" prompted Robert.

"AGF Serval jeeps, Motorrad motorcycles, Heckler & Koch P8 handguns. And can I see a few MP7 rifles, tucked away in the jeep there?"

"So?" Robert was tempted to add how scary it was that Bill recognised that kind of weaponry and equipment now; his interest in military aviation had extended further over the past couple of years.

"*So*," said Bill, "they're all German issue, Rob. Don't that strike ye as a bit odd?"

Robert considered Bill's words for a moment. Was this kind of equipment freely available over here? He didn't have a clue. But yes, it did seem strange that it should *all* be German. He didn't know what that meant just yet, or what connection it had with the Widow's people, but he intended to find out.

And where to begin was with the prisoners they'd bagged today. Like Mary, the Rangers had them all by the balls.

They'd just twist until someone started talking.

Germany, thought Robert, as he began to give the orders to round up the Widow's men.

Germany.

CHAPTER TWO

IT HAD WAITED a long time to become the rightful seat of power once more.

Constructed to house the parliament of the German Empire, the Reichstag Building was formerly opened in the late nineteenth century. It existed solely for that purpose until 1933, when a fire – supposedly part of a Communist plot, though some suspect otherwise – ravaged the place, paving the way for new masters to seize control. After the Second World War, the parliament of the Federal Republic of Germany decided to meet in the Bundeshaus in Bonn, but it wasn't long before the Reichstag Building was made safe again and partially refurbished in the 1960s.

It would take the reunification of this country, though, before the building was itself fully renovated, at last becoming the meeting place of the modern German parliament, the Bundestag.

Then the virus struck.

The parliament itself had been just as helpless as the rest of the world's politicians. Nations blamed other nations back then, arguments raging while the clever few got themselves to safety and hid away. No-one really knew what happened to them, but they'd never been seen again. By the time any kind of plan had been agreed on, it was too late. The virus was killing anyone who didn't have O-Negative blood, and what few safeguards were put in place to try and halt the infection proved ineffectual.

Inevitably, the survivors ran amok. Months, years of anarchy followed – of gangs on the streets of all sizes and allegiances, from small youth groups to much larger and more organised armies. Several attempts were made to take over the entire country, of course: those with lofty ideas looking to Russia for their inspiration, and tales of an all-powerful Tsar – now rumoured to be dead, but quickly replaced to prevent the fall of the system.

There had even been an attempt by a Frenchman called De Falaise, who had, in the end, travelled to England to try his hand there – with just as much success.

Failed; every one of them.

Until he came along.

Loewe patted back his slicked-down hair, taking in the scene from one of the levels of the huge glass dome that sat atop the Reichstag Building. He'd had any cracked glass replaced a long time ago, so it wouldn't spoil his enjoyment of the 360-degree view of Berlin. Or his enjoyment in watching the troops that he'd amassed outside, along with the many tanks, jeeps, Tiger and NHI NH90 helicopters, Tornado fighter planes, Skorpion minelayers and so on. Not a bad little defensive force from which to move outwards – and upwards.

Not bad, especially for a monumental conman like him.

Loewe began his walk back to the command centre he'd established. "With me!" he snapped, and the two magnificent Alsatians that went everywhere with him dutifully came to heel and trotted alongside. As he walked, Loewe came across various members of his staff, soldiers and military brains alike, nodding to each in turn. All wore the muted grey uniform of his legion, the Army of the New Order: its emblem a variation of the Mursunsydän symbol, overlapping squares in a very familiar shape.

God, not even he'd thought he could pull the trick off, managing to convince those few who still believed in the old doctrines that he was the guiding light of a new force – one which looked simultaneously to the past and the future – when in actuality he didn't give a shit about their dogma. He wasn't a neo-Nazi and never would be. But that didn't mean he couldn't *use* them to get what he wanted. After all, hadn't his whole life been a tissue of lies and deception?

From an early age he'd discovered that you could get more by hiding things than coming right out with the truth.

("Was that you who trailed that mud into the house, Achim?" "No Mütti, I swear. It was the dog." His mother thrashed that animal to within an inch of its life, while it looked at him accusingly.)

In his teens Loewe found that the more he lied, the more women would fall at his feet. He dumped them when he'd had his fun, usually after he'd taken them for their money. That fun soon ended when he was drafted into the armed forces, though he'd pulled a fast one to make sure he was given light duties; the doctor at his medical taken in by his protestations about his bad back. He had to admit he'd learned a lot during his time in the military, however, like where the real money was. When he eventually left – without permission, naturally – he took a stash of weapons with him and sold them all on the black market. It was enough to fund his escape from Germany, and further operations in Belgium, Switzerland, Hungary and further afield. His reputation, under an assumed name, as an international thief spread throughout the criminal underworld.

He'd stumbled into the world of terrorism quite by accident, after getting involved with a woman called Letty who'd introduced him to her cell: fighters against the injustices of the world.

"So what do *you* believe in?" he was asked, and he'd told them exactly what they wanted to hear. There was money to be made here, he could smell it. To prove himself, Loewe had to plant a device in the lobby of a certain office building with links to slave labour in the third world. He'd tried to convince them to blackmail the company, but they'd gone ahead and detonated the bomb instead. What a waste. Not of human life, but of an opportunity. And he really hated that.

Once he'd ingratiated himself with the people really pulling the strings, and had got bored with Letty in the bedroom, Loewe planted another device which took out the cell. Then he convinced the organisation that expansion was the key to taking over the world, and to do that they'd need money. "For the cause, you understand," Loewe insisted – embarking on his schemes to blackmail other businesses, banks; even holding entire towns and cities to ransom. Sometimes he was paid, other times he wasn't; then, he'd had to follow through, or the next time he'd have no leverage. It didn't bother him.

Loewe amassed a small fortune in that time. He would have lived comfortably off the profits of his extortion for the rest of his life, had it not been for the small matter of that damned disease. What use was money then? You couldn't buy yourself out of a bullet in the head, not when the monetary system had collapsed. He didn't even count himself lucky that he was immune, just cursed whatever gods were up there for taking away his luxuries.

Once again, he'd had to think fast, and talk faster. Because he knew the place better than anywhere else, Loewe had returned home. And it was as he observed the situation there that a plan formed in his mind. It was obvious – and should have been all along – who the most organised groups belonged to in his country. They'd been biding their time, waiting for something like this to occur. But they'd also been waiting for a leader to emerge, someone to bring them all together under one flag, and finally under one roof. Someone like General Loewe, military hero – just check his (forged) records – and bringer of terror to the Motherland's enemies.

He told his faithful followers, who'd soaked up his fake promises like sponges, that they should take up residence in the place that once raised Hitler to power. It had waited, just as they had, to be put to use again. Not as the home of a democratic parliament, but as *their* home, *their* headquarters from which to plan their next move. Indeed, hadn't Hitler promised there would be a special place for the building in his Welthauptstadt Germania renovation of Berlin after his 'assured' victory in World War II: a key structure in his vision of a World Capital, a reward for services rendered? Now they would make good on that promise.

His growing legions had lapped it up, helping him to take the place from those who were already in residence – hopelessly outmatched amateurs playing at being soldiers. The skirmish had lasted less than five hours.

Now his forces owned not only the building, but most of Berlin. And he was working on the rest of Germany; already they had stretched into Hamburg, Magdeburg, Leipzig and Dresden. He might not be as big as the Tsar yet, but it was a start. As with the terrorism, it was all about expansion, which kept not only his troops occupied but also ensured a comfortable standard of living for him. It might not be about money anymore, but he had people at his beck and call. What's more, he was safe, in a world where that word no longer had much meaning for most people. Loewe knew that any number of his men would willingly give their lives for him; were already doing so out there.

He descended the levels with his dogs, hands behind his back, heading towards the main control centre. Striding inside, he noted the maps on walls with dots on them, the table with a miniature landscape built on top: models of tanks, jeeps and soldiers covering it – everything Loewe imagined a command centre *should* look like, in fact. He, of all people, knew how important it was to look the part. Men in uniform were busying themselves, some on radios, others looking at the charts and discussing how their plans to take over the country and beyond were going. Because they weren't a force the size of Russia's, they couldn't just invade a country outright. No, they had to play things a bit more subtly. At the moment his Army of the New Order had its fingers in a lot of pies, covert agents in every country you could think of. But Loewe wasn't doing this to take over the world; rather to take out any other opposition before they came looking for *him*. It was all about security again. He'd made himself a target over here, and it was only a matter of time before the Tsar or another warlord came to challenge him. The only thing that had put them off so far was that Loewe talked a good battle, spreading rumours that they were much better armed and equipped then they actually were. That and the fact they were committed fanatics. Nobody would be stupid enough to go after the Nazis unless they absolutely had to, or were completely assured of a victory.

The men all stood to attention when they saw him, and he told them to be at ease. He walked through the area, pretending to be interested, peering at a few maps and nodding. Really, he just wanted to get to his office on the other side. It amused him when the men parted to let his dogs through, standing well back so that they wouldn't even brush against the dangerous-looking creatures.

Loewe's spacious office had been furnished to his specifications – lined on one side with books he would never read, on the other with a well stocked bar. A huge oak table had been positioned near the window, with a reclining leather chair behind it and an antique globe of the world not far away, which he would spin whenever he got bored. He had been inside only a few minutes, having just had time to sit down – the dogs taking up positions on either side of the desk – when there was a knock at the door. Loewe spread out papers in front of him and picked one up to study it, before shouting, "Enter!"

It was his second, young Schaefer, who dealt with the day-to-day running of the New Order. Behind those eyes, shielded by thick-rimmed glasses, was a frighteningly large intellect. Loewe was more than happy to let the man deal with organisational matters and supervise military operations, just as long as he was kept in the loop every step of the way. Which was what Schaefer was doing here now.

"I was just about to send for you," Loewe lied. "I wanted an update on the situation in –"

"Sir, I come with grave news about –"

"Schaefer!" screamed Loewe, sitting bolt upright in his chair. He may only have been pretending to be their leader – and wasn't really interested in an update on *anything* at the moment – but if there was one thing Loewe couldn't stand it was being interrupted. "Never speak before I have finished, is that understood?"

Schaefer remained silent, until he realised Loewe was waiting for him to give his answer. "Yes, of course, sir. But I bring bad news about the campaign in England."

Loewe raised an eyebrow. *England*: one of their oldest enemies.

That is, Loewe didn't give a shit about the country either way, but his men felt especially passionate about taking control of the isle, which was why they didn't complain – not that they dared anyway – about his use of so many resources over there, when they still had much of Germany to secure. This *was* potentially serious.

"*You* bring bad news?" asked Loewe.

"Er, actually..." Schaefer dragged in a second man, this one not familiar to Loewe; after a while all the uniformed people blurred into one. "Mayer here was the messenger who brought the news." Schafer pushed the other man into the room, closing the door behind them. "Tell the General what you told me," he ordered.

"Sir, I..."

Loewe rose, and his dogs raised their heads. "What is it, man? Spit it out, for God's sake!"

Mayer was looking nervously from Loewe to the Alsatians.

"I said *spit it out!*" Loewe snapped. The dogs began to growl.

"I-it's about the Widow's venture."

"The venture we have been *funding*, sir," clarified Schaefer, adjusting his glasses. That word took on a different meaning in this day and age, from the one Loewe had been used to at any rate, but it amounted to the same thing. They'd been supplying the woman with vehicles and equipment in order to cause the maximum amount of trouble. Something had obviously gone very wrong, though, by the look of Mayer. *He's practically shitting himself*, thought Loewe.

"The venture *you* convinced us to fund, Schaefer," Loewe reminded him, then addressed Mayer again. "Go on."

"T-there was an attack yesterday," Mayer informed him.

"The Widow lost a number of men," Schaefer added, "but also, regrettably, several jeeps and motorcycles, not to mention guns, ammunition –"

"*Our* jeeps, motorcycles, guns and ammunition," Loewe reminded him. "Who was responsible for this attack?"

Schaefer prodded Mayer in the back to get him to answer. "Hood," said the man, his voice breaking. "It was Hood, sir."

Hood. Yes, Loewe had heard the tales just like everyone else, about a man who dressed like a folk take and fought using a bow and arrow. Loewe almost had to admire the conman's audacity; it would be like him donning a toothbrush moustache and insisting they all called him the Führer. But that man had also, it was said, depleted the Tsar's forces – another reason why they hadn't attacked the New Order yet. In any event, if this Hood character was tackling the Widow, then reports were correct and he was doing just as they were, spreading out across his own country. It was a dangerous thing, because it meant that at some point their paths would cross. Someone like Hood, who had managed to convince his followers he was on some kind of damned crusade against evil, might get the bright idea of coming after them in Germany.

"How did it happen?" Loewe asked through gritted teeth.

"He and his Rangers were lying in wait, hidden in a convoy the Widow's men were raiding."

Loewe slammed his fist down on the desk, which hurt, making him madder. "The silly bitch! We give her all those weapons and she loses them to a bunch of fucking comic book characters." He walked round the front of the desk and his dogs rose again. Loewe tapped his lips for a moment, trying to look thoughtful. He already knew what had to be done. Picking up a large silver letter opener that had been resting on the wood, he touched the tip, testing its sharpness. "Mayer, have you ever heard the saying about messengers and bad news?"

"Please, sir." Mayer held up his shaking hands.

"You're a member of the Army of the New Order, man! For Heaven's sake act like it!"

Mayer attempted to show a little backbone, but there was still a quiver in his voice when he said, "It wasn't my fault. I was not even there, sir. Please don't –"

"Don't what?"

Mayer looked at Schaefer, then back again at Loewe. "Don't kill me."

Loewe laughed; it was all part of the act. "Oh, I'm not going to kill you. Why would I do that? I wish you to deliver a message to the Widow."

Mayer let out a relieved breath.

"However, I would like the message to be of a very specific nature. Do you think you can manage that?"

Mayer nodded, almost smiling.

"Good." He clicked his fingers. The Alsatians bared their teeth, and Mayer's eyes widened.

"But you said –"

"I said *I'm* not going to kill you. And I'm not," replied Loewe. He snapped his fingers a second time and the dogs were across the room in seconds, leaping at Mayer. The first jumped up on its back legs, slamming Mayer in the chest with its paws and causing him to stumble backwards. The second took hold of his arm, clamping its teeth around the wrist and shaking it violently. Mayer's scream was loud and piercing.

Loewe watched Schaefer's reaction; it was largely for his benefit that he was doing this. There was no real reason to set the dogs on Mayer. The man was right, it wasn't his fault. If anything, it was Schaefer's, but Loewe needed him. Sadly, for Mayer, if Loewe was to play the part of their General without drawing any kind of suspicion, he had to make it look convincing. Failure should not be tolerated by someone in his position. His men expected this kind of behaviour, so that's what he gave them. Schaefer would be his witness and word would travel fast through the ranks.

The tearing sounds drew Loewe's attention back to Mayer, who had managed to turn but was on his knees. To his credit, and quite unlike what Loewe had expected, he was showing signs of being a *true* fighter. This soldier was someone who actually deserved to be in the New Order. Loewe couldn't believe what he was thinking; *he* didn't even believe in the fucking New Order himself! But this was starting to be quite entertaining, and would relieve some of the boredom for a little while.

Schaefer, pulling a face, stepped out of the way as Mayer – now with both dogs attached to him – crawled towards the door. His hand was shaking for an entirely different reason now, as it reached for the handle, then managed to turn it. In a last ditch effort to be free, Mayer flung it open and collapsed in the doorway – both dogs biting and clawing at his body; one ripping off an ear and eating it as blood poured from the wound.

This was good – now there would be more witnesses. As Mayer's screams faded, some of the soldiers from the room beyond came to see what was happening. They gaped at the Alsatians savaging the man's prone body, then up through the open doorway at Loewe.

"I trust you will see that the Widow is sent the remains," he said to Schaefer, loud enough for those watching to hear as well.

Schaefer nodded.

"This Hood problem: I think we need to look into it further," he told his second.

Another nod.

"I would hate for it to interfere with some of the other projects we're involved with over there," Loewe continued, and almost added 'projects you also initiated, Schaefer,' but felt his point had been made. "Perhaps we need to find someone to deal with him." He knew Schaefer understood what he meant and would leave him to it, the example of Mayer spurring him on to succeed. But if he failed, would Loewe be able to go through with the punishment, as he'd done when blackmailing his targets back in his 'terrorist' days? He needed Schaefer too much. Maybe another pawn could be sacrificed. After all, Schaefer was too damned clever to put himself directly in the firing line: he'd always have a fall guy standing by.

Loewe clicked his fingers and the dogs returned to him immediately, Schaefer mirroring the men from the command centre, standing well out of their way. The dogs' mouths were covered in gore as they took their places flanking Loewe. He gestured for Schaefer to clear the corpse away, then shut the door.

Loewe returned to his seat, tossing down the letter opener and adjusting the position of the chair. As he lay back, he thought again of Hood and what he'd done, and hoped the man could be stopped before he really did become a threat.

THE PLANE REMAINED high, circling the area like a carrion crow.

When it finally descended, the small craft came in fast and low, making good use of the fading April light. Like its pilot, it was more at home in the shadows than the glare of daylight.

He'd managed to find a patch of grassland some distance from his chosen goal, near to a place called Creswell Crags. Deftly, he manipulated the sombrely-painted Cessna into position for a landing. He hardly felt the ground as the wheels touched down and carried him under the trees. The man opened up his door and climbed out, bringing his bow and arrows with him.

His dark clothes and long black hair, tied back in a ponytail, made him resemble that which he loved so much; his weathered skin completing the picture. It was the reason he had taken that name, the one he went by these days.

Shadow.

He began to camouflage his transportation, bending thin branches and layering foliage over the wings and main body of the plane. Before leaving her, he patted her cooling side. She had served him well during his long trip, admittedly punctuated by stops to replenish her fuel. Fuel supplied by those who'd employed him.

Shadow made his way stealthily through the Crags themselves. When he broke into the rundown visitor centre there, to search for a local map of the area, he noted that one of the caves not far away was named after his quarry – the original version, at any rate. According to books he found, under all the cobwebs – those that hadn't been destroyed by vandals – it had been called this because it was rumoured to have been used as one of his storage holes. But for thousands of years before that, it had been used by hunters just like Shadow's own ancestors. There was evidence of stone weapons and tools fashioned from animal teeth.

He dug out a map that showed him his destination within walking distance. So, quiver on his back, along with a handmade rucksack – knife and hawk axe already at his hip – he set off for the place where his 'mark' had once made his home. Nowadays, of course, the man spent most of his time in the city.

Shadow knew a great many things about him, simply from communing with higher forces, listening to his spirit guides. Even before he had set off, visions had revealed much about the Hooded Man and his forest. Prepared him for the task ahead.

Shadow contemplated the events that had led him here, the bargain he had struck. It had been necessary, like most things in his life. Part of him respected the hunter this Hood was. In another time, another world, they might even have been blood brothers. But, here and now, fate had forced them to cross paths as opposite numbers: Hood the person he must 'deal with' – isn't that how they'd put it? – in order to receive his reward.

Did he feel any guilt? Some, perhaps. Though they looked alike, it was not Hood's people who had murdered his brethren, taken their land and left them a minority in their country. Or was it? Hadn't it been that man's own ancestors who'd crossed the ocean and begun to colonise, begun the war that had lasted so long? His blood was their blood, wasn't it? So how could they *ever* be brothers? Though the natives of this country were worlds apart from those across the Atlantic, they were still cousins. They still had the same ways.

Many of Shadow's kind had banded together, forming a United Tribal Nation in order to take back what was theirs from the white man. They judged these post-virus times to be the perfect catalyst; thought the Great Spirit had granted them this opportunity. Shadow had always gone his own way, though, and used his own methods. He felt certain that they would achieve better results than the entire UTN affair.

It was why he was on his way to Sherwood, running at a pace that would see him reach the outskirts within the hour. Even though Hood appeared to have turned his back on it for now, in favour of building his army to police this land, the forest was still his seat of power – and it had waited so long for the rightful heir to come along.

Now Shadow intended to take that power away from the Hooded Man.

It was the only way to defeat him.

The only way to win.

He couldn't sleep.

The aching in what had once been his hand was keeping him awake again. Not that he slept soundly anyway; the nightmares of the battlefield saw to that. Bohuslav understood it wasn't possible for the hand itself to be aching, because it wasn't there anymore. He understood it was just the nerve endings from the stump of a wrist, extending out into nothingness – perhaps even missing the lost appendage? Was that it; was the wrist, like him, still in mourning? None of which stopped it feeling real. He felt the pain, just as surely as he felt hatred for those who had done this to him.

He was grateful for the fact that the weather was starting to turn slightly warmer; you could never *truly* call it warm during these months. The 'hand' ached more than ever in wintertime, and the winters in Russia were invariably brutal.

Bohuslav pushed himself up on the enormous bed. One of the benefits of his position was occupancy of the Presidential Suite of the Marriott Grand; the only occupied room in the whole hotel. Back before the virus, he would have had the full five star experience. Even today there was a team of staff dedicated to giving him everything he could possibly desire. That included bringing him certain luxuries he craved. Certain 'items': living items. Male or female, it didn't matter which. Not for sex, or anything like that. Bohuslav's desires ran much deeper. It was a way of taking him back to the days before all this, when he would hunt his prey on the streets.

At first they'd just brought them to him, knocking on the door and leaving the meat standing there quivering. Where was the sport in that? He'd soon grown bored when there was no chase, no excitement. Then he'd struck upon the notion of letting them loose in the hotel. If they could escape him, they went free. If not...

None had ever escaped.

He closed his eyes and could imagine the weight of his sickle – once handheld but now attached to his stump – as it slashed and gutted. A smile played across his face. The memories of all that bloodshed, before – when he had been one of the most wanted serial killers in this country – and after the virus, came back to him all at once. It made him want to grab the sickle right now and slide it in place. Go out hunting and –

Bohuslav sighed. He should really try and rest. He had responsibilities beyond the ending of individual lives at his... hand. Inherited responsibilities from the man who had once been Tsar, who now rotted away in a distant land – killed by Hood.

It was no use. Bohuslav flicked on his bedside light, powered – like so many things these days – by generator. He padded across the room, yawning. When he reached the door that would take him into the spacious living area, he paused, remembering a meeting here more than a year ago.

Remembering the huge, olive-skinned bastard who'd got them into all this, persuading The Tsar to mount an offensive against Robert Stokes. Tanek. The name brought bile to his throat. If De Falaise's former Second had never come here, things would have continued as they were. They would still be at full capacity with their troops and armament – instead of building forces back up again – and would now be thinking about a strategy of moving against other, more important enemies. It was what other countries were now doing, like Germany, from what Bohuslav was hearing.

Hood may have dealt the blow, but Tanek brought them all together. And, while it was true being the new Tsar of Russia did have its benefits, Bohuslav would still prefer to have been more behind the scenes.

Pulling on a robe, he walked over to the bar and poured himself a generous measure of Smirnoff; he preferred this to drugs when his stump was aching. By the second glass, the pain had dulled considerably.

Even after the alcohol, he heard, and felt, the person outside his room before they knocked. The sickle attachment was back in the bedroom, but Bohuslav never answered a door unarmed, even if there were guards out in the hall. He settled for a nearby ice-pick, concealing it behind his back as he looked through the spyhole.

It was a member of his staff – Klopov – but still Bohuslav kept the pick hidden as he opened the door.

Klopov smiled inanely as the new Tsar bid him enter. *It's obviously good news*, thought Bohuslav. If it wasn't, the man might have been more reticent. Bad news ran the risk of enraging him. And very bad news meant the same for the messenger. It was how any military dictator would act.

"Sorry to call at such a late hour," Klopov said.

"Yes, yes," said Bohuslav. "What is it?"

For a second an image of stalking Klopov through the corridors of the hotel flashed through Bohuslav's mind, the pulse at the man's neck exciting him. *No, concentrate. Listen to what he has to say.*

"I thought you'd like to know that he's there."

"Who is where, exactly?"

"The arrow," replied Klopov, then added for good measure. "The arrow has landed, sir."

Now it was Bohuslav's turn to smile. The first part of his plan had been put into effect. The Native American was on British shores. "Excellent!" If all went well, he would soon be celebrating his revenge, or at least part of it. There would be more to come eventually.

It would be perfect. Bohuslav looked down at his stump for the millionth time since losing the hand fighting Hood and his men. "Would you care for a drink, Klopov?" He nodded towards the bar.

Klopov smiled again, then nodded.

Bohuslav was happy now, and ordinarily that meant he would leave the messenger be. It had indeed been good news; the *best* news in fact. But as Klopov moved towards the bar, once again the new Tsar's mind was filled with things he'd like to do to him. The way he might wish to celebrate.

The blood. The flesh. The ineffectual pleading of the victim.

Bohuslav smiled and followed him, pick still behind his back, having yet to decide whether the messenger would leave this room alive.

CHAPTER THREE

FROM THE OUTSIDE, it was a spectacular sight.

From the inside, it was even more impressive. Opened in 1999, this stadium marked the end of one millennium and the beginning of another. A fresh new start for everyone, but nobody could have guessed just how radical that new beginning would be.

He'd come here often once upon a time to watch the matches; brought by his Dad – though only after his eldest son, Gareth, had died from leukaemia. It was home to their national rugby union team, after all. He remembered their matches in the Six Nations, mainly their victories: the crowd going wild, that tribal thing of territory against territory. Mimicking his father, he'd cheer on their team. "It's all about that," his Dad repeatedly told him, pointing to the national flags some supporters were waving. Then he'd chorus with the crowd nearest to him: "We are dragons! We are dragons!" But he was a poor substitute for Gareth, who'd always been Dad's favourite. Still was, to this day.

When they lost Gareth, his Mam and Nan turned all their attention on him, as if they might lose him too at any moment. They'd feed him up, putting massive meals in front of him: cooked breakfasts, sausages and mash or fish and chips for dinners, and all kinds of treats in-between. All while his Dad looked on, the obvious disappointment in his one remaining offspring apparent. It wasn't even as if he had any skills, like Gareth's knack of fixing things. Gareth had been training to be a joiner when he became sick; would have made a good one, too. Gareth excelled at school, especially Maths and History. While he, the younger brother, excelled at nothing, failing all his exams and claiming dole when he left school early. "Nobody'll ever take him on, you know," he'd overheard his father say once to their mother. Straight away, she defended her little darling. "He's just a late bloomer, that's all. One day that boy will show everyone, Ryn, just you see if he doesn't."

He'd been a lot slimmer back then. Obviously, at eighteen stone, nobody could accuse him of being svelte, but compared to now... Actually, he'd lost a bit of weight during the Cull. Thankfully, it hadn't ended like Gareth. They all pulled through. But they'd also had to evade the men in yellow suits when they came to torch the infected houses and streets. It didn't seem to matter to those bastards whether people were alive or dead!

His family had turned to him, because he'd shown no signs of getting ill at all. Bizarrely, he'd ended up the strongest of the lot. Sure, he was scared to go out, but his Mam and Nan had looked after him all those years, fed him and kept him safe – it was the least he could do in return. So, onto the streets, bringing back what food he could find, as well as other supplies. His Dad accepted the help with bad grace, grudgingly accepting the mantle of Alpha male had passed to his youngest. All his life, he'd wanted to make his father proud, wanted to be half the man he was. Now the burly ex-miner was reduced to relying on him. There was a certain irony to that.

His Mam worried, of course, and she was right to; it was dangerous out there. But he was lucky for a while, managed to get away with foraging. Until that day at the supermarket on the outskirts of the city: one he hadn't hit yet – this was back when there were actually stocks left of food and other essentials. He'd made sure there was no-one inside before entering, watched it for hours before venturing into the storeroom. Halfway through his labours, he'd been interrupted by a gang of youths wielding makeshift weapons.

"Hey, Porko, if we let you take all that, there'll be nothing left for the rest of us," the leader – a tattooed guy who spat when he talked – had said, making a snorting noise. Whether this was just his normal breathing or he was doing an impression of a pig, there was no way of telling.

"The rest of *the country*," added the pasty-faced girl by his side, sniggering.

"Or the world," another member of the gang chipped in.

He'd clutched the plastic bags to his chest, the tins inside rattling. "It's for me Mam and me Nan," he'd told them, only adding afterwards, "and me sick Dad."

"Jesus, there are *more* like you?" said the leader, spittle flying from his lips. "Are they *all* your size?"

He shook his head. No, he was the only one prone to putting on weight. Especially now; hardly surprising, when they'd had to share what resources he could scrounge up.

"I bet it's not," said the only other girl, this one dressed in a leather jacket she'd attempted to do up over her ample chest. In fact she was ample all round, so wasn't really in a position to criticise. It didn't stop her, though. "I bet he's gonna eat it all himself."

He shook his head, but the other members of the gang just laughed. "You're right," said the lad who'd originally made the joke. "He's goin' to scoff the fucking lot."

"No, he bloody well isn't," the tattooed leader announced as the gang fanned out. Gareth had backed up a few paces before hitting a wall, and the gang encircled him. He felt like crying, but knew that would do no good. Neither would shouting out for his Mam, nor his Dad – even if they had been nearby, the man couldn't fend off a flea.

"Come on, Porko, show us what you've got," said the boss, holding up a meat cleaver. And as they moved in, he flashed back to all the bullies at school who'd ever called him Porky, or Chubster or Wide Load. Flashed back to his Dad at those rugby matches, to what he was trying to tell his wimp of a second son.

"We are dragons," he whispered. *"I am a dragon."*

"What?" asked the pasty-faced girl, but it was already too late.

Before he realised what he was doing, he'd grabbed the tattooed thug, evading the cleaver blow by inches, and swung his attacker into the wall. The youth's shoulder cracked loudly and he let out a cry. He'd turned to the joker and butted him with his stomach, sending him backwards into a pile of boxes. The rest of the gang went down in the same vein. It was as if a switch had been flipped. He even began to enjoy the violence, taking years of abuse out on them. A golf club struck him on the hip but he barely felt it, pulling his enemy in, throwing him to the floor and then stamping hard on the lad's pelvis.

Looking around, breathing hard, he found there was nobody left but the two girls. The larger one fancied her chances and, it had to be said, she was probably more of a match for him than all the men put together. She tried to kick him in the crotch, but he sidestepped her, then punched her in the face. Bits of cartilage exploded across her cheeks, blood splattering over his own face. The girl sank to her knees and he brought down his fist again, this time hitting her on the top of the head with the base of his fist. There was another *crack* as the weight of the blow fractured her skull, and she toppled sideways.

The pasty-faced girl stared in disbelief, unable to move as he approached. Christ alone knew what he must have looked like with all that blood covering him. When he reached her, she suddenly darted, but his hand was out, clamping around her arm.

"Let go! Let me –"

"Shhh," he told her, pressing a finger to her lips. If the other members of the gang had represented all the bullies who'd ever called him names, then this girl, her flesh quivering beneath his touch, represented all those who'd ever spurned him romantically. The Kaiyas and Denises and Aimees and Brennas from his class, who he'd fantasised about, but who looked at him like he was the scum of the earth; at the same time draping themselves over the boys with model good looks. Well, he'd show them all now, wouldn't he?

The things he made that girl do, before snapping her neck... It was a sort of catharsis.

He eventually picked up the bags and walked back through the streets to his family, not caring now if anyone saw him. In fact, a few people did spot him, but didn't come anywhere near. Perhaps it was his appearance, perhaps it was just his demeanour. When he arrived home, his Mam and Nan looked at him funny, but didn't ask about the blood. They were probably afraid to.

"Where have you been?" asked his Dad, then shut up promptly when his son glared at him. He could see it, see that he was a dragon. Maybe even *the* Dragon. And maybe his father realised that he himself was no longer one of those creatures. The older man took the food gladly this time, tucking in.

There was even a *thank you*.

From that day on, there was never any fear about going outside. Anyone stupid enough to tackle him soon regretted it. He attracted a gang of his own: those who not only respected the way he handled himself – his size a plus rather than a drawback – but also his allegiance to the flag. Just like in those matches so long ago now. It was every nation for themselves, and they knew if they stuck with him, there was a chance of making theirs great again.

It took a lot of time, but eventually the gang became a small army, then a larger army. Just as his family had done, they all looked to him to take care of them. Which he did at first, until they became big enough and tough enough to begin looking after him again. Why go out on scavenging trips – further and further afield – when you could send bands of your own men to do it? The food was shared equally, *after* he and his family were taken care of. And why fight, when others would fight for you – to *protect* you?

Soon they were much too big to occupy any one building, so about six or seven months ago he'd struck upon the idea of the Stadium. The place that had inspired him, the place where the Dragons used to meet. The place where this Dragon would rule.

There was just one problem. While he had been gathering his forces, others had been setting up shop in the area. Recruiting the local populace with promises that they would be safeguarded. Using these lies, a regional division of something called the Rangers had been established. It only took a little digging to discover where they came from and how they'd come about. Some prick masquerading as Robin Hood had managed to convince enough people to follow his lead, to create a peacekeeping force – what could easily be seen from the outside as a personal militia, hellbent on taking over Britain.

Well, they wouldn't fucking get Wales; he'd see to that. No matter what it took.

Understandably, as the Dragon was wheeled along the corridor, two of his elite guardsmen pushing what could only be described as a padded sled – complete with troughs filled with food on either side – he was eager to begin today's proceedings. He was about to make an example of these Rangers, make them understand in no uncertain terms that they were not welcome in this country. And the punishment for those born here who'd joined their cause would be severe.

The Dragon sat back and enjoyed the final stages of the ride to his private box – a viewing place his Dad could only dream about, but which now belonged to his son. Inside, he found more guards, with sub-machine guns and pistols. They wore green and white uniforms, with the Dragon symbol emblazoned across the chest. A symbol of power and unity, under his command. His Mam had been right all along; he *had* been destined for greatness. It had just taken the death of ninety per cent of the world's population before he saw it.

Also in here were some of the new members of his private harem. Girls brought to the Stadium, some willing, others who'd required more coaxing to enjoy everything his hospitality had to offer. They were wearing a variety of revealing outfits, in silk, satins and lace. The Dragon noted one of the newest, sitting on a velvet couch near the window, wearing a baby-doll nightie. She looked away from him, her blonde hair cascading over the milky skin of her shoulders, strands falling down between her pert breasts. He licked his lips, then reached for a chicken leg out of the trough and took a bite. He'd settle for sating at least one of his massive appetites for now, because he wanted to get on with the game. Later, he'd turn his attentions towards the women. The one woman in particular who'd caught his eye.

With a waving hand, he motioned for the guards to manoeuvre him closer to the gigantic window and peered out at the pitch, which he'd insisted they clean up when they arrived. There he saw more of his men leading bound figures onto the freshly mown grass. The prisoners were dressed in darker green, hoods down at the back; there were about a dozen or so of them. His guards pushed them into the middle of the grounds at gunpoint.

It had been a decent swoop, he had to admit. Sending his troops into the very heart of the local Ranger's nest, where they'd encountered very little resistance. Taken by surprise, swords and arrows were no match for heavily-armed men storming a building. These were the only ones left alive. It was still very much a fledgling operation in this locality, and that told him Hood had a way to go before he was a force to be reckoned with outside his native Nottingham.

What was about to happen today would make him think twice about a foothold here. Either that, or make him mad enough to come here *en masse* – in which case they'd devastate his numbers and send them packing back off to where they belonged.

"The microphone," he demanded through a mouthful of chicken. "And some doughnuts."

One of the guards passed him the mike, while another guard called for more food to be brought, which arrived just as the Dragon began addressing his captives. The young man who brought it was another new face to him, and one that didn't appeal much. His soapstar good looks reminded him a little too much of the boys from school. He shooed the servant away, noting that the lad held back to watch the proceedings from behind. Well, let him. This would serve as a lesson to his own people just as much. You do not cross the Dragon.

"Your attention," The Dragon said, nodding happily at the sound of his amplified voice. The Rangers on the pitch turned and looked up. "That's right, I'm up here," he said, sighing. "Now, I expect you're wondering what you're doing in this place? It's very simple. Your actions have marked you out as not only an enemy of my country, but also of me. I offer you the chance of freedom, though. I am nothing if not a fair man. You are familiar with this nation's favourite sport?"

The Rangers on the pitch did and said nothing.

"Even if you're not, you know the idea is to pass this" – he waited while one of his men produced an oval-shaped ball – "forward, either by carrying or kicking. Then reach the other end of the pitch and score a try without the other team taking it from you. Got all that?" Silence again. "I'll take that as a yes."

His men began to cut the Rangers' bonds, guns still trained on them. Given any opening, these men were sure to retaliate. The Dragon noted that his new blonde odalisque – it was a word he'd 'borrowed' from the Turks, who knew a thing or two about their harems – was watching events unfold below with increasing interest. It was time to move things along so he could become better acquainted with her.

"Be aware that you are playing for high stakes," he told them. "If my men should win and score, then you will lose not only the game, but also your lives." One of his guards motioned for the Rangers and his own men to form a haphazard scrum. There were about the same amount of the Dragon's men facing them, which meant that theoretically they *could* win.

The Dragon nodded for the ball to be tossed into the heap of figures, who immediately began scrabbling for it. They were a blur of reds, whites and greens. Light and dark, limbs out at all angles, they moved like a giant human spider. All were punching and kicking – not exactly within the rules of the game, but then neither was a death sentence if you lost. One of the Rangers suddenly emerged, holding the ball up. When he knew his comrades had seen him, he tucked it under his arm and began to run. Both the Dragon's men and the remaining Rangers started after him, one side to offer support, the others to attack. One guard dived, but missed the Ranger, then spun over and over on the grass. The Dragon pulled a sour face.

The Ranger with the ball could really run, had possibly been some kind of sportsman in his former life. But so had a few of the Dragon's men. They were catching up, and he was looking for one of his mates to take the ball. He spotted another Ranger advancing on his right. The Dragon's fingers dug into the arms of his seat. He needn't have worried; his men knew exactly what to do.

Just as the Ranger was about to toss the ball, one of the guards in pursuit pulled out a pistol and fired at the man who would have received it. The bullet blew away most of the Ranger's left kneecap, splattering redness across the grass.

There was an intake of breath from some of the harem watching, and the Dragon smiled. He looked across at the new woman, who was fixated on the 'match' and now had her hand to her mouth. God, she was magnificent. Whoever chose her would be rewarded well, he'd see to it. She realised he was watching and glanced at the Dragon out of the corner of her eye. Then she returned her gaze to the pitch, as if what she was witnessing there was preferable.

She'll look at me later, he thought to himself. *I'll* make *her look*.

The Dragon turned his attention back to what was happening below. The Rangers appeared shocked that one of their team had been gunned down, hanging back in case the same should happen to them. Then, suddenly, one Ranger put on a spurt and ran as fast as he could ahead of the pack. He was small and quick, dodging around a couple of the guards. Another one of the Dragon's men pulled out a gun, but a Ranger barged into him, spoiling his aim. The guard turned and elbowed his attacker in the face, knocking him to the ground, but the delay left smaller Ranger racing ahead.

The man running with the ball kicked it across quickly. The smaller Ranger fumbled with it, but managed to get it under control, tucking it under his arm, making a sprint for the end of the pitch. Behind him, four guards were on his tail. He looked over his shoulder to see them drawing their weapons.

He was about to get a bullet in the back, when a couple of his comrades dived on the armed men, tackling them from behind. They all went down. Then there was the flash of gunfire, and the Dragon's people were standing again – leaving the bodies of the Rangers on the grass.

He'd told them he was a fair man, and some might say this game was anything but. However, it was his stadium, his game, his rules. The Dragon didn't like to lose.

But it looked like that was about to happen. The small Ranger had his head down, the finishing line in sight. Those Rangers left were sprinting too, catching him up, leaving the Dragon's guards behind.

No: the guards were retreating. They were actually pulling back. Running in the other direction! A couple of the harem women were looking at the Dragon, wondering what was going on – but not his new favourite, she was leaning forward, one hand on the glass. Even the young slave who'd brought his food had moved forward to get a better view.

The Dragon chuckled. Yes, watch and learn.

The smaller Ranger dived with the ball and planted it on the grass, scoring the try that he thought would save them all. His team-mates joined him, still not having put two and two together. They jumped in the air, celebrating. They'd beaten the Dragon's men, they'd –

The explosion wasn't a big one – no mushroom cloud or mortar – but large enough to make sure anyone within a twenty metre radius was caught in it. The harem girls screamed; the servant boy stepped forward again, sucking in a sharp breath. The blonde girl had both hands on the glass, then she turned. The Dragon was holding a radio transmitter in his right hand, thumb still on the trigger that had detonated the device inside the rugby ball. The girl was definitely looking at him now, intently – in fact, she couldn't take her eyes off him. *Was* it fear that he saw? Was it repulsion, like the first one, the pasty-faced girl? No, it was something else. Could it be pity; if so, who for? The Rangers or him? There were definitely tears in her eyes. He saw them just before she looked away again.

Why? He'd offered those men their freedom, hadn't he? And he'd delivered. They were free – they couldn't be *more* free. The Dragon looked down on the smouldering crater in the pitch – that would have to be fixed before he played the game again – at the various body parts, and one full torso. He spoke into the microphone, telling the guards to pick one of the two Rangers still alive: a choice between the guy with no kneecap and the one who'd been elbowed in the face. "We need one survivor to send back, to tell Hood about what happened here. Kill the other one."

There, that look again. His latest odalisque was staring at him, her eyes still moist. Now that the match had reached its conclusion, it was time for other distractions. He'd teach her now to look at him in another way. Or Heaven help her.

The Dragon gave the order to be wheeled away, and for the guards to bring the woman. "Just her?" they asked, as often he asked for several at a time. The Dragon nodded and she was grabbed by the arm. At first he thought she might resist; there was just a flash of 'fuck you' in those tearful eyes. But she thought better of it, thankfully.

As he was taken away, the Dragon glimpsed the Ranger who'd been knocked to the ground get shot in the head; they'd chosen the man who could barely walk to release. He approved. The Ranger's wound alone would serve as a warning.

Today had been a good day, he thought to himself. And it was about to get even better.

In his head, he heard those crowds again back when there used to be real matches here. But instead of chorusing with them, he changed his own contribution to:

I am a Dragon! I am the *Dragon!*

He could do nothing but watch.

Stand and stare as those innocent men were slaughtered by that slug. Gazing down at the devastation. One last act of cruelty: a Ranger shot in the head, while his colleague with the shattered kneecap was set free. It was doubtful whether he'd ever walk properly again, let alone run as he had been doing when the bullet struck him.

What kind of sadist was this?

He was half tempted to make a move right then and there, but he'd have ended up just as dead as the Rangers in that explosion. Might have been worth it, just to take this so-called Dragon with him.

Dale turned away from the window in time to see one of the women in the slug's private collection get dragged to her feet. She was crying, had been since the killings. But he saw a strength there also, a determination and resolve. And... something else. Something he couldn't quite put his finger on. Briefly, he caught her eye and the look lingered – far longer than any glances between her and the Dragon. Again, he almost sprang into action, fully aware of what would happen to the girl when those doors shut behind her. When the Dragon got her back to his lair. For some reason the thought of that happening to this one girl in particular turned his stomach.

He looked around at the others on display, all wearing skimpy outfits to tantalise the fat pig. *How is it any different from what you've done in the past?* he asked himself. The way he sometimes thought of women, as disposable, as objects. As meat? Dale shook his head. He might not be the settling down kind, but he was nothing like this. The Dragon forced them to dress this way, to do... *things* with him. He'd never forced anyone to do anything in his life. So what if he'd never been in love, never had a relationship that wasn't based on sex? It didn't make him the kind of monster he was dealing with here.

It did make him lonely, though, and sad that while people like Robert and Mary were getting hitched, while Mark and Sophie were getting it together, he still had nobody apart from the occasional girl in a village or town he was patrolling, or at a fête like the one they held last Christmas at the castle.

If he wasn't careful, he really would end up like his father: not able to commit to Dale's mum, chasing women left, right and centre.

What was the difference between the women sitting around him, and those he'd looked at in lad's mags? In those strip clubs he'd frequented? You could tell yourself that they were getting paid, that nobody was holding a gun to their head – like they were, literally, here – but what if that was the only work they could get? *Do you honestly think that they enjoyed it?*

Now really wasn't the time or the place to be thinking about that, but he couldn't get the blonde woman out of his mind. Couldn't stand thinking about the Dragon pawing at her. It wasn't right. Just wasn't –

Rangers have died here today, he reminded himself. Some of them he knew, albeit briefly. Even though he'd taken the name from their flag, that man wasn't representative of this country, any more than the Tsar was representative of Russia's population. Those men down there, who'd been trying to bring peace and stability to the region – they were the *real* heroes of Wales. And it was about time this sick son of a bitch who thought he was in charge was driven out.

That's what Dale was doing here, that was the mission – or part of it – given to him by Jack. The Welsh contingent of the Rangers were well aware of what the Dragon could become, so they'd asked for help. Dale had been sent in undercover to gather information, to find something they could use to take down the Dragon's organisation. He'd only been around a couple of days when they'd attacked the Ranger HQ; he'd heard about it from some of the other servants, but never thought he'd see the survivors of that massacre exterminated in such a sick mockery of what this place was built for.

Again he couldn't help thinking about the girl with blonde hair.

Dale squeezed his eyes shut. Stop the Dragon, you stop the killing, *and* stop what was happening to these women. It was up to Dale. Jack was relying on him. Wouldn't do anything about the attack on the Rangers until he'd heard back from his mole. He wondered if they could even muster a force to take on all the Dragon's people in one go. There were more than they'd imagined, or the Welsh Rangers had suggested. And with Robert's troops spread out now more than ever, the man himself having answered a distress call from Bill up near Scotland, perhaps it really was down to Dale to do something.

This certainly wasn't as cool as Jack had made it sound. "It'll be just like *Mission: Impossible*, kid," the large American had promised.

Mission: Impossible? Mission bloody unbelievable more like – as in how unbelievably bad his luck was. What exactly would Tom Cruise do now in his position? Off the bad guy, blow up his base and get the girl.

He sighed; that really did only happen in the movies. This was real life and sometimes that stank.

"Hey, you," said one of the guards. He touched his chest. "Yes, you. What you still doing here? Clear off back to the kitchens, this isn't a peep show."

Dale nodded. No, it was more like a flesh farm. No doubt these men wanted to be left alone with the harem women for a reason. Only look but don't touch, because they belonged to the Dragon.

No woman – no man, either, for that matter – should belong to someone else. If Robert had taught them anything, it was that. He'd taught the lesson to De Falaise, the Tsar and countless other thugs who didn't seem to know it already. His men followed him not because they had to, but because they *wanted* to. Because they believed in what he did, in liberty and the right to a peaceful existence.

Impossible or not, Dale would find a way to bring that to these people again. He had to.

Reluctantly, he left the women behind with the guards.

But still couldn't shake the picture of the one girl who'd gone off with the Dragon from his mind.

CHAPTER FOUR

IT WAS AMAZING to think how, over the last year especially, this place had become like a home to him.

The Reverend Tate even had a place where he would go to pray, a quiet place he'd blessed himself down in the Lower Bailey. He was there now, talking to God; thanking Him for the new day, for keeping his friends safe, and asking Him to keep a watchful eye on them. Especially Robert, who never seemed to take a bit of notice when Tate told him to be careful. And asking the Lord to look after His humble servant, trying to bring His word to those who were building this new world.

As Tate got up, relying more heavily these days than ever on his stick, he began his slow, steady walk back up towards the castle, and considered the rebuilding they'd done here after the Tsar's attack. That had been a horrible time.

While Robert and his men had been going through Hell on the battlefield, Tate, Jack, Mark and Sophie had been trying to keep invading forces out of the castle grounds – and failing miserably. If it hadn't been for Dale arriving with more Rangers, this place would look very different. Russian troops would be guarding the walls and the gate instead of Rangers, and they'd probably all have been hunted down and killed. Tate liked to think it was the power of prayer that had helped Robert recover enough to finally defeat the Tsar.

Whichever way you cut it, they owed the Almighty a big one... two, actually, if you counted that other battle for the castle when they'd put an end to the Sheriff's reign.

But it seemed as though no sooner had they tackled one insane dictator than another cropped up. The Widow in Scotland, for example, or the potential threat of this Dragon character across to the west. In this post-virus world, everyone was staking a claim on their own territories – and other people's. The only thing standing in their way was people like Robert and his Rangers.

As Tate hobbled further up, joining the path, he remembered what the castle had looked like the previous year. The gardens torn up, the castle pock-marked – even a hole in the wall where Adele, De Falaise's traitorous daughter, had left her mark.

The attack had left the castle and its grounds devastated, and their souls as well. Left them questioning if they were actually doing any good, or just fooling themselves. Luckily, God had shown them the way. Drawn more people to their cause, who wanted to join Robert's police force. Brought folk with even more useful skills, or given them the ability to learn them, to repair the damage done.

The physical damage, that was. Spiritually, it was another matter.

Yet some of his friends and, yes, family – since that's how Tate thought of them now – had thrived in the months after the attack. Mark and Sophie, for example, had finally acted on their feelings for each other. As if on cue, he saw the boy, walking with his new girlfriend.

Boy. You couldn't really describe him as that these days, he'd grown so tall. Tate could remember the first time he'd met Mark, back when Bill had been running the floating markets. He'd only come up to the holy man's chest then, and he wasn't exactly tall himself. Mark had also filled out somewhat since he'd started his Ranger training, working out whenever he wasn't spending time with Sophie or practising archery and the sword. By all accounts, the youngster was turning into a pretty decent Ranger, modelling himself on Robert, of course – still going with him on those private trips to the forest.

Tate raised a hand and both of the young people waved back. They looked so happy. For Mark and Sophie, things had actually improved since the Tsar's attack.

The same was also probably true of their older counterparts, Robert and Mary, who were closer than ever. Tate cast his mind back to their wedding the previous summer, a small affair but attended by all those who mattered. Tate had presided over the ceremony, where the old bandstand was, and everyone had clapped when he'd finally said: "I now pronounce you man and wife. Robert, you may kiss the bride." There had been little time for a honeymoon, as a spot of trouble with a new wannabe gang in Chesterfield had required their attention, but both had gone off to tackle the problem together. Tate firmly believed that now they were fighting side by side, they couldn't be happier.

Most residents had been left gloomy and miserable by the events, though – Jack, for one, who even now stewed about Adele and how he'd fallen for her. How he'd betrayed their whereabouts because he thought Adele would harm Mary.

Tate, too, had found it a struggle at times – having lost the place he had once called his home, and finding himself estranged from the person he'd failed so miserably to protect not once, but twice. Gwen, who'd been the Sheriff's plaything once upon a time, snatched from the village of Hope after her partner Clive had been brutally murdered. Who'd returned to the village after the birth of her son at the castle – Clive Jr, who she still maintained was fathered by his namesake, but as he grew bore more and more of a resemblance to the Frenchman. Gwen, who'd said she never wanted anything more to do with Tate again. His own fault: assuming he knew what was best for her, sending for her because he'd thought she'd be safer at the castle, then putting her in even more danger. When he'd found out that she'd almost been assaulted by Jace, one of De Falaise's former soldiers, Tate could scarcely forgive himself. So why should Gwen? The castle held many terrifying memories for her, and they all must have come rushing back when that thug –

The man was dead now, killed by Gwen or someone else, they hadn't been able to determine which. The woman was certainly capable. She'd gone after the Mexican, Major Javier, the man who'd shot Clive, finishing him off during the very first fight for Nottingham Castle. But Tate had a feeling she'd had help this time. Gwen had become even harder, if that was the right word, in the time since all this happened. For the most part she'd hidden herself away in New Hope – turning the place into a veritable fortress, its inhabitants into soldiers.

Tate had only seen her once since the Tsar's men had invaded, a few months ago when they'd held the Winter Festival at the castle – an attempt to put a smile back on the faces, not only of the people who lived here, but also those in the outlying regions. Gwen had come only because some of her own villagers had heard about it. The Festival itself – with live music from Dale – had been a roaring success. But it had been the inroads Tate had made with Gwen that proved the most successful from his point of view.

At first she still hadn't wanted to know. In fact Tate thought, when he approached, she might just walk off, turn her back like she had when he'd tried to visit New Hope. But something about that time of year, about peace to all men and forgiveness, must have touched her heart. It was the Lord working His magic again, he suspected. No, more than suspected, *believed*. For the fact that she'd spoken to him at all must surely have been some kind of miracle.

They'd left it open, with the possibility of talking again at some point; the friendship thawing a little. She no longer sounded like she wanted to rip out his throat, anyway. Tate had planned to visit New Hope again soon after and see how the land lay, but up till now things had been so busy at the castle. He'd resolved to definitely go there within the next couple of weeks, though, as spring took hold, because there wouldn't *ever* be a perfect time. He didn't want to waste the opportunity he'd been given back in December. They'd rebuilt the castle, and he had to now rebuild a few bridges.

He'd talk to Robert when he returned, ask for an escort. Once he'd resolved to do it, he found he was actually looking forward to seeing Gwen again. To talking with her, and maybe, just maybe, persuading her to abandon the path of hatred and anger she was currently on.

To return her to the fold of Christ, where she might actually find tranquillity again.

"JESUS H. FUCKING Christ!"

Gwen ducked back down as the bullet ricocheted off the wall she was hiding behind. The wall she and the other people of New Hope had built for just such a reason – to keep out intruders.

Like the men who'd shown up here today and were attacking her village. She'd sensed there was something wrong, to be honest. Every now and then spotting unusual movement in the woods flanking New Hope whenever she was on watch; fleeting glimpses of... she couldn't tell what. Gwen had the feeling that someone was watching their little community, but it wasn't like before. Like last year. Back then she'd felt safe, as if they were being watched over, protected. This time she just felt threatened.

These were only feelings, suspicions, so she hadn't mentioned them to the rest of the villagers. She couldn't be sure of anything, couldn't prove anything. But still she had skipped out on the last couple of foraging missions for new weapons, relying instead on Graham Leicester. Once an ordinary, gentle guy who'd worked in a garden centre, Graham had, like her, been changed forever by what happened when the Sheriff's men came to call. Now he was more soldier than agriculturalist. Gwen had seen him strip clean a Colt AR-15 machine-gun in minutes, putting the pieces back together like he was doing a jigsaw puzzle. He knew what he was looking for out there, knew what they needed to defend themselves. The weapons she'd stolen from Robert's castle had given them a head start, but they were always searching for more.

The wall – a huge brick affair, strengthened by sheet metal on the outside – had been young Darryl Wade's idea. Darryl, whose father had been a handyman and had passed on much of his expertise. He'd been helping Clive fix up the school when Javier and his men had –

Gwen had to keep stopping herself from thinking about that day, those painful memories. While it was true at certain times they'd given her strength, now they twisted her guts up in knots. If she didn't have Clive Jr, son of the man she'd loved so much, she didn't know what she might do. What those memories might drive her to. But she did, and that child was the only thing driving her these days.

She'd got her first proof that the village was being observed five hours ago, when Graham had returned from his latest foray in her jeep. He'd unexpectedly drawn fire from several locations in the woods. Andy Hobbs, another founding member of Hope, shouted for her to come quickly – which she'd done, leaving Clive Jr in the capable hands of Dr Ken Jeffreys, who'd joined them from a group in Worksop. When she got to the lookout post on the wall, shouldering her M16 rifle as she climbed the ladder, she saw why Andy was so concerned.

Flashes of light from the woods, bursts of automatic gunfire spraying the jeep Graham and his team were in. The vehicle was barrelling down a country lane barely big enough to accommodate it, and Gwen watched as Graham leaned out of the side, returning fire. Whoever was shooting at her people was dug in well, using the woodland for cover. It was only what they did themselves, the countryside concealing them from unwanted attention. Javier had been a one-off; they'd never encountered another wandering army like that here since. It crossed her mind briefly to wonder whether the shooters out there had come specifically for them.

"Unlock the gates!" Andy shouted down, pointing to the wrought iron monstrosities that were also Darryl's brainchild.

"Wait," Gwen said, brushing a strand of auburn hair out of her eyes. "What do you think you're doing?"

"We have to risk it," he replied.

Andy was right, of course, she knew that. Graham was one of them, she'd known him almost as long as she'd known... would have known Clive. But there was still that nagging part of her wanting to keep the rest of them – wanting to keep Clive Jr – locked up behind those gates, behind these walls. Risk was a thing she had a problem with when it came to her son's life.

"It's Graham," Andy said, as if that was all he needed to add.

Gwen nodded, allowing the men below to unbolt the gate.

"Get ready," called down Andy. If this was to work, they had to open them at just the right time. The jeep had sped up and was now pelting towards the gates, trailing fire behind it. Andy held up his hand; it was shaking. "Ready..." he repeated and she heard the catch in his voice. "*Now!*" he barked, letting his hand fall.

The men below swung open the gates, just in time for the jeep to come crashing through the gap. It scraped the side of the opening and, for a second, Gwen feared it might collapse them completely. But Darryl's handiwork was stronger than it looked. Everything held, and the doors were shut behind the jeep – bullets pinging off the metal. Gwen hoped their enemies didn't have anything that could ram those gates down.

As she got to the bottom of the ladder, Graham was stumbling out of the jeep. He dropped his gun and fell to his knees, his khaki jumper stained red at the front. "Oh, no," she heard Andy say behind her. "Fetch the doc."

By now several of the residents of New Hope had emerged from their homes to see what was going on. Gwen waved to Darryl, told him to get Jeffreys, and to stay with Clive Jr. A few minutes later, the medic was examining the man's wound.

"He's been lucky, it went right through, just missed his lung. But he's bleeding badly. We need to get him to my surgery, as quickly as possible. Here, keep pressure on the wound." Four people picked up Graham, and set off down the road with him. Jeffreys turned to Gwen. "What's the devil's going on? Are we under attack?"

"Yes," Gwen said.

"We're not sure yet," Andy broke in, looking at her.

"Tell that to Graham."

The sound of gunfire was still echoing loudly from outside. And it wasn't long before more lookouts confirmed there were several shooters at the back wall as well. These too were keeping out of sight, but if anyone stuck their head above the parapet, they were setting themselves up as a target. In fact, shooters had been positioned around the whole wall, it seemed – either a few men circling, or quite a number of them in fixed positions.

"We're under siege," Gwen stated after they'd called an emergency meeting in the Red Lion pub. Clive Jr was nearby, happily banging plastic bricks together in a playpen.

"But why?" This came from Karen Shipley, a thirty-year-old ex-receptionist who'd joined them about six months ago. "I don't understand."

"Do people need a reason anymore?" Darryl answered, and she looked stung by his remark. Everyone knew she had a crush on Darryl – everyone except the young man himself, apparently. "They see something others have built up, and they want to take it, destroy it." He was quite obviously talking about their experience when Javier had rolled into town; Gwen could empathise. It was the kind of thinking she'd used to motivate these people.

"Hold on. Look, we still don't know what we're dealing with here," Andy commented. "How many men, how well armed they are."

"Pretty *well* armed going by the state of that jeep," Jeffreys chipped in, as he took another look at it through the window. "Put it this way, I'm glad *it's* not my patient." He'd managed to stabilise Graham. New Hope had boasted a small local practice, even before the name change. The doctor's trainee assistant, a young Indian called Sat, was keeping an eye on Graham while Jeffreys attended the crisis talks. He'd alert him if anything happened.

"Agreed," said Gwen. "And there's something else." She told them about her suspicions that someone had been watching them for a while now.

"You didn't think to mention this before?" Andy asked.

"What was I supposed to say? I didn't know anything for certain. What good would it have done to worry everyone needlessly? Besides, it's not the first time I've thought people might be keeping an eye on the village."

"What?" This was Jeffreys.

"It's okay, I think they were here to help. It's connected to how I got away from the castle last year." Gwen saw that they didn't understand, and shook her head. "You know what? I'm not even going to try to explain. What's happened has happened. But these people obviously aren't friendlies. And they aren't going away anytime soon."

"How long can we hold out for?" asked Jeffreys.

"Food-wise, a week. Maybe two," Darryl informed them. "It's ammo we're running short of. Graham brought back a few more supplies, but not nearly enough. If those guys keep pushing and have more than us…"

"They obviously want *something*," Jeffreys said.

Andy sighed. "Yeah: us, dead. And they might just get it, too."

Gwen glanced across at her son, playing without a care in the world. "That's not going to happen." She walked towards the door, then opened it, ignoring protests from the people inside. Gwen strode across the village to the front wall and climbed the ladder. Taking hold of her rifle, she crouched down on the ledge. Gwen stuck her head up over the top, and it was then that bullets raked the wall, causing her to duck again. "All right," she whispered to herself, "if that's the way you want to play it." She swung around and returned fire with the M16, targeting the flashes. "You like that, eh? All right, have some more, then." Her teeth were clenched as she fired, spraying until the rifle clicked empty. Still she kept her finger pressed on the trigger, breathing hard.

There was silence outside. The only sound she could hear was the pounding of her heart in her chest. The hand on her shoulder made her jump, and she almost turned the weapon on whoever it was.

"Gwen, that's enough." It was Andy, his expression full of concern.

"No, I –"

He took the rifle from her. "They're camped out. It's a waste of our ammo."

She stared at him, then said quietly, "We can't let them take us, Andy. Not again. We *have* to fight back." Gwen looked down and saw that some of the others had followed her out of the meeting. She saw the worried faces of Darryl, Karen, a half dozen more. Some of them knew what it was like to be invaded, some had no idea – yet.

Andy took hold of her, attempting to rest her head on his shoulder. "It's okay. We won't let that happen." Then it was his turn to tense up.

She pulled away. "What?" Gwen followed his gaze, peering at an angle through the gap in the wall.

"I think you winged one," he said.

He was right. One of the shooters had broken cover, staggering about in the open. He was clutching his leg, rifle falling from his hands.

"We need to get to him, get him inside," Gwen told Andy. If they could question this guy they might get a few answers.

"You can't be serious?" said Andy.

"I am, and I know exactly the way to do it."

For the first time that day, Gwen broke into a smile.

CHAPTER FIVE

S<small>HE HADN'T DONE</small> badly for herself, she had to say. Though, obviously, she'd seen it coming.

And while most little girls' childhood fantasies revolved around living in a castle, it had never been hers. This had been an adult fantasy, something that occurred to her later in life when she realised it actually could be achieved. She'd always been a realist, even from an early age.

What attracted her the most was not the fantasy life of living here, but how well these surroundings fitted her persona. A medieval backdrop to match her outlook. Yet she was also a dichotomy, because however much she loved the old fashioned nature of where she now resided, she was still connected to the modern world. The castle had power, it had running water; all right, people who would run and *fetch* her water. It was protected by the weapons of the 20th and 21st century: tanks, jeeps, machine-guns and mounted rocket launchers. Her men might well carry the swords of their ancestors, had changed their names according to the old Celtic ways, but they were also armed to the gills with guns.

It made her laugh to think that if she had been around back in the days when this place had been built – the rock itself had been occupied as far back as the mid-second century – she would have been burned at the stake. Not just because of the modern weaponry – just how would you explain a Weasel 2 light anti-aircraft defence system to a primitive? – but because she studied the ancient arts.

Ancient and modern, it was a curious mix. But one which she found most appealing.

She pondered this again as she sat before her cards. Looking around the faded red walls, then up at the original hammerbeam roof, her gaze settled on the suits of armour flanking the fireplace.

Each now held Heckler & Koch MG4 5.56 mm light machine-guns at her insistence. There was something *right* about the combination.

But that was her all over, as many had commented in the past.

The past. It wasn't very often she looked back there – preferring instead to look into the future. Now it had crossed her mind, spurred on, no doubt, by the reading she'd just done, and she thought back to how her life had taken this turn.

Maybe she hadn't dreamed about castles and crowns when she was little, because the reality of her situation meant there was no point believing in fairy tales. How could she when she was forced to survive on whatever food her mother could afford, gristly scrag-ends begged from the butchers? After seeing her mother stab her violent, abusive father right in front of her eyes? Her dad had come home stinking of beer and her mother had asked if he had the rent, because the landlord had been round again.

"Dinnae bother me, woman," he'd shouted in her face, then turned away. When her maw tried to get him to listen, he'd brought his fist round in an arc and caught her with a back-hander that sent the woman sprawling across the floor. He didn't seem to care that his five-year-old daughter was in the room, watching. She remembered seeing her mother spit out blood, getting to her hands and knees as her father turned his attentions to the screaming child in the corner. "Shut yer fuckin' trap, or so help me I'll…"

She'd run when she saw her dad approach, scooting past and making for the kitchen. She'd been looking for a cupboard to climb into, when her father grabbed her by the scruff of the neck. "I'll teach yer to run from me, lass!"

"Git away from her," came her mother's voice from behind.

The large man dropped his terrified child and turned. It was then that she saw what her mother had in her right hand. A kitchen knife; meant only to scare him perhaps, to warn him off – stop him from beating them both to a pulp. And if he hadn't tried to wrestle the thing from her grasp, perhaps it wouldn't have slid into his stomach like that. But it was what happened afterwards that really shattered her illusions about fantasies. Her father staggering backwards, clutching his stomach, holding up his red hands and calling her maw a 'fuckin' houk.' Her mother's face contorting, then the knife plunging into him again and again, even when he was on the floor; the years of cruelty at his hands all coming out in those thrusts.

If it hadn't been for that, her mother might have got away with self defence, or at least shown that she was only protecting her baby. As it was, the judge said what she'd done, the wounds inflicted, indicated it was a conscious, perhaps even premeditated, act. Lawyers tried to argue mental instability due to the abuse at the hands of a psychotic drunkard, but the courts hadn't bought it. Her mother died in prison long before the virus came along, managing to hang herself with some bedsheets.

If only I'd been able to see it coming.

It was a dangerous thought that had plagued her throughout her childhood in care, then into her adolescence. One which finally became an obsession. She'd consulted the libraries, but didn't have much joy finding a way to achieve this – and back then there hadn't been an accessible 'net. So she'd turned to someone who might be able to teach her. There was an old fortune teller called Evelyn who operated not too far away from the home they'd stuck her in, making a meagre living from consultations. Whenever she had any spare time, she'd visit Evelyn, who live on her own and welcomed the company. The old lady taught her much about the different methods of seeing into the future: the crystal ball, the runes and, of course, the cards. But she also told her something else.

"You have a gift, dear," Evelyn would often say. "A real gift. It's only just starting to emerge, as often they do at this time of life, but it's there. And it's strong."

She became the closest thing to a daughter the woman had, or more like a granddaughter. On Evelyn's shelves, in her back room, were row upon row of books on magic and the occult, which she'd borrow and read, often without permission or Evelyn's knowledge. When Evelyn passed away at the age of eighty – she'd found her one Sunday, after letting herself in: eyes closed in her favourite armchair – she'd taken some of these books before calling the authorities. For safe keeping, she told herself. Well, Evelyn had no family; what would happen to them otherwise?

The cow who ran the home eventually discovered them, however, although they'd been hidden away in the back of her wardrobe. She'd thrown out the 'filth' and given her charge a lecture on morals. Angry, and remembering enough to perform one spell in particular, she'd put a curse on the bitch, who'd crashed her car about a week later. It might have been coincidence, but she doubted that very much, and it scared her. She'd never in a million years thought the magic would work. It taught her to have a newfound respect for the forces she was dabbling with.

"You have a gift."

She used to look at those girls at school, into the Goth scene, or kids involved in roleplaying games, and think: *You really don't know a thing, do you?*

When she was old enough to leave care and school, she got a job in a local fish and chip shop. For a while she tried to live an ordinary life, mainly because she fell in love with the owner's son. She'd always sworn she'd never get involved with anyone, never let her heart rule her head – never let herself get into the same mess as her mother. But the emotions she felt whenever she saw Alex were impossible to ignore. There was such a connection, such a pull, and they had so much in common. He was strong, but gentle with it, and said that he loved her too. She believed him. He was *so* different from her father: for one thing, he never touched a drop of alcohol, and there wasn't a violent bone in his body. It was rare to find someone like that, she knew. So rare, that she'd said yes when Alex proposed.

In spite of everything she'd once said, all she'd once learnt, she didn't even *try* and look into the future this time. She didn't need to, because Evelyn had told her about Alex. Told her that one day that special, perfect man would come along and she'd have everything she ever dreamed of. Someone with whom she'd share a special bond. "Where love's involved, it's difficult to see your own future; it... clouds things, makes them unclear," the old woman had warned, then held up one card in particular. A man sat on a throne, holding a sword: 'The Emperor.' "But I see it. I see it all. He'll come along, your king. You just wait and see, sweetheart. You'll almost be as one, the same. Then it'll be happy ever after."

She should have known better than to believe it, though. Happy ever afters only happened in make-believe. She'd been gutted when she found out Alex was cheating on her after only a year as her husband. Not just with one woman, either, but with several.

"I got bored," was his only defence when she confronted him. It was that night she discovered there were more ways to hurt someone than simply hitting them. "Look, it was a mistake to get hitched. We rushed into it."

"Please, Alex, darlin'." She was tugging at his shirtsleeve – Christ, she could hardly believe that now.

"Lemme go. I-I just don't love yer or fancy yer anymore, all right?"

It was far from all right. About as far as you could get.

"I'm leaving now – and tomorro' I'm getting a divorce."

It was at that point she realised just how similar she was to her mother – and her father, too, ironically. She still had hold of his shirtsleeve, his arm. If she couldn't have Alex, then nobody else would; certainly not those whores he'd been sleeping with. Pulling him round, she dragged him over and shoved his face into the vat of boiling fat. His scream was piercing – she almost stopped what she was doing. But she glimpsed the ring on his finger, felt it brush against hers on the hand she was bending back. He'd worn that every time he'd fucked one of those tarts, the promises meaning nothing.

She'd pushed him even further into the fat, until he went limp and stopped screaming altogether.

It was only afterwards she realised the severity of what she'd done. But there'd been no witnesses. The blinds at the front of the shop had been drawn and it was too late for anyone to be in the clothes store or electrics shop on either side.

That left the question of what to do with the evidence. Then she recalled reading something in one of those occult books about an ancient ritual; about how to take the hurt and pain away, and empower yourself with the spirit of the one who'd done you wrong in the first place. Something to do with ancient tribes. She'd turned her nose up at it when she'd first read it, found it disgusting, but –

The more she thought about it, the more it made sense. A way to dispose of both the evidence, and for a part of Alex to be with her forever. To make her stronger.

And she hadn't eaten all day.

It had taken some building up to, even more determination to continue – to finish as much as she could. But before she knew it she was stripping him, putting the rest of Alex into the fat and turning up the heat. Cooking him until the meat practically slid off. And do you know what, it tasted much better than the gristly scrag-ends she'd survived on as a child.

The rest of the remains she'd disposed of in a secluded spot miles away. But before leaving, she'd packed both lots of clothes and left a note for Alex's father saying that they needed some time away together, to remember what was important in the marriage.

She hadn't returned until after everything went crazy in the world.

The next few years after Alex, she'd spent travelling – Romania, Haiti, China, New Orleans – reconnecting with more than just her dead husband. She'd sought out other people who could help her hone the skills she'd abandoned, and gotten herself into trouble more times than she cared to mention. Not all of her tutors had been as nice as Evelyn, not all of the places they operated in quite so reputable. At one underground club, she'd had to fight off three guys who insisted on more than just cash as payment for their knowledge. One would never walk again, another would never see again, and the third would never have children.

The ones she found the most useful, the most adept at the black arts, she beguiled. Sometimes simply with her body, other times helped along with a spell of attraction. She'd marry them, often not legally, then take their power, too. She literally ate men alive, in the end revelling in the nickname some gave her: the Widow. To most that simply meant she'd lost husbands in the past and had a penchant for black, but she couldn't help thinking just how appropriate it was to be likened to the spider.

Had she ever loved any of the men she'd wed, then killed? She'd been fond of some, it had to be said. But loved? She hadn't felt love since Alex, hadn't *let* herself; it made you weak. She'd just needed their energy, their abilities, that's all. Fashioning herself into something that could survive the coming storm.

She'd known it was on the horizon, even before the first person died of the virus. The Widow had seen it, was prepared for it, knew that she would live through it. Even knew she'd end up here, returning to her homeland and leading an army of men. Knew she'd take the castle once she had enough of them to fight for her, to wipe out those few remaining members of the 52 Infantry Brigade and Royal Regiment of Scotland still protecting Edinburgh Castle. Knew she'd choose her own colours for them to wear, giving them traditional names to further emphasize the marriage of ancient and modern. And knew that she'd be crowned queen of all she surveyed by way of the Stone of Destiny.

She laughed, running a hand through her wild hair.

"Something amusing?"

The voice came from the shadowy archway over to her right, but didn't startle her. She'd been expecting his return, knew her men wouldn't stop him from gaining entrance. Nor should they, because the pair of them had business to discuss.

"Just thinking about destiny," she told him. "Fate. The future."

"You will not *have* a future if you continue to make such mistakes."

"Why don't you come out, man? Come out where I can see yer."

There was a second or two's hesitation, but the tall figure did just that, walking cautiously into the hall. His looked wary, as though expecting an attack. This was not a trusting person, but then she'd always known that as well, hadn't she? Even before they'd met.

"Now, what were you sayin' about mistakes?" she asked.

"I think you know already." He wasn't referring to her power; it was pretty easy to guess the topic of conversation. What some might call her recent failure. "I assume you received the message from our mutual friends abroad? The ones who loaned you those little toys to play with."

Toys? Yes, she supposed they were. Just like the men she used. But this was a game on a grander scale than most. "I did. Just didn't want tae make a meal of it."

The man raised an eyebrow. "With your reputation, you surprise me."

The Widow rose from her seat. "Credit me with some... taste," she said. "The man looked like he'd been half eaten already. By animals." There had been no power to gain by devouring *him*. He had no power to give. But this man in front of her, now he was different.

"He had," said her intruder. "There's a difference?"

The warrior in front of her didn't – couldn't – understand. She knew what he must think of her, what most folk out there thought. But they were wrong. They didn't have the first clue what she was all about. "Aye. Want to find out?"

"I'll pass."

The Widow grinned. "So, I presume yer here to follow up?"

The man said nothing, just watched as she came closer. And was he... yes, she caught his eyes roaming over her body. Perhaps she could work her magic on him yet.

"Forget your mind control tricks," he said, as if reading her mind. "They won't work on me."

No, she doubted very much that they would. His was not a weak mind, and he had purpose. He also had a connection to someone who'd passed over. Someone who had given him a mission to fulfil.

"Why d'ya keep on pretending you're their lackey?" she asked. "Yer nothin' of the kind. You have other motives. Doesn't take someone with my abilities to see that."

"Your 'abilities'?" He gave a throaty chuckle.

She scowled. "Dinnae mock me, I'm warnin' yer."

He laughed and she felt the rage in her rising again. She no longer wished to subdue him the fun way, now she wanted to teach him a lesson. The Widow reached behind her back and brought out a sharp, golden knife with a jewelled hilt.

"It would be the last thing you'd do," said the big man.

She stepped forwards, and he brought a crossbow up, letting off a couple of bolts.

She avoided them easily, knowing where he would fire, then continued with her attack. Snarling, he lunged to meet her. But as he did so, the Widow brought up her other hand, which had been clenched. She opened it and blew the contents in his direction.

Like the seeds of a dandelion, the dust drifted into her opponent's face. He coughed, dropped the crossbow – then froze. The Widow smirked. Relaxing, she walked slowly towards the large man and tutted.

"All that pent-up aggression. When was the last time yer released any of it in another way... my Hermit?" She knew the answer to that already; it had been a long time, back before the virus even. Someone no-one else knew about. Someone he'd loved and lost, who'd betrayed him. Someone he'd killed.

She brought up the knife, tracing the tip down the olive-skinned man's cheek – not hard enough to make it bleed, but enough to make her point. Now she was this close, she looked him up and down, just as he had her. Oh, to take him – then take his power. She licked her lips, running her free hand over his chest, over his arms, feeling the bulge of the muscles there. The Widow knew he could feel it too. She'd only prevented him from moving, not *feeling*.

Then lower. She looked him in the eyes, but he didn't blink. He couldn't, even if he'd wanted to. *You can't do it, not yet. You need him*, she told herself. "Look, I understand why you want Hood dead. I know what he did. I know what you've lost at his hands. It's common knowledge, you're going to say. But I know more than yer average bystander. I know about yer promise, Tanek."

His eyebrow twitched, in spite of the paralysis.

"Keep his child safe, isn't that what was asked of yer?" She smiled. "I won't tell. Yer secret's safe with me. Nothing that has happened so far has happened by chance. Everything's in a state of constant balance and flux, Tanek, do you understand? But if you know the outcome of certain events, you can... manipulate that balance. Tweak the future in yer favour. I've given yer a sample of that today. Believe me when I say the sacrifice of those toys, as you call them, was necessary. It's all part of my plan. A plan you and those you claim to serve couldn't possibly hope to understand."

She paused, studying his eyes, trying to work out whether or not her words had sunk in. She'd had this selfsame conversation with Ceallach when he'd returned from the raid, when he'd demanded to know why she hadn't seen the trap Hood had sprung. The Widow could understand how angry he'd been at seeing their men captured, at losing those weapons and vehicles, but it was all for the greater good. Ceallach had seen that after some gentle persuasion, and a night or two in the Castle Vaults. Tanek would see it as well. He had to, because she needed the weapons those he worked for supplied. And she had no wish to anger them, even if she did know what would happen to that nation in the long term.

"Now, I want you tae deliver a message back for me. Tell them they have tae trust what I'm doing. They will get what they want, and so will you. Hood will come here, and when he does, we – I – will be ready for him. It has all been foreseen, Tanek."

The Widow removed the knife from Tanek's cheek.

"So, yer have a choice. Leave now, do this for me, and I swear yer'll get what yer want. Hood out of the way and De Falaise's offspring. I think yer know what will happen if you choose otherwise. Do we have an agreement?" The Widow continued to scrutinise his face; she saw the twitch again and smiled. "Good!" She backed off, and when she was far enough away said, "Oh, aye, yer can move now."

Tanek stumbled forwards, shaking his head.

"Take it easy for a minute, the magic's strong."

"Fuck magic. You mean poison."

The Widow sighed. "Believe what yer want."

Some people just didn't have the capacity to think beyond the everyday. Tanek believed in what he could see, in what he could feel – and fight. She couldn't really blame him, but at the same time it soured the idea of taking his power. There were other strengths than the purely physical, and she understood he would never be one of her conquests. That didn't mean she couldn't still use him, of course.

Tanek stooped to pick up his crossbow, raising it again. The Widow didn't even flinch. He was just testing her, to see if she knew his intentions. She did. "Time yer were goin', isn't it," she said. It wasn't a question. "After all, there are others to see."

The larger man's eyes narrowed, then he nodded. "Very well. But we shall see each other again, soon."

"Somehow, I doubt that," the Widow said after him, but she was talking only to his lengthening shadow. She returned to the table, shoving aside a tarot card showing *The Hermit*. She reached instead for the one she'd been seeing time and again throughout her life.

The Widow examined it, and tapped it against her lips. Then she placed it back down.

On it was a picture of a man sat on a throne.

CHAPTER SIX

THE MAN KNOWN as Shadow sat crossed-legged on the ground, gazing ahead and waiting.

This place had tried to repel him from the moment he'd entered. He could feel it. The whole forest was somehow against him. Its inhabitants as well; the creatures that called this their home. Birds flapping up in the trees, their song shrill and piercing instead of beautiful. Things scuttling about in the undergrowth. And the trees themselves had done their best to get him lost, even when light broke, making one part of this place look like another.

Then came the open attack. He'd only just managed to dodge the vicious charge – and as it was he'd been whipped sideways, a sudden pain in his side causing him to wince. He'd glanced down to see blood seeping from a tear in his clothes caused by the animal's antlers.

Rising slowly, he'd found himself facing a large stag. Shadow stared at it, losing himself momentarily in those black eyes. When he hadn't listened to what the forest was telling him, this creature had been sent to encourage him to leave.

He wasn't about to.

The stag charged again. Shadow dove out of its way, but crouched on his knee this time, ready with his bow – nocking an arrow in seconds. But his aim was off – impossible, his aim was never off! – and the arrow flew wide. Thankfully, when the stag came by for another pass, Shadow was able to draw his hawk axe and deliver a blow to the back of the animal's neck with the blunt side. Crouching next to the felled beast, he placed a hand on its side and felt the rhythm, the pumping of its heart.

He is you and you are him, Shadow said to himself.

His true quarry was linked to this animal somehow, in a way he couldn't explain.

Show me, he said to the creature. *Show me this place's true heart.*

It defied him, of course, but the sudden flash Shadow saw in his mind was enough. He'd recognise the location even if it took weeks to find it.

In the end, it didn't. He stumbled upon it by accident, a clearing he doubted whether he'd find if he'd been actively looking for it. And sincerely doubted he would ever leave again if this didn't work.

After stitching up his wound, Shadow set to work; time was growing short. This forest was attempting to expel him, like a body fighting a disease. But he wasn't going to be defeated.

First he built his fire pit. Then he placed wood – logs he chopped with his axe – in the bottom of the hole. By the time he'd completed the pit, it was a good five foot by seven, the sides forming a kind of semi-circle and strengthened by rocks.

Next he chopped more fire wood, ignoring what sounded like screams in his head. Lies, tricks. Telling him this wasn't his to cut, to burn. It belonged to Hood. Only he could use it. Shadow was trying to evict the guardians, or at the very least subdue them, as he had done with the stag. It wasn't theirs at all; it belonged to the universe, to the Great Spirit. He would show them that.

He kept on ignoring the screams as he chopped wood for the framework of the small lodge: facing the fire pit, with an opening at the front. He covered it with hides he'd brought with him, stitched together in the traditional way and weighted down with rocks. Tied inside the lodge were pouches filled with tobacco as offerings. Using some of the longest logs he'd cut, Shadow built a box about three feet square, which he then built up, filling it with kindling, before building up a dome of rocks – then more wood until the pile was quite high. He had problems getting the fire to light, the wood refusing to respond to the spark of rock, the kindling unwilling to burn, but finally nature took its course as he knew it would. Soon a roaring fire was going.

It took some time for the rocks in the pit to grow hot enough for his purpose. Shadow removed anything metal from his person. He also made sure he had the bottles of water he'd brought with him, for drinking and for wetting the rocks he'd be using.

He also set up an altar made from dirt found in the hole. On this he placed several items personal to him as offerings, including ashes from previous sweats – through which his mission had been imparted.

Shadow stripped to the waist and began his spirit calling ceremony. He started by chanting words known only to him, the lodge preparing him for his journey to another plane of existence. Once there, he would call forth those who watched over *him*, to do battle with the ancients of this place. The prize would be the forest, for he needed to sever the link with Hood before he could defeat the man. Sherwood's favourite son fought with old gods on his side, but so did Shadow. It was just a question of which were the strongest this day.

To help him on his way, Shadow smoked the pipe he had prepared. While it was in his hands, it represented a conduit through which the universe and the creator's power could flow. It would help him to commune with those he sought.

Shadow felt it flowing through him, felt the rhythms of this place just as surely as he had the stag's heartbeat. He begged the spirits he worshipped to come: to cleanse not only him, but the forest.

They appeared in a miasma of colourful scenes, taking on shapes: wolf, the bear, the buffalo. The creatures of this forest were pitted against them, led by the stag, not felled as its body was, but strong and majestic, a symbol of the old god's power and dominance. For now. It was a battlefield unlike any other, way beyond anything ordinary humans had ever witnessed. Beyond guns, tanks and helicopters.

Mighty hawks swooped and fought with owls, spinning over and over in the technicoloured clouds. The stag rammed its antlers into the bear, just as it had done with Shadow, only for the wolf to leap on its back and begin tearing at it. Even the smaller animals, like badgers and foxes, fought – pitting themselves against the creatures of the desert, like the rattlesnake.

Shadow marvelled at the complexity of it, then at the simplicity: a glorious contradiction. The fight seemed to rage for hours, but there was no telling the passage of time. The only way Shadow realised it was over was when the bear picked up the stag and held it aloft, delivering it to him.

Shadow gave thanks to the Great Spirit, just before the connection was severed. He managed to crawl out of the lodge – staggering a few yards with a bottle of water he'd grabbed – before collapsing.

But he knew that no harm would come to him now. He was protected by the new keepers of Sherwood. And Hood was soon to find out exactly what it was like to be the prey instead of the predator.

A trap would be set before long, and as Shadow drifted off into unconsciousness, he realised exactly where he would find the bait.

CHAPTER SEVEN

SOMETHING WAS VERY wrong.

It had started with the dreams. It sounded crazy, but he'd accepted that the forest was giving them to him. They hadn't begun until he'd moved to Sherwood. Then he'd moved out of the forest and into the castle to run the Rangers, and the dreams had deserted him for a spell – which had almost cost all their lives. The forest had also – and this sounded even crazier when he thought about it – *healed* him at least a couple of times, even brought him back from the brink of death.

He'd come to realise that he needed to return there every now and again, to recharge. His excuse was the trips he took young Mark on to teach him hunting skills, but wasn't the lad starting to feel the forest, as well? He'd certainly spoken to Robert about strange dreams he'd had while he'd been there.

More and more, though, over the last year especially, Robert had come to understand that he always carried a part of that special place with him wherever he went.

In fact, that was literally true these days, since he'd struck upon the idea of making himself a little reminder of home. His true, spiritual home. In the pouch he wore on his belt were twigs, earth, stones, grass, bark and leaves he'd gathered from Sherwood – and copying him in all things, Mark had insisted on making one as well. When travelling or on a mission, and in times of great stress, he'd find himself clutching the bag unconsciously. It eased his mind. And while he'd been carrying it, the dreams had never deserted him again.

Until now.

It had happened last night while he slept, out under the stars with Mary beside him. He'd refused the offer of staying at a hotel Bill had commandeered for himself and the rest of the Rangers. Instead,

Robert and Mary had found a local park and bedded down there; she was more used to sleeping outdoors now, since the Christmas surprise he'd given her of a night out in Sherwood. So, falling asleep with the pouch in his hand, it hadn't taken long for the dreams to visit Robert.

His eyes opened and at first he'd thought he was still in the park. But the sheer mass of trees and greenery soon told him otherwise. It had to be the dreamscape, and it had to be Sherwood. He was walking through familiar surroundings, enjoying being back once again, when there was a disturbance in the trees up ahead. At first he thought it was some kind of animal, but when the trees themselves began falling he realised it was something much bigger. Flashes of red appeared between the trunks, then the trees directly in front of him parted.

And he saw a monster.

It looked like a dinosaur, but was nothing so mundane. Robert recognised it from the tales he'd read as a kid. It was a dragon, its scaly crimson hide tough and impenetrable. And it was huge: as tall as the trees in Sherwood.

It breathed out fire, burning the trees.

But this wasn't the only monster in Sherwood. Another parting of the trees and on Robert's right was a giant black spider, its multitude of eyes bulbous and glassy, regarding him with both hatred and longing. The dragon saw the spider and roared; the arachnid, for its part, made a series of clicking noises and weird shrills. Somehow Robert instinctively knew it was female, and although he was no expert he would have bet his life on the fact that the species was a Black Widow.

These were the opponents he and his men were facing at the moment, or at least that's what they represented. Gaining power, becoming bigger and stronger, they would take over soon unless something was done to stop them. No sooner had he thought this than Robert's Rangers flooded the scene, loosing arrows at the two behemoths and swinging their swords. Robert looked on as the Dragon crushed a couple of his Rangers underfoot, while the Widow stopped others in their tracks with webs they couldn't break. She then turned on one poor soul and began to eat him, starting with the head. Robert winced at the sight, but didn't – *couldn't* – move.

Faces he recognised now were tackling the threat: Dale and Jack on his left, leading the attack against the Dragon; Bill, Azhar and Mary on his right, trying to avoid those webs and deadly mandibles. Mary turned, urging him to join the fight. They couldn't do this without him. Robert tried to move again, but still couldn't.

Then he saw it. Something, some*one* striding out between the two creatures, ignoring them as if they didn't matter. A man, but not quite a man – indistinct and shadowy, his body like fog. He was carrying something above his head. Something with antlers.

The stag. The thing Robert had often become himself in the dreamland. Was that meant to be him there, defeated? Dead, even? There was blood dripping from the body, he could see that now. As the man came closer, his features grew clearer. He looked Native American, but Robert didn't have long to take in the sight of him.

Everything happened so quickly. The Dragon and the Widow shrank back, diminishing as something else was revealed behind them – an unclear shape, pushing, or manipulating, them. Next, the shadow man started to grow, becoming stronger, more significant. As he did so, the stag he was holding caught fire – perhaps from one of the Dragon's blasts, Robert couldn't tell. The stag burnt fiercely for a second or two before raining down on the ground as ash.

Robert thought something terrible might happen then. Often the dreams had shown him his own death, in an effort to try and prevent it. But what actually occurred was that everything went black. It was like a TV being put on standby, the picture telescoping away into nothing. At any second Robert thought he might wake up, but he didn't. Nothing happened. He'd lost the connection somehow, the information out of reach.

He awoke not long after, Mary stirring when she heard him.

"What is it?" she asked, half mumbling.

"Nothing," he lied.

She rolled over, snuggling up to him. "Good. Go back to sleep, love."

It was good advice, and he tried, for a long time. He'd finally nodded off before dawn, long enough usually to bring back the dreams. But again there was nothing but darkness.

Over breakfast back at the hotel, Robert was agitated, but refused to discuss it with Mary. She'd come to understand that Sherwood was a special place for him, but still didn't really get *how* special. Nor how much of a role it played in keeping them one step ahead of their enemies. When she looked hurt, Robert had given her hand a squeeze and told her not to worry; he didn't want her thinking he was shutting her out again. But at the same time he wasn't in the mood to talk about what was going on with his dreams.

"So," Bill had asked, "any idea what we're going t'do about the situation?"

They'd questioned the captured raiders and found out more about the Widow. The conclusion they'd drawn was that her men were devoted to the woman, fanatically so in fact. She was power hungry and, not to put too fine a point on it, completely insane. The raiders didn't mind telling them about her, in fact they quite relished it, fuelling the rumour that she ate human flesh, that she was into black magic and that she could never die. They were less forthcoming about her defensive capabilities. Loyal even under pressure – if not the kind of pressure De Falaise and his goon Tanek put their prisoners under – they gave Robert and Bill nothing in the interrogation sessions, apart from the location of their base: Edinburgh Castle.

That had been when Mary stepped in with the sodium pentothal. Picked up during routine searches of medical facilities for supplies that she and the trainee nurses back home could use, Mary was the only one allowed to administer this drug, and even then only in extreme circumstances. It was surprising how much looser their tongues were then, spilling information about lookout positions dotted around the city, guard changes, patrol patterns.

"This German connection wi' the jeeps, bikes an' guns still bothers me," Bill concluded.

Robert nodded. "This whole thing goes beyond simple raiding parties. We're going to have to stamp on the Widow before she gets out of control."

"What exactly did you have in mind?" said Mary.

What he had in mind was getting inside the castle for a closer look at their operation, perhaps even tracing the Widow's support to its source. If they were facing another invasion, then forewarned was forearmed: a hand-picked strike force, led by himself, would ascertain the level of threat, and eradicate it if necessary. He thought Mary might argue about him going, but she didn't. All she said was that if he went, then she was going too, which was fair enough. As much as he still felt that twinge of dread whenever she wanted to accompany him on a mission, he knew she'd be feeling exactly the same about him. If one of them was going, then both should. And, as he'd observed on many occasions, Mary was one hell of a fighter. She'd saved his skin at least as many times as he'd saved hers – more, probably. If anyone was going to watch his back, Robert wanted – *needed* – Mary.

"Right, when do we leave?" Bill wanted to know.

Robert shook his head. "I want you to stay here."

"What?"

"I can't afford to have all my best people on this. I need you out here, Bill, in case we run into difficulties." Robert didn't call Bill a loose cannon – often literally, with that shotgun of his.

Bill argued a little – "I was the one who bloody well brought ye into all this!" – but in the end he grudgingly accepted the logic of Robert's decision. That was probably a first. *Must be mellowing in his old age*, thought Robert.

"And Bill," he said, "if we do need backup, promise me you won't kit the Rangers out with machine-guns or whatever. No heavy stuff. Let them fight how they were meant to. How they were *trained* to."

Bill folded his arms.

"Promise me," Robert insisted.

"Aye, all right," Bill said reluctantly. "But I still think ye're bloody crackers."

Robert grinned. "Nothing new there, then."

Using maps of the castle, Robert had outlined how they were going to play this: entering the city just as they had done when taking Nottingham Castle the first time, only this time knowing exactly where to avoid, and under cover of darkness. He knew his Rangers could move silently, unseen, through the urban forest just as he had done through Sherwood. When they were close enough, they'd split into three teams of a handful each: one, led by Azhar, making an assault up the rocks on the north side, climbing over the wall at a point just down from the Argyle Battery cannons. The second, led by a Ranger called Annie Reid, would do the same on the south side, gaining access up and into the grounds near the old Scottish United Services Museum. The third group would take out the guards outside the Gatehouse, replacing them with Rangers dressed in captured raider uniforms, who would then let in the rest of that team. Later they'd regroup within the castle boundaries.

"The good thing is, the Widow doesn't have nearly as many men as either De Falaise or the Tsar at the moment," Robert informed his troops. "With a bit of luck, we should be able to get in there, get the job done, and leave again without anyone having seen us."

Robert and Mary would be leading the frontal assault. "It'll be just like old times," she said to her husband, thinking of when she'd walked through the gates of Nottingham Castle to confront the Sheriff.

"Let's hope not," Robert replied. "I don't want to take on her entire army just yet."

Preparations were made and they'd set off on horseback for Scotland's capital in the afternoon, timing it so they'd reach the castle itself by nightfall. Everything had gone well, they'd managed to avoid the Widow's people watching for signs of intruders in the city, and tethered their mounts once they were close enough to make it on foot. They moved as one through the streets, and even Robert was impressed by the way his people conducted themselves – all those hours of practise had paid off. He felt proud as they pressed themselves up against walls, checked around corners. They couldn't have been better trained if they'd been on the police force with him all those years ago.

When the time came, they'd branched off: Azhar skirting round one side with his team; Annie taking her group round the other, keeping to the shadows at the base. And near the Esplanade – where jeeps, tanks and other armoured vehicles were stationed – Robert and Mary held back with the others. Two of their Rangers, dressed in the Widow's tartan, handled the guards at the Gatehouse. They could have taken them out with arrows, but didn't want to risk raising an alarm; guards suddenly keeling over at the same time was sure to cause suspicion. Better to take them out at close quarters and replace them almost immediately. Robert looked on as the Rangers crept silently up towards the Gatehouse, sneaking behind the guards simultaneously, hands over mouths, knocking them out and taking their places.

Once the nod was given, the rest of them moved forwards just as stealthily, finding whatever cover they could to reach the arch. "Good work," Robert whispered to his troops now standing guard, as they let them all in through the front door, flanked on either side by statues of Robert the Bruce and William Wallace. Robert couldn't help thinking that Scotland deserved the kind of freedom those men had fought so hard for, not the slavery this Widow obviously had in mind.

Inside, they remained in the shadows, making their way up towards the Portcullis Gate, the second line of the Widow's defence. They waited patiently for confirmation that Azhar's team had taken out the guards here, which came when the lethal-looking gate was raised.

Nicely done, Azhar, thought Robert, waving to the figures up in the building above them.

He motioned for his team to move forwards through the gate, into the castle grounds proper. This place was much larger than their castle, but that meant there were more places to hide between its many buildings: St Margaret's Chapel, the rounded water Reservoirs, the large War Memorial. No sooner had they entered than they had to conceal themselves as a dozen or so of the Widow's men walked past.

"That was close," Mary said.

He nodded, but found himself frowning at the same time. It was about now that the sense of unease really hit him: his own instinct telling him something was wrong. As good as they were at this kind of operation, this was all a bit too easy.

Robert registered more jeeps outside the New Barracks – which housed the bulk of the Widow's troops – as they moved back and round towards the Royal buildings where the woman herself would be located.

He looked around as they entered the Crown Square, then tugged on Mary's arm. "I think we need to get out of here."

"What is it?"

"This smells like –" He was about to say 'a trap,' but by then it was obvious. Lights kicked in from above and they were surrounded by armed guards, swarming from every conceivable nook and cranny. Ranger Madison, at Robert's side, raised his bow and felled a couple of the Widow's men, and was shot dead at point blank range for his trouble. Mary's Peacekeepers were out, but Robert put an arm across to stop her from firing. It was no use, they were hopelessly outnumbered and in a confined space. Their only hope was that Annie Reid and her team might come to their aid, but that was soon dashed when Robert heard a voice from one of the open windows above.

"Welcome to our home, Robin," said the woman with the wild hair. "I know what you're thinking, but yer other teams are a little bit tied up right now." The crowds parted to show them the other Ranger groups, including Ahzar's, captured: their hands bound behind their backs. "Who do yer think let you in at the Portcullis Gate?" She laughed, and it echoed around the square. "I knew you fellas were coming even before you did."

It crossed Robert's mind that he could pick her off with just one arrow. Her men wouldn't be able to stop him in time.

"I wouldnae try that," she called down. "It'd just be a waste of an arrow – and yer life."

Lucky guess, had to be. It was what anyone in this position would be thinking.

"What is it that you want?" said Robert, perhaps hoping to negotiate, but knowing full well this wasn't a woman who could be bargained with.

"Yer come here in the dead of night and ask what *I* want? It seems obvious *yer* wantin' *me*. You want to know ma secrets. That's okay, because what I want is *you*, Hooded Man, so I'd be more than happy tae oblige."

CHAPTER EIGHT

THE MORE HE explored of the place, the more he realised just how dangerous this man's outfit was.

Take Cardiff Arms Park, for example, next door. Dale had managed to sneak a look from up high in the stadium and saw that it was filled with all kinds of jeeps, tanks, tracked and eight-wheeled armoured vehicles. They must have widened or knocked down the entrance to get them all in. And more seemed to be arriving every day, enough to take on the rest of Wales, maybe even sometime soon the rest of what had once been Great Britain. Where they were coming from, he had no idea, and he was no closer to finding out.

So here he was, alone and cut off from the outside world: a spy in the Dragon's den. He needed to get to a radio – the Dragon must be keeping in touch with his units that way, same as they did – but he didn't have all that much to report at the moment. Just his observations about how powerful this Welshman was becoming, how the rest of this country would never shift him if they didn't act soon.

He'd never felt so unsure about what to do in all his life. When he was younger, he'd always been focused on the music, always known he wanted to be a musician. Surviving after the Cull, on the streets, he'd been confident that he'd get by, travelling with his guitar and fending off anyone who fancied their chances. But right now he just didn't know which way to turn.

It wasn't even so much that he was on his own here, because he'd always felt that way deep down, like he shouldn't really get too close to anyone. That was probably why he could never really connect with the opposite sex. Even after he'd found Robert and his Rangers, joined them, been accepted into their clan, Dale still saw himself as being something apart from that too. A maverick. No, his anxiety rose from being out of his depth; he wasn't used to all this masquerading. Dale preferred to be upfront, to fight his enemy face to face, not pretend to be something he wasn't in order to find out a potential weakness.

But it's not the first time you've pretended to be something you're not, is it? He'd done that all the time with the women he'd dated – if you could call one night stands dating. Pretended he'd call them, that things might go further, just to get them into the sack. *This is different, and besides, I've changed.* Or at least he wanted to change, but hadn't quite got it yet.

All this was just to stop him thinking about what to do next. And a distraction so he wouldn't think about –

A radio; he should at the very least check in with Jack, let the man know he was still alive. If Dale knew Jack, he'd be monitoring the frequencies for a call. That man knew the airwaves like the back of his hand, having had an interest in radio since he was a kid – the only way he could keep in touch with anyone, cut off in upstate New York.

Cut off, just like Dale was now.

When he was sure he could slip out without being noticed, Dale grabbed a tray and exited the kitchens in the stadium, praying that another big order wouldn't come in from the Dragon while he was searching. He made his way up one corridor and down another, almost bumping into the man himself, being wheeled along towards a set of double doors.

Dale hung back, but followed for a little while, trailing the Dragon to a set of lifts – actual working lifts! – where he descended with his personal guards. Maybe that was where he took the women from his –

You weren't going to think about that, remember? Well, at least if he was heading there, he wouldn't be asking for food again in a hurry. Dale swore under his breath, thinking what the cost might be for buying him some time. It was too high a price. Much too high.

He got on with his task of looking for a radio. It wasn't easy; he couldn't just stop and ask one of the Dragon's men where it was. Bit of a giveaway for a budding secret agent. On the plus side, only certain key locations inside were lit with proper electric lights; obviously the work of whoever had rigged up the PA system and lifts. If he just carried the tray around with him, none of the guards said a thing, simply assuming he was on his way back from delivering the Dragon's latest meal, or fetching and carrying for the rest of the troops. Dale had the run of the place. Now all he had to do was –

There!

One of the Dragon's men was coming out of a well lit room, the door swinging open a crack behind him. Dale spotted a radio on the table inside. There was another guy still in the room, speaking into the mouthpiece. Dale looked left and right. If he took out the operator, it was sure to be discovered eventually, and before Dale was ready to get out of this place. Maybe he should just wait for the bloke to leave. But what if he never did? What if the other one came back, and he had to wait for both of them to vacate the room? Dale was conscious that he'd been absent from the kitchens for a while. People would begin to notice soon, if they hadn't already. He had to do something, or just give up on contacting Jack altogether.

The man inside yawned, stretched and looked as though he was about to get up. Dale smiled. He was in luck, the bloke was about to follow his comrade. But no, instead he rested his head on the table. He was having a fucking nap! There was no way Dale would be able to use the radio with him in there kipping.

Dale had crept further towards the door to watch. It was only now, when a hand came down on his shoulder, that he realised he'd given himself away. A good spy should never be caught snooping in doorways.

He started, almost bringing the tray round and smacking the person in the face – assuming it was the second guard coming back. But Dale held himself in check, as well as holding his breath. It was a good job; when he turned, he saw a face he recognised.

"You're going to get caught sneaking about like that," whispered the girl with the milky skin and blonde hair. The girl he hadn't been able to get out of his mind since the Dragon took her away. Dale's had never been lost for words in his life, but he was now. "Caught, or killed," the girl said, her voice betrayed a faint Welsh accent, like she'd been born in this country but had lived further east for a while.

He stepped back, taking her in. She was still dressed in a flimsy outfit; the baby doll replaced by a chemise. Dale suddenly found his voice. "What are *you* doing here?"

"*Not* getting caught," she replied, and he realised that his first assessment of her had been spot on. Back in that VIP box he'd noticed her obvious compassion for those murdered Rangers, but also an inner strength he really admired. It reminded him a little of Sophie, of Mary. "I hope, anyway." The girl pulled him to one side so they couldn't be seen from inside the room.

"Caught doing what?" Dale's curiosity about her had overcome any surprise or awkwardness; now he just wanted to know what she was up to.

"The same as you, I'm guessing. Something we shouldn't be."

She had him there. He definitely shouldn't be sending a radio message out or thinking about whacking one of the Dragon's men to do it. "Okay... Look, just who are you?"

"My name's Sian."

"Dale."

"All right, then, Dale, you obviously want to get into that room to use the radio. But you can't with that big lug snoring over there. I want information. We can help each other." Sian skirted around him and made for the door.

Dale grabbed her by the arm. "What are you doing? You can't!"

"Out of the two of us, I reckon I'm the one that can," she said, removing his hand from her arm. She smiled. "Don't worry, I came prepared." She raised her other hand, holding most of a bottle of whiskey. "Loosens the tongue."

Suddenly Sian was gone, walking into the room and rousing the Dragon's man. He heard the guy ask gruffly what she was doing there, but he didn't catch her reply. The rest of what they were saying was muffled. Although he couldn't see from this angle, Dale figured the guy would be looking at her, his eyes trailing over her body just as the Dragon's had. Just as his own had.

Not the same, not the same thing at all!

Dale held back as long as he could, but when he heard laughter he edged closer to the door. Sian was explaining to the man that she'd been sent here with a little present for his hard work, that the Dragon had said to enjoy it. Dale wasn't sure whether she was talking about the booze or her; the thought made him want to retch. He heard gulping as the man drank and felt grateful he couldn't see what else he was up to. Dale waited as the man drank more, and more. It was only when he heard him telling Sian what he'd like to do to her, his voice slurring badly, that Dale couldn't restrain himself any longer.

The next thing he knew, he was inside the room and had brought the tray he was holding down on the back of the man's head. The operator slumped forward.

"What the hell do you think you're doing?" Sian snapped.

"Giving him a hangover he won't forget in a hurry."

"And what if he remembers? What if –"

"Look, he was about to, you know, try it on." He couldn't believe he'd just said that. This was the woman who'd been dragged off by the Dragon, had done Christ knows what with him, and he was worried about a drunk radio guy getting a bit fresh.

"He was in no condition to try *anything* on! God, if you've screwed things up for me –"

"Screwed things up... what are you talking about?"

Sian let out a weary sigh. "I came in here looking for my Aunt Meghan. We've been together ever since... well, you know. The Dragon's men took her a few weeks ago. She hid me away safe when they found us, I think she thought she could talk her way out of it. But they took her, Dale. They took her. So I *let* myself get captured."

"Jesus. I'm really sorry." If anything, that made what Sian had gone through all the more upsetting. "Did you get anything from him?"

Sian shook her head.

"Listen, I'll help you look for her. But first, I really need to send a message out on that radio before his mate comes back."

"Won't be back anytime soon. This one made it very clear we'd be alone for a good while. They just got a message through saying some big foreign guy the Dragon's supposed to be meeting is almost here. His mate's gone off to look after him personally, give him a tour until the Dragon is ready to meet up."

"What big foreign guy?"

"Funny sounding name: Tunic or something."

Dale placed his hands on her arms. "*Tanek?* Was that the name?"

"Might have been."

"Be certain, Sian. This is important!"

She nodded. "Yeah, I think so.

"Shit!"

"What? I don't understand."

Dale ignored her, flipping switches and attempting to dial up a signal. "Please be out there, Jack," he said.

Now he really did have something to report, but he wished with all his heart he didn't.

HE REALLY WISHED he'd never sent the kid in there.

Jack ground his teeth as he sat in what was left of the Welsh Ranger headquarters. He and his squad had arrived too late to do anything to help the troops stationed there, and as Jack had looked over the devastation – the bodies of Rangers, men and women alike – his guts tied themselves in knots. It was these people who'd alerted them to the problem in the first place, but they hadn't described anything on this scale. Another wannabe dictator, maybe, who was still building up his forces, but with nowhere near the capability to do something like *this*. These were trained fighters, damned well trained. He'd trained some of them himself back at Nottingham Castle.

Now they were dead.

Jack had felt his hands tightening around the staff he always carried as he took in the blood, the glassy eyes, the expressionless faces.

"Sir!" one of his squad had alerted him to the approach of a vehicle. A jeep, travelling at speed on the horizon. He didn't need to order his Rangers to hunker down and find cover. If this was a clean-up crew of the Dragon's men, coming to pick off any survivors they'd missed, then they'd chosen the wrong day.

As the jeep came closer, however, it was clear that they had other intentions. The vehicle skidded, doing a handbrake turn as it reached the former HQ. Then two men threw a bundle out of the back... a living bundle, though it was a poor excuse for a human being. In fact the body they tossed out looked in worse shape than some of the corpses surrounding Jack. But from the hood and dark green garb, it was another one of his Rangers. Where he'd been and what had happened to him, Jack had no idea, but he was guessing it hadn't been pleasant.

As the jeep began to drive off again, Jack broke cover and ordered the others to see to their fallen comrade. He had a score to settle.

He began to run. Although he wasn't as young as he had been when he'd done the circuits as a professional wrestler, he'd kept himself in good shape with exercise and training. Not to mention actual combat. In the last couple of years, he'd been in more scrapes than he ever had in the ring, been in more danger than he had been against Big Bud McCardle or The Terror from Tallahassee. There still wasn't an ounce of fat on Jack 'The Hammer' Finlayson's frame, and it meant that before too long he was catching up with that accelerating jeep. He had also attracted the attention of those in the back. Those within reach of a pretty lethal-looking mounted machine-gun.

He saw one of the men pointing, then the other pulling the weapon around and firing. Jack dodged sideways, only just avoiding the bullets raking the road.

The gunman aimed, but again fired wide – Jack leaping just in time. He bent and ran even faster at the vehicle, his baseball cap flying off, pressing on until he was almost level with the jeep. Before either the gunman or his partner could react, Jack was using his staff to pole-vault into the back. He lost his grip on the stick, but didn't need it now. When the man closest tried to draw his pistol, Jack clipped it out of his hands and grabbed hold of him by the collar.

"Let's see how you like it, pal!" he roared, picking the man up and heaving him from the vehicle. There was an audible *crack* as one of his legs broke, and he tumbled head over heels. The other man yelped and scrabbled to get away, but a huge hand on his shoulder stopped him, twisting him around so that Jack could take hold of his head with both hands, and then bring it down onto his raised knee. The man toppled backwards, over the side. He must have fallen under the wheels, though, because the whole vehicle rose up in the air momentarily; when Jack looked behind him, he saw the man's body flattened against the road.

Jack clambered around on the outside of the jeep as it continued to speed up, the lone driver perhaps thinking – bizarrely – that he could escape that way. Jack reached in through the open window and grabbed at the wheel, pulling pulling them off the road and towards a house. The driver attempted to wrestle the wheel back, but there was only one wrestler present. When Jack was satisfied they were on a collision course, he let go and jumped free.

Unlike the two men from the back of the jeep, Jack did know how to fall. As he rolled to a halt, he watched with satisfaction as the jeep rammed headlong into the house, pitching the driver through its windscreen.

"*You* have just been Jack-Hammered," he uttered in a low tone, but there was none of the usual glibness. This had been revenge, pure and simple, for the Rangers killed back at the base, and for the one they'd dumped by the roadside. Jack only hoped he got a chance to explain how he felt to their boss.

He picked himself up and began his walk back along the road, retrieving his staff and his cap along the way. The man who'd been run over was dead; the other was alive, but badly injured. Jack quizzed him about what had happened at the HQ, and back at the stadium, standing on the damaged leg whenever the man refused to answer. Robert probably wouldn't have approved, but their leader wasn't here. Hadn't seen what these men had done. The injured man told Jack how the Rangers they'd captured had died. "You sick sons of bitches," Jack said. Then he thought about Dale. "Have you seen a young guy back at the stadium? About yay high, good looking? You know if he's still alive?" The man shook his head. "Okay," said Jack, and began walking off.

"Wait, you can't just leave me here," screamed the soldier.

"Our man comes first. Then maybe I'll send someone back for you." Or maybe he would just clean forget. *Things slip your mind sometimes*, Jack said to himself. For now, all he wanted to know was how the fallen Ranger was doing, and if Dale was all right.

His squad were attempting to patch up their colleague, who Jack could now see was suffering from a bullet wound to the leg. "He'll be lucky if it doesn't get infected," a Ranger called Chadwick told him, out of earshot of the patient, "even with antibiotics. And he'll never be able to walk properly again."

All the battles, all the fights he'd been in; nothing compared to this. Slaughtering his Rangers in their home, promising freedom then blowing them up, leaving just one alive but crippled for life. And he'd sent Dale into that maniac's domain. Sure, the kid could handle himself, but Jack still felt as though he'd signed his death warrant. This wasn't the movies. Bad things happened to good people and there were never any guarantees of a happy ending.

So in the time since then he'd sat by the radio. Waiting for a sign that Dale was still alive, that he hadn't simply been shot in the head for the Dragon's amusement. Once or twice he'd heard a crackle of static, but it had only been ghosts whispering down the line.

Then Dale's voice actually came down the line. *"Green Three Leader, come in. Green Three, are you out there? Please respond. Jack, answer the radio, will you? Over."*

Jack picked up the receiver and spoke. "This is Green Three Leader. Dale, is that you, little buddy? Over."

There was another crackle of static, then: *"Well it's not bloody Bono, is it? Over."* Jack smiled, but could hear the panic in Dale's voice.

"Are you okay? Over."

"Yeah – for now. But I don't have much time. Listen, there's been a development. The Dragon's working with a guy you might have heard of. Big fella, olive skinned. Likes crossbows. Over."

Jack couldn't believe his ears. "Tanek?" The last time Jack had seen that man, it had been as his torture victim, while De Falaise's daughter, Adele, cheered him on. Robert said that he'd escaped after they'd taken down the Tsar in Sherwood, but nobody had seen or heard about him since. Like that proverbial bad penny, he just always seemed to show up – especially when there was something big going down. But what was his connection to the Welsh Dragon? Whatever it turned out to be, this wasn't good news at all. "Do you know what he's doing there, Dale? Over."

"Not yet. But stuff's been arriving all the time I've been here. Weapons, vehicles, most of it kept in Cardiff Arms Park. I think he might be involved in supplying it. Over."

Jack rubbed his chin. That would make sense; first Tanek allied himself with De Falaise, then the Tsar, now the Dragon. Anyone he thought might be able to seize power. *But there must be a third party involved if that pond scum's the go-between,* he reasoned.

"Listen, Dale, I want you to get out of there. You've done all you can, now I want you to report back to –"

"What's that? You're breaking up."

"I said get your ass out of there, Dale, and that's an order!" The radio died. Whether it was just a loss of signal, someone had found Dale, or he'd just run out of time, Jack had no way of knowing. But it made him more aware than ever that if something happened to the youth it would be on his head. Jack slammed his fist against the wall, swearing. When one of the Rangers came in, he barked at them that he wanted to be left alone.

After a few minutes, he nodded to himself, then muttered, "Okay, so you're not coming out. Maybe it's about time we came in."

DALE CLICKED THE radio off. He'd heard Jack's orders, but there was no way he was going to pull out just yet.

"Green Three..." Sian said. "You're a Ranger, aren't you? One of Robin Hood's men?"

Back before the virus that would have sounded so stupid, but Sian said it with complete seriousness. Robert's reputation, and that of his Rangers, had spread far. No-one was laughing, least of all his enemies. Dale shrugged, then nodded, feeling slightly embarrassed; what was wrong with him? He wasn't usually shy about blowing his own trumpet. But with Sian it was different. He wasn't out to impress.

"God, why didn't you say something?"

"Didn't really seem the time or place."

The radio operator moaned. There wasn't much danger of him waking up yet, but it was time they made themselves scarce.

"I think we'd probably better get out of here." Dale said.

Sian nodded, but touched his arm as he made to leave. "Why did you do that just then?"

"What?"

"Cut off... what was his name, Jack? Cut him off when he was ordering you to get out of here."

Once more, Dale felt the blood rushing to his cheeks. He looked down as he answered. "Because I didn't want to leave you here. And you won't leave until you've found your aunty... So..."

Sian looked at him, then, suddenly, kissed him on the cheek. "Thank you, Dale."

He shrugged a final time, feeling as though his cheeks were on fire. Then, as much to hide this as anything else, he nodded towards the door, gesturing for them both to leave.

There was still much to do before either of them could get out of this madhouse.

CHAPTER NINE

THE CAPTIVE'S HEAD rocked with the sheer force of the blow.

"Come on, talk, damn you!" Gwen brought her hand back and hit the man again, almost tipping over the chair he was tied to.

The prisoner – his features pinched, hair closely cropped – spat blood and grinned, teeth stained crimson. Gwen punched him in the side, where her bullet had winged him, and Dr Jeffreys gave a wail of protest.

"You'll pull out the stitches!"

Gwen took no notice, striking the man again. He gritted his teeth, bubbles of red saliva bursting as they escaped his lips.

"I said *talk!*" she screamed into his face. "Who sent you? Who do you work for?"

The man smirked again, even laughed.

Gwen brought her hand back once more, but felt someone grab it. She turned to find Andy holding her wrist. "Take it easy, Gwen. The guy's obviously not going to play ball."

She looked at Andy, then back at their prisoner. Play ball? This wasn't a game. Gwen pulled her arm away. After all they'd risked to get this dickhead here, she wasn't about to ask nicely. The guy had been shooting at them, for Christ's sake. He'd put her son at risk, why did he deserve any kind of compassion?

The answer was, he didn't. She smacked him again, perhaps just to spite Andy. He might be okay with waiting for New Hope to be overrun by armed men, but she wasn't going to just sit here and let it happen.

Andy had been against going out there to fetch the prisoner in the first place. "You're joking," he'd said when he heard Gwen's plan. "You're going to get yourself killed. *Then* what'll happen to little Clive?"

It hadn't been the smartest thing he'd ever said. Clive Jr was the reason for *everything* she did. It was precisely because of him she'd risk venturing out to get the fallen gunman, even with more of his friends still in the woods. "It's almost dark. If we use the warren –"

"What if those nuts have night-vision or whatever? Have you thought of that? Hell, I can't be a part of this madness," Andy had said, holding up his hands and walking off.

"Okay," Gwen had said after him. Thankfully, there had been others willing to go with her. Darryl for instance, who they had to thank for the warren in the first place. When designing the wall, he'd had the foresight to include a back door in case of just such an emergency. The warren was exactly what it sounded like, an underground tunnel leading from the back of New Hope up and out into the woods, the exit covered over with foliage and bracken. If Graham had been fit enough, he'd have volunteered as well, if only to pay back the sods who'd shot him, but he was nowhere near. In fact, Jeffreys had reported earlier that his situation was deteriorating, in spite of the drugs they were giving him.

"All the more reason to go and fetch one of them, bring him inside," Gwen told the doctor.

So, she and Darryl had climbed into the warren and made their way up and out into the woods. Rifles primed, they'd crawled along on their bellies as silently as they could to where Gwen guessed the man had fallen. She'd posted a watch on him, and not one of his friends had come to get him or see how he was. Loyalty obviously wasn't part of their agenda.

Just when they thought they weren't going to find him, Gwen spotted a boot in the undergrowth and tugged on Darryl's arm. He nodded, following her. Jeffreys had given Gwen a tranquiliser to subdue the guy, but as it turned out he'd lost so much blood that he barely put up a fight. As they started dragging him away, however, bullets splintered the trees surrounding them. The fuckers had been using him as bait. "Quick, move!" Gwen ordered; they didn't have time for messing about. She and Darryl hauled the man back, and it was only now he started to cry out, risking giving away their location. Gwen put her hand over his mouth as they pulled him along, racing towards the hole in the ground. They reached it ahead of their pursuers and scrambled back down inside the warren, yanking the trapdoor shut and locking it from inside. They heard boots, but the shooters trampled overhead, running past, oblivious to what was hidden under their feet.

Darryl emerged first at New Hope, greeted by the sight of Karen Shipley pointing a pistol at him. As instructed, she'd been keeping it trained on the open black square since they'd entered, just in case they had any unwanted visitors. When she saw Darryl poke his head through, she let out a whoop of joy, hugging and kissing him on the cheek, much to his surprise.

"Oh, thank God!"

Yes, she'd been pleased to see the man she was clearly sweet on. But Karen had also never shot anyone before. Gwen knew the woman might have to if things carried on the way they were going, but felt only a small twinge of sadness about the loss of her innocence. After all, Gwen's had been snatched away a long time ago.

They'd taken the prisoner to Jeffreys, who'd patched up the wound and given the man a transfusion. At first no-one had volunteered, but when the doctor pointed out he'd die without one and they'd get nothing from him at all, Darryl once again stepped into the breach. Who'd have thought she'd come to rely on him so much? *He* was the very essence of lost innocence, yet Gwen couldn't have done all this without him. "Hook me up, doc," Darryl had said. "Least we know we're the same group."

Unbelievably, that had been four hours ago, and as the prisoner had recovered steadily, Gwen sat studying him. When she judged he was fit enough to be questioned, she'd taken him at gunpoint – virtually carrying him to the Red Lion – ignoring all of Jeffreys' and Andy's complaints. She was still ignoring them.

"What's happened to you, Gwen?" Andy asked after the last blow. She gaped at him. "Do I really have to answer that?"

"You're killing him."

"Hopefully not until we get what we want."

"This isn't the way to treat *anyone*. He's still a human being."

"A human being who's been shooting at our home, Andy. Who wants us dead. Those were your words, not mine. Weren't you the one who greeted me with a rifle when I came back here with Tate? Why was that exactly? Because you thought men like Javier had returned, right?"

Andy said nothing.

"Well, *he's* a man like Javier, like De Falaise. His lot don't understand kindness, Andy. All they understand is this." She held up a fist in front of his face. "And this!" She grabbed her pistol and waved it under his nose. "They see anything else as weakness, do you understand?"

"Oh, I think I'm starting to. Have you ever thought that maybe by doing all this, we attract men like him?"

"You've got it backwards. All we wanted to do here was live in peace and then… Everything changed."

Andy was silent for a moment: "This isn't what Clive would've wanted. He would've –"

Gwen struck Andy with the same hand she'd been using to hit the prisoner. And with just as much force. She hadn't meant to do that. It was the mention of her dead lover's name that provoked her. How *dare* Andy tell her what Clive would or wouldn't have wanted? Clive was dead, and they would be too if they listened to Andy.

He stepped back, his fingers touching the cheek she'd slapped, which was reddening nicely. Andy said nothing more, just glared at her before storming out of the pub. Gwen looked at the others present – at Jeffreys, at Karen – waiting for them to say something. They didn't, and she knew why. They were scared of her. And were probably right to be.

She turned back to the prisoner. Could she see the faintest glimmer of fear in his eyes? Gwen bent and whispered in his ear: "One way or another, you're talking to me." She raised the pistol, pressing it against his head. "You just have to decide how you want to do this."

"All right," said the man. Gwen was a bit shocked to hear his voice. He had a distinct German accent. *So*, she thought, *at last I know* something *about you. About the people out there.* "I will tell you this. The men out there *will* find a way into your little village, one way or the other." He laughed. "It is for you to decide how *you* want to do this."

Gwen struck him on the cheek with the butt of the pistol. "Who are you people, what do you want?"

He spat out more blood and a tooth, which landed on the carpet not far from her feet. Gwen waited for the answer to her query. "That is very simple. We want your son." He smiled again, a chilling sight. It was Gwen who felt a rush of fear now.

"And I can assure you, we are *not* going to leave without him."

CHAPTER TEN

SHE KNEW THE Rangers were being interrogated, and tortured; Mary could hear the screams throughout the building, throughout the vaults. What she didn't know was whether one of them was Robert.

Another scream, and Mary – shut away in one of the cells of the French prisons – curled up on the hard wooden bed, putting her fists to her ears. The thought of Robert undergoing such a horrible ordeal at the hands of someone like Tanek was too much to bear. A mental image of her husband on the rack flashed through her mind; his limbs stretched, the veins at his neck standing proud.

"No! Stop this! Stop it!"

Mary didn't know if anyone could hear her, but nobody came. Another thought crossed her mind. What if it was the Widow herself doing the torturing? Was she standing by as Robert's ruined body was whipped or cut to ribbons, enjoying his pain?

It might not even be *Robert*, said David. She'd been wondering when he would crop up, the voice of her long dead brother, killed by the disease that had liberated her, granting her freedom from the farm where she'd lived as a virtual recluse. The disease that had brought her Robert, the Hooded Man.

And what if it *wasn't* Robert – did it make things any better to know that it might be Azhar being tortured, or Annie Reid, or any of the Rangers they'd come here with? Soldiers, but also friends. She'd laughed with these people, danced alongside them at the summer fête and winter festivals, treated their wounds and their illnesses, been a mother figure to some. At least it wasn't Mark in there, she thought: the boy – the *man* now, who she'd adopted. Who she and Robert had adopted.

I was just trying to look on the positive side, Moo-Moo, said David. She wasn't in real trouble yet, because he wasn't calling her by her full name. *No, it's not you who's in trouble at the moment,* he observed as another scream reverberated throughout the prison.

"Look, that really isn't helping," she told him, and not for the first time she tried willing David away. Mary knew deep down it had to be her own subconscious talking to her, but why did it always have to use David's voice?

I keep trying to tell you, it's me, Moo-Moo. Honest. How can I prove it?

"Get me out of here. If it's really you and you're really a ghost, then open up that prison door and get me the hell out. Do something useful for a change."

She regretted the words as soon as she'd said them. Ridiculous, really; if it *was* her unconscious mind talking, then the only feelings she could hurt were her own. Nevertheless David had helped her plenty of times in the past, rousing her when she was knocked out or half dead.

But that wouldn't be good enough this time. She was already wide awake. How was she supposed to sleep knowing those screams could belong to –

Mary chastised herself; she was going round in circles. "David, if you're really real, and you love me, get that fucking door open."

Language, Moo-Moo.

"Are you going to do it, or aren't you?"

It doesn't work like that. There are rules.

"David!" she insisted, her tone hardening. Was it her imagination or did she hear him sigh?

"David, please." Mary couldn't believe she was begging her own *id* to do something she knew was impossible. But she scrunched up her eyes and prayed anyway.

Mary opened them in surprise when she heard the sound of bolts being drawn back.

"*Yes!* Thanks so much, David, I –"

The door opened and there were two of the Widow's men, dressed in that same black and tartan uniform she'd first seen during the raid on that convoy. Her heart sank.

"Yeah, thanks a bunch," she said quietly to herself. David didn't answer. But then what did she expect him to do? He was no more likely to open that door and let Mary out than he was to appear in front of her covered in a sheet and rattling chains.

The men came inside, guns trained on her. She struggled with them, making life hard for them, as they drag her from the cell. Probably on her way to be tortured like the other Rangers.

They pulled her back up and along corridors she'd been hauled down after they'd been captured, turning her around several times until she didn't know where she was – the sound of screaming still in her ears. Then they opened a final door and shoved her inside, where she landed awkwardly on the floor.

It was dark in this room, lit only by a few candles. Mary got up off her knees, looking over her shoulder to see that the men hadn't gone anywhere. They were covering the doorway to prevent her escape. Was this all part of the torture?

She heard breathing, coming from the other end of the room. "If you're going to do something to me, you'd better get on with it," she snarled. "I'm not a patient woman."

"Now, we both know that isnae true," said a voice she knew, although she'd only heard it the once.

The Widow appeared in front of her, in a black corset and skin-tight trousers. "Yer can be *very* patient when it suits."

"What would you know about it?" snapped Mary.

The Widow smiled her feral smile, which somehow complimented her face. Her backcombed hair highlighted the effect. "More than yer'd think. For example, I know yer waited patiently on that farm, waiting with yer Dad and brother. Waiting in more ways than one. But fer what? I dinnae think you could even tell me."

Mary rose slowly. How could she possibly know that? Must have got it from some of the Rangers. But how many knew that much about her past? Only Robert, and even he didn't know all of it.

"Then yer waited for *him* to come, the Hooded Man. Waited for him tae get over his dead wife and child. Even now yer still worry that he loved them more than he does you, or Mark."

No, couldn't be Robert. He'd never talk about private stuff like that with this trollop. It wasn't his way. God, Mary had enough trouble getting him to open up, getting past that macho bullshit he used as a shield. But there were ways to get information out of people; just look at what she'd done to the Widow's men to get them to talk. What if the Widow had drugged him somehow?

David, whoever, wherever you really are, she said to herself, *I could really use your help right about now.*

"Aye, call on David," said the Widow, circling Mary. "I talk to the dead as well, y'know. They're inside me, all of ma husbands. They can give yer power, Mary. They have knowledge that we don't. Well, most of us. They know things and, if we're only willing tae listen, they'll tell us. In that way we're not that dissimilar, you and I."

Mary screwed up her face. "You're delusional. I'm *nothing* like you!"

The Widow threw her head back and laughed. "Am I? Or perhaps I'm the only sane person left in this world. I see things as they are, or as they *should be*."

"Doubtful."

"Suit yerself. Anyway, where was I? Oh, aye, patience. Yer waited for Robert. I don't blame yer, he's very special."

Mary felt herself bristling. "You leave him alone," she warned the Widow.

"Or what?"

"I won't be responsible for what happens," was all Mary could think of. That earned another cackle from the Widow.

"It's a bit late anyway," the Widow said from behind her. Mary spun around. "See, while yer been waiting again, I've been getting' t'know him better. *Much* better. I had to be sure. Certain it was really *him*." The Widow produced what looked like a playing card, its back facing Mary, and stared at it. "Quite a man, isn't he?"

Mary took a step towards the Widow, drawing back her fist at the same time. There was the clack of machine-guns being cocked, the guards raising their weapons. But the Widow held up her hand for them to lower their guns.

"Give it yer best shot," the Widow said, grinning.

Mary didn't need to be told twice. She swung her punch, but hit nothing: the space the Widow had occupied only a moment before was now empty. Mary felt someone tapping her on her shoulder and spun back round, lashing out as soon as she saw the Widow again. For a second time she struck nothing, and the Widow was now to the side of her. Mary saved her strength. The woman was too fast for her.

"Finished? Now, can we talk sensibly? Woman tae woman?" The Widow stood in front of Mary. "As I was sayin', that's quite a man yer have there. Or should I say, *had*. I've been waitin' a long time fer someone like him. Someone wi' his strength and power, who will live on forever." Mary frowned at that remark, but let it pass. "Someone wi' the sight, like me."

Now she did feel the need to speak. "What are you talking about? What sight?"

The Widow chuckled. "Yer really don't know him at all. How can yer call yerself his woman, when he keeps so much hidden? When yer choose not to see the blindingly obvious?"

Mary was sick of these mind games. She wanted to know what the Widow was up to. What she wanted with Robert.

"I have special plans for him," the Widow informed her, again seemingly reading her thoughts. "A long time ago I was promised something, Mary. Ma king. Ma Emperor. Thought I'd found him once, too." There was a real sadness to the Widow's voice, and Mary almost felt a little sorry for her. The feeling only lasted a moment, however, when she remembered what the Widow was after. *"What I want is you, Hooded Man."*

"And even when I began to see Robert," the Widow continued, "feel his presence, I still didnae dare hope, Mary. But bein' in the same room as him; now that was different. No denying it then. Our... connection."

Mary laughed. "You and Robert? In your dreams."

"Actually, in *his*. He's seen me, just as I've seen him. He sees a lot of things before they happen. Just like I do."

What was she saying, that Robert was some kind of psychic? All of this was completely ludicrous. "He wouldn't look at you twice. What we share you couldn't possibly understand."

The Widow shook her head. "It's the bond Robert and I share that you cannae understand. You and he were never fated to be together, Mary. That's why when the Frenchman's daughter came along –"

"You shut your filthy mouth."

"That's why he was tempted, if only for a wee while. Yer can't possibly make him happy, don't yer see? Not really. Yer might have some ability, but yer deny it. Don't believe in it. I, on the other hand, embrace it. And Robert can see that."

"I'm not having this conversation with you. You're a lying cow."

"Dinnae take my word for it. Robert..."

The Widow beckoned, and Mary saw who had been standing at the back of the room in the darkness. It had been his breathing she'd been able to hear; the man she loved more than life itself. He'd been watching, listening to everything, and never said a thing.

Robert moved forward slowly. His hood was down, and he regarded Mary strangely, like he wasn't really registering her presence. "Tell her," the Widow said. "Tell yer 'wife' how you *really* feel."

He hesitated for a second, then said: "I'm sorry, Mary. What she's said is true. We shouldn't be together. My place is here."

"Robert..." She turned to the Widow. "You fucking witch, what have you done to him?"

"Nothing. Except talked to him, explained things. Got him to see reason. See the link between us and how much stronger we are together than apart. We were never supposed to be enemies."

"I take it back, you're not delusional – you're barking mad. Robert, sweetheart..." Mary came forward, but Robert took a step back.

"Please, Mary, don't make this harder than it already is," he told her. "There are things I've never shared with you, that I didn't think you'd understand. But now I've found someone who does. She's promised to help me get back what I've lost."

Mary shook her head. "Lost? I don't understand."

"His focus. His dreams. His link to forces beyond ours, Mary. A link he'll get back through me. Now, Robert, don't yer have something tae do? We cannae go ahead with our preparations until it's done."

"Preparations?" None of this was making any sense to Mary, and it made even less when Robert reached out and grabbed her left hand. She tried to pull away, but he held on tightly. "Robert, no, you're hurting me." Mary looked into his eyes, but there was no response. This wasn't the man she'd first met at the farm when she'd saved his life, wasn't the man who'd saved her from De Falaise or spent the night with her for the first time after the summer fête a year later, or made those vows in front of Reverend Tate to love and cherish her for the rest of his life. This was someone else, a warped image of her husband created by the Widow. And he was taking back the ring he'd placed on her finger that special day, tugging and pulling so hard she thought he might snap her finger off just to get at it. Mary beat on his chest, but he didn't let go. "Stop it. I said: STOP IT!" She pushed him away, but as she did so the ring came loose and Mary fell back onto the floor.

Robert returned to the Widow, satisfied now that he had what he wanted. He smiled, and it was the same kind of messed-up grin the Widow had plastered all over her face. Feral. As much as Mary hated to admit it, right now they did make the perfect couple. Then, as Mary lay on the floor, Robert took the Widow's left hand and slid the ring onto a finger.

"Not exactly legal, or recognised by the eyes of *yer* God," the Widow told Mary. "But then I never really cared for the law, or for *Him*." She held up the hand with the ring on. "He's mine now, and I'm his." She pulled Robert close, crushing her lips against his.

Mary let out a howl and scrambled to her feet. Before she could get anywhere near them, though, she felt the hands of the guards restraining her.

The Widow broke off the kiss long enough to say, "Take the woman back to her cell." The guards began manhandling Mary towards the door. She lashed out, raking one man's face with her nails, but it didn't get her anywhere.

"I'll kill you!"

"This was all preordained," the Widow called after her. "If yer don't believe either of us, ask yer brother. The dead have knowledge that we don't, so ask him."

As Mary was escorted out of the room, the last thing she saw was the Widow all over Robert. She screamed as she was dragged back down the corridor, louder than any of the Rangers had done while they were being tortured.

Ask David? Ask the dead? She didn't need to. Because as she'd fallen backwards onto the floor she'd seen the strange symbol painted on Robert's wrist, snaking up his arm. Talked to him and reasoned with him, her arse! The Widow had done something to Robert. But that fact didn't make it any easier to take. What Mary had waited so long for – Robert's affections – the Widow had managed to secure in hours. And she couldn't get the image of them together out of her mind.

She hadn't asked for it, but David chose that moment to speak up. When she was thrown back into her cell, tears flowing from her eyes, he said in a quiet, serious voice:

I'm really sorry, Moo-Moo. But she was telling the truth. She's not controlling him, he's doing all this of his own accord.

"Shut up!"

This was all meant to be, it had to happen this way.

"Shut up! Shut up! Shut up!" she repeated, convinced she was finally going crazy. But she could also hear the Widow's voice:

"The dead have knowledge that we don't. They know things and, if we're only willing tae listen, they'll tell us."

SOMETIMES HE COULD hear what the dead were saying.

One person, at any rate. And not directly, but through the people closest to him. It didn't matter what he did, what he'd achieved, he'd always be compared to someone who'd died long before this fucking virus had come along; killed by something else entirely, though still tied to the blood. His brother's problem had been with his white blood cells. That's what had done for him, and yet in a way he got to live on forever in the memories of his mother, grandmother and father. His father especially. He'd been the one who'd doted on Gareth, to the point where it might have seemed to the outside world that the man *had* no other child. The golden son, who'd shone so brightly he'd burned out – leaving the patriarch of the family with no alternative but to grudgingly acknowledge his younger offspring.

A younger offspring who now catered for the man's every need, even though he didn't get so much as a "thanks."

"I don't know why I still bother," he said to his father, who was practically bedridden – or who preferred to stay in bed anyway, being waited on hand and foot.

"You bother because you're a good lad. A good son. You always have been." This was his Mam talking, lowering her romance novel – one of many he had to constantly supply her with. She was next to his father's bed, keeping him company, although it was becoming increasingly obvious that her husband couldn't stand the sight of her these days. The Dragon's Nan wasn't far away; sat in the corner with her knitting, clacking away.

How long had it been since any of them had been outside? He couldn't remember. Must have been back during the early days, when he'd got them safely away from all the fighting, the rioting, the burning houses. Got them somewhere safe so he could look after them. Even when they'd moved to the stadium, they'd been transported in the back of an armoured truck. Only his dad had complained, as the Dragon's most trusted aides had hefted him into the lift, taking him to the floor where a home away from home had been constructed. "Mind what you're doing," his father had shouted at the men, still not grateful that he was being looked after, taken to a place of safety.

His Mam and Nan had been more appreciative, settling well into the routine – "Ooh, look, isn't this nice. At least we can get a decent cup of tea." They hadn't really gone out of the house much even before the Cull, whereas his Dad had at least been able to escape down the pub or to the rugby. The Dragon had thought – mistakenly – that his father might approve of the new venue. "When things calm down a bit, I'll arrange for you to watch some matches," he'd told him. Still stupidly trying to gain his approval, even though the Dragon had shown who was really in charge a long time ago. His Dad had looked at him like he was filth.

Like he wasn't Gareth.

But he still visited them as often as he could, given his hectic schedule. He'd fitted in this quick call after meeting with Tanek, who represented some of the Dragon's associates. "Associates?" his Nan had said. "Your grandfather fought a war against their kind, you know." Her knitting needles were going like the clappers. "Nazis."

"That was a long time ago," the Dragon's mother had said, standing up for her son. "I'm sure our boy knows what he's doing, and what he's getting himself involved in. Don't you?"

His father had huffed at that one.

"You got something to say?" the Dragon asked point blank; he was done pussyfooting around.

"Only that you'd never have seen our Gareth –"

"Fuck him!"

"Now dear, there's no call for –"

"No Mam, *fuck* Gareth. He's not here, I am! I'm the one who looks after you, clothes you, feeds you. Without me where would you be, eh?" He was aware he was breathing hard, his pulse pounding in his ears. "*Of course* I know what I'm doing! Anyway, they're not *really* Nazis," he said, turning on his Nan.

She said nothing, just continued to knit.

"They're a means to an end. Once we have enough weapons and vehicles, we can push them out of the picture altogether."

"And they're just going to let you, are they?" his Dad said.

"They won't have any choice."

"Listen to him. They're supplying *you* with stuff and you're talking about taking them on and beating them. They could wipe you out like *that*, lad." His father snapped his fingers.

The Dragon growled. "We could take them. Just like we did with Hood's men."

"That's going to come back and bite you on the arse, as well."

"How so?"

"They won't be best pleased when they see what you did to their headquarters."

"That was the whole idea. That's why I released one of them. When Hood sees what I've done, he'll think twice about moving against me."

"You're underestimating him."

His mother nodded. "He does sound like a very rough customer to me."

The Dragon sighed.

His Dad continued: "Remember all those stories about what he did. That man pretending to be the Sheriff of Nottingham, the Russian fella? He's someone who's not frightened easily."

"And what would you know about military strategy?"

"Please, can we stop arguing?" his mother pleaded. "I hate it when you two don't get along."

Ignoring his wife, the Dragon's father pressed on, "What do I know? Only what I learnt on the rugby pitch, boy."

"Hmmm, you mean the way no-one would tackle a larger opponent, someone who seems stronger, you mean? Someone filled with enough confidence to make people think twice? That's exactly what I'm banking on."

"I think you're out of your tiny mind," his father stated, finally.

"Oh, you do, do you? Well –"

A knock on the door interrupted the dispute and they all looked at each other. Then the Dragon remembered he'd asked for lunch to be brought down. "Enter!"

The woman who came in didn't meet his eye as she wheeled in a trolley carrying a silver soup tureen, bowls and fresh bread on plates. The Dragon gestured for her to serve each of his relatives with the soup. The servant was actually not doing such a bad job. He remembered seeing her for the first time, when the men brought her before him as part of a recent haul. She'd been a little too old for his tastes compared with some of the others – that silver-blonde hair a turn off. By no means bad looking, but she reminded him a little too much of some of the teachers back at school. But he'd decided she was ideal to run about after his family, as some of the younger girls just weren't cut out for that kind of thing. It transpired she'd worked in a nursing home back before the fall of mankind, so he'd set her to work washing his father daily, changing the sheets on his bed. As much as his Mam wanted to help, she was getting on a bit herself and it was too much for her. Besides, why have servants and do the work yourself?

Meghan, wasn't it? Yes, that was the woman's name. He watched as she set the soup down first beside his Nan, then his Mam, who both thanked her – they didn't get the whole concept of personal slaves – and then on the table beside his father. The older man said nothing, but struggled to sit himself up.

"What are you waiting for?" the Dragon said to Meghan. "Bring a tray across and put it over his knees."

The Dragon's mother nodded, smiling. He knew what she was thinking: *See? A good boy to his Dad after all.*

As Meghan set up the tray, her hands were shaking a little. But it was as she served his Dad's soup that she spilled it on the bed, catching his leg with the hot liquid. The man cried out and Meghan stepped back, hand to her mouth. "I-I'm sorry, I –"

"You stupid bitch!" shouted the Dragon. "Look what you've done!"

She grabbed a cloth and started mopping up the soup.

"Now dear, it was only an accident," said the Dragon's mother, trying to keep the peace.

"I'll have you killed!" the Dragon screamed, and Meghan burst into tears.

"There's no need for that," his Nan told him. She'd never really liked his father. "The lady's been doing a good job."

And the more the Dragon thought about it, the more the idea of his Dad getting a little burned did appeal. A lesson for arguing with him. Perhaps he had overreacted, annoyed that his father had personally witnessed one of his staff cock up. But there was no actual harm done, save for a bit of scalding maybe. His Nan was right: this woman *had* done a good job up to now.

But the Dragon couldn't be seen to be too soft. "Get out," he told Meghan. "Wait in the hall, while I think about suitable disciplinary action."

She left, still in tears, closing the door behind her. The Dragon's father was glaring at him.

"What will you do to her?" his mother asked.

"I haven't decided yet. She'll be punished."

"Like you do to all those other women," his father hissed. "The ones you think we don't know about."

"Ryn!" snapped the Dragon's mother.

The Dragon ignored them both, and called for the guards to come and wheel him out. It always made him feel uncomfortable, the things they knew. How they knew was anyone's guess; quizzing the guards, quizzing the slaves who saw to them? The Dragon dismissed all this from his mind, as his guards brought him out into the corridor. There was Meghan, as he'd instructed. She was still sobbing. And something about that, the mixture of her tears and her resemblance to some of his old teachers, made him wonder if he'd been too hasty in relegating her to simple menial chores. He'd discipline her, yes, as he had never had the chance to do to those teachers who put him down when he was young.

Then, who knows.

"Like you do to all those other women," came his father's voice again, echoing in his mind.

It went without saying, but he could also hear the man suggesting that Gareth would never have done such a thing. He wouldn't need to do things like that to women, because he'd have had his pick – if he'd lived.

Dead, and still speaking to him.

The Dragon decided to take his mind off his problems for a while.

CHAPTER ELEVEN

IT HAD TAKEN some time to recover.

The sights that he'd witnessed had exhausted him, mentally and physically. He was convinced no human had ever witnessed anything like it, so in one way he felt privileged. In another, it made him feel small, inconsequential: a tiny cog in a massive machine. He had his role to play, obviously, and a duty to perform that they couldn't possibly complete in his realm. But in the grand scheme of things...

Shadow kept checking that the pouch was still at his hip. Its contents were an important part of pulling this whole thing off. After he'd woken, and after he'd drunk a *lot* of water, he'd gathered the ashes at the place where the forest gods had been subdued. With that taken care of, it was time for the next part of his plan to be put into effect.

That would involve travelling to the Hooded Man's other home. The castle at Nottingham. Entering the city would not be easy, he'd anticipated that. Hood's Rangers patrolled the territory and didn't leave much room for manoeuvre. But there were always ways into places. Shadow felt brave, he felt lucky; with such forces guiding him, how could he possibly fail?

The Rangers were good at concealment, he'd give them that. But he'd sniffed out their presence from a mile away, enabling him to avoid patrols, keep away from the lookout posts and sneak into the city as the sun fell at his back.

He'd studied and memorised maps of the city before leaving for these isles, and it stood him in good stead when it came to negotiating his way to the castle. Once again, Shadow was conscious of the parallels between him and the man who might have been, given different circumstances, a brother in arms. How many times had Hood done this to creep up on an enemy, taking out their defences and leaving the way clear for his Rangers? That wasn't Shadow's intention today. He was just one man, and, in spite of the backup he had on the ethereal plane, he had no army ready to move in once he opened the gates.

What he wanted was not to bring about the downfall of the castle, unlike other visitors in the last few years. He wanted something from it. More specifically, *someone*. It wasn't the Hooded Man himself, because Shadow knew he wasn't here. When he'd severed Hood's link to his beloved forest, Shadow had sensed that the man was quite some distance from both Sherwood and Nottingham. But there were others, people important to Hood, still present at the castle.

It was one of these Shadow was stalking.

He leapt across rooftops, he darted through streets, his agility second to none. Not one patrol or guard spotted him and not one alarm was raised. Pretty soon Shadow came to the castle walls. Scaling the cliff was one option, and held the least risk of detection. Then there were the caves at the Brewhouse Yard, although they were sure to be guarded and he would have to incapacitate the Rangers there. Unfortunate, especially if someone happened to stumble upon them while he was still inside.

That left the walls, which were patrolled regularly, or the main gates. Not an easy decision, but he was running out of time.

As he was waiting, Shadow observed an unusual amount of activity just beyond those gates. Several units of Rangers mounting horses, readying themselves to leave the grounds. There must be something going on, some kind of emergency. This was good timing, and good news in two ways: there would be fewer Rangers inside, which slashed the chances of him being seen, and it suggested a way to gain entrance. Quickly, he made his way across the roof he was on, swung over the edge and began climbing down, just as the gates were opening and the first batch of Rangers were departing. The noise and confusion of so many horses and their riders leaving the castle at the same time was excellent cover, and Shadow was able to slip through the gates easily. He pressed his back up against the wall while another stream of Rangers flowed through. Shadow became his namesake; entering silently and unseen, keeping to the pockets of blackness where the torches illuminating the castle grounds didn't extend. As invisible as the wind, he began exploring. It was an interesting experience. Even at night the castle was a place of safety, a haven for those living under Hood's protection. He was no evil overlord, rather someone trying to bring back balance to a world that had tipped too far over the edge.

Handfuls of Rangers – men and women alike – laughed and joked as they toured the grounds; there were families here, children. Shadow almost envied these people their existence. He had never known a proper home, never felt that he fitted in, not even with his own people. Shadow shook himself. He couldn't let thoughts like this distract him from his task. Making his way silently through the grounds, he discovered a set of steps leading to the castle itself. Then, looking left and right, he entered without making a sound.

MARK SAT STARING at the radio, trying to get his head round everything that he'd been told in the last twenty-four hours. The airwaves had never been so busy, communications coming in from Ranger groups on routine assignments, from Bill, from Jack. And there was something to be said for the old adage – no news is good news – because everything they'd received had been bad: pure and simple.

First, Bill had informed him that they'd heard nothing from Robert and Mary since they'd taken a team of Rangers to Edinburgh Castle to check out this Widow. What had happened, no-one yet knew, and although Mark still held out some hope they might return, it was looking increasingly likely they'd either been captured or –

To take his mind off that, Mark recalled what Jack had said earlier on that day – relaying information about the Dragon from Dale. He'd been sent inside to spy on the man; a mission Mark had actually argued *he* was ready for, but Jack and Robert had vetoed him as usual. Even after everything he'd gone through in the field, Mark knew when they looked at him they still saw that kid with the dirty-blond hair they'd first met when De Falaise invaded England. He'd changed so much since those days. Mark was an adult now, even had a girlfriend – the lovely Sophie – which he had to admit had taken up a lot of his time in recent months. Sooner or later the others were going to have to accept he'd grown up.

Hadn't he shown them he was ready for combat? What did Mark have to do to prove he was worthy? Even the dreams he'd been having since starting those trips with Robert into the forest had suggested he should be given more responsibility. He'd learnt to interpret them quite well, the symbols and meanings; talking to Robert about them, because he knew his adoptive father had them as well. The last one Mark experienced had seen him running through the forest, too close to the ground to be on human legs. His running was awkward, not coordinated – at first, anyway. But Mark found that the further and faster he ran, the stronger those legs became. And then he could see them beneath him, a browny colour with white specks. The legs of a young fawn, but one that was growing fast.

Soon enough, Mark found himself at the lake at Rufford, where he stared down into the water at his reflection. There were antlers there now, budding now, but growing at the same pace as the rest of him. Something was wrong, though; droplets of red in the water, falling from a wound Mark couldn't see. He looked up and saw a grown stag across the water, looking at him. Behind the creature was a man dressed in red, with a sickle for a hand. In one movement, he drew that blade across the stag's throat, allowing a jet of red to shoot out across the lake. Mark tried to scream, but a shadow fell across the lake from behind him.

Mark hadn't had time to register anything else, because he'd been woken out of the dream by Robert calling him for breakfast by the campfire. If nothing else, the analogy about growing up was clear. Mark was almost there, and he deserved the right to be treated like a grown man. He should be –

Mark stiffened. There was someone behind him, just like in the dream he'd had all those weeks ago. He pulled off the earphones, rising from the chair at the same time; his heart going like a piston. He let out a sigh of relief when he saw Sophie standing there with a plate, holding a beef sandwich.

She smiled. "Sorry, didn't mean to startle you. Just thought you might like a bite to eat."

Mark smiled back. That sandwich did look good. "I'm sorry. Just a little on edge is all. Ta." He leaned over, took the plate gratefully, and gave her a kiss. Taking his face in both her hands, she pressed her lips harder against his. When she pulled away, his smile grew even wider. "What was that for?"

"Do I need a reason?"

Mark laughed. "No, I guess not. And I'm *so* not complaining."

"I just haven't seen much of you today."

Mark pointed to the radio. "Been stuck monitoring, in case anything else came in. You heard about what's going on, I suppose?"

Sophie nodded. "I'm worried about Robert and Mary."

"Me too. At least when we were fighting the Sheriff and the Tsar, we were dealing with them one at a time. Now we seem to be split between tackling these Dragon and Widow loonies."

Sophie leaned on the table next to him. "What exactly did Dale say about the Dragon?"

There was a time when Mark would have felt threatened by that question; by the implication that Dale was on Sophie's mind. But way too much water had passed under the bridge for that. He felt secure now about how Sophie felt, knew she only saw Dale as a mate. In fact, he'd got to know Dale a lot better himself over the past year, and once that initial jealousy had evaporated, Mark actually found himself liking the guy, too. "You mean what did he say about our mutual friend?"

Sophie nodded again, more sombrely. She remembered fighting Tanek last year as well as he did – it was one of the things that had brought them closer together. "I heard he was acting as some kind of go-between, supplying weapons and vehicles. But didn't Bill also say that the Widow was being supplied with arms from somewhere?"

"He said the weapons they took from her raiders were German."

Sophie looked at him seriously. "You don't think there could be a connection, do you?"

"What, Tanek dealing with both the Dragon and the Widow? Working with the Germans?" Mark bit his lip. It was a thought that hadn't occurred to him, but now Sophie had put it in his head, he couldn't shake it. And it terrified him. "God, I hope not."

"Isn't that what he and De Falaise used to do before? Gun-running?"

"Amongst other things." The more he thought about it, the more he wanted to fire up that radio and ask Jack and Bill's opinion. Sophie had definitely struck on something. Mark jotted down a note on the pad by the side of the radio as a reminder to broach it when Bill and Jack next checked in. He picked up the sandwich Sophie had brought, considered taking a bite, but found he'd lost his appetite.

"So what are Jack and Bill going to do?" she asked.

"Jack's requested more Rangers, in addition to those who left this afternoon. They've just been sent. I think he wants to go in and sort the Dragon problem before it gets any worse. Reading between the lines, he also wants to get Dale out of there as quickly as possible."

"Understandable. And Bill?"

Mark shrugged. "Don't think anything's been decided yet. For one thing, if we send any more men up there, we'll hardly have anyone left at the castle. And the last time we did that, it didn't end well."

"So Lord knows what could be happening to Mary and Robert, and we just have to sit here?" Sophie said, folding her arms.

"That's about the size of it. Welcome to my world."

Sophie reached over and stroked his hair, brushing a strand off his forehead. "Your time will come, Mark, you'll see."

Man, he loved this girl – and as he thought it, he rose and kissed her again. She responded in kind, wrapping her arms around him. More than anything in this world, Mark wanted Sophie right then. But it was her that broke off the kiss.

"Not like this, Mark," she said, looking into his eyes, then looking around. She knew what he was thinking, because she was thinking it herself. If they didn't stop now, they never would – and on the table of a radio room was not the most romantic place for your first time. Mark was surprised they'd been able to hold off this long, but he hadn't wanted to rush Sophie. They'd talked about it, sure, and been on the verge several times, but somehow never quite got it together. Mark sensed that tonight they were both ready.

"How about I get someone to take over here?" he suggested. "Then we can find somewhere a bit more private."

Sophie smiled again, then nodded enthusiastically.

Mark kissed her a final time, excited but petrified. Emotions were coursing through him, and doubts about whether he'd be any good, what Sophie might think of him afterwards... But none of that would matter once they were shut away alone.

It was as he was heading towards the door that he heard it. Sounds of a scuffle outside. Punches being thrown and a cry.

Sophie looked at him. "What was that?"

"I don't know," Mark replied, realising that the chances of him and Sophie being alone right now had just taken a massive dip. "Let's find out."

REVEREND TATE HAD just rounded the corner when he'd spotted the intruder.

Dressed in muted colours, in clothes that looked handmade, the figure almost blended in with his surroundings – making good use of the dim lighting in the hallway. Tate doubted very much whether he would have spotted him at all, but the man had sacrificed the shadows in order to spy inside a room to his left: the radio room. Tate had heard the reports about Robert and Mary going missing, the Dragon being in league with Tanek. It had made him more vigilant. Usually when things like that started happening, someone, somewhere made an attempt at the castle.

And perhaps this man in front of him was part of the first wave? Tate took in the rest of the fellow. He didn't seem to be armed with any kind of modern weapon, no machine-guns or pistols. There was a bow and quiver at his back, and what looked to be an axe and knife on his belt. Tate couldn't see the man's face at this angle, and given the length of his black hair. Though it was hard to tell, the man's skin tone was slightly darker than his; perhaps from the Middle East? Tate hesitated, reminded of a moment in his own past...

Now wasn't the time.

He definitely spelt trouble. Gripping his stick tighter, Tate made an effort to get nearer. He wasn't the most practised at this kind of thing – not like Robert or Azhar, say – but he had his moments. He could still remember how to sneak up on an enemy.

The intruder didn't seem to notice him – he was transfixed by what was being said inside the room. And Tate could now hear voices: Mark and Sophie's. They were discussing the day's events, unaware that everything was being overheard.

Then Tate was behind the intruder. He realised he hadn't thought the rest of this through. Would he just hit the man over the head with his stick, or confront him, try and find out what he was doing here? Or maybe that should come later when they had him locked up?

In any event, he didn't get the chance. The man whirled, ready for him. He'd heard Tate's approach all along, just wanted him to get closer so he wouldn't have to make as much noise incapacitating him. Or maybe he just wanted to see who was stupid enough to think they could take him down. In the instant Tate had time to register what was happening, he finally saw the man's face. The arching eyebrows sheltering intense, dark eyes; the distinctive shape of the nose, cheekbones and mouth. He hadn't seen many of this man's kind, but he recognised the features immediately: a Native American.

Tate didn't have any more time to consider this, because as the man turned he also brought round a fist. The punch would have knocked him clean out had the holy man not been quick enough to block it with his forearm. The intruder tried again with his other fist, but Tate blocked that as well. This was one of the things in Tate's favour, it seemed; the Native American hadn't been expecting him to fend off the first blow, let alone the second. He'd done as most people had, to their cost: underestimated the Reverend, written him off as just an overweight cripple with a stick. That was their first mistake.

They didn't usually get a chance to make a second.

This man did, blocking Tate's own swing with the stick – catching it between two hands and attempting to force it out of the Reverend's grasp. But Tate was stronger than he appeared and, with a grunt, held on to the only weapon he ever carried.

The stranger kicked out unexpectedly in a move Tate had never come across before. It caught him unawares and he only just had time to step back and avoid it. As he did so, his opponent drew the axe on his belt. He held it high and swung it, forcing Tate to bring his stick up lengthways. The edge of the axe embedded in the wood, but then the man got in a swift punch to the chin with his free hand.

Tate took the blow with practised ease, rolling with it so as not to cause too much damage. The next one came so fast, though, he couldn't help but let out a small cry as the man's fist slammed into his cheek. Tate slid back against the wall, dropping slightly. The Native American yanked his axe out of Tate's stick. Still reeling, Tate released the stick with one hand and swung it like a club at the intruder – who ducked, coming back up and batting the stick away with his elbow. He then slid it under his arm so that Tate couldn't use it, pulling backwards and at last disarming the holy man.

Tate just had time to see Mark at the doorway before the stranger swivelled, using the priest's own stick against him; striking him on the side of the head. Everything went black as Tate felt himself slide down the wall.

He vaguely heard the exchange between Mark and the stranger, but couldn't hold on to consciousness any longer.

As he always did in situations like this – when he felt helpless and he'd done everything he possibly could – the Reverend Tate prayed.

SHADOW HAD BEEN aware of the man behind him even before his opponent reached the corner.

Yes, he'd been focused on what the teenage boy and girl were saying, not because the information meant anything to him – Shadow cared nothing about what happened in Wales and Scotland – but because it might hold ramifications for his mission. As soon as he'd heard them mention Robert was missing in action, he'd tuned in. That could affect his plans. How do you lure someone into a trap when they've already been caught by somebody else? This Widow, it seemed, had the Hooded Man in her web, which might potentially mess things up for Shadow.

Nevertheless, he had to press on – trust that forces with more vision than him had things well in hand. That meant handling this situation. Shadow came out from the darkness, let himself be seen – and at the same time saw the overweight man out of the corner of his eye. It would have been comical if it were not for the seriousness of his predicament. The local was hardly worthy of his attention, had it not been for the fact that he needed to complete his task, hopefully without drawing undue attention to himself.

Shadow had to admit, the older man had surprised him. He'd fought admirably. There was more to the stocky individual than met the eye; he'd drawn Shadow into a fracas he had neither the time nor the inclination for. That was what had made him draw his axe, to get it over and done with. His misdirection had worked and Shadow had finally been able to floor his enemy.

It was only as the man slid down the wall and his jacket opened that Shadow saw what he was wearing beneath: the black shirt buttoned up to the top, the dog collar. He'd been fighting with a religious man. All right, not *his* religion, but a religion all the same. It was another surprise, from an opponent who had astounded him already. The Reverend had fought like a soldier, but stood for the doctrines of peace and goodwill. Shadow was still thinking about this when he heard the boy say from behind:

"Reverend Tate? Hey, get away from him!"

Shadow turned, holstering his axe and looking the boy up and down – not that he hadn't seen him before in the room, but now he was assessing how much of a threat he would be. He'd been wrong about the priest, and didn't intend to make a snap decision this time. The figure in front of him might only be a kid, but could well be highly trained.

"Who are you?" asked the boy.

"That is not important," Shadow told him, stalling for time as he glided forward, leaving the felled clergyman. Shadow saw the boy's eyes flash sideways, about to call out, sound an alarm and cry for help. Shadow couldn't let that happen. He dove at him, pushing the boy back into the radio room.

The boy grabbed Shadow's wrists, taking him backwards in an attempt to throw him over. More a wrestling move than anything, which made Shadow wonder just who had trained him. He was good; but Shadow was better. He resisted, letting the boy hit the ground, but tearing himself away and standing upright.

The girl with the freckles made a move to attack. Turning her lunge back on her, Shadow put an arm around the girl and had his knife at her throat in seconds. It stopped her from struggling, and gave the boy on the floor pause for thought. He would not do anything stupid while there was a blade at his woman's throat.

"What do you want?" asked the young man as he started to rise again.

"That is not *your* concern. Which one of you means the most to the Hooded Man?"

"Me," said the girl quickly. "I'm his daughter."

The boy on the ground opened his mouth to contradict her, but Shadow could tell the girl was lying anyway. "Try again."

"It's me," her boyfriend said. "I'm his... son." There had been some hesitation, and it was true that in trying to save the girl he might well say anything. This wasn't Hood's flesh and blood, Shadow sensed that much, yet it *was* his son.

"You will come with me," Shadow said.

The girl was about to scream until Shadow increased the pressure of the blade.

"Don't," he warned her. Then, once he was sure she would keep quiet, he shifted the knife to her side, still keeping the pressure there. He instructed the boy to rip a sleeve from his shirt, and forced the girl to bind him with it at the wrists. With another strip, taken from the bottom of the boy's trousers, she gagged him.

"You won't make it out of here," she promised him. Shadow took no notice. He turned the knife around and brought the hilt down on the back of her head, and she slumped to the floor. The boy began to growl something through the gag, and Shadow realised that it wouldn't be nearly enough to shut him up as they exited the castle. So he did the same to the boy – a glancing blow to the side of the head, rendering him unconscious.

He went back out into the corridor and dragged the priest into the room, leaving him and his stick lying next to the girl. Shadow spotted the notebook and pen on the table and scribbled something on the paper, below what had already been written. A note for the Hooded Man, when he returned.

Finally, he hefted his unconscious prize onto his shoulder and, checking the corridor, stepped out and closed the door behind him. Shadow allowed the pockets of darkness to cover both him and his captive, until they were outside the castle, where it consumed them completely.

CHAPTER TWELVE

HE'D BEEN LOATH to split up again; in a place like this, you had to ask yourself if you'd see the other person alive again. But, as Sian had pointed out, she was meant to be in a certain area, and so was he. If they didn't return, it could raise suspicions.

"I have to get back to the other girls," she told Dale. "You should be in the kitchens."

Reluctantly, he'd agreed. They'd already taken a risk with the radio operator – though they'd poured even more of the booze down his throat, and left him leaning back in the chair. He wouldn't be waking up anytime soon, nor remembering much when he did. Concussion and whiskey would see to that. He'd probably be reported, too, when he was discovered, for drinking on the job; put somewhere to dry out... or worse. Dale doubted the Dragon took very kindly to that kind of behaviour.

Splitting up would mean they'd double their chances of finding out something about Sian's Aunty Meghan.

"Can I ask you something?" Dale had said just before they parted.

"Sure. Anything."

"I have to ask about... you and The Dragon."

"You *really* want to know what happened? What happens when he takes a girl away?"

Dale wasn't sure that he did, but the question was out there anyway. It had been hounding him since Sian had been dragged off, and even more so now that he'd gotten to know her a little. "I couldn't stop thinking about you and that creep."

"I think I got off lightly compared to some. He... he made me dance for him a little; told me what he'd *like* to do to me. But, well, in the end he couldn't."

"What?"

"You know: the *big* couldn't. To tell the truth, I don't think he's actually been with a woman. A girl can just tell these things sometimes."

"And what happened then?"

"Then he sent for the guards to take me away."

"So he's not really got what he wanted from you?"

"With a bit of luck, he never will."

Dale had to be content with that, and hope that while they were trying to find Meghan, Jack was planning something major on the outside. He'd considered taking a quick look around before heading back to the kitchen, but apart from the time factor – it'd already taken quite a while to find the radio room and send the message – he had no idea where the meeting between the Dragon and Tanek was taking place. The only good thing was that at least Dale and Tanek had never met, so he wasn't likely to recognise him as a Ranger, even if he bumped into him accidentally. Convincing himself there wasn't much more he could do, Dale figured his time was probably better spent helping Sian.

Thankfully, the Dragon didn't have much call for food overnight. It gave Dale some leeway, and after grabbing a couple of hours of restless sleep, he was up and about and looking into Sian's aunty. And praying the Dragon didn't call on the girl in the meantime.

That morning, he asked around some of the members of staff he'd become friendly with, people who liked to gossip. It was surprising how much, actually, seeing as they were supposed to be in fear of their lives. But people were people whatever the situation, and talking about folk behind their backs was still a popular pastime even in this post-apocalyptic age. A middle aged woman called Sally, who did a lot of the cooking for the Dragon and his soldiers, had been of most use. She told him that there was a maid called Meghan who their boss had drafted into his innermost personnel.

"I'm surprised you haven't seen her yourself," she told him. "She comes to collect food and drink most mealtimes."

"For the Dragon?" asked a puzzled Dale, who did recall seeing a woman wheeling a trolley away from the kitchens from time to time, but hadn't paid much attention to her.

"Don't know and haven't asked. Best way, round here."

He'd kept an eye out, around lunchtime especially, but Dale almost missed her when he was roped into fixing sandwiches for some of the Dragon's men, back from patrol. As he looked over again, trying not to draw attention to himself, there she was finally – wheeling in an empty trolley to be loaded up. There was definitely a resemblance to Sian. The woman had a purple bruise flowering on her right eye.

Dale finished up the sandwich he was working on, then went over on the pretext of lending a hand. He made sure he caught her attention as he was placing the food on the trolley – there looked to be enough for three people there, but that was nothing new with the Dragon. Dale waited until it had all been piled on, then offered to keep the door open as she backed the trolley out.

"I need to speak to you," he whispered when she was close enough.

Meghan glanced away, nervously scanning the room, then said, loud enough for everyone nearby to hear: "Would you mind giving me a hand getting this into the lift?" Dale nodded, flashing what he hoped was a reassuring smile. He began to speak in the hallway, but she shook her head sharply as two of the Dragon's men walked by. Dale took hold of the other side of the trolley, and when they eventually reached the lift, Meghan motioned for him to enter with her. However, so did another of the Dragon's soldiers, squeezing in just before the doors closed. Meghan asked the man what floor he wanted, then pressed the number for them all to descend.

The man got out a couple of stops before them, but when Dale began again, Meghan pressed a finger to his lips. The doors finally opened on their level and Dale helped her out with the trolley.

"Okay, it's safe to talk now."

"Safe?"

"His eyes and ears are everywhere. We should keep walking, I can't be late delivering this stuff."

"To the Dragon?"

Meghan shook her head. "To his family."

"He has *family* here?" This was a new one on Dale, and information he could probably use later, especially if Jack and the other Rangers showed up.

"Mother, father and grandmother. I'm basically their slave."

Figures, thought Dale. The Dragon saw people as his property, so why would his family act any different? It was probably even their fault. "That who gave you the eye? His father?"

Meghan shook her head, and he could feel her hand shaking as she pushed the trolley. "I spilt some soup on his Dad, though. Had to be punished."

Dale couldn't tell whether she actually believed the last bit. Had she been here so long that it felt normal to be beaten for spilling soup? Jesus, look what that fat bastard was doing to these people. For a second Dale wondered if the punishment had involved more than just the punch, but didn't ask; he was afraid to. And more than a little afraid that Sian would get similar before too long.

"Look, I'm going to get you out of here. You *and* Sian." Meghan stopped the trolley, a look of complete surprise on her face. "That's right, she's here as well. I'm meeting her in a bit. She came to find you. Don't worry, come with me and –"

"Nobody escapes from here. He kills anyone who tries."

"I don't doubt it, but you have to trust that I'm going to get you both away from this... this..." Dale struggled to find words to describe the place and failed. He'd witnessed more depravity here than all his time on the streets and as a Ranger put together.

"You'll be killed. We all will. He's insane!"

"Look, you have to trust me, Meghan."

"I-I've got to deliver this. If I don't he'll send his men to find me."

That was true, it would arouse more suspicion than ever if the Dragon's family didn't get their grub. "Okay, but I'm coming with you."

"No, you mustn't. It's –"

"Not inside. I'll wait in the corridor. But now I've found you I'm not letting you out of my sight."

Meghan's hands were shaking again, but she nodded. When they arrived at the corridor in question, he let Meghan walk down it alone. There was nobody else around that he could see. Pretty weird in itself, but Dale reasoned that the Dragon probably wanted privacy for his family. He wondered if most of the guards even knew about them. Meghan looked back over at him just once before knocking, and he smiled again to try and reassure her. Then she was inside, and all he could do was wait for her to come out.

He wasn't standing there long, though, when he heard the first of the screams. It was definitely Meghan. Dale raced up the corridor to the room she'd entered. He threw open the door and was already inside before he realised something was wrong. The room was in semi-darkness. There was no sign of Meghan or the trolley, let alone the Dragon's family. Just a bank of monitors throwing out the only light. Dale wondered how they were still working, but then the Dragon had all kinds of electrical stuff rigged up. He looked at the monitors more closely, seeing what they were displaying – various parts of the stadium: guards walking up and down corridors; the pitch outside; the entrance; even the lift he'd just been in. A damned CCTV system!

He'd noticed the cameras all around, of course he had, but he'd assumed they weren't on. Dale hadn't seen one of these in operation since before the Cull. But if the other stuff was working, why shouldn't these be as well? *Stupid, stupid!*

There was the *clack* of a machine-gun being cocked behind him, then another, and a third. Dale froze. A switch was flipped, flooding the room with light. The Dragon was wheeled around in front of him by Meghan.

I don't believe this, thought Dale. She'd led him right into a trap. How could he have been so –

The Dragon suddenly grabbed her arm and threw her violently to the floor, where she knelt, crying. Dale could see now that her lip was split and bleeding; those screams had been for real. "Why don't you come further in?" he said, his voice making Dale squirm. "Come on, don't be shy. After all, you haven't been, during your time here, have you?"

Dale was prodded forwards with the barrel of a rifle.

"Oh, I've been keeping tabs on you for a while now, all your little excursions. Quite innocent to the casual observer, but you did keep cropping up here, there and everywhere. Sort of like a really crap Jason Bourne." The Dragon laughed. "Except the spy was being spied on himself. I like that, don't you? And then last night... Oh, last night. I didn't catch the show live, of course, because I had other things to attend to, as you probably already know. But thankfully everything was being recorded and I watched it all back today. Made for very interesting viewing. Nice touch trying to frame the radio operator, by the way, but very sloppily executed. Unlike him." The Dragon leaned forward. "What I still don't know is who you are and who you're working for. You see, some of the cameras have picture, but no sound. Who exactly were you contacting on the radio?"

"Nobody."

The Dragon held up his hand. "Save the bullshit. When I saw those pictures, who do you think I spoke to first, eh?" He pointed to one of the screens behind him. Right next to the one showing the harem's showers – in use right that minute, to Dale's disgust – was Sian in a room, strapped to a chair, head back and unconscious. "But she wouldn't tell me anything either, even under... duress."

"You fucking shit, I'll –"

"Be realistic; you'll do nothing." He kicked out at Meghan, who was attempting to stand. "That's why you shouldn't think so badly of this poor cow. Oh, I know exactly who she is, now; don't I, sweetheart? And I do so believe in family loyalty. That's why she brought you here, although you didn't need much persuading, I have to say. I just showed her what was on that screen, said her precious niece would be cut up into little pieces right in front of her if she didn't do exactly what I said. Actually, be thankful my foreign friend isn't still around; he would have enjoyed doing that, I think."

I'll bet he would, thought Dale.

"The stupid bitch still tried to warn you, though." Another kick and Meghan was pitched forwards on her hands and knees. "Unfortunately for you, the audio works just fine in the lift and corridors in this section." He grinned.

Now Dale thought about it, Meghan *had* tried to stop him, even though it would have put both herself and Sian in danger.

"I'll come with you."

"No, you mustn't."

She'd tried to tell him about the cameras, too: *"He has eyes and ears everywhere."* Dale had just assumed that she was talking about his men.

"It's funny, I was warned about a danger from within, but this still came as a bit of a surprise."

"Warned?" Dale said before he could stop himself.

"My family. Ever since the virus, they come out with things... the strangest things."

"Please! You have to do something!" Meghan said to Dale. Tears were streaming down her face. "He's crazy. His family are –"

Before she could get another word out, the Dragon had hefted himself a couple of inches forward, the front wheel of his sled rolling over the woman's hand. Dale heard the cracking as the bones broke under that weight, then another scream from Meghan – much louder than the first. Dale winced. The Dragon ignored the cries.

"Tell me what I want to know, or this is only the beginning. I'll make them both suffer. And from what I've seen already, you're not a man who'd enjoy that." The Dragon paused, eyeing Dale up and down. "Or are you? Hmm? Perhaps you enjoy seeing women get hurt? Perhaps you've hurt a few in the past as well?" The Dragon rolled off Meghan's hand and she clutched it to her chest, howling in agony.

Fucking mind games, Dale said to himself. The Dragon didn't know the first thing about him. *Concentrate.* Meghan was right, he had to do something to stop this. But what? There were at least three men behind him, and so many more outside these doors. He'd often wondered what the scenario would be if he got caught. Bourne? More like Bond, complete with the psychopathic villain. All the Dragon needed was a cat. It'd be funny if it wasn't so real.

Dale looked over at the screens again, seeing Sian there, helpless.

Two damsels in quite a bit of distress, and he couldn't help either. And then his eyes caught something else on one of the screens. Something everyone in the room seemed to have missed. Movement between the seats out in the stadium itself – brief flashes, tiny but unmistakable. Hoods, the tips of bows, a flash of metal. The Rangers – his friends – were here. If he could just hold on a while longer...

But he'd have to do something to make sure nobody saw the screens just yet.

Dale's mind raced. *Okay, you want mind games, mate. I'll give you mind games.* "I guess that's all you can really do, isn't it?"

"I'm sorry?" said the Dragon.

"Hurt them, get them to perform for you. It's not like you can do anything else with them, you limp-dicked chubster."

The Dragon's face reddened. "What?"

"I bet your men don't even know that, do they? All those women you collect and you can't even get it up when you're alone with them, can you?"

He stared at Dale, fuming. "Shut your mouth."

"Some Dragon. Some leader of men. You're not much of a man at all, really, are you? All you can do is watch, perv over them and wish you were more like some of these guys who fetch and carry for you. Who protect you."

"I said shut the fuck up!"

"I bet it's all recorded somewhere as well, all those times you've made women do things, but haven't been able to satisfy them. Bet the proof's right there for any of your men to see."

"If you don't shut your mouth –"

"What is it, the weight? Or something else? Don't tell me, you have issues with strong women, don't you? Mummy's boy, were we? Is that it? Or maybe even your Dad? Was he the problem? Was he a *real* man, Dragon?"

"I. Said. *SHUT UP!*" roared the Dragon, leaning forward so far in his sled it was rocking.

"Well, come on, if you think you can take me. You don't need these guys to fight your battles as well, do you? Come on, then!"

The Dragon raised himself up, and it was at that moment the sled wobbled over, crashing sideways to the floor. Dale used the distraction to drop to the ground, as the men behind opened fire – hitting some of the screens, shattering the ones chronicling the Rangers' progress. Dale rolled backwards, taking the guards' legs out from under them. Sending them sprawling in all directions.

He was up first, elbowing one in the face to keep him down and snatching his rifle. The second he shot in the leg; the third he took out with the butt of the rifle. Even if he wasn't as slick as Bourne or Bond, he fought like them: hard and fast, getting rid of the Dragon's men in here, at least.

But not the Dragon himself. As Dale rose, the man was charging towards him – faster than Dale ever would have thought. He'd probably been even quicker in the days before piling on all that meat, but was still quick enough to slam Dale backwards into the wall.

"Not a man, eh? We'll see about that," he grunted as he swatted Dale's gun aside with a flabby arm.

Dale had no room; when he threw his punch – hard, in the kidneys, which should have crippled his opponent – it simply sank in, having no effect whatsoever. The Dragon might have been overweight, but he knew how to use that to his advantage, crushing Dale against the solid wall, gripping him by the throat.

Dale kicked out, but that had no more effect than the punch. The Dragon squeezed his opponent's windpipe harder. "Who. Sent. You?" he shouted. "Tell me!"

The sound of an explosion came – it was distant, possibly even in the next building. But a second and third followed, and this time they rocked the room they were in. The Dragon looked up at the ceiling as dust fell.

"Y-you really want to know?" gasped Dale. "You'll get to meet them soon. They're here, Dragon... and they're not... very happy about what you did to their HQ. Or their men."

"A Ranger," breathed the biggest of the two men. "I should have known."

Dale grinned again, but soon stopped when the Dragon lifted him up and shoved him hard against the wall, banging his head. Everything went fuzzy for a moment.

The last thing Dale remembered after that was an angry red face, a face that almost did resemble a Dragon in his muddled mind.

Dale fell; fighting for breath and losing his grip on consciousness.

He could still see only red as he lost both battles.

Then the redness turned to black.

CHAPTER THIRTEEN

How EXACTLY HAD he got into this mess?

He was dangling, suspended, above a fire in what had once been the castle's reservoirs.

He thought he'd been so clever, but like always, he was really only making all this up as he went along, trying to turn something hopeless into a fighting chance.

Maybe this was his punishment for hurting the woman he loved more than life itself. And, in his defence, the Widow's mumbo jumbo did have an effect on him initially. Some kind of weird hypnosis or mind control. The best way he could describe it was like having a waking dream, where you were doing and saying things you wouldn't normally, but had no control over. He cast his mind back to when they'd first been alone together, back in the Vaults where he'd been chained to the wall. She'd had him stripped naked and he'd assumed there would be some kind of torture involved, especially surrounded as he was by the implements. Maybe it was just his turn, he thought. Both Mark and Jack had suffered at the hands of Tanek – Mark coming away missing a finger, while Jack's mental scars ran deeper. If they could brave it, then so could he. He'd had to face worse: up against tanks, jeeps, helicopters, armed with only a bow and arrow.

But torture had been the last thing on her mind.

"I do admire a man who's not afraid of being in the raw," the Widow told him as she'd scrutinised his body, approving eyes passing over his taut muscles. "I've been waitin' fer you to come. Expecting yer."

"So you said. Some kind of tip off."

The Widow might have suspected they'd strike sometime, but couldn't have known *exactly* when without some kinds of heads-up.

"Could say that." The Widow laughed. "But no the kind that

you'd believe. Not yet, anyway." She'd approached him, and placed a hand on his chest. "Good, strong heartbeat," said the Widow, then ran her hands over his torso. Then her hand moved downwards and she gave an approving, suggestive smile.

"Would you like me to cough?" Robert spat.

"Sense of humour. I like that. A perfect man in a lot of ways: fit, strong. Yer know, a lot of men have disappointed me over the years, Robert."

"You do surprise me."

"Something tells me *you* won't disappoint."

He strained against the chains that held his wrists and ankles. "Don't fight it. You and I both know something more powerful than either of us has brought us together. There's something special between us, something we share."

"And what's that?"

She leaned in and breathed: "A kind of magic. 'Course, yours has been weakened, but I can help get it back. Helps me with what's about to follow." The Widow told him it was all in the cards: he'd come, and they would one day rule this country – the world – together.

"With the help of German ingenuity, I suppose," said Robert.

She waved away his comment. "Means to an end. Right now, our countries need each other. But who knows what's around the corner?"

"You do, apparently."

"That's right." The Widow produced a tarot card: a man sitting on a throne, wearing and crown and holding a sword. "This is you, Robert: The Emperor. *My* Emperor. The one I've been looking for my whole life. This is who you will become when we've... joined."

"Are you for real?"

"Aye. An' I knew it was not going to be easy to persuade yer, but I must try."

Then she drew strange markings on the floor and walls around him. Burning odd-smelling incense and candles, leaving them under him so he had no option but to inhale. Robert fought their effects, but it was no use. They made his muscles relax and he hung on the wall like a puppet. She chanted in a language he didn't understand: the words overlapping, tumbling into each other at one point. Robert recalled the Widow lifting his chin, pressing her lips against his, saying something about needing to be sure.

And he remembered the painting she'd done on his body, markings and symbols to complement the words she spoke. He felt drunk, more drunk than he had even on his stag do, just before marrying...

Joanne.

He saw her face, those beautiful eyes, those lips. But it was morphing into someone else. He saw Mary, remembered what had happened, how lost he'd become in the forest when Joanne and his son, Stevie, had died from the A-B virus. How Mary had made him feel human again, her love, her –

Then both faces were replaced with the Widow's, the only person he could see, the only voice he could hear. Over and over, telling him he was hers – that they were destined to be together.

He hadn't even realised he was nodding, until he was doing so. Suddenly it had all made perfect sense, what she was offering him. Though they'd only spent a short time together, those minutes had become hours, days, and somehow he knew this woman better than he ever had Joanne or Mary. So much so that he'd agreed to talk with the latter. The Widow freed him, once she was certain he was under her control, dressing Robert so that he could come with her to meet Mary, to convince *her*.

Even as he'd come forward, walking through that dream haze, speaking words that were his and yet weren't, he'd semi-believed it. Robert told Mary the Widow was going to share her magic, replacing what he'd lost, what had been stolen from him. He believed it all so much he'd taken the ring from Mary's finger.

And then it happened.

Robert recognised that look. He'd been responsible for it once before, when they'd been arguing, drifting apart, when Adele had been on the scene. When there had been doubt in Mary's mind, although Robert had been faithful throughout. That look, that hurt. He'd sworn there and then he'd never do anything to cause it again.

Memories came back to him of all the time he'd spent with Mary, his wedding day, last Christmas. It hit him like a slap in the face, smashing its way through the fog and clearing his mind.

But now was not the time to strike. Robert was still heavily outnumbered, and the Widow had armed guards trained on Mary. The only way was to make that harlot think he was still under her control. The fact that she wanted him so badly, that she thought he was some long-promised love, might just work in his favour. So he'd gone along with the kiss, this time responding as the Widow covered his lips with her own – trying hard to ignore Mary's wails and hoping she might understand if – no, *when* – they finally got out of this.

Mary had been taken back to her cell, and at least out of harm's way. The Widow had held up the hand on which she now wore Mary's wedding ring. "I'll have tae think about changin' ma name."

Afterblight Chronicles: Hooded Man

Robert had smiled, playing along. The spell was definitely broken, but he couldn't allow the woman to see that. Now, it was simply a question of biding his time until he could incapacitate the Widow. That wasn't going to be easy. Even alone, she was a force to be reckoned with.

The question was, how far would he take his performance? Because the Widow was keen to consummate their sham of a marriage. "Come on, lover, I'll show you ma chambers," she'd said, batting her dark eyelashes and pulling on his arm as she dragged him through the halls. There were armed soldiers on every corner, no opportunity for Robert to act. Perhaps he'd stand a better chance when they were alone together in her bedroom.

And what a room it was. Located inside the Royal Palace, it was certainly fitting for a king and queen. The Widow removed her skin-tight trousers, leaving just her corset and a thong on, then lay back on the four poster bed, beckoning him.

Okay, now what? thought Robert. There was no way he was going to go through with this – even if Mary hadn't been in the equation, the Widow was just too damned… scary. No wonder the men in her past had disappointed her. Now here she was, expecting him to step up to the bat, her perfect man.

The Widow patted the bed beside her. "What yer waiting for? Come here." There was a powerful edge to those words, and if he hadn't been such a strong-willed person, Robert might not have been able to resist. More tricks of the mind, and drug fumes from the candles and incense sticks. As it was, he moved forward, almost involuntarily, but still in command of his own body. He was walking stiffly, though, finding it hard to conceal his true feelings. By the time he reached the bed, he could see the Widow suspected something was wrong.

To throw her off the scent, he took off his top and sat down on the mattress.

The Widow propped herself up on one elbow, placing a hand on his chest. "That strong heart's racin'."

"With excitement."

She smiled. "Aye. Let me calm yer down a bit." Her hand snaked lower, but before it could reach its destination, Robert grabbed her wrist. Rather than fighting him, the Widow seemed to enjoy it. "I just knew yer liked it rough," she growled. He grabbed her other wrist, pushing her back down against the bed. But she wrapped her legs around Robert, forcing him down on her her. Obviously her idea of foreplay, but it was more like some of the wrestling moves Jack used.

"Aye, that's it, that's…"

Robert pulled away from her. She gripped him by the shoulders, attempting to draw him down on top of her, but he couldn't help resisting. Almost without warning, the Widow let go of him.

Dammit, she knows, thought Robert.

"There's one link left. She still has a hold on yer, doesn't she?" said the Widow. "Aye. I can see it. I can *feel* it."

Robert said nothing.

"I saw this, as well," the Widow confessed, and now he really knew he was in trouble.

"I-I'm sorry," he offered. And part of him actually was. Because behind those hard eyes of hers, under the exterior – the bravado she put on – was a woman who just wanted to be loved. Who wanted on some level what he and Mary had, who'd been filled up with nonsense about a perfect man when one didn't exist. And certainly wasn't Robert, could never *be* Robert.

"Aye, well, there's only one thing for it." The Widow looked at Robert expectantly, then replied for him. "For me to become yer new Empress, *you* have to kill the former one. Don't worry, there's nothing tae it. I've murdered more exes than yer've fired arrows."

Of course, that woman who just wanted to be loved was also an utter lunatic. Before he could do anything, she was already calling for the men guarding her chambers – ordering some to fetch Mary, while the rest escorted Robert and the Widow to the Great Hall.

So he had to play along again, part of him relieved that the ordeal of the Widow's bedchambers was over, part of him concerned about what was to come next. It had been necessary for the Widow to believe, he knew that – her blind faith that he was the man from the card, her chosen one, was the only thing seemingly stopping her from focusing. It was a weakness he could exploit, he just wasn't sure how yet.

As they waited in the Hall, though, the Widow impatient to get this over with so he could be totally hers, Robert kept an eye on everything around him: from the positioning of the guards – six on either side of the room, dotted between suits of armour with machine-guns, an eclectic touch – to the space around him and what he could use to initiate an escape; plenty of archways, which would be either a help or hindrance. When Mary was brought in, he attempted to act cool, but what he saw made his heart ache.

She'd obviously been crying, but Mary seemed resigned to what had happened, that Robert belonged to the Widow. Her head was bowed; her body spoke of a woman who'd given up.

"All right, let's get this over and done wi', shall we?" said the Widow, and produced a knife, which she handed to Robert. *A sacrificial dagger*, thought Robert. Meant to represent the sacrifice not only of Mary, but of their whole relationship.

Not going to happen.

"Well, go on, then," encouraged the Widow, nodding towards Mary. "Yer know what must be done. I cannae do it for yer, Robert."

Yes, he knew exactly what to do. Robert approached Mary, hoping to convey what his plan was. But she wouldn't – couldn't – look him in the eye. *Come on, Mary, look at me.*

"Kill her, Robert. Kill them both," urged the Widow.

Robert paused. Mary raised her head.

"Both?" said Robert.

"Aye, her and the child. The last link. Yer rejected her, now do the same with the creature growing inside her."

Robert's mouth gaped and he stared at Mary; she stared back. Her hands went to her stomach, a look of astonishment on her face. What the hell was the Widow talking about? He could see Mary had no idea either. Something to gauge his reaction, to test whether he was still loyal? Or perhaps to make him rethink what he was planning to do next? But if it were true... If –

"*Do it, man!*" screamed the Widow.

Robert exchanged a look with Mary, all that was needed. "I'm sorry," he said, approaching her with the blade held high.

"I know," she told him.

"Now!" he cried, and twisted – flinging the dagger back towards the Widow. Mary brought up both her arms. The guards obviously hadn't been expecting any more resistance after half-carrying the defeated woman from her cell, and were taken completely by surprise when she elbowed them both in the stomach. They crumpled up, but Mary didn't wait to draw breath. Grabbing them both by the back of the neck, she knocked their heads together. *Hard.*

As the blade flew towards the Widow, Robert was also diving to attack one of the Widow's men. The man's reaction was slower than Robert's and all it took was a blow across the windpipe to incapacitate him. Robert dragged the soldier around, using him as a human shield as the guard opposite opened fire. The first one took the bullets, his body jerking as they exploded into him. Robert glanced up to see what had happened with the knife.

The Widow had caught it and was turning it around.

"Mary, run!" he shouted, snatching the guard's claymore and

belt-knife before letting him drop. The knife he hurled at the soldier shooting in his direction, and this time it did find its mark.

The Widow was rushing forward, preventing any of her men from getting a clean shot at Robert. Mary looked left and right, back towards the door she'd been brought through, then at Robert. "*Run!*" he yelled again, but it was already too late. The Widow had almost reached her, dagger ready to do what Robert couldn't.

He was about to hurl himself at the woman, when he remembered the other guards. He ducked in time to escape the machine-gun fire, rolling over and bringing his sword up into the first. Robert offloaded the impaled man onto the guard directly behind him, who was racing towards his companion. Wood splintered around Robert as the guards opposite trained their weapons on him.

Which also meant that the Widow had reached Mary.

Robert rolled again, rising and throwing his claymore at one of the guards like a javelin. He snatched another belt-knife from the closest felled guard and tossed it at another guard diagonally opposite. Ducking sideways, he grabbed one of the suits of armour, pulling it in front of him for protection against yet more machine-gun fire. Bullets sparked off the armour, dislodging the rifle it held, but did at least allow him to move back toward Mary, and the Widow.

To Robert's dismay, the archways were indeed proving a menace, as more guards – attracted by the noise – came dashing in. Pretty soon the whole damned hall would be filled with reinforcements. He had to take out the Widow right now.

Robert ran at her, throwing the empty metal suit – the only weapon he had. As good as his aim was, the armour hit nothing, crashing across the floor and into the opposite wall. The Widow had already circled around behind Mary and was holding the dagger to her throat.

Weapons were being readied behind him, new soldiers swarming into the Hall. But Robert didn't care. For one thing he was in the direct line of sight of the Widow – any stray bullet might hit her as well, which he knew they couldn't risk – for another, he was more concerned about the golden blade pressed up against Mary's neck, the edge already drawing blood.

"Wait, no!" he begged. "Stop! I'll do anything you want. Just please, please don't kill her." There were tears in his eyes. The Widow looked at him and froze. Was there still some compassion in her? Something that recognised Mary was the one for him, not her?

"All right," she told Robert. "And you'll agree to *anything* if I let her live?"

He nodded.

"Robert, no!" said Mary.

"There is still a way we can be together. It wasnae what I wanted, though." The Widow ordered her men to restrain Robert. He held up his hands willingly. He and Mary were marched out into the open, the light suddenly blinding. Out, up and round to the reservoir buildings, then in through a door. The Widow had been busy here, the place already set up for its new purpose, away from the prying eyes of her army. She allowed two men inside with her, then she bolted the door.

In front of them was a large funeral pyre. Some kind of pulley system had been rigged up, attached to the walls and ceiling. Robert and Mary exchanged worried glances as they cottoned on to what was going to happen.

With guns on both him and Mary, Robert had no choice. One way or another the Widow was finding a way for him to be her King, to make his strength her own so they could be together forever. Then she went over to a trunk, bringing out several bottles of liquid. She proceeded to coat his skin with this, mixing the solutions generously.

"Cooking oil?"

She didn't reply. There was a distinct air of disappointment in her expression, like he *should* have killed Mary – and his child, if what she'd said was true.

"You and I have lived many lives," she told him. "And we *will* live on forever, whatever happens. We will *be* together."

She nodded at one of the men, who took Robert by the arms, wrenching him away from Mary when all he really wanted to do was kiss her, say goodbye. In all the scenarios he'd played out in his mind, after all the adventures and dangers he'd faced, he'd never once pictured this. Being eaten alive by a crazy Scottish woman who thought they were soul mates.

As he was pulled across to the ropes, his hands shoved inside them – then hauled upwards and across – he realised that the Widow had actually done worse to Mary than kill her. Now she would have to witness her husband being cooked alive and devoured.

On the Widow's orders one of her guards lit the fire, as she began her damned chanting again. Must have been part of whatever process she thought would give her his soul.

He looked over at Mary. She was crying, trying to look away but not managing it. Wanting to capture his face, remember the moment – the last time she'd see him alive.

And once again, Robert wondered how he'd gotten into this mess.

CHAPTER FOURTEEN

SO FAR, IT was going according to plan.

Usually everything turned into such a mess. But not now, not this time. Twice he'd had to suffer defeat at the hands of his enemies. No more. As he drove along the road in the Eagle Armoured Vehicle, Tanek thought back to his meetings with the Widow and the Dragon.

Both had gone well enough, the latter more so. That Widow was going to be trouble eventually; she'd already *been* trouble as far as he was concerned, with her magic tricks and supposed clairvoyance. More co-operative had been that bloated excuse for a human being, the Dragon. Tanek had radioed in to say he was close to the man's headquarters, and, after a tour of the weaponry and vehicles, he'd been escorted to the meet. The Welshman had quite an impressive set up, Tanek had to admit, funded by the people he himself represented. Tanks, armoured vehicles, guns, all supplied by the Germans.

Both were only playing at being dictators, though. Neither the Widow nor the Dragon had the foresight, nor the clout, to pull something off like De Falaise, who'd swept up the country building an army as he'd gone. Nor did they possess the vision of the first Tsar.

If the Dragon and Widow had pooled their resources and teamed up, however, it might have been a different story.

His thoughts switched to the dreams the Widow had spoken of, the promise he'd made to his former leader to watch over his child. Tanek had assumed that was Adele, who'd come out of nowhere and almost caused Hood's downfall. She'd been shot by Hood's woman, Mary, and had died in Tanek's arms – in spite of his best efforts to save her.

"Take it slow," he'd told her as the bullet finally took its toll.

"No, I must... We have to save... He made me promise. My father."

"Promise what?"

"Save —"

"Save who?"

Her grip on his arm had tightened: "His child. My brother. My little brother."

A brother? Could it be? Somewhere out there, another child of De Falaise's existed? Tanek would have bet anything – back when betting actually meant something – that there were lots of little De Falaise bastards out there, providing they'd had his O-Neg blood. If he'd conquered women like he conquered territories, then Tanek would have quite a search on his hands. The kid – if, indeed, it was still a kid – could be anywhere.

Tanek had done as he had before, after De Falaise's death: retreated abroad. He figured he stood a better chance of tracking down the Sheriff's child if he scoured Europe first. After all, that had been De Falaise's playground for quite some time. Tanek had even tried searching back in Istanbul where he'd first encountered the Frenchman, but things had changed significantly while he'd been away. So many tin-pot dictators, exactly like the Dragon and the Widow, it was unbelievable. He couldn't move without getting into a fight, or having to prove to the people there exactly who he was; though part of him was very flattered his reputation had spread.

If he hadn't been on a mission, he might have stayed and showed them a thing or two, perhaps taking over a couple of their operations and building a force of his own. But it would be nothing compared to the armies already established in places like Germany.

He'd heard the rumours, just as others had heard rumours about him. There was some kind of new Reich starting up, not that he was any great fan of the Nazis – the whole Aryan race thing put him off – but if nothing else they were organised. And this version's belief system was slightly more flexible than the old guard.

That was the impression he got and the confirmation he received when he made contact with the Army of the New Order. He hadn't been able to gain access to the man in charge, but found himself talking to sympathetic members, one of whom had given him this gig, based on the tales of him almost taking out Hood, twice. The stories didn't go into detail, thankfully, about how everything had gone to shit both times – just told how the upstart woodsman had nearly got his comeuppance at Tanek's hands. He hadn't corrected them.

As always, Tanek had been able to use that misplaced trust to his advantage. Yes, he would consent to oversee the distribution of the New Order's property in the north and west of Britain. Yes, he would make sure they used it wisely, with one eye on trying to eradicate Hood – an extra bonus as far as he was concerned, just so long as he got to do the deed himself. But in return he also required men and equipment to implement one of his own projects.

Because, in the time between leaving England and hooking up with the New Order, Tanek had also heard rumours about a woman De Falaise had once been acquainted with. A woman called Gwen who – for reasons beyond Tanek's comprehension – had held some appeal for his former leader. Tanek couldn't believe he hadn't worked it out before, the amount of time De Falaise had spent alone with her.

Tanek had lost track of the woman, but it didn't take long to pick up the trail again. He couldn't quite believe she'd been stupid enough to go back to the place where she'd first been kidnapped. Who would do that? Apparently it was because that was where the man she'd loved had been from, the man she – falsely – believed to be the father of her child. But Tanek felt sure that the son she'd borne belonged to the Frenchman. The timing, everything; it all fitted.

It hadn't taken much effort, with the resources now at Tanek's command, to pinpoint her village. And while he'd been travelling round checking on the Widow and Dragon, his men – sequestered from the New Order – had laid siege to her home. No questions asked, which was the way he liked it.

That was where he was driving to now, cross-country from Wales. It had taken a good few hours, but he hadn't encountered any trouble. Driving the Eagle ensured you fairly safe passage.

In that time, he'd been in contact with the men on the ground – finding out what had happened during the siege. They'd begun a day or so ago, bedding in and using sniper fire to take out anyone coming and out. One jeep in particular returning from some kind of recce had been hit badly, along with a villager who'd fired on them. Ever since then they'd kept the place pinned down tight.

"I'm waiting for the 'but,'" Tanek had said to the mercenary in charge, Brauer.

"Sadly, one of our men was captured."

"Tell me that was a joke," he spat down the handset, although his German comrades very rarely made those.

"I wish I could. But regrettably it is true."

"How did he get captured when your men are surrounding the fucking village?" Tanek snapped. Static was his only reply, which just made him angrier. "Just tell me you're making progress wearing them down?"

"We will be inside within the next day. I'd stake my life on that."

"Choose your words carefully," Tanek warned him. He had killed people for much less. He had killed people for pleasure, for that matter.

"There will be progress before you arrive, Herr Tanek," he was promised. That would have to be good enough for now.

Even with the capture of one German – who knew relatively little in the great scheme of things, save for the reason they were there – Tanek felt oddly optimistic. Everything was pretty much going to his plan, the second phase of which would begin as soon as he reached New Hope.

And there was nothing and nobody to stand in his way this time.

GWEN WAS DETERMINED not to let anyone stand in her way. Not Andy, nor Jeffreys, not even the memory of her dear, sweet Clive. Nobody was going to take her son away from her. If it meant fighting to the death, then she'd do it. The rest of them could go screw themselves.

Ever since the German prisoner had told her what they were after, she'd been like this. His confession that they weren't going to leave without Clive Jr had sent her into overdrive. And if she'd been hard on their captive before, that knowledge had pushed her over the edge.

"Tell me!" she'd demanded when she got over the shock, raking his cheek with her nails. "Tell me *why* you want my son!"

When she'd begun to tear into the wound in his side, the one that Jeffreys had spent so long stitching, Gwen had to be pulled away.

"Now that's enough! He's not going to talk," Andy said in her ear as he and the good doctor dragged her away from the man. "You can see he's not going to give you anything more."

"He will when I've finished with him!" But, given a chance to calm down, Gwen realised the truth was, he probably wouldn't. Not even under the kind of torture she'd love to inflict.

Torture, for Heaven's sakes. Can you hear yourself? This wasn't her, this *really* wasn't her. But it was; nothing in the world was more important to her than her son, and these arseholes had come here specifically to take him. Why, she had no idea – and probably wouldn't find out until it was too late. Until he was gone.

"What the hell's going on?" Darryl had asked, rising from the couch as she'd returned home, slamming the front door behind her. He'd stayed there to keep an eye on Clive Jr, and because he was still wobbly after giving the German his blood. She felt a twinge of guilt when she saw how pale he still was, because she'd been ready to drain every last drop of blood from that German in order to uncover the truth. Then again, she knew Darryl would understand – he was probably one of the few who would. He'd only volunteered for the transfusion in the first place so they could ask their captive questions. Clive would have been proud of the courage and self sacrifice the young man had shown tonight. Gwen vowed to tell him that, when she got the chance. When the time was right.

"No guts, none of them," she grumbled under her breath. "They won't do what's necessary."

"Easy, Gwen, sit down."

She ignored him, pacing up and down, explaining what had happened during the interrogation. "I just don't know what to do, Darryl. I won't let them take Clive Jr."

"Course not, none of us will."

"I'm not so sure," she said, voice wavering. Before he could ask her what she meant, Clive Jr appeared in the doorway to the living room, wearing his pyjamas and clutching a teddy. He'd been in the other room asleep when Gwen came in. She went to him immediately.

"Oh, I'm so sorry for waking you sweetie, sweetheart," she cooed. "Let's get you back to bed, little man. You need your sleep."

"He's not the only one," Darryl told her. "You look knackered."

"Thanks a lot," she laughed.

"I'm serious," he said, concern etched on his face, and it was then that she realised just how much he cared about her.

Gwen shook her head. "I can't, not with all this going on."

"You're no use to anyone like that, especially him," Darryl said, nodding at Clive Jr.

He did have a point. How could she fight for her son when she was exhausted? She wouldn't be able to think clearly if she was half asleep. "I'm not even sure I could, even if I tried," she protested, but was already yawning in spite of herself; coming down off the adrenalin high she'd been on while questioning of the prisoner.

"You'd be surprised. Now go on, take him back to bed and get some rest yourself."

Gwen nodded, holding Clive Jr's hand. She turned back before heading upstairs. "Thanks Darryl. For everything."

He smiled and waved a hand for her to get her head down. Which she did, taking the pistol from the back of her jeans and putting it under the pillow, then curling up with her son. She watched him nod off again, then watched him some more, her own eyes drooping.

She dreamt of *him*. The man who'd once saved her from almost certain death at Nottingham Castle – at the very least rape and who

knows what else at the hands of that thug Jace. A Hooded Man, but
not the one that everyone knew about. He wore a *red* hood, this one,
over a face painted to resemble a skull – practically indistinguishable
from the rest of his clan, though *she* could tell him apart instantly.
She'd called him Skullface once, but now understood what an
inappropriate name that was; used only because she knew nothing
about him, not even his real name. Some would probably have said it
was Servitor, because he served the Fallen One, but Gwen wasn't so
sure about that. He'd shown her only kindness and compassion, and
at no other time since Clive's death had she felt so safe.

In this dreamscape, he came to her again, exactly when she needed
him. Gwen reached out and pulled down that crimson cowl, stroking
the painted face. The face of a dead man, because hadn't he once
died? She didn't know *how* she knew that, but he'd also been reborn
in flames. She felt the rough edges of the tattoo on his forehead: an
inverted pentangle and cross. Her hands went even higher, feeling
the bristles of his shaven head, and she wondered what he'd looked
like before all this. What he looked like without the painted skull,
with his hair grown long. And suddenly her question was answered,
because standing there in front of her was a man who looked almost
exactly like Clive. It wasn't him, of course, could never *be* him. But
the resemblance was uncanny. This man had felt the same kind of
pain as her – somehow she knew that as well. He'd lost people he
cared about: a lover... no, a wife. And a child.

It was the kind of bond which could only be shared through loss.

Gwen felt herself falling into his eyes, pools of sadness coaxing her
in. Then suddenly they were holding each other, arms wrapped about
each other, clinging like they were drowning. When their lips met it
was with a hunger she'd never felt when she was with Clive. There
was an urgency this time, as if at any moment this would be snatched
away from her, as it was before. Gwen closed her eyes...

Their mouths parted and his tongue found hers, dancing with
it, at first tentatively, then with that same driving need. They were
exploring each other's bodies. Gwen's hands ran down his naked
back, feeling the strength of him and holding him closer as they
kissed: faces locked together until there was no differentiating them.

Gwen lay back and let him kiss her neck, butterfly kisses which
ended at her nipples. She moaned, loudly now, as he took one into his
mouth, sucking and biting.

But that sensation was nothing compared to what came next. He
was inside her, even though she hadn't felt him slide in. She could

feel him there, and it was beyond anything she'd ever experienced before. They kissed again, tongues lapping at each other as he moved backwards and forwards on top of Gwen. The motion increased along with the intensity of feeling. His thrusts were hard and gentle at the same time, lifting her higher and higher into this feeling. Breaking off the kiss, she was moaning in time with those thrusts. Her hands at his shoulders willing him on.

She felt like she was going to explode. It was only at the very point of finishing, when she couldn't hold back any longer, that she opened her eyes. To see something from her worst nightmare.

The Sheriff, De Falaise. Labouring away above her, sweat pouring from his brow, his yellow teeth glinting in the light. A memory from when she'd been held against her will at the castle, used like some kind of sex toy.

Gwen's cry of ecstasy became a scream.

She woke suddenly, just in time to hear explosions breaking the silence outside.

PHASE TWO OF the plan started when Tanek reached the woodland on the outskirts of New Hope.

As he pulled up in the Eagle, he was greeted by Brauer, who saluted him. That made Tanek smile. It was good to be in command of men again, even if it was only for this one mission. It was the respect he'd earned, the respect he'd commanded when he'd been De Falaise's right-hand man. He'd never felt fully in charge during his time with the Russians – too many people looking over his shoulder, including the Tsar himself. Here he was alone, with a small army who were under orders to obey him, whatever the cost.

The first thing Tanek wanted to know was how they'd allowed one of the men to be taken.

"How did any of the villagers get out in the first place?"

Brauer shook his head. "We have all possible entrances and exits covered, sir."

"Not *all* of them, apparently." But he wasn't going to expend valuable time and manpower searching for them. Tanek needed to step up the siege, force the people inside to give themselves up.

Or give up the child.

The woman the boy belonged to would never surrender herself – she'd die rather than see him fall into the hands of the Sheriff's former second. But the others might, with the correct motivation.

They'd already been shot at from every conceivable position around that damned wall they'd erected – a troublesome obstacle, but a good idea, Tanek had to admit. It prevented them from leaving, in theory. Now it was time to show them that he and his forces would be coming in soon, whether they liked it or not. The only thing that had prevented him from blowing the shit out of them in the first place was that they might accidentally hurt the boy. None of them had the first clue where he was being kept, and a stray mortar fired into the village might just hit a building with him inside.

But that didn't prevent a barrage against the wall.

"Ride with me," he told Brauer, and the man saluted again.

They drove towards the gates of New Hope, and the Eagle began to draw fire from a gunman positioned on the wall. The bullets bounced harmlessly off its armoured exterior. Tanek parked and slid out, using the vehicle as cover. He ordered Brauer out, to give him a hand with something he had in the back, under the camouflaged canvas cover.

Brauer barely batted an eye when he saw the huge GMG automatic grenade launcher. A look of understanding passed across his hard face as he realised why Tanek had asked him along. Resembling a very large M-60, it fired grenades in place of bullets, fed through a belt. The gunmen from the wall continued to fire at them as they set up the mount, Tanek fixing the gun into position. A ricochet sparked off the side of the jeep near his head, but he barely even twitched, concentrating on the task in hand.

"Ready?" Tanek asked Brauer, who nodded, holding the grenade belt. The larger man pivoted the barrel of the GMG and aimed for the wall. The blast almost knocked Brauer backwards, but Tanek remained rooted to the spot. The grenades exploded against the wall, which shook with the impacts.

Tanek shifted position, relying on Brauer to move with him, and fired several more along the length of the wall. *Should get their attention.*

There was no return fire, at least for a few seconds. Then it came again; the bullets, pathetic compared with the GMG's load.

Okay, thought Tanek. *Let's try this.*

Leaving Brauer with the canon, he made his way round the side of the Eagle, picking something up from the back seat as he went. Tanek walked out into the enemy fire, standing there as if daring any of the sentry's bullets to strike him. And indeed they refused, hitting trees, foliage and the dirt track. Then Tanek raised his repeater crossbow, as accurate a weapon as any you could wish for, and loosed bolts into the gaps on the top of the wall.

The gunfire stopped. Tanek stood there and grunted with satisfaction.

"People of New... *Hope*," he shouted "You have something we want. A boy belonging to a woman called Gwen. Your leader. You are cut off. Give us what we came here for, or suffer the consequences."

"Do you think they will listen, sir?" asked Brauer.

Tanek didn't reply; he just looked out over the bonnet of his vehicle, up towards the wall. He saw a brief glimpse of auburn hair.

And now he really was tempted to grin.

GWEN HAD WOKEN from the dream feeling flushed and disgusted at the same time, but hadn't had the opportunity to reflect on it thanks to the explosions.

Several *bangs* in quick succession, all coming from beyond the wall. Clive Jr slept on, oblivious, so she'd retrieved the pistol from under the pillow, hurried downstairs, then asked Darryl to watch her son.

"What is it, what were those noises?" he said as she opened the gun cabinet near the door. Gwen took out a Colt Commando assault rifle, one of the haul she'd originally brought with her from Nottingham Castle.

"Trouble," she replied, locking the cabinet again and tossing him the key.

The first thing she noticed was that it was fully light outside, dawn having broken while she'd slept. Another blast hit as she was running towards the wall – followed by gunfire – and she was joined by more villagers who'd been roused by the noise, including Karen and Dr Jeffreys.

Gwen saw Andy lying on the ground at the base of the wall, not moving; the rifle he had been using was a few feet away. For a moment or two she thought he was dead, and mixed emotions surged through her. How she'd once been great friends with this man, but had found herself at odds with him of late.

She was relieved when she saw him move, until she got closer and could see what had done this to Andy. Two crossbow bolts: one in the shoulder, the other in the chest. She slowed her pace. Only one person she'd ever known used a weapon like that.

Then she heard his voice and it sent a shiver down her spine. He was calling from beyond the wall, telling them it was Gwen's son they'd come here for. She still couldn't understand why, unless after all this time Tanek had decided to believe the bollocks about Clive Jr being De Falaise's child. It was something Tate, Robert, maybe even Mary believed – but a mother knew her own son, in her heart. The boy was Clive's.

Jeffreys was attending to Andy, so she ascended the ladder. Crouching on the ledge of the wall, she risked a peek at her foe. How he'd got his feet under the table with the Germans was anyone's guess, but then mercenaries flocked together, didn't they? It was how De Falaise and Tanek had hooked up in the first place.

Just look at the arrogant sod, standing there like he's indestructible. But like her dream lover, hadn't Tanek come back from the dead once, after the battle for Nottingham Castle? Come back with a fleet of Russian soldiers as his allies. *Working his way around the fucking countries.*

She could see Tanek watching from behind his vehicle, and ducked back out of sight. Gwen wasn't about to give him the satisfaction of knowing she was there. Of knowing she was shit scared about what they were going to do next.

It had been bad enough when she thought the Germans were on their own; now, who knew how many more troops might come? They were just villagers with guns, not well trained, either. Some hadn't even fired a gun before, in spite of her best efforts to prepare them. Some, like Karen, had never taken a life and she couldn't rely on them to begin now.

It was time to start being realistic. In most cases they would have been able to fend off what came down that road. If Javier, the man who'd killed Clive, had trundled up now, they could have at least have sent *him* packing. But Tanek was a different kettle of fish. *Face it, you need help,* Gwen told herself.

Tate.

Gwen hated herself for even thinking it, but the Reverend – her old friend, who'd left her a prisoner of the Sheriff for so long, who'd put her in danger again when the Tsar had attacked – was probably their only hope.

At the castle was Robert, and wouldn't he just love to see her begging for their help? But there were also the Rangers. Well trained specialists who'd be able to take those Krauts down without breaking a sweat. With them on the outside, and her lot fighting from within, they might yet stand a chance.

Gwen caught sight of the villagers below. They were looking up, some accusatory – blaming her for bringing this to their doorstep – but most looking to her for a solution.

There was only one thing she could think of to do.

Gwen got down, motioning for someone else to take her place on the wall. Hardly worth it, probably, but they still had to make an attempt to defend New Hope.

"Okay," she told the assembled crowd, "here's what we're going to do..."

CHAPTER FIFTEEN

"Wake up. Oh, please, wake up!"

He heard the muffled words, but didn't want to. They sounded like his mother's cries as she tried to get him up out of bed on a school day. "You're going to miss the bus, if you're not careful."

But this wasn't his mother's voice. It sounded familiar, though, like someone else he knew. The same inflections, though maybe a little deeper. Lyrical in tone, almost like music – and if there was one thing he knew about it was that.

Then he saw a face in the darkness.

Sian.

She was in his mind, just as she'd been in his thoughts since he'd first seen her.

"Please, whoever you are, wake up!" The words were sharper now, more acute. More real. He was fighting against the dark, raging against it. Time to get up or he'd miss the bus.

"D-Dale..." he croaked, not caring for the sound it made in his head. He tried to ignore the pain, and hoped that fat git hadn't damaged his voice permanently when he grabbed hold of his neck. He should have been grateful he was still alive. As it was, he was simply glad he might get a shot at revenge.

Not very Ranger-like thoughts, he told himself. But then, hadn't Robert himself exacted his own revenge – twice – on people who'd hurt the woman he loved?

Love. It was an alien concept to him. It was something he always thought he'd feel one day, that he hadn't been able to feel for any other girl he'd ever been with, as much as he'd liked to. He just hadn't been built that way. But the way he felt about Sian... it was either love or something very like it. Dale knew that when he saw what that slug had done to Sian, he'd do anything he could to save her. That's why he *had* to wake up.

Dale opened his eyes, his vision blurred. And the picture of Sian's face he'd held there became that of her aunty, Meghan.

"Please... Dale. You have to help her."

Dale moved, and regretted it instantly. He ached all over from the beating the Dragon had given him. From somewhere he heard the sound of gunfire. Meghan looked up and out through the open door. Dale blinked and his focus returned enough to see what the Dragon had done to her hand, which she was holding against her chest as she knelt next to him.

"Please, we have to hurry," she said.

"Where..." Dale croaked again. "Where is he?" There was no sign of the Dragon, just the men Dale had put out of action before the real fight began.

"He left, maybe to see what was happening out there – with your friends?" Meghan winced as her hand moved; whatever he'd been through, he was in better shape than her, Dale reminded himself. That hand needed looking at, and soon. But Meghan hadn't finished talking. "Then I saw him on the screen back there, the one Sian had been on." The screen had a crack across it, but still showed a picture. The chair Sian had been tied to was empty. Dale's heart sank.

"Where is she?" he asked.

"He took her," said Meghan.

Dale didn't want to make things worse by saying that Sian had come here to rescue her.

"I was only trying to keep her safe!" Meghan told him.

Dale tried to get himself up, one hand on the floor. Meghan stood to help him with her good hand. "Do you have any idea where he might have gone with her?" Dale asked. He didn't need to ask *why*. The Dragon had seen the Rangers in action out there and wanted some leverage. A hostage who meant something to one of them.

"Somewhere he'd feel safe, where his family are."

"Right," said Dale, picking up the rifle he'd been brandishing when the Dragon came at him. It wasn't a Ranger's weapon, but was the only one he had to hand, and he wasn't about to go up against armed men with nothing. He began to make his way outside, but would have toppled if Meghan hadn't steadied him. What was he thinking? He was in no shape to take on the Dragon. He'd get them all killed.

Dale could hear the sound of gunfire out in the corridor – then another explosion. There was a battle going on, and usually Dale would have wanted to be a part of that. Not this time. He let Meghan take the lead to the Dragon's family.

They turned a corner and were confronted by two or three of the Dragon's men, who opened fire on them before they'd had a chance to identify themselves. *Nerves and hair-triggers,* thought Dale as he pulled Meghan back behind the wall for safety. *Not a good combination.* The soldiers were seeing enemies everywhere.

Bullets pinged off the wall and Dale swore. He stuck out the machine-gun and returned fire, but drew even more in return.

He didn't have time for this. For all they knew, the Dragon could have already killed Sian, and –

No, she was still alive. She had to be! Dale sprayed another burst of bullets in the direction of the Dragon's men, this time chancing a look around the corner as he did.

There were even more now. He checked his magazine; there wasn't much ammo left. Certainly not enough to take on all those guys.

He looked at Meghan's terrified face and couldn't muster any reassurance.

But if he didn't do something, and fast, a young woman that they both cared about would be in serious trouble.

THE CASTLE HAD sent all the reinforcements they could, but they were still heavily outnumbered.

But one trained Ranger was worth at least a dozen of the Dragon's men, which evened it out somewhat. They also had the element of surprise on their side. Jack deemed the risk necessary. Had done since he'd learned of the connection between the Dragon and Tanek.

If that sadistic son of a bitch was back on the scene, then this outfit needed crippling sooner rather than later. Before another Sheriff or Tsar could come along and take advantage. For all they knew, the Dragon might have the credentials himself – he was certainly psychotic enough. What he'd done to their Welsh HQ, to the survivors he'd taken back to the Millennium Stadium, was proof enough of that. And although revenge shouldn't have been the motivation for the attack, Jack's mind kept flashing back to those bodies, to the Ranger who'd been dumped on the road by the Dragon's men.

And the idea that Tanek might also still be around was too tantalising to pass up. Jack had a major score to settle with that man. On two occasions, he'd been bested by him – although the rematch *almost* went his way. And that was before the torture he'd put him through.

Still, he'd thought long and hard about this: putting even more Rangers in the line of fire for some kind of personal vendetta wasn't what they were all about. But when the men and women had come to him themselves, saying this was the right thing, that they wanted payback for their comrades who'd died at the Dragon's hands, that had settled it. Each one of them knew what they were letting themselves in for once they put on the Ranger uniform. It hadn't stopped them before, and it certainly wasn't about to deter them now. Far from putting them off, the Dragon's actions had simply put fire in their bellies.

Then there was the small matter of one of his Rangers being inside. A man he'd personally sent there.

"I'm not one for speeches," Jack had told the collected troops just before they'd headed off. "Robert's the one you want for that. But I do know one thing: whatever happens today, you're doing the Rangers proud. Now good luck to all of you, and let's go and kick some butt!"

His people knew exactly what they were doing, which ensured he could rely on them to crush the lookouts on the outskirts of the Dragon's territory without fuss and without them getting off a warning. Jack had watched one squad through binoculars from a deserted house, with equal amounts of anticipation and pride. The hooded soldiers slipped through the streets, coming up on the lookouts while the Dragon's men chatted amongst themselves. If the guards had spotted trouble they might have sprung into action, but they were oblivious – and before they could even get off a shot, the group of half a dozen soldiers dropped silently to the ground, taken out by a mixture of arrows and bolas. Jack had allowed himself a slight smile, but there was a bigger test to come.

They'd moved through the city using the buildings, just as Robert had taught them. Nobody from the stadium would have seen their approach, and when they were close enough, teams of Rangers were deployed as planned, surrounding the stadium. There were a handful of Rangers present with scuba diving skills; they were not only well trained fighters, these men and women, but sometimes had hobbies from the old days that came in useful. They used the River Taff to approach the building, after Jack had sourced the equipment from a shop which used to sell tanks and gear before the virus. It would be just like the beginning of *Goldfinger*, he'd told them, but without the dinner jackets underneath their wetsuits.

Any guards they spotted were felled with arrows or bolas, some even with throwing knives if the Rangers were close enough. A team had been sent out to deal with the problem of the vehicles and weapons stashed at Cardiff Arms Park. As Robert had done during his battle with the Tsar's men, they'd be using chemically-treated arrows to deal with this – the tips carrying a concentrated explosive. They'd shoot them into the smaller stadium, with catastrophic results for the Dragon's defences.

A couple of teams had entered via Park Street and Scott Road in a pincer movement. There were emergency doors here – Jack had done his homework – next to the old media access area, which could be used to gain entrance after any guards had been dealt with.

Meanwhile for other groups, including Jack's, the architecture of the stadium itself was a gift: struts and poles for climbing, perfect for ropes attached to arrows shot onto the roof. Jack had to admit, he didn't relish the prospect of the climb, but he did all right keeping up with some of the younger Rangers. There were absolutely no guards up on top, as Jack had figured – nobody would be stupid enough to camp out there – so the Rangers were able to climb down inside, again using all those metal struts and poles to their advantage. Hanging from the rooftop inside, they could pick off any obvious guards, leaving the way free for the rest of them to abseil down directly from the roof. That one was inspired by *You Only Live Twice*.

Jack and the others watched as the Rangers disappeared under the roof on the opposite side. They waited, and waited. Then the all-clear signal was given; a faint whistle which could be mistaken for birdsong unless you were really listening for it. Jack nodded for them all to begin their run, and looked over the edge at the pitch below. Even with a head for heights, this was not something he was looking forward to. "Well, here goes nothin'."

Holding the rope steady – his staff jammed under his arm – he lowered himself over the edge of the stadium's canopy. Jack pushed himself off, swaying as he dropped, and let out the rope. He glanced over at other Rangers doing the same, spotting those who had already climbed up and under, now crouching between the rows of seats; quietly making their way downwards.

They'd been lucky so far, but that wouldn't last. Sooner or later someone, somewhere, would spot the ropes dangling into the stadium. They had to move quickly.

Jack heard shouting. Raised voices that didn't belong to his troops. That was it. But the timing couldn't have been better.

Loud bangs sounded from the smaller stadium next door, then explosions as the Rangers' arrows found their marks – blowing up stationary jeeps and motorbikes, tanks and trucks... and ammo. A chain reaction ensued, the ground and the stadium shaking with the ferocity of it. The distraction bought them some time, but not much. Machine-gun fire came from Jack's left, and he dropped a few yards. The other dangling Rangers, rather than waiting to fall to the pitch, swung into the rows of seats, detaching themselves as soon as they could. Their bows were out seconds later, trained on the source of the machine-gun fire.

Jack did the same, using his momentum to swing across. Bullets missed him by inches and he spotted the gunman. Holding on to the rope with one hand, he let his staff fall into his free hand and flung it at the Dragon's guard, hitting the man squarely in the chest. The guard fell backwards, then flopped forwards over one of the blue plastic seats. Jack swung himself across, letting go when he was over the steps between seats. He landed well enough, but had to duck more rapid gunfire from another shooter.

A Ranger Jack recognised as Beth Garrett popped up between the seats and put an arrow in the guy; Jack nodded his thanks and went to retrieve his staff. He knew that inside, his other troopers were fighting their own battles – bow and arrow against hot lead. But Jack's money was on the Rangers.

Heavy weapons fire suddenly drew his attention and he looked across the stadium to see a fixed mounted gun the size of a bloody cannon, spitting out... yes, dammit, those were grenades. A couple exploded near to one of his Rangers and Jack watched, horrified, as the hooded figure flew up into the air along with wrecked seats.

"Hawkings!" he shouted, pointing to the weapon, and was gratified to see the Ranger had already lit one of his chemical arrows. He shot it in the direction of the cannon, and the resultant blast spread across the Dragon's men and set off the grenades they'd been feeding into the weapon.

Jack nodded with satisfaction. "How'd ya like them apples?"

Another skirmish had broken out on the pitch below, Rangers taking on guards with their swords. Rolling to duck bullets, they hacked at legs – cutting into shins and thighs. No guard would be getting up after that.

In doorways and from behind the seats, his Rangers continued to hold their own, loosing arrow after arrow, some explosive, most not needing to be. About twenty of the Dragon's men, all armed to the teeth, were taken down in seconds by arrows; clustered together, they'd made it easy for his Rangers to wound and incapacitate.

Some of the guards were fleeing, retreating back inside the stadium. It wouldn't do them any good, because already the Rangers were spreading throughout this place: down corridors and on stairwells, checking every room and crushing any resistance.

He made his way up towards a door, but as he did so a guard came through it, brandishing a pistol. Jack flicked his staff up and knocked the gun out of the man's hand, then whacked him on the temple. There was the sound of boots to the left and right, and Jack dropped immediately, just as the machine-gun fire from two groups of guards on either side opened up. "Chumps," muttered Jack as he rose again and saw the bodies. The Dragon's men had shot each other.

Leaving his forces to carry on their clean-up, Jack slipped inside through the entrance ahead of him.

It was a big place, and it was time to begin his search.

After all, he had more than one person to find.

"WHAT NOW?" ASKED Meghan.

"I'm thinking, I'm thinking," Dale replied. It wasn't easy when you were pinned down and bullets were sparking off the corner next to your head. He looked around frantically for an answer.

Then he saw it. Their way out of there. Dale smiled.

"What?" asked Meghan.

"Here, hold this." He put the gun in her good hand, then ran across the hallway.

"Dale...?" came Meghan's worried voice. It was obvious they hadn't returned fire in a while and she was thinking that perhaps they should. She was right, but not with bullets. Or not *only* with bullets.

Dale wrenched the red metal cylinder from the wall and joined her again. "Okay, you might want to duck," he told her as he relieved her of the machine-gun. She did as she was told and Dale pressed himself up against the wall, closing his eyes. "Fingers crossed."

He set off the fire extinguisher, jamming the mechanism so it continued spraying clouds of white as he flung it around the corner. When Dale heard the men coughing, he broke cover and fired wildly into the gas. He'd been intending just to hit the men, but one of his bullets hit the canister itself and it went up in the middle of the guards, achieving exactly the opposite of what it was meant to – starting a fire instead of putting one out. It sent them sprawling in all directions. The blast also knocked him back against the far wall, reminding him of the injuries the Dragon had only recently inflicted.

But it had been worth it. All the men down at one stroke.

No, not all of them. One guard, blackened from the smoke, emerged. His face was blistered, one eye looked as though it was either gone or had skin stretched over it. There was a lump of metal sticking out of his shoulder.

None of this seemed to be bothering him too much. He grunted and brought his machine-gun to bear. Dale, still holding his, pulled the trigger.

It clicked empty.

In spite of the pain he was obviously in, the man laughed, guttural, deep and throaty, in keeping with his nightmarish appearance. He raised his gun and Dale closed his eyes, waiting for the end.

He heard a dull thump rather than the *rat-ta-tat* he'd been expecting. "You've just been Jack-Hammered, buddy," said a voice that made him open his eyes immediately.

The guard was on the floor, but there was still no sign of Jack. Then, through the smoke, came the end of the staff that had struck the guard on the head. Jack's face followed, and he adjusted the cap he always wore as he looked down at his handiwork. When he noticed Dale, he looked just as surprised to see him.

"Dale?" said Jack, unable to disguise the delight in his voice. "All that worrying and you're here sitting on your ass."

"You know me. Always slacking."

Jack laughed. "And getting yourself into trouble. I just had to follow the sound of gunfire."

Dale was having trouble getting up; Jack came over to help, as did Meghan, appearing from around the corner. Jack raised his staff, but Dale held up his hand.

"She's with me. Civilian. There are more dotted about this place."

"I see." The large man lowered his weapon, smiling tentatively at her. She smiled back. He'd had a problem with women ever since what had happened with Adele, although Dale couldn't really talk – he'd thought badly of Meghan too, when it looked like she'd set him up. Then Jack spotted her hand.

"Why, you're hurt as well, little lady." That wasn't Jack being patronising, it was just what he called most women – and there was a certain respectful charm to it, which Meghan appeared unused to.

"The Dragon," said Dale, by way of explanation about her hand.

"We need to get that examined," Jack said, moving closer and placing his hand underneath hers. "We have some Rangers trained in first aid."

"I-I'll be all right," she said shyly.

Jack smiled, then turned and addressed Dale. "I'm guessing he did that number on you, as well."

Dale nodded. "We're on our way to him right now... well, we think. He's got Meghan's niece."

"Okay." Jack handed him the guard's machine-gun in exchange for his exhausted one, then got him to his feet. "So, what are we waiting for?"

As they got moving, Dale asked how their side were doing. "Creamin' em, kid," said Jack. "Tanek still around?"

"Sorry," Dale told him. "He headed off after the meet, by the sound of things."

Jack's face fell. Then he turned to Dale and asked, "Listen, this niece we're on our way to save. Are you and her... Y'know?"

Dale didn't say a word, but his expression must have told Jack everything he needed.

"Figures," said the big man, rolling his eyes. "You really have got to get another act, kid."

Dale thought about telling him he had; that this girl was different. But Jack probably wouldn't believe him, and he couldn't blame him for that.

The point was they were on their way to try and save her. Sian.

Dale just hoped they were in time.

CHAPTER SIXTEEN

ENOUGH WAS ENOUGH.

He couldn't take any more of this, it was insane! He'd only been up there a short time, but Ceallach could smell Hood's flesh beginning to cook. It made his stomach churn.

Not long ago, he would have gladly cheered at the death of this man. The one responsible for his band of raiders losing that haul with the truck. The one who shot arrows at Ceallach himself as he rode alongside on his motorbike, watching as Hood dispatched most of his companions. Hadn't he himself even ordered Torradan to shoot through the roof of the van and kill Hood? But, when all was said and done, the woodsman had defeated them, pretty much single-handedly.

Ceallach had been thrown off his bike during the course of the scrap; or, more accurately, when Hood jammed his sword in the wheel. That had hurt. But afterwards, when Ceallach had dragged himself back to the vehicle to make his escape, Hood had also been the one who'd allowed him to escape. Ceallach had seen him in the smashed mirrors, preventing the guy with the shotgun from shooting.

The trip back to the castle hadn't been easy. Knowing he was leaving so many of his friends behind stuck in his craw. But if those captured Rangers were telling the truth, then they were at least being treated humanely. Ceallach had heard in the past about Hood's hotel prisons – sounded quite nice actually, better than some of the accommodation here.

And, after he'd returned to tell the Widow what had happened – still hurt and angry that her reputed vision hadn't shown her what would happen – what had she offered in reply?

"Aye, I knew Hood would be waitin'."

Just like that. Which told him one of two things. Either she couldn't see shit, and all the voodoo bollocks they believed about her was just a crock, or she'd let them walk into a trap. Neither option made him warm to her. Why exactly would the Widow knowingly send them into an ambush? She hadn't shared her reasons with him – simply sent Ceallach to the Vaults to be punished for answering back. Re-education, she'd called it. That had hurt more than fucking falling off the bike. Some of the stuff they did to people. He'd thought it was only reserved for their enemies, but apparently not.

Well, he'd been re-educated all right. It had definitely made him think twice, but not about questioning the Widow's motives. More like what the fuck he was still doing here? He'd pretended the experience had done him a favour; the Widow didn't generally try that conversion thing on people like him if they turned against her. She just had you killed; less trouble. He played along, all nice like. He knew how to do that from before, when he'd been one of Freddie Banks' guys, pulling bank-jobs and other robberies. You did the work, you took your cut; you smiled, said thanks. That's what he'd done after he'd finished his stint in the Vaults. The Widow usually asked to see you afterwards, to look you in the eye, check out whether you really *were* sorry. And he'd been scared of that, he had to admit, if not as scared as before. See, he was starting to lean more towards the opinion that she was a fake. This Widow could no more see into the future than his testicles were going to sprout wings and fly away, waving a cheery goodbye to his dick.

As it turned out, he hadn't needed to pass the test, because that was when Hood was captured. He'd had mixed feelings about that. On the one hand, he'd wanted to find him and punch him in the face. On the other, it showed that not even this man, the living legend, was immune to the Widow's power. If only those people who'd believed Hood's press over the past couple of years could see him now; naked and helpless as a baby while the heat roasted him.

Ceallach knew what she had in mind next. He'd known ever since they'd called him to help escort these prisoners to the Reservoirs – re-enforcements, after something had happened in the Great Hall. What the Widow had planned was something the men always talked about, but no-one could confirm. Something she'd done to men she'd been fond of, but was bored with, or who'd betrayed her. Seems she'd had designs on Hood, from what he could make out, even used that mojo of hers on him; the symbols were still painted on his glistening skin. But he'd spurned her, so now she was going to cook him.

Then eat him.

Again, Ceallach felt his stomach lurch. He'd seen some weird shit in his time at Edinburgh Castle, heard tales about so much more. But this wasn't him. Not this. If most of the fellas here knew what was actually going down, they'd feel the same – which was why she'd only allowed a couple to remain, locking the door behind her. Ones she felt sure were loyal to her. Ceallach had only just undergone re-education, so was unlikely to want to go there again in a hurry. The other guard across the way, Artair, lived up to the name she'd given him; stone-like, unmoved by what was occurring.

Which was more than could be said for Hood's woman. Little wonder, when the Widow had just told them she was up the duff, and now her husband was being treated like a suckling pig on a spit. The Widow was licking her lips at the prospect. Salivating.

This was too much; too much. He'd done some bad things in his time, but a line was being crossed here. Could Ceallach just stand by and watch? He had to do something. Ceallach – no, that's the name *she* gave you, a Celtic name meaning *war* or *strife*; your name is Tommy Neagle, remember? Tommy gritted his teeth, knowing that he was going to regret this, but the time had come to test his theory.

The time had come to see if this bloody madwoman really could see into the future.

He turned his machine-gun on the Widow.

"Let him down," Tommy told her. "Or I'll shoot."

At first he didn't think she'd heard him. She didn't turn or even look. Then, slowly, she shifted her gaze from the fire, and Hood, to Tommy. She frowned, perhaps thinking he'd gone insane, unable to see that the only crazy one around here was her. "And what exactly do yer think yer doin', Ceallach?"

"Tommy," he grumbled under his breath. Then, louder: "My name is fuckin' Tommy! Now let him down, for God's sake."

"God?" The Widow didn't move, but he saw beyond her that Hood's wife had begun to look hopeful.

When Tommy looked back at the Widow, she'd moved closer. He raised his machine-gun higher. "Don't move, I'm warnin' yer!"

Then everything seemed to happen at once. The Widow leapt forward again, and Tommy fired. At the same time, Artair turned his gun on Tommy, which this was all the distraction Hood's woman needed to strike. She spoiled Artair's aim by grabbing the rifle and twisting, then delivering a punch across the face that any heavyweight boxer would have been proud of. But she hadn't finished yet. With the flat of her hand, she smacked Artair squarely in the face. There was a loud *crack* as his nasal cartilage shattered, was driven up into the man's brain.

That didn't help Tommy, though. The Widow was no longer in front of him, where he'd just fired. She was off to one side, blowing something in his face. He coughed, spluttered; then attempted to move.

He couldn't.

Fuck.

He heard the Widow laughing in his ear. "Time to meet yer God in person, Tommy." She showed him the golden dagger; held it under his nose, in fact, to taunt him. Then it was gone, and Tommy felt a sharp, stabbing pain in his side as she slid it into him – holding his shoulder to stop him falling over. He would have screamed, except that his jaw had locked up completely. And he would have dropped to the ground, but his knees were fixed in position. *Should have called me Artair,* he thought, but there was no humour to it. He was dying and he knew that. Tommy felt the blade being removed, and then he saw why.

A blur in front of him, another crazed woman – this time out to save her man from his terrible fate. She grabbed hold of the Widow, and started pummelling her face. "Bet you didn't see *that* coming!" shrieked Hood's woman, her words fuelled by hatred. The Widow responded by shaking her head, wiping her nose, and lashing out with the bloodied dagger. The blood that had saved him, when everyone else had died of the virus. Tommy attempted to roll his eyes down to his belt, but Hood's woman wasn't looking. Thankfully, she'd thought of the same, and turned to face him, unsheathing both his claymore and his belt-knife.

Yes! thought Tommy, now actually rooting for Hood's woman. She was only just in time to block an attack from the Widow, bringing up both weapons she'd taken and crossing them to prevent the dagger from plunging into her chest.

The Widow was still fast, but the unexpected punches had hampered her a little. More evidence, Tommy thought, that she couldn't really predict what was about to happen.

Unless she'd been too close to this whole thing? a voice in his mind said. *Maybe it had clouded her judgement?* It didn't matter now; he wouldn't be around for much longer. But he was holding on to see who would win the grudge match between the two women.

On the face of it, that should have been obvious. The Widow had bested bigger and better opponents. But Hood's woman was fighting with such determination and rage, he wasn't sure. She pushed back the

Widow's lunge, kicking out at the Widow's midriff. His former leader crumpled, taking a couple of steps backwards, but soon straightened. Hood's woman swept the claymore around in an arc, and the Widow only narrowly avoided having her head separated from her body.

The Widow's response was to sweep her leg up, knocking the sword from the woman's hand and sending it spinning across the room. That left them with just knives. Both women hunkered down, trying to anticipate each other's moves. The Widow still looked sluggish from the blows to the face, or Tommy was sure she'd have been on Hood's woman in seconds, and her enemy wouldn't have stood a chance. As it was when they clashed, it was Hood's lady who had the distinct advantage, her knife slashes fast and furious while the Widow seemed to be having trouble avoiding them.

Tommy watched as the Widow began to mumble something in that unknown language she'd been using before. But whatever spell she'd been trying to muster either didn't work or she didn't get time to finish it, because Hood's woman brought down the knife – forcing the Widow to grab her wrist with her free hand to stop it from entering her shoulder. Hood's woman had to do the same to avoid getting stabbed in the ribs, and the pair staggered around like this for a few moments, each looking for an opening.

It was the Widow who was losing ground, having to find her footing again and again as Hood's woman heaved her back, but on the very last push, the Widow used her opponent's momentum against her, dragging her around full circle and flinging her to the ground. She struck the floor hard and Tommy looked on in dismay as his knife flew out of the woman's hand, clattering across the stone. The Widow followed up with a kick across the jaw which sent the woman's head whipping sideways and saw her flat on her back. The Widow laughed.

"I was goin' tae let you watch what came next, but I suppose the time's come for doin' what Robert couldn't. Killing you and that little maggot inside yer. Cuttin' all links to ma intended." It was then that Tommy realised how completely mental the Widow was. She was still talking as if she was going to marry Hood or something, rather than eat him. The Widow held the dagger high, ready to bring it down into the woman's stomach.

Tommy was aware that his vision was fading as his body went numb. He'd hung on for as long as he could, but it seemed that the woman's fate was sealed. Just like his. It would have been nice to have seen his death avenged, even if Hood's woman hadn't known she was doing it. But everything was growing black, even though he couldn't close his eyes.

Then something happened that made him fight for every second he had left. The Widow was just about to strike when a pair of legs appeared, wrapping themselves around her shoulders and neck. Using all the effort he could muster, Tommy raised his eyes to see that Hood had swung over using the rope and grabbed the Widow, locking her tightly between his legs.

Again, the Widow seemed shocked – and before she could think about bringing the dagger up and into Hood's leg, he was straining on the ropes and pulling her backwards. Tommy was amazed at the resolve he was showing – perhaps there was something to the legend after all, if he could pull victory from the jaws of death like this. Or just sheer bloody-mindedness? The muscles in the man's taut body were bulging, thighs pressing against the sides of the Widow's head, causing her obvious pain. But he was also pulling against the ropes, his biceps fighting against the Widow's efforts to stay put.

With a last concerted effort, gritting his teeth, Hood pulled her backwards and off her feet. Turning, she realised too late what was about to happen and again began chanting in that strange language, as if that was going to save her.

It wasn't. Tommy watched, with a certain degree of satisfaction, as the woman was pulled onto the pyre. It seemed only fitting for a witch to be killed that way. Hood used whatever strength remained to pull his legs and feet up out of the way of the flames as they caught the Widow's body, drowning her in a fiery sea.

Tommy was aware of banging at the door. They didn't have long before the rest of the Widow's men would be inside. But Hood's woman was already climbing to her feet, limping across to the rope that held the man she loved suspended above the fire.

He didn't see her get him down or what happened next, because Tommy's life was pretty much at an end. But as his vision went completely and his heart stopped, he celebrated this small victory at least. The Widow, the woman who'd killed him, had been defeated.

But Tommy also knew that this was far from the end of Hood and his woman's problems.

THE VEHICLES HAD pulled up, the driver of the largest nervously gripping the wheel.

This had been a stupid, stupid idea and was bound to fail. How on earth had he let himself get talked into it? Because the people inside there had put their lives on the line for such as him. He owed them. They all did. The least they could do was try and free them.

But Jesus, was this the wrong way to go about it. They'd never get away with it. They'd been lucky that they'd managed to get past the check-points so far, although a couple had needed taking out when they got too nosey. That, to his mind, didn't give them much time before their subterfuge was discovered. Weren't check-points supposed to check *in* every now and again? What happened when they didn't? Was a radio screw-up blamed, or did it mean another ambush awaited *them*? At one of the security checks someone had mentioned radioing in, but then a guard had said that the Widow was engaged in urgent business and wouldn't want to be disturbed. That gave him some hope, at least, that they might make it to the castle.

And they had enough captured uniforms and vehicles to make the Widow's men think twice about firing in case they really were on the level; though reason also told him that they knew they'd been stolen a few days ago, so might be expecting such a trick. After all, Hood and his team had gone in there and never come out again. If *they* could be taken...

Matt Jamison could hear Bill's voice even now, knew what he would say in reply to that. "Show some bloody backbone!" Well he was here, wasn't he? When they'd been told of what had happened, about the Widow taking Robert's group prisoner, he and his friends had volunteered to make up the numbers.

"I just heard from Nottingham Castle. Some kind of big push goin' on in Wales," Bill had explained, "so we won't be getting any re-enforcements. But I've decided to mount some kind o' rescue anyway, with the few Rangers we already have."

"It's suicide," one of the traders had said, and Bill had flown at the man.

"They'd do the same for me, or for ye. They've put their lives on the line more times than I've trodden in cow dung. So if ye think I'm just going to wait around here playin' with mysen, think again."

Bill was right, of course. Whether or not Matt agreed with how they'd gone about scuppering that raid – he still said they should have warned the drivers – the Rangers had come to help at Bill's request. They'd also saved lives that day, and who knows how many others, by taking those raiders into custody. Even now, they were being guarded in makeshift prisons by other volunteers from the trader community, most of whom now pledged their support for Bill.

Just like Matt had done.

It was then that Bill had told them about his scheme. In a way, Matt shouldn't have been that surprised. The Rangers were known for their brass balls when it came to things like this – God in Heaven, how Robert and Mary could have gone to Edinburgh in the first place like that was beyond him. *Asking* to be killed, all of them. But they'd felt the need to do more digging, perhaps even take out the Widow quickly and quietly. That plan had failed, so what made Bill think this one would fare any better? The men at the castle were much better armed and greater in number. Bill was asking Matt and his trader friends to go up against that when most of them hadn't seen any combat in their lives.

Again, Bill's probable answer echoed in Matt's head: "Then it's about time, in't it?" They were living in a different world these days, had been for a while. A new and dangerous world, one which Robert and his men were trying to enforce and police – as impossible as that might seem. That's what they'd been attempting to do up here, and *that's* why Matt had agreed to all this, he reminded himself. Now he was beginning to regret his decision.

Matt had swallowed when he saw all the vehicles on the grassland either side of the Esplanade; enough to win a small war, he reckoned – though Bill assured him Robert and co. had faced worse. He was waiting for things to kick off at any moment, as there was no way they could continue getting away with this. For one thing, wasn't this damned Widow supposed to know everything that was happening in advance? A stupid rumour, but one that had started somewhere. Indeed, even as he thought it, Matt saw the Rangers in the jeeps up ahead being flagged down – those riding bikes pulling up also. They were dressed in the Widow's tartan, had the same attire as those people telling them to halt, but they'd surely be marked at any time as impostors. Matt watched anxiously as one Ranger pointed down the convoy line; clearly trying to convey what a great catch they'd made and how full all the vehicles were with foodstuffs. If nothing else, the Widow and her lot were greedy beggars and might let them in purely because of what they could be carrying.

There was also the distinct possibility that the people in charge at the gatehouse were going to want to search the vehicles – which is what they looked like they were about to do. Matt spotted raiders heading down towards the armoured vehicles on the grass, perhaps getting ready to go out on a routine patrol, but maybe in anticipation of something else occurring? If their enemies chose to attack from both sides, then Matt and his friends would be caught in the crossfire to end all crossfires. And where the devil was Bill? Not here in the trenches, that was for sure. "Don't ye worry," he'd told them, "I won't let ye get caught with ye britches down."

Matt gripped the wheel even harder as the Widow's men traipsed down the line of vehicles. If Bill had thought they could just waltz in here, he was dreaming. But then he saw something else.

Men, crawling underneath the vehicles in the convoy – Rangers who'd climbed out of the backs of carts and the other vehicles, making their way beneath to reach the gatehouse unseen; pausing if any of the raiders walked by.

As one of the guards passed by, Matt gave him an uneasy smile and salute. The man paused, and for a moment Matt thought he was going to ask something. He didn't – just continued up along to the tail end of his truck. Matt watched him in the rear view banging on the side of the truck. "Open her up!" he called down to Matt.

"Well, Stacey," he told his truck as he prepared to get out, fingers curling around the handle of his baseball bat, "this is it."

From somewhere came the sound of a helicopter. Matt looked sideways and saw something black coming in fast and low: a beast of a thing that meant business. It was armed to the teeth with missiles, and – as it got closer – what looked like machine-guns.

It took just one of those missiles to cause complete and utter pandemonium. Detaching from the helicopter, the projectile whistled into the banks of armoured vehicles to the right of Matt and the convoy. He watched, mouth gaping, as a couple of jeeps flew up into the air with an explosion loud enough to almost deafen him.

Matt saw the guard at the back of his truck fling himself to the ground as the helicopter flew over them, so close he could have jumped up onto Stacey's cab and hitched a ride. As it passed by, Matt caught a glimpse of the painting on the side door – a cartoon shotgun which had just gone off, the sound effect 'Blam!' written next to the red and yellow explosion.

"Bill," Matt said to himself as the chopper came about on the other side of the convoy. It fired another missile into the vehicles there, taking out jeeps, tanks and bikes. It was all the distraction the Rangers near the front of the convoy needed. With practiced skill, they reached into their jeeps for bows and arrows; those riding bikes pulled out bolas which they flung at the gatehouse, causing whatever was inside them to explode on contact.

The Rangers who'd been crawling under the convoy sprang up to pick off the guards defending the entrance. Arrows were shot over the walls, followed by Rangers scrambling up them and over onto the other side like ants into a hill. Matt could do nothing but watch and marvel at the efficiency of their attack. More exploding bolas and arrows struck the Gate and suddenly it was open, free for the Ranger-manned jeeps to enter.

There was no way Matt was getting inside there with his truck, but Bill had thought of that, too, it seemed. As soon as his men had cleared the Esplanade and gatehouse, another – smaller, targeted – missile hit the entrance and expanded the opening. Matt winced at the damage, but the history of the place wouldn't have crossed Bill's mind. The tourist days were over for this castle, and it was time to worm out the woman who'd caused so much havoc in the region, no matter what the cost.

Matt put Stacey into gear and began to move forward. Carrying his payload into the castle, up towards the portcullis gate.

"SHOT!" BILL SAID in his rough, Derbyshire accent.

What he'd just done to the gatehouse was regrettable, especially to students of history, but he'd needed to create an opening for Matt and his truck to get inside. The Widow's people would have no qualms about doing the same, just as the Tsar's folk hadn't with their own castle back home. The Widow had picked this spot because it was easy to defend, and the gate there was *part* of that defence. Which was why it needed to be obliterated. Thoughts of rebuilding would come afterwards, *if* they won – right now, all Bill could think about was taking this place back from the thieves and murderers who'd made it their home, returning the castle to its true heirs: the locals who'd had to put up with the Widow's shenanigans for too long. Scottish people like those traders who'd chosen to fight with the Rangers today.

From his position, Bill could see his men making their way up towards the portcullis gates, in jeeps, on bikes and on foot. He could also see the number of guards on the other side, in the castle grounds. Roused by the explosions and machine-gun fire, they were flitting about: especially near the building Bill knew to be the New Barracks; arming and generally gearing themselves up to repel boarders.

There was no way of telling from up here where Robert, Mary or the other Rangers might be – *if* they were even still alive. That would be the job of those on the ground to ascertain. There were some good Rangers down there, all of whom had been trained to the best of their abilities. But, in Bill's opinion, you couldn't beat some top of the range firepower on your side. He knew what Robert would say, and if he'd been around he would have prevented Bill from using the Black Shark at all – which he'd lovingly restored after the battle Robert fought with the Tsar's men, including re-arming her with spares from other wrecked Black Sharks that had been taken down that day, and making a number of modifications himself. But Robert *wasn't* here. He'd gone and got himself and his team captured, so it was up to Bill to try and sort this muddle out. He hadn't been able to obtain any more men or weapons from Nottingham because Jack had bloody well requisitioned all they could spare – and Bill fully intended to have words with the big, dumb lummox about that later. So what else was he supposed to do? They needed a way of taking out some of those armoured vehicles down there, and this was the only option he could think of.

The fact that he'd been dying to try this baby out in combat since he'd fixed her up was neither here nor there.

"That's my girl," he said, nudging the one-seater craft to one side. She handled like a dream, even better than his old Sioux or Gazelle, and she definitely packed more of a bite. In all honesty, Bill reckoned he could probably take on the whole of the Widow's mob single-handed, decimating the castle and everyone there, if it weren't for the fact his friends were somewhere inside.

He opened up the cannon on a group of the Widow's men, his targeting system so precise he could put the wind up them without having to kill. The vehicles were another matter, and fair game as far as he was concerned, so he loosed another couple of missiles into what was rapidly becoming a vehicles' graveyard, twisted metal jutting up from the ground like bones.

Something was moving to his left, and Bill manoeuvred round to see a Gepard anti-aircraft tank emerging from the smoke, massive twin guns being raised in his direction. The Germans who'd supplied all this kit had obviously thrown in a few driving lessons for the Widow's men. The brute trundling over the green, up and onto the Esplanade itself, was the first thing he'd seen which could give him a run for his money. Both 90 calibre guns spat at once, armour-piercing rounds which could tear through the Black Shark's torso like paper. Bill pulled back on the control stick sharply; perhaps a little too sharply, as the Black Shark protested.

"Bear with me, girl," he said to the chopper, angling her round. The fire from the Gepard was still reaching into the sky. Fortunately the men aiming the guns were lacking in practice, and Bill had done nothing *but*, even if he had saved most of the live ammo he'd salvaged for just such a occasion. He fired an anti-tank missile and grinned as the laser-guided projectile found its target, giving Bill plenty of time to get clear of the blast zone. The Gepard opened up like one of those old bangers in a black and white slapstick movie.

Coming about, Bill flew over the top of the castle once more, noticing a Ranger jeep about to ram the portcullis gate, the driver inside throwing himself clear at the last moment. The vehicle slammed into the gridded obstacle, knocking through it before grinding to a standstill. The other vehicles behind drew up, Rangers climbing out of jeeps or from bikes, while Matt's truck – too wide to get any further – was opened at the back.

A mass of men – traders and Rangers, men and women – leapt from the trailer, rushing forward through the portcullis. They'd meet the guards heading in their direction any moment, so Bill decided to even the odds a little. He sprayed a covering fire in front of the Widow's forces, enough to make them pause. Some even fired up at the helicopter, but hit nothing. Then his troops were there, on the ground and tackling the soldiers. His lot may be outnumbered, but Bill was proud to see the guards falling first and fast, spinning round to reveal arrows in shoulders or thighs. And yes, there was Matt himself, having climbed out of the cab of his truck. He was putting his baseball bat to good use, whacking enemies as they came round one of the corners near the portcullis gate.

More had taken up positions along the wall, to shoot at his people from above. Bill wasn't having that, and so spun the chopper around, splattering them with gunfire and causing the guards to fall back from the walls. But it was as he did so that he felt something strike the side of the Black Shark to his right. Bill craned his head to see the old cannons from the Argyle battery had been pulled around and raised up to fire at the chopper. The mixture of old and new weaponry obviously extended beyond those claymores they fought with.

Two more fired at him, one hitting the tail end of the Black Shark. "Why, you little –" began Bill, but before he could say any more, he was being fired on from the left as well, ducking heavy cannonballs. Bill attempted to dodge them, but he'd flown in too close, assuming, wrongly, that the old relics didn't work anymore. His control panel was lighting up like a Christmas tree, emergency alarms wailing in his cockpit. "Damn and blast it," he said, narrowly avoiding another blast from a cannon which would have downed the Black Shark there and then if it had hit.

Bill searched for a place to put her down, and quickly – only now spotting smoke from one of the reservoir buildings and wondering what it was. But he didn't have time to dwell on that. The square next to the palace appeared to be the only open-plan area nearby to attempt an emergency landing. He dipped the nose, hopping over the War Memorial and almost catching the back end of his helicopter on the roof. His landing was rough, to say the least; only some of his gear responded when he flipped the switch.

"Easy," he said, tapping the roof of the helicopter from the inside after he'd set her down, calming the thing like it was some kind of pet. He didn't have much time to check on the damage, because he was already being fired on by the Widow's men. Bill risked using his cannon: the aim was totally shot, but he hoped he could scare the gunmen enough so he could effect an escape. He pressed the trigger, but only one round went off, hitting the building in front of him and kicking dust up from the stonework.

It would have to do; he grabbed his shotgun, opened the cockpit and dived out. Rolling, he balanced on one knee and let off both barrels into the group of approaching soldiers. It scattered them, but a couple still came at him on the left. They fired and some of the gunshot sparked off the pilot's helmet he was wearing. "Judas Priest!" he shouted. With no time to reload, Bill turned his gun around and hit one on the side of the head, sending him toppling. The other he grabbed by the collar and pulled in close, settling matters with one punch. He snatched up their machine-guns in both hands and sprayed the other guards with bullets, left and right.

Then he ran across the yard, looking for a way inside, using the wall of a building for cover. "Might as well start searchin' while I'm 'ere," he said to no-one in particular.

And, with that, he ducked inside the building that would take him to the castle vaults.

CHAPTER SEVENTEEN

"You, um, need to know something before we go in," said Meghan.

They'd almost reached the area of the stadium where she delivered food. Dale hoped so, because he was sick of the chase. It was nowhere near the place he'd gone with her the first time, but then he guessed the Dragon hadn't wanted the ambush to take place anywhere close to his family. Probably hadn't wanted any of them seeing what he liked to look at on those screens, either. *I'll bet he kept that very quiet*, he thought, *unless they're all as twisted as him, of course.*

"What is it?" asked Dale as they made their way down along yet another corridor, nearly at the end of their journey.

"I-It's his family."

"What about them?"

"They're, well, it's hard to explain, but –"

Jack shushed them both as they came to the corner. "Guards," he said, pointing.

That meant the Dragon *had* to be inside that room. Even with everything going on, with his empire crashing down around his ears, that creep could still command some kind of respect – still command his men. There were a couple of the Welshman's guards outside, and Jack motioned for Dale to take out the one to the right of the door. "But quietly. We don't want to tip off whoever's inside," he told Dale. "You up to it?" he whispered, scrutinizing the young man.

Dale stood a little straighter, hiding the discomfort he was in. "When have I ever refused an invitation to party?"

Jack grinned. "So let's dance, kid."

The trick was to incapacitate the guards before they could get off a shot or a warning cry. Jack rounded the corner first, jabbing a guard with his staff. Dale followed close behind, putting the butt of his machine-gun first in the second guard's belly, doubling him over, then to his temple, putting him on the ground. When the man started to get up, Dale delivered a blow to the back of the neck for good measure. He looked across at how Jack was getting on: the bigger man was disarming his opponent. The machine-gun clattered to the ground, a little too noisily, and from Jack's expression Dale could see the element of surprise had already been lost.

The guard then foolishly attempted to grab the former wrestler around the neck. Jack bent and threw the guard over his head, then gave the man an almighty kick, knocking him into the door and knocking the *door* down.

Jack was inside first, but his reward for being so eager was a smack in the face from a waiting guard. Dale stepped in and felt the barrel of a pistol against his temple. "Drop it," he was told, so he let the machine-gun fall to the ground. These were two of the Dragon's most trusted guards; they had to be.

As Jack was rising, a machine pistol trained on him, he was relieved of his staff. And now he saw what Dale was looking at, too.

The room was laid out almost like a bedsit; a living room area with chairs and a bed. There were people sitting in the chairs, and one lying in the bed, Dale could see, but there was something wrong with them. They were much thinner than they should have been, in spite of all the food Meghan must have delivered. In fact, they were malnourished, with stick-like arms that hung limply at their sides – although one was attempting to knit. The Dragon's grandmother, Dale supposed. The figure in bed was sitting up, leaning back against the pillows. Dale guessed he's been injured at some time.

His mind wouldn't let him see it at first, *couldn't* let him see what was in front of him. Because the truth was too hideous to contemplate. That someone could do this, even after everything else he'd witnessed at the Dragon's hands, was too much. It threatened to bend Dale's mind, just as something must surely have bent the Dragon's long ago.

"Dale... they're..." Jack obviously had as much trouble processing the information as him. "They're all –"

"Dead," finished Dale. All three of them. They'd been dressed up to look as though they were still alive, positioned carefully. The gran was knitting, the mother had a magazine on her lap open at some celebrity gossip that had long since failed to have any meaning. The father was just staring out in an accusatory way at everything in front of him, including Jack and Dale. Or he would have been staring if he'd still had eyes. All of the corpses were in a distinct state of decay, the flesh rotted from their bones, eyes long since gone to jelly, leaving empty black sockets behind. Dale wondered how they all still had hair, but then noticed the artificiality of it, especially the tight curls of the mother and gran. Wigs taken from a hairdressers or fancy dress shop.

There wasn't the usual stench associated with death – and Dale knew this all too well, from his time walking the streets post-Cull. The air smelt quite sweet, thanka no doubt to large amounts of air-freshener being pumped into the atmosphere.

Dale turned as much and as slowly as he could and saw Meghan being ushered in by one of the recovering guards from the doorway. "You brought *them* food?" he asked.

She nodded. "I had to, and change their clothes. I did everything for them." Tears were in her eyes again and Dale shuddered at what she must have gone through as their personal slave.

"And don't think we didn't appreciate it, dear," came a voice from the back of the room. It was female, and appeared to be coming from the mother.

"That's right," said another feminine voice, this time sounding much frailer: the grandmother. "We don't know what we would have done without you."

Dale frowned, searching for the source. He didn't have to look far. There, at the back of the room, now stepping out from behind a partition, was the Dragon. He was half dragging, half holding up Sian, the girl's head drooping as it had been on the screen in the other room. Probably drugged, Dale suspected, or just worn down by her interrogation.

Dale took a step forwards when he saw her, forgetting about the gun until it was cocked. "Let her go!" he shouted.

"He really should, shouldn't he," said the mother, and now Dale could see the Dragon's lips moving. Christ, how long had he been having conversations with his dead relatives? "But she's such a sweet young thing. The only girlfriend he's ever brought back to meet us."

"I wonder why." This voice was gruffer, a thick Welsh accent. The Dragon's father.

"Now, don't you two start again," said the mother.

All the voices sounded real. Drawn from real life, Dale imagined; honed over years.

"I really like this one," the Dragon said in his own voice, and for a second Dale didn't even recognise it. This was the first time he'd spoken since they'd discovered his little secret.

Dale tried to look to the side, at the guard, but the barrel of the gun was pressed harder into his temple. "Look, can't you see what's happening here? The kind of man you're protecting?"

"Your boss is a Grade A fruitcake," Jack added.

"I am *not* a –" the Dragon began, then smiled. "You're only jealous, all of you."

"Of what?" Dale spluttered.

"My family survived. I'm guessing most of yours didn't."

"They're not looking too healthy for people who are supposed to be alive," Dale argued.

"What's he talking about, sweetheart?" asked the mother.

"I feel as fit as a fiddle," the Dragon now said in the grandmother's voice. "Never felt better."

"Don't know what he needs a girlfriend for anyway," the father piped up. "It's not like he'd be able to do anything with her."

"Ryn!" snapped the mother.

"Well, look at him. Even if he wasn't such a pansy, he's the size of a bloody house."

"This is crackers," said Dale, stating the obvious. "Let her go right now, you sick fuck, or –"

"Hey, boy, don't you talk to our Owain like that! Little prick."

The Dragon looked sideways, at the dead body that had once been his father. "Dad?"

"You're still my son. Might not be anything like Gareth, but you're still my flesh and..." The Dragon hesitated, some small part of his brain realising the significance of what he was saying.

If they had exactly the same blood, then his father would still be alive. Or had the man died after the virus? Dale wondered. Whatever the case, the Dragon had stopped; had realised. It was probably also the most touching moment he'd ever shared with his father, and it wasn't even real. Dale might have felt sorry for him, if he hadn't caused so much death and destruction. If he didn't still have Sian in a vice-like grip.

"It's time to end this," Jack said. "Right *now!*"

Dale moved quickly, ignoring his pain, ducking and elbowing the guard holding the gun to him in one movement. The pistol went off, deafening him, but he couldn't allow that to stop him; too much was at stake. Dale grabbed the guard's gun arm, pulling it down and forcing the man to pull the trigger again, to shoot himself in his foot. Dale barely heard the muffled howl of agony. He looked over to see Jack wrestling with his own guard, having already disarmed him – a final head butt saw the man sinking to his knees. "The girl," Dale just about made out from Jack's lips, while the larger man concentrated on the guard holding Meghan. The guard pushed her to the floor, readying himself for Jack's second attack of the day.

As Dale moved forwards, though, the Dragon pulled Sian into a headlock, as though to twist it off if he came any closer. "Let her go," Dale repeated.

"No! She's mine."

There were two gunshots in quick succession, and Dale – wrongly – assumed they were the result of Jack's tussle with the final guard. But then he noticed the two bullet holes in the Dragon's chest. Dale turned around, and was surprised to see Meghan holding the first guard's pistol, the one that had been pressed against his own temple. She was on her knees, her wounded hand hanging by her side, but the other was outstretched, still holding the smoking gun.

Dale often thought back to that day, and wondered if Meghan had just been really lucky not to hit Sian, or if the size of the Dragon had helped with her aim; after all, there was so much more of him than her niece. Meghan didn't know either, and she'd never fired a gun in her life before, as she'd explained afterwards. Something had just made her pick it up and shoot. Something guiding her hand. An instinct that had tried to keep Sian safe long before the Dragon came along.

Sian dropped from the Dragon's grasp as he tottered backwards. Dale went across to her, keeping his eye on the big man as he went. The Dragon was looking down at the holes, the blood. His eyes were wide as he dipped his fingers inside, not daring to believe he'd been hit.

"I can't," he said. "I'm..."

"Oh, Owain, let us have a look at that. I'm sure it'll be all right if we put some antiseptic on it and a plaster," he managed in his mother's voice – though Dale noticed the tremble of fear.

Then Owain said one thing in his father's tones: "Prat."

Dale began pulling Sian away from the scene. The Dragon clutched at his wounds, and his hands came away scarlet. He rubbed his face with them, closing his eyes.

Dale shuddered as the Dragon opened them again, looking more like his namesake than ever. "I... I am..." he said, then stumbled forwards. He held on to the back of his father's bed for support. Dale watched him reach down, lifting the pillow.

"Do you remember, Dad? When you brought me here?" The Dragon's voice was weakening as he brought out the object he'd hidden there. "D-do you remember those rugby games?"

"Jesus," said Dale. "Jack, Meghan, we have to get out of here!" They looked at him, puzzled, so he thumbed back towards the Dragon – now holding a rugby ball. "It's a bomb!"

That did the trick, and Jack helped Meghan up, pulling her out through the door. Dale followed closely behind with Sian, struggling to hold her up and knowing they only had a few moments left. His ears had finally stopped ringing and he clearly heard the last words to come from inside the room.

"Do you remember what we said, what you taught me? Say it with me now. We are Dragons. Come on…" He sounded like he was half crying; but to Dale, right at the end, it also sounded like there was more than one voice. "We are Dragons. I. AM. A. DRAGO –"

The explosion blew them halfway up the corridor, but the walls protected them from much of the blast. It had to have killed the Dragon, though, even if his gunshot wounds hadn't – not to mention the other men who'd chosen to guard him. Everyone else in there had been dead a long time ago.

As the smoke cleared, Jack and Meghan rose, and Dale picked Sian up. She was starting to stir a little, thankfully, even tried to smile when she opened her eyes and saw him. He smiled back, brushing hair out of her eyes.

"Come on," Jack said, "that's enough of all that." He realised he was still holding onto Meghan, and let go. He coughed. "We'd better check what's happening in the rest of this place. It ain't over yet, kid."

But compared with what they'd just gone through – what he, Sian and Meghan had been *going* through for a while – how could the battles raging upstairs be any worse?

THINGS WERE ABOUT to get much worse.

Robert thought it as Mary freed him from the ropes at his wrists. Oh, his legs were scorched in places, but it could have been so much worse. And they'd had some good fortune: take the guy who'd confronted the Widow, now standing like a statue, quite clearly dead from the knife wound she'd inflicted on him. Robert felt sure he recognised him, had seen the man somewhere, but couldn't place him. Why had he done it? They'd probably never know, but they *had* been lucky. But that luck was about to run out. Apart from the veritable army about to knock down the door, Robert still had his wife – his *real* wife – to face. And apologise to. "Mary, listen –"

"Later," she told him.

"But..."

She placed a finger to his lips as she helped him up. "I know what you were doing," Mary told him. "Buying us time. Trying to fool her. You weren't the only one acting back there, you know. Oh, I didn't want to listen at first, but then someone close forced me to."

He was about to ask what she meant when she kissed him, long and hard, on the lips. It was as she was doing so that the first of the explosions went off. "Did the earth move for you?" she asked.

"Always."

They kissed again, the explosions and gunfire a million miles away. But when they broke off, Robert frowned. "Can you smell –"

"Burning!" Mary screamed, pushing Robert away. Coming at them was a flaming figure, risen from the bonfire like some kind of phoenix. The Widow rushed at them, flailing her hands, still wielding the sacrificial dagger that meant so much to her. For a moment Robert thought that the words she'd been uttering as he dragged her back onto the flames might have worked; that instead of burning her alive, they'd somehow made her more powerful. But if it was black magic keeping her alive, it didn't last for long. She dropped to the ground after failing to either share the fire with the couple or stab them.

As she fell, she let go of the dagger and Mary promptly kicked it away, out of reach. The flames went out quickly, leaving her body blackened and crisp. Still the Widow struggled to rise, climbing to her hands and knees. Robert thought then how much she resembled the thing he'd seen in his dream: the spider that was her namesake.

She toppled over onto her back, her breathing shallow. Only her eyes and her teeth now shone white. Though it was clearly agony for her to do so, the Widow gestured for Robert to come closer. He remained where he was, and she whispered something inaudible.

Robert took a step nearer.

"Robert, *no!*"

"She's trying to speak," he told Mary.

"Just be careful. She's dangerous."

There was a laugh from the Widow at this, followed by a pained moan. Robert leaned in, close enough to hear but not near enough to be grabbed if she decided to pull a stunt.

"W-won't hurt yer..." breathed the Widow. "Just wanted to tell yer, we will meet agin... Robert, ma Hooded Man. I'll see yer agin..."

Robert shook his head. It was highly doubtful, but then hadn't he seen De Falaise and the Tsar again after their deaths? After he'd *taken* their lives?

"It's... it's fitting..." she told him. "What I deserved... but it is not the end... You'll get yer magic back, Robert... This I promise... And we... we *will* see each other again." She reached up now, too quickly for him to pull back. She grabbed his arm, pulling him closer. Mary made a move, but he held up his other hand.

The Widow smiled, eyes closing. "Tae bad," she whispered, "It could have been... somethin' quite special." Then she collapsed back to the ground.

Robert looked at the thing in his hand: a blackened card, but he could still make out the picture of the Emperor on its surface. He shook his head.

Mary said nothing. She just crouched down on the other side of the Widow, wrapped her fingers in the edge of her top and pulled off the golden ring on the third finger of the woman's left hand. "Mine, I believe."

They'd been so caught up in the Widow's final moments that they hadn't noticed the escalating gunfire and explosions outside. The banging on the door continued nonetheless, those loyal to the Widow still trying to get in.

Robert barely had time to stand when the door finally caved and in rushed several raiders. Mary helped him to his feet, not knowing what either of them could do. But then they saw the guards lowering their weapons. "Robert? Mary?"

He squinted, trying to see beyond the goggles and masks. One pulled off his headgear to reveal a face he recognised. "Saxton!"

The others came inside and Robert saw there were more Rangers dressed like the Widow's men, but bringing up the rear and shouting for them to let him past was a voice he recognised all too well. "Come on, move aside. Let the dog see the..." Bill paused when he saw Robert. "Well, I didn't really want to see *that* much!" he exclaimed, nodding at his friend's nakedness. Mary stood in front of her husband, at least until she could find something to cover him with.

"Bill, you came for us," said Robert, giving him a weary smile.

"Aye lad, in the Black Shark. Didn't ye hear me?" Bill laughed, until he caught the glare Robert was giving him. "Ahem, but look who I found in the Widow's dungeons," the ex-farmer said, changing the subject. He stepped back to reveal Azhar, Annie Reid and some of the other Rangers from Robert's original strike force.

Robert's smile widened. "What's happening outside now?"

"The battle's still going on, but we're holding our own, with the help of the traders I brought with us. Won't take long to settle now we're all back together again. It's the Widow we're really after, mind. Fix her and you fix the probl –" Bill suddenly stopped, as if only now seeing the blackened thing between them on the ground. "What's that?"

"Consider the problem fixed," Mary told him, putting her wedding ring back on now that it had cooled.

CHAPTER EIGHTEEN

SHE'D BEEN ON the move for hours. Her legs ached, her feet had blisters, but she marched on. She didn't need the torch anymore, since the sun had started to rise. *Nearly there,* she kept telling herself. *Reach the outskirts and you'll be spotted. They'll take you to the castle and you can explain everything. You can do your bit.*

Walking through the woodland at night had been the hardest part – all those strange sounds and movements in the undergrowth. After finding the dirt track to the main road, it was just a matter of following the map to the city. It reminded her a little of the walks her parents would insist on taking when she was younger, out every weekend into the country, boots and backpacks on, striding out over hill and dale. If nothing else, that had prepared her for a hike like this. And she'd kept herself fit during her adult years, going to the gym three nights a week, keeping her alcohol consumption down. *Yeah, only because you never used to go out anywhere at the weekend; even the walks with your folks were better than the marathon weepie sessions with a chick flick and a box of Kleenex.*

Approaching thirty and still a virgin, stuck in a dead-end job as a receptionist with a boss she hated, fancying male employees but never having the courage to ask any of them out. Karen Shipley, hopeless romantic with no-one to lavish her affections on. It had taken most of the population of the planet being wiped out before she stood even the remotest chance with a guy.

Karen hadn't really wept for anyone during those early stages of the virus, because she didn't have anyone she loved as such – her parents had died in a car accident long before that. Perhaps they'd been the lucky ones? Neville from Human Resources didn't count because he was creepy, and she'd only snogged him under the mistletoe that

Christmas because she had given in to the booze at the office party. It had taken her so long to stop him from trailing her around the place that she was almost grateful for the virus... No, that was terrible. Poor Neville. Poor *everyone*. She didn't like to think the only reason it had happened was so she could actually get herself a man.

Yet it was looking like that might be a happy by-product. The one ray of sunshine in this whole, stinking mess. It wasn't her fault the virus killed all those people who didn't have O-Neg blood like hers. The more she thought about it, the more it made a kind of sense; it was the duty of those left behind to hook up and try and repopulate the planet, wasn't it? Karen knew exactly who she wanted to start her own particular repopulation with, as well.

She'd known from the minute she set foot in the village, after being picked up by a scout party from New Hope. Karen had convinced them she had skills they'd find useful – typing counted, right? By the time they discovered she didn't have anything to offer, she'd already made herself indispensable fetching and carrying, working hard on whatever needed to be done. Like the wall and the tunnel, for example; both his ideas. The man she planned to marry someday: Darryl.

Karen had spotted him as the jeep drew up, younger than her definitely, but extremely hot – especially with his shirt round his waist like that, sweat covering his muscles. He'd noticed the jeep arriving, breaking off from his labours working on the first few sections of the wall, and trotted across to greet the new arrivals. As usual, she'd made a complete arse of herself and tripped over her words. But she'd smiled at him and he'd thrown her one of his casual smiles back. The kind of smile she'd walk a million miles – never mind this piddling distance – for.

That's why you're doing this, she reminded herself every time she felt her feet hurting, or her legs aching. *For Darryl. Because he'd volunteered again to do this, but you wouldn't let him. And to keep him safe. To fetch help, making sure those Germans didn't get to him and kill him.*

It had been Gwen who'd come up with the notion, who'd wanted to go herself – trusting only Darryl to look after her son, Clive Jr. Karen didn't care much for the bond between Gwen and Darryl, but they had known each other a long time. Besides, Karen didn't see her as too much of a threat; she was always banging on about that dead father of her child, the guy who'd founded Hope and got himself killed for his trouble. Gwen wanted to slip out again using the tunnel, this time to fetch help from Nottingham Castle even though there was some kind of stupid feud going on between her and the Hood. "They'll help once I've explained," Gwen had assured everyone. "It's what they do. It's *all* they do." But Darryl had played the hero again, putting himself forward.

"You can't, Gwen. We need you here," Darryl had said. "*I* need you."

Karen winced inwardly at that one, but chose to read it as him needing her leadership. Dammit, even after the hug when he climbed back up through that hole, he still didn't seem to get it. Which was why, when Darryl said that he was going instead, Karen had piped up, volunteering herself.

He'd looked at her oddly, then, like he was seeing her for the first time. "You?"

"Yes," she said. "Why not? I'm a lot more resourceful than I look, matey. I'm quick and used to walking long distances, have been since I was a kid." The fact she hadn't walked more than a couple of miles in one go during the past ten years was irrelevant.

Darryl smiled, but wasn't there a tinge of concern there too? Did he realise, just a little bit, that she was doing it for *him*? Yes, Karen thought that he did. "If you're sure, then?"

Karen nodded emphatically. "But when I get back, I'll expect another hug," she told him. Probably the boldest thing she'd said or done in her life; even bolder than Neville, and she'd been drunk then.

Darryl had smiled again, a little awkwardly, but she'd take it. He'd also exchanged glances with Gwen, probably to see whether she was okay with Karen taking this on. Gwen had looked concerned as well, but shrugged. "If you're sure that's what you want. Thanks, Karen."

So she'd set off, armed with a pistol, carrying a map and torch. Gwen had issued orders and instructions, especially about not being seen as she emerged from the tunnel on the other side of the wall. Karen had nodded, not really taking any of it in; she was too busy watching Darryl in the crowd of people who'd come to see her off. "But most of all, hurry," Gwen said. "We don't know how much longer we can hold them off now Tanek's here. And Graham and Andy aren't getting any better." Andy had been badly injured by Tanek's crossbows on the last attack, and now resided with Graham in the surgery. Both were growing weaker by the hour. Karen had nodded, taking at least that much in.

"Hurry. Got it."

She'd left amidst the 'thank yous' and 'good lucks,' a bit disappointed that Darryl hadn't come across personally to say goodbye. But she knew he'd see her in a different light if she pulled this off. All she had to do was bring back help and *she'd* be the hero of the hour. Then she'd get that hug, and more besides.

Karen had listened at the trap-door for a good while before opening it, and then only a crack. Once she was certain nobody was about, she'd come up and covered the door back over again. Keeping low, she'd moved what she thought had been stealthily. She'd had one scary moment when it looked as if a German soldier had spotted her, but she'd carried on away from the area – away from New Hope – undetected; unscathed. And she *had* hurried, to begin with. But her lack of fitness soon began to tell on her.

Nevertheless, she'd trudged on to the main road – then followed it along, keenly aware of what might be coming along it from either direction at any given time. Thankfully tanks and armoured jeeps were quite easy to spot and hide from. Hardly surprising it was on the last leg of the journey that she'd flagged, having to stop every few yards at one point.

It was then, as she'd stumbled along one of the smaller roads on the way to Nottingham, that she'd been seen. She hadn't spotted anyone herself – but then, that was what these Rangers were good at, concealing themselves. All of a sudden she was confronted by three of Hood's people, all pointing bows and arrows at her.

"Lose the gun," one told her, and she'd cautiously taken her pistol out of her jeans, tossing it on the floor.

"I need to see Robert," she'd told the Ranger who'd spoken. "Or Reverend Tate. It's about New Hope – the place is under siege."

The Rangers exchanged glances, and one detached a walkie-talkie from his belt to radio in. The next thing she knew she was being marched up into the city. When she'd complained about how far she'd tramped already, arrangements had been made for a horse to be brought. Karen had never ridden before, and it was a strange experience to do it for the first time through the empty streets of Nottingham. It took an age, and just when she thought they'd never get there, she was led up one final street and the castle was in front of them.

She'd never visited it before, having opted to remain at home when the Winter Festival had been going on here, probably because Darryl had stayed behind, too. Karen had no idea whether this was the norm, but there didn't appear to be many Rangers in evidence as she was taken through the gates. She was greeted by a portly man she hadn't seen before, walking with a stick. But she knew immediately who he was from his dog collar. The man who used to live at New Hope, but who Gwen threw out for his actions. The holy man who'd left her at the castle during De Falaise's reign; who'd coaxed her back and almost got her killed during the Tsar's invasion.

"Welcome, my child," said the bald fellow. "Welcome to Nottingham Castle. I'm Reverend Tate."

Karen was helped down off the horse and shook his hand. "Karen Shipley. I'm from New Hope."

"So I gather. The men here mentioned something about a siege?"

"Germans are shooting up the place. Gwen told me to tell you Tanek is with them."

"Tanek? She's certain?"

"There are injured people, too. Look, I need to see him. Robin... Robert... whatever he prefers to call himself."

The Reverend sighed, then rubbed his chin.

"Is he here?"

There was another pause. "He *is*, just got back after we managed to get hold of him. But you couldn't have picked a worse moment."

It was then that Karen noticed the bruises on the holy man's chin and cheek; he'd recently been in a fight, and looked like he'd come off worse. Still, Karen had a mission. "*Please*, I need to see him."

Tate nodded and took her up the long path towards the castle. They ascended a set of steps, the Reverend appearing to have trouble with them. Karen took his arm and he thanked her. He led her inside the castle itself through a set of double doors, then up some more stairs and along a corridor. She could hear raised voices even before they reached the room Tate was zeroing in on.

"...even if you do go," Karen heard someone say, a woman's voice.

"You read the note." A man's voice. "He wants *me*, Mary. Alone."

Tate knocked on the door, which was ajar, then pushed on it when he heard: "Who is it?" The woman – Mary, Karen assumed.

Tate entered first, leaving Karen waiting in the doorway of the small room. "Someone to see Robert."

Karen could see the pair now, the woman with her dark hair tied back; the man in his trademark greens, that famous hood hanging down his back. His face was stubbled, as if he'd been away from home for a while. "Can't it wait?" This was Mary once more, looking past Tate. Directly at Karen.

"I'm afraid not."

Robert came forward. His movements were slow, as if he'd been injured. But he had a bow in his hand and looked like he was either packing, or getting ready to go out again. "Reverend, you of all people should know this isn't the time for –"

"This lady, Karen Shipley," Tate interrupted and moved aside so that Robert could see her, "has come from New Hope."

"You'll forgive me, but that place is the last thing on my mind right now," snapped Robert. "I've just rushed back here after being held prisoner and nearly roasted alive, because my son's missing. Kidnapped. His girlfriend's frantic, blaming herself for not doing more to prevent it. The man who took him says he wants me to come alone to Sherwood. I don't know whether Mark's alive or dead, and you're asking me to listen to someone Gwen's sent?"

Tate was silent, then said: "Yes, I really think you need to hear what she's got to say."

Karen came forward, not waiting for the answer. She was sorry for what had happened here, but *they* needed help too – if not from the Hooded Man himself, then at least from his Rangers.

"Please, Mr Hood," Karen began, "our village has been surrounded. Armed soldiers, Germans. They came a couple of days ago."

"How did you get out?"

"It wasn't easy. I don't know how much longer the other people there can hold on."

"Thought that place was like Fort Knox now?" Robert said.

"These men are professionals. If they want in, they'll *get* in." Karen was beginning to see what Gwen meant about Hood. He wasn't the easiest of people to talk to, and she had caught him at a spectacularly bad moment. "People are injured, they're dying."

"Dying? I've just come back from a battle to take Edinburgh Castle from a cannibalistic witch woman, a battle that some of my Rangers lost. I've heard my other troops in Wales have suffered casualties, as well, trying to remove another crazed dictator from power. We only just made it back alive, and now you're asking me to help a village that pretty much turned its back on *us*?"

Karen wasn't around when the bulk of this bad feeling had built up, so she couldn't comment. She said the only thing she could. "I understand what you're going through with your son, and I really do hope you get him back safely. But Gwen has a son, too. A son these people want to get their hands on for some reason."

Robert frowned, then looked at Tate.

"Tanek is with them, Robert," said the Reverend. "There's definitely a link between the Germans there and what's been happening in Wales and Scotland."

Karen could see Hood thinking about it, brought up short by the mention of Tanek. Then he waved his hand. "I don't have time for this. I need to get to Sherwood. Mark's been missing for over a day now as it is."

"Even if you can't come yourself, could you at least spare some of your Rangers? Then we might stand a –"

"Look around you! Most of my men are still in the North and the West. The castle's practically defenceless, and you want me to send more of them away with you?"

"Robert," chastised Mary.

"I'm sorry, but Gwen and her lot have made their own beds as far as I'm concerned. She's repeatedly ignored our warnings about what would happen if she carried on arming herself to the teeth, poaching people from other communities just because they're useful to her. She's also point blank refused any protection from us in the past. Gwen likes to do things her way, and look where it's got her!" Robert turned to Karen. "I don't care for or condone the way you people operate. Like attracts like, Miss Shipley."

"Please, you *have* to help us."

Robert pointed a finger at her. "Give me one good reason why I should."

There was silence for a moment, then Karen said: "Compassion."

He looked into her eyes, then hung his head.

"If you won't send anyone else, then I'm going anyway," said Tate. "I've let Gwen down twice in the past before. I will not do so again."

"That," said Robert, "is your choice. I'm going to try and save my son."

Tate took Karen's arm this time. "Come on. Robert, I pray for you and that you will bring Mark safely back home. I'm only sorry I couldn't stop the man who took him."

As the Reverend was walking out of the room with Karen, she heard Robert call after them. "Take a dozen Rangers with you, but bring them back in one piece." Tate smiled at her, as if knowing he'd do that all along.

Karen felt less reassured, though. A crippled Reverend and a handful of men. What good would they be against the German troops and that giant they called Tanek? She was almost embarrassed to be returning with them.

"Don't worry," Tate had said as they'd made their way back out of the castle. "It's going to be alright this time. I'm going to make up for everything."

Karen hoped to God that the holy man was right.

CHAPTER NINETEEN

ROBERT RODE LOW on his horse, trying not to think about the events that had forced him here.

But he couldn't help it. That had always been his trouble, dwelling on things. His mind harking back to the past. In his early days at Sherwood, it had been the life he'd led with his former wife and son. Now it was the events of the last few days, and hours.

After Bill had shown up at Edinburgh Castle, freeing the other members of his captured team – rectifying Robert's first, but not his only, major mistake of late – the resistance had soon been quashed. Once word spread through the Widow's men about her death, it hadn't taken long. Even the depleted Rangers on their side had been enough in the face of these thieves and yobs. Bill had already destroyed most of their heavy armaments in his initial run with the Black Shark, and though Robert had to openly disapprove of these actions – having denounced modern weaponry in all its forms – there was still a part of him that was glad they didn't have to tackle these with bows and arrows after what he'd already gone through.

The victory had been hard won, but satisfying, leaving the way clear for the local Rangers to set up their own HQ at the castle in the future. Securing a way of life for the Scottish people which didn't involve bowing down to that mad woman. They'd once said no-one could ever take away their freedom, but hadn't banked on one of their own trying it. At least now the bare bones of a free Scotland – protected by a Scottish contingent of Rangers – looked more likely.

Then, when most of the fighting was over, the message had come in about Mark. That someone had broken into the castle the previous evening and taken him, leaving a handwritten note by the radio which read:

Hooded Man. You will come to the forest alone if you ever want to see him alive again. Send anyone else and I will kill him. I will wait for you there.

It had been signed simply 'S.'

Tate had described the intruder as being Native American, which didn't give Robert much to go on. But the very fact the holy man had been bested by him spoke volumes. Though at first glance Tate might look like he was a helpless old cripple, he could actually handle himself extremely well in a fight.

That Mark hadn't been able to take the man, either, further emphasised that his kidnapper was a professional. Mark had been coming up in the ranks over the last twelve months. He was no longer the boy Robert had first met at an ad-hoc market three years ago; he was a fully grown man – however he might be treated sometimes by them – and had been training with the Rangers for a long time. He'd handled himself excellently during the Tsar's invasion and had even started to have the same prophetic dreams Robert had, especially during their frequent visits to the forest he was heading towards today. He was becoming everything Robert had anticipated he would. But then he'd heard this, and it took him right back to that day when De Falaise had taken the boy. To when that bastard Tanek had cut Mark's finger off.

In the time since, Mark had become every bit as much a son to Robert as Stevie once was, and would always be. In fact he liked to think Stevie might have grown up to be something like Mark. Obviously if the virus hadn't happened, then Stevie would have aspired to being something other than a Ranger; but that was another life, an alternate Stevie, living happily in an alternate universe. The important thing was that Mark was his own man, and he'd *chosen* to follow in Robert's footsteps. In fact, Robert liked to think that Mark might well take over this whole operation one day. But he couldn't do that if he was dead. Robert needed Mark, probably as much as his son needed him right now.

But as much as Mark was now his son, Robert couldn't help thinking about the Widow's revelation – that Mary was pregnant with his baby. They'd yet to confirm or deny it, but Robert had the weirdest feeling it was true. As did Mary, going by her words when they'd found out about Mark. "You might have another child," she'd said – not to suggest that Mark wasn't theirs, because he was, no matter what. But Robert knew that she'd said this to remind him the

Widow was right; that they *might* be having a baby together. And that if Robert got himself killed she'd be bringing it up alone. The Widow could just have been playing another mind game, granted, but there wasn't time to find out one way or another.

Ultimately, weakened and wounded as he was, Mary knew Robert had to do as the message said. She hadn't said anything more as he'd prepared to leave, other than pointing out the obvious, that it was a set up. She was worried about him; they'd almost lost each other up in Edinburgh, and hadn't even had time to draw breath before the next crisis. Then the woman had arrived from New Hope.

Robert had conflicting feelings about that place. The last time he'd seen Gwen properly, to talk to, not simply across the way at the Winter Festival, she'd made it quite plain what she thought about him. He might as well have been to blame for leaving the woman there at the Castle while De Falaise had his way with her, although he hadn't even known her at the time. Robert's forces weren't anywhere near organised or strong enough to tackle the Sheriff when Gwen was taken, but when Mark and those other villages had been taken and threatened with execution, he'd been forced to act. The simple fact was he hadn't been able to do anything about Gwen's situation, as rough as it had been for her, just like he couldn't do much for the people of New Hope now. His Rangers were scattered all over the country; even letting Tate take half a dozen with him was leaving the Castle open to serious trouble. But he'd done it anyway, because of what that Shipley woman said. Because of what the Rangers *should* stand for: the compassion she'd spoken about.

Would Gwen show the same if Nottingham Castle came under attack and needed a return favour? Robert seriously doubted it. But then, didn't Tate say they should always turn the other cheek?

All this and more was racing through Robert's mind as he raced towards his former home – the one he'd retreated to after the Cull, been talked out of by Tate, and remained estranged from to this day.

When he came to the outskirts, he decided to leave his horse tethered there, rather than come in through the more obvious entrance: up through the Visitors' Centre and into the forest that way. It was asking to walk into some kind of ambush. Robert instead entered the forest the way he had when he'd first come here: through Rufford. He was acutely aware of his lost connection to this place, but he still had tracking skills he could rely on, and his enemy had left a trail even a blind man could follow. But as Robert crept through the forest, he almost fell into the most rudimentary of traps: a concealed hole underneath him. He felt the ground slip away, just quickly enough to grab the side of the pit, scrabbling up and back onto terra firma. God, that hurt! It was a sign that his enemy had left the trail on purpose. And also proved his opposite number had the upper hand. Back in the old days, when Robert had lived here, *he* would have been the one setting the traps, Today, he knew he was walking right into one.

Picking himself up, Robert stumbled further into the forest that had once felt so familiar. He didn't have far to go before he saw a figure tied to a tree, slumped against the trunk as if drugged. Or beaten. And as Robert crept closer, he saw that yes, it was Mark, head lolling, a red welt on his temple. He had no idea whether the lad was still alive or not, but knew he had to find out. Find the man responsible.

Robert crawled along, using the woodland as cover, just like he always used to do. But he didn't feel at all confident this time. Felt that somehow the grass and trees just weren't on his side anymore. That it was revealing snatches of him where once it had hidden his presence completely. Robert might as well have a neon sign above his head telling anyone on the vicinity that he had arrived.

Undaunted, he pressed on. He had to reach Mark, free him, ascertain what injuries he had sustained. Robert was almost at the tree when he heard a rustling to his right.

"Dad, look out!" This was Mark shouting – at least he was still alive. Robert rose and brought his bow and arrow to bear.

Standing directly opposite him was a man. Dressed in black, dark-skinned, with dark hair to match his attire. He looked more like a shadow than a man. As Tate had described him, he was Native American in appearance, had a backpack over his shoulder – containing his quiver – with an axe and knife at his belt. He had his own bow drawn, aimed at Robert. For a second or two both men stood their ground, fingertips pulling back on their twines. The bows shook slightly with tension.

Each man had one eye closed, leaving the other open to judge the distance to his target. But with that one eye each was also judging his opponent. What he might do, when he might loose his shot.

It was Robert who released his arrow first, sending it flying towards what should have been the stranger's head. The man moved out of the way, though, allowing Robert's arrow to embed itself in the tree just behind him.

"Impressive," came the response, even as the stranger was shooting himself.

Robert saw the arrow coming and dived out of the way, feeling its wind brushing his ear. The other man's arrow thudded into an oak several metres behind him, causing Robert to flinch. Already both bows were nocked again and ready to shoot.

"What do you want?" he asked, more to stall than anything, although he was genuinely curious.

There was no reply, except for the release of another arrow, again flying directly towards Robert. He flopped to the ground to avoid it, the missile whipping over his hood and sailing off into the woodland beyond. Robert's answer was to shoot from the ground, the arrow aimed at the Native American's head. But, again, the stranger was quicker; sidestepping this shot with ease and allowing it to disappear off into the forest.

The pair exchanged a couple more shots like this, pulling arrows from quivers and letting them loose, as Robert managed to get to his feet. Then they wound up where they'd first began; staring each other down. Both men with bows primed and aimed at the other.

Time this was ended, thought Robert, searching for a sign the Native American was going to shoot. When he found it, he released his own arrow.

Both pieces of wood and metal twirled in the distance between the men, heading directly for each other. They met almost head on, but it was the stranger's that had the advantage while Robert's suddenly flew way off course. The stranger's projectile struck Robert's left shoulder, lifting him up off his feet and back into one of the oaks he'd once considered his only true friends. The arrow carried on through the shoulder and into the wood behind, pinning Robert there.

"Dad!" screamed Mark, struggling to free himself from his bonds without success.

Robert dropped his weapon, writhing in agony. It was now that he knew exactly what had happened – somehow this man in front of him had *stolen* his advantage. Taken away the protection the forest once afforded him, leaving him defenceless against this new threat.

"How?" shouted Robert. "How have you done this?"

He could tell by the Native American's face that he understood the question. But he didn't answer. Just walked over with a satisfied smile on his face – so slight it would have been missed by the average person – and stood in front of his impaled prey.

Robert reached for his sword, but the stranger grabbed his wrist, pulling the length of metal out of its sheath and flinging it away. There was a part of Robert that wondered if it was because of his exhaustion, the burns he'd suffered at the Widow's hands. But he'd endured more in a shorter period before – and it wasn't just the fact that he was getting older, either. This man had taken something from him, of that Robert was certain. Not just the dreams, but the almost superhuman strength he apparently drew from this place. If he'd faced the Tsar's men at this point and fallen in battle, there was no way he'd be getting back up to finish what he'd started. If the stranger chose to end this now, then Robert – the Hooded Man – would be dead. No two ways about it.

But that wasn't his intent. It *never had been* his intent. The stranger examined the arrow, nodding. "Clean wound. You'll live."

"D-do what you want with me," Robert said, breath coming in sharp gasps. "But let my boy go."

The stranger regarded him with those dark eyes. "That was always my intent. This was never about him."

That's what this man had in mind all along. Like him, he was a hunter. Mark had been the bait, obviously, but this stranger had never wanted to kill either Robert or his son. Especially not the latter.

"Then what's this about?" asked Robert.

"That is not for me to tell, but rest assured, I will free your son now I have you. There is nothing he can do to stop me, anyway."

"Stop you from what? Who are you working with: Tanek? The Germans?" Robert's questions went unanswered once more.

"It is time," said the stranger, then he took something out of a pouch at his belt. He emptied the contents – which looked like tobacco – into the palm of one hand, then grabbed Robert's chin with the other. *Not again*, he thought. *I'm not being drugged again!*

"This will help the journey pass more quickly," the stranger told him, forcing the weed into his mouth. Robert spat the first lot back into the stranger's face, but he just squeezed harder on his cheeks, forcing more into Robert's mouth, clamping his mouth shut. Though he didn't chew, Robert felt some of it slide down his throat. The weird concoction was dissolving on his tongue. In his own way, this stranger was just as much a magician as the Widow.

No, have to fight it, Have to –

But already the stuff was having an effect. The stranger's face looked to be melting, the whole scene falling away in front of Robert. He tried to look over at Mark, but couldn't focus.

"Sleep now," he heard the stranger say.

It seemed like such a good idea. He was exhausted, and it *had* been a gruelling couple of days. Some sleep would do him the world of good.

Robert felt his eyelids closing, then there was blackness.

But there was also the total absence of dreams.

CHAPTER TWENTY

SHE'D BEEN GONE for hours now. And while they all knew the trip to Nottingham was quite a trek, things were growing desperate at New Hope.

People were sick of the periodic attacks on the walls since Tanek arrived – scared that at any moment, the Germans would just come crashing inside – and their friends were dying. Graham and Andy weren't doing well at all, in spite of Jennings' best efforts. One of the bolts Andy caught had caused internal injuries that the doctor couldn't do much about. "We need to get him somewhere we can operate. Otherwise I don't think he's going to make it."

Gwen had gone to see Andy, at his request, and they'd talked: about the old days, about what had happened to New Hope, about the direction she was taking. "Y-you have to promise me," Andy said, "that you'll turn away from this course you're on."

"I don't know what you're talking about," she'd told him, avoiding his eyes.

"There's so much hatred inside you now, Gwen. This..." Andy winced. "This isn't what Clive would have wanted for you."

She'd said nothing. She wanted to get up and leave when he started talking like that, but she owed him her time. Owed him the opportunity to get whatever this problem was that he had with her off his chest. Regardless of how things were with them now, Andy had done a lot for New Hope. He'd been there with her and Clive right from the beginning, just like Darryl, just like Graham. And this might be the last chance he'd get to say his piece.

He'd reached out for her hand and she'd let him take it. "You promise me, Gwen. Don't let it eat you up inside. I'm worried about you."

"You don't need to be. I'm fine."

"No, you're not," Andy insisted. "You –"

"Listen, I should go and see what's happening out there. You get some rest." Gwen removed her hand and let Andy's flop back down on the bed. "Look after him," she told Sat, the doctor's assistant, as she left. She looked back just once to see Andy staring at her. He didn't believe for one minute she was all right, but she didn't know what to do to convince him. More than ever, she felt guilty for striking him when they were interrogating the prisoner. And, in a way, Andy had been right; they'd gotten nothing more out of the man, even after she'd gone back again.

During the last session overnight, she'd dismissed the guards keeping an eye on him and got down to business. "Just you and me now," she'd told the soldier. "I know who your boss is, outside."

The man had laughed. "You know nothing." That earned him a punch in the face which broke his nose. He hadn't been laughing then.

"Me and him go back quite a way, did you know that?" Gwen said. "There's not much love lost between us."

"Go to Hell, *hure!*"

"You first, fucker!" She'd kicked him hard in the side, where his injuries were, and smiled as he'd howled in pain.

They'd gone on like this for about an hour, until Gwen was satisfied she'd get no new information. In the end she'd wound up kicking the chair over, placing her foot on his windpipe and threatening to crush it just to try and get some answers. "*Why* does he want my son?" she'd spat into the German's face. He'd remained silent, either not willing to say or because he didn't know.

Gwen left the room, calling the guards back in and giving them specific orders not to fetch Jeffreys when they saw the state of the prisoner. "We might still be able to use him if push comes to shove, but it won't matter what condition he's in. He's alive, that's good enough."

Was there a part of her that connected Andy's words with her actions? No, she felt them entirely justified. She was protecting her village, protecting her son at all costs.

When she looked into the faces of those villagers, however, she didn't think that they felt the same. Yes, they wanted to keep this place safe, but she wasn't convinced they wouldn't just fling Clive Jr over the wall to save *themselves*. She'd thought about telling them: "I know Tanek. He'll kill you all anyway, then, just for fun. The only thing keeping you alive right now in fact is that he wants my son and daren't risk storming in and harming him." But they wouldn't have listened. She'd need to keep a close eye on them, especially when it all hit the fan. Darryl was still the only one she trusted to keep watch over her child, and she was pleased to see he'd almost fully recovered from giving his blood to the German.

Gwen had been on her way from seeing Andy when she heard her name being called. "Come quickly," came the cry, and when Gwen reached the part of the wall it had originated from, she got a sinking feeling in the pit of her stomach. It was the section directly overlooking the opening of their tunnel's hidden trap door. The man who'd called her across – Henry Collins, a middle-aged ex-veterinarian who helped look after their livestock – was crouching, holding his rifle and jabbing his finger in the direction of the secret entrance. Gwen climbed the ladder to join him, not liking the stern look on his face.

"What is it?"

"See for yourself," he told her, taking off his glasses and rubbing his forehead with the back of his hand.

Gwen peeked out through the gap, and spotted it instantly. A group of German soldiers at the opening. They'd uncovered the camouflage Karen had replaced and were pointing down at the door. One was running some kind of wire from it.

"They're getting ready to blow it," Gwen said.

Henry nodded. "Bingo. And guess where they're going once they have."

Up the tunnel and into this damned compound. How had they found out about the door in the first place? Must have been Karen, the stupid idiot! Someone must have seen her. Or maybe the Germans had just stumbled on it by accident? Gwen hoped that was the case, because if anyone had seen Karen then it meant she'd either been followed, or killed, or both. In spite of herself, the first thing Gwen found herself thinking was not about Karen's death, but that they shouldn't rely on any help from the castle now.

More important even than that, their enemies were about to step the siege up a notch. If the people of New Hope weren't going to give them what they wanted, their enemies had just discovered a way to come inside and get it for themselves.

TANEK WAS HAPPY.

For the first time in a long while, he was really, truly happy. And he was *never* happy. It didn't happen. There was always something that came along to balls things up. Not this time. Luck was on their side for a change.

Even before they'd made arrangements to begin the next phase of this campaign, they'd been given an unexpected break. Determined to get to the bottom of how his man was snatched, Tanek had ordered a thorough – if covert – search of the perimeter. It was then that they'd discovered the trap door. It hadn't been concealed properly, and was almost definitely the way they'd snuck in and out. It could have been used to go and fetch help; Tanek had to move now. They'd forced his hand. But they'd also given him the perfect way to gain entrance.

And while the villagers were dealing with German soldiers coming up through that tunnel into New Hope, Tanek and his team would concentrate on breaking in through the front door, sealing this locality's fate. Once they were inside, they'd see just how fast the woman and her child were given up.

That moment had now come, his men preparing to blow the lid on that secret door. Tanek felt satisfied this was going to end well.

But more than anything else, he was looking forward to seeing De Falaise's woman again.

They still had unfinished business.

GWEN HAD POSTED at least three people on the tunnel door in the village grounds. Like Karen before them, they had orders to shoot whatever came through that didn't look like one of theirs. The only person out there was Karen, and no reports of her return had been made, more's the pity. Even if she had come back alone, then she wouldn't be able to get past the Germans to crawl through the tunnel.

"Chances are it'll be unfriendlies," she warned. "Don't give them the chance to fire on you first."

In the meantime, Gwen had gathered the rest of the villagers and handed out weapons to anyone who wasn't yet armed. Whether they'd have enough firepower was another matter, but they'd bloody well try to fight those bastards off. Gwen would, at any rate – she still wasn't sure about some of her fellow villagers. Would they turn their guns on her to hand over Clive Jr? Would she have to shoot the very people she'd been trying to look after all these months? People she'd lived alongside, fought alongside?

She'd find out soon enough, because the word came down from Henry that the hatch door had been breached and men were climbing inside the tunnel. Gwen made sure Darryl was *extremely* well armed – a rifle, a shotgun and two pistols – and told him to stand guard over both her house and Clive Jr, while she waited out in the street. It was the longest wait she'd ever endured; even those hours back at the castle when she'd been De Falaise's prisoner hadn't been as bad as this.

Gwen shook her head; such thoughts made her angry, made her want to put a bullet in every one of those men invading her home, and distracted her at a time when she needed to be focused. She gripped her Colt Commando rifle, holding it across her chest like a shield.

Although they were expecting something to happen, the loud *bang* still came as a shock. But what happened next, none of them could have predicted. The door to the tunnel on this side was blown clean off its hinges, but what came out of the tunnel wasn't men. At least not at first. Grenades were tossed up, causing the villagers defending it to move back. They began coughing, as multi-coloured smoke – some of it yellow, some orange, some blue – got into their lungs.

"No, stay where you are!" shouted Gwen, running towards it. But that was easier said than done when they could hardly breathe.

The next thing they knew, German soldiers were inside. Nobody saw them climb up through the hole, they just appeared wearing gasmasks, striding through the smog, rifles held high and zeroing in on the villagers surrounding the trapdoor. Several shots were fired and men and women fell straight away. Carol Fawkes was shot point blank in the face.

Gwen opened fire on the advancing soldiers. They were spreading out, some heading to the nearest cottages and taking up covering positions – or maybe searching them? – others crouching in order to pick off the sentries up on the wall. Henry was one of the first to buy it, standing and firing on the men and being riddled with automatic rifle fire for his efforts.

Gwen barely batted an eye; she didn't have time. The soldiers were getting closer and closer to her house – to Darryl and to Clive Jr. Hefting the rifle up to her shoulder, Gwen aimed at one of the soldiers and got him directly between the eyes. She'd become so much better with a gun than when she first used one to kill Major Javier, the man who'd slaughtered her beloved Clive.

She turned, shooting another German who was coming up on her left. Then she fired at a group on her right, breathing hard – relishing the feel of the rifle as it pumped out bullet after bullet. A smattering of machine-gun fire forced her to pull back behind the wall of a house, but she immediately bobbed her head back round the corner, firing again.

Screams filled the air, but some were taking her lead, realising that if they didn't fight, they'd die. Two or three had taken cover behind a notice board. The wood splintered as German troops fired at them, but they ducked and returned fire, causing the soldiers to try and find shelter now. One didn't make it; shot in the legs as he ran.

Gwen grinned, targeting the fallen man and putting a bullet in his chest to make sure he was out of the picture.

"Fall back!" she heard someone shout, and for a moment Gwen thought it might be the Germans. No such luck: it was another team of villagers, being driven into doorways by an advancing squad of enemy soldiers. They just kept on coming out of that hole. Gwen needed to put a stop to it. She moved up, sliding along the wall of the house she'd been using for protection. Then she ran across, making the most of the thinning smoke cover. She could see the tunnel entrance, and put several bullets in a German using his elbow to climb out. Gunfire raked the ground ahead of her and she dived out of the way, rolling and coming up shooting. She clicked empty and sprinted towards the bench just ahead of her, leaping over and ducking behind it as more bullets followed in her wake.

She ejected the magazine, grabbed another from her pocket, slapped it in place. Then she got up and rested on the back of the seat, firing in the direction the bullets had come from, shouting in triumph when she saw one German soldier fall to the ground.

Just when she thought they might stand a chance, there was an explosion at the front wall.

Jesus, Gwen thought. *What now?*

She wished she hadn't asked when she looked over and saw the gates flung wide as Tanek's armoured vehicle smashed through.

"Shit!"

Villagers fired at the jeep, but their bullets just zinged off. One man was caught in the vehicle's path, turning as it was upon him; he fell under the wheels and was crushed, head popping like a melon.

More German troops entered behind the armoured car, picking their targets, not wasting a round. How did she ever think they could stand a chance against professional fighters like these?

Then there he was, climbing out of the jeep. He was even bigger than she remembered, but that dour face, that olive skin was the same. He'd only been out a few seconds and he'd already put two crossbow bolts into someone. Tanek was coming for her son, but she was damned if she was going to let that happen.

Gwen came out from behind the bench, heading back in the direction she'd just come from: heading Tanek off at the pass before he could reach –

"Shit!"

The giant was striding across, busting in door after door and killing whoever resisted. He was checking every house for Clive Jr, and he didn't have many to go. Sam Coulson came up behind Tanek, rifle raised. Gwen held her breath, watching as Sam was about to pull the trigger, but Tanek had already sensed his presence and was spinning, so quickly Sam didn't have time to fire. The weapon was knocked clean out of his hands and Tanek grabbed him by the throat, lifting Sam into the air as though he weighed nothing. If Gwen had been closer – and if there hadn't been so much noise – she probably would have heard the cracking of the bones in Sam's neck as Tanek squeezed. Sam's eyes bulged, his tongue flopping out as he dropped to the ground, legs giving out beneath him.

Tanek looked around, hardly flinching as bullets ricocheted off the building behind. It was then that he saw her. His eyes narrowed and he pointed, as if to say 'I'm coming for you.' Gwen had to admit, she was scared. Probably the first time she had been since the castle. Not for herself – for her son. Because she could see now that De Falaise's old second in command was on a mission, and he wasn't about to let *anyone* get in his way. Without looking, he held his crossbow out to the side and shot another villager – a young woman this time – twice. One bolt between her breasts and another in her temple.

So much death. Too much, thought Gwen. But this wasn't over yet.

She was distracted by Jeffreys being dragged out of the doctor's surgery. He was pleading with the soldier who had hold of him.

"Where is the boy?" asked the German.

Jeffreys said nothing, so the soldier shot him in the shoulder. Jeffreys screamed and clasped his hand to the wound. The soldier put the gun to Jeffreys' head. "The boy!"

Jeffreys glanced over to where Gwen was standing, and she gave a small shake of the head, pleading with him not to do it. But she could already see in his eyes he'd made the decision. He pointed at Gwen's house. "In there. Please don't –" His final words were silenced by the *blam!* of the pistol as it blew his brains out.

Gwen felt nothing at his death, the betrayal still stinging. She couldn't even consider what she might have done in his position; could only think about the fact her son's location had been given away. The German was already motioning towards Tanek.

"No!" shouted Gwen, training her rifle on the soldier who'd just killed Jeffreys. She opened fire, the bullets smacking into his body, so many he was lifted off his feet. Perhaps she thought that by killing him she could somehow turn back time; erase what had just happened.

But *nothing* could do that and, as Tanek began to head towards her home, Gwen ran. She was halted by a rain of bullets from a semi-circle of soldiers who appeared out of nowhere. Gwen fired into them, but such was the intensity of the return fire that she had to duck back behind a wall. If she fell here, then Clive Jr was as good as Tanek's.

Gwen peered round the corner and let off a few more rounds. Then she was empty. There were no more magazines left, so she dropped the rifle and took out her pistol, cocking it. She reached down for the knife she kept strapped to her ankle.

She came out, making every shot with the pistol count, taking out four soldiers with the first volley. Gwen threw herself down and slashed at another soldier's calves with her knife, causing him to drop to one knee. Then she plunged the knife in his ribs. He toppled over onto his face, twitching.

Gwen rose with one eye still on Tanek, who was about to enter her house.

"Gwen! Watch out!" she heard, and then she was being pushed out of the way, falling to the ground and landing awkwardly on her shoulder. She looked up as bullets hit her rescuer. It was Andy, who'd staggered out of the doctor's, perhaps in the vain hope he might be able to help Jeffreys. Instead he'd taken about a dozen bullets for her. He turned towards her, an expression of disbelief on his face.

"Andy!" she cried. But it was too late. He was beyond hearing her.

Squeezing off a few rounds in the direction of the German machine-guns, she didn't waste the opportunity he'd given her. She raced after Tanek, just as someone came crashing through the living room window of her house. The body was covered in shattered glass, and rolled a few times before stopping. Darryl.

"No... Christ in Heaven, no!" she wailed.

Tanek emerged from her place, carrying a crying Clive Jr – holding him by the scruff of his T-shirt and brandishing the crossbow as if daring anyone to take the child from him.

"*No!*" she screamed, running forward. Then, suddenly, she was aware of the fact that she wasn't moving anymore. Her leg had given out, and a white hot pain spread through her thigh. Looking down, she saw the bolt there, embedded deep. She began to crawl, holding up her pistol with a shaky hand but not daring to fire in case she hit her son. Gwen was a good shot, but not *that* good, especially in this condition. Then another bolt slammed into her shoulder, causing her to drop the gun altogether.

Machine-gun fire continued unabated all around as the pain kicked in, and she realised that no one was going to ride in and save the day. Not Robert and his Rangers, not anybody. He'd probably left her to it just to spite her, assuming Karen had even made it to the castle.

"If only De Falaise could see you now," Tanek shouted over the noise.

"L-leave my son alone, you bastard!"

"Sorry, I made a promise."

What promise? Gwen didn't understand what all this was about. Wasn't really interested – all she wanted was her son back. She would give anything for that.

Tanek raised his crossbow once again, aiming at her heart. "And now your role in the story ends."

It was at that moment Clive Jr began to wriggle and kick out. Tanek pressed the trigger, and the bolt went off target, but still hit Gwen, just below the ribs. She sucked in air through her teeth as it sank in.

At the same time there was a hissing sound. More smoke bombs had been thrown into New Hope, but they didn't originate from the hole. And it didn't appear to be the Germans who'd set them off. They looked at each other, mystified, as red smoke filled the area. Tanek looked over, frowning.

Gwen squinted, catching glimpses of figures in the smoke, moving through the German troops. Taking them down with the kind of skill her villagers would never possess. Professional fighters, even more professional than the Germans. Gwen grimaced from the pain, but started to feel a glimmer of hope, especially when she saw a hood. *Karen made it after all!* And it looked like she'd brought back company.

There was only one thing wrong. Where were the arrows? Where were the bolas those men favoured? She saw a flash of metal. Yes, swords: they used swords instead of conventional weaponry. But, when one of the hooded figures appeared beside a German soldier, bringing down his blade across the man's wrists and severing his hands, Gwen knew this wasn't Robert and his men. Blood pumped from the soldier's wrists as he raised them, looking uncomprehendingly at the stumps. He didn't have to suffer for long, though, because the hooded figure twirled and cut off his head in one quick, clean stroke. It was as the blade lowered that Gwen saw it wasn't a broadsword he was holding, but a machete.

And the colour of the hood had nothing to do with the red smoke that plumed around the figure, because the material was red to begin with. *Morningstar Servitors!*

Tanek recognised this, he'd spent long enough working with them when they'd allied themselves with the Tsar. They'd thought the Russian was their chosen leader on earth or something, but had abandoned him soon after the fight for the castle.

Here and there, Gwen saw snatches of what was happening out in the crimson smog: a German soldier firing into the mist, but hitting nothing, only for a machete blade to appear in the centre of his chest; another German firing a pistol off to one side, arm outstretched, and then the next moment a blade coming out of nowhere, hacking his arm off at the elbow. It was a similar story everywhere you looked: a leg here, a hand there. The Servitors – and yes, there were definitely more than one – were everywhere and nowhere at once. Finally, Gwen saw one German staggering through the smoke, his rifle held close, eyes darting left and right – when a hooded figure materialized behind him and planted his machete deep into the man's head, practically slicing it in two.

It was clear the Germans didn't know quite what had hit them, and they were rapidly losing the battle. Tanek shot a couple of bolts at the approaching men, but in spite of his precision they didn't end up anywhere near the targets. As they moved forwards, holding their machetes in one hand, they removed their cowls with the others, revealing those skull faces Gwen knew so well. Tanek shot again, but found he was out of bolts. To change the magazine, he had to drop Clive Jr. Her son began crying even louder as he was dumped unceremoniously on the ground. Tanek reloaded quickly, loosing a couple of bolts – hitting nothing. But when he reached down to retrieve the child, Clive Jr had disappeared. Gwen hadn't seen him vanish, either; perhaps he'd got up and toddled off into the smoke?

Whatever the case, Tanek had other matters to deal with. The Servitors were closing in, and no matter where he shot, Tanek didn't seem to be able to land a hit. It was like he was attacking the fog itself.

Slinging the weapon over his shoulder, he brought out his knife and prepared for hand-to-hand. The Servitors rushed him as one, machete blades swishing. Tanek avoided the first of the blows, grabbing one Servitor – not so insubstantial now – and throwing him into three of his brethren, who tumbled to the ground like bowling skittles. But one of the machetes caught Tanek a glancing blow across the forearm and he roared.

Gwen attempted to move, to crawl forward and search for her son, but her whole body cried out in agony. She tried to call his name, but doubted whether he could hear her. "C-Clive, sweetheart, where are you? It's... it's Mummy."

She gritted her teeth, severely hampered by her wounds but

desperate to find her son. Suddenly, in front of her, was a set of feet. Gwen looked slowly up, and there he was, hood removed.

It was the man who'd saved her once from the castle, this time without his skull make-up. He was here again to save her. And he was holding Clive Jr in his arms, safely returned to her. Gwen couldn't help herself; she began to cry. "Th-thank you," she whispered. She didn't know what else to say, there weren't the words to express how she felt. Gwen held up a trembling hand to take her child. But the man she'd once known only as Skullface cocked his head, frowning. It was then that she saw it: the tears tracking down his face, the humanity she'd sensed in him before. Yet still he held on to her child...

The smoke was clearing a little. The circle of Servitors remained, but there was no sign of Tanek, and there were more new arrivals. At first Gwen thought they were Servitor reinforcements, but these people in hoods were on horseback, and were armed with bows and arrows. Karen was with them, riding with a shocked-looking Reverend Tate, who immediately ordered the Rangers to shoot at the Servitors. "No, wait!" Gwen wanted to shout, but didn't have the voice anymore. It came out as a croak.

Tate had dismounted and was leading a team across the square. A couple of the Rangers had engaged the Servitors in swordplay. The Reverend was limping towards Gwen and her saviour, calling for the man to release his hostages. Gwen wanted to explain, to tell him he'd got it all wrong, but even if she had the strength Tate probably wouldn't have believed her. The man who'd come to her aid looked from Gwen to the Reverend, and finally let Clive Jr down to be with his mother.

Then he ran, calling for the other Morningstars to retreat as well. Tate attempted to stop him, swinging his stick, but the man easily dodged it. In moments, the robed figures were gone.

Though it was agony to do so, Gwen put her free arm around Clive Jr, growing weaker by the minute. That final bolt had done something to her, torn something vital inside, she realised, and part of her wondered if that was why the Servitor was crying? She couldn't help looking at the bodies of the fallen all around, clearly visible now the smoke was gone, and thinking that soon she would be joining them. Gwen cried again, not because she'd been reunited with her son, but because she'd have to say goodbye to him shortly.

As Tate came over – concern etched on his face and calling for medical assistance – she also wondered if Clive Jr would have been better off with the man who'd *really* saved them? It was clearly what the Servitor himself had been considering right at the end.

But one thing comforted her as she lay there, bleeding out from her wounds.

At least she knew her boy wasn't with that bastard Tanek.

TANEK WONDERED WHAT exactly had happened.

One minute everything had been going brilliantly, according to plan. The villagers were being worn down, they had pretty much been removed as any kind of real threat. The woman Gwen was on her knees in front of him, where she belonged, and De Falaise's child was his for the taking.

Then... *they'd* arrived, out of nowhere. The Morningstars. Tanek simply couldn't get his head around it. He'd not seen a single one of those freaks since the battle at Nottingham Castle; they'd fucked off and left the rest of them to it, abandoning the Tsar to die at Hood's hands. Now this. Why had they stepped in? What was their argument with him? Or the Germans, for that matter?

It just didn't make sense.

But Tanek believed in the evidence of his own eyes. Back there, with those Servitors all around him, machete wounds in at least half a dozen places, he hadn't questioned the fact that they were there; that they were attacking for no reason. He'd fled, ensuring his own survival. If he lived, then there was always another chance to capture the boy. A good job he had, too, because he'd only narrowly avoided a run in with some Rangers on horseback, riding in like the fucking cavalry. It was definitely time to beat a hasty retreat, put some distance between him and the Morningstars, *and* the Rangers. Once, he might have actually stayed and slugged it out with both, despite the superior numbers, but Tanek was on to a good thing with the Germans. And he'd figure out another way to get to De Falaise's child at some point.

His way had been blocked to the jeep, so he'd had to escape on foot, losing himself in the woodland around the village. Tanek kept looking over his shoulder as he went, nursing the cuts on his arms and torso, trying to stem the bleeding for fear of leaving a trail.

Tanek didn't like being the hunted, didn't even think of himself that way now. He wasn't some vulnerable prey, and even if they caught up with him they'd wish they hadn't –

There, in the trees: a noise. Tanek stopped, bringing the knife up and shrugging his crossbow off his shoulder.

There was definitely someone... Yes, movement. *There!* Tanek loosed a bolt, then set off in the opposite direction. There was a rustling from behind, the sound of someone coming after him. One or several? He couldn't tell. Tanek was a good distance from New Hope; they must have been determined, to follow him this far. But who was it, the cultists or the Rangers? Maybe he should just make a stand, get this over with, use the cover the woods afforded him to turn the tables on his –

The ground suddenly fell away, and Tanek found himself tumbling. Down into a deep hole; concealed, like the secret entrance to New Hope. Whoever had created that must have made this one, he thought as he hit the bottom, hard. It wasn't the Morningstars' style to do something like this.

It was more like Hood's.

Tanek shook his head, attempted to get up, but found he couldn't. He touched the base of his skull and his fingers came away wet. He didn't have long before he blacked out.

A lone figure appeared at the edge of the pit he'd fallen into. Tanek made to raise his crossbow, but both that and his knife must have slipped out of his grasp during the fall. It didn't matter, he couldn't focus properly on the man anyway. What he could see, though, was that he wasn't wearing red or green. He was wearing black, from head to toe. In fact, as Tanek gazed up, it looked to him very much like a shadow was standing there.

"Hello, Mr Tanek," said, with a strange, distinctive accent. "I have been waiting for you."

Tanek attempted to reply, but found his grasp on language was about as good as his grasp on his weapons.

And now he was falling again, into another deep pit.

Filled with darkness.

Filled with shadows.

CHAPTER TWENTY-ONE

"CAN'T THIS THING go any faster?"

Jack's driver – a Ranger called Doherty – shook his head. He was already coaxing all the speed he could out of the jeep, one of the few German vehicles that survived their attack on the Dragon's power base. Jack gritted his teeth, and slammed his fist on the dashboard. "Damn!"

"I'm sure he'll be okay, sir," Doherty told him.

Jack appreciated the sentiment, but there was no way of knowing. Nobody could see the future, except that mad bat up in Scotland that the others had just seen off, if the rumours about her were true. There wasn't much to choose between her and the Welshman, by the sounds of things. Just thinking about it sent a shiver down Jack's spine. In all their years of doing this, standing up to people like the Sheriff and the Tsar, Jack had never come across somebody as deranged as the Dragon. Someone so unbalanced he kept his family's bones as some sort of puppet show, to convince himself they'd never died. There were so many horror movie references he could have made – the Dragon gave Norman Bates a run for his money, for starters – but seeing that in real life... Fact was stranger than celluloid.

Thankfully, they'd seen the last of him, and the rest of the operation had just been an exercise in clearing up. With a decent number of Rangers to hand, it hadn't taken them long to seize control. And because the Dragon had deprived the Welsh Rangers of their HQ, it seemed only fitting that they should take over the Millennium Stadium now instead.

"Think of the training you could do on that pitch," Dale had said, after commenting that he'd loved to have played there when it was still used as a concert venue. Dale had been a marvel throughout; not only during his undercover work, but afterwards, offering to stay and help with setting up the new Ranger base. How much of that was to do with Sian, Jack couldn't say – or indeed whether they'd be seeing Dale back at their own HQ in Nottingham again anytime soon – but the lad deserved a break. Why shouldn't he spend it with that pretty gal? Jack reckoned she'd been through just as much; maybe they could make each other happy.

"You know, I think Meghan's taken quite a shine to you as well," Dale told him.

"Hey, now –"

"All I'm saying is think about it, mate. She's really nice." And he had a point. She'd even come down to the entrance to see Jack off.

"I hope things work out okay," she told him, then kissed him on the cheek. "I don't know how I can ever thank you and Dale for what you've done."

Jack had felt his face reddening, just as it had once done when he'd helped rescue Adele from the Morningstars. It was those kinds of memories which held him back, forced him to keep Meghan at a distance. Not that he was saying she was a traitor or anything; she was far from that. But Jack still had trust issues and they weren't going away anytime soon. "All in the line of duty, ma'am," he told her, "nothing more."

But he'd spent the first few miles regretting that cool response. Hoping maybe someday he'd get to put that right. Perhaps get to know Meghan better, become friends, then – No, he wasn't about to jump in again. His poor heart couldn't take another battering like the last one. But Jack was lonely, and had been for some time.

Not that any of this was a priority at the moment; just something to take his mind off his real concern of the day. It was funny; all that fighting, everything that had happened with the Dragon, and the disappearance of just one boy could send him into a tailspin. But then Mark was a very special young man.

They'd always had a connection, Jack and Mark. He remembered their first meeting, when Robert had mistaken Jack for an intruder in Sherwood. It had been Mark who'd recognised him as The Hammer, a former professional wrestler who the boy had followed on the circuits. Robert had taken Mark's word when he vouched that Jack was one of the good guys, and a good fighter to have on board. Jack had returned the favour by teaching Mark, training him whenever Robert wasn't able, taking him under his wing and showing him all his own moves, and a few more besides. Mark was family, like Sian was to Meghan. Jack had always thought of himself as an uncle to the boy. Which was why, when he'd heard about the kidnapping, he'd told Mary he was on his way back to the castle ASAP.

"Bill's already been told," she explained over the radio, "and he's coming back here. Jack, we need you."

"I'm already there, little lady."

Except he wasn't. It was taking forever in this piece of shit, made more for protection than speed. It wasn't just the fact that Mark was missing, although that was bad enough. Robert had gone in after him, alone; heading to Sherwood, like the note said. Who the Sam Hill was 'S'?

"I'm coming with you," Dale had said when he heard, but Jack had shaken his head.

"You're still getting over being pummelled by the Dragon. No, you stay here and do what you said you were going to do: look after Sian and get things in motion for setting up the base."

"But –"

"You're more use to me here, Dale," he'd insisted, then clapped the lad on the shoulder. "Please." Jack had put him through enough already, sending him on this mission; he didn't want to be worrying about him all over again. They'd hugged and Dale had told him to look after himself. The kid was worried about Robert and Mark, just as much as he was. Now that they'd got over their difference of opinion about Sophie, those two had become quite good pals.

The radio crackled into life and Jack looked at Doherty. *You know what they say about the best laid plans, Jackie-boy.* He picked up the receiver and identified himself. It was Mary again, calling from the castle, but he was having trouble hearing her.

"Say again. Over."

"Found... I repeat... Mark... unharmed..."

"Sounded like you said Mark's been found? Over."

"Affirmative."

"*Wahooo!*" Jack removed his cap and slapped it on his thigh. If he'd been out in the open he might have thrown it into the air. But he was celebrating too soon.

"...missing now..."

"Didn't catch that, Mary. Could you repeat? Over."

"I said..." And he could hear the tears in her voice. "Robert's missing... same... took him... Over."

That wiped the smile off his face. They'd been given one member of their family back, only to lose another. Mark had been the lure all along, it seemed, and Robert had been the real target. But what did this 'S' want with their leader? He had a lot of enemies at home and abroad, but why now, and why take him rather than kill him? Jack wasn't sure he wanted to know the answer to that. There was a distinct possibility that whoever the kidnapper was, or whoever he worked for, wanted to have a little fun with Robert before finishing him off. A slow death. Jack said nothing about this to Mary, but she'd probably already thought of it.

"Took him? Took him where?" asked Jack. "Do we have any leads? Over."

There was silence at the other end, static at his. Then Mary said: "Maybe. Over."

Maybe was better than nothing. She wouldn't be drawn on the rest, preferring to wait until Jack was home so she could report in person. It was probably wise – this frequency might well be monitored by third parties.

When he hung up the radio, Jack looked out at the open country roads stretching before them, and then across at Doherty.

"Hey man, can't this thing go any faster?" he repeated.

CHAPTER TWENTY-TWO

IT WAS THE smell that roused him.

Cold as it was, this place stank of sweat. There was also the coppery stench of blood, and another scent that was harder to pin down, distinct and sharp.

Death. That was it. This place smelled of death.

Robert had smelled it many times before in battle. It was rank and he couldn't stand it in his nostrils for long without opening his eyes. It took a few moments for his eyes to adjust. He felt the ache in his shoulder where the arrow had passed right through; still blinking, he reached up to touch the wound. It had been stitched. The stranger had obviously wanted Robert in one piece before delivering him God knows where. Robert also felt as though he'd slept for decades: drugged, obviously, but at least he felt rested.

He shivered. Robert had been stripped down to just his vest and combat trousers, he realised. He blinked a few more times then heard the noise, the sound of people all around – not saying anything, remaining as quiet as they possibly could, but giving themselves away with their breathing.

He put a hand beneath him, feeling concrete. Where in Christ's name was he?

The first thing he saw were people, surrounding him. Lots of people. Some dressed in uniform, some in little more than rags. They were staring at him, and all had that same tired, resigned expression on their faces. The hard lives they'd lived were reflected in every downturned mouth, every crease of the brow. These people were pissed off, Robert just didn't know why.

If it was with Robert, he was in trouble. Kidnapped and dumped here to be pulled to pieces by an angry mob. He couldn't hope to fight off a fifth of them, especially without his weapons, which – yep – he checked again and confirmed he definitely didn't have.

And why was it so bloody cold? Even the harshest spring in England was never this chilly.

There was a groan from behind, and Robert was suddenly aware of someone else on the floor with him. Someone not that far away. He looked around, though it hurt to do so.

The other man was face down on the ground, also just waking up. Robert couldn't see his face yet, but could see a bandage on the back of his head, cuts on his arms that, like Robert's wounds, had been stitched. *Our Native American friend's been busy*, he thought. *Glad it's not just me that he's been dicking around with. Why should I have all the fun?*

It did beg the question: what did he have in common with this other prisoner, and could he use that to his advantage? Shadow had nobbled both of them and brought them to this place; that demanded a little payback, didn't it? If nothing else, Robert might have someone to stand alongside as the mob closed in on him and –

The man on the floor put an elbow underneath himself and raised his head. Robert's face fell. He'd seen that face on two occasions in the past – when he and Bill had flown into the middle of the fight for Nottingham Castle, and then at Sherwood a little over a year later. This was one of the most dangerous people on the planet, and that was saying something these days. Robert would rather face a dozen Widows than this man.

"Tanek," he said.

The giant shook his head and opened his eyes. "Hood," he snarled – not looking at anything else, not the crowds surrounding them, nor the armed guards now dotted here and there. Armed, Robert noted, with AK-47s; meant to keep the people in line, but also maybe to stop him and Tanek from escaping.

When Robert looked back at the large man, he found he was already up and ready to charge at him. Robert rose too, only just avoiding Tanek's assault – but made the same mistake a lot of people had in the past. Assuming that Tanek's size made him slow. When Tanek swung round, striking Robert on the back with his laced fists, it felt like a battering ram hitting him. Robert was sent hurtling across the pit. He fell and rolled, wincing when the ground caught his injured shoulder.

Woozy as he was, Robert staggered to his feet. He couldn't afford to be lax with this big ape after him. And, sure enough, Tanek was lunging towards him again. Robert faked one way and slid the other, bringing his fists down between the bigger man's shoulder-blades. It actually hurt his hands, the man was so solid, but it did unbalance Tanek enough to send him tumbling head over heels. Robert looked around: the crowd was going wild. They weren't here to attack, they were here to watch him and Tanek fight. There was even a cordon, almost totally obscured by the throngs of people. Keeping them out and the contenders in.

Tanek was on his feet once more. "I'm going to kill you!" he shouted, rushing towards Robert.

"You and whose army? Oh, that's right – you tried that *twice* already."

It had the desired effect, making Tanek's next move clumsy, easier to avoid. Robert rolled under the punch his opponent threw, barging into Tanek sideways and almost pitching him over with the giant's momentum. It was the only way he'd be able to keep avoiding Tanek, but he couldn't keep it up for long. Already the giant was lunging back round again, delivering a kick that practically flipped Robert over in mid-air. He landed on his front, winded for the second time in as many minutes.

The crowd was cheering with delight, and Robert felt Tanek standing over him, about to deliver a killing blow. Though it took just about all the strength he could muster, Robert shuffled backwards and out of reach as Tanek's fist came down. Instead of grinding Robert's head into the dirt, the giant punched the floor and growled with pain. Robert scrabbled back further away from the man.

Tanek was about to leap on him again when a sharp banging from above interrupted. It reminded Robert of old courtroom dramas, of a judge striking the bench with his gavel.

"Enough!" came a voice. Robert recognised the accent, and sadly recognised the voice, too. He looked up for the source, spotting a ledge with a railing. Part of what had once been an overhanging office, stripped bare to provide a viewing platform.

It was then that Robert matched the voice to the face, and the face to the name. "Bohuslav. This day's getting better and better." The new Tsar of Russia, crowned after Robert had killed his former master. Bohuslav was dressed in what looked like a red velvet uniform with yellow piping – replacing the previous Tsar's leather – and a flowing cape. In place of the hand that Dale had taken from him was Bohuslav's favourite weapon, the sickle, and in his other hand a heavy metal hammer with which he'd struck the edge of the rail. He was a living embodiment of the Russian flag.

Robert glanced over at the man who'd been about to kill him and saw that Tanek was equally surprised to see their captor.

"Do not kill each other so quickly. I have gone to great pains to arrange this. I want to savour it," Bohuslav said with a wide grin.

Great pains, thought Robert. *Now I understand.* He could see the Native American on that viewing platform as well. He was looking on with interest, arms folded. A satisfied Bohuslav turned to one side, now, nodding to one of his personal guards, who gave the man in black a bag. His payment for services rendered. Robert wondered what was inside; thirty pieces of silver would get you nowhere nowadays. Had to be something else, something –

"I will kill you!" This was Tanek, now addressing Bohuslav, who turned back to face them.

"Not before you've killed Hood, surely? You just said that was your intention." His broken English was exactly how Robert remembered it. The last time he'd clapped eyes on this nutter it had been when his Rangers had defeated the Tsar's not inconsiderable forces. If Dale hadn't come to the rescue... Robert had assumed the man had been killed by the wounds that lad inflicted, but obviously not. And the new Tsar wanted revenge, not on the man who'd mutilated him, but on the man responsible for the Rangers in the first place. The man who'd killed his lord and master.

When Tanek said nothing, Bohuslav laughed. "So, kill him, and we will talk about what happens after that. On the other hand, Hood might kill you. He has just as much of an axe to grind." The new Tsar nodded to a guard below, who tossed a weapon into the area of combat: a large, double-edged axe. "If I remember rightly you, Tanek, favoured the pollaxe the last time you were here. Yes, Hood, Tanek has an advantage over you. He has fought in this place once before." And with that, a staff with a lethal-looking blade on the end landed near Tanek's feet. He looked at it, then up again at Bohuslav.

The Tsar banged his hammer on the rail again, before tucking it into his belt. "Go on, pick up your weapons. If you do not, then your opponent might gain the advantage."

Robert was about to say something to Tanek when the bigger man grabbed his pollaxe and tested its weight.

Okay... thought Robert, snatching up his axe. A large net and a round shield were also thrown into the ring, for whoever picked them up first.

Tanek made it to the shield, so Robert had to settle for the net, winding the thick rope around his hand and wrist. Just in time, because Tanek made a swift lunge with the pollaxe, which Robert snagged in the netting, attempting to swing the larger man round. Tanek held his ground, however, raising the weapon and almost taking the netting with it. Robert held on, feeling himself being lifted along with the mesh. He used it to his advantage, swinging forward and bringing his axe around in an arc to try and hit Tanek. The giant was forced to lower the pole, and in doing so both of them wound up on the floor.

"Tanek," said Robert, catching his breath. "Tanek, listen to me. He's playing us both off against –"

The big man was up and swinging the pollaxe at him again. Robert sighed, ducked, then rose to block the next swing. The wooden hafts of both his own weapon and the pollaxe juddered with the strain, but Tanek was just too strong. Robert had to defect the blow sideways or risk being struck full in the face by the business end, which would have cleaved his skull in two.

"Tanek, dammit, listen to me! You know he'll kill whoever's left when –" Robert had to step sideways to dodge yet another attack, but this time he clambered onto Tanek's back, kicking as he used it as a springboard. The larger man lost his footing and ended up on the ground, while Robert landed awkwardly and turned. "He'll just kill whoever wins," Robert finished.

"He will not get the chance," Tanek said, sneering. Then he righted himself and came at Robert once again. He lunged with the axe, but then twisted and brought round his shield, using that as a weapon instead. Robert barely had time to lean back, falling over in an effort to prevent the edge of the shield connecting with his windpipe.

Damn and blast, the bastard's stubborn, thought Robert. "Unless we work together, it'll –" Robert rolled to the right, missing another stroke with the axe. He couldn't believe this; it wouldn't be his first choice to try and work with one of his greatest enemies either, but Tanek was too obsessed by the idea of killing him and Bohuslav to see clearly. To see how they could win. There was only one way Robert could convince him, that he could see.

That was to beat him.

Robert hunkered down, trying to ignore his body's protests and waiting for the next strike from Tanek. When it came, he clumsily swung his blade – but hit the handle nonetheless and splintered it. Then he cast the net, but instead of tangling up Tanek's weapon, he laid it on the ground, so that Tanek would step into it, pulled forward by his momentum. Robert put the end of the net over his good shoulder and tugged as hard as he could. Tanek wobbled, but didn't fall – so much for that plan – so instead Robert ran around the big man, tangling him up. It was then a matter of batting the axe out of Tanek's grasp as it poked up through the net, leaving Tanek with just a shield that was bound up with him and couldn't be shifted.

Robert saw a newfound respect for his fighting abilities in Tanek's eyes. With shaky hands, he lifted his weapon aloft, blocking out the cheers of the crowd. "The only way we're going to do this is *together*," Robert said, close enough that only they could hear. "Remember that."

He brought the axe down, but veered off at the final moment, cutting through the netting to free Tanek. As far as the onlookers – and indeed Bohuslav himself – were concerned it simply looked like he'd missed, but what he'd done was not lost on the olive-skinned giant. Again, Robert could see in his eyes that an understanding had finally been reached.

Which was why he was surprised when the big man got up, leaving his shield on the floor and grabbing the pollaxe, lashing out again with it seconds later. Robert blocked him with his own axe, but this time he could feel there was no real tension. Tanek grunted, as they drew closer together in a struggle with the weapons. "I will settle with you later," he promised Robert, then suddenly turned his back, and thrust his axe into the nearest guard.

Robert himself jabbed the blunt end of his axe into another guard's stomach, bringing it up and knocking the man backwards, taking him down without serious injury. He refused to do as Tanek had and just kill the armed men surrounding them. That was the difference between them, and always would be.

There was gunfire as the remaining guards attempted to get the gladiators to move back into position. To fight each other again, not them. Robert ducked and rolled, lashing out with the handle of the axe to knock a rifle out of a guard's hand. Then he whacked another over the head with the flat of the blade. Twirling, he saw a gunman draw a bead on him and fire, so he raised the axe, holding his breath as the bullets pinged off the metal. "No, you idiots!" Bohuslav screamed from above. "I want them alive. If they will not kill each other, then *I* will have the satisfaction of ending both their lives!" He ordered one of his personal troopers to gun down the pit guard who'd fired on Robert. At least that would work in their favour, thought Robert; the others wouldn't dare shoot to kill now.

More gunfire, this time from behind him. Tanek with the first guard's rifle, spraying bullets into the air, sending the crowd into a panic. It provided necessary cover, but then he shot at more guards on the lower level, hitting chests, heads and stomachs.

"No! *Wound* them, Tanek. Just –"

Another burst told Robert the giant wouldn't listen. Life meant very little to Tanek, and it was too late to try and change him. For a second Robert wondered what would happen if it came down to him and the giant? If he couldn't take him alive? Would he himself do as he'd done to De Falaise, to the Tsar? Kill, to rid the world of another monster? And wasn't there more than a hint of good old-fashioned revenge, as well? Didn't he want retribution for all the things Tanek had done to them, to Mark and Jack in particular?

Another smattering of machine-gun fire, now targeted at the viewing platform. Robert looked up to see the Native American withdrawing; this wasn't his fight. But Robert needed something from him, wanted back what the man had taken.

He looked around and saw Tanek's discarded shield on the ground. He slipped it along one arm until it covered his shoulder, then made a play for the platform, ducking beneath the cordon. Robert pushed through both the guards and the crowd.

"Hood!" roared Tanek. "Leave him!"

Robert cast the axe aside and began to climb towards the ledge. It was a struggle, his muscles and shoulder on fire, but he had to get up there and follow the man in black. It was more important right now than anything else, even getting his hands on Bohuslav.

Bohuslav's guards were now leaning over the rail, firing at Robert. He pulled his arm across, letting the bullets bounce off the shield. They sparked around him and he wondered how much more the metal could take. In the lull of changing magazines, he urged himself upwards. The threat of being shot at again was a distinct incentive.

Just as one guard was about to open fire, Robert put on a final spurt and grabbed the barrel of his rifle, pulling him over the ledge. Another man turned and aimed at Robert's head, but was slashed across the back of the neck by Bohuslav. He wanted to kill his captive personally, which was warping the Tsar's judgement, and for that Robert was grateful.

"Hood!" he heard Tanek shout up again, and risked a look over his shoulder. He saw the giant making his way through the panicking throng.

Robert pulled the shield down to his forearm and struck an oncoming guard full in the face, sending him crashing onto his back.

There were now only a couple left – and Bohuslav. Robert bent when one of the remaining guards attempted to restrain him, lifting the man and pitching him over onto the ground before kicking him across the face. The final one he dispatched by bringing up the shield again and catching him under the chin.

There was a swishing sound and Robert leaned to his right as Bohuslav's sickle came down. Then he ducked a sideswing, aiming to catch him across the face. "I was intending to savour this, but I should just get it over with," Bohuslav told him. "Now, where did we leave things last time? Ah yes, I was about to end your life." The mad Russian lashed out again and Robert brought up the shield to block him.

"Hood! He's mine!" came Tanek's distinctive rumble from beneath them. It said a lot for what Tanek thought of Bohuslav's chances against him.

Robert brought up the shield again, deflecting another blow. "You can have him," Robert answered, then pushed forward, taking Bohuslav to the very edge of the rail.

"No... Wait..." said Bohuslav, but Robert shoved again, harder this time, tipping the man over.

Bohuslav managed to grab one of the bars, his cape flowing behind him. Robert placed his boot on Bohuslav's fingers. "You two deserve each other," he told the man, then removed his foot. "Happy landings!"

Leaving Bohuslav to fall, Robert headed off through the doorway of what had once been the office, in search of the Native American.

It led out into a corridor, and Robert now realised he was in some kind of abandoned warehouse. Checking doors left and right, holding the shield up in case there were more guards with guns inside, he ventured up the corridor, following the trail of the man who'd brought him here. The man in black had a head start, that was true, but Robert had to hope he'd just carried on in a straight line, since his tracking abilities were all over the place at the moment. For all the Native American knew, Robert was still occupied downstairs; with a bit of luck, he hadn't tried to hide his trail too much.

And suddenly there he was: up ahead, a shadow amongst the shadows. Like the professional he was, the Native American *felt* Robert behind him, casting a quick glance over his shoulder, then picking up his pace. There was a bend coming up, which the Native American negotiated quickly.

Damn, I'm going to lose him, thought Robert, speeding up.

When he rounded the corner, he found the man in black had waited. The first blow struck Robert across the chin; a warning. "Do not follow me."

"Like Hell. You have something that belongs to me."

The man grimaced, then came at Robert again, this time with a knife suddenly in hand, slashing furiously. Robert could do nothing but use the shield to fend off the attack. The blows rained down hard, knocking the battered metal from his arm. "My quarrel is not with you," the kidnapper told him.

"You should have thought of that before," Robert replied, grabbing the Native American's arm, bringing it down on his knee and forcing the weapon out of the man's grasp.

The response was a fighting move Robert hadn't come across before, somewhere between wrestling and kung fu. It took Robert's legs out from under him, coupled with a swift elbow to the stomach. "I will not say this again. Do not follow me."

Robert was getting ready to rise again, so the man in black gave him a kick to keep him down.

"Hey, you," Robert heard a voice. "I think we've got unfinished business." A fist slammed into the Native American's face, hard. It knocked him back against the corridor's wall. Robert couldn't see who'd delivered it at first, until a hooded figure stepped out, following up his first move with a roundhouse kick. "I owe you this!"

The figure pulled back his cowl and it was Mark, his son, last seen tied to a tree, his head covered in dried blood. Robert didn't question it; he got up, and while the man in black was still disoriented, Robert snatched his bag he'd been carrying – the one the Tsar's guards had given him. Mark had his bow and arrow out already and was covering the Native American at close range, the tip of the arrow pointing directly at the man's head. "So much as a twitch," warned Mark, jabbing the weapon even closer. "Go on, try me."

Robert smiled; the boy had come on in leaps and bounds since his training had begun and, given the circumstances, he was proud. "Now, let's see what this was all about." Robert opened the bag and looked inside. He looked up, puzzled. Then he took out the single object inside: a stone.

"This is what you sold us out for?"

"I don't expect you to understand. You do not even understand your *own* heritage."

"I understand enough. What did you do, out there in the forest? How do we put things back to... to normal?"

It seemed a strange thing to say and Mark glanced at him, but they both knew what he meant. It wasn't exactly normal to dream about things that were going to happen, to have a connection with nature that gave you strength and health, but it was *their* normal. If Robert had been a superhero, then this man had found his weakness. He looked again at the stone he was holding. "Is this it? Is this the way to put things right again? Destroy this?" Robert made as if to drop it on the floor.

"No!" shouted the Native American, holding out his hand. Mark drew back his bow even further. "No... please don't do that."

That got his attention anyway, thought Robert. "Okay, so tell us, or I really will break your precious stone."

Shadow sighed, slumping back against the wall. He reached down to his belt. Mark tensed, but Shadow held up one hand to show that he was only reaching for another small pouch.

"Easy, mate. Nice and slow. We've both seen what you keep inside those things. I don't fancy another nap."

"You asked for the way. This is it," explained the man. He threw the pouch to Robert, who looked inside.

"Looks like ash. What is this?"

"You must take it back to your forest. Release it there and the spirits, your gods, will be freed." When they both frowned, he continued: "It must mix with the essence of your spiritual home. Now, hand me back what *you* have taken."

"How do we know this will wor–" Robert didn't finish the sentence; gunfire filled the corridor. Russian soldiers were approaching. Everyone ducked, and Robert tossed the stone over to the man in black to free his hands, then shoved the pouch of ashes in his pocket. Mark shifted his aim to fire on the Russians, which left their enemy free to nock his own bow, after tucking away his prize.

At first, Robert thought the man might actually shoot at them. Instead, he let off a couple of precisely aimed arrows at the guards. Robert nodded to him and the Native American nodded back. But then he was off, running towards the Russians, leaping over their heads. Mark was about to shoot at him when Robert placed his hand on the boy's shoulder. "Let him go. We have other problems."

They certainly did, as automatic fire raked the walls. Rounding the corner, Mark pressed himself up against the pock-marked plaster and shot at the men. Robert had already grabbed the shield to protect himself from the barrage and joined him. "Now what?" asked Mark.

"Fall back," Robert told him. They backed up the corridor until they reached one of the rooms Robert had checked on the way. "Inside. Cover us."

Hiding behind the doorframe, Mark continued to pull arrow after arrow from his quiver. Robert called for Mark, pointing to the window. His son loosed a few more arrows to buy them some time, then followed Robert as he ran at the window, using the shield to break the glass and then plummeting towards the ground.

Robert hit the concrete below badly, but it would have been much worse were it not for the shield and the thick snow covering the street. Tiny shards of glass followed, sprinkling Robert as he watched Mark bend and take the strain on his much younger knees, dropping perfectly beside him. They were somewhere round the side of the warehouse, in a deserted alley. Deserted, that was, apart from what looked like frozen statues lying on the ground. The slowly decomposing dead, who thawed in warmer weather, then refroze when the snow returned.

"Come on," Mark said, helping him up and looking above him to where the Russian soldiers were now taking up firing positions at the window. "Time we weren't here."

Robert couldn't agree more, but as they rounded the corner of the building they were stopped dead in their tracks. Assembled at the front of the warehouse was a vast collection of jeeps, tanks and other armoured vehicles, and dozens of soldiers with rifles. And they were all trained in Robert and Mark's direction.

The air filled with the *clack* of weapons being cocked, as Robert saw the new Tsar stumble through the main doors of the warehouse. What had happened to Tanek, he had no clue.

Bohuslav grinned slyly when he saw the scene.

"What are you waiting for? Execute them!"

CHAPTER TWENTY-THREE

THE FIGHT HAD been a vicious one, but it had been he who'd been victorious.

He'd often wondered in the time since their last meeting – in the time since their *first* meeting, as a matter of fact – who would be the eventual winner. Both of them were sadistic bastards, quick to kill by whatever methods were available. But also, if time allowed, keen to savour the act of extinguishing life itself.

That hadn't been an option today, but Bohuslav didn't care. He'd tried to do this the slow way, to make Tanek and Hood perform a little before their deaths. But now it was over for at least one of them, he felt good. And he felt all the better for having got it over and done with quickly.

When Hood pushed him over that ledge, he'd thought that was the end of it. The bastard had practically kicked him off into the lion's den. Luckily, Bohuslav knew how to fall – and *who* to fall *on*, making use of a couple of guards and civilians below. He'd walked away relatively unscathed, but that had just been the start of it.

Tanek had been rushing towards him by the time he found his feet again. Bohuslav had just about managed to dodge the first attack, stumbling over the bodies he'd fallen on. As he rose, Bohuslav wielded his hammer, aiming for the big lug's fingers. Tanek had let out a cry as they opened in pain, his axe flying out of his grasp. With his good hand, Tanek grabbed the length of the hammer and tugged, pulling Bohuslav in for a head butt. It was a glancing blow which opened up a cut over his right eye, disorientating him long enough for Tanek to yank the hammer from his clutches.

Tanek swung it, but Bohuslav ducked, slashing at Tanek with his sickle and inflicting a wound on Tanek's side. The giant snarled, bringing down the hammer on Bohuslav's shoulder and almost dislocating it. Bohuslav lashed out with the sickle again, slicing open Tanek's forearm and forcing him to drop the weapon. The larger man dived on him and they rolled over and over, the floor relatively empty now that the crowds had thinned. People were racing for the exit now that the majority of guards were either dead or wounded.

When they came to a stop in the middle of the fighting pit, Bohuslav found himself on top. Before he could embed his sickle in Tanek's flesh, though, the giant had thrown him off, flinging the Tsar onto his back.

As Tanek was getting to his feet, Bohuslav was already crawling around him. He slashed at the tendons at the back of the big man's ankles, severing one and cutting almost all the way through the other. Tanek dropped onto his knees, but still whirled grabbing at Bohuslav.

The Tsar had discovered the axe Hood had abandoned. Seizing it as he climbed to his feet, he ran at Tanek with the weapon. The big man grabbed it just below the blade, squeezing the wood. Bohuslav could feel the power in that hand still, even after he'd struck it with the hammer. Tanek was threatening to break the handle in his grip, or at least snatch it away from Bohuslav. It was time to finish things.

"I *will* kill you," Tanek said.

Bohuslav jerked sideways suddenly, causing the end to snap off, but he'd put enough weight behind the move that the wooden shaft carried on moving... into Tanek's chest, rammed through a good few inches. The big man opened his eyes wide, looking down at the wood. "Just... just like the Sheriff..." he said, a slight smile playing on his lips. Lips that were growing redder by the second. "No... I must live... the promise... the –"

Then he fell and Bohuslav stood over him, watching as he breathed his last. To make sure, he bent and cut the man's throat open from one side to the other. "Goodbye, Tanek," he spat. Then he began hobbling towards the door, leaving the body of the giant behind.

Bohuslav made it to the main entrance, the last person to leave, and was stunned by what he saw. He'd assumed Hood had already fled, that he'd have to send out a search party to bring the escapee back: one dead, one to go. But here was the man himself, in pretty bad shape by the looks of things, being helped by one of his lot; a lone man sent in to free him. Ridiculous, the arrogance of those Rangers!

What made the picture perfect, however, was the forces already summoned to tackle him – a guard must have sounded the alarm.

Even Bohuslav was impressed with the speed with which his men had assembled, the sheer force of vehicles and soldiers that had gathered.

Looking across at Hood and smiling, he gave the order to kill them.

It was only then that Bohuslav noticed the men were not wearing the grey uniforms of his own army. Yes, they were similar – *very* similar, in fact – but there were subtle differences. For one thing the symbol worn on the shoulders of their uniform was different. A symbol from history, familiar yet updated, formed of overlapping squares. A shape that had struck terror into millions during the 1930s and 40s. And the vehicles weren't of Russian origin either. Not the standard issue they'd used against Hood back in England, nor those he'd been building up since. Bohuslav had become quite an expert in scavenged military gear, and he knew which army had once used these vehicles. Which country.

The deciding factor had been when their commander had ordered for the troops to turn on *him*: turning their guns away from Hood and his Ranger, towards the Tsar.

"Wait," said Bohuslav, holding up his hands. "Wait a second –"

The commander shouted for them to open fire.

Bohuslav barely had time to breathe out, "God forgive me," before the soldiers pulled their triggers.

ROBERT AND MARK'S mouths fell open.

They'd thought this was it. That death had finally caught up with them. Staring down the barrels of so many guns and cannons, how could they possibly cheat death again this time? Robert felt more sorry for Mark than for himself; the boy had never really had time to become a man, to become the great Ranger Robert knew he would someday. Now all that was about to end.

And now Bohuslav had somehow got away from Tanek and had come to watch. Had ordered their deaths, in fact; obviously too tired and pissed off to want to savour it anymore.

Robert held his breath as Bohuslav told his men to execute them, then let it out, amazed, as all the guns were trained in the Tsar's direction.

It was only now, with the luxury of not having those guns facing them, that Robert took in what was really happening. Who those forces actually belonged to. He and Mark looked on as another order was given to kill Bohuslav.

Robert couldn't watch beyond the first salvo of bullets, keeping

Bohuslav upright long after he should have dropped to the ground. The gunfire seemed to go on forever. After the last *crack* sounded, Mark touched his arm and Robert jumped, the noise still ringing in his ears. He looked, but couldn't see Bohuslav – just a red smear against the whiteness of the snow: all that was left after the weapons had done their worst. Robert shivered again, but it had nothing to do with the snow all around.

The German soldiers turned back in their direction. What had happened with Bohuslav had been merely a stay of execution, it seemed. There was no bargaining with the Germans, either. If anything, it made things worse, because he and Mark had just been given a preview of what would happen to them.

As Robert steeled himself, he felt something touch his arm. He assumed it was Mark again, but when he turned his head he saw a rope dangling from above him. "What..." began Robert, looking up, but there was no time for questions. Mark grabbed him, then shoved his foot into a loop at the bottom before winding his hand around the rope already lifting them. Robert grabbed on himself so Mark didn't have to carry him. He followed the line of the rope up towards a shape above – something dark in the sky; something huge. A helicopter.

The Germans were about to fire, and probably still would have blown them to pieces – had the Russian forces not turned up at that point. Too late to save their Tsar, they nevertheless engaged the Germans on the ground level, their own jeeps and tanks approaching through the streets, soldiers with more AK-47s opening fire. Now the Germans had more on their plate than a couple of escaping men on a rope. One vehicle exploded as Robert and Mark were pulled up and away from the scene – they had no idea whose side it had belonged to. While the rope was being wound back into the helicopter, the battle raged below, and looked like it was going to for some time.

Next thing they knew, the pair of them were at the back door of the chopper, being helped in by familiar faces. Jack was there, taking his hand off the winch lever to grab Robert's own hand, while Sophie clapped her arms around Mark, planting a huge kiss on his lips.

And there, in front of Robert, was Mary. She smiled and ran to him. The helicopter lurched and he and Mary fell against one side. Robert grabbed onto some netting. He heard a garbled apology from the front of the craft. "Hold on, I'm tryin' to pull 'er out of range of those bigger guns below, before they drag us into their fun and games."

"Bill?" shouted Robert. "Where in Heaven's name did you find *this*?"

He heard a chuckle, then the reply: "Like it? Thought I'd upscale a little. Amazing what those locals up North had kickin' round at their flyin' museum. They let me borrow their Chinook for a while. Whoops."

They lurched again, this time to the other side, but Robert held Mary close. "And how did you know where to find me?"

"That was Mark," she told him. "Said he thought he remembered overhearing something about Moscow and the Tsar when he was kidnapped. Wouldn't tell us the rest. Insisted on going in alone, that he was the only one who could find you." Robert studied Mark's face, and knew full well that nothing had been overheard. The Native American wouldn't have been that careless. But Robert fully intended to get the truth out of Mark later on.

For a third time the helicopter lurched, but now they heard a noise from the open back, a whooshing sound as a missile flew past. Bill had lost it. Robert thanked God it wasn't a heat-seeker.

Next came machine-gun fire, but it was too close to be coming from the ground.

"Look!" Sophie was pointing at two aircraft, jet fighters with crosses on the side: formerly of the Luftwaffe. They were flying in as low as the chopper, on their trail while the rest of the Germans were otherwise engaged.

"Tornadoes," Jack called across to Robert, frowning.

"Blast," Robert said. "Just when I thought we might be out of the woods." That phrase, that sentence, connected with him and he suddenly had an idea. He took out the ash the Native American had given him, and then he shouted for Mark to hand him the pouch on his own belt. The pouch, like Robert's, which contained foliage and twigs from Sherwood. Well, if he couldn't get to the forest... Mark handed it to him and Robert quickly mixed the contents.

"What are you doing?" asked Mary, but he didn't reply. He was too busy willing this to work, praying that, although they weren't in Sherwood, it might be enough.

"What kind of weapons have you got back there?" asked Robert.

Jack looked at him sideways. "Nothing that can stop those, chief." But he went to fetch Robert's usual selection: bolas, arrows – some chemically tipped, Robert was pleased to see – a bow and his sword.

"Robert," Mary began, starting to look worried. "What are you going to do?"

"What I have to," he said, strangely starting to feel better as he hooked Mark's pouch onto his belt.

"Whatever it is, you might need this." Jack tossed across his hooded top. "Your uniform."

Robert put it on, then found Mary clutching at his sleeve. "Robert, listen to me. There's something you need to know before you do anything stupid. The Widow was right, Robert." She touched her stomach as she whispered the words. "Do you hear me? The Widow was right."

Robert paused, smiled, then kissed her on the top of the head. That was all the more reason to do this, to keep them safe. "I'll be back," he assured her, strapping on his weapons. He was feeling more invigorated by the second, the aches and wounds of the past few days fading – might have been the adrenalin of what he was about to do; might have been something else. Robert wasn't about to analyse it.

"Let me come with you," Mark said, but Robert held up his hand. "You've already risked enough today. I've got this," he told his son, glad that Sophie was pulling him back, and that Mary was not trying to do the same to him. Robert took hold of the line from the winch, opening up the loop and slipping it around his waist. Then he pulled up his hood.

And he was gone, racing towards the open end of the Chinook. He heard the cries as he jumped, the line slackening as he dropped.

Robert swung out, falling towards the first of the nearing fighters. When he was just yards away, he reached for his bow. Then there was another smattering of machine-gun fire, and suddenly he was dropping much faster than before.

He looked over his shoulder: the line had been shot through. Gritting his teeth, Robert threw back his shoulders and angled himself towards the first jet.

He slammed into the plane, just behind the cockpit, rolling over onto the right wing. He'd had just moments to register the shocked look of the pilot as he tumbled past. Robert hadn't been prepared for just how fast the wind would be coming at him, though; he gripped the edge of the wing as the pilot attempted to shake him.

When the plane righted itself, Robert slid across and onto the main body of the craft again, so that the pilot couldn't see him. The man could only turn his head so far, and he didn't try to bank again, presumably assuming he'd shaken the hooded lunatic. The pilot began firing at the Chinook once more. Robert began crawling along the spine of the plane inch by inch until he reached the cockpit, then drew his broadsword and, pulling it back as far as he could – the wind almost taking it from his hand – he rammed it through the glass and into the pilot. The plane took an immediate dive, and Robert found himself sliding over the edge – hanging on only by the sword's handle, embedded in both the cockpit and slumping pilot.

He looked down to see the other Tornado below, rising swiftly. Robert waited until he could judge the angle, then dropped. As he fell, the first plane dipped suddenly, then banked. Robert barely looked; he was too busy pulling the bow from his shoulder, nocking one of the incendiary arrows and preparing to fire at the second Tornado. He had a split second to do this, so his aim had to be dead on. Ignoring everything around him, he targeted one of the missiles the plane was carrying.

The wind suddenly took him sideways, and his aim was spoiled, the arrow going wide. Robert continued to fall, passing the Tornado now on his way down. He could see the pilot smirking, then opening fire himself, but Robert pitched himself forward, torpedoing down and underneath the jet.

Flipping himself around and onto his back, coasting on the breeze, he drew another arrow and shot upwards. This time it struck its target, the chemicals igniting the missile, and the plane carrying it, seconds later.

As Robert continued to fall, down and down, his only compensation was that he was leaving the Tornado as a burning wreck to fall from the sky. He continued to fall, letting his bow go as he closed his eyes. There was no way back to the helicopter, the rope well out of reach.

He resigned himself to the fact that this really was his final act, but that he'd kept all those he loved safe from the missiles and guns. He'd done the task that he set out to when he first left the forest. The Rangers would be in good hands with Mark.

The one regret he did have was that he could never tell Mary again how much he loved her, how much finding her had meant. Would never feel her in his arms again. Would not see his child born, or grow.

Robert felt himself still falling – there couldn't be more sky left, surely, he was going so fast.

Then he hit something. Not the ground, which he was rapidly hurtling towards. But something soft. Some*one*.

He opened his eyes again to see Jack swinging on the rope, his cap long gone. The length was still dropping; the wrestler had hitched a ride and gone down with it. Now the larger man was matching

Robert's descent, and had closed in on him thanks to Bill's skilful flying. As he swung again, Jack reached out and grabbed Robert by the hood of his top. He heard the big man yell as he took the strain; Robert doubted there was another person alive who was strong enough to do that.

Robert turned and again took hold of the rope, gripping it tightly as the winch lever was thrown up in the chopper. They stopped in mid-descent, and started being winched back up.

He'd been given *yet another* chance. His life extended, watched over by the spirits the Native American had been talking about.

But he also knew that his luck really would run out one day.

And as Robert was pulled back up to the Chinook, looking forward to holding Mary again – something he hoped to do many more times – he couldn't help dwelling on that thought.

Wondering if when that day came, he might not be wishing that Jack had simply let him fall.

CHAPTER TWENTY-FOUR

LOEWE WAS FUMING.

It hadn't been a good week. Usually, he couldn't care less about what happened out there in the real world; he was safe and sound in the Army of the New Order's headquarters. But the setbacks his organisation had suffered this week had a knock-on effect, threatened what he had established in Germany. As a leader of these men – even if he was only a fake leader – it was his responsibility to take action, to punish those responsible for losing all those vehicles and equipment in Scotland and Wales to Hood's men. His lifestyle was in jeopardy; he was frightened. And when Loewe was frightened, he got mad.

"On top of all that," he bellowed at young Schaefer, "you okayed a mission to Russia, which has practically sparked a war."

"I thought it necessary to retrieve the man responsible."

"Tanek. A man *you* hired, let us not forget. Did you succeed?" Schaefer was silent.

"We lost tanks, jeeps, countless men – and *two* aircraft in the process!"

"Hood was –"

Loewe skirted the edge of his desk, fists clenching and unclenching. The Alsatians rose as well, snarling. "Hood! Fucking Hood! I'm sick to death of him! This whole thing has been a catalogue of disasters from start to finish." He wagged a finger at Schaefer. "And I'm holding you responsible." This time he had to; Loewe had no choice. It had been Schaefer's idea to supply the Widow and the Dragon with arms, his idea to have it overseen by that olive-skinned idiot.

"The Russians are in disarray themselves, sir, now that the Tsar is dead."

That was something, at least, but it also meant they might be after revenge; might want to carry on this war until both their sides had nothing left. And besides, it didn't make up for the humiliation. Someone still had to pay. Loewe's reputation as a ball breaker was at stake. As much as he relied on the bespectacled man in front of him, it was going to have to be *his* head that Loewe took.

"I'm sorry it has come to this," he told Schaefer. "Guards!" Two members of the New Order were inside the room immediately, and Schaefer looked worriedly over his shoulder at them. He knew what was coming next, knew that the men were here not only to stop him from getting away but to witness what came next. He'd seen it happen with Mayer not long ago. A trickle of sweat ran down his forehead, dripping onto the left lens of his glasses. Any moment now Schaefer would be on his knees, begging Loewe not to set the dogs on him. Any moment he would –

Schaefer began to laugh.

Loewe's brow furrowed; that was not the reaction he'd expected. He'd seen men cry, whine, shit themselves in this position; never *laugh*.

His mind must be gone, thought Loewe. *All the more reason to put this sorry excuse for a human being out of his misery.*

"You're sorry. *You're* sorry?" Schaefer was shaking his head, the laughter still pouring out. The Alsatians' growls were getting louder; Loewe would let them off the leash in a moment. The young man wouldn't be laughing then. "You complete and utter moron," said Schaefer. "You haven't got a clue what's going on, have you?"

"How dare you talk to me that way!" Loewe said. Now he was livid. "You've asked for this." Loewe clicked his fingers for the dogs to attack.

Nothing happened.

Loewe clicked his fingers again. The dogs continued to growl, but remained where they were, flanking the desk. "Get him! What are you waiting for?"

Schaefer laughed harder now, so hard he had to take off his glasses and wipe his eyes. "You can't see further than your office, than all this." Loewe was clicking his fingers frantically, but the dogs were still ignoring him. Schaefer whistled sharply, and at last they sprang into action; not leaping to attack, but coming to heel. The young man replaced his glasses. "Who do you think oversaw their training, Loewe? Who has overseen *everything* around here?" He touched a hand to his chest. "Because you're good at the talking, but not so great at the strategies, are you?"

Loewe licked his lips, realising he was on thin ice but knowing there were still two guards in the room who could shoot the dogs if necessary. Schaefer's little back-up plan hadn't succeeded quite yet. "Like the strategies you fucked up this week?"

"I'll give you that one. Things haven't gone exactly to plan. But there's always the future, hopefully. One, sadly, that you will never witness."

"Men!" Loewe roared. "Shoot him, right now!" The guards, like the dogs, did nothing. Now Loewe began to worry, to grow even more frightened.

"You see, I know who you really are, *General*. I have done for a while. And now the men know as well; I've told them. Your loyalty is not to the cause. It is to yourself, pretender."

Loewe opened his mouth, the mouth he could rely on nine times out of ten to talk him out of a scrape. This must be the tenth time.

"The New Order was never meant to be yours." Schaefer took a step forward and the dogs followed. "My choice of liaison wasn't an accident, either. Poor Tanek once knew my cousin, Henrik. He was part of De Falaise's army. Hood killed him."

Loewe found his voice again, sensing an opportunity to turn this against the young upstart. "So, this was about revenge?"

Schaefer shook his head again. "No. Family is important to me, but so is my country. Hood presented... *still* presents a threat. But enough of this chit chat. Let's get on with things, shall we?"

Loewe backed up against the desk, holding a hand in front of him. "Listen, please... Guards! Men!" he called beyond his office, to the control room, into the HQ itself, but nobody came. Schaefer was in charge here. The *real* conman. "Please, we can talk about this. Work it out and –"

Schaefer gave two sharp whistles and the dogs leaped forward, one springing for Loewe's throat and the other his privates. He felt pain like he'd never experienced before. As he lay back on the desk, the Alsatians' teeth were everywhere, ripping chunks out of his arms, legs, hands and feet in a feeding frenzy. He tried to reach up, but the dogs were weighing him down. All those times he'd given the order for them to attack, he'd never once considered what it might be like on the receiving end... until now.

"What is it they say?" he vaguely heard Schaefer comment, through ears that were being ripped to shreds, but realised now quite how insane he was. "Cry havoc and let slip the dogs of war, General!" There was laughter again, before his young second concluded: "Well, I would love to stay and watch these final moments, but I have places to be. I would like to say it has been a pleasure, but that wouldn't be true at all. So instead I will simply say *auf wiedersehen*."

Loewe didn't hear any more, only felt a few more seconds of torture before passing out. His last thoughts were of his very first lie, about the dog he'd blamed for trailing mud into the house.

"Was that you who trailed that mud into the house, Achim?"

"No Mütti, I swear."

Remembered its whine as his mother had thrashed it.

And he thought about how, in the end, the dog had finally got its own revenge.

Finally had its day.

FIRST A WEDDING, now a funeral.

Not for one person, but many. The Reverend Tate had presided over the internment of all those dead at New Hope, even the Germans, who were buried out in the woodland. The villagers who'd been killed during their brave offensive had found their ultimate resting place in the graveyard, with Tate leading the prayers for them. It had been a touching and poignant day, the service attended by those still left alive, as well as many from Nottingham Castle – including Mary and, yes, even Robert, though he seemed embarrassed and ashamed to be there.

Probably because of what he'd said to Karen Shipley, even though he'd relented and sent Rangers to assist. She'd been there on the day also, pushing a recovering Darryl in a wheelchair to pay their respects. Doctor Jeffreys' assistant Sat had been able to stem the bleeding from his wounds after the battle, until they could get him back to the castle for proper medical care – along with Graham Leicester – but could do nothing for Andy. Nor for Gwen, ultimately.

It was her grave Tate was standing over today, mourning the loss of the courageous woman, who'd died after Tanek had shot her. She'd died cradling her beloved son, Clive Jr, who Tate had saved from a Morningstar Servitor himself. The cult had gone to ground again after being defeated here by the Rangers – those taken captive during the fight having already committed suicide, as was their way. He had to admit, it had been a shock to see them there as well as the Germans, and Tate had reported the fact to Robert immediately upon his return from Russia; while the rest of the surviving German prisoners – including a very battered captive they'd discovered in the Red Lion – were being locked up in Nottingham's hotel jails.

The Reverend doubted they'd see the evil cultists or Germans again anytime soon, but just in case, Robert had allowed a contingent of Rangers to remain in New Hope to make sure.

"I'd like to stay as well," the Reverend had informed him. "These people need my guidance, Robert. They've lost their way a little."

Robert had agreed, but was sad to see Tate leaving again, especially when he was so settled now at the castle. But he also recognised the fact that the holy man had been there at the village's birth, that he'd been best friends with the man who founded it. Perhaps it was time to take the place back to that original vision, under the Rangers' protection. Tate also owed Gwen – buried beside that man, who she'd loved with all her heart – because he'd been too late once more. And this time it had cost her dearly.

As for Clive Jr, Darryl and Karen had offered to bring up the child. "It's what Gwen would have wanted," Darryl told him. Tate had a feeling Karen was only helping out to get closer to the man she quite clearly adored, but then maybe that wasn't a bad thing. In time, perhaps they'd become the family that Clive, Gwen and Clive Jr should have been. And while Tate was on the scene, he'd make sure that not only were the villagers brought back into the flock, but Gwen's son was taught right from wrong according to the Good Book.

Tate wiped a tear from his eye, saying the words he'd said every day for a month now. "I'm sorry, Gwen. So sorry."

As he turned away and began his walk down the path of the graveyard, Tate paused and looked back over his shoulder. Was it his imagination, or had he felt a presence? Just for a second seen a glimpse of a figure. Someone on the periphery of the graveyard itself? Someone who might also have come to pay their respects, but hadn't ventured inside for whatever reason?

Tate shook his head. Just his imagination, he told himself.

That was all.

THE TREES HID him from view as he sped through the forest.

He was alone today, but then he needed to be. He would spend time with Mark here soon enough, spend time with Mary elsewhere, but first Robert needed to reconnect with Sherwood. Needed to feel the grass beneath his feet, hear the birdsong; needed to fly.

All was well back at the castle, and reports were coming in that the establishment of both the Welsh and Scottish arms of the Rangers was going very well. Dale had asked to remain as liaison in Cardiff, ostensibly to help with that regional chapter's growth, but reading between the lines he'd fallen for this girl Jack had told them about. It also appeared to be catching, because the big man himself had talked quite a bit about the girl's aunty, Meghan. Robert hadn't met her yet, but there was talk of the woman coming to visit Nottingham. Hopefully she would help Jack get over the heartache of Adele.

Tate was the only one sad at the moment, thanks to the way things had gone at New Hope – to not being able to save Gwen. But, helping to piece that community back together was at least taking his mind off things.

And their enemies, including the Morningstars, Germans and the Russians, seemed to be out of the picture for now, thankfully, either lying low or fighting each other. What would happen in the long term, though, was anyone's guess.

He'd been thinking about that a lot recently: the future. Thinking about what Mark would become. The young man had told Robert when they were alone that he'd seen the Tsar in a dream, back when they'd been camping out in Sherwood, before the Native American did his thing. "I just *knew* where I'd find you," Mark said. "Don't ask me to explain, because I can't. And definitely not to anyone but you. That's one of the reasons I couldn't tell the others. And I wanted to return the favour by saving *you* this time."

Robert also wondered what his new daughter or son might be like, whether they'd have the same kind of insights eventually. He supposed he'd find out in time.

Robert's legs pumped harder. With his hood up he was like a green blur streaking through the forest. It was as if he was getting to know it again, everything fresh and new – and that was re-energising him. He should have felt old, worn out, but right now he felt young.

He'd found evidence of the man in black's presence in Sherwood, primarily the sweat lodge he'd constructed and used to tame the forest somehow. Robert had released the contents of the pouch here, a formality, but one which he knew he had to go through for things to get back to normal. For the magic – the dreams – to return. They hadn't so far, but he figured that was only because they were granting him a desperately needed respite. He'd been through so much over the past few weeks and he was far from ready for any more emergencies.

It was strange, but he still felt the Native American here today as he was running. Felt like he might be behind the next tree about to spring out, or watching from a distance. Robert scrutinised every single patch of blackness as the day was waning, in case it might be him. No, the Native American had his own agenda. Something to do with what the Tsar had given him.

Just a stone, Robert told himself, but he didn't believe that for a minute – and he also wondered whether there were more where it had come from.

As if to prove him wrong, the shadows ahead lengthened and he saw movement behind one of the oaks. Robert stopped, his bow primed in seconds, ready for another duel if necessary.

But it hadn't been *the* Shadow. Robert eased back on the tension when he saw his old friend. The creature he'd left alive all that time ago, now walking through the forest towards him. Not scared at all, not worried Robert was going to hunt or kill it. Because the stag *was* him. He'd seen that so many times in those dreams.

It was wounded, or had been – red stains on the back of its neck. Robert was only guessing, but perhaps the animal had been trying to defend Sherwood against its intruder, in lieu of him being around.

They regarded each other, just as they'd done that first time – an understanding passing between them. They were guardians of worlds: both real and imagined. They were the stuff of legend, just like this place.

The stuff of song, of words and of deeds. They had always been here and always would be.

And really, their story was only just beginning.

THE END

ABOUT THE AUTHOR

PAUL KANE has been writing professionally for almost fifteen years. His genre journalism has appeared in such magazines as *The Dark Side*, *Death Ray*, *Fangoria*, *SFX*, *Dreamwatch* and *Rue Morgue*, and his first non-fiction book was the critically acclaimed *The Hellraiser Films and Their Legacy*.

His award-winning short fiction has appeared in magazines and anthologies on both sides of the Atlantic, and has been collected in *Alone (In the Dark)*, *Touching the Flame*, *FunnyBones* and *Peripheral Visions*. His novella *Signs of Life* reached the shortlist of the British Fantasy Awards 2006, *The Lazarus Condition* was introduced by Mick Garris, creator of *Masters of Horror*, and *RED* featured artwork from Dave (*The Graveyard Book*) McKean.

As Special Publications Editor of the British Fantasy Society, Paul worked with authors like Brian Aldiss, Ramsey Campbell, Muriel Gray, Robert Silverberg and many more, and he is the co-editor of *Hellbound Hearts* for Pocket Books (Simon and Schuster), an anthology of original stories inspired by Clive Barker's novella.

In 2008, Paul's zombie story 'Dead Time' was turned into an episode of the Lionsgate/NBC TV series *Fear Itself*, adapted by Steve Niles (*30 Days of Night*) and directed by Darren Lynn Bousman (*SAW II-IV*). He also scripted the short film *The Opportunity*, which premiered at Cannes in 2009.

Paul's other novels include *Of Darkness and Light* (with cover art from the award-winning Vincent Chong) and *The Gemini Factor* (with an introduction from Peter Atkins, screenwriter of *Hellraiser II-IV* and *Wishmaster*). His website, which has featured guest writers such as Stephen King, James Herbert and Neil Gaiman, can be found at www.shadow-writer.co.uk.

Paul currently lives in Derbyshire, UK, with his wife – the author Marie O'Regan – his family, and a black cat called Mina.

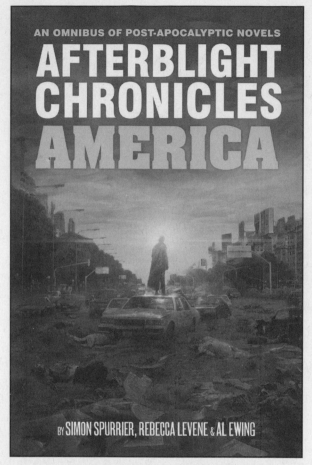

AN OMNIBUS OF POST-APOCALYPTIC NOVELS

AFTERBLIGHT CHRONICLES AMERICA

BY SIMON SPURRIER, REBECCA LEVENE & AL EWING

ISBN: 978 1 907992 14 8 • $12.99/$14.99

It swept across the world like the end of times, a killer virus that spared only those with one rare blood type. Now, in the ruined cities, cannibalism and casual murder are the rule, and religious fervour vies with cynical self-interest. The few who hope to make a difference, to rise above the monsters, must sometimes become monsters themselves.

An English soldier, killing his way across America to find the one hope he has of regaining his humanity, which he'd thought lost in the Cull; a doctor at the precipice of madness, who'd taken a Cure, in the last days, that may prove worse than the illness; a maniac who'd never had cause to care about anyone or go to any lengths to help them, until now.

Three stories. Three damned heroes.

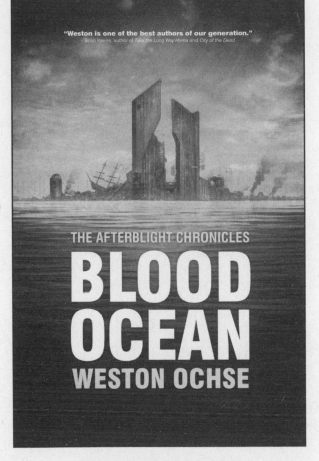